Defying Shadows

By
Ashley Townsend

Ink Smith Publishing
www.ink-smith.com

Formatted by: VJO Gardner
Cover design by: Lisa M. of The Elegant Stylus

Printed in the U.S.A, 2016

ISBN: 978-1-939156-79-2

Ink Smith Publishing
710 S. Myrtle Ave Suite 209
Monrovia, CA 91016

www.ink-smith.com

To all the Sarahs out there:
I hope that you find the strength and courage to never give up. When one dream dies, keep pressing until you discover a new one. And may your story live on in the hearts of others for another thousand years.

Prologue

"Wandering between two worlds, one dead
The other powerless to be born."

Matthew Arnold

The morning dawned gray, casting a hazy light over the land. It was always dreary here in the small province of Ridlan, and the fog that rolled in from the north settled in thick waves between the mountains, placing the town in perpetual gloom. Undeterred by the bleak setting, the town was already coming awake, abuzz with activity as they set to work opening their shops and perusing the vendor carts that would roll in for the week to sell and trade goods with the townsfolk, who were few in number—merely a thousand citizens lived in Ridlan, and only a few hundred of them men to protect and defend the small city.

But although the town appeared diminutive in size when compared to the thousands of beings occupying Serimone, it made up for its deficiency with the iron working forges set deep in the valley between the rolling hills. Their few men and these forges were their only defense, but it was enough. Protected by the constant veil of mist that hung in the air between the rising knolls in the distance, the men worked hard to produce the tools and weapons that Ridlan was revered for. Their weapons were also the reason why the small and seemingly unprotected province had never lost a battle, remaining untouched for over a hundred years.

The sound of metal-on-metal echoed through the valley as the men labored tirelessly to keep their city safe with a storehouse of arms. They did not just produce their weapons; Ridlan men were also trained fighters, practicing fiercely for hours on end with their tools in the hidden hills. The surrounding provinces had every right to fear a potential attack from the deceptively dormant town.

The intense, vengeful thoughts that sparked such interest in the province came from a man who was, at present, nursing a headache inside a quiet inn located at the heart of town. He rolled over on his firm mattress and stood, waiting for the room to cease spinning before throwing on his robe. Squinting against the harsh sun that glared through the heavy clouds, he stared out the window. The stony castle loomed in the distance, set just before the hills, and was partly shrouded by the mist that clung to the air. He imagined his warm, soft bed behind those walls in the guest wing with the other nobles, the room he had been granted as a representative of Serimone.

Planting his lips against a closed fist, Cadius considered the townsfolk below his window, who appeared as easily squashed as any other pest, but he knew that was not the case. Many kings had tried to overthrow Ridlan and take control of its countless armaments stored in the veiled hillside, and each one had failed. He stared into the distance, trying to make out the valleys where these powerful weapons were stored, but it was impossible to see beyond the hovering clouds. He imagined a small troupe of fearsome warriors emerging from the fog and attacking anyone who dared take control of their city, and then receding back into the mist when the battle was won. He had heard the tales of short-lived battles with great loss on the side of kingdoms that invaded Ridlan, the fearsome province.

And he wanted its power for himself.

Cadius dressed quickly and exited the inn with no true destination in mind. The tavern next door was quiet in the morning hours as he passed it, and he gritted his teeth against the pulsating ache behind his temples—the result of a night spent in his cups. A day of loathing his life and coveting that of his brother had turned into a night of pondering how to improve his presently dismal circumstances; yet the answer had not been found as he nursed cup after cup of honeyed wine.

It had been a chore to make it to the bordering inn after he was done licking his wounds and had finished his final tankard of spirits. Paying the owner of the run-down inn had been an interesting affair as Cadius attempted to count the correct amount of coins, and he knew he never would have made it to the castle sans incident. The manservant Josiah had allowed him to take along doubtless hadn't taken note of his absence, since the youth never bothered to check in on him unless prompted.

Cadius ground his teeth in vexation as he considered how his brother had allowed him a single blasted servant. One prolonged illness that kept Cadius from his duties, and everything was stripped from him in an instant. Instead of Cadius succeeding to the throne, his younger brother received all he had ever desired: the reverence of his people, the control of a thriving kingdom, a wife that adored him.

His hands balled into fists when he thought of Alexis, smiling and laughing with him as she had in their youth. Those tender memories turned sour in his throat when Cadius imagined her now, older but no less beautiful, touching and smiling and lying with another man. His brother. Their marriage had cemented a political alliance between Serimone and Ridlan, from which she hailed, and had caused the kingdoms to draw up a Peace Pact that prevented any discourse from breaking out between the neighboring provinces, provided that a king of Serimone was married to one of Ridlan's most prominent daughters.

Through it all, Cadius had remained silent, falling into his position as the king's advisor, a role he detested. Yet it also gave him a sense of power, believing that he could sway his brother's mind as he wished, if only

Josiah were more malleable. His true reason for maintaining his position, though, was that it kept him near his dearest Alexis—the girl who had openly returned his affections and now the woman who remained reticent in his presence, despite countless pleas from the man who was still mad for her.

Although she and Josiah had never borne a healthy child, having lost several in pregnancy and two children to illness before they saw their first year, Alexis had sworn that she had grown to love Josiah and would remain faithful to her king. Over the years, Cadius tried to sway her affection his way once more, and he persisted even when his love seemed to have fallen out of love with him. It was only now, after decades of effort and countless professions of love, that he knew he had no chance.

Before he left on this political meeting, Alexis had told him, in no uncertain terms, that she would never love him again. Gently, she relayed that she could never again think of him as she once had, because she knew the man he had become and saw the darkness that rested inside of him as his envy for his brother grew. Cadius had scoffed when his beloved said she feared for his soul, but in truth, he had never felt so rejected, so certain that whatever tryst they'd had in their youth was truly over.

A shoulder rammed into him from the side, jostling Cadius from his stupor. He glanced up sharply and cursed. The young blond man spun as he jogged backward, shouting out his apology. "Sorry, sir. I'm late for work!" And then he was off, rushing down the street and dodging startled passerby.

Cadius considered chasing after the irritating youth, but his head had started pounding again, and the youth was hardly worth the effort. He pretended to flick invisible dirt off his shirtfront, allowing for time to collect himself, and saw that the blond man had dropped something in his haste. Curious, he bent down and grabbed the leather band, not even entertaining the notion of returning it to its owner.

"How strange," he murmured to himself, rubbing his finger over the glossy metal side of the inset. The square sitting between the two bands of leather was completely black and impossibly thin. An odd piece of jewelry, he thought to himself as he meandered down the street. It wasn't very attractive, with no gems or adornment of any kind, really. Perhaps it was foreign—the young man's accent had seemed peculiar.

Leather-soled boots slapped the dirt path, heading toward him. Cadius looked up sharply and caught that same man hurrying through the crowd once more, his eyes moving over the ground with frantic movements.

Smoothly, the aging man concealed the sought-after item with a closed fist and moved into an alleyway nearby. The youth ran past the opening between buildings, disappearing from sight. Cadius couldn't say precisely why he did not simply return the leather band to its rightful owner, but he had never been fond of making another's life easier.

Unlike his brother, who had received everything at the hands of another and at Cadius' own expense.

His palm began to tingle with the faint and sudden thrumming coming from the item he held. Removing his thumb from the sleek square, he stared in surprise as the blackness in the center shifted, brightening and coming to life with numbers and letters that made no sense to him. At the top of the contraption was what appeared to be a chart of sorts, with latitudes and longitudes and other indecipherable codes a seaman might utilize.

"What the devil—?" His voice faded as the numbers changed, revealing the outline of a province he did not recognize. A black dot blinked on and off near the edge of the map, and, as if in a trance, Cadius reached out a curious finger and gently tapped the flashing speck.

The world changed, and his body was thrown to the side, though he never felt the ground. He gasped at the overwhelming brightness that surrounded him, instinctively clutching the object in his palm. A tingling sensation began in his feet and progressively worsened, turning into a searing pain by the time it worked its way up to his skull. He fell to his knees, grinding his teeth in agony as he pressed his fists to his temples against the excruciating feeling of being split apart. The sensation left him so abruptly that he crumpled onto his side, gasping for breath as the phantom feelings left every limb trembling.

When at last he felt he could move, Cadius slowly pulled his aching body from its prostrate position and groaned as his shaky limbs obeyed his command. Now on his feet, he blinked the glaring dots from his vision and took in his surroundings, eyes widening at the strange equipment he saw before him, at the desk laden with a menagerie of tools and the stacks of paper covered in cramped script and diagrams. The writing was foreign to him, as were the instruments and the enormous silver box in the center of what was clearly a workroom of sorts.

Different colored ropes stretched out from the contraption, and the thick, chorded mass slithered across the gray surface of the floor. The end of the line disappeared inside a domed object sitting on the ground a few feet away, a single green ember fading in and out on its side, and that foul-looking object was connected by another gray rope to a small white rectangle low on the wall.

He suddenly became aware of the two forms in the room on the other side of the large contraption, and he gave a start. One was a graying man with two clear orbs hovering over his eyes, and his hands rested on the girl's shoulders. She looked young, with long red hair and heightened color in her cheeks, accompanied by a youthful sparkle in her green eyes. They were clearly peasants, with no formal garb on the man or ornamental vestment of any kind, and the girl wore nothing but a short shift and . . . trousers? Neither seemed to have spotted him, or they had lost all common decency and were ignoring his sudden presence.

Yanking on the end of his elegant coat in vexation, Cadius stepped forward. "Where am I, and who are you?" he demanded. But they took no notice of him, and both continued to smile stupidly at that ridiculous, bulbous object.

"We did it, Professor," the girl whispered, shaking her head with a laugh. "We finally fixed the glitch."

The older man gave her shoulders a squeeze and, though she could not see it, gave the top of her head a look of total adoration. "I couldn't have done it without you, my dear girl."

More disgruntled than ever over being ignored, Cadius tried again, using the tone that struck fear in lords around the country. "What the devil is going on? I demand an explana—" The room lurched, throwing him off balance. He landed prostrate on the ground, slamming his knee into the smooth, rock-hard surface.

Cadius glared up at the two, sure they were to blame for his fall, but the reprimand stuck in his throat as he witnessed them disappear, shifting and fading into dim orbs that were replaced by—yes, the girl was still there, smiling. But the old man was gone, and in his place stood a man and a woman, clearly the girl's parents by the likeness between them. The walls changed color, an enormous fur rug replaced the cold stone beneath Cadius, though he could not feel it, and his mind continued to register stone against his palms. He could see it, but it was as though he could not truly touch this world.

His eyes returned to the man and woman perched on the settee below the large window draped with sheer fabric, laughing as their red-haired daughter tore into the brightly colored parcel in her lap. She squealed in delight as she produced a leather-bound book and threw a huge smile over her shoulder. Cadius realized the older man was, indeed, still in the picture, sitting quietly in the corner and watching her antics with a smile of amusement.

"Thank you, Uncle Charles! I love it!"

That man chuckled and nodded once. "I thought you might."

"Does this mean I can help you with some of your experiments?" The hopeful look in her eyes caused the older man's smile to soften. Their gazes had yet to register the foreigner lying on their floor, though their sights would graze over him now and again. Cadius was too startled to speak up, not that he could have, as his tongue appeared too heavy to make a sound.

"I believe I've given that up for a time, my dear. I think I need to focus on my teaching just now."

The girl quirked a brow. "One too many electrical shocks to the head?"

A chuckle. "Perhaps."

The sound of the group's laughter turned warbly, as though they were underwater, and the images before him began to dissolve again, turning back to the older man and the girl in the cellar. The throbbing in Cadius' skull increased as both realities vied for attention, fading in and out and sometimes lapping over the other, as though his mind couldn't decide which one was true. Suddenly, the object he'd forgotten he held turned unbearably hot in his palm, scorching his skin. He released it with a hiss of pain and didn't bother to retrieve it, too distracted by the baffling images.

The voices became unintelligible, blending together in a cacophony of sound as an onslaught of images came at him: the girl laughing as she threw a stick to a small dog, then crying with the older man as she stood over two gravestones; the redhead just waking in the backseat of a covered wagon and screaming as her father lost control, shrieking in delight as she played with her parents at a lake. It all blended together, the sounds and feelings of hope, agony, and joy flashing before him in brief glimpses of someone's life. But whose?

Was this what losing one's mind felt like, to be drowning inside yourself, to feel split between two worlds? He pressed his face against the ground, squeezing his eyes closed against the swirling images, the sobs and shouts of delight. What was happening to him?

Abruptly, the hard surface beneath him softened, and the cold stone turned warm and soft, brushing his face and tickling his nose.

Cadius jerked his head up, startled to see that he was clutching grass. His frightened heart rate slowed and his roiling stomach settled when he realized he must be back home, in Glendale Forest, or Thornwood, perhaps. Had he fallen asleep? But then he recalled that he had awoken in Ridlan not more than an hour before.

His eyes landed on the wristband he had previously clung to and now laid half-forgotten by his fist. By God, was it possessed with an evil spirit that had caused him to fantasize the entire episode? But while the mysterious contraption and what it had been able to accomplish was terrifying, Cadius felt strangely drawn to it, intrigued by its power. Hesitantly, he touched a finger to it, bracing himself for another uncomfortable journey or the searing heat he had experienced before. But the surface was cool, and he snatched it from the ground before he could second-guess himself.

Getting to his feet, he stumbled through the forest until his legs felt sure once more, and then he ran, hoping he could find his way out of this blasted woods before nightfall. But the trees here were thin and sparse, and he abruptly burst through them and emerged into daylight. He froze.

Scantly clad children were laughing and playing in the dirt, a little girl in a bright pink shift was swinging through the air on a strange apparatus attached to a colored rod, and a young lad with a scraped knee was calling for his parents, who were sitting on an iron bench nearby. Where the devil was he?

He blew past them, eyes like that of a frightened deer, and received wary looks from a few of the adults and curious stares from the little ones.

He ignored them all, stumbling past the onlookers, beyond the strange, malformed pieces of iron on which the children were playing. Before him, Cadius made out the stretch of black, cobbled road, and he released a gusty breath. Civilization, he thought in utter relief, breaking away from the barbarians behind him.

But when he reached the cross-section of the street, he froze in his tracks. The black road was not made up of stones, but was a flat surface, stretching and weaving as far as his eyes could see in all directions. He was alarmed to find that the "road" was alive with activity—people jogging and walking every which way, a group of women in trousers who walked past, laughing mockingly, without modesty or restraint, as their eyes boldly took in his long formal vest and covered legs.

And there were enclosed, horseless carriages, too many to count, that careened across the street at shocking speeds, blowing past him and passerby seemingly without concern for the packed road. Cadius jerked in surprise when a young man dressed in short trousers ran across the street, and one of the transports emitted a long, blaring sound as it swerved around the lad.

Stumbling along the gray walkway next to the road, he shoved people aside, unconcerned if they were male or female. He only had one thought—air. By God, was his heart going to give out?

He could see grass up ahead in front of an enormous structure and ran to the open space, panting as he jogged past the large sign with bold script that he had no mind to read. The large elm tree shading a wooden bench called to him, as it was away from the youths socializing about the grass. With quick strides, he made his way to it, sucking in a deep breath as he collapsed onto the bench, reassured to be away from the mass chaos near the main pathway but still fighting panic as he took in the strange sights and sounds around him.

The entire front of the building was made of pristine glass, and he could see countless people within, sitting at desks and padded chairs, reading and talking and drinking steaming beverages from white cups. The noises surrounding him were nearly overwhelming—loud chatter, boisterous laughter, shouting, a constant buzzing or jingle that would only be silenced once a youth began speaking into a small colored box they held to their ear. And there was a man and a woman lying on the grass together, being far too intimate for modesty's sake. What manner of place would allow such a spectacle?

"You appear lost."

Cadius glanced up sharply, not having noticed the man who had stopped before him. He forced his breathing to calm, but the perpetually baffled looked on his countenance refused to fade. All pretense of authority was impossible at this point. "I believe I am."

“Well, you’re at the university.” The dark-haired man eyed him up and down with a look of vague amusement. “Are you with the theater department?”

Cadius blinked. “I don’t quite understand the question.”

Now he was watching him with a look of suspicion, though the grin on the man’s face remained in place. “Your silly costume. I assumed you were part of the production.”

Outraged, Cadius replied crossly, “I beg your pardon! This is not a silly costume, as you put it. I happen to be on a royal errand.” Peasant, he thought disgruntledly, though the man’s tan trousers and matching coat were far more formal than that of the young people wandering about the area.

Holding his hands up defensively, the man’s grin returned in full force. “Forgive my impudence,” he said grandly, rolling a hand in the air as he dipped his head. Cadius had the sense he was being mocked. “You just didn’t seem to know quite what to do with yourself. Can I direct you somewhere, my liege?”

Cadius shot him a quick glare and hefted his chin, then his shoulders slumped as he realized he had no idea where he was and was unsure if he could find his way back to Ridlan. “I don’t quite know,” he whispered. Opening his palm, he watched the midday light glint off of the sleek, now lifeless, face attached to the leather band. Had this small piece of enchanted jewelry truly done all of this? It was the only explanation, but surely that notion was impossible.

When he turned his gaze upward, the man’s eyes were fixed on the object he held. “How did you—did someone give that to you?”

A spark of hope shot up his spine. “Do you know what this is?”

“Yes,” the man whispered, studying him anew and paying greater attention to his dress this time. “I know precisely what it is, I just can’t believe he managed it.” Suddenly, his hand was held out to Cadius, who shook it dazedly. “My name is Guy. I’m a professor at this university.”

Most of what was said was lost on Cadius, save for the vague inclination that he might be able to get him out of this tragically horrid place. “Cadius, advisor to the king of Serimone. Can you tell me what has happened to me?”

Guy smiled, taking the seat next to him. “Yes, I believe I can. But it will be quite shocking.”

Cadius grimaced. “How shocking?” Had he not already endured too much?

With a sly, secretive grin that caused Cadius to swallow nervously, the man replied, “Suffice it to say that history as you know it need not be set in stone.”

Chapter One

"The beginning is always today."

Mary Shelley, *Frankenstein*

Students were already clearing out of the dorms and heading home for Christmas vacation, though finals had only been just yesterday; it seemed they couldn't get out of there fast enough. The campus was like a ghost town, the cafeteria mostly devoid of life, and the dorms held a few leftover students who were saying goodbye to friends before they booked it out of there. It seemed that everyone was eager to return home or leave for vacation after the stress of finals, looking forward to exciting trips.

That is, everyone except for Sarah.

She stood over her bed, stuffing a few last-minute items into her duffel bag. Her roommate, Clara, lay sprawled over her own bed, eyes closed, humming a high-powered electric guitar beat and air-strumming to her tune.

Sarah glanced over her shoulder in amusement. Her roommate's eyes were closed as she continued in her intense musical solo, and the hazy light coming in through their single window glinted off the row of studs in her brow and the single hoop in her right nostril. Sarah had been a little surprised at her appearance when they'd first met, but after a few weeks of living with the amusingly dramatic Clara Somers, she'd realized that her façade was just that—a front to keep people out. Sarah had made it her mission to make their living arrangement as comfortable as possible, and her roommate had warmed up to her over time. Sarah now considered her a friend, one she certainly needed in this new environment.

"What are you doing, Clary?" she asked, using the nickname the girl had given herself, insisting that Clara was "too prissy."

"I'm providing a dramatic backdrop to your life," Clara answered, sounding bored. Then she added, "I still don't get why you don't want to come with me and my brother to Cabo over vacation. You know Todd likes you, and you'll only be more appealing if you keep playing hard-to-get."

Sarah sighed at her roommate's persistence. Clara had been trying to get her to agree to the trip for over a month, and she had yet to budge. "Yeah, I'd love to hear that conversation: 'Sorry, Mom and Dad, but I can't visit my elderly grandparents because I'll be in Cabo with a boy. What's that? Oh, no, his parents are in Seattle over Christmas, so we'll be unchaperoned when Clary isn't around.'"

Clara sat up, the springs in her mattress squeaking in protest. She pretended to flip the short ends of her blond, pixie-cut locks. "Fine, I get that. But at least consider agreeing to go out with him the next time he asks." She hopped to her feet in one fluid motion. "You know he'll try again. He can be irritatingly persistent."

Wincing, Sarah turned back to her bag, stuffing a shirt into the already packed duffel. "He hasn't really asked yet."

"Oh, puh-leez." She imagined Clara rolling her eyes. "'Do you want to study together?' 'Let's grab a cup of coffee.' 'Would you like to have my children?'"

Sarah gut-laughed at the last one. "Okay, that never happened. And you're also crazy."

"That's what they tell me." Grinning in satisfaction, she added, "And he's going to be on campus for another week—something about finishing up some sort of flooty wooty project he's working on with one of the professors." She waved her hand in the air in a dismissive gesture. "I didn't totally get it. But you could grab some casual 'friendship' coffee with Todd while I pack the rest of our stuff for vacation at the house. The trip back to Wyoming is sooo boring, not to mention that the state itself is a dud. He'd better hurry it up here so I'm not stranded at home for too long and can get on my way to some semblance of a tan."

"I hate to be the logical one and point out that you could stay here for the week with him while he finishes up and leave for the house together to pack, but . . ."

"That would mean dwelling in this institution a minute longer than necessary. Uh-uh. I'll take my chances in Wyoming." She swung her backpack over her shoulder, grinning as she moved toward the door. "Just keep Todd in mind. He's weak and tired from finals right now, so the time to overtake and mold the baby gazelle is now, my friend. At the very least you can get a free meal out of it. Capitalize, girl! It's not like you have anyone holding you back."

Sarah's expression stayed frozen on her face, though she was tempted to grin with her secret. Not necessarily.

"Well, see you in Cabo, dah-ling!" Clara called grandly over her shoulder, leaving the door open as she breezed into the hall.

Sarah grinned, not even trying to dissuade her. Her roommate didn't take no for an answer, anyway.

Clara's dramatic background music had only drowned out the sounds coming from Sarah's CD player on her nightstand. She hummed along to the upbeat tune as Relient K sang about the difficulties of college life. Sarah could relate—she had been poisoned, had nearly been burned alive, and spent a portion of Christmas in Serimone running for her life, and finals week had given these dire straits a run for their money.

Grabbing her brown leather boots from the mound of clothing on her bed, the pile slid precariously, and some clothing and books fell to the floor.

With an exaggerated huff, she bent to pick up her leather-bound copy of Frankenstein and tossed it onto the mattress, seeing a note beneath it. She snatched it up automatically, and the thick paper was crumpled as if it had been removed from the trash, though its wax seal was still intact.

Sarah's mind stopped her hand from opening it out of curiosity. Her fingers trembled, and she sat heavily on her bed, paying no mind as Frankenstein toppled to the carpet. She had her own monster to deal with.

The wrinkled paper glared at her, the thick glob of red wax a stark contrast against the slightly yellow parchment that she knew contained Damien's writing, though she hadn't been able to bring herself to slit the seal after months of holding it in her possession, unopened but never far from her mind. They were some of his final words to her, and she imagined they would explain his actions and apologize for dragging her into the murderous scheme he himself had fallen into with Cadius. But she would never know what he had penned that day until she decided to open it.

Her hand twitched as she slid a finger under the seal with careful movements, the wax cracking and lifting as she did so. She held her breath when the seal broke and the letter unfolded an inch. She ignored the smaller piece of paper, crinkled and yellowed with age—either because she'd left it in her dirty laundry for months or because it was nearly a thousand years old—that fell to the floor. She carefully held open Damien's letter. His tight, beautiful script filled the entire page, as though he'd needed every inch for his thoughts, his looping a's painfully familiar. Her eyes scanned quickly, unseeing, over the whole of the letter and then returned to the top, to the three perfectly sculpted words that looked like he had penned them with painstaking care: My dearest Sarah—

Abruptly, she snatched the smaller note from the floor, stuffed it between the pages of Damien's letter once more, and smashed the paper between her hands, balling it in her fists and chucking the offending letter across the room with a screech of annoyance. It hit the frosted window and fell lamely to the floor atop a mound of clothes Clara had left behind.

It was an overreaction, but it felt good, as though Damien could see she still held onto her anger at what he'd done and offense that he thought a single letter could make up for it all.

How dare he still have that kind of power over her that she should care what he had to say! However fancy and pleading his words might be, it wasn't like it would change what he'd done, the fact that he had lied to her and taken part in multiple murders and killed Edith. The death of her friend had been an accident, but she would never forgive him for it, and it upset her that a small part of her wanted to.

Feeling restless in her dorm room, where the air had suddenly become too thin to breathe properly, Sarah grabbed her heavy vest off the mattress and slipped her arms through it. She shoved her feet into her boots and booked it down the stairs, needing fresh air. A girl she vaguely recognized smiled at her in the foyer, saying a friendly, "Have a great vacation!"

"You, too," Sarah managed, too distracted to make small talk.

She immediately felt refreshed once she stepped outside into the cold. The afternoon air was crisp after the storm they'd received in the night. Layers of soft, white fluff covered the dead grass and piled up on the trees, which had been decorated with colorful lights in the Christmas spirit.

Sarah wrapped her arms around her middle as she meandered down the grassy knoll leading from her dorm, her boots crunching over the snow as she trudged without purpose. Two girls overtook her slow progress as the ground leveled out, both shouldering backpacks that bounced up and down as they jogged toward the parking lot, passing a couple of freshman boys carrying a mattress between them. The bleached-blond called flirtatiously over her shoulder, "Looking good, guys!" And then she and her friend burst into a fit of giggles, leaving the grinning boys behind.

Aside from those few bodies currently inhabiting the grounds, campus was otherwise deserted, Sarah realized as she let her gaze wander the snowy landscape. Hardly another soul in sight.

That was why her eyes found his so easily.

Sarah stopped dead in her tracks, arms falling to her sides in surprise. A dark-haired man stared back at her, and she could see, even from this distance, that his wide eyes were a deep blue. She imagined that she could make out the lighter blue ring surrounding his indigo irises, how the shadow along his jaw would feel against her fingertips. She blinked, sure he was a mirage, but he was still there when she opened her eyes. He looked exactly as she had last seen him—handsome, tall, and dressed for a different age—though he was also strangely like a ghost at the same time. It wasn't that she could see through him, but there was something off about his appearance that was so subtle, Sarah wondered if she might be imagining it.

Will's lips parted when their gazes met, mouth working almost in slow motion as he shook his head. She squinted, trying to make out the words but too distracted by the fact that Will was in Oklahoma, on her campus, in the twenty-first century. Every instance they'd spent together slammed into her, washing over her in a flood and bringing out the ache in her chest that had become a constant companion these past months, one that was tactfully ignored but always there, like a quiet, throbbing pulse. The sight of him reminded her just how much she had missed him, how she cared for him, and how he should not be here.

He took a step, eyes as big as saucers as he moved forward, motioning with one hand for her to come his way. He looked alarmed as he advanced toward her, though his movements were off somehow, slow and wavering. The boys walked in front of him, the mattress blocking him from view. She stood on tiptoe to see over it, eyes searching.

"Miss Matthews."

She bit back a shriek and spun to find her professor behind her, smiling cordially. On instinct, she whipped her head back to see the mattress bobbing along, but Will was nowhere in sight. She blinked, swallowing over how silly she had been to think he was here and not a million miles away, though she couldn't keep her eyes from roving the grounds for another moment in deluded hope. He had looked so real. . . .

Her heart rate returned to normal, though the pain in her chest, lying dormant for so long, throbbed noticeably now. No, she told herself dully, Will is dead to this world, and you'll never see him in it.

With a small exhale, she turned back to the man. "Professor Demetrius, what are you still doing here? I'd have thought you'd be just as eager to go on vacation as the rest of us."

He grinned pointedly. Most girls on campus were in love with the professor of medieval history, a class Sarah had quickly added to her course list after her most recent trip to Serimone. Demetrius was younger—in his mid-thirties—with dark hair and chiseled features, and had a British accent that was smooth enough to cause several girls in class to sigh dreamily whenever he spoke.

"And yet, here you are, as well," he commented.

She smiled in return, knowing he'd caught her, though her heart had yet to quiet.

"Your final assignment on the tyrannical reign of Prince John was quite fascinating and rather passionate, for a creative essay. What made you decide to write on the subject, if you don't mind my asking?"

"Let's just say I felt connected to the topic and the era." Understatement of the century, she thought, masking her grin by brushing a finger under her nose. She'd had to do a little rearranging to make Cadius' evil plots and storyline fit in with Prince John's, but it had practically felt like journaling as she penned her "fictional" paper.

"Whatever your inspiration, I appreciated your thoughts. It felt as though I was reading a biography from someone who had been there during the Holy Wars." Sarah hid her smile, and Professor Demetrius dipped his head in farewell. "I suppose I should be going. I have a dissertation to get through that might take until the next turn of the century," he said wryly.

Sarah chuckled. "Have a nice break, Professor."

He smiled, giving her a slight wave as he walked down the sidewalk toward his car, greeting Todd as the younger man made his way onto the school grounds. They stopped to chat—to see how Todd's scientific "breakthrough" was progressing, no doubt.

With a cringe, Sarah spun on her heels before the science genius spotted her and hastened toward the campus café. She could hide out in there until he went inside the science building where he and a few of the professors were working on lengthy projects during the break.

Keeping her head down as she jogged across the grass, she wrapped her arms around her middle and peeked over her shoulder. No sign of Todd, or her Will-delusion.

Sarah yanked open the door to the coffee shop/bookstore, upsetting the bell above the door, and stepped into the warmth. Stomping her boots on the large entry mat, she chastised her wayward mind for letting herself think for even a moment that Will could have traveled into the future, or that he did so to see her. It was foolish to entertain thoughts of him following her to her time and being content to leave behind the only home—and era—he had ever known.

Why was she thinking about him now? Not that she had ever managed to push him from her thoughts for an entire day, but why the sudden, entirely realistic hallucinations? She knew that's what he had been; he had seemed as perfect as she remembered and yet somehow too strange to be tangible, as though he wasn't moving in line with the world and he might dissolve if she touched him. Will had appeared too perfect and unexpected to be real.

It was a ridiculous line of reasoning, but Sarah knew that it was an appropriate description for her fantasy, since there was no possibility of Will ever coming to her time. But she would see the genuine version of the man soon enough, she reminded herself.

Sarah gave her boot one final stomp and made her way to the register, ordering a drink and drumming her nails on the counter while she waited. She kept shooting anxious glances over her shoulder, out the glass window, over the room, at the vacant chairs in the corner by the bookshelves. The barista gave her an annoyed look as he handed over her coffee, and she stopped her thrumming on the laminate. "Sorry," she mumbled.

Taking her pick of the vacant chairs in her favorite reading nook, Sarah plopped down on the oversized wingback chair and sank into the plush cushion. Surrounded by bookshelves and the smell of coffee and pressed ink, she stared out the floor-to-ceiling window, mind wandering without her realizing it.

Fingering the tree-shaped pendant she always wore, she wondered why Karen hadn't come for her yet. It had already been a couple months since Sarah had left winter in Serimone and returned to the heat of August in Oklahoma. She would have assumed the spring wedding Karen and Seth had planned would be happening by now, and Karen had promised to come for her. Had something happened that prevented her from jumping into the future? Was she all right? Had Cadius gotten to her for taking part in the investigation?

But Sarah was already shaking her head and quickly reminded herself that they had sent Cadius to the gallows for planning the assassination of his brother, the king. And Damien had been transferred to solitary confinement, so he wouldn't be bothering any of them, either.

Sarah took a sip of the steaming beverage to mask her cringe as she recalled her part in putting her supposed "friend" away. He would spend the remainder of his days in a 12x12 cell, thanks to her, and that reminder still pained her.

Stop it, she chided herself. He had a hand in killing the king, and he murdered Edith. He doesn't deserve anyone's sympathy.

But the words meant to console her conscience only made her heart ache. Each day was a confusing tangle of emotions—anger at him for betraying and using her, pain as she recalled his concern that she would be harmed, and a small flicker of warmth in her heart when she thought about his smiles and the joy he expressed when they were together. Although a portion of their friendship—and whatever else it might have turned into—had been a lie, her affection for Damien and his feelings toward her had been genuine. As hard as she'd tried to wipe away the memory of their time together, trying not to think about him only caused his face to stay at the forefront of her mind. She hated to admit it, but she feared Damien was . . .

Sarah breathed a sigh, closing her eyes in pain. "Unforgettable," she finished aloud, her words a small breath of noise in the silence.

The bell on the door jingled, and she opened her eyes. Sarah froze in shock, and then a slow, bemused smile tugged at the corner of her mouth as the redhead in jeans, moccasin boots, and a short-waisted fur coat breezed into the café. Sarah had set her coffee on the table and was already on her feet by the time Karen spotted her.

Karen squealed and ran the rest of the way to her, squeezing her tightly for someone so small.

"How did you find me?" Sarah asked, pulling back.

With a shrug of her slender shoulders, Karen said, "GPS led me to the college, as close to your watch as it could get, but I've been wandering around for an hour trying to find you."

"Oh." Sarah paused. "I thought there might be a cooler explanation than latitudes and longitudes."

Karen laughed. The sound always reminded Sarah of wind chimes swaying in a summer breeze. She wiped a happy tear from the corner of her eye. "It's good to see you, too, Sarah," she remarked teasingly. "It seems like forever since we've been able to talk."

"You should really consider getting a cell tower in Serimone."

Karen guffawed in surprise at her joke. "I'll get right on that and beat Ben Franklin by discovering electricity several hundred years earlier. That won't affect history at all."

Placing a hand to her heart in mock surprise, Sarah gasped and fell to the loveseat by the window. "Sass from Miss Ashmore? Oooh, I'm gonna tell Seth on you. He needs to know what he's getting into."

Karen's green eyes sparkled, and she bit her lip to contain her growing grin as she sat down beside her. "After seeing me nearly everyday for a couple years, I think he knows more about me than he'd like to—the good, the bad, and the ugly."

"Pshaw." Sarah flicked her hand in the air. "I've never heard that man speak one bad word about any woman, especially not you, even if he could find a fault."

Karen looked ready to add something when Sarah gasped. "Wait, is it spring there yet? You two were planning for spring. I didn't miss the wedding, did I? Did you reschedule?" Almost immediately, Sarah pictured Seth and Karen standing together before a large gathering of guests and family, Will among them to greet her. . . .

"Actually," Karen replied, nearly sing-songing the word, "that's why I'm here. I had to wander this enormous campus asking around after you because I didn't want my maid of honor to miss her best friend's wedding tomorrow."

Sarah gaped at her and then gave such a high-pitched squeal that her voice nearly cracked. The barista shot her a dirty look, but she ignored him, planting her fists beneath her chin in excitement and grinning like a fool.

"So it's tomorrow? You're getting married tomorrow? As in the day after today?"

Rolling her eyes, Karen replied, "Yes, that is the general meaning of tomorrow."

"Wow. So soon." Sarah inhaled a deep breath and eyed her friend's expression. "I know you love Seth, but are you sure you don't want to wait a couple years until you're older? You're only nineteen. That's pretty young to be making plans for forever."

A look of such utter peace and contentment passed over Karen's features that Sarah relaxed her shoulders, reminding herself that her friend never would have made such an important decision in haste. "I've thought about that, too, believe me, and Seth and I have discussed it several times and prayed about it. But it's different in Serimone: Marriage is an eternal commitment that isn't taken lightly, and Seth and I are committed to one another for the rest of our lives." Sarah thought she suddenly looked far wiser than her nineteen—maybe it was twenty now?—years should allow. "And I know that we're mature enough to pledge faithfulness to our union and remain true to our marriage."

Karen shrugged, the corner of her mouth tipping in faint humor as she added, "Seth will drive me bonkers with his ridiculous jokes, and my stubborn independence will send him up a wall, I'm sure. But in the end, we're both sticking with each other for the rest of our lives, come what may."

Swallowing at her passion for her union and husband-to-be, Sarah gave a wobbly smile. "Maybe you and Seth can swing by the future to counsel newlyweds on commitment."

Raising a red brow, Karen shook her head. "That could be a tad difficult to explain to Seth, and you know he isn't good with speeches."

Sarah laughed. "Yeah, I see your point, although he might die seeing you in this getup. In a good way, of course."

Karen pulled at the tight fabric of her jeans with a grimace, squirming in her seat. "How do you even breathe in these, anyway? It's like a meat casing around my thighs. I think I can actually feel the absence of blood in my lower extremities."

Chuckling, Sarah remarked, "I think it helps if you buy a new pair as you grow."

"Oh." Karen frowned, seeming to realize that she might have grown out of them as they lay unused in her trunk stashed in the Joneses' barn. Brushing the topic aside, she asked, "So what are you drinking?"

"Funky Monkey." Sarah picked up the paper cup from the table and choked on a laugh when she caught Karen's expression. "Hot cocoa with espresso, banana syrup, and caramel. Don't worry—no monkeys were harmed in the making of this beverage. My dentist, however, might stage a coup."

"Sounds like a sugar coma waiting to happen." Sarah had to chuckle at that. A look of sweet contentment passed over Karen's fair features. "I've missed laughing with you."

"Me too." The friends smiled at each other, and it seemed that no time had passed between them, though the gap in eras that separated them was vast.

Karen suddenly noticed Sarah's gray sweater beneath her vest. Her expression turned incredulously amused. "Are those salamanders riding kites on your shirt?" She narrowed her eyes. "And I think that one it tossing a cowboy hat in the air."

"What? He's excited because he's riding in the clouds! And they're turtles, not lizards." When Karen looked ready to laugh, Sarah felt the need to add in defense, "Turtles are cute."

Karen bit her lip to mask her giggles. "They're adorable, especially when they're riding a kite like it's a horse."

Sarah feigned indignation and huffed. "I'm going to wear this sweater forever so that you learn to love it."

“I’m sure I would, in time. Where’s your watch?” Karen asked suddenly, voice quavering with repressed laughter.

“It’s back in my dorm room. Why?”

“Well, it wouldn’t be very wise for us to let my maid of honor get stranded in a foreign land.” She smiled. “And we’d better hurry; I can’t be late for my own wedding, now, can I?”

Chapter Two

"True friends are always together in spirit."

L.M. Montgomery, *Anne of Green Gables*

The two young women ran across the grass, rolling clouds escaping their lips the instant their breath encountered the crisp air. Sarah glanced over her shoulder at the tree line, her stomach a jumble of nerves. A shadow moved through the trees, and she grabbed Karen's hand, dropping them both into a crouch at the side of the building.

"We can't let him see you," Sarah whispered, sucking in deep gulps of air. "It will ruin everything . . . if he spots you."

Karen nodded mutely beside her, trying to quietly fill her lungs.

They watched in silence as the man moved from the woods and toward the structure they hid behind, boots crunching over patches of half-frozen tundra. He was going to spot them if they didn't move, but there was nowhere else to hide.

Sarah looked over at her friend and knew she couldn't let her be discovered. Launching herself to her feet, she stepped out of the shelter the building offered and glared at the man before her. "Don't come any closer!"

He stopped, surprised to find her lurking in the shadows. "What are you doing here?"

"Protecting Karen's future. I told you it's bad luck to see the bride before the wedding!"

Seth chuckled. "Your theory is absurd. . . . So, she is with you, then?"

Sarah planted her hands on her hips. "Like I'd tell—"

"Hi, honey!" The invisible girl waved her hand around the side of the Joneses' house.

"Karen!"

Seth chuckled at Sarah's outburst. "I knew you were hiding back there. How are you, beautiful?"

"Ready to get married."

Sarah huffed at the sky. "Why do I bother? Seth, you knew that we were going to get ready at the house this morning, so you and Josh were supposed to go for a long walk and then wait in the barn. Your mom hasn't given you the 'go' sign, has she?" She tapped her foot on the ground, awaiting his response.

Seth's easy grin appeared to be a permanent fixture on his face that day. He covered his eyes with a big hand. "Are you pleased? I haven't seen my bride-to-be, so no harm done to the sanctity of our marriage, according to your silly fable."

"I guess not," Sarah responded slowly, eyeing him suspiciously. He waited there, expectant smile in place, which caused her own grin to appear. "She isn't coming out until you lock yourself inside that barn, but nice try. Where's Josh?"

"I lost my escort in the forest." His nose twitched in humor beneath his palm.

Sarah couldn't help it. She guffawed at his pleased expression, knowing he'd been hoping to catch a glimpse of Karen before their nuptials. "You're relentless."

He gave her an enormous smile to let her know her assessment pleased him. She was just winding up with a sassy retort when Joshua came bounding through the trees, panting as he searched the clearing.

"Josh!" Sarah called, motioning him over. Seth's younger brother threw his hands in the air when he spotted them.

"I tried my best, but this oaf had me running in circles." Joshua jogged up to them and punched his brother good-naturedly in the arm. Seth grinned unrepentantly beneath his hand. "Is the plan foiled?"

Sarah began shoving the half-blind Seth toward the barn. "Not if you can keep him inside until we get Karen ready. Your mom will come for you both when you can move about freely."

Joshua came up beside her and whispered uncertainly, "What's the point of this again?"

"It's so he doesn't see Karen before the wedding and ruin their marriage with bad luck." Seth was already shaking with laughter, and she rolled her eyes. "Oh, forget it. I can't explain it to boys. Just keep an eye on Seth until someone comes and gets you both." She walked away, muttering to herself, "Honestly, is it so much to honor tradition?"

"I'll see you soon, lovely," Seth called over his shoulder, still covering his eyes like an idiot.

"'Bye." Sarah could tell from the way her friend's voice wobbled that she was laughing.

"I honestly don't know how you're going to live with him," Sarah remarked, coming around the corner and helping Karen to her feet. She tried to sound putout even as she felt a smile tugging at the corner of her mouth.

Karen chuckled. "He'll definitely keep our marriage interesting, that's for sure."

Hurrying her inside the house before Seth did another impromptu peek, Sarah retorted, "Well, there won't be a wedding if we don't get you ready in time."

Her friend's light laughter filled the space. "I feel like you're more eager for this wedding than Seth and I."

"I doubt that." But Sarah was looking forward to it more than she could say at the moment. Last night at supper, Seth had casually mentioned that Will would be standing by him during the ceremony, and when little Leah jumped into the conversation—something about flowers and garlands—the whole family joined in a discussion about the upcoming nuptials. But Sarah missed every word.

A stampede of horses ran circles around Sarah's middle with the reminder that she would see Will again—the first time in months that they would lay eyes on each other. Did he look different, older? Had he changed? Had she?

But now wasn't the time for fantasizing about the moment when she would breeze down the staircase and he would smile at her and toss her onto his horse, where they would ride off into the sunset. Although that doesn't sound too bad, she mused to herself. Right now it was time to get Karen ready for her wedding, and Ruth and Leah Jones were already sweeping the bride-to-be into the main room, where they had a plethora of cosmetics and jewelry littering the square table they'd had the men bring in earlier that morning.

Taking a deep breath, Sarah joined the others, determined to make this a memorable day for her friends.

ꟼ

Pursing her lips, Sarah twirled a strand of silky red hair around the iron that Ruth had heated over the fire. Karen's tresses were too silky to hold much of a shape, and she had to heat each strand twice before it came out half as good as she wanted.

"This is a bit trickier than the plug-in curlers I'm used to," she muttered. "I'll try not to burn either of us or make you bald."

Karen laughed, sounding a little more jittery than she had earlier. "That would be much appreciated."

"So how is it that you two are having such a casual wedding?" Sarah could tell her friend's nerves were getting to her, and she hoped talking would calm her. "I wasn't sure if it would be allowed."

"I wanted our wedding to be more traditional in the way that I'm used to—a maid of honor, a father walking his daughter down the isle, an outdoor wedding—and Seth understood that." Karen was still talking quickly, but at least her hands had stopped shaking. "You know that most ceremonies can only be conducted in the Church, but after all you guys did in discovering the king's murderer and turning Cadius and everybody else over to the court, Will was able to call in a favor to King Adrian and the queen for us." She laughed in delight, but Sarah was taken aback.

"Prince Adrian has already been crowned king?" Sarah asked, surprised.

Karen nodded, and one stringy, half-curl fell over her eye. "It's been nearly a year since King Josiah's death, and Serimone couldn't be left without a ruler for too long. The coronation occurred shortly after you left and was entirely uneventful, although Will was invited to attend. Speaking of Will," she added slyly, "when Queen Meredith heard that he was a friend of yours, she immediately secured a priest who would be willing to conduct a ceremony outside of the Church. That ivory hair comb is a gift from her; Will delivered it."

Biting her lip to keep her sudden smile at bay, Sarah shot a brief glance at the gorgeous hair accessory lying on the table and remarked, as evenly as she could manage, "That was thoughtful of him to do all that, and I'm glad it worked out for you."

Karen seemed to sense that her words tactfully lacked any emotion, and she turned a saucy grin her way. "As soon as we had the arrangement set, I told Seth that where I'm from, the bride and groom both pick someone to stand by them. I had no idea he would choose Will. I hope it isn't too much of an imposition."

"I think I'll survive." But the wait was horrible, and the butterflies seemed to multiply each second. She could only imagine how the bride felt.

Pulling the last curl free of her silken red hair, Sarah put a few pins up to her mouth and held them between her lips as she arranged the loose waves on Karen's head. She tried to pin the strands strategically so they fell in a waterfall of red that flashed streaks of deep gold when they caught the light from the open window. Leaning back with a mouthful of pins, she surveyed her work and frowned. It was unbalanced, pieces hung limply amidst the pile, and pins were popping out everywhere.

Karen patted her head. "Does it look all right?"

The left corner of Sarah's mouth twitched in dissatisfaction, and she pulled the pins from her mouth and dropped them on the table. "It's just too much, and I didn't do it right. And it makes you look plastic-y." She hesitated. "Have you ever seen Toddlers and Tiaras?"

The petite girl squinted in confusion and then chuckled. "No, but I get the general picture. So this style is out?"

"I just don't think I can get it to stay." Sarah began sliding pins from the strands, tossing them onto the table with the others. Karen's hair fell in soft, uneven waves against her back, and Sarah tapped her fingers as she tried to think up another fashion that would suit her friend.

"Plan B it is, then." Karen reached behind her head and separated her hair, tugging and tucking the strands into a thick braid.

Smiling, Sarah handed over a thin strip of leather for her to tie off the end. "That looks more like you. Although"—she picked up the intricately carved comb and gently slid it into Karen's hair, angling it just above the top of the twists she'd made—"this makes it look like you're going to your own wedding. It's a small difference, but subtly is everything, darling."

Karen fingered the curved base of the ivory hairpiece. "I love it." Swiveling in the chair to face her, she whispered, "I'm so glad you could be here with me today."

"Me too." Sarah smiled. "It's kind of amazing to think that we were thrown together by some random circumstance. Imagine if you hadn't dropped your watch in that puddle." So much would be different. But she didn't want to think about life without these people, because envisioning a future without their warmth seemed dismal and terrifying. She knew it was only scary because it was possible. One day she would leave this place for good, and she couldn't take any of these beautiful people home with her.

Leah suddenly burst through the front door, saving Sarah the trouble of explaining why she looked so upset all of a sudden. The tall young girl left the door open behind her, hurrying toward them with an armload of flowers atop a small wrapped parcel, wearing a huge smile. "I want to sprinkle some on the ground outside." When she looked at Karen's hair, her smile dimmed somewhat. "I thought you were going to put it up. Wait!" she cried, shuffling over to them. She emptied her load unceremoniously on the table and selected a few of the smallest pink and yellow wildflowers. Handing several to Sarah, she explained, "We can use the stems to weave them into the braid."

Smiling with fondness at the young woman, Sarah nodded, slipping and tugging one long stem at a time through the looped strands. Leah helped her arrange them, and in a few minutes, the job was done and Karen's tresses looked like a silky red flowerbed.

Leah let out a tiny squeal of delight. "It's marvelous."

"Indeed." Ruth Jones smiled at the girls as she preceded her husband into the room, his arms loaded with layers of thick fabric, though the weight was no trouble for the big man. "Over there," his wife, the self-appointed director of the wedding, motioned with a flick of her hand to the chair in the corner. Samuel laid the dresses over the back of the chair he'd handcrafted with more gentleness than a man his size should possess.

He turned and surveyed his daughter-in-law to-be and grinned. The expression caused him to look so much like Seth that Sarah bit her lip to keep from smiling. "That looks like our girl."

Sarah couldn't be sure, but she thought Karen's eyes might have sparkled with joyful tears before she ducked her head.

"Thank you, dear, but the ladies must dress now," Mrs. Jones said, the petite woman shooing her grinning husband out the door. The three girls shared a look before she spun around with a huff of satisfaction and went to the chair in the corner. Picking up the white gown and leaving the green one slung over the chair back, she held it up for Karen's inspection. "You haven't seen it since the alterations were made. What do you think?"

The dress was simple but perfectly elegant, with drooping eyelet sleeves that brushed the floor as Ruth held it. Karen nodded and barely managed to whisper a quick "It's wonderful" before the older woman snapped her fingers—no easy task, as she still held the gown—and told the girls to help the bride out of her robe. Karen stood in her underdress by the fire, trying to keep warm as Mrs. Jones and Sarah helped to slide the dress over her head, taking care not to crush the flowers woven throughout her braid. The fabric slid down over her hips, clinging in all the right places and hanging off of her delicate shoulders. It brushed the floor, barely covering Karen's tried-and-true boots that she'd refused to give up, even at Ruth's insistence.

The older woman worked to tug the sleeves into perfect order, and Leah handed the white sash to Sarah. She tied it around Karen's slender waist, letting the loose ends fall to the floor over her hips, and she couldn't help smiling. Karen was stunning. "You look like a real bride," she remarked.

"Thanks." Karen took a deep breath. "You need to get ready, too."

Sarah glanced down at her plain gown and whispered so only Karen could hear, "It's not like I brought anything from home to change into, not that any of my dresses would be era-appropriate, anyway." Now that she knew Will was somewhere outside, probably getting ready with Seth, she wished she'd thought to purchase some spectacular medieval gown back home and showed up in Serimone dressed to impress.

Her shoulders stooped a little. It wasn't the end of the world, she knew, but she had at least hoped to look her best when she met Will again after months of separation and prayed he hadn't built her up in his mind, only to be disappointed when he saw her in this drab gown.

"I have you covered," Karen whispered back, breaking into her haze.

Confused, Sarah began, "What do you—?"

"Sarah, dear, do get ready." Mrs. Jones stood behind her future daughter-in-law, smoothing invisible stray hairs back into order and adjusting the flowers in her hair. "Karen already picked out your dress—it's over there on the chair. I will fix your hair, if need be, but make haste about it!"

Closing her mouth and biting back her grin, Sarah moved over to the corner to inspect the other forgotten dress Sam Jones had brought in earlier. The velvety fabric was a deep green, with detailing lining the sleeves and decorating the sections of the bodice that closed over the gold under-dress.

"Can I help?" Leah was suddenly behind her. Together, the two girls managed to unstrap Sarah from her gown and down to her plain gray shift. Even with the younger girl's help, Sarah still had to wriggle herself into the green ensemble, though once past her hips, it fit like it was made for her. The extra length of fabric fanned across the wood floor, creating a short trail of green behind her. She yanked the flared sleeve over her wrist to hide the watch she wore, having decided that the safest place to hide the contraption was on her person. But she needn't have worried about Leah questioning the presence of the modern device; the girl had already gone to work cinching the fabric closed, crisscrossing the green leather ties over the golden bodice, and her attention was occupied with restricting Sarah's breathing.

She clutched her abdomen when the girl yanked the strings tighter. "That might be a bit much."

Catching her grimace of pain, Leah winced in sympathy and loosened the ties. "Sorry. Is that better?"

"Much," Sarah answered on a grateful breath. Leah finished tying a long, thick band of gold fabric around each of her biceps and nodded when she finished. "Do you need help arranging the rest of the flowers?" Sarah asked her. While Mrs. Jones had spent most of the day indoors preparing the food with the assistance of a few other women, Leah had been working outside for most of the day, helping to move benches into place and decorating the seating with fresh-cut wildflower bouquets. She'd planned to cover the aisle—the short stretch of patchy earth between the benches—with flower petals.

Leah shook her head. "I'm nearly finished." She went over to the table, picked up the remaining flowers they hadn't used for Karen's hair, and then skipped toward the door. Peeking outside, she shot a toothy smile over her shoulder and sing-songed, "Guests are arriving."

No one but Sarah seemed to notice the spark of trepidation that shot over Karen's pale features.

"Oh, heavens!" Ruth cried, appearing suddenly panicked. Her Irish accent, faded with time, thickened as she began giving orders, seeming to tick items off a mental list. "Finish with the flowers quick as ye can, Leah. And tell Joshua that the guests must be directed to their seats. The Muelsons cannot sit next to the produce vendor; they might be poor, but they stick up their noses at—"

"Dagwood's invited?" Sarah perked up a little at that. She had only met the man a few times, but she instantly pictured his kind eyes and quick, weathered smile.

"And his son, Richard, too." Leah looked more interested in this fact than she had in anything the whole day, which was saying a lot, since her level of enthusiasm had been at an all-time high for the past six hours.

Mrs. Jones gasped. "And the pies! They need to be removed from the fire. Tell Brigeeda—oh, never mind, I shall do it myself." She gave Karen and Sarah a grave look. "Do not go outside." And then she was moving, hustling Leah out the door and closing it behind them.

Soft giggles floated on the air, and Sarah turned to find Karen covering her mouth, shoulders shaking. Sarah couldn't hide her grin. "Has she been like this ever since she found out that you and Seth were getting married, or is this a recent development?"

Karen's laugh was a gust of pent-up anxiety being released. "I've been letting her plan the entire thing. I think she needed to feel like an integral part of her first child's wedding, and you know how she likes to take care of everyone and everything."

Smiling in agreement, Sarah remarked, "That was really selfless of you to let her take over, though, and plan her dream wedding for you two."

"Thanks, but I didn't mind letting her handle all the details—actually, I was relieved she wanted to delegate tasks and make lists and plan everything down to a T, because it means more to her than it does to me. All I really care about is getting married outdoors to the man I love and"—she linked her arm through Sarah's—"having you standing by my side."

"You know I wouldn't miss this for the world."

Karen's look turned suddenly wicked. "You told me once that Will likes green, so you're welcome in advance, though I'm not even sure that he'll notice what you're wearing. He's so incredibly transparent in his eagerness to see you, though he tries not to show it—"

"You've seen Will?" Sarah shook her head. "Of course you have. You told me he and Seth have gotten close again. . . . So, does he ever mention me?"

Karen's lips tipped knowingly. "It's not so much that he talks about you often. But he'll become suddenly alert if someone mentions your name at the table when he comes over for dinner, or he'll casually ask questions about whether or not we've heard from you. And sometimes when Seth's mom would bring up the wedding, Will would just stare off into space, and I could tell he was thinking of you." Sarah bit her lip to mask her smile of pleasure. "In all honesty, I think he's been looking forward to today as much as Ruth."

Sarah laughed, though she hoped her friend's words held a kernel of truth. "Then good choice on the dress."

"I just wanted to remind him of what he's been missing for five months."

Ducking to hide her grin behind her hair, Sarah took a better look at herself. The gold dress whispered lightly against the wood as she moved it from side to side, watching as the natural light coming through the cracked window reflected off the fabric. Gold designs and scrolling lined every edge of the green overcoat, which hung off her shoulders and dipped into a V that showed off her pendant. The sleeves were two-toned, with the green fabric ending just above her elbows and turning into gold sleeves that flared slightly around her wrists. The thick band of gold ribbon nearly dragged on the floor when Sarah's arms were relaxed at her sides, hiding the intersection of the two tones of material. The entire ensemble looked terribly expensive . . . and familiar.

Wrinkling her brow, Sarah asked, "Haven't I seen this dress before?"

"Hmm? Oh, yes, it's from your room at the castle. All of your dresses just stayed in the wardrobe after you left. I can't remember if they were going to throw them away or recycle them, but Will managed to convince the queen to give them to us to keep for you here when you visit. They were all yours, technically, since Damien had them all brought to you, and so I guess she had no problem with you keeping what was rightfully yours. The fact that Will was asking probably had something to do with it, too."

"So they're all here?" Karen nodded proudly. "That was nice of him to think of it." Blinking away thoughts of Will before they could take root in her mind and grow, Sarah voiced a concern that had been on her mind for months. "I left so quickly after what happened, and I barely saw everyone after my fall in the lake."

"You mean when you nearly died?" Karen suddenly looked grave.

Sarah nodded, scratching anxiously behind her ear at the reminder that she had come close to losing her life. "I just never heard what they thought of my staying at the castle or everything that went on while I was there."

"Well," Karen began slowly, "the thing is that they were definitely curious about what you'd seen and heard during the excitement, since you were the one who came back and told us about Cadius' conviction in the king's murder, but they never seemed to consider that you actually had a part in putting him away."

"So you didn't tell them about Damien?"

"There isn't anything to tell, is there?" Karen asked carefully.

Sarah sighed. "No. Not really. I was just curious if they were aware that I'm partly the reason Damien's in prison."

"Only if you want to tell them."

"No, I'd rather keep it between us. The less I talk about him, the farther away he seems, which is for the better." Sarah nodded her head, the action decisive, but she wasn't sure her heart was in her words. She worried her lower lip, which Leah had painted with crushed red berries earlier that day, and stopped abruptly, hoping she hadn't smudged it.

Karen watched her expression closely. "You don't still feel guilty over what happened to him, do you?"

"A little," she answered honestly. "I have no doubt in my mind that I did the right thing, but I'll always have a little part of me that wishes I could have fixed him. Silly, I know." She fingered a small arrow on the table, rubbing her thumb back and forth across the forest-green feather.

Karen wrapped an arm around her shoulders, offering comfort. "I hope that one day you can forgive yourself, because you did nothing wrong."

Sarah's voice was quiet. "I know that." But I could have done things differently, that ever-present voice reminded. Then maybe . . . It was no use, though. Sarah had worked out a hundred different scenarios over the past few months, and each one ended in Damien being sentenced as he'd been or executed for all to see. She wasn't sure which one he would consider the crueler fate.

Karen caught the way her fingers played with the little arrow. "That is a little wedding gift from me to you. I found it in the marketplace a few weeks ago and thought it might remind you of your adventures with the Shadow. And it goes perfectly with the dress, if I do say so myself." Her voice was unnaturally chipper, and Sarah knew it was for her.

"Wait, I'm sorry, is the bride-to-be trying to cheer me up and give me counseling on her big day?" she quipped, following along with the lighter topic.

"Yes," Karen answered with a single bob of her head. Her mouth tipped. "I can't very well enjoy 'my' day when my best friend isn't one hundred percent."

Sarah cringed. "I wasn't thinking." Straightening, she said determinedly. "I am not going to put a damper on this wedding, and we're only talking happy things from now on."

"But I don't mind discussing it."

Sarah raised a hand to stop her, knowing her words rang true. "We are not spending your last few minutes as a single woman talking about past issues of mine. Nuh-uh. Today is about the union between you and that big loveable baboon you're marrying." Karen chuckled.

"Only smiles and joy are allowed at this wedding," Sarah added, "and there will be no more serious talk today. We'll have plenty of time to catch up later." Though she wasn't sure that was true. She pictured the small cabin that Seth had built for the two of them, visible from the Joneses' garden—a temporary home until they could find land of their own to build on. When that happened, Sarah knew there would be no middle-of-the-night talks with Karen in the loft, because she would be miles and years away.

Karen's mirth faded a little. "You know we'll still see each other, right? I mean, you can come to me anytime. We can just kick Seth out of the house for the day."

Shaking her head, Sarah grinned, though a heaviness still clung to her heart, tangling with the joy residing there over her friend's happiness. It felt impossible to think that they had known each other for a few months, but in that time Karen had become her best friend, and she had a difficult time considering life completely devoid of her presence. The fact that her two friends would be united was both elating and also gave her a sense that she was losing a piece of her friendship with Karen, one that would be given to Seth, instead.

"Sounds like a plan," Sarah said at last, mustering a genuine smile for her friend. "Now, let's put the focus back on you, future-Mrs. Jones."

Karen giggled. "Can I at least do your hair before the ceremony? Please? I guarantee it will make me feel superbly happy."

Sarah succumbed with a roll of her eyes. "If the bride wishes it."

"I do." Pulling another chair over by the fire, Karen set to work on her auburn waves, pulling a few of the curls away from Sarah's face and creating a loose bun at the back of her head, leaving the rest of her hair flowing freely down her back and about her shoulders. Karen used one hand to hold the curly twist in place and reached for the small arrow, stabbing it into the bun so that it held. She gently ran her fingers through the length of hair that cascaded down Sarah's back to separate her curls.

"Finished," she announced happily, loudly kissing her fingertips in a self-satisfied way.

Sarah gingerly touched the tip of the feather. Karen had said she'd given it to her to remind her of the Shadow, but she couldn't have known it would hold meaning for both her and Will. When she slid her fingers down to make sure the twist was secure, she suddenly remembered Will touching the ends of her hair with reverence that time in the forest when Damien had been fast on their heels. Biting her lip at the feelings the memory stirred up, she mumbled past her grin, "It's great, Karen. Thank you."

The front door suddenly burst open, and both girls turned to find Leah, flushed and wearing the largest smile Sarah had ever seen. "It's time. Mama said that you're supposed to meet me at the front by Seth, and then Karen will come down after we're in our positions. Oh, and you're supposed to open that package before the ceremony." And with that, she flitted out into the yard, leaving the door open.

Karen picked up the forgotten parcel on the table and untied the ribbon. The napkin unfolded, revealing a carefully twined wreath of white daisies resting, unharmed, in the center. It took Sarah a moment to remember walking in on the intimate scene of Karen teaching Seth to make flower crowns, and she wondered if that moment marked the day that he realized he was in love with the girl who lived in their barn.

Pale fingers reached out to stroke one of the petals. "I can't believe he remembered," Karen whispered.

"I guess all those lessons finally paid off." Gently removing the crown from the folds of fabric, Sarah set it atop her friend's hair and smiled. "There. Now you look like the angel you are. . . . Wasn't that what Seth said before?"

Karen giggled. "Something like that. It isn't too much with everything?" But she didn't wait for an answer. She took a deep breath and exhaled slowly. "I guess that's the final touch, then."

Despite her struggle for calm, Sarah's pulse raced nervously for both she and her friend. "Are you ready for this?"

Karen's smile was angelic. "I've been ready for centuries. And you?"

"You're the one getting married, and you're acting like I'm the anxious one."

Quirking a brow, Karen remarked, "Well, you are. I'm as calm as . . . things that are calm. Like a cucumber."

Sarah wished she had one tenth of her poise and confidence. She thought about standing in front of a group mostly comprised of strangers and of walking down an aisle toward a man she hadn't seen in months, and her stomach did a full flip. Taking a deep breath that her tight bodice barely allowed, she clutched her necklace for strength and said dryly, "As ready as I'll ever be. Let's just hope that neither of us trips before we reach the end."

Chapter Three

"But now, you are twain, you are cloven apart,
Flesh of his flesh, but heart of my heart."

Algernon Charles Swinburne, "The Triumph of Time"

The majority of the snow had melted, and the sun was out, though the barest chill of winter still clung to the breeze. Sarah sucked in a grateful breath of the crisp afternoon air as she rounded the house, her feet feeling like lead. Her train dragged behind her, making a soft *shh* sound against the small tufts of grass that had fought to come early that May.

Pulse racing and tongue suddenly thick, she came around the corner and spotted the dense trail of flower petals that Leah had used to mark the aisle. Bouquets of wildflowers had been tied to the end of each bench with pink and white ribbons to decorate the plain wood seats that were occupied by the small gathering, not much more than thirty townsfolk, who had all turned around in their seats to stare at her. This type of procession must be new to them, and Sarah ducked her head a little in embarrassment at being the center of attention, counting the seconds until she reached the opposite end of the aisle and it would be Karen's turn to be ogled, as she rightfully should.

Sarah had been unbothered by her friend's choice to nix the bouquets, but now she wished she had something to hold onto, something to keep her nervous hands from twitching awkwardly at her sides as she walked. Sarah told herself to lift her chin, and she caught Seth's coy grin, though it wasn't for her. Following his line of sight, she glanced to his left—past an anxious-looking Joshua—and her heart and stomach lurched at the same time.

William Taylor stood there in the flesh, wearing a new coat and gray tunic, and his chest rose and fell, seeming to suck in a deep breath when she looked at him. His wavy black hair—shorter than she remembered—had been tamed, though that wayward lock had ignored his ministrations and fell stubbornly over his forehead. But it was his eyes that caught her attention, as perfectly dark blue as she had imagined and trained, unmoving, on her.

Seth glanced at Sarah, grin still in place, and raised his eyebrows knowingly. She felt a blush steal over her cheeks, but she didn't care as she returned Will's stare, her mouth tipping unbeknownst to her as she gave a tiny, almost imperceptible two-finger wave for him alone. He caught the gesture, and his eyes narrowed a little as his lips curved slowly. When she realized it was impossible to hold back her nervous smile, she bit her lower lip and dropped his gaze, telling her pulse to slow and her mouth to stop tipping upward.

Taking her place beside Leah, whose smile could not get any bigger, she turned around and faced the spot where she knew Karen would appear, forcing her eyes to stay glued to that place in the grass even as they itched to return the gaze she felt on her.

A hush stole over the murmuring gathering as Karen made her entrance, moving gracefully over the grass. Sarah shot a quick glance at the groom and saw Seth swallow hard, muscles in his cheeks twitching, looking as though he was trying not to cry. She accidentally caught Will's gaze again, full of things she didn't quite understand and that made her heart lurch, and quickly trained her eyes back on Karen.

The girl-turned-woman was a vision in her white gown, her red braid spilling over one bare shoulder, a stark contrast against the pale and colorful flowers woven into the knots. She moved slowly down the aisle, a contented smile on her lips as she and Seth locked gazes. Neither seemed to notice his smiling family or the way Mrs. Jones blew her nose softly into a handkerchief, or any of the others gathered to celebrate their union. There was no music—the small band comprised of local musicians had been reserved for the gathering after the ceremony—but Sarah thought she might have heard Karen humming the wedding march softly to herself as she neared the end. She appeared completely at ease and so sure of herself that Sarah relaxed at the front, reminding herself that everyone was captivated with this lady in white.

Karen took her place beside Seth, who had to quickly wipe the corner of his eye before grabbing both small hands in his and kissing the backs of each one before letting their clasped hands fall between them. The large, tender-hearted farm boy sucked in a shuddering breath, and Sarah caught him mouth the words, "You look stunning, my bride."

Karen's smile grew, and the whole gathering could hear Ruth's sniffle of joy.

The priest, borrowed from the royal church, looked rather putout to have been ordered to deign to perform for such a small gathering outside of the holy sanctuary. However, he seemed to stiffen his shoulders, appearing suddenly professional, and told the couple to face him and kneel. They did so, but kept their hands clasped together at their sides, remaining linked throughout the ceremony as the priest began a slow speech in what Sarah presumed to be Latin. Though the words were lost on her, the two being united appeared to understand their meaning, nodding every so often in agreement.

Their eyes conveyed the promise of a future, and Sarah felt her throat tighten over how perfect they looked together, how certain they appeared in their decision to unite their lives. Two futures had never seemed so clear.

After several minutes of confusion for Sarah, the priest conveyed some final, indiscernible message that seemed to announce them as husband and wife, and the bride and groom rose to their feet. Though she hadn't understood a word said during the ceremony, Sarah was almost positive there had been no "You may now kiss the bride," but Seth did anyway, much to the surprise of the crowd. He bent down to plant a soft, half-grin, half-kiss on his bride's lips. Sarah was the first to let out a *whoop* of delight, clapping her hands together in encouragement, and this seemed to crack the uncertainty that had settled in the air. After a split second passed and their shock wore off, the crowd joined her, cheering uproariously and making quite a bit of ruckus for so small a gathering.

Karen pulled away, blushing and laughing. Seth appeared rather pleased with himself, grinning roguishly at his new bride. The crowd cheered, Mrs. Jones shed tears of joy, Joshua heartily clapped his hands, and the priest looked as though this relatively tame hoopla was the very reason why he didn't perform ceremonies outside the Church.

Samuel Jones stood to his full height, silently calling attention to himself as he turned to face the gathering. Everyone quieted. "Thank you all for coming," he began, his deep, calm voice somehow reaching every ear. "We are moving this celebration for Seth and our new daughter, Karen, to the barn. There are chairs, food, and drink both inside and outside, and a band already waiting to perform for those who dare to dance." A light chuckle rippled through the crowd.

His expression, generally bordering on calm amusement at all times, turned at once earnest, his eyes trained on Karen. "And I would like to say how blessed this family has been in the presence of this girl. Daughter, you have been a light to us, filling our house—but usually our barn"—he and Karen shared a secret smile over her sleeping arrangement—"with such warmth. To know that you will flood your own home with immense joy and faith, and that you will spend the rest of your days with our eldest son, acting as a partner in this union as God intended, encouraging and leaning on one another through hard times . . . Well, there is nothing that I want more." He grinned. "And speaking as his father, Seth can certainly use an accountability partner to ensure he abstains from trouble."

Seth rolled his eyes, though he smiled good-naturedly as everyone laughed. Sarah's gaze darted over the crowd, and her eyes caught in surprise at the sight of Charles Ashmore, Karen's adoptive father and the inventor of the time watches. He had been held at the castle by Cadius as a sorcerer, and Sarah was surprised to find him there. Then again, she reasoned, with Cadius out of the way, there wasn't anyone who would try to keep him in servitude at the castle, and she doubted either Queen Meredith or Prince—King—Adrian would hold him against his will.

She gave him a tiny wave when he glanced in her direction. His head bobbed once in acknowledgement, a small smile causing his salt and pepper beard to twitch, before he looked back to the man giving the speech. He squinted his eyes to near slits, probably to see better, since he refused to wear his glasses in public. Sarah tried to gauge his expression, but the man was hard to read. Though she knew he was not overly affectionate, she was still taken aback to find the professor sitting calmly with the others, since he hadn't walked Karen down the aisle.

"But truly," Mr. Jones continued. Sarah dragged her attention away from the professor to find Samuel's face serious once more as he looked at Karen. "I never thought I could be so happy to have my son marry, but the fact that it is to you that he has willingly given his heart gives us immense joy." He placed a large hand on his wife's shoulder, and that woman nodded her head in agreement, beaming through her tears. "Daughter, we love you, and though you were already a part of our family, this day declares what we have felt in our hearts for years. Welcome to the family."

The townsfolk clapped over his beautiful speech, some wiping their eyes, and Karen gave a wobbly smile to him, obviously holding back tears as Seth kissed her knuckles. Sarah knew how much Samuel's words meant to her, declaring her their daughter, as she'd lost her parents when she was young. But there was no denying that on this day she had become part of a tight-knit family that cared for and pestered each other, something she had craved for so long. Sarah had to wipe the corner of her eye when she thought about how full her friend's heart must be, and her own was nearly bursting with happiness for Karen and Seth.

She looked past the couple and saw Will quickly swipe a thumb under his eye; it appeared that not one attendant had been unmoved by the speech. He caught her glance and gave a small smile, taking a step toward her. At that moment, the crowd suddenly surged forward, blocking his path as they surrounded the couple to bestow their good wishes and congratulations on them.

After so long spent hiding in a barn, Karen appeared uncomfortable with all the attention focused on her. But Seth took it all in stride, thanking them for their kindness as he slowly pulled Karen through the foray and out into the open. When it appeared they would pursue them, he looked to Sarah and announced a little too brightly, "I don't believe you have been introduced to our good friend, Sarah Matthews. She has traveled quite a ways to join us."

He shot her a saucy grin as she gaped at him and pulled his laughing bride toward the barn, urging her into a jog before the well-wishers had a chance to follow. Half of the crowd shadowed the couple as they meandered toward the barn, but those remaining turned on Sarah, converging on her to ask questions and pester her about her personal life, where she was from, how she knew the family. Seth had known full well that an outsider was like fodder to these gossipmongers, and Sarah had been his sacrificial lamb. It might be his wedding day, but Seth was in deep trouble.

"Have you seen how they've decorated the barn? Simply charming," one woman commented, pulling her along with the group to see for herself. Sarah didn't bother to mention that she had been the one to help set up earlier in the day and knew precisely how it looked. She glanced over her shoulder at Will in desperation, though his expression was conflicted; he didn't appear to know whether he should be disappointed or laugh at their poor luck.

They had been apart for months, and Sarah had built up their reunion into some grand encounter that ended with him declaring his mad, unending love for her once again and with her being able to express the feeling she'd felt building in her heart as each day ticked closer to their meeting. Yet they hadn't spoken a single word to each other, and already she was being carted away from him. That hardly seemed fair.

Another second ticked by, and Will's lips parted ever so slightly, tipping at one corner to reveal a sliver of white teeth and causing that dimple in his cheek to appear. He lifted his shoulders in a shrug as if to say, "This wasn't how I planned it, either."

The younger woman who was clutching her arm leaned in conspiratorially, though the other women could plainly hear. "The bride and groom are planning to live nearby, in a tiny cabin on a hilltop. Can you imagine, being so far from civilization?" She feigned a shiver. "It's unfathomable. I certainly would have been smart enough to postpone my wedding until better preparations could be made."

Sarah blinked at her, shocked that she would speak so freely against her friends' choices. Hadn't she noticed Sarah standing beside Karen at the alter? She couldn't be so dense as to insult the bride in front of her best friend.

"Excuse me?" Sarah hadn't meant to sound snippy, but the young woman was far too forward for her liking, and she had already decided she didn't like her one iota. "Who are you, anyway?"

Giggling, she squeezed her arm. "Oh, dear, I completely neglected to introduce myself. I'm Marjorie Hernstock, and I cannot tell you how excited I am to have another young woman with whom to share stories."

The "snooty, uppity gossip" Leah had warned her about, Sarah realized as the small troupe stepped past some guests mingling near the tables set up outside the barn. She'd been informed that Marjorie had only been invited because her father owned the butcher shop and her mother was an old friend of Mrs. Jones. Leah had received a scolding from her own mother at hearing her call the girl snooty.

"Well, she is," Leah had whispered the instant her mother turned around, as though the fact of the girl's unpleasantness should be obvious to all who knew her.

Gently disentangling her arm from the girl's as they entered the building, Sarah gave her a smile that felt like plastic on her lips. She hoped her words, dripping with false pleasantness, conveyed her distaste for Marjorie's gossip. "Well, since my good friends are incredibly happy and in no way came to this decision lightly, I feel that I can't be anything but delighted that they can be together. Perhaps some people have the ability to find happiness in their present circumstances, rather than relying on petty things like large houses and diamonds to bring them joy. Now, I think I'll take my leave to go find my friend and her new husband." Sarah caught the way the girl's lower lip dipped in surprise before she spun on her heels and went in search of Karen.

Some people had no filter. Of all the nerve!

She spotted Karen and Seth speaking with a group of individuals, some of whom Sarah vaguely recognized from her time spent in town. Karen caught her gaze, and a look of utter relief washed over her features. "There you are." She excused herself and Seth from the small gathering. Her wide eyes conveyed that Sarah had saved them from a tiresome conversation.

Seth was chuckling by the time they reached her, looking like he was greatly enjoying himself. However, Karen's pale cheeks were flushed, and she looked uncomfortable with the eyes that followed the couple as they moved. "I didn't think we had invited so many people," she hissed when she reached Sarah's side.

Sarah couldn't help smiling. "There are maybe forty people, including our group, who are all here to wish you well and bless you guys." She leaned in so only Karen could hear. "It was nearly a year ago—no one is here to convict you of anything, so relax and enjoy your wedding day," she said, referring to the fact that Gabriel Dunlivey had accused Karen of witchery many months before. Unbeknownst to her, Will had disguised himself as the Shadow to save her from that fate, and Karen had been taking precautions ever since, always looking over her shoulder everywhere she went. But it had been so long ago that Sarah doubted anyone would recognize her, and the man who had accused her was now dead, taking his suspicions with him to the grave.

Fiddling with the end of her silky red braid, Karen nodded, whispering, "You're right, but it just feels odd to have so many paying attention to me. I think I prefer being invisible."

Sarah could think of another resident of Serimone who felt the same way.

"Have you spoken with him yet?" She jerked her head to look at Seth, whose ever-present grin took on a knowing glint.

"Who?" Sarah lifted her brows, feigning a casualness they all knew was forced. Seth's cheeky grin grew, and she quickly shifted the conversation before he could begin teasing her about her clear interest in seeing Will again. "The ceremony was beautiful, although I couldn't understand a word of it," she admitted on a laugh.

"Wasn't it perfect?" Karen smiled at her. "Thank you for helping out so much. I know we threw you right into the middle of the last-minute preparations, but I appreciate you being here."

Sarah gave her an Are you kidding me? look. "Of course. That's what a maid of honor is for. And I must say that you two look pretty cute together."

Seth smiled down at his bride, draping a thick, work-muscled arm over her delicate shoulders. "I'd like to think so." He glanced at Sarah then, look turning playfully regretful. "You know it never would have worked out between us, dearest: two stars shooting in opposite directions, different paths to take. Even with the bet going between us, I knew my heart belonged elsewhere." He sighed dramatically for effect, and Karen rolled her eyes at his antics. He was obviously on an adrenaline high from the ceremony and it was leaking out in waves, heightening his silly nature.

"Wait." Sarah narrowed her eyes at him. "What bet?"

"The one Taylor and I had agreed upon." At her dumb look, he went on slowly, as though she should know this already. "Will and I placed a bet that one of us would win your affections. It was while you were first staying with us. He didn't tell you it was a race?" He winced as Karen elbowed him.

"I can't believe you two would do that!" she whispered harshly. Her eyes turned cautious and sympathetic when she looked at Sarah. "Are you okay? You know that's not why he's here now, right? You can't fake that kind of sincerity." She hesitated. "You're not upset, are you?"

Sarah closed her mouth, absorbing this info. No, Will had never mentioned it to her, but she knew for certain that he hadn't done and said all that he had because of some stupid bet he'd made with Seth months ago. If he chose to be with her now, it was because he wanted to be, and that warmed her insides a little.

Lifting her chin, she said, "First of all, Seth, that is extremely childish and I'm not something to be bought or won."

"Agreed." Karen nodded her head decisively, giving her husband a stern look. He simply grinned, glancing back and forth between the severe expressions of the two girls.

"And second," she went on, pausing mid-speech to lay a quick, gentle slap on the forearm not around Karen's neck. She tried to sound putout when she spouted, "You couldn't have tried a little harder or given me bigger gifts? I mean, I thought I was at least worth an expensive picnic or a sparkly new wagon or even a goat. Sheesh."

Seth howled with laughter, the sound echoing off the rafters and drawing the attention of a few nearby guests. "He will have his hands full with you."

A blush stole over her cheeks, though she couldn't hide her hopeful grin. Seth's own mirth grew. "So you are considering long-term plans with Will. My wife mentioned you have doubts, or there was some obstacle to be overcome, but I am relieved to see you two have been able to work it out. I didn't believe you would lead him on, anyway, but you never can be too sure—"

Karen gave a hard yank on the hand hanging over her shoulder, giving him a disbelieving and reproachful look. "What?" Seth appeared genuinely surprised. "What did I say?"

Scratching her ear to hide her discomfort, Sarah admitted, "Actually, we haven't been able to talk and sort all of that out. Mostly, I might add, because you"—she waved a finger at the big man-boy—"threw me to the wolves out there. I barely managed to get away from that Marjorie girl. Leah told me about her, but I didn't know who she was until it was too late and I got sucked in."

Seth grimaced, the first look of genuine distaste he'd worn in the time since she'd been back. . . . Or ever, that she could remember. "Ah, yes. She can be quite the handful, especially when she sets her mind on 'sharing' with someone." His cheeky look returned, and he gave her an adorably pleading expression. "It is my wedding day, though, so might we call a truce?"

It was impossible to stay mad at the big puppy dog, and Sarah nodded once decisively. "Cease-fire accepted."

"Excellent!"

A man was heading toward them, and Sarah's gazed landed on Professor Charles Ashmore. She had seen him earlier at the ceremony, but she hadn't heard a peep from or seen him since. He looked uncomfortable as he sidled up to the small group, shoving his index finger up the bridge of his nose as though readjusting a pair of invisible glasses. Though he needed them, he had once told Sarah that he could never wear them around town, as it might spark some chain reaction in the space-time continuum if people could enhance their vision too early in society.

The professor was brilliant enough to discover a tear in the fabric of time, but he was also paranoid and just plain eccentric.

He nodded in recognition at Sarah and then reached out to shake Seth's hand. "The groom, I presume?" Sarah tried not to blanch, amazed that the two men were meeting for the first time.

"Seth, this is my father, Charles Ashmore," Karen supplied, smiling at the man with the salt-and-pepper beard.

Seth's eyes brightened, and he shook the smaller man's hand heartily, which seemed to startle the professor. "A pleasure, sir. Karen has told me so much about you."

Gray-flecked eyes widened at once with concern, though Karen subtly shook her head, and Sarah imagined the exchange was over his fear that she had told Seth about where they came from. But Karen wanted to live a normal life here, unburdened with time travel, and Sarah knew for a fact that she had no intention of telling Seth that she was from the future.

"Well." Charles cleared his throat and hiked his non-existent glasses once more. "I just wanted to offer my congratulations before I left."

Karen appeared to deflate before their eyes. "You're going? So soon?"

"I must get back. Science waits for no man." He forced a chuckle, obviously sensing her disappointment.

Sarah raised her brows in surprise. "You're still working at the castle? But Cadius is gone—you're free to go."

"You'll recall I mentioned that I can learn so much here." The professor appeared like he wanted to say more on the subject, but then he shot a pointed glance at Seth that seemed to say, Not in front of the outsider.

Sarah resisted the urge to roll her eyes at his paranoia.

"But you haven't had any dessert yet, have you, Professor?" Karen tried again, sounding cordial enough, though she looked as though she was trying to mask her desperation to keep him there. "Have you met Seth's family? You must meet them before you leave."

"Perhaps another time." He paused, his speckled eyes filling with warmth, and Sarah thought they might have glistened with tears. Leaning down to plant a quick, fatherly kiss on Karen's cheek, he whispered, "I am proud of you, my dear girl." He looked uncomfortable speaking the words but appeared glad to have them out, though Karen's flattened expression didn't change.

"All right, then." She gave him a wavering smile. "I'll see you soon."

He nodded jerkily and moved quickly through the crowd and out of sight as he exited the barn.

"Guess he's still not great with sentiment," Sarah muttered. She regretted her words when she caught Karen's expression.

Her gaze was heavy, and she stared at the ground with a slightly pained look over his abrupt departure. Seth watched his wife's face for a moment, sympathy etching his kind features. Seeming to decide that it was best to divert her thoughts, he quickly pulled his wife in for a tight hug against his side, appearing at once suspicious as his gaze scanned the crowd. "Now our goal is to move through the room to greet the guests without encountering the town gossips."

Karen perked up at once at his effort, and Sarah was glad that he could distract her from the pain of having a father who didn't know how to show love. "A near-impossible task, but one I think we can accomplish," Karen returned playfully. She broke free of her husband to give Sarah a tight hug, whispering in her ear, "I'm so glad you came to be here with us, but now it's time to get your happy ending. Go find him, Sarah, and stop bringing your doubts into each moment with him."

Sarah's throat tightened, and she squeezed her back. "Okay. Also, your husband has gotten weirder."

Karen's delicate laugh caused her to smile. They released each other, and the redhead took hold of Seth's hand and together they made their way through the gathering. Sarah watched them go, the feeling in her heart bittersweet.

Seeking distraction from the excited apprehension in her stomach at the prospect of finding Will, she made her way to one of the tables she and Joshua had moved into the barn earlier. The women had been hard at work in the kitchen, and it was now laden with pies and custards and cakes and little treats that Sarah had never seen before, but that had been donated by several of the guests to contribute to the event.

She selected a small morsel covered in white powder, savoring its lemony tang on her tongue and grinning in delight at her options. She had enjoyed desserts like this at elite castle parties; however, she hadn't expected the lower classes to be able to replicate such delicacies with their meager supplies. She smiled a little, knowing they weren't just fancy sweets, but were a sign of their love for the couple as they represented an investment of time and grand effort.

Her smile slipped from her lips when she glanced up from her musings and caught the eye of Marjorie. Sarah quickly jerked her head down, but not before she saw the girl step in her direction. Blast it all! She quickly reached for a wooden cup and ladled cider into it, hoping to look casual and avoid conversation.

Marjorie came up alongside her, and Sarah managed to hide her cringe as the girl idly picked up a small apple tart, turning it in her hands to examine it, and then placing it back on the platter as she perused her options. Her voice held a casual air when she spoke. "I must apologize for my words earlier. I had no notion of you being in such good company with the bride and groom."

Sarah widened her eyes in annoyed disbelief at the dessert table, doubting that very much, though the girl didn't appear to notice; her expression said that their previous conversation was water under the bridge and that they were back to being friends. Why had this girl latched onto her? Sarah turned around with her glass, leaning against the table as she surveyed the crowd, hoping to think of some polite excuse to leave. Her heart gave a little skip as she spotted Will enter the barn, eyes roving the crowd.

Marjorie leaned toward her, invading her personal space. Sarah shifted another inch to the right. "That man there, the one who stood up with the groom, is the town blacksmith. Not much of a conversationalist, from what I hear and have experienced myself, but he is rather pleasant to look at, as you've noticed. Yet he is established and still remains single, almost insistently so." Her voice turned hushed, as though speaking of his singleness might bring about some unexpected consequence. Her expression said that she believed she was providing the new girl with some tasty information to process.

Sarah held back her grin, and she didn't have to try too hard to look interested in the story as she watched Will's not-so-casual search of the crowd. He was interrupted now and again by some of the townsfolk, and he was attentive to their brief conversations, but the instant they left, his eyes began searching once more. "You don't say," she murmured distractedly, waiting for the moment he spotted her.

Encouraged, Marjorie's voice lost its false indifference that poorly masked her interest in the subject. She leaned closer, keeping her excited tone low. "I heard there was quite the scandal last year with Mr. Taylor and a girl, and then she disappeared after not more than a week, only to return later that winter. Although nothing ever came of it, he is clearly not completely through with her." Her voice turned musing. "I believe her to be a foreigner, though no one appears to know who she is, precisely. "

"Is that so?"

"Yes." She sounded rather putout over it, and Sarah hid her smile behind her cup as she took a sip of the warm cider. When she lowered it, Will's eyes had found hers, and she could hide her smile no longer. She set the cup on the table.

"Please excuse me, Margie. I see someone I need to reacquaint myself with." She made her way through the small gathering, cutting a straight path toward Will, resisting the urge to look back and catch the woman's expression. Though she imagined, with a small spark of pleasure, that Marjorie's jaw had dropped to the hay-covered floor as she realized she'd been speaking to the girl around which her gossipy tales had been centered.

Chapter Four

"To burn always with this hard, gem-like flame."

Walter Pater

She couldn't get to him fast enough, her anticipation and nervousness increasing with each step as she wove her way through the partygoers. But all too soon she arrived before him, wishing she had moved at a slower pace so she had more time to think of what to say. Then again, she'd had months of pretend conversations with Will, and she still had no clue what her first words should be to him after their prolonged separation.

"It's wonderful to see you," he said at last, appearing calmer than she felt. The corner of his mouth twitched in a tiny gesture that came and faded.

Sarah didn't think he knew he was smiling as he took in her full appearance, as if assuring himself that she was truly here. She grabbed a fistful of her skirt to dry her suddenly damp palms. "Hi, Will. It's really great to see you, too." You look incredible. I missed you. You smell amazing. Her thoughts crashed together in her head, embarrassing her at how rapidly they came. When she caught Will's startled look and sudden grin, she realized, much to her mortification, that she had mumbled her last observation aloud.

"Why, thank you."

Heat swept up her neck like wildfire, and Sarah resisted the urge to fan her cheeks, which pulsed in embarrassment. "Is it warm in here? They must have a fire lit somewhere," she said, hoping to blame her heightened color on the suddenly hot room. She cleared her throat.

"You do look flushed," he observed, feigning seriousness. "Would you care to go outside?" She nodded eagerly, grateful he didn't tease her further.

They ducked outside and slowly wandered the gathering there, neither having a destination in mind but both grateful to be together.

"The ceremony was beautiful," Sarah commented to fill the empty space between them.

"Mm. It was at that. They make a lovely pair." He paused to chuckle. "Though I imagine they will both have their hands full taming the other." Seth had said the same thing about her and Will, and she suppressed a grin.

Will seemed to relax a little more in the open air. He was always more comfortable outdoors, and his ease in her presence caused Sarah to drop her anxiety and try to get back to where they'd left off—comfortable and with their feelings out in the open. Or, at the very least, not masking them with small talk.

Sarah's shoulders softened and she unclenched her fists, his calm, steady presence easing away her anxiety. "I'd like to think that some people are made to run wild together."

He looked down at her, his steps slowing, and his eyes softened. Sarah sucked in a breath and turned her head away at the depth of emotion she saw there. Though she loved seeing his honest feelings for her, she was still unused to that open look on his features. Her tone turned mildly playful, changing the topic since she had forgotten what they'd previously been discussing. "So, I was having a rather scintillating conversation with Marjorie in there. About you, interestingly enough."

Will groaned. "That girl. Honestly, if she was not the butcher's daughter, I don't believe half the town would put up with her, and the other half already feeds off of her gossiping tongue enough as it is."

"She is definitely a lot to handle, I've already realized, although she said some curious things." She tried to sound casual, though her grin belied her expression.

"Like what?" They had neared the back corner of the barn, away from the crowd, and he took both her hands in his and pulled her behind the building.

"Oh, just this and that." Sarah nudged a clod of dirt with the toe of her boot, ducking to hide how his touch affected her. "And she also mentioned that you seemed a little hung up on this girl you met last summer. Seems she might have stolen your heart, or something." Though she tried to sound teasing, her tone held a note of hope.

He gave her hands a gentle pulse. "Nothing was stolen, love, because I gave it freely."

Sarah tipped up her chin to look into his eyes, seeing the sincerity there. "I missed you, Will. I don't think I realized how much until this moment, but I missed you like crazy."

Tugging gently on her grip, Will pulled her close, wrapping his arms around her and holding her like he'd never let go. That was just fine with her. She slipped her arms around his middle, savoring the feeling of his strong arms and breathing in that earthy scent she remembered.

His tone was playfully thoughtful as he placed his chin on the top of her head and said slowly, "You know, I do believe those are the best words I have heard this century."

She laughed, pulling back to see his face. "Come on, I was being serious."

Will's expression turned at once sober as his eyes roved her features, the barest of smiles tipping one corner of his mouth when he spotted the tree pendant he had given her. "As was I. It seems impossible, but I managed to carry you with me every moment of everyday and miss you all the same. It was unbearable to be without you for so long."

She grinned in pleasure even as his words caused her to melt a little. "You're a very good multitasker, Will Taylor—both having and missing me at the same time." A laugh echoed through the air, and the sounds of the gathering drifted back to their little bubble of quiet. How long had they been away?

With a begrudging sigh, she said, "We should probably join the others before we're missed."

His arms tightened around her. "Not yet." She blinked in surprise, and he explained, "I have managed to gain five minutes alone with you away from prying eyes and gossips, and I don't plan to waist a single one."

Laughing, Sarah shook her head. "So you went through the trouble of luring me back here just to catch up? We could have done that at the party."

"Not quite," he murmured. Leaning down, he gave her a soft kiss that sent her heart into marathon-mode. It was nothing more than a gentle brush of his lips against hers, but Sarah's hands flexed unconsciously at her sides as electrical currents coursed through her extremities.

She felt him smile just before he pulled back—all too soon for her liking—that sweet smile in place and making him look more like a boy and not a man with a haunted past. "You are so beautiful." She ducked her head, feeling suddenly shy, but he gently hiked her chin with a calloused finger. His eyes were earnest. "When you were walking down that aisle toward me—well, I mean no disrespect to Karen, but I knew I would be unable to take my eyes from you for the rest of the evening. I told you I thought of you each day, but seeing you again reminded me that my memories pale in comparison to the genuine article. And this"—he tapped the arrow that held her bun in place, grinning—"is absolutely perfect."

"It was a gift from Karen. She's the one who picked out the dress, too," Sarah added unnecessarily, reeling a little at how close he was as he spoke such sweet words. She could see in his eyes that he was thinking the same thing—their escapades together, firing arrows and riding off into the forest to escape danger. They had survived and accomplished so much working side-by-side, and she couldn't help the bubbling of joy she felt over this team reuniting.

"Remind me to thank her profusely." He slid his free hand down the side of her neck and entwined his fingers with a few of her curls, smiling softly. "Certainly no substitute for this," he murmured, appearing perfectly content to fiddle with her hair and hold her for the rest of the evening, and Sarah was tempted to let him.

She couldn't believe this was the same man that she had met in the livery that day so long ago. He had been cut-off and distant back then, and it had taken her awhile to break through his façade and discover the compassionate man beneath. And when she had left Serimone without a word only to return months later when Karen needed her help, she'd had to earn his trust all over again. To see him so open and honest and happy was a surprise, to say the least.

Standing on tiptoe, she wrapped her arms about his neck, shaking her head. "What happened to you?" He blinked, and she hurried to explain before he took offense. "No, what I meant was just that when I first met you, you could barely look me in the eye, and now you're saying the most beautiful things and are so sincere; I can hardly believe how far we've come. I mean, what changed?"

"I did," Will answered honestly. His thumb brushed over the pulse in her neck, expression thoughtful. "Once I opened myself up to you and as I expressed my feelings for you more and more, it simply became easier to do with each passing day. I was forced to look outside myself, and once I chose to do so, I began to see that others had gone through similar traumatic events to the ones that caused me to cut myself off from them. I have never been entirely social or outgoing, and I would still rather spend my time in the forest than at a festival"—Sarah grinned at the honesty in that statement—"but I no longer feel disconnected from the townsfolk. It's as though the instant one wall came down and I allowed myself to feel one thing, then all the other borders I had built around my heart crumbled, as well. You did all that for me."

Drawing in a deep breath to steady her quivering lip, she shook her head, pride surging through her. Not for herself, but for him. "No, Will, you chose that all on your own."

He played with her fingers, dragging his back and forth across the tips of hers. "I suppose I had a little help." With a begrudging breath, Will placed her hand in the crook of his arm and began guiding her back toward the sounds of music and laughter. "I am certain we will be missed if we don't return."

They moved slowly along the ground, neither in much of a hurry to join the others, and boisterous laughter greeted them as they came around the corner. The band was playing a lively jig, and several couples had created a dance floor out of a patch of dry, even dirt, swinging one another around and clapping to the beat. Karen and Seth were leading the group, dancing in the middle of the circle, and Sarah wondered why everyone appeared so entertained as she and Will sidled up next to the rest of the guffawing onlookers. And then she caught a glimpse of Seth dancing.

He was honestly and truly an awful dancer. He was awkward, his legs were stiff, his feet appeared to stomp wherever he went, and he couldn't glide to save his life. It didn't help that he towered over his new bride, who appeared petite and delicate as he swung her 'round and 'round the "dance floor." Karen was jerked back and forth, here and there, with absolutely no rhythm to the music, but she glided along with him, sometimes throwing her head back and smiling at the early stars in the sky.

A few of the guests, some of Seth's friends from town, Sarah assumed, called out gibes about his lack of agility and questions over how he ever managed to snag a girl as lady-like as Karen. Sarah was about to say a few choice words to shut them up, but then she noticed that neither Seth nor Karen seemed bothered by the laughter.

Grinning hugely, Seth stomped to the right, jerking Karen along with him and dipping her backward, nearly losing his balance in the process. But Karen laughed at his efforts, kicking up one leg as he lowered her almost to the ground. The sound of her laughter caused Seth's boyish grin to widen, and he pulled her back up and launched them through the crowd, pumping their arms up and down. The newlyweds looked like they were enjoying themselves immensely and appeared pleased at the crowd's laughter, looking happy to entertain them.

Sarah placed a hand over her mouth to keep her laughter at bay, because she knew that she wasn't the best dancer, either. But Will had already released his own mirth, throwing his head back and letting out a throaty laugh of surprise at his friend's embarrassing dance. The sound, so rarely heard, made her smile.

A hand suddenly gripped hers, and Will dragged her into the midst of the dancers. Sarah laughed as he pulled her close and they tried their best to move in sync to the fast-paced music. They looked far from elegant or skilled as they took on the difficult jig, but they were having fun as they laughed at their mistakes and bumped into other dancers. It was so different from Sarah's experience with the cultured, stylized dancing she had participated in at the balls held at Serimone Castle, but it was wonderful to dance wildly around with the group—most often out of sync, with no rhyme or reason. Sarah couldn't help thinking that it felt marvelous to break free and know that they were all letting their inhibitions go for the night.

"That's it, you've got the idea!" Seth shouted as he jerked his bride in their direction. Karen was pink-cheeked and laughing as she bounced along with him. "But I could teach you a thing or two, William."

Will laughed aloud at that notion and pulled Sarah a little closer as they shifted from side to side. She could feel his heart beating rapidly as he laid her hand on his chest. "I appreciate the offer, but I do believe I already have a far more pleasant partner."

Seth shrugged good-naturedly. "Suit yourself." He hummed loudly as he yanked his and Karen's hands up and down to the "beat" that didn't quite appear to match up with what the band was playing.

Feeling sillier and freer than she had in a long time, Sarah said loudly to be heard over the music, "So, Seth mentioned the bet you two made up to deceive me and win my heart."

The two men stopped in unison, both looking surprised as dancers spun around their still forms. "Why would you tell her that?" Will asked his friend, whose mouth was opening and closing silently in his defense.

"I—it's not as though—" Seth looked at her, eyes wide. "I thought you had forgiven me, and now you try to get him to pommel me? Do you want me dead on my wedding day?"

Sarah and Karen exchanged glances and then burst into peels of laughter. The men blinked in surprise and then gave slow, hesitant smiles, as though they weren't quite sure what was happening.

"You aren't upset with us?" Will hedged.

The song came to an end, and the dancers and onlookers all cheered. "Not at all. Besides," Sarah added, smiling at their little group, "I think we all won, anyway."

ଔଔ

They danced until dusk, much to the amusement of the crowd, and kept swinging around the dance floor until the handcrafted barrel fires were brought out to light the gathering. When Sarah felt she'd have a hard time standing if they danced any longer, she breathlessly told Will that she needed a break. They moved away from the rest of the group and saw Joshua heading their way. Sarah had noticed him dancing with Leah earlier and then a young girl from one of the local farms, but she hadn't spotted him in the last hour and had assumed he'd been readying things for the couple's departure.

"Sorry to break up all the fun," he said, grinning in a way that made him look like his brother. "But, Will, I need your help. One of the mares is giving me trouble and won't let me hitch her to the Marriage Carriage." Sarah bit her lip at the ridiculous name he and Leah had given to Mr. and Mrs. Jones's wedding gift—a wagon Seth and Karen would use to leave the gathering for their own home.

Will looked down at her. "Do you mind?"

"Not at all. There's actually someone I want to see again." He nodded and followed Joshua into the barn.

Sarah scanned the crowd for Dagwood and Richard, hoping to speak with them. A shadow standing in the tree line caught her eye. It was almost too dark to make out his face, but Sarah thought he looked so familiar. Curious, she moved away from the gathering to investigate, and the man lurched behind the tree at her approach.

She squinted against the growing darkness and whispered his name in confusion as she neared. Peering around the trunk of a tree, she found him with his back against it, looking as though he was trying to camouflage himself against the peeling brown and gray bark. "Robert, what are you doing hiding back here?"

Will's assistant looked wide-eyed at having been caught, his piercing gaze tearing right through the growing darkness. "Sarah, I didn't see you there."

"You do realize that you're wearing a white shirt? If you're going to hide, then you need to learn to blend in more."

Sighing, Robert dropped the casual pretense and ducked his head forward, shaggy blond hair falling over his eyes. "I didn't plan on coming here," he mumbled.

Sarah bit her lip. "Why are you here? You aren't thinking about barging in on the wedding, are you? Because Karen and Seth are married; there's nothing you can do."

He winced as though she had slapped him, but he shook his head. "I never intended to interrupt the ceremony, but I couldn't stay away. I just needed to know that she was happy." He swallowed thickly, though a small, reconciled smile touched his lips as he met her eyes. "And she is. Seth's a good man and will take care of her."

Sarah softened, seeing that he was truly glad for her happiness. She could tell that it had never crossed his mind to break up the marriage, only to make sure that Karen would be safe with Seth. Karen had once admitted that she'd felt girlish love for the man years ago when he had been the professor's assistant, but that had faded as her love for Seth grew. What was the harm in reuniting old friends?

"Robert," she began thoughtfully, "do you want to see her? The ceremony is over, and I know that she loves Seth, so it wouldn't do any harm."

"Won't do any good, either," he retorted with a pained grin, revealing perfect teeth surely corrected by braces when he was younger.

Sarah was taken aback by his response. "But she hasn't seen you for years, ever since you attacked her with that proposal on the beach." He grimaced, and she winced, realizing how her words must have sounded. "Sorry. I just meant that she'd love to see you and know that you made a life for yourself. You probably have a million time travel stories you could share with each other." Her left eye narrowed at the odd truth of it.

Robert appeared to consider it, but then he shook his head, just once. "I'd rather her forget until I'm nothing more than a memory to her. I don't want there to be any possibility of her holding back from her life with the farmer because she wonders if there might have been something between us, or because she feels guilty and questions if she hurt me. So long as I know she'll be all right and live a great life, then maybe someday I can feel free to move on, too."

Watching him closely, Sarah felt herself smiling. "You're very gallant, you know."

A roguish grin suddenly appeared on his handsome features, though she could tell it was a little forced. "Feel free to spread that around with the ladies."

"And he bounces back quick enough," Sarah retorted with a laugh.

Robert pushed off the tree and glanced over his shoulder one last time at the bride and groom. "Just don't tell her you saw me. Like I said, I'd rather her forget all about me."

"But doesn't she deserve to know?" she asked softly.

Sighing, he shook his head. "It's better for all of us if I just disappear from her life. For good this time."

"So you were just going to leave without saying hello?"

They spun in unison to find Karen in her wedding gown, hands planted on her hips and a playfully stern look on her face. Robert's mouth worked silently, taking her in up-close. Sarah's eyes went wide as she looked between the two of them, trying to gauge how she should react. "Uhh, Robert, Karen—Karen, Robert," she supplied lamely, unsure if she should pretend that she didn't know of their history together.

"How did you know?" Robert whispered, then cleared his throat. "It's great to see you."

Karen was grinning now. "You were always terrible at hide-and-seek when we were younger, and I saw you earlier. I was waiting for you to finally join the party. Why didn't you just come over and say hello? Everyone's dancing, and there are a few eligible ladies who need a partner." She giggled, clearly riding on adrenaline from all the hoopla.

He blinked in utter shock. "You aren't even just a little bit curious about how I'm here or when or why?"

Sarah whipped her head around to catch her friend's response, but Karen was already shaking her head. She didn't respond directly to his question, just smiled up at him. "It's good to see you, too." She raised her brows at Sarah. "And you obviously knew more than you were letting on, but I'll get the full story out of you later."

Laughing, Sarah raised her hands in surrender. "I may or may not have been sworn to secrecy over his presence here, but I am sorry for keeping that from you."

"I've known he was working at Will's shop for weeks; I already mentioned he's terrible at blending in."

Robert and Sarah balked at her flippant tone. This appeared to be news to them both. "Why didn't you say anything?" he asked when at last he'd recovered.

Karen raised a brow in challenge. "Why didn't you?"

His face relaxed, and he shook his head. "Still as feisty as ever, I see."

Softening, Karen asked, "Won't you join us? You can meet Seth and his family, though Professor Charles already left. You know he was never much for crowds," she added quietly, and they shared a sad, knowing look.

But he was already shaking his head. “No, I can’t. I really must get back, seeing as my employer is a little occupied,” he added with a meaningful grin in Sarah’s direction. She rolled her eyes, trying to hide her own smile.

“Well, don’t be a stranger this time, all right?” Karen stood on tiptoe, surprising him as she wrapped her arms around his neck in a quick, friendly hug. Sarah caught the way his arms hesitated and then slowly coiled around her middle as his eyes closed tight.

Pulling back, Karen beamed up at him. “It really is wonderful to know you’re here.”

To Sarah, it looked as though Robert had just fallen in love with her all over again, though Karen didn’t appear to see it as she looked at him in obvious brotherly-adoration. “Congratulations, Pickle,” he said softly.

Karen rolled her eyes. “Ugh, you know I hate that nickname.”

“That’s why I keep it in my arsenal.” He grinned and swallowed. “Just remind that farmer what a lucky man he is.”

She bobbed her head once, her look cheeky. “Everyday.”

His laugh was genuine then, and Sarah’s heart broke a little as he waved over his shoulder to them, giving Karen one final, poorly concealed glance of longing. And then he seemed to take a deep breath, and he didn’t look back again.

Karen watched him go, her look pensive. Sarah didn’t want her sweet friend to dwell on his tortured expression for too long, so she wrapped an arm about her shoulders and guided her back to her wedding party. “I do believe you have a husband who is waiting to trip over you on the dance floor again.”

“He is terrible, isn’t he? But he’s my terrible,” Karen announced proudly, causing Sarah to laugh.

“Yes, he is.”

They joined the gathering once more, and Karen was immediately swept up by a group of crowing women. Sarah was left to scan the crowd for Will, and she found him speaking with his uncle, Thomas. Both men looked seriously involved in conversation, and she wondered what had been said to put that solemn look on Will’s face after all their gaiety that evening.

Not wanting to intrude on their serious exchange, Sarah wandered through the partygoers in search of someone she recognized. Her eyes landed on Marjorie as that girl turned, and Sarah quickly ducked to the right, lest they make eye contact and she get sucked into another one of the girl’s gossipy dirges. In her haste to avoid her, Sarah nearly smacked right into someone, and she exhaled in pleasant surprise as Richard’s own shock at the near-collision melted into a friendly smile.

“Lady Sarah, I was wondering when we might meet again.” His voice was still smooth and cultured for a peasant, his manners impeccable as he dipped his head in greeting. His golden-brown eyes glowed in the torchlight. "I am pleased to find that you have not been trodden upon by any horses this day."

"Well, it's still early," she remarked, recalling their first encounter and how he had rescued her from nearly being run over by a foul-mouthed horseman.

"True enough." He motioned someone over, and Dagwood pushed his way through the small crowd, beaming.

"Lovely ceremony, it was." He clasped Sarah's hand between his own, smiling at her, his kind gray eyes shining with warmth. This man had a way of acting like he had known and cared about you for years, and to Sarah, it had felt natural to trust him and call this kind man a friend. "You cut quite the figure in that dress, I must say, Lady Matthews."

Sarah laughed as Richard winced at his boldness. "Dagwood," he began, but the older man was already waving him off.

"Oh, we're in the country, my boy, and you don't have to be so stuffy when we're among old friends." He craned his neck to see over Sarah's head as someone caught his eye. "Ah, there's Samuel now. I haven't yet had a chance to congratulate him." He gave Sarah an apologetic glance. "Would you mind terribly if we spoke again later this evening, my dear?"

Sarah nodded eagerly. His presence reminded her of their mutual friend Edith, and for the first time, Sarah could enjoy her memory without a pang of sadness over her loss. She smiled at the man. "I'd like that."

Giving her a quick wink that made one bushy eyebrow twitch, Dagwood jogged off in the direction of Mr. Jones, whose face lit up. The two men embraced in a friendly, entirely awkward looking hug—Samuel Jones was a good head and shoulders taller than the gray-haired man—and Sarah grinned at their strange looking friendship.

There was a moment of sudden, uncomfortable silence between she and Richard as he fiddled with the wooden lion pendant that lay against his shirt. Sarah was tempted to grab her own necklace just for something to do, and she broke the quiet first. "So, how's business?"

"Good, very good," he supplied, looking eager to have something to say. He released the necklace. "The castle kitchen has been placing several orders a week, which keeps us well enough in business as it is, but now everyone wants our produce because it's the same as Queen Meredith and the young king are enjoying." He chuckled.

Sarah smiled. "I'm glad to hear you and your dad are doing well."

He appeared surprised by her remark, and then his expression cleared. "Oh, Dagwood is not my true father." Sarah's eyebrows lifted in surprise. She had always thought it odd how he referred to Dagwood by his given name, but this was still news to her. Richard went on to explain. "Half the town assumes that he is, but he only took me in when I was just a babe. Never knew my real parents," he added softly.

"He adopted you?"

She didn't quite understand his secretive grin. "Something of the sort." He hesitated. At her confused stare, he clarified, "Actually, Dagwood says that I was dropped on his doorstep in a little basket with a pouch of coins. I was clutching this in my hand." He fingered the necklace and shrugged. "Dagwood had never married, so he hired a wet nurse from town and then raised me as his own. I suppose the rest is history."

Sarah didn't know if she should apologize, congratulate him on having such a great father, or change the subject entirely. She was saved from having to do anything as Will sidled up beside her, his uncle just behind him. Their previous conversation seemed to be forgotten, and Sarah's face brightened at the sight of Thomas, glad to see the man who had patched her up and aided them in convicting Cadius of his crimes. He smiled fondly back at her.

Will shook hands with Richard, and the two looked friendly with each other. "Glad you could make it. I was sorry to hear about the break-in at your farm, and I hope nothing important was taken."

"'Tis nothing, truly. Only a few documents were found missing, but nothing of significance." Richard shrugged. "Dagwood seemed a little putout about what wasn't recovered, and I imagine he was more upset over the whole ordeal than he let on. I shall tell him you inquired after the matter."

"So you know each other, then?" Sarah shook her head at the obvious answer. One was the blacksmith, the other worked with the produce vendor—they were bound to encounter each other in town. "Of course you do. You two probably see each other all the time in the square."

"Actually, we spent our youth together," Will explained.

"Our misguided youth," Richard added with a smirk.

Thomas scoffed. "I believe you're both recalling those years with a blind eye. All William did was brood and practice his archery. And you, Richard"—he nudged him good-naturedly—"were just accident-prone and went about lamenting and droning on about the 'injustices of the world.' I do believe they are making their growing up years seem rather grand and mysterious for your benefit, my lady."

Sarah bit her lip to hide her grin. Both men looked a little putout over being thrown under the bus so quickly.

"Some of the things we did were exciting," Will muttered, looking like a reprimanded schoolboy who was embarrassed over being ousted.

Leaning his head closer to Sarah's, Thomas said in a mock whisper so that the others could hear, "Yes, like nearly burning down my cabin because William was too occupied with his practice and Richard was completely engrossed in his book of dirges by some grim saint or another, and neither remembered that I had told them to put out the fire before they left the house."

Sarah giggled, holding a hand over her mouth. "They didn't."

"Oh, but they did." Thomas raised a brow at the two grown men, who were shooting each other nervous glances like boys caught with their hands in the cookie jar. "These two had to rebuild the entire main room over the summer, seeing as they were the ones to reduce it to a pile of rubble."

"Uncle," Will interjected, looking a little slighted at the less than stellar account of their childhood. He turned to Sarah with a sudden grin. "We weren't entirely terrible children, as my uncle would have you think. We play-acted rescues, where squirrels mainly played the maidens in distress, and we staged prison escapes where we were Vikings trying to get back to our ship."

"Sounds very grand," Sarah said with a smile.

Richard shifted toward them, lowering his voice. "Speaking of escapes, I wanted to get your opinion on the most recent one, Taylor."

Sarah watched his eager expression in confusion and then turned her gaze to find Will giving a slight, frantic shake of his head. He immediately stilled when she glanced his way and pasted on a very fake, innocent look. "What's he talking about?" she asked.

"You should have said something sooner," Thomas mumbled under his breath to his nephew.

"It's nothing," Will replied hurriedly, shooting Richard an unreadable look. Apparently, Richard didn't understand what it meant, either, because he looked entirely nonplussed and was narrowing his eyes in confusion, shaking his head.

"How can you say it's nothing? Half the guard is out looking for him! A convicted felon on the loose—heaven knows where he's got off to."

Will shot him a clearly unmistakable glare. Blinking, Richard seemed to understand whatever went unspoken between them, and he nodded slowly, darting a quick glance at Sarah. "Why don't I go in search of Dagwood?" he suggested.

"I'd like to see him myself, if you don't mind." Thomas raised a reprimanding brow at his nephew before he and Richard slipped off into the crowd.

Silence rang between them, tickling the air with the electricity of what went unsaid. Finally, Sarah blurted, "What are you keeping from me?"

Will sighed heavily, raking a hand back through his perfectly styled hair and upsetting it so that his waves stuck out in all directions. "Uncle said I should have told you sooner, but I wished for you to enjoy the party without . . . this hanging over your head. Let me just preface by saying I am sorry for keeping this from you and that Uncle Thomas mentioned you would not hold it against me, and I believe he is right, but I was worried—"

"Will," she prodded nervously. "Just come out with it already. I'm sure you're making it seem worse than it is."

He swallowed and drew her a little ways from the group and the fires. It was colder away from the press of bodies, and she shivered. Quietly, he said, "It has recently come to my attention, and apparently many others, that there are still a few at the castle under Lisandro's employ."

Sarah's lips parted in confusion. "He has connections from prison? How is that even possible?"

Grimacing, Will shook his head, looking pained to admit his next words to her. "No, that's just it: the transport carrying the Spaniard to his permanent prison arrived empty. Sarah, Lisandro has escaped."

Chapter Five

"The human heart has hidden treasures,
In secret kept, in silence sealed;
The thoughts, the hopes, the dreams, the pleasures,
Whose charms were broken if revealed."

Charlotte Brontë, "Evening Solace"

The sounds of the party faded away, and Sarah's stomach dropped. "How? When?"

"I don't have all of the details," Will admitted quietly. "But my understanding is that at least one guard that accompanied the Spaniard on his journey from the castle to the prison bordering the Ridlan territory was paid off, either by Lisandro himself or someone else—not much is certain at this point. All we know is that the transport arrived at the prison minus two guards and one prisoner, and the only thing left inside the carriage was a key and his chains, which didn't seem to have held him for long."

"He can't—but he was supposed to go away for life. . . ." Sarah's throat constricted. Her mind was fighting between shock, relief, and fear as it tried to process the fact that Damien was free, roaming Ridlan. Maybe he planned to come back to Serimone, or maybe he was already here. "Have they spotted him here yet?" she had to ask.

Reluctantly, Will admitted, "Not a soul witnessed him escaping the transport, which means the last place he was seen was Serimone Castle."

The future could be different for us. . . . I've come for Sarah. . . . Keeping you close meant ensuring your safety. . . . Don't think I'm letting go.

Damien's smooth voice rang in her ears, so clear with remembrance that it was as though the wind had actually carried his words to her ears. She shivered, wondering if he had actually said that last thought or if her fear was playing tricks and clouding her memories of him, making her think that he was more sinister than he had actually been.

She shook her head at her jumbled thoughts.

Will clasped her hand in his. "I can tell you are thinking a hundred things right now." He paused and then asked, "Would you like to share one of them?"

"I-I don't know what I'm thinking," she answered honestly, her emotions too tumultuous to distinguish any single one. She shrugged her shoulders in annoyance at herself. "First I feel angry at Damien again for everything he put us through, his hand in Cadius' plan, killing Edith. Then there is this two-second, completely insane moment where I'm actually relieved that he's free and won't spend his life in a freezing cold cell. How messed up is that?"

Will gave her hand a reassuring pulse. "You never wanted him there to begin with."

"What I wanted was for him to be different in the first place," she muttered dismally, then realized she had said something similar to Will before. "No, he deserves to be there, and I think even Damien would acknowledge that." Then she recalled that they had been discussing his escape and sighed. "Or maybe he doesn't and that's why he broke out. I don't know."

He watched her face closely. "Is that all?" he urged, knowing her all too well.

Scuffing the toe of her boot against the earth and grinding a dirt clod into fine brown powder, Sarah avoided his eyes when she spoke. "I know it sounds ridiculous, but knowing he's out there is also a little scary. I really don't think he would ever hurt me—if he'd wanted me dead, he had plenty of opportunities to do it—but Damien acted kind of obsessed and protective of me." She groaned and threw her eyes heavenward. "That makes me sound so narcissistic. I know that he would never come back to Serimone just for me, if he is, in fact, here. But I had a lot of time to overthink scenarios like this, and he managed to nab me in every one. Though I never actually thought it could happen," she muttered truthfully.

The hand holding Sarah's tightened, and Will closed the distance between them. Her skirt, wrinkled from dancing, wrapped around his legs as he came to stand toe-to-toe with her. "You needn't fear; I will not let you out of my sight."

"What about tonight?" she pointed out gently. "Or tomorrow, or the next day, and every night after that? You can't expect to protect me forever."

Something flickered in his gaze, and Sarah thought there might have been an instance of hurt that flitted across his vision. But it was gone in an instant, replaced by that fierce determination she recognized so well. "I'll be cursed if I won't try."

There was no use arguing with him when his mind was made up. She thought about the way that Will had been willing to die to save her from Damien, and a spark of worry shot through her. Sarah gave him a half-hearted smile, trying to look encouraging. "I'm probably overreacting. Damien's a city boy, and I bet he's still wandering the forest near Ridlan, trying to find his way out." She forced a laugh, but her phony amusement quickly wavered.

Will's smile was just as uncertain. "I suppose you are right." She knew he'd rather have Damien fall headfirst into a bear trap than have him on the lam, but he didn't say anything else on the matter.

He placed her hand in the crook of his elbow. "Shall we join the others for a dance? I believe Seth's hazardous footwork has left a clear opening for us to sneak in."

Sarah nodded, ready to forget their conversation, though she imagined that a little gray cloud of worry would hang over her head until she returned home, a place where he could never find her.

ꕥ

The party stayed late into the night and they didn't bid farewell to the newlyweds until almost the next day. Karen waved back to friends and her new family as Seth flicked the reins to get the horses moving. She was still waving and calling out her goodbyes as the wagon disappeared from view.

A few of Mrs. Jones's friends stayed to help clean up and put away the leftovers as the men tore down the tables and lanterns, packing everything away in the barn or in wagons to be returned to their owners. The instant the party had concluded and every last soul went home, Ruth seemed to deflate, all of her liveliness leaving with her guests. After investing every ounce of effort into this event for so long, once it was over, she didn't seem to have an ounce of energy left.

Appearing on the verge of collapse, she scrubbed down the kitchen with the tears of someone who is emotionally and physically spent. Samuel gave his wife a pointed look. When she shook her head, insisting there was yet work to be done before she turned in, he simply scooped her into his arms, bade them all goodnight, and took her up the stairs.

Ruth sniffed back her tears and whispered brokenly, "Our little man has grown up." Her husband's murmured response was unintelligible as he closed their bedroom door with his foot.

That had been over an hour ago, and now it was just Leah, Joshua, Sarah, and Will who remained awake in the Joneses' household. It was quiet, save for the gentle clack of wood on wood as Sarah tossed the eight-sided dice. They rolled across the hand-carved board and stopped on double X's.

"Yes! That's six spaces for me," she announced happily, moving her wooden horse across the board.

Sensing they were all too wired to turn in after the party, Joshua had suggested a quick game after their parents turned in, and the game had been a blessed distraction from Sarah's doubts and emotions. But that game had turned into three once Sarah got the hang of it, and Joshua—"the master," as he'd called himself—had to keep playing to try and beat her.

Now he groaned aloud. “Again? I’m telling you, Will, I’ve never regretted teaching someone a skill in my entire life, but this is absurd.”

“You’re simply too good of an instructor,” Will assured him, giving him a sympathetic look. He shot Sarah a grin as he rolled his own dice, and she bit her lip to hide her smirk.

As Will shifted his piece across the board, Sarah glanced over at Leah, who sat by the fire holding an old, worn book. “What are you reading, Leah?” she asked from her rather unladylike, cross-legged position on the floor. Dice clattered against the board, and Joshua cursed softly under his breath—another poor combo, Sarah imagined.

Leah glanced up in surprise, and then her eyes lit up. “Mama and Papa had it made for me years ago. It’s a compilation of family histories, fables, and old family legends that were written down on scraps of lambskin, and then they put it all together for me. Since neither of them knows how to read, I taught myself just so I could enjoy my gift.” She giggled. “I nearly have it memorized by now.”

Sarah was taken aback, and then she remembered something from her history course about only the wealthy elite and monasteries owning hoards of real books, and even fewer actually knowing how to read them, but she still had a hard time believing it. Her smile was genuine, though, at the thought that this family would try so hard to fill their home with words and stories for their daughter’s entertainment, even if they didn’t understand it themselves. “That’s really lovely.”

“A-ha!” Joshua cried triumphantly. She turned back to find him smiling coyly at her. “I do believe your piece is in trouble.” Folding his arms across his chest and looking rather satisfied with himself, he nodded to the board. “And it’s your turn.”

Raising her eyebrows in challenge, Sarah picked up the dice, rolled them between her palms, and flicked them carelessly onto the wood surface covered with shapes and carvings that meant little to her. Joshua gaped at the roll, though she cringed in confusion. “I forget—is that squiggly line a snake or a river?”

Joshua threw his hands up in the air, looking to Will for help. “She doesn’t even know what they are!” The other man just gave him a helpless shrug, smirking unapologetically. “I thought we men were supposed to stick together,” Joshua muttered. He glanced at Sarah, sighed, and then said lowly to the other man, “I mean, I understand your reasons.”

Will chuckled. “I thought you might.” He turned to Sarah, smiling with what looked like pride and amusement. “You won the game.”

“Again,” Joshua added grumpily. Sarah scratched her upper lip to hide her grin.

“Oh, don’t be such a poor sport, Joshy,” Leah admonished, not even bothering to glance up from her book as she turned another page.

He looked like he wanted to argue with his sister, but she rubbed her eyes with a fist, looking suddenly tired and very young. He hesitated and a slow, accepting grin emerged. “She’s right. Well played, Miss Matthews.”

“Thanks for teaching me. I had fun.” And it had been wonderful to not think about where Damien was, whether or not he would come for her, and also served to perk her up after her relationship with Karen changed tonight forever. They would always be friends—they’d established that early on in their complicated friendship that stretched the centuries—but it would be different now with her living on a completely different piece of the Joneses’ land. And then when she and Seth moved somewhere else? Sarah hadn’t really thought that far ahead, and she felt a quick pang in her middle, pushing aside the saddening thought.

Leah rubbed the corner of her drooping eye again and tried to concentrate on her reading, her shoulders slumping in exhaustion. It was late, and though she had done her best to keep up with the adults that night, acting the part of a mature hostess as she entertained at the party, she was still just a girl who looked as exhausted as her mother had.

Joshua seemed to notice this, as well. He rose to his feet, stretching his arms out to his sides and feigning a yawn. “It has been quite the day, and I think it’s time we both turned in for the night, don’t you think?”

Glancing over at him with foggy eyes, her reaction delayed by a few seconds, Leah nodded once. “If you need to, brother.” They all hid their smiles as she rose from her chair with unnecessary grace and sophistication, laying her book down on the vacated seat.

Joshua wrapped an arm around her shoulders and kissed the top of her head. His expression turned at once from warmth and fondness into an instant look of consternation. “And you, Will, must leave. I am now man of the house, and—”

“What about Papa?” Leah reminded him wryly.

“Aside from Father,” he amended before stretching his neck to lend an extra inch to his height. He sounded very self-important when he spoke, though his changing voice belied his authority. “I cannot leave Sarah unchaperoned with you in our house. I hope you understand that it isn’t you, precisely, but it would not be proper.”

Sarah quirked a brow and rose to her feet, grimacing as the blood returned to her legs. She had to resist the urge to rub her numb backside after sitting on the hard floor for hours. “I can take care of myself, Josh.”

Glancing at Will, she could tell he was holding back a look of amusement as the corner of his mouth trembled and the muscle in his jaw twitched. But he didn’t look as though he wanted to embarrass or belittle Joshua in his new self-appointed duties typical of the man of the house. Will managed to pull a serious expression, and he nodded gravely. “I understand perfectly. You are looking after her well-being, and I shall go at once.”

Sarah shook her head, grinning. "I'll walk you out, then." She and Will turned toward the door.

"You'll stay with me tonight, won't you?" Sarah glanced back to find Leah looking unsure in her brother's arms, and she realized that a lot of changes had occurred for her today, too.

Sarah gave her a reassuring smile. "Of course. I'll be up in a bit."

The girl appeared relieved at her promise and then focused a suddenly shy look on Will. "'Night, William."

He smiled fondly at her. "Pleasant dreams, Leah."

Her cheeks turned a little pink before her brother guided her upstairs. It looks like Will has made quite the impression on her, Sarah thought, her heart going out to the girl. But she recalled plenty of crushes on older men when she was younger, so she was hopeful the girl would move on quickly, for her young heart's sake.

Sarah glanced up at Will as they walked outside into the cold night air and knew she would have fallen in love with him if she was Leah's age and he was around all the time, spending his days with her family and treating her well. You're half in love with him now. The thought came out of nowhere, and she quickly averted her gaze, afraid he might read her mind. He had already declared his feelings for her and revealed his love in everything he did, but she was more cautious, feeling she had more to lose if she fell in love with him.

Frowning, she realized that was selfish and untrue. He was the one with the broken past and yet chose to let her in and put his heart in her hands, completely confident that she would care for it. She felt that she was a coward for being too scared to love this man fully or allow herself to consider her true feelings, which she knew ran deep. But a part of her reluctance was the fact that she did care for him. Because if she did, in fact, love him, then wouldn't that make her a terrible person to give him hope and then squash it when she walked away for good someday, leaving him a thousand years in the past?

Maybe you should consider what he wants, a little voice reminded. Sarah almost started, surprised at the thought, and then she frowned as she considered this. She imagined he would want whatever time he had with her, but was it what was best for him?

"Your thoughts are louder than the thrushes." She jerked her head in Will's direction and found him smiling curiously. He planted his forearms on the porch railing Seth and Mr. Jones had worked on over the winter, waiting for her to join him.

"Sorry." She leaned against the wood, shoulder nearly brushing his, and stared at the heavens. The moon was bright and huge, and the stars dappled the night sky like white bursts of light against a blue-black canvass.

Sucking in a small breath of wonder, she whispered so as to not disturb the birds' night song, "We definitely don't have stars like these back home." Too many lights, she wanted to add, but, of course, he couldn't know about that part of her life. Yet one more secret she had to keep from him.

Will was silent for a long minute, and she glanced at him. His brows were drawn together in contemplation as he studied her face. "Would you care to share what has your mind in such a fit?"

Sarah dropped her gaze to the patch of fresh grass growing just below them, searching her brain for something to say. The only thing that came to mind was the truth, and she was tired of anxiously wondering what the future held. Planting her hip against the railing so that she could face him, she blurted, "Aren't you upset that I haven't said I love you back?"

That clearly had not been what he'd expected. Will blinked slowly, lips parting in surprise. "I told you before that I would not rush you, and I won't." He frowned. "Is that what has you so upset? Because I am not."

"But you have to be," she countered, knowing she sounded a little desperate and ridiculous as she tried to probe his true feelings from him. "You bare your soul, and in response I drag my feet because I'm scared over how we can make this work, and you've been understanding and perfect and haven't pushed me at all. You're not supposed to be so patient."

"Oh, can't I?" He was smiling softly at her, appearing unfazed by her anxious countering. Actually, he was watching her with an expression akin to amusement.

Her shoulders slumped as she shook her head in confusion. "But you must want to hear me say it back." She hadn't meant to sound so lost and small as she said it, but now the words hung between them.

Will straightened slowly, his expression tender and sincere. Placing his hands on either side of her face, his thumbs brushed over her cheekbones as he studied her features. "You know I want that more than anything," he answered honestly. "But I want you to mean it when you say those words. Do you remember what I said to you when you last left Serimone?"

Scanning her memory for what he might be referencing, Sarah tried, "Something about being patient and not wanting to pressure me?"

He nodded, face serious. "I will not influence you toward any feelings you do not want for yourself. However, if there is the smallest glint of hope for us, then I shall wait for as long as it takes and do my best to earn your love. As I have declared before, I have no intention of giving up on us." He grinned lazily, gaze roving her features like a loving caress. "You've expressed your concern for my heart, but the only one I am focused on is yours. Looking into the future, I honestly believe that our greatest regret would be letting what exists between us wither before it has a chance to fully bloom, come what may." He planted a tender kiss on her forehead and breathed against her skin, "Simply be here with me now, all right? I am tired of missing you."

A part of her had sensed what he would say, but hearing him speak the words aloud eased the tension between her shoulders and unknotted her stomach. Sarah's heart filled to bursting, feeling as though a huge weight had been lifted at his words, reassuring her that he was invested in this now and that he wasn't stressing the future, as she had been. The unknown still hung over them, but Sarah recalled the promise she had made to herself at the ball that she wouldn't be afraid of falling anymore and would just enjoy the time they had together. These next few days could either be the greatest memory of her life or the biggest regret of her soul. It was her choice.

When he pulled back from her, she felt a small surge of recklessness and placed her hands on his broad chest, standing on tiptoe to press her mouth to his. She felt him start before his lips softened against hers. Hands moving to encircle her waist, he pulled her close until her hands were pressed between their two bodies. Sarah loved the feel of his strong chest beneath her palms, of feeling secure in his strength as he held her like she was something precious and loved, and she shoved aside her uncertainty to relish this moment.

The kiss was slow and sweet, and a little contained on his part, and Sarah slid one hand up around his neck to pull him closer. She felt his heart hitch and quicken beneath her other palm in response, which caused her own heart to beat against her ribcage like something trapped and trying to fight its way into the light.

He whispered her name breathlessly, breaking the kiss for a brief instant. She opened her eyes, feeling lightheaded, and caught his close-lipped smile as he tilted his head to the side, kissing her once more. Her body unconsciously mirrored the curve of his own as he leaned down, whispering her name against her lips, his own moving slowly over hers in a beautiful dance of words and breath and silent promises.

The kiss wasn't fast-paced or uncontrollable, but rather soft and beautiful and sustained by the tenderness that passed between them; it expressed emotions that Sarah didn't know how to articulate on her own, and she imagined it held more meaning than wild and passionate interludes. She felt light as air, as though the slightest breeze could pull her away if his arms weren't there to keep her on earth.

This is what love should feel like. The realization took her by surprise and stole her breath as much as the kiss had. She was falling in love with him and had only just realized how deep her feelings for him ran. Heart filling with warmth that spread to every limb, Sarah lost herself in his kiss.

Just as she felt her awareness slipping away, and with it the careful control they had been practicing in those tender moments, Will drew back from her slowly, unwillingly. She wavered on her feet, lips still parted, and swallowed as she opened her eyes to find a goofy sort of smile on his lips.

"Oh, umm," she mumbled, voice sounding strange to her own ears. She felt suddenly self-conscious, but when she looked at him, she knew she needn't be.

He enveloped her in his arms, hugging her tight against his chest. Kissing the top of her head, he exhaled against her hair. "I missed you desperately, you know." His voice was deep, raspy.

Sarah felt a shaky breath leave her own chest. "You said that already." He released her with a contented smile. When he shifted, blue moonlight revealed a small nick on his smooth chin, and she reached up and rubbed her thumb gently over it. "What happened here?"

"Oh." He averted his gaze in a tell-tell way. "I might have nicked myself trying to get a close shave. For the event."

Hiding her grin, she nodded as though she understood completely. Giving that stubborn lock on his forehead a gentle tug, she commented innocently, "Your hair's shorter, too."

Will rubbed the back of his neck. "Well, I also might have gone into town to have it trimmed." She could hide her playful grin no longer as it tickled the corner of her lips, knowing for a fact that he hadn't paid someone to cut his hair in years.

At her look, his eyes widened almost imperceptibly. "To look more presentable by Seth's side, of course," he added quickly, as though just realizing his mistake. It was terrible, she knew, but Sarah thought he looked so adorable when she caught him off-guard, which didn't happen very often.

"Will," she said slyly, voice cajoling, "did you get your hair cut because you knew you'd see me today?"

"Would it matter if I had?" he asked, his words laced with hesitation as he leaned his arms against the railing, turning his head to watch her so they were at eye level. His gaze met hers, and he looked both shy and embarrassed, though she could tell he tried to mask it. "For once I wanted to appear a gentleman and not the ruffian that you remember."

Sarah let out a surprised laugh. "What?"

"When we parted last, I was bruised and battered from my scuffle with the Spaniard, and I didn't wish to remind you of that day." He scuffed the toe of his boot against a pebble, pale light cutting across his broad forehead. "And I must also admit that I wanted to make a good impression after so long, to not cause you to wonder if you were returning to a lout."

From this angle, Sarah saw the small scar on his brow that he'd received when he fought with Damien. She hid her wince, recalling how both men had been covered in blood and bruises and how she had tended his wounds. The sight of Will so broken and injured was something she definitely wished to forget, but they had also accomplished so much that day that she couldn't ignore it completely.

"I think you're forgetting that we solved the mystery, put away the king's killer, and righted the kingdom that same afternoon. When I think of that day, I'm reminded of how you rescued me from Damien and fought gallantly for my honor and my life." She paused and admitted, "And I gotta say, you're probably the most handsome guy I know, even when you're covered in bruises after being so chivalrous."

"Truly?" Will asked, his grin a little roguish and his eyes sparkling in pleasure. He took her hand, and his thumb brushed over the faded scar that Allan had given her so long ago. The scar was a reminder of what they had overcome, and Sarah had become rather proud of that little white ridge on the back of her hand. They both had scars, but they had come to this point in spite of them.

"Yes," she returned honestly, and then thought to add, "But I will slap you if you ever try to do it again. I don't like having to patch you back up."

His eyes were alight with promise. "Although I swore to protect you and this land at any cost, and I will honor that promise, I assure you that I will do my best to abstain from imprudent actions."

"Fair enough," she answered with a soft smile, knowing that was the best she could get out of him. His entire being cried out against injustice.

Will's gaze suddenly brightened. "I forgot that I have a message to deliver from the queen." Her own eyes widened in surprise as he continued. "When I requested from Queen Meredith and King Adrian that the priest should conduct the ceremony for our friends out of doors, your name came up." He squinted, looking like he was searching his memory. "I can't quite remember how, but when she heard I was a friend of yours, the queen asked that I relay to you her hope that you will visit her during your stay."

"That would be wonderful!" Sarah said eagerly. Queen Meredith had been kind to her at that horribly awkward dinner with Damien, the former prince, and the castle guests—an event at which Cadius had practically threatened her, though it hadn't been the last time he'd made it clear she was poking her nose where it didn't belong, endangering her life by snooping into his affairs. But the queen had expressed genuine warmth and kindness toward her, and Sarah itched at the opportunity to speak with her again.

Will's grin turned suddenly bashful, and he picked at a splinter near his elbow, avoiding her gaze. "Perhaps you can meet with her on the morrow. You see, I was at the castle because the king had requested my presence." Sarah raised a brow. "He mentioned that he desires to honor me for my service in bringing Cadius to justice and wishes to have me knighted tomorrow in the royal court. He even expressed his apologies for having waited so long to do it." He sounded cavalier about the whole thing, as though he was embarrassed over the hoopla.

Sarah gaped a little at him before she had the sense of mind to smile. "Are you serious? That's a huge honor! Why aren't you more excited?"

"It is an honor, and one I could not refuse, coming from the new king," he admitted, his Adam's apple bobbing nervously in his throat. He sighed. "Before I became the Shadow, as a boy I dreamt of being knighted and riding off in the Crusades, of wielding swords and wearing armor. I can't say exactly why I feel hesitant about it all, but it feels entirely surreal to be thrust into a new identity. Please, don't misunderstand; I am grateful. I simply—I don't know."

"Will," she began, watching his expression carefully. "Are you embarrassed over doing something honorable to protect the town and being recognized for it? Is it the attention for your good deeds that makes this so intimidating?"

He exhaled again. "Perhaps. But you and my uncle did as much, if not more, than I. Why should you not receive such an honor?"

She chuckled and placed her hand over his, grateful that his good heart prevented him from buying into the backward ideas of women that this era upheld. "I've never considered myself much of a knight, so don't worry about me, and I don't think your uncle would want you sapping the joy out of this moment. Be proud of yourself, Will. I know I am."

Smiling slowly, he whispered, "Thank you."

They leaned against the railing, side by side, watching the stars, neither in much of a hurry to say goodnight.

Sarah thought about tonight, the joy on her friends' faces, the kind family who had taken her in. They had become her home away from home, and she missed them sorely when she wasn't here. It wasn't like the castle had been, stuffy and proper and all about social etiquette. This family was real and inviting and so perfectly wonderful that it was impossible not to feel warm when she was around them. She caught Will's steady gaze and acknowledged that it wasn't just the sweetness of this family that had her insides melting.

Looking suddenly aware that he had been staring at her profile, Will straightened. "I should go." But he looked hesitant to leave her, and she knew part of it was the unknown whereabouts of an escapee that had him rooted to the spot.

Remembering her promise earlier, she assured him that she would be careful. "You don't have to worry about me tonight. He doesn't know exactly where the Joneses' live; I never let him take me all the way to the house, so I'm safe here." She reminded herself that with his connections, it wouldn't take Damien very long to figure out that they were just a little ways down the road he had dropped her off at, but she didn't feel the need to remind Will of that. "Just don't tell the family about him escaping. I don't want anything to taint the joy of this week and get them worrying that we're unprotected at night."

Reluctantly, he admitted, "Actually, I was going to ride my horse around the perimeter of the forest until everyone fell asleep, and then I planned to make bed in the barn."

Sarah gaped, then surprised him by laughing. Shaking her head, she said, "You are the craziest and most endearingly overprotective man I have ever met, and I love that about you."

His head perked up, eyes suddenly bright. "What was that you said?"

She squinted in confusion and then her eyes widened. "Oh, no, I—no. I just meant that I really like that you take care of me. I appreciate it." She winced, wishing she had thought her words through before they came pouring out.

Though she was sure he was disappointed, he hid it well. Face suddenly teasing, he said, "Oh, well, that is quite the distinction."

It was obvious he wished to say more as his false mirth faded, and she knew he wanted to hear her say those three words she wished would come to her lips. She felt her throat tighten and swallowed. "Promise me you'll go home and get some rest; it's been a long day," she added, genuinely concerned that he would spend the entire night on horseback patrolling for Damien, though she was also attempting to steer the conversation in a different direction.

Sensing her distress, Will lowered his gaze and smiled softly. Instead of declare the love that she saw in his dark eyes, he simply bent down and planted a sweet kiss on her cheek. Giving her a smile that made her weak at the knees, he whispered, "Until the morrow, my darling."

Swallowing the lump that threatened to hold back her words, Sarah blurted out his name. He turned, expression open. "Yes, love?"

This was it—her opportunity to tell him she was falling in love with him—but the words lodged in her throat, refusing to come. She shouldn't be afraid of him refusing her, since he had been the first to express his love. Yet she still hesitated, feeling uncertain and a little embarrassed that she'd only just discovered her true feelings now, after he had told her he wouldn't rush her, and she felt cautious of speaking her emotions too soon. She needed time to think about her newfound feelings for him before she blurted them to the world, and she didn't want him to think his sweet words and their even sweeter kiss had convinced her that she was falling in love. It had merely helped her realize what she should have recognized long ago, though she had been too scared at the time to admit it to herself.

Sarah smiled, knowing that the only things she felt certain of was Will and the fact that there was plenty of time to discuss such things. "Nothing. I'll see you tomorrow."

He gave her a heartwarming smile in return. "Always."

Chapter Six

"All brave men love; for he only is brave who has affections to fight for."

Nathaniel Hawthorne

Sarah half expected to find him sleeping at the bottom of the stairs when she descended late the next morning. She had dressed in one of the gowns she and Leah had brought into the house the night before, so at least she was presentable . . . barely. Her hair was uncombed, her limbs stiff from so much dancing the night before, and she kept rubbing her eyes groggily, trying to clean away the grit clouding her vision. She was almost glad when she discovered the main room devoid of life, knowing that she must look like the Ghost of Weddings Past.

She did, however, find Will already in the dining room/kitchen, shadowing Mrs. Jones as she handed him dish after dish to place on the table. Joshua was sitting down, his chin propped up by a fist, elbows planted on the table, eyes drooping. Apparently she wasn't the only one who had collapsed after the adrenaline of the night had faded, and Leah had still been asleep when Sarah snuck out of the room they'd shared.

At the soft sound of her bare feet padding across the wood, Will glanced up, his smile causing her heart to skitter around in her chest. She tucked a wild curl behind her ear, wishing she had thought to put it back with the arrow she had spent an hour fiddling with last night. He didn't look tired at all, though—in fact, his eyes were bright, his gaze clear as he watched her enter the room. His hair was damp and curled over his forehead, and she realized he must have washed it sometime this morning.

"Well, good day to you, idle-bones," Mrs. Jones chirped brightly, seemingly recovered from the emotions of the previous night. The Irishwoman planted a quick, motherly kiss on her cheek as she passed with a steaming platter of eggs and potatoes. "Where is Leah?"

"Asleep," Sarah mumbled, hesitating in the doorway, feeling uncertain if she should give Will a kiss on the cheek, a hug, or if Mrs. Jones would find it wildly improper. She settled on shooting him a small, meaningful smile before plopping down next to Josh at the table. They both seemed to have the same glazed expression, and she needed an ally against the unnecessary brightness the other two carried with them.

Grinning, Will came up behind her and planted a polite kiss on her cheek. "Good morning, love," he said quietly but contentedly against her skin. Then he went back to arranging platters on the table.

Eyes wide, Sarah tucked her chin to hide her flaming cheeks behind her hair, but she wasn't fast enough to mask her look of embarrassment from the other two in the room. Mrs. Jones appeared surprised, and then her expression immediately shifted to a look one might expect from someone who had discovered buried treasure or the trick behind a magic act, or that chocolate was 75%-off after Valentine's Day.

"Well, this is lovely to see," she announced gaily, looking perfectly pleased. It was obvious Will was biting back his grin as he moved to the counter to finish slicing the bread. Sarah found she liked seeing him so domestic and relaxed in the Joneses' home, but she was a little perturbed that he had caught her off-guard—just to watch her blush, no doubt—and she didn't feel like applauding him for that fact just then.

She turned her head and caught Joshua's suddenly alert gaze and raised brow. "I suppose I was right to send him home early last night," he teased, grinning wickedly.

Rolling her eyes, Sarah plopped her chin in her hand as she'd seen him do earlier. With bleary eyes, she watched Will and Ruth bustle around the kitchen as she asked him to pass this or chop that. "Wow. Sorry for leaving you alone with these two morning people for so long."

"I thank you for your sympathy." Joshua's look was wry, and then he groaned as he watched them. "Something must be wrong with them, because I feel as though I could die at any moment."

Sarah gave a small, tired laugh. "We'll perk up once we get going," she said against her fingertips as they curled over her chin, wishing that coffee was a household item in the twelfth century. Her eyes scanned the table as Will set down the bowl of homemade bread. "Wow, this looks great, you two."

The petite, flushed woman came over and reached high on her tiptoes to pat Will on the cheek, her look adoring; there was no sign of the tears from last night. Sarah felt her lips curving, knowing that the two of them needed this mother-son relationship right now. "William has been quite the study and so attentive. It has been marvelous to have him around so often."

"Mama's been teaching him to cook," Joshua said quietly to Sarah, feigning a shiver. "Better him than me, since men should never be in the kitchen—OW!" Mrs. Jones swatted his shoulder as she breezed past, chin hiked.

"You could take a lesson on manners from William," she remarked, shooting her middle child a look that has been perfected by mothers since the beginning of time. She disappeared from the room and they heard her call Mr. Jones in from the barn for breakfast.

Will took the seat on Sarah's other side. "I live on my own," he explained to her, "so I must admit that it has been rather nice to make myself something other than venison stew."

"Ah, but you did it so well." She smirked. "Actually, I think it's really nice that you're learning a new skill."

Joshua made a quiet gagging noise, and she elbowed him in the ribs, receiving a grunt in return. "We're breaking the fast this morning, not my body, Miss Matthews," he rasped, rubbing his side and slumping dramatically. "She's all yours, Will."

Chuckling, he said, "Sounds perfect to me."

Mrs. Jones bustled back into the room, followed by her husband, who grabbed a cloth from the counter and rubbed the dirt from his hands. He bade them all good morning, seemingly in as good a mood as his wife.

Sitting at the head of the table, he waited for Ruth to take her place beside him before reaching out to grab the hands of those nearest him. Everyone followed suit, and then Mr. Jones gave a short prayer over their food and blessed the hands that had been used to make it. Curious, Sarah cracked one eye open and glanced over at Will to catch his reaction. His head was dipped obediently but his eyes were open, staring at his empty plate with a blank expression, looking purposefully detached from the blessing Mr. Jones spoke. She imagined he did that every time they prayed over the meal.

Sarah's shoulders slumped a little, and she quickly closed her eyes, wishing she hadn't looked at all. Seeing how deeply unaffected Will was by the sincere prayer caused a pang to shoot through her chest. Make it real for him, she prayed silently, unconsciously holding his hand a little tighter. She added a quiet "Amen" with everyone else. Everyone except for Will, that is.

The family ate in companionable silence, piping up with occasional remarks or to-dos for the day. Sarah chewed the delicious meal, partly prepared by the man at her side, contemplating their situation. Last night, she had promised him and herself that she wouldn't overthink it, but it was nearly impossible when every rational bone in her body reasoned against falling for him. There would be no coming back from loving this man, and no recovering from losing him.

"—be leaving before the hour's up," Will was saying. "Sarah is supposed to meet with the queen later, as well."

Sarah started at her name and glanced up from the food she had been shuffling around her plate. "What are we talking about?"

"He told you of the ceremony held in his honor, I'm sure." Mrs. Jones gave him a look of a proud mother, and he appeared suddenly bashful.

"It's not so much a ceremony," he corrected modestly. "It will only be a quick, customary procedure."

"Procedure?" Sarah grinned at him. It was exciting to be honored in such a way, and he made the whole thing sound so boring and sterile.

Will shrugged one shoulder dismissively. "I simply meant that it isn't as thrilling as you seem to think. The actual knighting will take place, which you will attend, and then I must stay behind to sign a royal decree that binds my loyalty to the true king, subject myself to a lengthy sermon on the duties of a knight, and meet with some aristocrats. It's quite dull and tedious. "

"Now, son," Mr. Jones began, his expression chastising, "it is an honor given to few, and you should be proud to be among them."

A cocky smirk tipped Sarah's lips as his words echoed hers from last night. "Yeah, Will, you should be proud."

A sleepy looking Leah entered just then, saving him from coming up with a reply. She gave everyone a groggy smile and then noticeably perked up when she caught Will's eye, looking at him with a suddenly bright and adoring expression. "You have a big day today," she commented as she took a seat and filled her plate.

Will rose, pulling Sarah's chair back for her to follow suit. "And we really should be going so we aren't late."

She stood, giving him a look of utter shock. "We're going now? But I'm hardly dressed for an event."

"You look lovely," he returned.

Shooting him a look that said he clearly didn't know what he was talking about, she jumped back from the table, accidentally knocking the chair over and almost taking out his legs, if he hadn't jumped out of the way in time.

Leah's jaw swung open, revealing a mouthful of bread. Her mother chided her poor manners, and she swallowed hurriedly. "She can't go like that."

"Thank you!" Sarah declared, and then narrowed one eye as she realized it hadn't been a compliment.

Dropping her half-eaten piece of bread onto her plate, Leah grabbed Sarah's hand and they rushed out of the room. "Give me ten minutes," Sarah called over her shoulder.

"Women—OW!" Joshua squealed as they ran up the stairs.

Leah worked as quick as she could to help Sarah dress in a gown of pale pink. She left her alone, the dress pulled only halfway over her shift, to grab a few hairpins and a small jar of pink goo from the table beside the mattress. Sarah was having trouble pulling the gown over her hips, since they hadn't taken the time to undo all of the laces, and she jumped, trying to hike it higher. Her foot caught in the folds of fabric, and she slipped, plowing face-first onto the low straw mattress with a shriek.

Leah spun around and gasped, trying to untangle her from the twisted dress and help her to her feet.

A knock sounded on the door. "Are you all right?" Will called out hesitantly.

The two girls gave each other horrified glances at the prospect of him seeing Sarah in this state. "Don't come in!" they shrieked in unison, struggling to get Sarah on her feet and making a ruckus as they bumped into things and gave commands to each other in harsh whispers. Sarah accidentally shoved the mattress against the wall with a bang when she gave a kick as she and Leah worked to get the dress up.

"Are you certain—?"

"I'm almost done!" Sarah called out anxiously, hoping she hadn't split the dress seams as she hurriedly slipped her arms through the sleeves. She shoved a few jagged hairpins between her lips, scooping her curls back into some semblance of a bun as Leah worked to cinch the dress together in the back.

"Quick, use this." Leah reached for the small arrow on the table and stabbed it through Sarah's chignon with more force than was necessary in her haste. She came around and opened the tin, dabbing some of the berry-tasting goo onto Sarah's lips. "Your cheeks are all flushed now, so we won't be needing much of this."

When she had finished, Sarah slipped on her boots, quickly laced them, and then stood for the girl's inspection. "Good enough?"

Leah nodded, looking pleased. "I wish we'd had more time, but you look really nice."

Sarah gave her a hesitant smile, not sure if that meant she looked good enough to meet with a queen that afternoon. "Wish us luck." She threw the door open and caught Will's surprised look.

"I'm sorry, but it sounded like quite the fracas was going on." He glanced past Leah and her too-bright smile and caught the rumpled sheets, the dresses littering the floor.

Sarah pasted on a casual look and grabbed his arm, trying to steady her breathing. "Just getting ready. Shall we?"

"The mysteries of women," he commented with a grin and guided her downstairs. The family was waiting for them by the door.

"Enjoy your time with the queen," sighed Mrs. Jones dreamily.

Mr. Jones clapped Will on the back in encouragement. He looked a little awkward at their attention, but he smiled in gratitude, taking in this family's love. "Thank you."

"Come back for supper so we can hear all about the ceremony!" Ruth called as Sarah and Will walked across the porch, and he promised they would.

"You appear to be enjoying yourself with the family," Sarah remarked as they moved across the lawn.

"Yes, I believe my presence came at the right time. Mrs. Jones has been especially attentive, and I believe it helps her to have an extra body in the house in Seth's absence." His expression turned faraway, thoughtful. "And having a mother figure after so many years has been better than I could have thought. I cannot believe I missed out on so many years with their family because of some forgotten disagreement between Seth and myself."

He hitched the wagon, which had been parked outside to make more room in the barn for the party, and Sarah realized he was wearing last night's clothes. Out of earshot from the family, she said as she climbed into the seat, "You're wearing the same thing you had on at the wedding. Please tell me you didn't stay out all night."

He hopped up beside her, shrugging as he grabbed the reins and got the wagon turned toward the road. "I only stayed for a little while to ensure the perimeter was safe. I knew I would get little sleep after such an eventful evening, and so I thought it might help to exhaust my mind, as well. However"—he gave her a placating look, his tone calm—"I knew you would be vexed if I stayed until dawn, so I did proceed home, after a time."

Smiling, Sarah placed a hand on his arm. "Thank you for caring enough to keep watch of me, though you do know you don't have to stress over my well-being all the time. You gotta have a little faith," she added in a teasing tone.

It had been said in jest, but the contented look on Will's face slowly fell away. She retracted her hand, worried she had offended him somehow. "I was only kidding, Will."

He sighed and shook his head. Casting her a sidelong glance, she saw the misery in his dark blue eyes. "You might have said it in jest, but I believe we both know that it is what you want—for me to have faith." Will sucked in a shuddering breath as he steered the animals onto the main road. "And I am trying—to believe the way my parents did and show the kind of faith in the Almighty and love for others that you exhibit in your own life."

Heart quickening, Sarah held her breath, afraid that the smallest sound might stop him from admitting those words she longed to hear. Just knowing that he was considering it . . .

"But it's not yet real for me," he continued, cringing as he shot a quick look her way, as if wary of her reaction. She did her best to mask how her heart sank past her ribs. Drawing his eyes back to the rode, Will went on, his words halting. "It's not as though I don't believe in God's existence, but I have yet to see His mercy or love in my own life."

"What about when I was dying?" Sarah reminded gently. "You told me that I was fading quickly from Allan's poison and that you prayed for my recovery. God listened to you then, so why would it be different now?"

But he already looked as though he had dismissed that instance. His tone was one of regret as he admitted, "It would be impossible for me to deny that He had a hand in your recovery, yes, but that's just it—your recovery. His mercy extended to you in that moment because you are blameless."

Sarah was so shocked over his conclusion that she was truly speechless for half a minute. Her laugh of surprise appeared to startle him. "I'm not some magical girl that has grace follow me wherever I go because I deserve it, if that's what you're getting at. I have screwed up countless times and continue to make mistakes; I'm nothing special. The only thing that sets me apart from other people is that I accept God's grace as it's stretched out to me, day after day—generally because I mess up in new ways all the time," she added wryly. "And I know that He loves and cares for me. If there is anything extraordinary in me, it's because of Him."

They'd had a similar conversation before, just prior to their parting last winter in Serimone, and he had worn the same expression on his face—that look of reluctance to believe that God cared for him when He had allowed Will's parents to die, and sadness that he couldn't have faith in something outside of himself. His restless heart was always searching—for security, for love—and she knew that he was looking in the wrong places.

Taking her hand in his calloused one, Will leaned over to plant a soft kiss on the back of her hand. "My mother was unique in the way she prayed aloud, as though the Almighty was in the room with her, and she expressed a similar tenacity in her faith." His lips curved in a small, wistful smile as he watched the road before them. "I wish I could trust as you both have."

"It's not about trust," she countered quietly, holding onto his hand as though the touch could make him feel God's love. "It's about having faith in the right people."

He turned his tiny smile on her and then looked back at the road without commenting.

Sarah was silent as they emerged from the forest and passed the town gate, and by the way Will's shoulders relaxed, she assumed he thought she had let the matter drop. But then she threw out abruptly, "I say this because I care about you, so don't take this the wrong way, but I hope that someday God puts you in a situation where your strength isn't enough and you have no choice but to rely on Him—that you'll be forced to acknowledge that He loves you and you're not guiltier than the rest of us."

"We always have a choice in what we do, though," Will whispered to his feet, his expression thoughtful, if not a little obstinate.

"Yes, we do," she admitted. Placing a hand on his shoulder, she gave it a quick, comforting pulse. "He gives us the opportunity to choose His love—the only thing keeping us from it is, well, us. But I promise to stop pushing you, because I know for a fact that it won't be real to you until you've experienced it for yourself."

Giving her a look of appreciation, though his gaze was still heavy, Will stepped from the wagon, causing it to shift jerkily in the absence of his weight. He helped her down and together they strode past the guards, through the inner courtyard, where the grass patches on either side of the stone pathway were beginning to grow back after a harsh winter. Will didn't need to announce their names to the guard stationed at the massive door leading into the castle.

The man's face lit up and he gave Will's hand a hearty shake. "Taylor, wonderful news about the honor King Adrian wishes to present you with, boy." He chuckled. "Though I suppose you are a boy no more."

Will shook his hand in return. "Lawrence, this is Lady Sarah Matthews." She had thought the guard looked vaguely familiar, and when she heard his name, she recalled seeing him at the ball she and Will had attended on her first trip to Serimone. They had snuck into the dungeons to see Karen after she had been accused of witchery, and Lawrence had nearly caught them as they attempted to rejoin the other partygoers.

Smiling to the man, whom she thankfully realized didn't recognize her, she bobbed her head in greeting. "Nice to meet you."

Lawrence dipped his own head and smiled in return as he opened the enormous door for them. "The pleasure is all mine, milady." Shifting his attention to Will, he commented, "Terrance will guide you to the room where you can change, then he will escort Lady Matthews to the throne room, but you had better hurry, Taylor—they're nearly ready for you." He paused, eying Will up and down. "I'm assuming you already took care of the ritual bathing," he muttered quietly.

Will cast an embarrassed glance in Sarah's direction, and then nodded in the affirmative. Lawrence bade him good luck, and she tried to hide her grin as they entered the castle, amused that the word bathe had seemed so immodest to Will.

The castle had few windows to prevent some of the cold from entering and help insulate the chilly stone building against the harsh winter winds as best they could, but it always kept the interior immersed in shadows and a depressing gray light. Torches were mounted every few feet to light the way and help stave off the chill that had settled into the stone walls.

"Washing is supposed to symbolize purification of the soul, right?" she commented, hoping conversation would make the situation less awkward for Will. She drew upon what little she had gleaned from Professor Demetrius' class and hoped she was on the right track.

"Yes," Will answered, eyes darting about their surroundings. "It's required before the actual dubbing can be performed by the king."

"There you are!" They both turned sharply to the left and saw Terrance hurrying toward them. The older man's smile brightened when he realized Sarah was there, and she gave him a friendly little wave, remembering how she and Terrance had both felt the loss of their friend, Edith.

"Lady Sarah," he said, sounding pleased. "This is a delightful surprise. The queen mentioned you might attend, but I was not certain you would be able."

"How are you?" she asked. It was strange that this kindly older man felt like a little piece of home, but he carried reminders of Edith with him. Now that the horrible sting of despair had faded over the months, it was nice to be reminded of her by someone who had cared for the woman as Sarah had.

Terrance took both her hands between his and gave them a fatherly pat. "Well, my dear, very well. But I truly must get Master Taylor changed. We are pushed for time as i' 'tis."

They quickly followed behind him along the lit corridor on the main floor, and he motioned Will inside a brightly lit room—there was only a small table with a pitcher atop it and a settee in the corner, and a haze hung in the tiny space from the burning torches. A pair of black trousers, a thick white vest, and a red robe lay across the back of the couch, waiting for him.

"Someone will come for you when you are finished," Terrance said to Will, who nodded blankly. The older man turned to Sarah. "This way, my lady." She gave Will a thumbs up, and he looked like he was going to be sick.

Quietly, she trailed behind Terrance down a long hall, past several open archways, and into the throne room, where many nobles had already gathered, conversing quietly amongst themselves. Sarah had only seen the living quarters and sitting rooms, and she had dined in the Great Hall once, and though these rooms were impressive, they were all a little dreary with the cold stone walls. However, the throne room appeared completely set apart from the rest of the castle.

It wasn't huge like the Great Hall, but it was opulent and long, with drapes of deep purple and red hanging from the high ceiling, some having been swept aside to reveal the beautiful tapestries on the walls that depicted scenes of war and seduction and court life. Pillars were dispersed along the walls as well, wrapped with golden chords and sashes and painted with leaves of the same color. A red velvet carpet ran the length of the room and ended at the front of the dais, the steps of which supported a large sword and shield with the royal crest painted on the face.

Sarah saw atop the stone platform two tall, plush throne chairs that were swathed in fabric, the backs having been decorated with beautiful carvings and intricate designs. Just beyond those chairs, at the back wall, hung an enormous painting for the royal crest—a sword stabbed through the heart of a crown with a lion crouched beside it. Three gigantic wooden chandeliers hung above it all, lighting the long room and making the oiled stone glisten. The gentle hum of conversation that bounced off the walls made the room feel full and alive.

"It's spectacular," Sarah whispered breathlessly, not meaning to say it aloud.

Terrance chuckled at her side, urging her toward the front of the room. "You will have to tell Her Majesty so."

Sarah suddenly recalled that she would be seeing the royals again, and she glanced down at her dress self-consciously, wondering if it was suitable for the occasion. The light pink fabric scooped off her tan shoulders, and thick ribbons of pink and peach had been secured to each shoulder, trailing past her knees over the solid, pale gray sleeves beneath. A small band tightened the colored fabric of the sleeves around her wrist to keep it in place and allowed the remaining cloth to flow freely toward the floor, waving gently each time she moved. A leather belt in the shape of an upside-down crown and the color of a ripe peach was tied around her waist, cinching the tiered folds of pink, peach, and gray that fell in thick layers to the floor. It was some of the most beautiful and rich-looking fabric Sarah had ever seen, and she reminded herself to thank Leah later for selecting it from the gowns Damien had bought her. Vaguely, she wondered if he would be pleased with how it looked.

She pursed her lips, chastising herself.

Just then, two forms entered the room from a side entrance near the back, and everyone turned suddenly silent. Sarah watched as King Adrian preceded his mother into the throne room and mounted the steps on the side of the dais. They took their seats, both looking regal, though the new king appeared exhausted and like a hollow shell of his former self. Sarah cringed at his sallow appearance and the shadows under his eyes, though he tipped his chin regally. She glanced around her and realized Terrance had gone, and when she looked back, the queen was smiling at her. Sarah might have imagined it, but she thought she appeared a little relieved to find her there.

Everyone turned at once, and Sarah followed suit quickly, her heart catching a little in her chest as Will entered from the back, looking resplendent in his knight-wear. His nervous look was gone, replaced by a solemn dignity as he slowly made his way down the carpet to the king and queen. A slow, proud smile spread across Sarah's mouth as he walked by in his white vest and red robe, which symbolized purity and nobility, if she recalled correctly. As he passed, Will's gaze flickered in her direction before quickly returning his eyes to what was before him. But the corner of his lips twitched, and she knew he was glad she was there.

He had reached the steps of the dais, and Will dropped slowly to one knee, placing his right fist over his heart in respect to the royal family.

King Adrian rose to his feet, tugging gently on the ends of his thick purple vest and sending a hush over the room. He walked to the edge of the steps, just above the sword and shield, and stared down at Will, whose head was bowed. "William Taylor"—once addressed, Will was able to raise his head and look at the man—"you are here today to receive honor from this court of Serimone, which is forever in your debt for your service in bringing justice to our land."

The young king paused and seemed to take a breath to collect himself. Sarah felt a pang of sympathy for him, knowing that he had lost his father to his uncle's callousness and was trying to live up to the greatness King Josiah had established in the kingdom. It couldn't be easy to live under a legacy like that.

King Adrian said in a grave voice, "This honor of knighthood shall be bestowed upon you with your acceptance of the chivalric code and the Oath of Knighthood. You must vow to live a life of dignity and to never involve yourself with traitors or activity traitorous to the crown; you must never give ill counsel to a lady and shall express respect for the fairer sex; and you shall swear to defend to your utmost the weak and oppressed, the orphans and widows, and shall be courteous in all of your dealings."

Sarah felt herself smiling, thinking that Will had already taken up the mantle of protector as the king went on. "Do you accept this Oath of Knighthood and vow to embrace the honor and duty that comes with it, knowing that should you prove false, you shall suffer divine retribution from the Almighty for your unfaithfulness?"

Sarah thought that was a bit extreme, but Will agreed without hesitation. "I do, my lord." His voice rang out strong and clear in the room.

A guard—or perhaps he was another knight, judging by the vest he wore similar to Will's—took up the sword on the dais and handed it to the king, who wielded it, tapping the blunt side of the blade to both of Will's shoulders as he said solemnly, "Then I dub thee, William Taylor, Sir Knight of the Royal Court of Serimone."

The crowd clapped heartily as Will stood. His robe was removed, and someone slipped a thin chainmail vest over his clothes. Another guard—or knight—wrapped a belt around his waist and girded the sword to his side.

Sarah felt immeasurably proud as she watched him receive the attention with an austere gaze, though she could tell from the swelling of his chest that this was more of an honor than he had let on. When he was properly dressed, the shield was handed to him, and he knelt once more, placing a fist over the crest on the shield where his heart should be. "I swear my fealty to the true king of Serimone." King Adrian smiled slowly, the first crack in his solemn facade.

Roaring applause filled the hall once more, and Sarah couldn't hide her smile. "You shall now retire to the Great Hall to honor Sir Taylor's valor with a feast," the king announced loudly to be heard over the hearty accolades, and his words started another round of cheers. Judging by the raucous sound, the guests were even more excited at the prospect of food and drink than they were over a new knight coming into their midst.

Will rose and turned to Sarah as the gathering dispersed, breathing heavily, eyes bright with excitement. Before he could join her like she knew he wanted, Queen Meredith descended the steps of the dais with elegance and stood before him, smiling regally. She placed her fingertips delicately on his shoulder. “You have honored this kingdom and my husband’s memory, Sir Knight, and you have my gratitude for that.”

Nodding gravely, Will merely said, “Thank you, Your Majesty.”

She dipped her head once to dismiss him and then moved toward Sarah, her court-trained smile turning at once relaxed and friendly. “I am so pleased you are here, my dear.” She placed an airy kiss on either of Sarah’s cheeks. “Come, you must join me at the feast while the king and Sir Knight confirm the ceremony.”

Sarah masked her grin. Sir Knight. She could get used to that.

Chapter Seven

"The truth is rarely pure and never simple."

Oscar Wilde, *The Importance of Being Earnest*

Sarah had attended two different festive occasions at the castle, and both had been opulent and filled with energy, but the atmosphere of the feast in Will's honor was exciting and electric.

The Great Hall was filled to the brim with nobles and aristocrats and a few of the better-known townsfolk. The sound of laughter from the lords and ladies, some having started early in the celebration and were half-drunk already, echoed through the enormous hall. Several long tables had been spread throughout the room, laden with meats and delicacies and sweets, tankards of honeyed mead and goblets of spiced wine. Sarah gave a startled laugh as a Fool lumbered past her, carrying a harp too big for his thin body, the bells on his silly hat jangling as he passed.

The queen chuckled lightly next to her. "You appear surprised," she commented.

Sarah nodded vaguely, amazed at the energized atmosphere and the complete lack of inhibition present in the guests as they laughed gaily, drank their fill, and danced around the tables to the music of the flute and stringed instruments played joyfully in the far corner. "I just can't believe they're all so . . . relaxed. Everyone enjoyed themselves at the balls I've attended, but this is something else."

Smiling at the gathering, Queen Meredith remarked, "Yes, I suppose it is quite different. You can sense a shift in the attitude of everyone present, can you not?" Sarah nodded affirmatively. "I attribute it to a feeling of security, knowing that the kingdom is at last set right after so long, with Adrian taking control as king and the death of my brother-in-law." Sarah watched her swallow thickly, noticing she didn't say Cadius' name. Hiking her chin a fraction, the queen added, "This ceremony serves as a reminder of Serimone's well-being, the fact that it is being cared for by noble and brave knights and men of strength."

"I guess they don't mind embarrassing themselves, then," Sarah muttered, but somehow the queen caught her words above the cacophony in the Great Hall, and her mouth quirked in a look of genuine amusement.

"They do look rather gauche, I am forced to admit, and many of them shall more than likely remain at the castle for the night after their amusements." Queen Meredith's golden-brown eyes lit with an idea, and she glanced up at Sarah hopefully. "I do hope you will do me the honor of taking a turn about the gardens this evening. The roses are coming in beautifully"—she looked back to the boisterous gathering with a wary eye—"and I find these events to be rather taxing and vain."

"I'd love to," Sarah replied quickly, feeling a small spark of importance that out of everyone, the queen wished to spend time with her. Meredith had not been raised for this life—her sister, Alexis, had—and maybe it took one awkward out-of-towner to put the queen at ease, reminding her that she was not the only one to feel alien here.

"Wonderful." The petite woman smiled brightly up at her, but it faded as she examined the crowd. "I am afraid that I must engage my guests now." A man nearby belched loudly, and she gave a small wince. "But perhaps I shall come for you before the feast is over."

Sarah grinned and nodded, watching the woman glide with graceful movements through the gathering. Unsure what to do with herself as she waited for Will to join them, Sarah observed the guests, hoping to spot someone she recognized. But the only noble she had truly known was Damien, and she definitely did not want to run into him now.

She made her way to the tables along the far wall to avoid as many jostling, overexcited, inebriated guests as possible. A clearly drunk man wearing a cap similar to that of the Fool, though it sagged off his head in a haphazard fashion, staggered in Sarah's direction and forced her closer to the wall. She quickly ducked to avoid one of the many hanging fire bowls that were spread about the area to provide warmth and light in the gigantic room. Luckily, the man passed out before he could upset the flaming bowl and fell into a dead sleep beneath it.

Shaking her head in annoyance, Sarah hurried toward the closest table, hoping to keep her hands and her mind busy by perusing the selection of delicious treats on the table. Hmm. No chocolate, she thought vaguely, eyes searching as she fiddled with her skirt.

Thunderous applause suddenly filled the Great Hall, and she spun around in surprise to find everyone's backs turned. Will had just entered the room, and he started at the noise, looking terribly uncomfortable with all eyes on him. When he spotted her familiar face after a frantic search of the crowd, his shoulders sagged in relief, and he hurriedly pushed his way toward her, accepting the hearty claps on his should and the shouts of encouragement with a pained smile. The shield and sword were gone—merely ceremonial ornaments left behind, Sarah assumed—but he still wore the chainmail over his white vest.

"My knight in shining armor," she commented brightly when he reached her, adjusting the metal vest he wore. "Is it heavy?"

"It isn't so much the weight, simply that it feels restraining," Will replied honestly, then lurched forward as a husky fellow slapped him on the back, calling out loudly, "Well done, lad!"

The man's wife eyed Will up and down with a far-too-familiar gaze. "I feel safer already," she remarked, gliding past in her portly husband's wake.

Sarah gaped after her. "Seriously?" she asked dryly, though a little too late as the woman was halfway across the room by the time she regained her voice. Sarah turned to Will, who was grinning down at her. "Don't give me that look. I wasn't jealous—she was being incredibly obnoxious and rude. I mean, honestly!" she huffed, at a loss for words.

But Will continued to look amused, and so she quickly returned the subject to his knighting. "That was exciting—the ceremony, I mean. I've never been in a throne room before."

"Nor I. It was quite the experience." He fussed with the end of the chainmail again.

"It's not going to get any looser," she commented in amusement.

He sighed disgruntledly and dropped his arms. "It simply feels different than I expected, is all."

Sarah wondered what he meant by that but didn't get the chance to ask as a short, stocky fellow sidled up to them, smiling broadly at Will. "Young Taylor, I was surprised when I heard that His Majesty was acknowledging you, but I couldn't be more pleased for you. I know your parents would be proud of the legacy they left behind."

"Thank you," Will answered quietly, his eyes serious.

The man glanced at Sarah and gave her a friendly sort of smile, though he immediately turned his gaze back to Will. She thought it was a little rude that he practically ignored her standing right there, though she tried to tell herself not to be offended, as most men in this era didn't treat women with as much respect as Will and the Jones family did. But it still grated on her nerves.

"I must introduce you to Landon Mallory," the man went on. "He is a noble who knew your father while he worked the castle. You were very young when he met you last, and I know he would enjoy seeing how you've grown. Come—come, come."

Will glanced at Sarah, appearing reluctant to leave her side. "Go make your rounds," she said with a smile, though she felt a little disappointed that he was leaving so soon. "I promised the queen I would join her later, anyway. Just come for me when you're ready to go, all right?"

Will nodded and waited for the man—who didn't even bother to bid Sarah farewell—to turn around before ducking his head and planting a quick kiss on her cheek. When he pulled back, she mouthed I'm proud of you, and her sincere approval seemed to mean more to him than all the praise in the room. With a nod and a small smile of gratitude, Will followed the man across the floor and through the sea of jovial party guests, who appeared to care less about the reason for the party than they did about having a reason for feasting and drinking.

Feeling once again a little lost and alone among the gaiety of the huge party, Sarah moved slowly through the crowd just for something to do. A few gentlemen—as well as some not-so-gentle men—asked her to dance or tried to engage her in conversation, but she didn't feel like talking with any of them. Will was across the room, speaking with a large group of men, and he kept shooting glances in her direction. She gave him an encouraging smile so he wouldn't abandon his duties as the guest of honor, and she moved on through the gathering.

Her heart quickened with relief when she saw the queen, staring with glazed eyes at the man who was speaking with animated hand movements to her and the young king, who both pretended to listen. Well, Queen Meredith did, nodding every once in awhile, while Adrian's gaze wandered aimlessly about the Great Hall.

Suddenly, the queen's eyes shifted and caught Sarah moving in their direction. She smiled at the younger girl and summoned her with a subtle gesture. As Sarah approached, King Adrian glanced her way, and up-close, his gray eyes were duller than she remembered. His eyes brightened a modicum with recognition. "Lady Matthias, is it?"

"Matthews, actually," Sarah corrected before she could stop herself. She paused, wondering if it was completely moronic to correct a king. But his mother was masking a delicate smirk of amusement, and the young king looked unbothered as he nodded.

"Yes, of course, you were Lord Lisandro's guest. Nasty business, that was," he added dimly.

Shockingly, the expression of the man with the strange looking mustache became even more animated at Adrian's words. He fixed his beady gaze on Sarah. "You knew Lisandro?"

"A little," she answered slowly, carefully.

"Such a grotesque scheme concocted by he and Cadius," the man went on. "To kill the king and try to steal the throne from the next monarch is unfathomable. The thought of that filth being a relation of our dear king, may he rest in peace, is despicable. Why I—"

"Silence!" King Adrian interjected harshly, eyes brighter than Sarah had ever seen them. He was breathing heavily, staring the shocked man down with a horrific glare. A few others heard him above the din and began whispering over his outburst. The young king looked like he wished to rebuke the man further, but his mother placed a light hand on his arm, giving him a subtly imploring look.

Turning her suddenly courteous gaze to their guest, she said smoothly, "Lord Chiffray, I am so sorry to depart, but you must excuse Lady Sarah and myself. I have promised her my attention this hour."

"Of course, My Queen, of course," Lord Chiffray replied heartily, shooting the still seething king a disconcerted look. He gave a quick, hurried bow to both royals before moving through the gathering, his short legs working rapidly as he tried to escape the king's displeasure.

Queen Meredith removed the hand from her son's arm. "Please, my dear," she whispered before leaving his side. Confused at the exchange, Sarah gave the king a quick curtsy, receiving a civil but strained nod in return, and joined the queen's side as they moved between bodies. The queen glided among the guests with a kind of delicate grace that Sarah could never hope to mimic.

"I know it is still a bit early," Queen Meredith remarked as they continued toward the open door leading from the Great Hall. "But might you consider departing for a bit of fresh air earlier than we had planned?"

Sarah tried to hide her smirk of relief. "The best words I've heard all day." She glanced over her shoulder and saw that Will was surrounded on all sides by a new group of gentlemen and ladies, and one man was clapping him jovially on the shoulder. Will still appeared uncomfortable with the praise, but there was a small, shy smile on his face as he received their blessings. He didn't appear in desperate need of saving just yet.

"I realize that it is the natural order of things," the queen was saying. Sarah quickly returned her attention to the woman and found her gaze pensive. The sounds of the gathering faded as they wound their way through the torch-lit halls. "Yet it is so difficult to raise a boy, to love him with your entire being, only to one day be forced to allow him grow up to be a monarch that makes his own decisions."

"How is he handling it?" Sarah asked, knowing he'd had plenty thrown at him at once: his father's murder, the betrayal and death of his uncle and advisor, becoming king.

With a sigh, the queen gave her a faint, pained smile. "It has been a challenge, I imagine, though he speaks little to me of the matter. But I know he and Cadius"—she flinched at the name—"had become close during the king's illness, and that bond only grew after his father's passing."

Her practiced mask slipped, and Sarah saw worry lining her features. "Adrian has changed so much in the past year, and it concerns me that he keeps everything inside of him." The queen gave a small start as she realized all she had revealed, and she uttered a tiny laugh. "I must apologize, my dear, for burdening you with such dreary tales. It is simply that I find my guard slips easily with you around."

Sarah's face was serious. "I'll take that as a compliment, but I hope you know that I won't share any of what you just told me. Your secrets are safe with me."

Looking content, the petite woman took Sarah's hand and placed it in the crook of her arm, patting it fondly. "I imagine so." They made their way to the servants' entrance, as it was closer than the main doors. Servants stared as they passed, some merely ducking their heads while others bowed deeply to their queen. She smiled at each of them in turn, looking them directly in the eye, and Sarah could tell that they all adored her. A scullery maid hurried to the door and opened it for them, bowing her head and holding a curtsy until they passed outside.

The queen seemed to breathe out the chaotic atmosphere of the feast and inhaled the crisp air around them. "Alexis was much better at these large social events than I," she commented suddenly with a small, self-deprecating smile.

"I have a sister, too. She's younger but sometimes I think she's smarter and more mature than I am." Sarah chuckled at the truth of that statement, but the older woman didn't smile.

"Alexis was very intelligent in all areas of life, except in those concerning men. Although she was raised to rule as a monarch and personified the perfect future heir in public, she rarely behaved as such among friends and constantly seemed to acquire new 'gentlemen companions,' as she called them." The queen frowned. "An assembly that included Cadius, I am afraid."

Sarah stared at her in open-mouthed shock. "Alexis and Cadius? But she married his brother." She suddenly recalled a conversation long ago with Karen about Cadius having been the rightful heir to the throne as the older brother, but she couldn't remember exactly what had happened, and Karen had definitely never mentioned anything about an affair.

The queen appeared surprised at her lack of knowledge, but then she nodded. "I forget you are not from Serimone. Yes, their romance was kept a secret, though the gossip quickly spread far and wide. For months Cadius seduced her—for his own amusement, I suppose—and Alexis informed me of their plans to run away together, but it was not to be. You see, after their father's death and when Cadius should have been crowned, he became terribly ill. When it appeared he would not recover, Josiah was declared the new king and Alexis was forced to turn her affections toward him, as well. So you see, both Josiah and I were unprepared to rule." She smiled softly. "Perhaps that is what bonded us so quickly."

"But if Cadius was the heir," Sarah said slowly, thinking her thoughts aloud as they came to her, "then that would mean it would have been Alexis and Cadius who were supposed to marry."

Queen Meredith nodded as she tread lightly over the dirt along the outer wall of the castle, and she let go of Sarah to hike her skirts away from a particularly muddy patch. "Yes, the heirs of Ridlan and Serimone were betrothed from infancy, but I am so relieved that it did not work out that way. My sister and Cadius were both too emotionally insecure and high-need together, and it would have been quite the disaster for the kingdom. It was difficult enough for Josiah and I, what with losing my sister, raising her child, and then losing one of my own—"

"You had a baby?" Sarah was so surprised she didn't even register how rude her question had been, nor the fact that she had stopped mid-stride. When her abrupt question registered, her cheeks reddened, but the queen didn't appear affected as she halted beside her.

"A boy not much younger than Adrian," she commented wistfully, her look faraway. "Oh, he was beautiful, with eyes like mine and a tiny shock of brown hair. He died nearly the same day he was born."

Sarah was reeling with this new discovery about how the regime had been broken down and patched together several times. She couldn't think of anything useful or inquisitive to say except a quiet, "I'm so sorry." And she was. She couldn't imagine her child dying shortly after the loss of her sister. The pain of that was unfathomable, and as Sarah watched the queen's face, she knew that she had to be an incredibly strong woman to have endured so much and still muster such grace and compassion.

"Thank you, my dear." Queen Meredith sucked in a wavering breath. "A mother never moves past the loss of her child, and I do not believe that her heart can heal quite fully in their absence. However, those moments I spent with my only child were some of the most fulfilling of my life, and I will never forget his face." Her wistful expression faded into one of guilt, and she gave Sarah an anxious look. "I did not mean it as it sounded. Adrian is, of course, my son as well, but carrying a child for months is simply . . ." Her voice drifted off, and she appeared at a loss for words.

"Different?" Sarah supplied with a tiny, sad smile.

The queen nodded, her eyes clouded with memories. "Yes, it is very different." She hiked her chin and gave Sarah a motherly, encouraging look. "But we must not dwell on the past and what can never be. We must always look to the future."

"But if you're always looking ahead," Sarah countered, "won't you miss what's right in front of you?"

Quietly and with a smile that looked forced, the queen said, "How right you are."

With a thoughtful gaze, Sarah glanced down the way and saw Richard rounding the corner and hurrying toward them, lugging a heavy sack in front of him. He smiled in what appeared to be pleasant surprise when he saw Sarah, and then he jerked to an abrupt halt when he spotted her companion and the delicate jeweled crown she wore.

"Your Majesty." He didn't quite appear to know what to do, and he stood there awkwardly for a full minute before slowly moving their way. "Just a, ah, delivery for the celebration. Cook placed another order." He raised the heavy sack to support his words, and it bulged with fruits and vegetables.

The queen smiled at him, and he stopped again, appearing surprised to be acknowledged by her. "You must be Dagwood's boy, yes?" Richard nodded mutely, and Sarah noticed he didn't correct her that the man wasn't exactly his father.

"This is Richard," Sarah supplied as the silence lengthened into an uncomfortable pause. "Uh, Richard, I believe you recognize Queen Meredith."

The queen's amiable look faded as she stared into Richard's face, watching his gold-brown eyes with a keen, distant look that Sarah couldn't even begin to decipher. The quiet stretched on, and Sarah wondered if Richard was waiting to be dismissed.

Queen Meredith blinked, appearing to return to herself. Whatever moment there had been was gone. "Yes, well, please tell your father that everything has been quite marvelous."

Richard nodded slowly, his brow knitting slightly in contemplation. "Of course, Your Majesty. Please excuse me." He ducked his head and hurried along the wall to the servants' entrance. Both women watched him go.

"Do you know Richard?" Sarah asked curiously, finding her reaction to his presence strange.

"Hmm?" The queen pulled her gaze from the closing door. "Oh, no, not personally. I have met Dagwood a few times when he has made deliveries or when I have toured the town, and he has spoken of his son many times." She paused, seeming to collect herself. "Now, where was I in the story?"

"Cadius and your sister were supposed to be together, but she and the king married instead," Sarah supplied, though she rushed on before the queen could continue. "But I've met Cadius before, and he was so cold and lifeless. And creepy," she added, muttering the words under her breath as she recalled the way he had threatened her, pretending to be civil as he compared her curiosity to that of the dead deer they stood by. Crazy, murderous streak aside, that encounter alone had left her with a negative viewpoint of him, to say the least. "How could your sister have ever fallen in love with someone so cruel?"

"Sometimes the eyes can see what the heart refuses to acknowledge." The queen looked far away, her expression clouded as she gazed off toward town.

"I suppose you're right." The woman started at Sarah's words and gave her a wavering smile.

"Yes, well, love can play tricks on us sometimes, and that was one of the things that prevented me from seeing how Alexis was stumbling. She had never been without her imperfections, but I looked up to her—so much fire and spirit and a mind of her own." Queen Meredith smiled fondly at her. "Qualities that I have seen in you, my dear, though only the good."

Sarah knew she had just been given an enormous compliment, but she didn't quite know what to say.

"Won't you return for tea on the morrow?" the queen asked suddenly, before Sarah had a chance to respond.

"Yes!" The queen laughed at her enthusiasm. Sarah tried to even her tone, masking her excitement over coming back to the castle and spending more time with royalty. But she was also looking forward to speaking further with the strong-willed woman who was helping to raise a country to its feet. "I'd love to come back."

"Wonderful." Queen Meredith gave her a sweet smile. "Forgive me for monopolizing the majority of our conversation, but tomorrow we shall share more about our pasts and our aspirations for the future. However, we must first return you to your dear knight; a few of the unattached courtiers looked rather hungry for a champion of their own, and I would hate for him to be devoured only a day into his new title." But Sarah only grinned, unconcerned that Will could be so easily taken from her.

Chapter Eight

"Fiction is the truth inside the lie."

Stephen King

The table was full of conversation and questions that night. The Jones gaggle, slightly smaller in the absence of Seth and Karen, were all eager to hear about the ceremony and feast and the new king and his mother. It had been hours of feasting and conversing with strangers before Will had broken away from the group, looking completely overwhelmed, and announced that he needed to depart. However, the crowd hadn't seemed to mind that the guest of honor was leaving their presence as they bid him goodbye and continued right on with the party.

Sitting at the table as they enjoyed dessert with the family, Sarah bit her lip to hide her grin. As Will told Joshua about the order of the ceremony and the oath he'd sworn, the sword and shield he had been given, Leah propped her chin on her hand, staring up at him with a dreamy look in her eyes, her pie left untouched as she listened to his voice. It didn't appear that Sarah was the only one who thought "knight in shining armor" was an attractive title.

"What is the matter with you?" Joshua asked his sister, his nose wrinkled as he considered her. "Did you fall asleep?"

Leah started from her trance, cheeks reddening as she struggled for a reply. Seeing her embarrassment, Sarah quickly jumped to her defense. "I think we're all still pretty exhausted after yesterday." Leah nodded eagerly, shooting her a look of utter gratitude.

"It is getting rather late," Mrs. Jones remarked, casting her eyes out of the dark window. "Leah, dear, perhaps you should turn in. Sarah can help me with the cleanup."

Leah looked torn, but she did appear genuinely tired. "You shouldn't have to do all that, Sarah."

But she was already shaking her head. "I don't mind." And she didn't—doing the dishes at home meant you were a part of the family, and she loved being part of this one.

"If you're sure," Leah said slowly. At Sarah's nod, she gave her a hug.

Sarah whispered so no one else could hear, "How are you doing tonight?" She knew the youngest Jones felt Seth and Karen's absence the most, though she tried hard not to show her loss.

Pulling back, Leah gave her a sad but reconciled look. “It’s natural that he should marry and leave home. It’s what’s done.”

“But it doesn’t mean you can’t be sad about it,” Sarah replied softly. The younger girl’s eyes immediately filled with tears, and Sarah quietly added, “Why don’t we stay up tonight and talk in your room? We can keep each other company.”

Leah nodded eagerly. She turned to Will and gave him a shy, angelic smile. “We’re really proud of you.”

“Aye, that we are.” Ruth Jones came over and reached high to pat Will affectionately on the cheek.

Her husband came forward and shook Will’s hand firmly. “You’ll come again tomorrow, won’t you, son?”

“I would not miss it,” Will answered.

“I’ll walk you out,” Sarah said hurriedly. Joshua shot her a wicked grin that she ignored as she and Will left the kitchen and stepped onto the porch.

“I’m proud of you too, you know,” she said quietly, leaning her back against the railing as he shut the door.

He shot her a smirk as he moved her way, bracing his hands against the handrail on either side of her to box her in. “So you’ve said.”

She could tell he was still making light of his accomplishment. “How can you be so cavalier after an entire day of hearing people praise you and being honored like that?”

“I suppose it hasn’t quite sunk in yet.” His voice was exceptionally low as he leaned toward her, and his gravelly tone caused her stomach to do a quick flip, though it did several rapid-fire somersaults when he kissed her.

“You are in a ridiculously good mood, mister,” Sarah said in surprise once he’d pulled away. He grinned roguishly at her breathlessness.

“I’m simply pleased to have you here with me, love.”

“Uh-huh.” She shot him a look that said she didn’t believe him. “You’re a total adrenaline junky right now, and I don’t want you to do something that you’ll regret because you were intoxicated from an emotional high.”

He placed a kiss on the tip of her nose. “What might that be, love?” he mumbled thickly, keeping his face close to hers. His breath brushed her skin, sending a tiny shiver up her spine.

She had thought up a hilarious comeback a second ago, but as he watched her with that piercing gaze of his and those deep blue eyes, all rational thoughts fell from her mind. His grin spread, turning wicked as her silence lengthened. She pushed him back from her with a huff. “Gah, you’re so distracting.”

He gave a quick, surprised laugh. “Me?”

"Yes, you," she replied shortly. "I'm not used to you being all open and direct and so . . . irresistible." She had meant to catch him off-guard with her candidness, but the second the word left her lips, Sarah threw her head back and groaned. Ugh. Kill me. "I didn't mean that."

Will looked entirely pleased. "But you said it—"

"Poor choice of words." She drew her eyes from the heavens to shoot him a stern look, shooing him away, toward his horse that was tethered to the barn. "Now, go before I embarrass myself further. I have chores to do." He backed down the steps slowly, grinning at her.

"You can tell me to leave when you find me so irresistible?" he asked, his look of wide-eyed innocence upset by his smirk.

Sarah's neck heated. "Go!" Self-satisfied smile in place, he turned around and jogged toward the barn, his laughter carrying through the darkness.

ઉ෴ව

"Thank you again for having me." Sarah accepted the cup of steaming spiced tea held out to her by a young servant girl.

Queen Meredith sipped delicately from her own cup and then smiled at her. "I appreciate the company."

Will had ridden his horse out to the Joneses' a little while after breakfast the next morning and drove Sarah to the castle in the wagon. Blessedly, he kept conversation light and didn't bring up her slip-of-the-tongue the previous evening, though he did shoot her a few knowing grins when he thought she wasn't looking.

Now, drinking tea with the queen in her sitting room, Sarah's mind was so caught up in the fact that she was drinking tea with the queen that she forgot all about last night.

"Tell me something about yourself, Lady Sarah."

She started from her perusal of the sitting room—the draping canopy above the settee in the corner, the roaring fireplace, the opulent rug at their feet and tapestries on the walls, the tea set on the table between them. Sarah gave a small, embarrassed shrug. Her life was definitely uninteresting compared to the queen's stories. "There isn't much to tell, really." Seeing that the older woman was going to wait until Sarah said something, she carefully started with, "Well, I told you about my younger sister, Lilly. She lives with my parents."

"But you do not," the queen added shrewdly, though there was a note of question in her voice.

"Ah, no." Sarah fought for words that would make sense. "I'm working on . . . gaining wisdom. An apprenticeship, you might call it."

Queen Meredith looked pleasantly surprised. She let her rigid posture slip, sinking into the back of her chair as she relaxed. "Educating yourself, are you? Well, I find that quite refreshing." She whispered conspiratorially, "We need more women who can think for themselves."

Sarah smiled in return, relieved. "Thank you." Their conversation about the tangled regime had kept her tossing and turning all night with the questions she wanted to pose. But in the light of day, they all seemed rude and probing, so she hesitated to broach the subject.

"Where were you raised?" the queen asked.

"Oh, well, it's very hot in the summer," Sarah answered carefully, though that gave away nothing.

Scrunching up her straight nose in confusion, Queen Meredith asked, "The desert of the Holy Land?"

"What?" Sarah laughed at their "language barrier." "No, it's much more humid than that. There's a lot of mist in the air," she supplied when the queen continued to look baffled at her explanation.

Expression clearing some, the queen nodded. "Of course."

"What about you? How did you and Alexis like growing up in Ridlan?"

"I handled it fine," the older woman replied, her tone dry. "It was Alexis who was always in search of something greater outside our province. That is why Cadius was so appealing to her on his political visits to Ridlan; he was dangerous and something 'foreign' in a world she christened as dull."

"She sounds like a bit of a rebel," Sarah remarked before she could stop herself.

"Oh, she was certainly insurgent." The queen hesitated, seeming to realize how harsh she sounded. "I loved Alexis, but oftentimes it was difficult to live in the shadow of a woman who did whatever she wished, while those around her imagined her to be perfect."

With a grimace of sympathy, Sarah said, "That must have been annoying."

"It was frustrating at times," the queen answered slowly, and then lifted one shoulder in a delicate shrug. "She was bred for the throne, and so certain behaviors and instances were overlooked, but we did have some marvelous adventures together and loved each other very much."

Rising from her chair, the queen moved toward the opposite end of the room, motioning for Sarah to join her. "I wish to show you something."

Sarah set her cup down on the tray and joined her as the queen opened a door leading into a private bedroom. She stepped inside hesitantly, uncertainly, wondering why it felt as though she was walking into a tomb. The room, though covered with furs and filled with furniture, appeared lifeless, as though it hadn't been touch in years.

"This was Alexis's private room. She and the king had separate bedchambers," Queen Meredith supplied at Sarah's questioning look. "I prefer her private sitting room to my own, and I come in here nearly every week. It sounds absurd, but it makes me feel close to her somehow."

"Oh," was all she said. If Lilly had died, Sarah wasn't sure if she would want constant reminders of the life lost, or if it would feel like wallowing in her pain, reopening the wound day after day.

Soft feet padded across the stones behind them, and they both turned. A girl entered the sitting room, and Sarah recognized Sevrine's blond curls and angelic features. The little French girl had been her maid while Sarah was at the castle, and when Sarah and Will were running from Damien, she had sent Thomas and the royal guard to their aid.

Sevrine's eyes scanned the empty room, and when she glanced up and saw Sarah, her beautiful eyes brightened. "Mademoiselle!" she cried happily, her accent as thick as ever as she hurried into the bedchamber. She saw the queen as she passed the doorway and looked suddenly alarmed before she attempted to wipe all expression from her face. Ducking her head subserviently, she missed the way the queen smiled fondly at her.

"What is it, my dear?"

The girl launched into soft but rapid-fire French, and Queen Meredith held up a hand. "English, little one."

"Oh, oui." Sevrine hesitated and then began in broken English, "The king is needing you . . . to come near him to speak of . . ." She searched for the words, appearing flustered as her fair cheeks turned pink, and then finished her message in hurried French.

Queen Meredith rattled off a few words in the girl's native tongue, and Sevrine nodded. The older woman gave her an encouraging smile. "Well done. Your English is improving." The girl blushed at her praise and dipped her head. Giving Sarah an apologetic look, the queen said, "I regret that the king requires my input on the next feast. It will take but a few minutes."

Sarah waved her hand dismissively in the air. "Take all the time you need." She gave the little girl a smile. The last time she had seen her, the two other girls who had acted as Sarah's maids, Beatrice and Jenna, had been rather cruel to the child. She hoped Sevrine wasn't working with them anymore, but the queen appeared to have a fondness for the girl, and Sarah sensed she would look out for her.

"It was nice to see you again, Sevrine," she said.

The French girl gave her a shy smile in return as she and the queen left the room.

Alone, Sarah shifted on the balls of her feet, wondering if she was supposed to wait in there for the queen or return to the sitting room. Uncertain, she moved another step inside, eyes roving the smooth bedcovers, the chairs and desk that looked as though they had been dusted frequently.

She rounded the room, gently fingering the soft, plush blanket as she passed on her way to the desk. She ran a finger over its glossy finish. Curious as to what she would find inside, Sarah opened one of the drawers, wondering what kind of person she could glean from the articles in the desk, but it was empty. Closing it silently, she peered inside the opposite drawer and found only a horsehair brush, with a few red-brown hairs wedged between the bristles.

Sarah grimaced. Creepy. She rolled her eyes at herself, realizing that she was the one snooping through a dead woman's things out of idle curiosity. Deciding she would wait in the sitting room for the queen to return, she slid the drawer closed. It made a strange, hollow *thunk* as it connected with something, and she winced.

"Please don't be broken, don't be broken," she whispered, opening and closing it again. It made the sound once more, of thick wood smacking together, and she frowned. It shouldn't have been that interesting, but Sarah let her curiosity get the better of her.

She pulled on the knob again and pulled out the hairbrush, setting it on top of the desk. Gently, she tugged on the corners of the drawer, trying to slip it out. The wood gave a high-pitched squeak as it slid off the track, and she cast a nervous glance over her shoulder, thinking how bad it would look if someone found her like this and wondering why she had even done it in the first place.

Hesitating, she considered putting everything back and walking away. But she was already holding the loose drawer in her hands and saw that the solid back was missing, which distracted her from thoughts of being discovered putting her nose where it shouldn't be. The drawer was also considerably shorter than the other one, and the wood at the back was splintered and peeling, as though someone had done a crude job of sawing it in half. But why? Sarah wondered.

She set the drawer on the floor and peered inside. Something caught the hazy light from the small window, but she couldn't make out any shapes. Curious, she reached a hand inside, and it didn't take her long to find the flat box at the back. She pulled it out, heart quickening as she examined the wooden box in her hands. There was nothing significant about it. It was flat and longish with a few small gems along the edges, but the fact that someone—Alexis—had gone through so much trouble to hide it meant something. And in light of all the secrets surrounding this family, it was certainly suspicious.

Shooting a wary glance at the empty doorway, Sarah opened the lid. Inside were several letters, all yellow with age and covered in water spots that looked strangely like teardrops. Although she had traveled through time and was living in the twelfth century at the moment, it dawned on her that these letters had been written nearly a thousand years before her time, by someone who had lived and had so many different stories to tell.

She tentatively ran a finger over the rough, discolored parchment. With careful fingers, she removed the uppermost letter from the pile and set the box on top of the desk. Pausing to listen for the sound of footsteps and hearing only her own breathing, Sarah reverently opened the letter, fingers shaking as she unstuck the broken seal. The ancient parchment crackled as she unfolded it gently, hoping it didn't disintegrate in her hands. Instinctively, her eyes roved the small letter quickly, catching glimpses of words that led her to believe it was a love letter, but her mouth swung open when she saw Cadius' signature at the bottom.

More curious than ever, Sarah's eyes eagerly scanned from beginning to end and realized that it was, indeed, a love letter, though she frowned in confusion at the words. Cadius had obviously manipulated them all, but this letter was genuine and heartfelt and impassioned.

Alexis,

Knowing that our plans have been foiled by your impending marriage to my brother is the acutest kind of torture. Yet the thought of you taking your own life, of my being forced to live a day without you in this world, is unfathomable. You have too much life in you to snuff out, and I beg of you, my heart, reconsider your betrothal. Even if we are not each other's possession, I shall see your face everyday and revel in the fact that Josiah will never have your heart, as I do.

Yours for eternity,
Cadius

With each word Sarah read, she found her belief that he had only seduced Alexis simply for entertainment, as the queen had assumed, slipping away. It was a side of Cadius that she had never seen in those brief instances she'd encountered him, and she doubted few others had glimpsed it. Then again, the bit that spoke of besting his brother by winning Alexis's heart first did sound like the Cadius who had his own brother killed in cold blood.

Shaking her head at herself but unable to resist, Sarah set the note back in the stack and pulled another out at random, quickly opening it before her conscience could prevent her. The note was a description from Cadius on how Alexis could fashion a secret compartment into the desk through which they could pass notes, and Sarah immediately discarded that one. The lettering on the next was askew, with large letters that made it look as though the writer had hurriedly scribbled his thoughts on the page. It appeared to be a response to something Alexis had written.

I know you are anxious over our circumstances, but know that I share in your agony. I might be the man in whose arms you spend your nights, but all the while I know that it is my brother who will spend his days with you. It has been a torment to see you at his side, though rare that occasion is as your affection for him wanes. My only consolation is the passing days marked by the growth of the child inside of you.

"Adrian," Sarah whispered, eyes hungrily scanning the page, though it ended quickly after that with a cryptic promise from Cadius to bring peace to their lives someday. Pausing only for a second to listen, she prayed the queen would take her time and forced aside the insanity of what she was doing as she greedily reached for another small folded letter, this one littered with cramped, meticulous script. It read:

We are nearing the end. You expressed your concern of my plans, but I assure you that I shall employ great care as my design unfolds. It will take time as I gather men who are willing to unseat the current monarch, but be patient, dear heart; I swear to you, we will be free of this gilded cage soon. I shall release our souls from the tyranny of my brother by releasing his soul from this life, as I promised you I would.

Sarah frowned down at the letter, brow furrowed in anger. Cadius had started plotting his brother's death over two decades ago. Knowing that malice had been in both their hearts—his and Alexis's—she no longer felt guilty over reading the letters of two dead lovers. With a freshly renewed hatred for the dead man and a growing annoyance with the selfish Alexis, she resumed her place in the letter.

Your time is near, and the pieces are falling into place as we planned. Patience, love—do not be so hasty as to try and rush our plan, as you proposed. All in due course, remember? Everything will go into motion once our child is born—

"No!" Sarah gasped in utter shock, leaning on the desk for support. Her hand connected with the box, which had been perched on the edge, and sent it clattering to the floor. She shrank back at the sound and the mess she had made as the letters fell to a heap in the rug, but she quickly ignored them.

Standing in shock and reeling from her discovery, she whispered, "Adrian is Cadius' son?" How was that even possible? She recalled the portion of Cadius' letter that spoke of he and Alexis "spending" their nights together and realized that it was actually quite possible. And since it sounded as though she and King Josiah hadn't had a very physical relationship, it would have been easy for Alexis to know who the father was.

She stared at the offending parchment as she set it down on the desk and quickly removed her hand from it. She found it difficult to believe that

Alexis had been in on the plot to kill the king—according to Cadius' letter, she'd even been the one to suggest rushing to the endpoint—but she only knew the woman from the queen's biased appraisal of her. The entire letter was incredibly incriminating against both the man and woman involved, and Sarah wondered if anyone had had suspicions of the affair and the early mutiny against the former king.

"It doesn't matter now," Sarah murmured calmly, trying to quiet her rushing thoughts as she stooped to collect the scattered letters. Alexis had died long ago, and Cadius had joined her, having been hanged for his crimes. Sarah's discovery meant little, since everyone involved was now dead.

Not everyone, she reminded herself, pausing from her letter gathering as she thought of the child Alexis had conceived. Did Adrian know who his true parents were, or had Cadius died before he could tell him?

The light padding of footsteps down the hall acted as a trigger for Sarah's shock-frozen limbs. At the faint sound, she immediately kicked into gear, hurriedly stuffing the letters into the box, slapping the lid closed, and shoving it to the very back of its resting place. Her heart pounded angrily in her chest as she dropped the hairbrush inside and slid the drawer back into place just as someone entered the sitting room. She froze in her bent position at the sight of the letter sitting at eye level on top of the desk, hesitating in a moment of panic. With a spark of alarm at the approaching footsteps, she snatched up the last note she had read and stuffed it into her sleeve as the queen rounded the doorway.

"I apologize for the delay," she said, offering an apologetic smile.

Sarah swallowed. "No problem." She tried desperately to sound as though she hadn't been running a marathon, but though her breathlessness was poorly masked, the queen made no comment.

"I hope you were not too bored while I was away," she joked lightly. Sarah nodded, not quite knowing how to answer that. "Shall we continue our discussion in the sitting room?"

Sarah's nervous gaze flickered to the drawer, and she could have sworn her forehead broke out in sweat. How was she going to get the letter back now? But she couldn't see any way out of it, so she simply gave a stiff nod, and the queen preceded her from the room. Sarah cast a longing glance back at the desk, the incriminating missive crinkling faintly in her sleeve.

They sat in their chairs once more, and Sarah tried to act normal and keep her mind off the contents of the letters, but it was nearly impossible. She had to stuff her hands under her thighs to keep them from shaking as the adrenaline made its way through her body.

"Is everything all right with dinner?" She winced at her breathless tone.

Queen Meredith gave a faint wave of her hand. "Oh, yes. We simply needed to discuss the menu, and Adrian was having difficulty deciding between lamb and venison."

Sarah nodded dumbly as the queen spoke, pretending like it was very important. "Adrian. The king. Right." She hesitated and then asked outright, trying to sound casual as she did so, "So, uh, Alexis—did she ever have any other children? You know, besides King Adrian?" There had to be another explanation. The letters were all missing dates, so Adrian could have already been born, and then Cadius and Alexis had their affair. Maybe their child had died before it was brought into the world—nobody would have found them out if there was never a child to discover.

Sarah frowned. But Queen Meredith had told her once before that Alexis had died right after Adrian was born, so she wouldn't have been able to have another baby in that time. Maybe in reverse order, then? Sarah thought quickly, trying to piece everything together as best should could. Their love child could have been born before Adrian came.

She looked up as the queen gave a faint shake of her head, as if dismissing Sarah's thoughts. "No, before she died, she conceived but once, as did I."

The expression on Sarah's face froze in place as her concerns were practically confirmed. Then that must mean that Cadius and Alexis were Adrian's biological parents! She became aware of the silence in the room and quickly said, "Ahh," knowing she had to give some kind of response even as her mind worked furiously. Had Cadius killed Meredith's child or interfered with the pregnancy to secure his son's—Adrian's—right to the throne? Luckily, the queen was reaching for a teacake from the tray and missed the way Sarah's eyes bulged in realization.

He isn't the true heir, she thought, amazed at the clarity of this fact. Adrian was illegitimate, since the former queen had conceived him out of wedlock, and so the proper right to the throne would have gone to Queen Meredith's son, if he'd survived. Cadius could have made sure the child didn't live a full day, and since no one knew of Adrian's soiled heritage, then he was next in line after the king.

"Are you all right?"

The queen was looking at her oddly, and Sarah realized her mouth was ajar. She quickly snapped it closed. "I was just thinking about your child," she said hurriedly, trying to mask the fact that she was still reeling from her discovery.

"Oh." Queen Meredith dropped her eyes to her hands, though there was a tiny smile of remembrance on her lips. "My mother told my sister and I of the bond that occurs between a mother and her child the instant she holds that tiny, squalling infant in her arms. I never quite understood her until the moment I held my son." She hesitated, eyes darkening with sadness. "Though I was only allowed a few hours with him before I was ordered to rest, I saw in him a lion's heart—fierce and dedicated."

"What happened?" Sarah whispered, watching the queen's eyes lower to the floor.

"When I awoke, Mr. Devlin informed me that the child had ceased breathing in his bed. There was nothing to be done."

"The old physician?" Sarah asked in surprise, thinking about the man Damien had sentenced to death on Cadius' order. That had been the start of his lies, and an innocent man had been sent to the gallows because of it.

The queen nodded. "He was a young physician then, but my time came on suddenly, and he was the most readily available assistance." She raised her chin a fraction, seeming to draw strength from the motion. "I was so excited for the arrival of my son that the instant he was born and I saw his inner strength, I requested a pendant be carved—a little flat piece of wood for him to play with until he grew into it." She paused. "He was buried with it instead."

A quiet, creeping suspicion gnawed at the back of Sarah's mind, something completely ridiculous that refused to go away and an idea that she didn't fully understand. Needing to hear her crazy theory refuted, she asked slowly, "The necklace—what was the carving on it?"

The queen smiled vaguely. "I fashioned it after his heart."

"Yes, but what did that look like?" Sarah hated forcing her to speak on the subject, but learning this small truth could change everything.

A single shoulder lifted in a shrug that said the matter was unimportant, though Sarah knew it meant the unraveling of history when she admitted, "On the face of the pendant was the impression of a roaring lion."

Sarah sat back in her chair, trying to keep the shock from her expression even as her mind screamed at her.

Richard is the lost heir!

Chapter Nine

"Ghosts don't haunt us. That's not how it works.
They're present among us because we won't let go of them."
Sue Grafton, *M is for Murder*

Sarah was still shaking her head as she left the castle an hour later, mulling this realization over and over until her head ached. The crackling of the parchment in her sleeve made her cringe guiltily, but there hadn't been an opportunity to put it back. Not that she had even remembered the letter until the queen saw her out; her mind had been too full of questions and answers that only presented more questions.

Had it been Cadius' intent all along to seduce Alexis and put their son on the throne? Did he have Meredith and Josiah's baby killed when that child threatened his son's right to rule? But they were all just questions, frustrating questions, with no one left alive to answer them.

Though winter's chill refused to allow spring to fully take over, the sun broke through the dark clouds to beat down on her head and shoulders, warming her as she strode quickly down the square to Will's shop. The horses and wagon were parked outside the livery, and she hurried past them and through the open door.

Robert turned as she entered and smiled in greeting. "Someone is here to see you, Taylor!" He called out as he selected a shoeing tool from the equipment hung on the wall.

"So," Robert said casually, pretending to examine the tool in his hand. "How is Karen settling in?"

"I don't really know just yet. I was hoping to visit her this afternoon." Sarah paused as a stall rattled closed at the back of the building. She lowered her voice. "Are you doing okay?"

Slowly, he nodded. "I think so, actually." He sounded surprised at the truth of it, and then he smiled at her. "Yes, I'm just happy that she's with someone who will care for her. Now," he said as Will rounded the corner and came into view. Robert backed up a few steps, quirking a brow at Sarah. "If you'll excuse me, I have to go remove the shoes from a devil horse."

"Darth Vader?" Will asked quizzically as he joined them. "He isn't so terrible."

Sarah bit her lip. "You named him Darth Vader?"

"It's the name Robert gave him." He looked confused at her grin. "He said it was German."

She and Robert shared a secretive, amused look before he moved to the back of the building. For a moment she forgot about the burden on her mind as Will helped her into the wagon and they set off.

"How was your visit with the queen?" he asked, shattering the illusion.

Sarah hesitated, wondering if what she had discovered would seem crazy to him. But she was dying to share it with someone, to see if she had jumped to conclusions in reading those letters and speaking with the queen. So she told him everything—of finding the letters, her conversation with the queen, Cadius' plot to put his son on the throne and his affair with Queen Alexis. She even pulled the letter out of her sleeve at one point during the story and read it to him.

Will listened intently, brow furrowing as the story progressed and he guided the wagon through the town gates.

"And there's more."

He shot her a wary glance. "What more could there possibly be?"

"I think Richard is the lost heir!" she blurted, wincing as she waited for his reaction.

His eyes widened, and he actually laughed. "That is the most ludicrous thing I've ever heard."

"Why?" she pressed.

"Because I have known him my entire life. He might act pompous at times, but he is no monarch."

"But think about his history," Sarah urged, pulse racing as everything became clearer now that she had said the words aloud. "Richard was an orphan left on Dagwood's doorstep with a pouch of coins and the lion pendant the queen—"

"There could be hundreds just like it," he countered.

"—had made for him," she finished, as though he hadn't spoken. "If someone was so poor they couldn't care for their own child, how could they afford to give away so much gold to a stranger?"

He shrugged and simply replied, "Perhaps they were well-off but didn't want another child."

Sarah gave him a disbelieving look. She thought of the queen and Richard's encounter, and her voice softened, though she couldn't mask her excitement. "But, Will, he has her eyes—seeing them side by side, they have the exact same eyes. And there was this moment between them, like she recognized him, or something."

Will leaned over to look her square in the face, and his own was sympathetic. "You're forgetting that Queen Meredith's child died. The entire kingdom mourned her loss."

But Sarah was already shaking her head, refusing to be so easily dissuaded. "The queen said that she was only told of her son's death by the physician." She paused, then muttered her thoughts aloud as they came. "I bet it was Malcolm."

"Malcolm Devlin?" Will clarified, sounding doubtful. Then his expression cleared, and he stared ahead at the road, clearly thinking. Almost musing to himself, he said, "Cadius did involve him in the king's death."

"Exactly!" Sarah's heart rate quickened. "What if Cadius blackmailed him into killing the child? Mr. Devlin was a kind man, and so maybe he pretended that the baby died and instead gave him away."

Will gave his head a faint shake. "Even if that is true, the physician, Cadius, the former queen and king—all are dead. There is no one left to reveal the truth."

Sarah's eager expression fell slowly as this realization sank in. Crestfallen, she slumped back in her seat, eyes fixed on her lap. Will reached over and gave her hand a squeeze, and she glanced up.

"I'm sorry," he said, giving her an unhappy look. "I wish we could find answers to this, but as it stands, the matter will have to remain unresolved."

Sarah started to nod in agreement, but then she froze, pulse quickening at a sudden thought. Will looked instantly wary of the expression on her face. "What are you thinking?"

She gave him a huge grin. "The queen and Richard—they have to know, they have to meet again. It's the only way to see for sure if he really is the lost heir."

"No, not possible." Will shook his head rather vehemently. "You cannot present something like this without evidence." She started to reach into her sleeve for the letter, and he quickly added, "Even with the letter, there is no date, nor is the illegitimate child named. And how shall we prove that Richard is the lost child of the king and queen?"

"He'll show her the necklace, they'll look into each other's eyes, and then they'll just know." Sarah said it so simply, as though it were the perfect plan. And she truly did believe it could be that easy. "The queen will remember what the necklace looks like, and a mother never forgets her child."

Will couldn't seem to hide his grin. He cast her a quick glance out of the corner of his eye, looking reluctantly amused. "I love your optimism." His expression turned wary once more, and he grimaced, returning his eyes to the road. "But I can't believe things would be that simple. And what about King Adrian? Will you simply unseat him from the only life he has ever known, declaring him the illegitimate son of the man he condemned to death?"

"Oh." She hadn't exactly been thinking about the repercussions. This revelation would change more than Richard and Meredith's lives alone.

"Precisely." He raked a hand back through his hair, sighing deeply. "I wish it were as simple as giving a mother back her dead child, but it isn't. There is an entire kingdom to think of, and there's no telling how the queen or King Adrian would react."

"But Richard is your friend," Sarah said softly, watching the trees pass by. She turned in her seat to face his profile. "You missed out on having a mother for so many years. Would you deny him the chance of having one for the first time?"

He winced. "That's hardly fair."

"What's unfair is keeping him from knowing his mother."

"And if it simply increases his hope and our suspicions turn out to be false?" he countered.

She let a moment pass and then replied softly, "But wouldn't it be worse to wonder?"

Pursing his lips, Will cast her a pensive look but didn't reply for several seconds. Finally, he sighed, guiding the horses around a bend. "I suppose you do have a point," he conceded slowly. "But," he added at her excited look, "I suggest we get a second opinion. Perhaps we are too close to this to see objectively."

"I was hoping we could stop by Karen's," she said eagerly. "She's been involved with so much of this—you remember that she was the one to turn me onto Cadius—and I think she might have some wisdom on what to do about Richard. Though Seth doesn't know anything about her imprisonment or involvement with Cadius' capture, so let's try to keep it quiet around him."

Nodding, Will kept the wagon on the path straight ahead, instead of veering off toward the Joneses'. "All right, let's see what she has to say. But I would like it noted that I still feel wary of this plan."

"Duly noted." She tried to keep the confident smile on her face, but it faded as she imagined how everything could backfire, how the queen could reject Richard, or if she did acknowledge him as her son, then Richard could unseat Adrian as king. And who knew how Adrian or the kingdom would react to that?

By the time the wagon pulled up to the newlyweds' cabin, her stomach was in knots. Sarah hopped down from the seat, and she and Will followed the sound of voices at the back of the narrow two-story home.

"You're going to fall and die, and I'll be left a young, lonely widow," Karen was saying loudly.

Seth grunted. "I would never leave you a widow, my darling—you wouldn't allow it."

"Well, at the very least you'll fall and break your neck, and then I'll be forced to remarry to support you." Karen's voice held a note of teasing, though it was high with anxiety. "So early in our marriage, too."

They heard his responding chuckle as they rounded the house. Seth was standing on a rather precarious-looking ladder that didn't quite meet the roof; it was perched against the side of the cabin and tipped awkwardly to the left as the ground sloped downward. Trying to hold the contraption in place was Karen, biting her lip worriedly as her husband stood on one leg and reached farther across the roof, grunting.

"I'm sure Joshua would be willing to help," Karen said hurriedly, wincing as one leg of the ladder lifted off the ground and she tried to correct it.

"He would have let me drop already." Seth paused, his face obscured as he hung over the roof. "Are you all right, though?"

"Fine." But her cheeks were pink with exertion and concern, and she looked up at his legs with a wary glance.

Seth resumed his straining, one leg flying out behind him as he lunged at something. "Wonderful. Fret not, my dearest!" he said grandly, grunting. "I shall have this vermin down in . . . but a moment."

"Oh, Lord," Karen muttered under her breath. Then louder, "You know I'm going to kill you if you survive this, so you're dead either way."

"That's the spirit!"

Rolling her eyes, Karen saw the newcomers headed toward them. Her eyes brightened. "Oh, thank heaven," she whispered, then called up to Seth, "Will and Sarah are here."

Will came up and took over her hold on the ladder, much to her obvious relief. There was a bit of a struggle above as Seth lowered himself a rung, and then he peeked over the roof, smiling. "Hello, company. I'm dealing with a bit of a badger situation at the current moment, but I'll be down for tea in a bit."

"He refused to ask for help," Karen whispered to Sarah, eyes flicking upward nervously. She took Sarah's hand and hurried her uphill toward the trees, casting a worried glance over her shoulder. "I know he can't reach it like this, but I had to steady the ladder and couldn't leave to get a stick to smack the thing off the roof." She reached overhead and grabbed hold of a branch the same thickness as her arm, yanking until it broke free.

They carried it between them as they walked back to the house, and from their elevated angle, they glimpsed the gray animal cowering on the roof, far out of Seth's reach. "Why don't you just let it die up there or find its way off?" Sarah suggested.

Karen heaved a disgruntled huff. "I tried that, but Seth said it will attract other vermin and animals if it dies, and he has no idea how it got up there in the first place, so he's not sure it will come down." Her speech halted abruptly, and she seemed to really look at Sarah for the first time. Lips quirking in a grin, she said, "Hi, friend."

Sarah gave the redhead a happy smile. "Hi back."

Karen gave Seth's flailing legs and backside a wry look. "Let's just make sure I'm not widowed before I'm married a week, and then we can talk."

The girls handed the long branch over to Will, and he took it, reaching high to offer it up to Seth, whose forehead was beaded with perspiration as he accepted it gladly.

"How did you manage to get a badger up there, Seth?" Will called up to him, looking amused. "There are no trees for thirty feet around your home. Don't have any raw meat lying around up there, do you?"

Seth muttered something under his breath at his friend's teasing.
"Sorry, didn't catch that," Will commented, grinning.

But Seth ignored him. "That's it," he cooed, trying to move the frightened animal toward him with the curved branch. "Come on, just a little—no, wait, NO!" The ladder wobbled when Seth jerked as he lost control of the animal, and Will barely corrected the old contraption. The two men stood frozen as the badger toppled over the side of the roof, giving a high-pitched squeal as it tumbled.

Or maybe it had been Karen's shriek when the animal fell directly overhead and she instinctively held out her arms to catch it. The bulbous badger landed in her outstretched arms, and she stared into its beady eyes with a look of horror. Sarah jumped back in surprise, and it gave another frightened scream that matched her own, thrashing wildly. Karen dropped it with a squeal. The badger plopped onto the ground, flipped itself upright, and then scampered off toward the trees.

"Are you all right?" Seth asked her, struggling to descend the ladder quickly as Will tried to hold the rickety old thing steady. "He got away from me." He paused, watching Karen's reaction, and then remarked slowly, "You look upset."

Her arms were held tightly at her sides, hands splayed, mouth open in shock as she stared at him. She took a moment to collect herself, looking like she wanted to scream after having held the oversized rat. Giving a small, convulsive shiver, all she could manage was a dull, "Ew."

Sarah bit her lip, but couldn't mask her chuckle. "I'm so sorry, but you should have seen your face."

The shock seemed to be fading, and Karen smiled. "Of course I was surprised—a giant rat fell on me."

"But you caught it!" Sarah countered excitedly.

"I know!" Laughing, Karen looped her arm through Sarah's and began guiding her around to the front of the house. "You boys can put everything away while we chat," she called over her shoulder to the men, who looked totally surprised at their quick recovery from the near-disaster.

There was a pause, and then they heard Seth say lowly, "I tell you, Will, as long as I live, I will never understand women."

߷

Sarah told her the story just as she'd told Will, letting Karen read the note and ending with her question on revealing Richard's heritage.

"I guess you could say it isn't a hundred percent certain," Sarah consented. "But everything leads me to believe that Richard is the missing link; the queen would be the only one able to confirm it." Hesitating, she added, "Will's concern is the repercussions of telling the queen and Richard. I mean, what if I'm wrong and it completely ruins both their lives and gives them false hope? Or I could be right and completely destroy Adrian's life in the process of trying to reunite the queen and Richard."

Karen's look was pensive as she contemplated this, waiting for the kettle to warm over the fire. The muffled sound of the men's voices could be heard outside, and something *thunked* against the side of the house, followed shortly by a similar noise on the roof. "But you're sure Adrian is the child of the former queen and Cadius?"

Sarah nodded firmly, then paused. "Well, pretty sure—like, almost completely positive. With the letter and Queen Meredith's statement that her sister only got pregnant once, it would have to mean that Adrian is Cadius' son. . . . Right?"

"They'd never allow an illegitimate son on the throne," Karen murmured. "The implications could be a disaster, especially since only some far-off French cousin would remain to rule over Serimone."

She joined Sarah in the "living room," which made up the entire first floor of the house and contained the kitchen and a small table for eating. "People would start digging into Adrian's past if another heir were discovered, and who knows what they would find? He might be immediately removed from the throne, with Richard taking his place, or someone else entirely."

"I know, that's the hardest part of all this." Sarah's tone was regretful. "I can reunite a son and mother, but it could ruin another man's life because of my speculations. I mean, it's all pretty obvious, but there's no real concrete proof; because, although the queen can confirm whether or not Richard is her son, I can't exactly prove that Adrian isn't the true heir." She slumped back in her chair with a sigh. "So what do I do? Is it the right thing to see if Richard is really the queen's son, or should I shut my mouth and let things go on as they are?"

"You mean with the queen thinking her son is dead and Richard living his life never knowing his mother?" One red eyebrow shot upward.

Sarah rolled her eyes. "Well, when you put it like that."

With a contemplative look, Karen stared at her lap. Then she said softly, "If I could have a child back that I'd lost, I'd at least want to try."

Sarah dropped her gaze, suddenly remembering how her friend had lost the ability to have children after traveling through an unsteady time stream too often. "I think so, too," she quietly agreed.

"I think the right thing would be to give the queen all the information, and then let her decide."

Sarah nodded slowly, thinking this over and knowing it was the wisest option. Then she groaned. "I guess that means admitting to the queen that I snooped through her dead sister's things." She frowned. "I hope she doesn't kick Adrian out when everything comes to light."

"You're forgetting that he's her son, too," Karen added gently. "He might not be her blood, but she loves him. I'm sure whatever happens, she'll make sure it goes as smoothly as possible for both her sons."

Drawing courage from her words, Sarah straightened in her chair, stiffening her resolve. "You're right. I can't keep the queen or Richard from possible happiness. I have to present her with what I know and hope for the best. For all of them," she added.

The corner of Karen's mouth tipped upward. "What?" Sarah asked.

"I've missed talking with you—for awhile now."

"Me too," Sarah replied with a soft smile. "Now, how is married life? We've talked enough about the drama in the kingdom, and I want to hear if Seth's driven you up a wall yet."

Karen laughed. "No, not yet, though today was certainly a step closer to that." She looked suddenly so content that Sarah had to smile at her. "Oh, Sarah, he's been absolutely wonderful, so attentive and kind and sweet these past months, and that hasn't changed since the ceremony. Yes, he is still our bumbling, hilarious farm boy," she added dryly, then her expression softened once more. "But knowing that he's by my side, whether day or night, makes me feel more secure than ever."

Sarah felt herself smiling at her friend, and she gave her head a faint shake of disbelief. "I never thought I'd see you—strong, independent Karen Ashmore—look this happy to have a man to protect her."

With a shrug, Karen grinned. "What can I say? I've seen the light of having Seth around." Sarah laughed, and Karen's look became suddenly curious. "And when are you and Will getting married—?"

Sarah held up a hand and shushed her. She paused to listen, ensuring that there was no hesitation in the conversation outside to indicate that they had overheard Karen's remark. Her shoulders relaxed. "We haven't exactly discussed that, thank you very much. But if you must know, I am allowing myself," she said carefully, "to fall for him. No holding back."

Karen grinned all the more at this. "Glad to see you've finally seen the light."

"And how do we always get started on my love life?" Sarah asked, scrunching up her nose in confusion.

Waving a dismissive hand in the air, Karen replied, "I'm an old married woman, and your life is way more interesting."

Sarah laughed at that. "Says the girl born in the 1990s and living in the twelfth century."

A reluctant grin emerged on Karen's shining face. "Well, I suppose that is a tad interesting."

A question Sarah had been pondering suddenly came to mind, and she bit her lip. "I've been wanting to ask you, but I haven't exactly had the chance," she added wryly. "But the watch—does it ever need to be charged? You've mentioned before that it's pretty self-sustaining, but I'd hate to be left in the dark with no way of contacting you about recharging it."

Shaking her head, Karen said, "You don't have to worry. As long as the stabilizer stored at my old house is functioning, then the watches never need to be charged. And even if power were to be lost or the machine was damaged, each watch has one single time jump stored. I told you before that the professor and I designed it as a type of security measure so we would never become marooned in any time."

Sarah nodded. "Okay. I'm not sure why, but I just felt I needed to be sure—" The front door swung open, and the men stepped inside. She snapped her mouth closed at their presence.

"It could have tunneled through the rafters," Will was saying. "Patching any holes could be a way to prevent re-entry."

Seth shook his head, closing the door behind them. "I checked earlier, and there was no sign that he'd forced his way inside. I suppose the only possibility is that he simply climbed up the side of the house."

"Wait." Sarah looked between the two as they came into the room. "Did you spend this entire time talking about how the badger got on the roof?"

They glanced at each other blankly and then said in unison, as though it should be obvious, "Yes."

Sarah and Karen shared a look, and the redhead rolled her eyes. They had spent the afternoon discussing the security and future of the kingdom, and Will and Seth had been thinking up ways an animal could have found its way onto the house.

They said their goodbyes a little while later, and Karen and Sarah shared a long hug. "Don't be a stranger," Karen whispered before they parted.

As soon as the house disappeared from view, Sarah blurted, "I need you to take me back to the castle."

Will started, shooting her a look of absolute shock. "You plan to tell the queen today?"

"No time better than the present." Sarah sucked in a shuddering breath. "She and Richard have waited long enough to know that the other exists, and I'm not sure how long I can keep this"—she waved her sleeve containing the letter for effect—"a secret."

Nodding compliantly, Will said, "All right. I'll take you."

The sky had darkened during their visit, and heavy clouds rolled in as they ambled through the town gate. They were just passing Will's shop when Robert ran outside, waving his arms and looking flustered. Will pulled back on the reins, and his assistant leaned against the side of the wagon, panting. "It's Vader, sir; he's going crazy and won't calm down. He's riling the other horses, and you seem to have a way with him."

Will had started to rise from his seat as the man spoke, and then he glanced back at Sarah with a wary look.

She waved him off. "I can make it to the castle myself."

Casting a suspicious glance at their surroundings, Sarah knew he was thinking of Damien, a concern that she just now realized hadn't been on her mind for an entire day. She lowered her voice. "Will, I'll be fine. I'll head straight to the castle, and it shouldn't take me very long to speak with the queen. You take care of this, and then I'll meet you back here and we can have dinner with the Joneses."

He still looked hesitant. Just then, a clatter sounded from inside the livery, and several horses whinnied loudly, one letting out a disgruntled shriek. Will cringed, and then nodded reluctantly. "I will see you back here in an hour. And good luck," he called as he hopped from the wagon and followed Robert inside to the sound of splintering wood.

Sarah watched him go and then made her way to the square, which was surprisingly quiet. Only a few townsfolk meandered about, most seeming on their way somewhere else as shopkeepers with mobile carts wheeled their wares under awnings or out of the marketplace altogether. Those with stationary businesses in the square and alongside other buildings threw tarps smeared with animal fat over their wagons or countertops. Spotting Richard, her stomach gave a small jolt of anticipation and she moved his way, not knowing exactly why she was doing so.

He glanced up at her approach, smiled, and placed the lid securely over the barrel of cabbage heads. Dusting his hands off on his pants, he walked the rest of the way to her. "Miss Matthews, what are you doing out on such a day?"

She shrugged one shoulder casually, fingers twitching anxiously at her side. The weather was the least of her concerns. "Oh, you know, just getting out to clear my head."

"Not exactly prime weather in which to take a stroll," he commented, pointing upward with a small grin.

As if to prove his point, a sudden rolling clap of thunder overhead caused Sarah to jump, and she glanced up at the darkening heavens just as they let loose with a light mist. "You did that on purpose," she said, laughing as the mist thickened and turned into small, intermittent drops.

"I swear I did not." Richard chuckled along with her at the perfect timing.

Sarah paused, knowing she should excuse herself and go on to her destination, but she was curious, and her curiosity was difficult to ignore. "I was just on my way to the castle, actually."

"Oh?"

Her toes curled inside her boots as the wind picked up, dragging her skirts along the cobblestones. "Umm, I wanted to ask you something the other night but didn't get a chance." She tried to keep her expression neutral, though she already wished she could take back the words. What did she expect him to say, anyway? To confirm that the queen was, in fact, his mother, and he'd known all along?

Richard's face was open. "Of course, but should we not find you shelter first?"

"I'm fine." She swallowed and pulled a look she hoped was something akin to casual friendliness. "I was just thinking about what you said at the wedding. You mentioned that there was a pouch of coins, er, left with you"—she stumbled over the words and took a breath to steady her nerves—"but there wasn't any kind of insignia on the pouch, or a note left with a specific seal? Nothing?" she said flatly when he shook his head.

"I'm afraid not," Richard answered. She tried to mask her disappointment. "I am only aware of the coins and this." He dragged the lion pendant up from inside his shirt for her inspection before quickly dropping it back into its hiding place, but not before Sarah examined the design and compared it to the queen's description of the one she'd had made for her son. As far as Sarah could tell, they should have been exact. "Why do you ask?"

Sarah quickly drew her eyes to his face, realizing that she was staring at the outline of the necklace under his shirt. Forcing a smile, she answered, "No reason, really." But if someone had saved Richard's life—if Cadius had, indeed, attempted to have Richard killed as a baby—then there had to have been something more than the letter she'd found. . . . Didn't there?

Or maybe you're just spiraling, Sarah reminded herself sullenly, wondering if this was just another one of her hasty assumptions brought about by too much free time and too many hours spent watching spy movies at the theater. Should she abandon her plan and turn back, give herself some time to think this through?

Her eyes darted back to the necklace she knew was under his shirt. Though such a small piece of evidence in the grand scheme of everything she would present to the queen, she felt that the little picture of the lion alone affirmed all of her assumptions and would secure the queen's confidence in Richard's heritage. She bolstered her courage, more certain than ever that the right thing to do was to give Queen Meredith what she knew and then let the woman decide.

Abruptly, she was pulled from her musings and realized that the rain had quickly turned to thick, heavy drops that splattered the ground at her feet. The square was mostly devoid of life and only a few folks were left to run for shelter.

"Do you need help getting somewhere?" Richard called over the sound of the rain splattering against tarps and cobblestones.

Sarah shook her head, not wanting to keep him out in the rain any longer than he had to be and also feeling a renewed eagerness to provide the queen with her discovery. "Thanks, but I can make it there on my own." When he looked reluctant to leave her at the whims of nature, she gave him a smile and a wave as she backed away. "I'll see you soon, Richard."

Holding her arm close to her body so the rain didn't soak her sleeve and ruin the letter stashed inside, she hurried across the street. Leaning against the corner of a building, she caught her breath for a moment, hoping Will didn't think she was trapped in the storm and that he wouldn't try to find her. Her shoulders were wet, her hemline dragging heavily with rainwater, and there was no point in them both getting soaked.

Sarah pushed off from the building and scurried to the next awning, peeking out from beneath to survey the deluge. If she played her cards right, she could hop from covering to covering and would only take the brunt of the rainstorm as she awaited admittance into the castle. Then maybe she wouldn't look completely drowned by the time she arrived.

Sighing over the fact that, however careful she might be, she would still look like a soaking vagrant when she saw the queen, Sarah sucked in a deep breath and stepped into the rain toward the next building.

Her mind was occupied with how she would present her theory to the queen, seeing the joy on her and Richard's faces when they met again with this new knowledge, the tearful embrace. She was so distracted that she didn't notice the hunched form that moved quickly from the shadows.

A hand snaked out of the darkened alleyway and caught her around the middle. Sarah instinctively let out a terrified scream as a gloved hand came around and pressed a wet cloth over her mouth, muffling her shrill cries. She coughed into the rank-smelling fabric, thrashing against her captor's firm grip around her waist. She tried to bite down on his hand, but the cloth was too thick, and so she reached behind her, frantically slapping and scratching at his face. Her vision swam, and she felt suddenly light-headed as she jerked her leg back to kick him. But it was as though her limbs were suddenly filled with lead. Her leg felt like jelly as it slid pathetically toward his foot rather than inflicting damage to his shin, the arm she had used to gouge out his eyes moving slower and finally falling limply over his shoulder.

Body flooding with panic, her eyes madly searched the empty square as the man retreated a step into the shadows. She put everything she had into one final, feeble scream that barely made a sound through the cloth, and she knew it was impossible that anyone had heard. Her head lolled, taking too much effort to keep it upright, and her legs gave way. She slumped forward like a jointless doll, and the man dropped the foul rag to grasp her around the waist with both arms, holding her upright. She groaned in protest, willing his hold to break and her legs to carry her away. But she couldn't remember where she was anyway, or how the man had found her, so what did it matter if she escaped?

The world turned, her eyes rolled, and she succumbed to the blackness. She was too far gone to realize that the rain-soaked form, who had been watching her from the shadows, waiting, was dragging her unconscious body into the descending darkness and silence of Bowler Street.

ꕥ

The rain fell in thick sheets now. Will jogged alongside the livery, trying to let the roof catch the brunt of the water falling heavily from dark, angry clouds. He hoped Sarah had made it to the castle before this let loose—neither had been dressed properly for the unexpected storm, though he had found a cloak that repelled water inside his shop and wore it now as he skirted alongside the building.

The horses pawed anxiously at the ground, thrashing their heads eagerly at his arrival and causing the wagon to jerk forward a few inches. Will grabbed hold of the reins, thinking to pull them inside and out of the deluge, when he spotted Richard jogging up the street past the buildings, glancing down each alley as he did. Will blinked as water ran into his eyes and saw him crouch just inside Bowler Street. He was the only soul, besides himself, foolish enough to be outside during the downpour.

"Richard?" he shouted, confused at the man's behavior as he spun around in a circle, as if lost or looking for something. "Rich!"

He turned at the sound of his name and then ran toward Will's shop, sliding once on the rain-slicked stones. "What are you doing out here?" Will asked when the man reached him, panting.

Richard swallowed and drew in a breath. His eyes were bright with concern, which caused Will's stomach to sink. "I didn't exactly see it happen, but I encountered Sarah in the marketplace." He stopped to drag in a lungful of moist air.

"Out with it, man," Will ground out, his apprehension mounting at the mention of Sarah's name.

Richard nodded, wincing as though what he was about to say would be painful for him to hear, which only increased Will's dread. "We parted ways when it began to rain, and I saw her moving near the alleys, trying to stay dry. I was packing things up when I thought I heard a woman's scream, but when I looked back to check, she was gone." He hesitated at Will's blank expression, his heaving chest. "There wasn't another woman in the marketplace when I had spoken with Sarah, and I immediately went to investigate. There is no sign of her, but I stumbled upon this."

Will's entire body felt frozen, but he mechanically took the soaked cloth held out to him. Bringing it up to his face, he took in the pungent, acerbic scent and wrinkled his nose, knowing that this particular plant extract was used to render someone unconscious.

"And I found—" Richard stopped, and then he reluctantly opened his fist in explanation. Sarah's tree pendant, the one Will had given to her months before, lay in his wet palm, its lock broken and chain twisted.

His panic-filled gaze met Richard's, and they both seemed to acknowledge the obvious. It was the worst possible scenario Will had imagined, a fear that Sarah had dissuaded him from that was now rearing its ugly head in reality. His heart thudded in panic. Dread, fear, and utter rage vied for attention within him as his world came crashing to a halt with realization.

"Heaven help me, he's taken her," he whispered, knowing it was true but unsure what he could do. It had happened again, and right under his nose. He should never have allowed her out of his sight, should have gone with her to the castle to ensure she arrived safely. This was his doing.

The rain was soaking through the gaps in his cloak, and he let it, hoping the cold would wake him from this nightmare.

ଔଓ

The world was a whirling pinwheel, and its sole purpose was to make her sick or kill her—she wasn't sure which.

Sarah moaned, head feeling like it was lolling back and forth, though she was keeping it perfectly still so it didn't explode. Reluctantly, she opened her eyes and instantly regretted it, hissing at the pain in her head as the lantern light blinded her burning eyes. Her stomach roiled, and she clutched her fists at her side, closing her lids and willing herself not to be sick. When the immediate urge to toss her cookies passed, she risked another peek at her surroundings, squinting until her eyes adjusted to the dim light and everything came into focus, her senses returning to her.

She'd been kidnapped, she was lying on her back on a thick blanket, and though her dark blue dress was mostly dry, she could still hear the faint sound of the rain outside. The blanket beneath her had been folded several times for her comfort, Sarah assumed. Why would her captor go to such lengths when he'd drugged her and—yes, she could remember him dragging her down the street. Everything else was a blur, much like her vision when she sat upright too quickly, reaching for the necklace that wasn't there, sudden panic flooding her.

She placed a hand to her aching head, sucking in deep, calming breaths so she didn't find herself yacking on the wood floor. Carefully, she moved her eyes over the room and saw that she was alone in a tiny rundown cabin, the walls sagging and bowing, some of the boards gapping to reveal slivers of moonlight. How long had she been out?

A spark of panic shot through her, and she touched her wrist where her watch was still nuzzled against her skin, safe and sound. Will's necklace was gone, but the watch might save her life. She exhaled in relief.

Gingerly, she rose to her feet, being careful to move slowly as she examined the shelves that lined the walls until her bleary vision landed on the door. Lethargic heartbeat picking up the pace at the sight of her exit, she walked the few feet to the other side of the room, past the lantern on the countertop, and glimpsed the tiniest flicker of moonlight beyond. Not caring how it hurt her head and thoughtless of who might be on the other side, she yanked on the handle, turning and sliding and twisting, but it didn't budge no matter what she tried. It was locked from the outside, she realized vaguely, still regaining all of her mental functions after they'd been sapped from whatever her captor had used on her—medieval chloroform?

She still felt too weak and nauseous to try and ram the door, so she cast her eyes about the small room, hoping for another exit. But she only saw walls, a locked door, and long shelves and a countertop lining one of the walls. Feeling a little helpless, she moved toward the light and examined the shelves, looking for something to jimmy the lock. But her brow furrowed as her confused gaze took in the knickknacks lining the shelves, things that Sarah couldn't even begin to comprehend. Her disbelief wasn't because they were foreign objects, but it was because of the fact that she knew exactly what they were that had her so baffled.

Mouth opening as her confusion mounted, her eyes roved the small stack of perfectly white computer paper, the rubber bands filling a glass jar on one shelf, the pencils and pens in neat rows on the countertop. Sarah peered inside a wood cup on the counter and saw a few erasers at the bottom; there was a heavy-duty flashlight sitting upright next to it, the glass end facing down, and she picked it up, pressing the ON button. Blinding white light flooded the room, and she quickly turned it off, laying it on the counter and waiting for her eyes to adjust once more.

Her incredulity turned to dread as her eyes caught sight of a small fabric collar, the type one might use for a small pet, and thoughts of her captor fell from her mind. With a shaking hand, Sarah used one finger to poke the tiny silver nameplate until the light revealed the name etched in the metal, one she already knew would be there, though it still came as a shock. "Chester," she whispered aloud. The name had been written in cursive script, clearly by a machine, and she recalled Karen's story of how her guinea pig had been the first living thing to travel back in time.

Sarah took a step back, eyes scanning the shelves littered with modern items—all made by machines—and then her gaze landed on the collar that had belonged to the pet Karen and the professor had used to test the early prototype of the time machine. Her body felt suddenly heavy with the aftereffects of the drug and her mounting alarm.

"Why am I here?" she asked herself aloud. Her muddled head and the constant patter of the rain kept her from registering the soft sound of a key turning in the lock or of the door moving inward.

"Because you are on dangerous ground."

Sarah froze at the familiar voice, at once disbelieving and fearful. She dragged her eyes from the shelves to the figure standing in the doorway. The man's face was cast in shadow, the moon illuminating the rain that fell in earnest behind him. He moved inside a foot so that he could shut the door and lock the inner latch, and Sarah retreated a step. The small flame of the lantern barely lit his face, but she saw clearly his grimace when her frightened gaze met his espresso eyes—ones she knew would be flecked with gold if he advanced toward the light.

Damien took another hesitant step into the tiny room. "Hello, Sarah."

Chapter Ten

"I know you despise me; allow me to say,
it is because you don't understand me."

Elizabeth Gaskell, *North and South*

Even in her confused, drug-muddled state, Sarah managed to take in every detail in the twelve seconds of silence that followed his entrance into the room.

Rain rolled off of Damien's shoulders and slipped to the ground, repelled by the oil or grease his cloak was coated with. His dark hair was plastered to his tan forehead, droplets of water falling from the usually perfectly styled strands and running down his straight nose, over his lips, and dripping off the end of a chin she knew had a little cleft beneath the line of tediously sculpted scruff running along his pronounced jawline. Aside from the dark circles rimming his under eyes and the fact that he was soaking wet, Damien Romeo Lisandro looked exactly as she had imagined him. But the most notable thing about his appearance was that he was most certainly here.

He took a tentative step toward her, as though she were a scared animal, and she knew her eyes must be huge as she lurched backward, banging into the shelves and sending a pencil rolling off the counter. Her eyes stayed locked with his, the gold flecks dancing in the lantern light, as she had known they would. He had stopped his advance at her shock and the apprehension she couldn't remove from her gaze.

"How are you here?" she whispered, shaking her head, holding one hand out before her to keep him at bay and clutching the counter at her back with the other.

"Allow me to explain." His voice was smooth like honey, just as she remembered. She waited for him to go on, but he just stood there, dripping wet, a perpetual grimace fixed on his face, forehead wrinkled in anxiety. He removed his cloak slowly, keeping his gaze trained on her as he did so, revealing shoulders that appeared thinner and less muscular than she recalled. He tossed the cloak into the corner.

Sarah flinched at the sound of wet fabric slapping against wood. "Why am *I* here?" She tried to steady her voice, to make herself seem more in control. Her intense fear was melting away, though the apprehension still remained—as well as a thousand other emotions his appearance had stirred in her. Seeing his face, she knew he wasn't there to kill her, but the problem lie in the fact that she still had no idea why *she* was there.

He took one step in her direction, but Sarah was already as far away from him as the small room would allow. Seeming not to know what to do, Damien shrugged his shoulders helplessly. "Because," he said quietly, his voice sounding husky from disuse. Then he sucked in a breath, cleared his throat, and tried again. "Because you are in danger."

After a full minute of silence that she hoped was wrecking him as he pondered her thoughts, she let him have it.

"What are you thinking?!" she screamed, then winced as her stomach lurched and her legs buckled, despite her best efforts to seem strong.

He closed the short distance in a flash, hands gripping her waist to keep her upright. Damien was so close she could smell the musty rainwater on his clothes and the scent of pine, saw the way his chest rose and fell faster at her nearness. His espresso-colored eyes grazed her face, like a loving caress that was searching for forgiveness. And though she was angry and annoyed and scared and confused, there was a part of her, too big for her liking, that was relieved to see him alive and looking healthier than the broken down, bedraggled prisoner she had imagined.

Sarah felt weak and confused and sick to her stomach, but she dragged in a ragged breath and managed to glare at him. She had no idea what had possessed him to kidnap her, and while some part of her was a little frightened that he was holding her hostage, she was ninety-percent ticked. Maybe it was the drugs that kept her from registering the seriousness of her situation and the fact that she shouldn't upset her captor, but she angrily shoved his hands away, making sure her face relayed her disgust. He let his arms drop to his sides, and she gave him a weak shove to put a few inches between them. "I should yack all over you," she whispered, secretly hoping she didn't do just that.

The corner of Damien's thin lips tipped. "I am pleased to see you haven't lost your spirit."

She blinked, ignoring him as she waited for her vision to clear, resisting the urge to slide to the ground like her wobbly legs were begging her to. "How long have I been here?"

"'Tis the middle of the night. You should sit down." He made a move toward her, and she swatted at his outstretched hand. She was supposed to have gone to the queen hours ago and delivered the letter—

Eyes widening, she jerked a hand into her sleeve and froze. The letter was gone.

Damien's face tightened at the movement. "Where is it?" she whispered, wondering if she looked murderous or frantic.

"Somewhere safe," was all he said.

She hardly believed him and wondered if he might have destroyed it, but her eyes still roved his layers of clothing, searching for some sign that he was carrying the evidence of Richard's heritage on him.

Raising his hands in submission, his eyebrows rose in that cheeky, challenging way she remembered too well. “You may search me, if you wish.”

Sarah threw daggers with her eyes, and his grin faded. He dropped his gaze. “It is safe,” he repeated, voice soft—with remorse, she realized.

“Give it back.”

Damien shook his head. “I cannot do that.”

Hesitating, she watched his face, which was turned toward the ground, assessing his reaction to the letter. Had he read it yet? Did he understand the contents, what they implied in regards to the kingdom? She tried to subtly examine the shelves, more thoroughly this time, wondering if it was hidden inside one of the discolored jars.

“It isn’t here.” Damien’s soft words caused her shoulders to slump.

“Where is here?” Her eyes flickered to the bowed walls and modern things littering the shelves and countertop. Stomach sinking, her gaze snapped back to his guilty one. She asked slowly, “How do you have these things?” Surely it was impossible that he was a time traveler—Karen would have told her. But then how had he discovered these items?

She drew her eyes back to Damien and found him cringing. “Consider it a temporary safe haven for us.” Vague, and it also didn’t explain how he’d come by these things.

Sarah eyed him warily, reaching back to rub a tender spot in her neck and feeling only bare skin. Her eyes narrowed accusingly. “Did you take my necklace?”

He appeared confused. “Wha—?”

“Did you take it?” Her gaze searched the floor, but the dim light revealed nothing. It was the only permanent object she had from Will, the only reminder she would have of him when she returned home.

“I took nothing.” She raised a brow at this, and he amended, “Nothing but the letter.”

She resisted the urge to roll her eyes, temporarily giving up her search so he didn’t see how much the necklace meant to her. A small shiver snaked up her spine as the wind picked up outside, seeping through the cracks. “There’s the lying, former friend I expected.”

He winced as though she had slapped him, and she shoved back a quick pang of regret. “I do not wish to mislead you, Sarah.”

“Don’t,” she hissed, tears pricking her eyes. She was exhausted and scared and hurt, and she was not in the mood for his petty, worthless apologies. “You do *not* have the right to use my name—you are not allowed to pretend that you care,” she whispered, repeating similar words she had said to him after discovering his betrayal.

Damien’s look was wounded, and she willed herself not to care. “I know my past is filled with mistakes and that I have hurt you, a fact that will forever haunt me.” She snorted, though it looked like he chose to ignore the disbelieving sound. "I have not earned it, but surely you must know that you can trust me."

"You broke me!" she shouted, chest heaving. "You convinced me to let you in and to trust you, and you destroyed every notion I ever had of you that was good and right." Her voice cracked, and she swallowed hard. That wasn't entirely true. Even after all he'd done, she still knew there was a modicum of goodness inside of him, enough that Will had managed to convince him to turn Cadius over to the court. She saw that softness inside of him even now, the same side that had caused her to befriend him in the first place.

Knowing she was on the verge of a breakdown, which she blamed on fatigue and whatever he'd used to drug her, she opted for sarcasm to keep up her defenses and keep him at arm's length. He had broken through her defenses once before—rather easily—and she had every intention of not letting him in again. Her stomach was settling, head clearing, and she was feeling more like herself, albeit more perturbed than usual.

She held up a hand when Damien took a step toward her, looking as though he wanted to comfort her or apologize. "Let's just go over the reasons why I shouldn't trust you, shall we?" Her voice was still thick with emotion, and she cleared her throat, ticking off the reasons on her fingers as she spoke. She held up her thumb. "The first offense was lying to me the entire time we were friends, which only happened because Cadius was paying you to keep an eye on me. Number two"—she added her index finger—"was murdering Edith in cold blood."

"You know I never meant—"

"The next," she went on as though he hadn't spoken, "was being a coward when Cadius was threatening my life." He winced, and she resisted the sudden urge to soften her tone. Aside from outright confronting Cadius, Damien *had* done almost everything he could to keep her out of harm's way.

Aware that her resolve was weakening, she stiffened her spine and hardened her tone, pulling out another finger. "Taking part in the murder of others is top on the list, and kidnapping and holding me hostage isn't exactly convincing me of your credibility. And there was also the time where you tried to kill Will, which *definitely* doesn't win you any trust points."

Damien's dejected gaze slowly lowered to her hem. He looked so wounded that it was difficult for Sarah to stay mad at him. She wasn't generally mean-spirited, and breaking his spirit hadn't improved her mood, but he didn't deserve to get off with a wrist slap after adding kidnapping to his list of wrongs. She thought again of her missing necklace, and an idea suddenly sparked a small ember of hope.

Hiking her chin, she said, "I was supposed to meet Will yesterday afternoon, and he's probably found my necklace by now." Damien's gaze jerked up to meet hers, and she allowed herself a small, satisfied smile as she realized that what she was about to say might be true. "I bet he already has a search party out looking for me."

"I am sure that is true," he agreed. His eyes searched hers. "The blacksmith—he will hunt for you, but he will never find you."

Sarah swallowed, the reality of her situation fully revealing itself to her clear head. She knew Damien would never intentionally do her bodily harm, but she was still trapped in here with him, a man who had killed and manipulated to save his own hide.

"Where's the key?" She had seen him lock the door but couldn't recall where he had placed the key.

He raised a brow in challenge, eyes bright and alive like she remembered. "My offer to search my person still stands."

She glared at him. "I'd rather eat my own toes. Now give it to me."

Damien appeared to consider this for a moment, and then he shook his head, the barest of grins curling his lips. He was enjoying this. She recalled a time when that look had melted her insides, but now it only fueled her ire. "There is no point in keeping me here. Just give. Me. The key," she ground out between clenched teeth. As an afterthought, she added, "And the letter. I need the letter."

Leaning his face so that it was inches away, he gave her one of his best, self-satisfied smiles. "No."

Sarah resisted the urge to slap him and then retreat into the corner to pout. She hesitated, staring at that infuriating grin that only grew with her silence, seeing the way his eyes dropped to her mouth, which was very close to his. "What is your decision?" he whispered, voice low.

Angry and feeling impulsive, Sarah did the one thing he hadn't expected her to do. She hurriedly shoved her hands into the deep pockets of his outer jacket, sending him off-balance. When that produced nothing, she quickly reached inside his shirt just as he was recovering from shock, searching for the letter but only feeling bare skin. In too much of a hurry to feel embarrassed, she plunged a hand into the front pocket that had been stitched into his trousers.

With a small noise of surprise over her boldness, Damien grabbed her wrists and held them at her sides. She tried to yank herself free and lift her knee, but he held fast, pinning her arms behind her back and using his body to press her back against the counter. Their chests rose and fell in unison.

"Good God, I wasn't serious." His eyes were wide, and she felt like grinning over the fact that she had taken him by surprise—even if she'd had to touch him to do it—but she was still too angry and trapped to find humor in his panicked gaze.

"Let go." She writhed, trying to get out from between the shelves and his body, which was way too close for comfort. But he held her fast.

"Just let—me explain," he hissed, trying to restrain her.

She stilled, glaring daggers up at him. "I. Don't. Think. So. And for the record, I didn't enjoy that."

Damien gaped at her, then the corner of his mouth twitched, a surprised grin breaking out. "I believe you might have."

Her mouth swung open. "Are you *joking*?"

His grip lessened on her wrists, but neither moved. He appeared confused. "Yes, I was."

He was taking her literally, which months ago would have caused Sarah to laugh. Now she could only glare at him. "Well, you can just stop pretending that we're so buddy-buddy. Will's coming soon to get me out of here, and you're going right back to that stone tower you should be in right now."

Slowly, his arms fell to his sides, his expression falling. Damien turned his back on her and moved a step away, but Sarah remained leaning against the wood, resisting a smug smile. "That's right. Any minute now, Will and a huge search party will come barging in here and arrest you. You know it's true; Will has always protected me, and nothing—"

He reacted so quickly that she barely had time to blink as he spun around and slammed his hands on the counter on either side of her. Jars rattled and the flashlight rolled an inch. His eyes were ablaze with fury and frustration. "The blacksmith will soon be gone, and he cannot protect you as I can."

Sarah recovered from her shock, snapping back, "You abducted and drugged me. How is that protection?" She paused as his words sank in. "And what do you mean he'll be out of the picture?"

"Does he know your homeland?" he asked abruptly, avoiding her question. His voice was hoarse with anger.

Sarah's first reaction was to retort with a snarky comment, but then she wondered if he really did know where she was from. But that was impossible. Her eyes darted nervously over the contents of the shelves. "I don't know what you're talking about."

"Look around you!" he practically shouted in her face. She shrank back, and Damien noticeably softened his tone. "Does he know everything about you, as I do? Does he know where you are *truly* from? Surely if you care for him and trust him so implicitly, then you must have shared this with him." His voice had taken on a bitter tone, and he raised his eyebrows at her stunned silence. "What? He is too dim-witted to have guessed that you are foreign to this place?"

Sarah blinked, too surprised to respond to the insult against Will. "How did you—?" She halted mid-speech, wondering how much she could give away. Carefully, she hedged, "What is it that you've discovered, exactly?"

Giving her a look that said he thought her aversion was unnecessary, he looked pointedly at the modern things behind her. Her back stiffened. "I am not the only soul to discover your origin. Others are watching you, and you can know that your precious blacksmith cannot save you from what he does not understand."

Her heart sped up. "Who?" she whispered. "Who else knows?" And what did they want with her? Were they watching Karen and Robert, too?

Damien shook his head. "It matters not. I shall watch over you until the threat can be eliminated and it is safe." His gaze softened in a tell-tell way, and Sarah's breath hitched as he took one hand from the counter, lightly brushing the back of his knuckles against her cheek. "I have missed you so these past months and have only thought of you," he whispered, his breath warm against her face in the chilly room.

Sarah felt frozen in shock and alarm. That is, until his head lowered toward hers as if pulled by a magnet he found difficult to resist. In one quick movement, she ducked under his arm and dove to the left, causing Damien to fall into the cabinet in the absence of her body, which had been supporting him. She made a beeline for the door, even though it was still locked, but her feet became hopelessly tangled in her skirts. She stumbled and fell, landing on the floor with a grunt. Damien was suddenly straddling her, and she shrieked, managing to roll over in an attempt to slap him and wriggle free.

"Just wait! Allow me a moment to explain before—" But his words dropped off as he struggled to stave off her flailing hands. He didn't fight back as she slapped his arms and punched him in the stomach and attempted to shove him away from her.

"Get off!" she shrieked when he barely budged, merely accepting her blows. Panicked, she landed a hard slap across his cheek, her nails digging in. They both stilled, and Sarah felt immediate remorse over the angry red cut that Damien touched in surprise. She frowned, knowing she shouldn't regret fighting off her attacker.

Someone *tsked*, and they both froze. "That was hardly necessary." Sarah stopped cold, eyes on Damien's face as they registered alarm. Her gaze dragged slowly across the floor, over the boots standing just inside the open door, up to the embroidered coat, to the key dangling from the man's hand. And, finally, her eyes came to rest on Cadius' cold, amused eyes.

"Yes, well, don't appear so astonished, child. I was never dead to begin with."

Chapter Eleven

"Hell is empty and all the devils are here."

William Shakespeare, *The Tempest*

Damien quickly moved to his feet and scraped his wet hair off his forehead as Cadius closed the door noiselessly behind him. Damien's gaze registered brief surprise and alarm at his former master's sudden appearance before he wiped his face clean.

Sarah scurried backward on the floor until she hit the wall and then used it for support as she rose to her feet. "Y-you're dead."

Cadius' stormy gray eyes, which were just as cold and accusatory as ever, rested on her. "It is rather inconvenient when one's plans are thwarted, is it not?" He gave her a pointed look that reminded her of the fact that she had helped foil his efforts for the throne.

"But you were executed," she said in disbelief, as though this fact would make his ghost disappear. "People *saw* you die."

Cadius examined his gloved fingers, and Sarah briefly wondered if there would be blood under the nail beds if they were uncovered. "It never happened." He rolled his eyes, looking as though he were dealing with a tiresome toddler. "Evidently."

A blink. Silence. Then Sarah said slowly, insistently, "But you *died*—"

"Oh, child," Cadius said airily, waving a hand. "Money and intimidation. A few carefully placed threats and coins, and the rope becomes just tight enough to prevent the neck from snapping, the fall a tad shorter than usual. Few attended, and it was rather too easy for my body to be secreted away."

"You've been hiding the entire time," Sarah breathed.

"Of course." There was a pause as Sarah absorbed the fact that he was probably still plotting to get on the throne. But knowing that Adrian was his son made his motives more complicated, and she was keeping her knowledge of Cadius and Alexis's past a secret until she absolutely had to use it.

"Why am I here?" she asked, her tone wavering more than she liked. The man appeared unarmed and hadn't done anything to harm her today—yet—but his cold, assessing gaze reminded her of the threats he had made before, of the fact that he had killed his own brother and countless others to get himself or his son on the throne.

Cadius tugged on the wrist of his right glove, making it snug over his fingers. His hair, mostly gray like his eyes, was barely wet. The rain pattered softly on the roof now, and Sarah realized it had begun to let up. "I am sure by now that you have noticed your surroundings," he said.

"We're in a shed somewhere," Sarah answered disgruntledly, eyes flicking between Damien and the older man. "I'm guessing in the forest."

A cold chuckle echoed through the small room, and Sarah shivered.

"No, child." He moved slowly across the room, picked up the flashlight, and clicked it on. A beam of yellow light shot to the ceiling, illuminating half the room and casting the other in shadows. Cadius' eyes became hollow sockets, and the glow highlighted his sunken cheeks and features that were more pronounced and bony than she remembered. "After your destruction of such carefully laid plans that took years to contrive and come to fruition, you can't possibly be as middling as I once believed you to be."

Sarah glared at him, knowing he was calling her something akin to slow and commonplace, but then he clicked the light off, and she was left blinking in the semi-darkness.

"So you have seen my collection, darling." She heard Cadius run one bony finger over the counter and waited for her eyes to adjust to the dim lantern light. Then his words hit her, and she inhaled audibly.

"These things are yours?"

"Did you know," Cadius went on, as though she hadn't spoken, his voice casual, "that there is a spot in the forest where strange objects once appeared. I first discovered a few pieces of pristinely dyed parchment, and then a week later, in nearly the exact same spot, there was one of"—he waved at the foggy jar of rubber bands, seeming to search for a name—"these stretchable entities. And so I came back, week after week, discovering new foreign items every time, and one day there was a sort of . . . large rat that was wandering the clearing. I kept him as a pet for some time."

He chuckled, as though greatly amused, and Sarah's eyes flickered to Chester's collar. She didn't feel like asking how Karen's pet had died, but she hoped it was from natural causes.

Clenching her teeth together, she drew her gaze back to Cadius as his eyes perused the shelves in a calculating way. She admitted nothing, knowing he couldn't pin her to any of this. Her eyes landed on Damien, who was staring at the floor, and she couldn't help wondering how much he really did know about where she came from.

"I was curious, naturally." Cadius dusted off his gloves and let his eyes rest on her, dark and dead in the low light. "I drew Gabriel into my confidence and allowed him to glimpse my collection, though he became obsessed with these unfamiliar items. It was one of the reasons why he was so curious about a young girl who appeared out of nothing, as if an apparition, in that same clearing one day. A girl whom I believe is an acquaintance of yours."

Sarah's stomach sank, her heart quickening in panic. Gabriel Dunlivey had been in on it, as well? He was dead now, so he wasn't a threat, but Cadius knew about Karen. Did he know where she was now?

Her voice was small when she spoke, though she tried to sound convincing. "I don't know what you're talking about. What girl?"

He looked tired of her evasiveness and narrowed his eyes. "Do not play games with me, girl. I have seen her face before, in your world, I believe." His lips curled in a cruel, triumphant smile at her wide eyes. "Yes, I have been to that horrible place you call home. When I recognized your friend after Gabriel brought her to me, I was concerned her hand would corrupt my plans, and so I set out to have her executed as a witch, something that Gabriel was already convinced she was. Simpleton," Cadius muttered.

Then he moved forward slowly, and Sarah slid across the wall, shrinking back into the corner. Cadius leaned toward her, his breath stale and cold against her face. "But she escaped, when the moon was at its height, the night before she was to be burned alive."

Cadius suddenly gripped her chin, his nails digging into her skin. Sarah shivered. She tried to keep the fear from her face and knew she was failing. "Do you know what it is like, Miss Matthews, to be forced to watch from your sickbed as history repeats itself, as your younger brother is crowned king once more and your lover is forced to marry him again?" He broke off, seeming to realize what he'd just said.

He released her with a look of disgust, and Sarah resisted the urge to rub her jaw. Her eyes found Damien, who had taken a few steps toward them. It was difficult to tell in the light, but the look on his face was something close to anger.

Sarah steadied her voice, feeling shaken after Cadius' nearness. "What do you mean that you watched it again?"

It was as though a mask had come over Cadius' features. He stared over her head at the door, his face turning instantly cold with remembrance, though he kept his voice indifferent and casual, as if they weren't discussing traveling through space and time. "Nearly two years past, I was on a political sojourn in Ridlan when the strangest thing occurred: I collided with a young man, and the action caused him to leave something behind—a watch, I have been informed. And when I touched this simple object, I was transported to your world, Miss Matthews."

Sarah found it impossible to keep her shock and alarm concealed. Robert had once told her that he'd lost his time watch in Ridlan, but she didn't think it possible that anyone had been able to make it work. "How did you get back?" She was done with pretense. Cadius knew who she was, and she needed to discover as much as she could about his trip to the twenty-first century.

A single finger rose into the air to halt any further questions. Cadius looked amused once more. "Tut, tut. Not just yet." He turned his back on her to pace a few steps away. Sarah's anxious gaze shifted to Damien, and he was watching her with a pinched expression.

"Something terribly strange happened when I first arrived in your world." Cadius leaned his back against the counter and folded his hands before him. "What I glimpsed, I've been told, was two realities—a glitch in the 'fabric' of time. One in which your young acquaintance was living a happy life with her parents, and the other where she and an alchemist created the machine which was necessary to return myself home. However, I found myself in a world in which the machine was unfinished, years prior to the realities I had witnessed. Stranded." His look hardened. "So you see, my dear, I did the only thing I could: I ensured that her parents were removed from the scene and that she found her way to the man's home, where she would encourage him to finish the contraption with which he was tinkering at the time."

He had killed Karen's parents. This realization shot through Sarah like a lightening bolt, and she threw herself at him with a cry. A hand snaked around her waist, and Damien held her back. "Sarah, *be wise*," he hissed close to her ear.

She tried to pry his hands from her waist, though it was no use; he held her fast, whispering low, cautioning words in her ear that she was too angry to understand. "They didn't do *anything* to you!" she shouted. Tears of rage and frustration and sorrow for her friend caused her voice to break. "They were good people. You destroyed all she knew for your own gain."

Cadius' eyes suddenly lit with an angry flame, and he advanced on them. Sarah thought the arms around her might have tightened protectively for a moment. "I did what I had to, and I suffered for it," he said, his voice full of barely contained fury. His breath fanned the hair around her face, and she shrank back against Damien's chest—the lesser of two evils at the moment.

Cadius leaned his face close to hers, and Damien pulled her back a step. "I returned to my world and found myself in a time that was years before I had departed; I imagined fortune had smiled down on me. You see, my brother was given my birth right because of a brief illness, and I thought I might correct the wrong done to me so long ago. Yet the journey wrecked my body, and I found myself worse off than I had been decades before, remaining ill for so long that even I wondered if I would recover. And Josiah won everything once more, *because* I had come back."

Seeming to collect himself, he straightened, giving her another cold look before taking a step back. She could feel Damien's chest falling and rising rapidly behind her back, and she wondered if he found the older man as intimidating as she did in that moment.

More controlled now, Cadius said, "I had the power to traverse through time, and yet I found myself powerless to correct a past that was worsening before my very eyes."

"Am I supposed to feel pity for you?" Sarah snapped. Damien's arms had slackened around her, and she shoved them away, though she stayed close to him. He had betrayed her, yes, but at the moment, she felt like he was the only thing keeping Cadius from ending her. She knew too much for him to keep her alive, and her snark probably wasn't helping Cadius' opinion of her. "You ruined someone else's life. . . ." For whatever reason, Cadius was telling her the entire story, but there were some things that she could tell he was leaving out. "You said someone explained everything to you, but who was it?"

"I encountered a stranger who believed me entirely in what I had seen, and he helped me find a way to return home." Cadius flexed his right hand, as though relieving pent-up tension, and his knuckles popped in the silence that descended over the room.

Sarah swallowed, her throat feeling suddenly dry after all her shouting. "But how did *he* know anything about it?"

Slowly, Cadius' lips curled in a mocking sort of smile. "Eager to understand, are we?" He let a moment tick by, then it seemed as though he was eager to reveal to her how little she really knew. "I was fortunate enough to stumble upon a man who had worked directly with the creator of that incredible machine. They had a . . . moral disagreement, if you will, and parted ways. He was more than willing to offer me passage home in return for certain compensation."

Sarah didn't consider asking what that favor had been; she was too intent on a conversation she'd had with Professor Charles about his scientific partner who had betrayed him. Did the professor know that this same man had tried to help Cadius change history? She doubted it, otherwise he would have mentioned something to Karen or her when they had spoken of the matter.

"Imagine my surprise when I discovered the man in question in my homeland," Cadius went on, his tone assuming that infuriatingly casual effect once more. "Charles, he called himself, the same man I had witnessed create this unimaginable ability. I waited months for him to design a new time apparatus for myself as I held him captive, but I soon came to realize that he did not have the proper tools to recreate such a thing. After that, I kept him on only for my own amusement."

Sarah barely restrained a gasp. The professor, Karen's adoptive father, had willingly been Cadius' captive—his "alchemist"—for all this time, only remaining because of his thirst to learn more about this period in time.

He hadn't even realized Cadius' original motive for keeping him at the castle.

Her eyes narrowed, turning suddenly accusatory as she trained them on Damien, whose face was devoid of emotion. "And, *of course*, you're working with him again."

"Yes, he is, my dear." Cadius held out his hand. Damien produced the letter from his back pocket and gave it to the man. His eyes flickered guiltily to Sarah's for a moment, looking like he wished to say something, but then he dropped his gaze.

"She hadn't a chance to read the contents," Damien said.

"I couldn't find it because I'm not a pervert," Sarah muttered under her breath, kicking herself for not thinking to check his back pockets. Then her heart sped up as she realized that Cadius held the evidence of his deeds against the king, his plot for the throne, and the implications of both Adrian and Richard's heritages. Her wide gaze watched his hand as it slipped the letter inside his coat, and he patted the spot fondly.

"It would appear that you have lost, my dear."

Sarah opened her mouth, readying a snarky comment, when the atmosphere in the room shifted, filling with sudden hostility.

Cadius pulled back his hand and slapped Damien hard across the face, the clap echoing in the small room. Sarah gasped the same instant that Damien sucked in a breath of surprise. "For your past mistakes and to be certain you make no more," Cadius hissed.

Color bloomed across Damien's cheek, the one she had already marked, and he swallowed hard, his eyes narrowing slightly as he stared at the man. Cadius inclined his head toward Damien, giving him a hard, cold look. His voice was so low that Sarah barely heard his threatening words. "Do not for one moment entertain the notion that she will desire you again. You are a black mark with one task—you belong to me, not this tempest. " He leaned back, eying him. "Is that understood?"

The gold flecks in Damien's eyes appeared to dance angrily in the lamplight. His nod was slow, strained, and Cadius smiled at the submissive gesture. Sarah was surprised at the pang of disappointment that shot through her heart, though she reprimanded herself for expecting more of Damien.

She clenched her hands at her sides, feeling anger over every single thing that Cadius had ever done, which now included, for reasons she didn't quite understand, assaulting her former friend. "So your entire intent for getting back here was to ruin your brother's life and steal his throne. You murdered someone's parents to get what you wanted"—she was careful to keep from using Karen's name in case he didn't already know it—"and when that didn't work out, you killed your own brother in cold blood when seducing his young wife didn't pan out. Did I get everything?" she asked, her tone dripping sarcasm.

"You know nothing." Cadius turned his back on her, fingers sliding idly over the counter, as if to distract himself.

Sarah scoffed. "Is that why you're revealing your entire plot to me, to keep me *informed*? You should know that it's always the bad guy's undoing; he takes so much time giving his diatribe that help arrives and they know everything they need to lock him away for good. Enjoy your freedom while you can."

"And who will find you? I selected this shed to store my secret items because of its isolated location on the outskirts of the forest." Cadius smiled slowly at her over his shoulder, one gray eyebrow lifting on his weathered forehead. Sarah's cocky look faded, even as she reminded herself that Will was coming for her.

Cadius clicked his tongue in mock pity. "No, I think not. You asked why, and I confess that my reason in revealing all of this, my dear, is in hopes that you will understand why I require your assistance."

"Oh, yeah, I'd *love* to help you out, but I'm not in the business of cavorting with sociopaths." Sarah folded her arms across her chest and bit her tongue, knowing her sass wasn't winning her any points with the man who could end her life any time he wanted, something she was surprised hadn't happened already.

A muscle in his neck spasmed. Cadius turned around, taking in her defiant look with a cold, amused one of his own, as though she were a pest he knew he could squash at any time. "Where is the girl?"

"What girl?" Sarah snapped back.

Cadius' cool expression altered as he advanced, and he glared down at her. His calm was only a facade, and a man fashioned from greed and anger lied beneath. "Do not play the fool with me, child. I had other provisions in place, but he may not return in time. I require information from the girl, and I believe you were the last to meet with her. So you *will* tell me if she is still in Serimone."

Sarah pinched her lips together, glaring at him. If he didn't know where Karen was, she would never tell. Her life was finally coming together after Cadius had broken it apart, and there was no way Sarah would take that happy ending from her.

Cadius seemed both annoyed and pleased with her silence. His voice was low, grating. "I believe you shall feel differently tomorrow."

"I highly doubt that," Sarah retorted saucily.

"You impudent little—" Cadius' stormy eyes flared, and he advanced a step, looking like he was ready to slap her. Sarah shrank back at the sudden movement, her courage failing, and Damien moved a few inches closer so that his shoulder blocked hers. It was the first act of defiance he'd exhibited since Cadius had appeared, and Sarah looked up at him, seeing the throbbing red handprint over the cut she'd made on his cheek.

Cadius' gaze flickered with surprise, and he stared at Damien's pinched expression and severe frown, which Cadius matched. "Do not think you will outlive your usefulness, Lisandro." He extended his bony hand once more, and Damien reluctantly gave up the key hidden in one of the inner pockets of his shirt. Cadius closed his fist around it. "Insurance," was all he said.

He directed his irate gaze to Sarah, and his voice dropped, turning low and menacing. "Understand this: when you next see me, that will be your final chance to spare your own life." He paused, his thin lips curling in a wicked grin. "And admitting my plan and past to you makes no difference. Before long, you will not be able to tell a soul."

With that, he shot Damien a final, indiscernible glance and then moved to the door. He gave Sarah a heartless look. "You have one night, Miss Matthews. I suggest you use it wisely." Then he slammed the door behind him, the key grating in the lock outside.

Silence pervaded the dark room. On shaky legs, Sarah moved to the corner and lowered herself onto her makeshift bed. She stared with glazed, unblinking eyes at the wall. Why did every vacation to Serimone turn into some horrible kidnapping situation or run for her life?

Damien moved toward her slowly, as though trying not to startle her, and then he sat on the floor a few feet away, leaning his back against the wall. "How much did you know about what he said?" she whispered, keeping her eyes on a small notch in the wood. At his silence, she glanced his way. He shrugged, meeting her eyes.

"A bit," he admitted with a grimace. "Mostly I was left with my assumptions and to piece it together myself. I heard talk of the impossible, but I have always believed that nearly anything is possible." His eyes met hers, softening. "And I knew that you had a part in everything, though I didn't realize how involved you were until this morning."

Sarah pulled her knees to her chest, shivering from the cold and the anxiety Cadius had stirred in her. "So you know I don't belong here."

He nodded slowly. "I've known for quite some time, though today only confirmed my suspicions. You will recall that when we first met, I said that you appeared out of place, as did I, and a little while later I realized *how* foreign you were to this land. It was my hope that we might escape together and disappear in your world." Damien dropped his head, his stringy hair falling over his eyes.

The angry welt flared on his cheek, and Sarah fought the desire to brush her thumb across it to remove the pain. She rubbed her burning eyes, knowing that a combination of anxiety, exhaustion, and being drugged was messing with her head.

"I know you detest me," Damien said softly, turning his bowed head to peak at her, and the action gave him an innocent, pleading look. "But I can protect you here."

"For how long?" she whispered, eyes pained. "He's coming back in the morning to kill me."

"I will not let him—"

"Don't you get it?" she fairly shouted, chest heaving. "I won't tell him a thing, and he's going to make sure I can't tell anyone else." She let that sink in and then added, her voice softer now, "I'll be safer if you just let me go."

He closed his eyes, leaning his head back against the wall. "I gave Cadius the key."

She frowned, having forgotten. "Then help me find a way out of here. Maybe there's a loose board or—"

Shaking his head, Damien asked, "And where would you go? You will never figure out where you are and would freeze before you found your way out of this forest."

"*Help* me," she urged.

"I cannot do that." The words escaped on a regretful breath.

Sarah's hope deflated like a balloon with a hole in it. Her voice turned bitter. "So you're still under his thumb, too scared to do anything against him." She shook her head, feeling renewed betrayal and disappointment. "I thought you had changed."

"But I have—"

"No, you haven't."

Damien huffed in vexation. "You've hardly given me a chance to explain. I must earn back his trust."

"And in doing so, you've lost mine. Again." She squeezed her eyes closed for a moment, steadying her emotions, which were quickly spinning out of control.

"Sarah, I—"

"It's 'my lady' to you." Angry with him and herself for wanting to believe in him again, Sarah laid down on the blankets on her side, giving him her back, and struggled to yank the covers up to her chin. She could see her breath now, exiting her lips in cold puffs of air. "I'm tired, but don't think I won't break out of here in the morning when that door is opened." Not that she would know which way to go.

She heard him sigh. "Fair enough," he whispered. "But you know I will do my utmost to stop you."

"Fair enough."

Damien expelled a tiny huff of a laugh, and if she hadn't been so hurt, she might have smiled along with him. But their friendship would never be the same, no matter what he did to earn back her trust. "Pleasant dreams, my lady."

Sarah grunted in response, dragging the quilt up to her chin to mask her shaking. Her body sagged in exhaustion, but her mind kept moving, heart racing as she felt his eyes on her. After a few minutes of silence, boots scraped against the floor, and one of the cabinet doors opened on creaky hinges and closed. She resisted a peek over her shoulder to see what he was doing, but when he cleared his throat loudly, she rolled onto her back and looked up at him. He stood a few feet back, holding a blanket in his own hands, a cautious look on his features.

"What?"

"It will be warmer if we—" Damien swallowed, and it looked like his tan cheeks had reddened. "What I mean to say is that we will be more comfortable if we are together for the night."

Sarah gave him a look that spoke volumes, then she rolled her face away from him, staring at the wall as she wrapped her arms around herself. Her dress had dried, but Damien was still wet from his recent trip in the rain, and she could only imagine how cold the night would be for him. She willed herself not to care as she curled in on herself to keep warm. "Wake me if someone breaks in to kill both of us or if you're dying of hypothermia, otherwise don't speak to me again."

There was a pause, and then she heard him sigh. "Have it your way, my lady."

ଔ

"Uncle, draw up a search party," Will commanded. "Dogs, horses, men—whatever we can acquire."

He and Richard had spent half the afternoon searching town and the surrounding woods for any sign of Sarah and her abductor, but the rain had ruined any trail left behind. When their search turned up nothing, he had gone to his uncle and explained everything—the fact that he knew Sarah had been taken, his fear that Damien had been the one to do it—and Thomas appeared to believe him and the seriousness of the situation. He had helped them scour the land for clues of Sarah's disappearance until the dark and rain made it useless to try any longer, and Thomas made them all turn in for the night.

Will had slept little, and what sleep he had was riddled with nightmares that, when he awoke, remained as nothing more than horrible, vague recollections of faceless creatures hunting in the night. But the feelings of guilt and fear stirred by his tortured dreams lingered. It tore at him to know that he was lying there in bed, when Sarah was heaven knew where and had endured, as Will was forced to imagine, unspeakable harm. That is, if she was, indeed, alive.

Unable to stand his idleness, he had arrived on his uncle's porch just before sunrise, pounding on the door until the man answered, looking groggy and unkempt.

At Will's words, Thomas shook his head, looking pained and regretful and a little exasperated at his nephew's demanding attitude. "Son, it's not as though we have the castle resources at our disposal, summoning them at *your* every whim; this is still a kingdom that needs protection. You know I will help in any way I can—"

Stiffening his resolve, Will hiked his chin in defiance as he strode inside. "A fine job the kingdom did of protecting Sarah when she needed it. But if this is your refusal of assistance, then allow me to plead my case to the queen directly. She is fond of Sarah, and I believe that she would give me the men I need if it would save Sarah from that fiend." His uncle still looked hesitant as he closed the door, and Will's head lowered, not in defeat, but out of respect to the man who had raised him, regretting having spoken so harshly. But he had spent half the night searching, and time was precious.

He softened his tone and tried one final time to make him understand. "It's Sarah, Uncle." Though simple words, they seemed to have the desired affect. "I fear too much time has passed already."

Thomas rubbed at the crease between his brows. "And why do you need me?" He sounded weary.

"I am a knight in title only and have no real power or sway in the kingdom, but you helped protect her once. *Please* help me save her once more."

With a great, heavy sigh, Thomas shook his head, but Will could tell his uncle had already acquiesced. His heart quickened in anticipation. After a pregnant pause, Thomas exhaled again. "I shall see what I can do."

Will's chest rose and fell in relief, though his anxiety still lingered. He knew it would never fully dissipate until Sarah was back in his arms. "Thank you, Uncle."

"I shall request an audience with Her Majesty and pray that she provides us with the resources we require." Thomas hesitated on his way to his bedroom to dress. He turned back to Will and asked carefully, "You don't truly believe he would hurt her after everything he did to protect Miss Matthews, do you?"

Will clenched his jaw. He had wondered the same thing himself. "I can hardly say, but I certainly won't stand idly by and allow her fate to be decided by the Spaniard's blood-stained hands."

Chapter Twelve

"No man chooses to be evil because it is evil;
he only mistakes it for the happiness, the good he seeks."

Mary Shelley, *Frankenstein*

Sarah woke with a start to find Damien's face close to hers as he crouched over her body, shaking her awake. She jerked back, slamming her shoulder into the wall. "What are you—?"

He hushed her with a finger to her lips, keeping it there even when she shook her head in displeasure. "Get up," he whispered urgently.

Blinking the grit from her eyes, Sarah gave him a confused, distrustful look, though he appeared genuinely alarmed. Hazy sunlight shone through the tiny cracks in the walls, and the small cabin looked even more dingy and run-down in the light. "What's going on?" Her voice was quieter this time and gravelly from sleep.

Damien dragged her to her feet, anxious gaze trained on the floor. He was paler without the night to darken his coloring, and the welt stood out against his skin, which was surrounded by a faint bruise in the shape of a hand. "He has brought friends this sunrise. It would appear our time is up, my lady," he added gravely, lips barely moving as he spoke.

Several pares of boots stomped across the earth, and a key grated in the outer lock. The door burst open, slamming against the wall. Sarah jumped, and Damien took a step in front of her as Cadius strode angrily into the room and right up to them. Two men, neither of whom she recognized, entered the room behind him, flanking the door on either side and making escape impossible. Each had a sword sheathed at his side.

Cadius' chest heaved, gray eyes turning the color of angry storm clouds getting ready to release havoc on the world. Sarah managed not to tuck her chin or show her fear, though she found herself clutching the back of Damien's shirt and pulling him just a modicum closer.

"You fool," Cadius hissed, his eyes trained on Damien's stoic face. "Where is it?"

Damien hiked his brows, appearing cool, collected, and curious, all facades that Sarah knew he had practiced well. But his color had faded at Cadius' appearance, though he was careful not to let too much show on his face. "You need to be more specific."

Eyes flaring, Cadius raised his clenched fist and threw a crumpled letter at Damien's chest. He watched the note fall to the floor before drawing his gaze back to the irate man before them. "I did not expect you to read it so soon," Damien said simply.

Sarah felt a little taken aback at the rebellion she saw in his eyes, in the hard set of his mouth and the defiance burning in his eyes. Was it because she had challenged him about being a coward that he was finally standing up to Cadius? She eyed the men guarding the door with a wary gaze, knowing her chance to run had yet to present itself.

Silence passed between them, and Cadius' nostrils flared. "That *dinner menu*"—he pointed to the wrinkled ball of paper on the floor as he ground out the words—"is not the missive I asked you to retrieve. Now, where is the letter?"

Damien said nothing. Sarah stared at his profile, realizing that he hadn't given Cadius the letter that had been in her possession. To his own detriment, no less, a fact that caused even greater confusion over his intent.

The angry, out-of-control look on Cadius' face shifted, turning cold—he always appeared more threatening when he was in control—and his eyes narrowed. "Perhaps I shall question the lady."

Damien reached back and grasped the hand that was just behind him. "It is out of her possession. She knows nothing."

Cadius looked like he was going to say more, or strike Damien, she couldn't tell which. Pasting on a look she hoped appeared both bold and assured, Sarah stepped out from behind Damien to stand at his side, unclasping their hands even though she was tempted to hang on for courage. Funny how she was turning to Damien for comfort after everything, but he was the best alternative she had at the moment, and she could always go back to loathing him again after they survived the morning.

"You should leave now," she said, trying to sound more confident than she felt in her bluff. "I'm friends with the queen and missed a meeting with her when I was taken; she'll have had a search party out all night looking for me. If you leave now, you might have a chance to get away before half the royal guard comes down on you."

"Oh, child." Cadius gave her an amused look that said how little her threats meant to him. "The only one who sought you out yesterday was that blacksmith, and he is no closer to stumbling upon this cabin than you are to escaping with your life before the day is out."

Sarah registered the threat, but then she realized that he knew Will, that he was aware of their relationship. Her face must have revealed her surprise, because Cadius smiled coldly, looking like a cat with a mouse caught in its paw. "Yes, I have been giving special attention to your lover for years to ensure he did nothing rash. Before everything changed, I attempted to draw the elder Taylor into my confidence nearly a decade past, but he wanted nothing to do with the plan he'd heard whispered about the castle by my men." Cadius examined his hands "His refusal concerned me, and so I had Gabriel eliminate the threat he posed to my plan before he could alert the king."

Sarah sucked in a breath. Will had always suspected that Dunlivey had been hired to kill his parents, setting fire to their house in the middle of the night, but he had never known why. When they had discovered Dunlivey's body, courtesy of Damien, it had been assumed that Will would never get an answer as to why he had been orphaned. And now Sarah knew. It shouldn't have come as a surprise that Cadius was yet again pulling the strings behind every tragic deed in Serimone, but it did. She just hoped that she lived to tell Will the truth and finally put his questions to rest, though she couldn't help wondering if drudging up the past would be wise.

"It shouldn't surprise me that you're so bloodthirsty," Sarah spat, trying to keep her mounting rage and fear from causing her to do something that would endanger her and Damien's lives . . . more so than they already were.

"You can prevent further bloodshed by simply *giving me the letter*." He directed his barely controlled anger at Damien, though he maintained his defiant silence. Cadius' eyes turned to mere slits. "Have it your way," he hissed. Pulling back, he collected his calm facade once more and gave Damien an unpleasant curl of his lips. "With you two out of the way, the letter matters not."

Sarah watched with wide eyes as he turned and strode to the door, where he paused. He raised his hand, poised as if to snap his fingers, a noise that she was sure would send his goons into action.

Panicked, the words flew out of her mouth before she could think about the repercussions. "I know Adrian's your son!" She froze, blood turning to ice as Cadius spun slowly to face her. She didn't know if she said it to distract him or buy them time—time for what, she didn't know. Or maybe it was to confront him with his horrible, dark self and make him feel regret for all his misdeeds, though she questioned if he even had a soul with which to feel remorse.

Cadius gave her a cold look. "And how, pray tell, might you know that?" He was testing her knowledge, and she planned on giving him whatever was needed, whatever would put just a few more seconds on her and Damien's clocks.

Instead of answering his question directly, she hastily added, "And I know you had Queen Meredith's baby—the true heir—killed so you could have a direct line through Adrian." Her voice wobbled, and she was careful not to mention that she thought the queen's son was still alive and living in town. She felt a moment's gratification at the spark of surprise that came over his features.

Collecting herself, she drew strength from his prolonged, stunned silence, stiffening her spine. Sarah could feel Damien's curious, surprised gaze on her, though he didn't try to stop her. He knew as well as she that this conversation was buying them precious seconds to think of some escape, even though the notion of getting out of this alive was looking very slim at the current juncture. "My only question is if you killed Alexis yourself after you were finished with her or if you had someone do it for you."

"I died with her!" Cadius burst out, advancing a step, eyes blazing.

Sarah barely kept herself from pulling back in response to the rage she saw. "Please," she goaded, scoffing. "You only went back to seduce her and get a direct line to the throne, and then you cast her aside like you do with everyone else when they outlive their usefulness."

"How dare you." Cadius' fists clenched at his sides, his knuckles turning white with strain. "Yes, my intent was to resume our romance when I returned and prevent her from directing her heart to my brother. Originally." He swallowed visibly, and his face softened a fraction as he remembered. "But then we fell in love, although she united with my brother once more when he became king, despite my intervention."

"And you were lovers in secret," Sarah added, lifting a brow. "Betraying the king yet again."

"It was not—" He glared at her. "He cared for her not, and it was *I* who tended to her heart. She was supposed to live a long, full life, as she had before, with my adoring shadow by her side." His features darkened once more. "Imagine my horror when I realized that this time around, it was the birth of *my* child that ended her young life, whereas she would be alive to this day in the other timeline."

Sarah was a little taken aback by his obvious love for Alexis, but she was more shocked by the fact that, according to Cadius, he had changed history by traveling back and had inadvertently brought about the premature death of Alexis. Could Sarah affect the past in the same way, bringing about events that shouldn't be?

She stiffened her spine against the thought and gave Cadius a look that said she didn't care about his plight. "The first death of many."

He exhaled slowly. A vein in his pale forehead pulsed, and his pursed lips tipped ever so slightly. "I hope you enjoy this century, Miss Matthews, because you will be here for some time." He spun on his heels, strode quickly from the cabin, and hopped onto the back of his horse. Grabbing the reins, he looked over his shoulder and addressed his two thugs. "They breathe their last here." Then he heeled his horse in the side, and it shot off into the dense forest with a disgruntled shriek.

"Wait!" Sarah shouted as the two men advanced, though she knew she would get no help from his retreating form.

Instead of waiting for the thugs to finish them off, Damien surged forward, catching the one on the right off-guard. He collided with the man before he could fully unsheathe his weapon, and the sword clattered to the floor, sliding a few feet away. The two men grunted, struggling over one another as they both attempted to reach the weapon first.

Eyes on the man who was advancing toward her, Sarah retreated until her back connected with the counter. He left the sword untouched at his side, probably thinking she was too easy a target to soil his boots with her blood. But she refused to go down without a fight, and when he neared with a confident smirk, she kicked and lashed out at the man's face with her hands. Her boot connected with his shin, and her nails managed to leave deep red gouges from his hairline down to his jaw.

His dark eyes flared with rage, and he wrapped his meaty hands around her throat, cutting her off mid-scream. He squeezed until her eyes bulged and her tiny chokes no longer made a sound. Her legs were useless with his proximity, but her hands still flailed madly, trying to buy her escape. But the man, whose grip didn't lessen, shook her so that her spine slammed into the edge of the counter, stealing what little breath she had, and pressed her back so that her head connected with the shelves.

Sarah's vision swam, stars dancing before her eyes, and she tried to pry his hands from her neck to no avail. She could feel her heartbeat pulsating in her cheeks now, and her sight was blurring uncontrollably, her lungs feelings like they might burst or shrivel to nothing at any moment. The sound of Damien's struggle was overpowered by the roaring in her ears.

Desperately, her hands searched the counter behind her in hopes of a weapon, knowing she was no match for the man's size. She was about to lose consciousness when her fingertips collided with something hard and cold, and she gripped it firmly. With all the strength she had left, Sarah drew it through the air and slammed it against the side of his head.

He staggered back, releasing her and closing his eyes as he touched the bloody mark on his temple. Sarah choked and sputtered, dragging in ragged breaths and filling her starved lungs as she stumbled out of his path. It eased the roar in her ears and her vision began to refocus, but she knew there was no time to enjoy the sensation of breathing. Already, the man was regaining his senses and had started to turn her way, and Sarah reacted out of fear and anger.

She swung the heavy flashlight around, and it connected with the soft part of his skull. His legs crumpled beneath him, and he fell forward, his temple colliding with the edge of the counter before he lay in a motionless heap on the floor.

Sarah stared in horror at what she'd done, waiting a moment to see the man's back rise and fall, indicating life, but then she spun around at the sounds of struggling behind her. Damien had been backed into a corner, and the man advancing on him wielded the sword now, though it looked as though he had received a few good blows in the process of retrieving the weapon. He jerked the sword back, blade poised toward Damien's chest, and Sarah ran up behind him on shaky legs and brought her only weapon down on the man's arm with all her might. He howled in pain and surprise as his sword clattered to the floor.

Sarah's triumph was short-lived, and she let out a tiny shriek, jumping back as he spun on her. But Damien's reflexes were quick, and he snatched up the sword and thrust it through the man's back with a cry. The blood-covered, razor sharp tip of the weapon tore through the man's shirt and protruded through his front. The man sputtered, staring at her with his widened gaze, and she threw her hands over her mouth to hide her cry of shock and revulsion. Turning her back on the grizzly scene, she closed her eyes to block out the image of the blade cutting all the way through him, through flesh and bone.

A wet gurgle issued from the man, and Sarah heard the sickening sound of the blade being ripped from his body. She turned around slowly, steeling herself, but the sight of the man's crumpled form surrounded by a pool of blood, which ceaselessly poured from the jagged gash in his back, was more grotesque than she imagined.

She dragged her eyes upward. Damien's chest was heaving, and he leaned on the bloodied sword for support as he stared at the man's lifeless form, a mixture of horror and rage on his face. Blood rolled over his knuckles, and a few drops splattered on the unstained wood at his feet. For the first time, Sarah noticed the tear in his sleeve and the wetness that stained the fabric around his forearm.

Exhaling a shaky breath, Damien met her frightened gaze and tried to put on what she assumed was meant to be an expression of strength, but his wild eyes and colorless face gave his own fear away. "We must go."

Sarah gave a vague nod, eyes trained once more on the man's body. The blood had stopped bubbling from the fatal cut, and the sight reminded her so much of the way Edith had died—also at Damien's hand—that she found herself unable to tear her horror-filled gaze away.

A hand gripped her arm, and her eyes jerked to Damien's, so close to her own. They seemed to understand her thoughts, and regret lingered in his determined gaze. "He would have killed both of us, if given the chance."

She shook her head, though she didn't know exactly why. "Did I kill him?" she asked quietly, casting a fleeting glance at the man she had knocked out. "Is he dead, too?" The men had been sent to kill her and Damien, and she told herself that she shouldn't feel so guilty or fearful of what her own survival instincts had driven her to do.

Damien took her hand. "I don't feel much like remaining to find out."

But as she stared, she thought the man's back moved an inch with breath, and his face might have barely tightened in a grimace. She breathed a sigh of relief, exhaling her guilt with it, but the sight reminded her feet to move.

They moved out the door and into the cool morning light, which brightened the forest floor with little patches of gold that managed to slip through the dense limbs overhead. Sarah glanced over her shoulder and glimpsed the small shack, which was even more rundown from the outside and was already being obstructed by the thick copse of trees that surrounded it. No wonder Cadius had thought it was a good place to hide his treasure; it was nearly impossible to discern the building from the surrounding trees.

Silence stretched between them as they worked their way slowly through the trees, and Sarah suddenly remembered that Damien was still holding her hand. Gently, she disentangled their fingers and let his hand drop. He appeared momentarily hurt, but he quickly recovered, breathing heavily as they journeyed deeper into the forest.

"I've never been as big a fan of flashlights as I am right now." She choked out a laugh, her body shaking. Damien didn't respond, and she eyed him questioningly. He wasn't *actually* mad that she wouldn't hold his hand, was he? Then she saw the color that bloomed over his waist and caused his shirt to droop heavily, and she knew it wasn't just his arm that had been wounded.

She stopped abruptly, and he faced her, chest rising and falling quickly, subtly using the sword for support. "You're hurt."

Damien shook his head, his shaggy hair falling over his forehead. "I am all right. Let's keep moving."

Eying him warily, she caught his stooped shoulders and colorless features, the sweat beading at his temples. "No, we need to stop for right now. You can't go much further."

But he was already moving, using the sword as though it were a cane. "If we stop, we're dead, to be sure."

Unable to stop him and knowing he was probably right, Sarah quietly returned to his side. She worried her lip at the trail of blood he was leaving behind. "Where are we going?"

"To see the one person we can trust," he panted, clutching his abdomen.

Annoyed at his pride and inexplicably saddened by the sight of him limping along, Sarah took the sword from his hand and silenced his irritated look by gently lifting his arm and wrapping it around her shoulders to support him. "And who might that be?" she asked, hoping to divert his attention from his wounded ego.

Damien leaned into her, though she could tell he was still trying to support most of his own weight as he navigated low-hanging branches and protruding roots in the earth. "Thank you."

"Don't think this means we're friends again," she replied, harsher than she'd intended. She softened her tone at his injured look. "Who are we going to see?"

"The person who is safeguarding that letter Cadius wants so desperately."

Sarah started. "You gave it to someone?"

He nodded, grimacing as he lifted his leg over a fallen log. "I delivered it to them just before you awoke. I did not want Cadius to find it on your person, and I had hoped that pretending to give him the letter would draw his suspicion away from how much you knew—perhaps allow more time to devise a plan. But he read the false missive sooner than I had anticipated." He ground out his next words. "It was why I brought you there—to get to you first and devise a plan before Cadius could lay his hands on you. If he believed I was still allied with him, then perhaps . . ."

Shaking his head, he said, "It was a foolish plan."

Sarah was silent for a long moment as she absorbed this. Up ahead, she could just discern the outline of a small cabin, and Damien pointed to it with a limp hand. Relieved, she quickened her pace as much as his wounds would allow, grunting as they climbed the steps. He pounded on the door with a grimace, and she quickly stepped away from him.

"Now that we're out of his hands, why don't we use the letter against Cadius?" she asked lowly as they waited. "Give it back to me, and I'll take it to the queen."

Damien shook his head, and her shoulders fell. "It is not enough evidence against him."

Frowning in annoyance, she said, "Then why try to keep it from him if it doesn't mean anything?"

"Because, at the moment, it is all we have, and I did not want to lose it."

Any reply died on her lips as someone unlocked the door from the inside, and a chain dropped against the wood just before the door swung open. Sarah's jaw followed suit.

Jade, who looked remarkably well for a dead woman, glared at the two of them. Though she was still gorgeous, with manicured features and long, dark hair flowing freely over one shoulder, she looked younger somehow. Maybe it was the lack of red-painted lips or rouge on her cheeks or charcoal lining her eyes that made her look sweeter, more innocent.

Then she spoke and reminded Sarah why she had never liked her.

Jade's eyes dropped to Damien's bloody hand clutching his stomach, and she raised a brow. "It's bad enough that I am forced to conceal your letters, but now I must hide and stitch you up, as well. I'm reduced to servitude once more after all my effort to disappear, is that it?"

Damien sighed. "We have encountered a bit of a disastrous morning. Will you let us inside?"

Raising one delicately arched brow, Jade asked haughtily, "And will *she* be staying?"

"Yes." Damien's voice was firm, his answer quick.

Sarah's gaze kept moving between the two of them, wondering how they knew each other, and trying to move past her bafflement that Jade was alive. "You went over a waterfall." The two dark-haired individuals turned to look at her.

Jade lifted a manicured hand and flicked a lock of hair from her eye. "So did William, pet, and he appears to be in good health."

"But your body was found—"

With a dramatic roll of her eyes, Jade said, "Obviously, it could not have been me, as I am in perfect health. Perhaps it was another tramp, eh?" She shot Damien a deadly glare that Sarah didn't quite understand.

He ground out in annoyance and pain, "Not that this brisk air isn't refreshing, but if you don't mind, Isabella, I would prefer to die inside my sister's home rather than in the dirt."

Chapter Thirteen

"The virtue of angels is that they cannot deteriorate;
their flaw is that they cannot improve.
Man's flaw is that he can deteriorate; and his virtue is that he can improve."

Hisidic saying

Sarah gaped at Jade. *She* was Damien's lost sister? "You're siblings?" she asked dumbly. She didn't know why she needed the clarification—the dark hair, straight noses, pointed chins, and identically shaped eyes were evidence enough. How had she not seen the resemblance before?

Maybe because Damien had said his sister had died.

Jade—Isabella?—blinked once, as if she couldn't believe her stupidity. "That is generally how it works when there are sisters and brothers involved. Do try to keep up."

Sarah was too shocked to take immediate offense, though she knew the comment would bother her later. "But you should be dead."

Jade gave her a demeaning look. "Yes, pet, we have established that. Are you asking me to die once more for your pleasure, or are you simply thick-skulled?"

"No." Sarah gave her head a small shake and bit back a nasty retort. "Though I can't exactly say I was broken up about your death," she muttered, then pursed her lips. So much for being the more mature woman. "I mean, Damien said that his sister *died*."

"Are you still telling that dribble, brother?" Jade gave him a reproachful look. To Sarah, she said, "When I announced that I was going into a more lucrative profession than that of a seamstress' assistant, Damien was hardly pleased. So you see, I suppose to him, his sweet, innocent little sister *did* die the moment she decided to sell herself—Isabella is nothing more than a ghost now, and only my brother calls me that." She frowned severely at Damien, who looked entirely uncomfortable with talk of Jade's former life. Or his expression could have been a product of the gaping wound in his abdomen.

"Might we discuss this at a later time when I am not watering your garden with my blood?" Damien's voice was dry, but pain laced every word. Sarah glanced at his side, and though it was hard to tell beneath his hand and the layers of stained fabric, it appeared that the blood flow hadn't slowed much.

Appearing to consider the condition they were in—Damien's wound and Sarah's bedraggled appearance—Jade huffed. "One night. And the weapon remains outside."

He sighed in relief. "Thank you, Isabella." She sashayed inside without another word, leaving the door open for them. Damien dropped the sword in the grass and leaned heavily on Sarah as she helped him up the steps and through the doorway. She quickly stepped back from him again once they were inside, closing the door.

Sarah's eyes adjusted to the small two-room cabin, and she saw that the wood floor, though weathered and peeling, was tidy. The long settee in the corner of the main room was old but the fabric was clean, and the table along the right wall by the fireplace was laden with a few goblets, two tankards, and a jug of what Sarah assumed was wine. Though it smelled a little stale and closed-up, overall, the place looked neatly kept, and though the tiny square window on the left wall was open, it was warm inside.

"I need to fetch a needle," Jade said as she moved past them, not having lost that old habit of swinging her hips wherever she went. "Don't touch anything . . ." She paused, glancing over her shoulder and pursing her lips as though trying to recall something. "Remind me of your name again." But she didn't wait for a response, only quirked a brow and moved along.

Sarah's jaw twisted to the side in annoyance, wanting very much to scream at her retreating form. She'd felt bad that Will had been plagued by the death of his old friend, and Sarah had experienced guilt over her lack of pity that Jade had died. But now Sarah wondered why she'd ever *wanted* to feel pity for the woman.

"Your sister is infuriating."

Damien chuckled at her abrupt appraisal. "That she is." Sarah turned from her staring at the open bedroom door and caught his thoughtful look. "But she wasn't always this way—you'll recall I told you of her sweetness and charity as a child. I believe that, beneath the hardened independence she has taken on to survive, some of that former child still exists."

She was tempted to disagree from what she knew of the woman, but that was just the thing: she had only met her a few times. And while Jade had been acerbic and demeaning with her each and every instance, Damien was her brother and knew her better than anyone. Though Sarah had her reservations about Jade's inner "sweetness," she knew she shouldn't be so rash to judge, especially considering the fact that Jade had good reason to hate her, if only because she imagined that Sarah had taken Will from her.

Damien was leaning heavily against the doorjamb, his face pale, chest rising and falling in what looked like controlled, steady breaths. He hadn't complained, but he appeared in considerable discomfort.

"I thought you had been trained to withstand pain from a young age," Sarah commented, reminding him of words he'd once spoken. "You barely appeared fazed by getting your arm seared back together and having a horrible nurse scrape your wound day after day." Though he did look amused by her remark on her poor performance as his caretaker, he appeared too exhausted to make much effort to smile.

She bit her lip, torn over her confusing desires to both comfort and rip into him for kidnapping her. She decided she could reprimand him for drugging her once he felt better; he was too exhausted now, and it would be like kicking a wounded puppy . . . that had kidnapped her. "You should probably sit down."

"Not on my sofa, you won't." Jade came back into the room carrying a stack of linens under one arm and a small, flat fold of leather that Sarah assumed contained her sewing equipment. "You can lie on the floor. There is more space for you to spread out, anyway." She tossed him the thin sheet that was slung over one of her arms, and he caught it with the hand that wasn't clutching his side.

Damien did as she told him. He carefully removed his coat and laid the fabric on the ground, grimacing as he lowered himself to the sheet with great care. Untying the strap from around the leather and parting the folds, Jade selected a pair of blunt scissors from among the various sewing tools.

"Your shirt is ruined," she muttered. Un-tucking Damien's shirt with jerky movements, she cut the fabric from the hem up to the neckline and laid the shredded folds aside. One half clung to sticky, partially dried blood, and she peeled the fabric back with more care, though the removal of the fresh scab cause Damien to hiss as his torso was exposed. Sarah tried to keep the surprise from her face, but the unwanted concern slipped through.

His ribs and clavicle were exposed from lack of food and his arms, though it appeared like he had tried to keep some semblance of his former athletic self, were devoid of the perfectly formed muscles that had distracted Sarah so long ago. His stomach was completely flat, and his skin, considerably paler than she remembered, caused the blood and bruises covering his torso to stand out. He had never been bulky like Will, though his tan body had once been covered with hard, lean muscle. But now, lying on the floor half-covered in his own blood, he looked sad and pathetic. The sight twisted her insides.

She wouldn't exactly call it emaciated, but seeing him go from a young, healthy looking heart-stealer to this thin escapee who clearly hadn't been treated well made her heart take a dive. And then there was the strange marking over his heart, the risen skin looking like a burn scar. Sarah observed it, trying to make out what the symbol was.

"Something you find interesting, pet?" She yanked her eyes away from Damien's bare chest and saw that the siblings were watching her—Damien with a curious, unreadable gaze, and Jade with a brow raised in challenge.

Sarah's neck heated at being caught and for Jade implying it had been more than a glance, and the heat spreading to her cheeks only embarrassed her more. Sarah glared at her. "No," she snapped. Jade pursed her lips in unbelief and then went back to tending her brother's wound, wiping the blood around the edges of the jagged cut at his side. It wasn't as deep as all the blood he'd lost had implied, but it still looked awful.

To keep her mind off Damien's current state, which Sarah knew would too easily earn her sympathy—if it hadn't already—she focused on her annoyance with Jade. The woman grated on her nerves, and even Jade's brief glances made her feel small, reminding Sarah that the woman had never thought much of her. Months ago, Jade had driven a wedge between Sarah and Will by implying that she'd had an "intimate" relationship with him while Sarah had been away, and the rumor she'd started had nearly ended Will and Sarah's fragile relationship. Distressed, Sarah had run right into Damien's arms to fill the void, and she might have stayed there if Will hadn't contradicted Jade's lies.

Sarah paused. Now that she knew the two were brother and sister, she couldn't help wondering if it had all been part of some plan to force her to bond with Damien. But an instant later she remembered the genuine, territorial look Jade wore when she discovered the history between Sarah and Will, her sorrow over being rejected by that same man, and Sarah dismissed the thought. No, Jade's motivation hadn't been driven by her brother's needs or to fill a gap in some grand scheme. Severing the bond between Sarah and Will had been purely for herself.

Suddenly, it occurred to her that she was spending "quality" time with her kidnapper and his crazy, formerly dead sister who seemed to take issue with Sarah. Though Damien had tried to protect her from Cadius and his goons and hadn't exactly done anything threatening toward her, he had still held her hostage in that shack, even if it had been part of a plan to draw Cadius' suspicion from her and Damien. Whatever the case, Sarah knew she couldn't remain a willing hostage, of sorts. She had to get back to Will and deliver her message to the queen—even without the letter Jade was hiding, if it came down to it.

She eyed the window, too small to squeeze through, and then considered bolting for the door, which was only a few feet away. Damien was in no state to chase after her, and she knew Jade would be glad to be rid of her.

"Isabella," Damien said quietly, muttering something else too low for Sarah to catch. With a scoff of annoyance, Jade swiped her red-stained hand on the sheet and stood. She ignored Sarah as she walked past her, reaching into her low-cut bodice to produce a key. Before Sarah could fully realize what she was about to do, Jade closed the iron lock on the door and turned the key.

Caught off-guard, Sarah hesitated, then she dove at her. Jade quickly dropped the key between her cleavage, and it disappeared. Sarah jerked to a halt, and Jade waved a finger at her. "Tut tut."

Sarah scowled. "Classy." She directed her steely gaze to Damien, who was leaning up on his elbows with a strained look on his pale face. "So I'm still your prisoner, is that it? I would have thought a guy who'd recently escaped would remember how that feels."

"I do," he whispered, and she felt a fleeting pang of guilt when she realized how horrible it must have been for him, if the bruises were any indication of the abuse he'd received while locked away. "But you cannot leave."

"Why not?" Sarah burst out, her voice echoing in the small house. Neither sibling flinched; perhaps they were used to outbursts. "I don't see why you need to keep an eye on me."

Damien rose to a sitting position, lips parting as he released a shaky breath, closing his eyes. "Because I can protect you." He used a towel to cautiously clean the shallow wound on his forearm.

"Look at yourself." He grimaced at her words, though they were softer than before. "You're in no position to be making promises to keep me safe. Give me the letter, and let me go so Will can protect me."

Damien's gold-flecked eyes flared with instant anger. He spoke quickly, his words low and sharp. "And what shall he do? Does he know every move that Cadius has made, what the man has in store? Because I do—I know everything he is planning that involves this kingdom and *you*, and I can predict his next move, which is why the letter remains here. Not even Cadius is aware of this cabin's location, but if you return to your precious blacksmith who is already under scrutiny, then how long do you think it will be until they find you? Hmm? A few hours before you both lose your lives? Cadius didn't succeed before, but he is a patient man who does not care for loose ends, and he *will* try again."

Sarah swallowed hard, pain turning into a band around her heart. "You don't know that." But her voice was small, unsure.

"The best thing you can do for either of you is to stay away from him." Damien was breathing hard, either from the stress his wound had put on him or because the topic raised his pulse. "For the time being, you have to consider your blacksmith as bait to get you into the open. Cadius wanted you for information before, but now he knows you will not give up your friend, and you are too dangerous left alive."

"But Cadius thinks we're dead," she reasoned. "He sent his men after us and didn't stick around to see if they finished the job; he's not going to expect either of us to pop up in town."

"And when they don't report back? He's sadistic, not a boob, and he will know you are alive if you *reveal* yourself." At her stubborn look laced with uncertainty she couldn't shake, he rolled his eyes heavenward. "Fine, if you are so assured he can fend off ten guards sent to kill him, then by all means, your freedom shall be granted. I wish you every happiness in your short lives together."

"Brother, stop," Jade chastised, kneeling beside him, her expression perturbed as she picked up a clean cloth and dabbed at the dribble of blood sliding from his sewn wound. "You will pop your stitches if you get so worked up." She directed her clear, assured gaze at Sarah. "If he says you are safest in his presence, then believe it. He might be a fool"—she shot him a look before returning her gaze to Sarah—"but a coward he is not. He will do whatever he can to keep you safe, and his knowledge of Cadius' plans will aid in that."

Sarah's chest heaved. She wanted to throw some snide remark back in Jade's face, to rebuke Damien for claiming that he could protect her when he was battered and broken. But her hope and defiance deflated when she acknowledged that what they said made sense—Cadius knew that she and Will had taken part in his "execution." He hadn't done anything to Will yet, but if he was having him watched and Sarah, who was supposed to be dead and had just openly defied the man who had tried to kill her, showed up, then Cadius certainly wouldn't make the same mistake twice. He would stick around this time to make sure they died properly.

"He'll kill Will if I turn up, won't he?" she whispered, hating to admit that it was true. Damien remained silent, but he'd already said as much. "Will's probably safer if I stay dead for a time," she went on quietly, half musing to herself. "And the only way for me to do so is to stay here for now, where no one will find me. So, in order to protect both of us, I'm literally having to room with the woman who launched herself over a waterfall to get Will's attention and the guy who tried to kill him and kidnapped me."

Sarah's eyebrows rose, and she stared across the room at nothing in particular. "This just took an ironic turn."

Damien hoisted himself to his elbows against his sister's protests. "Sarah—"

"Uh-uh." She held up a hand to stop his look of tortured sympathy. "You don't get to play the reasonable friend card—you cashed that in a long time ago when you murdered Edith and hurt Will. You can lie and beg for my forgiveness until your lips fall off, but I'm not here for friendship; I'm only staying to keep Will safe and to be near that letter until we can figure out some other concrete way to stop Cadius for good. As soon as it's safe, our business is finished and you go back to prison, where you'll be guarded by people who don't speak English so you can't make a deal with them to release you."

Jade gave Sarah a dull look. "A bit dramatic, don't you think, pet?"

Sarah spread her hands, shooting a look of acute annoyance at the ceiling. "Jade, if you don't want me to throw caution to the wind and take an axe to one of your walls to escape, then I suggest you keep your claws and unhelpful remarks to yourself." She felt a small triumph at Jade's flabbergasted look over her outburst. Before the woman could throw back a snide retort, Sarah added, "Now, I'm going to lock myself in the back room, but please let me know when all of this has blown over and I can resume my life."

An unreadable look passed between the siblings, and it looked like they were debating. Finally, Jade ground out to her brother, "No. I am allowing you into my home, but I draw the line at giving up my bed." She cast her haughty gaze toward Sarah. "You can sleep out here when night comes—the bedroom is mine."

Sarah considered stomping like a petulant child to show her displeasure at being stuck with these two for a minute longer than necessary. But instead, she clenched her jaw and slid down the door, resting her arms on upraised knees and staring off at the far wall, blinking the grit from her eyes and trying to maintain a steely gaze. She was tired, annoyed, confused, and scared at the idea that Will was being watched by Cadius' men. Add to that her frustration that she couldn't go to Will and fear that if she did, his life would be in great danger. It was a wonder that she hadn't burst into exhausted tears yet, though she imagined that was due to her resolve to not give Jade the satisfaction of seeing her cry.

It took another twenty minutes for Jade to finish cleaning and dressing Damien's wound, and Sarah's eyes flickered to his bare skin once or twice in that time. But she willed away the compassion and protective anger she instinctively felt at the condition his body was in. She recalled the way those feelings had stirred within her when she had been the one to dress his wound, or listen to stories of his father's cruelty, or when she had held his hand as he endured horrible seizures, unable to do anything but offer comfort and assurance that she was by his side. Damien had always been able to get her to feel something for him, even against her will, and he had a terrible knack for understanding her.

But it was like she'd told him: she was here for protection, not friendship, and she needed to do a better job of distancing herself from these people until she could leave.

"Quick question." Sarah's voice abruptly cutting into the silence seemed to startle the siblings. They both watched her curiously. "If I'm trapped in here, then how am I supposed to find further evidence against Cadius so that I can leave? Seems like a catch-22 to me."

Damien screwed up his nose in confusion. "I don't know what that means, but it is a bit of a paradoxical situation."

Sarah gave him a look. "That's what I just said."

"Oh." He frowned. "Well, I had an idea to use my connections to do some careful investigating without revealing our whereabouts. I assure you that you shan't be stuck in my presence forever." His bitter words were laced with disappointment.

"So you can investigate in the open air, but I can't? Seems fair. Maybe I'll die of asphyxiation before Cadius can finish me off." She knew she was being intentionally petulant, but she didn't feel like acting reasonable just then.

Damien looked momentarily flummoxed. "I am only leaving to . . . I have *connections*, remember?"

"So do I!" she burst without thinking.

He gave her a droll look. "Oh, yes, you can trap Cadius with your sardonic retorts and cause him to admit his entire dastardly plan to the royal court. And if that fails, the blacksmith and the farmers you live with can fend off his men with their pitchforks. We are saved!" he exclaimed mockingly, then winced as the effort strained his side.

Sarah's eyes widened in surprise, unable to recall Damien ever openly insulting her, but she'd goaded him into it; he was trying to protect her, in his bizarre way, and she was acting like a child and lashing out. She couldn't blame him for getting angry, since that had half been her intent, but it wasn't like she was okay with being insulted. "Well, your men left you to rot in prison for months," she retorted lamely.

Damien gave her a *That's all you've got?* look and opened his mouth to reply.

"That is enough, I can't do it anymore!" Jade rose to her feet and hiked her skirts, stepping lightly over her brother's body. "You two can argue or scheme or break the fast together, I truly do not care. But I am going for a walk. Neither of you goes into my room," she added. To Sarah, she said almost as an afterthought, "If he faints from lack of blood, slap him twice—once for each of us."

Sarah jumped to her feet and quickly moved out of her way as Jade reached down into her bodice and produced the key, opening the front door. Sarah felt a moment's desire to shove her out of the way and bolt through the door to freedom, but then she remembered that she would only be endangering Will if she left the confines of the cabin. The door closed behind Jade and was locked from the outside, making her decision for her.

The room was completely silent except for Damien's labored breathing and Sarah's own rushing pulse as it pounded in her ears in the wake of words she wished she hadn't spoken. She turned from the door slowly and found him watching her, his face pale and filled with an expression she could only describe as guilty. He gripped his side and pulled himself into a sitting position, twisting his body on the ground so he could lean his back on the settee. The muscles on his stomach bunched, body tensing with pain he tried to mask.

"I am sorry." His words were quiet but sincere, his eyes hooded like that of a regretful puppy.

Sarah gnawed her lip and then begrudgingly admitted, "I sort of am, too. I don't want to hate you, though I'm not saying we're friends." She paused, exhaled her pride, and then said haltingly, "I am grateful . . . for your protection right now."

The corner of Damien's mouth trembled with repressed humor. "Careful. My ego shall grow ten times with such appreciation."

Annoyed at how easy it felt to fall into their old friendship mode, Sarah did her best to hide the returning grin she was tempted to give. "It was a thank you," she said evenly. "But don't push your luck. And I meant what I said about leaving as soon as it's safe."

His face fell. "I suppose it's more than I deserve after everything I have put you through." He folded his hands in his lap and played with his thumbs, brow furrowed.

She wanted to contradict him, to say none of it had been his fault, but too much of it had been because of his involvement, so she bit her tongue. Her prolonged silence caused him to cringe.

After a moment, he motioned to the sofa at his back. "You didn't get much sleep last night—or rather, this morning. You may sit, if you like."

Warily, Sarah eyed the space, so close to his bare torso and shoulders. At her scrutiny, his hands rose casually, and he feigned scratching an itch on his neck—which looked awkward with both hands—but she saw the action for what it really was: embarrassment over his condition and an effort to hide it from her view.

"It's cold in here, is it not?" It was actually perfectly comfortable . . . temperature-wise. Sarah casually moved across the room and grabbed the multi-colored blanket from the back of the settee and handed it to him. "I don't know if Jade has any clothes that will fit you, so this will have to do to keep you warm."

Damien hesitated and then accepted it with a look of thanks. He draped it over his shoulders and then paused, grinning. "I will have to take care not to get any blood on it, or Isabella will have my head."

Sitting on the sofa against the opposite arm to put as much space as possible between them, she said, "Did I mention you have a great relationship with your sister?"

He let out a genuine laugh. Both seemed to have let out some of their pent-up tension during their disagreement, and the strain in the room had dissipated. "I suppose our dysfunction surprises you."

"No," she answered truthfully, and he angled his body slightly to look up at her. "But the fact that Jade and Isabella aren't dead was a little surprising . . . and that they're the same person."

Damien dropped her gaze, and she asked softly, "Did you really disown her like she said? I mean, it kind of explains why there's so much animosity between you two."

Shaking his head, he replied, “No. I mean, yes, of course I disapproved of her selling herself to men for mere stipends and living such a public life; it would have shattered Mother’s heart, God rest her soul.” He swallowed and turned his head away so she couldn’t see his face. “I was trying to provide a life for us, and she worked as a talented seamstress. I encouraged her to marry when she was ready, a future I knew both of our parents would approve of. But she saw every man as a threat to her freedom, including myself. They were all viewed as controlling dictators like our father, which is ironic, considering her most recent profession.”

Damien sighed. “I’ve always wondered if some part of why she went into such a life was not only to ruin the lives of other men, but also because it was something that our father never would have approved of and would have sullied his reputation—one giant act of defiance, even if he was not alive to be affected by it.”

Sarah could see his profile and the way the pulse in his neck throbbed, how he swallowed thickly. “Why didn’t she stay with you and not marry? You said you were making money for the both of you.”

“She called it blood money,” he whispered, wincing at the phrase, and Sarah knew he was referring to when he started working for Cadius. She couldn’t contradict the accurate description. “The instant she discovered how and from whom I was earning my income, she moved out on her own, refusing my help.”

Sarah was surprised to feel a dash of respect for Jade’s brave decision to go out on her own when she learned the underhanded way that Damien earned his keep. *So Jade does have a speck of a soul.*

Pausing for a thoughtful moment, she said, “Jade was the woman you were talking about.”

“Hmm?” Damien turned to look at her.

“When I locked you up in that cell—you said that part of the reason you were working with Cadius was because he might hurt ‘her.’ It was your sister, wasn’t it?”

“Yes.” He lowered his gaze. “Although she did not wish for my assistance or protection, I had to keep her safe. She put herself in harm’s way each and every night by taking on certain clients who would help her learn things about Cadius that would allow me to escape from under his thumb.” He inhaled a deep breath, and the scar on his chest stretched. “We might appear at odds, and she can come off as antagonistic, but we are all we have left, and we will do whatever we must to protect that.”

“She didn’t seem too eager to help us,” Sarah reminded tartly.

“Yet she did. Have compassion, Sarah. My sister has seen much darkness in her life.”

She frowned. “But you shared an awful dad and experienced a horrible childhood together, and *you* don’t seem to be making excuses for yourself. You and Jade have the same demons.”

"Not quite," was all he said.

Sarah was left to ponder his response as the latch clicked and Jade entered the room, cheeks flushed from her walk in the cool morning air. She surveyed their closeness with a lifted brow.

"I suppose it doesn't take you long to forgive and forget," she commented, closing and locking the door. Sarah fought off the urge to relocate from the couch when she realized how close she was sitting to her captor . . . of sorts. But she wouldn't give Jade the satisfaction. Damien might think that Isabella was still in there somewhere—the sweet, obedient little girl that he remembered so well—but Sarah was having a difficult time finding one iota of humanity in the woman. She might have had a terrible past, as Sarah knew from the stories she'd heard from Damien, but those events had shaped Jade into a cold, unpleasant woman who was only in this life for herself.

Jade spun around, her dark hair falling like silk over one shoulder. She saw the blanket hanging loosely over Damien's shoulders. "If I find blood on that, I will turn you both out of here without a second thought." Then she hiked her chin and breezed past them into her room, shutting the door soundly behind her.

Sarah jutted her chin in annoyance and glanced at Damien. She splayed her hands and held them toward the door, as if to say, "See what I mean?"

Be patient, he mouthed, though Sarah wasn't sure all the time in this world or hers would cause her to find a friendly bone in Jade's body. She didn't plan to be there for very long, anyway, but for the sake of Damien and Will, who had once been friends with the woman and had amazingly found *something* good in her, she would try.

Chapter Fourteen

"Dreams are true while they last, but do we not live in dreams?"

Alfred, Lord Tennyson, "The Higher Pantheism"

The day dragged by. There was absolutely nothing to do in Jade's small cabin—no games or books or even random brick-a-brack to entertain her. And the lady of the house hadn't opened her bedroom door after shutting herself in that morning, so Sarah couldn't even explore that part of the cabin. She spent the majority of the day wandering the main room, examining the sparse cookware and sniffing the decanter of wine—which was so strong she nearly gagged—sitting on the couch, and then popping back up to resume her aimless pacing when it looked like Damien might say something.

She didn't much feel like engaging him in conversation; he too easily broke down her defenses. He was offering her temporary protection, and the Christian thing to do would be to forgive *and* forget, but Sarah felt rebellious against doing either one. It wasn't because she felt entirely cold toward him, but rather because she was scared to find that there was still a place in her heart reserved for him and that she *wanted* to forget the bad things he had done. It frightened her to realize that she was so weak toward the lost boy she saw in him, and so she did her best to avoid him altogether.

Jade came out at one point during mid-afternoon, carelessly dropping a pile of blankets on the floor as she walked. Sarah and Damien watched her silently as she went to the short counter on the far wall and lifted the cover off a wooden platter, revealing a half-eaten loaf of bread, cheese, pieces of dried meat, and some over-ripe fruit. She selected a hunk of bread and some of the meat, gave her brother a silent, unreadable look, and then went back into her room. The door closed behind her once more.

Damien exhaled. "I suppose that means we can have supper."

"Thank God," Sarah muttered, pushing off the wall she had been leaning against. "I'm starving." When was her last meal? Had it been breakfast with the Joneses? Lunch? She couldn't even remember, but it didn't matter now, because there was *food*.

She found two small plates on the counter and filled both with a medley of everything she could find. Realizing she'd unconsciously dished one for Damien, she clenched her jaw and handed a heavy-laden plate to him, and then sat Indian-style on the floor. The meat was chewy and salty and had probably been some unsuspecting deer out for a stroll, but it was heaven to Sarah's empty stomach.

As the sun fell, they ate in silence—much like the rest of the day had been passed—and for a time there was only the sound of chewing and thick swallows. But when they finished, the cabin descended into total, uncomfortable silence once more. It was almost a relief when night fell and it came time for everyone to turn in, which was at least something to do.

"Do you think it's all right if I sleep on the couch?" Sarah asked sardonically, her voice sounding loud in the quiet that had stretched on for nearly the entire day. "Or will I wrinkle the cushions?"

Damien shook his head and rose to his feet, holding his arm close to his side and almost managing to mask his wince of pain. The blanket fell to the floor, and Sarah dropped her gaze to save him embarrassment, though it wasn't like she could see his torso perfectly—the light had faded hours ago, and there were no candles or lanterns in the room to stave off the darkness.

"This is ludicrous," Damien muttered, surprising her. He went to Jade's door and pounded on it.

"What?" she snapped from the other side.

"It would only be for a few nights, Isabella. Be realistic." His sister's reply was muffled by the thick door, but his brows rose in shock at whatever had been said. Then his eyes darkened. Voice lowering, he whispered, "You know that is not the case." All Sarah caught from Jade's next muted remark were the words *Sarah's reputation* and *your issue, not mine.* Ah, so Jade did remember her name.

Damien sighed and turned away from the door, the conversation clearly finished. He rubbed the back of his neck, an uncomfortable look suddenly on his face. "It would appear we have a bit of a predicament concerning, er, the, ah, sleeping arrangements."

It took her a moment to calculate that the rooms-to-people ratio was awkwardly numbered.

"She's going to make you sleep out here?" He didn't answer, and Sarah swallowed. "I hadn't really thought about that before." Taking a deep breath, she huffed. "All right, whatever. We slept together last night, so it shouldn't really matter." She glanced up to find that Damien's eyes had now become saucer-like, so large that she could make out the whites of them in the darkness.

With a roll of her eyes to cover her own embarrassment when she realized how her remark had sounded, she snatched one of the quilts from the ground, leaving the majority for Damien; Sarah had the thick folds of dress fabric to keep her warm, whereas he was still half-clad and would need the extra warmth, especially since he would be sleeping on the floor.

She flopped onto the couch and threw the blanket over herself, curling up and rolling onto her side to face the back of the settee. She was taller than it allowed and was a tight fit, but the couch would have to do for now.

She heard Damien shuffling around as he made his bed on the floor. "It'll be fine," she mumbled. "You keep to your side, and I'll keep—" She glanced over her shoulder to find him close, layering blankets directly in front of the settee she was on. He caught her eye and ceased his movements.

"What are you doing?" she asked slowly.

He was quiet for several heartbeats, and then he tried to explain himself. "I did not want you to escape in the night, and I wished to be near enough that if you should need anything—"

"I'm not going to escape." She sighed, rolling back onto her side with more flair than was necessary. "Forget it."

He exhaled, the breath coming out like a gust of defeat. Softly, he said, "Good night, my lady. I will be here if you need me."

Sarah bit her tongue, remaining silent while he made his bed nearby, close enough to touch.

ଓ଼ଃ

He heard the shouts as he made his way back from the field that bordered their land. Knowing that his father must have returned from the tavern for the second time that day, he considered remaining out of doors until night fell to keep far away from the man's pent-up wrath. He had been subject to it once already that day, when his father had been cutting wood in the yard and had drunkenly swiped at him with the axe. It had glanced off the boy's side, leaving behind only a small trail of blood on his skin, and his sister had tended to the wound.

His blood turned cold as he remembered that she had remained in the house, and he ran as fast as his lanky limbs would carry him. Knowing his father was in such a foul mood, he should not have left her alone, but the boy had not expected the man to return so soon. He prayed that the girl had thought to hide herself in the cupboard when she heard their father returning.

A shrill, female scream reached his ears, and the sound of loud sobbing punctuated the calm morning air. His heart stopped at a sound he knew too well.

Leaping over the short fence that separated their yard from public lands, he bounded up to the house and threw open the back door. He paused, breathing hard, listening for any sound in the large house. Had they gone? But then he heard a shout and the sound of pounding against wood, followed by another high-pitched scream.

The boy ran past the sitting room and down the hall, skidding to a stop at the stairwell. He sucked in a breath of shock at the sight of his father lying on the floor, his form crumpled and twisted, his neck and limbs bent at odd angles; a small trail of blood was spilling from his skull, staining the rug. It looked so much like how he had discovered his mother not so long ago, her body broken, that the boy was suddenly transported back to the horror of that moment after his father had beaten her to death.

"Damien!" His head jerked upward to find his sister standing at the top of the stairs, shaking uncontrollably, eyes huge, hair an unkempt mess around her round face, like a dark halo.

He stepped around his father's body and bolted up the stairs, wrapping his arms around her as she sank to the floor. "Isabella, you must tell me what happened. Please, darling."

"He hurt me," she whimpered, holding up her arm. A bruise in the shape of their father's hand was already forming on her forearm, and her right cheek was an angry red. Damien knew he had slapped her, and his body shook with rage, at the dead man and himself for leaving her alone.

"Forgive me, Bella, I should never have gone—" He bit his lip and closed his eyes, resting his quivering chin atop her shaking head. "Tell me."

It was silent expect for their shaky breathing and the occasional hiccup from Isabella. Then she whispered in a trembling voice, "I forgot to hide. Damien, I'm sorry, I forgot what you told me."

"Shh." He kissed the top of her head, trying to be brave for her, but they were only children, and the sight below frightened him to his very core.

"He saw me and kept calling me by Mama's name. And then he started hitting me, and when I tried to run"—she hiccupped and her voice lowered to a mere whisper—"he grabbed my arm too tight. I was scared and just wanted to be free, and I-I shoved him. He lost his balance and let me go, and then he—" She shook her head quickly, as though to rebuke the memory. "I was so scared."

He swiped his thumb under her eye to catch a tear she didn't appear to realize she had shed. "I should have been here for you, Bella. I should have saved you from him long ago."

"I'm glad he's dead," she whispered, face ashen as she stared blankly at their father's bloody, crumpled form. "He killed Mama, and I'm glad he is gone."

He had never seen such a cold, deadened look on his precious Isabella's angelic face—normally so full of joy and life—and it broke his heart to see her like that. He was supposed to protect her and lead her away from harm; instead, he had left her behind to fend for herself, which left her to do something unimaginable that he was sure would haunt her forever.

Young Damien bit back a sob, knowing he had to be strong for her, but they were alone now, and he couldn't stand the thought that their father had sapped her last ounce of joy from her. She had been a light like their mother, but at that tragic moment when Damien realized they were orphans, he couldn't find that light anywhere in her features. What Isabella had done had been an accident, but there were some things that one simply cannot return from, and he feared she might never be the same.

"We will be all right, sister," he whispered, stroking the hair back from her face. He wanted to remove her from the macabre sight, but he found he could not move. "We have each other, and that is all we will ever need."

"But we can't be the same, Damien." She buried her face in his chest, sobbing. "No one can ever forgive me for this. Oh, Papa, what did I do to you?"

"I forgive you, Bella." His arms tightened protectively around her. "You didn't know what you were doing. You cannot blame yourself for what you did not intend to do."

"But I did," she whispered, shivering against his side. "And I know I would do it again to free us of him, which is what scares me the most."

ꕥ

Damien jerked awake, breathing heavily. Something tickled his face, and he shrank back from it, instant fear sparking through him. "Damien, wake up—you're having a bad dream." Sarah's familiar voice, whispered near his face, washed over him, and he realized it was her hair that was brushing his cheek as she leaned over him from her position on the settee. She placed a hand on the side of his neck, her thumb gently brushing his jaw as if to soothe him, so soft and comforting. Her whisper calmed his spirit after his nightmare, and he found he believed her when she breathed quietly, "It's okay, I'm here."

It was a painfully familiar scene, and Damien recalled her sweetness, her soft touch and concern, when she had found him convulsing in his room—a lingering gift of his father's cruelty that overcame him sporadically. With no sign of hesitation, Sarah had cared for him, remaining with him until he fell asleep; her mere presence had reassured him, as it did every instance that she was near. No one but his mother had ever shown such tenderness toward him, not even his sister, whose kind and affectionate spirit had been hardened through the years.

Though Sarah was only comforting him because she thought he was asleep, it was the most affection she had shown him in months—the most physical contact he'd *had* in months—and he allowed himself a brief moment to enjoy the sensation of her cool palm on his bare skin as it slid down to rest over his pounding heart, racing in the aftermath of his nightmare and at the presence of her soft touch. Her thumb traced the rigid scar, and he felt a moment's embarrassment over his rough appearance, wishing he had not looked quite so damaged upon meeting her again. But then he remembered that out of everyone in this world full of darkness, even when she was full of anger directed at him, her tender, compassionate heart made her the most likely to accept his scars, to take him as he was: a man broken and in need of a purpose.

Damien could see the irritation and reluctance burning in her eyes whenever she looked at him, knowing she was reminded of their history. Yet there were instances where she glanced his way, seeming torn between holding onto her anger and trusting that he had changed; those moments gave him hope that there was the possibility of saving the last threads of their friendship. He felt most assured that she would never love him as he did her, but perhaps someday she would not be torn between antagonism and amity, reluctance to believe in him and acceptance that he wished to change—that he *had* changed.

"Oh, Damien," she breathed, and he thought—perhaps wished—that there might have been a slight hitch in her voice.

Because he was an absolute fool when it came to the woman who hovered over him, whispering nonsense as she touched his broken body with such gentle fingers, he imagined how it would be to wake up to her every morning. What would it be like to have a nightmare, as he did most nights, and know that she would be there to comfort him? He told himself that she would encourage him each and everyday to be the man he wished to be, and he would never leave her side, protecting and remaining faithful to her until he breathed his last. Though Damien had given his heart to her long ago, he found himself questioning what it would be like to be entrusted with *her* heart and know that his would be safe in her careful hands. Most of all, he wondered how it would feel for someone to accept and love him, scars and all.

But although he hoped that someday she would wholly forgive him, he knew he would never be deserving of her pardon for his crimes. It was pure torture to imagine a future that would never be, and even if it provided temporary bliss, it made the return to reality so much more agonizing.

"I am awake." His voice sounded as though he had eaten gravel for supper, and he swallowed. Sarah ripped her hand away from his chest and tucked it safely under her, as though she could erase the sweet, lingering sear of pain it left on his skin.

"Oh. . . . Are you okay?" she said softly, keeping her voice quiet so Isabella could not hear on the other side of the door. "It sounded like you were having a pretty awful dream."

"Yes." He stared at the ceiling, his wounded side throbbing beneath the dressings, sweat making the blanket stick to the portion of his stomach that was bare.

A pause. "Do you want to talk about it?"

He couldn't tell if she truly wished to know or if she was simply asking out of politeness, but the dream weighed heavy on him. He had suffered many sleepless nights under the horrible memory of that day and countless others, and never with anyone to share the burden with.

Sighing thickly at his own weak will, he dragged the blanket down to his waist and let the cool air dry his chest. "It is not very pretty," he said, wishing to give her the opportunity to choose whether or not she wanted to listen.

"Bad dreams rarely are," she whispered back drolly.

Damien found himself smiling, though it faded quickly. He told her about the dream—the memory—though he expounded little on his emotions over seeing his father's lifeless form at the base of the staircase.

"I told you before that we left shortly after my mother died," he said, "which was true, although the honest reason for our flight was because I feared the repercussions if someone discovered what Isabella had done." He fingered the bandage on his side. "It must have been my wound that triggered the dream—Father gave me a similar one earlier that day."

Sarah was silent for one very uncomfortable moment, leaving him to wonder at her reaction. They had discussed his unstable past before, but so much had happened between the two of them since then, and he was uncertain as to what her response would be now that she knew Isabella had killed their father.

"I'm sorry," she whispered at last. Damien found himself exhaling a breath of relief that she had finally disrupted the silence, even if she sounded as though she were trying to hold back some of her compassion. To protect her heart, he knew, feeling his own sink a modicum at her reserved response. But he deserved nothing more. "I can't imagine—" She broke off, sighing.

"I am glad you cannot imagine it." And he was. Damien never wished for her to experience first-hand what an evil soul like his father was capable of, nor the regret of killing someone you cared for. No matter that they were cruel and practically unlovable.

There was a moment of silence on her part, and then she said, "I still think your sister is cranky and could learn some social manners, but I can understand why she has a chip on her shoulder."

Damien stared at the shadows overhead. "Some days I can almost convince myself that she did not intend for him to fall or break his neck, that she simply wished to get away from him. But the look in her eyes—" He stopped, pondering the fact that it felt wonderful to share something with another human being after so long in solitude, even if it was a tale of murder. "She changed after that, and I could see a little of the life drain out of her each day. Isabella was the optimist of the two of us, full of energy and joy; Mother took some of that unabashed hope with her when she died, but Bella was completely altered when she killed Father. I have told her countless times that I forgave her, but I believe she imagines herself to be beyond redemption."

He heard Sarah shift on the settee, and her hand reached out slowly toward his chest, as if to touch him and offer comfort, and his heart leapt at the movement. But then her hand froze, and he knew she had thought better of touching him as she gripped the edge of the sofa instead. Damien went back to staring at the ceiling.

"No one is beyond grace." Her soft, thoughtful words brought his eyes back to the faint outline of her face.

"I told her as much—that it was not her fault and that she had my undying love and forgiveness." He pursed his lips. "But I doubt she has ever truly forgiven herself, nor does she believe anyone else could."

Silence reigned in the room for a full minute before Sarah said, "I didn't mean to notice, but the scar on your chest . . . It looks like a symbol or something."

To cover his shame at the reminder that she had seen his poorly kept body, Damien remarked coyly, "Ah, so you *did* notice the fact that I was half-naked earlier. I was not certain."

He could see the way her mouth worked silently, and his cockiness faded. "I should not have teased you. Forgive me." He took a deep breath, causing the tense muscles under the bandage to stretch uncomfortably. "The scar is in the shape of a T; I was branded with it when I was sentenced. It marks me as a traitor to the crown, though I suppose I deserved far more than a simple brand," he admitted shamefully.

Sarah shifted on her bed again, and he desperately wished he could see her face; he did not like losing the ability to read what she was feeling in her features. "Oh."

Oh? Damien deflated a little, though he knew he could not ask more of her. How did he expect her to react to information she already knew, in part? She was aware of his criminal history, but he also hoped that someday she would see he no longer wished to dwell in that past, that he regretted every moment of it. "I suppose this brand serves as a well-deserved reminder of what I have done. Perhaps one day I will find the courage to do something worthwhile with my life."

"You know that includes you too, right?" she asked.

Damien blinked, surprised at her curious tone. "What?"

"Forgiveness. You said how you wanted your sister to feel forgiven for, um, *accidentally* murdering your father, but you refuse to forgive yourself. Or allow someone else to do it for you."

He didn't quite know what to say to that and heaved a heavy breath. "But Isabella . . . Father was one man, and a cruel one at that. How many lives have *I* allowed to be excommunicated from this earth, either at my own hand or due to my silence?" He shook his head. "No, I have gone too far to come back."

"You're never too far from grace," she whispered again. She paused, then muttered as though she hadn't meant for him to hear, "If I had a nickel for every time I said that to Will . . ."

Damien's jaw clenched. "If it reassures you, I am sure the blacksmith is closer to redemption than I."

He made out the faint shake of her head in the darkness. "We're all sinners, Damien—every last one of us—and sometimes we totally blow it as human beings. Believe it or not, God's forgiven people for worse than you've done."

"You speak of the Almighty as though you know him personally," Damien remarked quietly.

Her voice softened, taking on a sweet note that caught something deep within him. "Because I do, and I know for a fact that His mercy and forgiveness are never too far from reach."

"And you? Do you forgive me?" he whispered, blind, pathetic hope leaking into his words. She need only say that there was a glimmer of forgiveness from her in the future, and he would hold out on that ounce of hope for however long it took.

She dragged a breath in through her nose. "I know I could forgive you one day, but our broken trust is another story. I just—I need time." She laid back, pulling the blankets up to her chin, masking whatever expression might have been visible in the darkness. "I'll see you in the morning."

Dispirited, he whispered, "Pleasant dreams."

Damien stared at the ceiling, his thoughts sluggish but the pain in his side—and his heart—keeping him awake as he listened to the sound of Sarah's breathing. After some time, she flopped onto her side with an indistinguishable mutter, and her arm fell over the side of the couch. Her cheek was pressed against the edge of the cushion, squishing her face as she snored softly. He couldn't help smiling with all the love he felt in his heart, even if she would never return it.

Damien hesitated, then weakened, needing to feel her touch even if she was unaware of the contact. He threaded his fingers through hers, the feel of her skin causing his heart to skip a beat—to him, it looked as though their palms were made to fit together. She didn't stir, and he placed the back of her hand over his heart, keeping their fingers knotted. Their joined hands rose and fell with each breath he took, and only then was he able to fall into a dreamless sleep.

❧

Jade closed her door softly so they didn't realize she had been listening in as they bade one another goodnight. She'd heard her brother cry out in the night and knew he was experiencing one of his night terrors, though he never told her what he saw when he slept, and had cracked her door open to see if she was needed. But the other girl was already comforting him, listening as Damien told her things he had never admitted to his *sister*.

Jade's feet padded over the cold floor, and she returned to her bed, her mind heavy with their conversation about forgiveness and mercy.

She scoffed into the silent room, realizing what she was doing. *Forgiveness*, she thought derisively. Then she remembered that she was alone and needn't keep up her indifferent guise, and she allowed her mind to drift back to their discussion. Damien had said that she had changed after their father died, and he was right.

Closing her eyes against the pain of that day, Jade wondered who Isabella would have grown into if she hadn't lost herself to fear and shoved her father down those stairs. Would she be a wife, a mother, run a business of her own, travel around the world? Maybe her life would have amounted to nothing more than it already was—an empty shell of what might have been.

It was too painful to dwell on the life she could have had, and it was foolishness to pretend that her decisions hadn't led her to where she was. She had killed her father in cold blood, sold herself to men for profit and information, and she had pushed away the only men who might have cared for her out of fear and pride.

No, her brother was right—there were some deeds in this world too horrible to pardon, and believing otherwise was simply entertaining a fairy tale.

"Oh, how I wish it weren't, though," she whispered into her cold, empty room.

Chapter Fifteen

"I love you as certain dark things are to be loved,
in secret, between the shadow and the soul."

Pablo Neruda, "I Do Not Love You"

Sarah's lids peeled back, feeling weighed down by a ton of bricks. Being woken up by Damien's heart-wrenching whimpers and having a deep conversation in the middle of the night, after a traumatic start to the day, left her head feeling like it had been stuffed with cotton.

She blinked slowly, her sluggish mind processing what she saw, and then she jerked her head up from its cramped position on the couch. Damien's head was turned toward her, his eyes closed, lips parted as his uncovered chest rose and fell rhythmically in sleep. Their hands were joined and rested on his stomach, moving up and down with each breath. When had that happened? Sarah couldn't remember grabbing his hand in the night, and though she hoped it had happened when they were both asleep, she doubted it.

Gently, she extricated her hand, stiff joints popping as she uncurled her fingers and slid them through his. Damien stirred, and she froze, waiting until he buried the side of his face into the folded blanket under his head and his body relaxed once more. Seeing he was fast asleep, Sarah allowed herself the opportunity to examine his features, to see how much these past months had changed him.

His body was thinner, as she had noticed before, and the scars and bruises covering his bare torso were new. And then there was the matter of the look of continual weariness on his face, as though he had seen and done too much to not carry each bad memory around with him like unnecessary luggage. But now, unconsciousness erased the hardness and pain from his expression, and that crease in his brow, though still visible, was fainter than it had been; he looked vulnerable and boyish as he slept, reminding Sarah of the charming, carefree man she had first met. She felt her heart opening up to him against her will.

She stared at the jagged T over his heart with a drawn brow. She wasn't sure if she was supposed to take a note from her own book—that no action could be beyond grace—and forgive him, or if she should use that scar as a reminder of what he had done. What concerned her was that it seemed easier to forgive him than hold onto her anger. Either he was still an excellent manipulator, or she could see enough honesty and sincerity in him to merit granting him her trust once more.

A creaking was heard at the back of the house, and Jade's door opened. Sarah looked up from her scrutiny of the sleeping man and saw the woman glide out of her room, looking well rested and fully dressed, her hair combed, though her face was devoid of cosmetics. She looked younger and more alert without it, and Sarah was a little envious of her good genes.

"For someone who claims to despise my brother, you spend a rather significant amount of your day paying him mind," Jade remarked conversationally, keeping her back to the rest of the room as she poured herself a goblet of water from one of the pitchers. "What do you see when you look at him?"

"How did you—?" Sarah sat up, annoyed that the only way off of the couch was to jump over Damien's sleeping form or get him to move, and she didn't want to wake him from his much-needed slumber. With last night's conversation of extending grace weighing heavy on her mind, she inhaled a breath as Jade turned, steeling her nerves. Fine, she could match Jade's bluntness and still remain calm. "I was just thinking what a difficult childhood he had—that you both had."

It was Jade's turn to look surprised, but she recovered quickly, adopting an indifferent expression. "I cannot think of anyone who has not," she replied tersely.

Sarah opened her mouth, then closed it as she shot a wary look at the man on the floor.

"He won't wake, if that is what concerns you," Jade said. She took a sip from her goblet and then set it on the table. "As a child, he could sleep through the house burning down around us."

Sarah glanced at Damien again and then sucked in a quick breath. "I just wanted to say that I'm sorry." Jade blinked and showed the barest amount of surprise. "I feel like there's been a lot of antagonism between us because of, well, things." She didn't feel that it would help their "bonding" if she reminded the woman of the fact that Sarah and Will were together.

Jade folded her arms across her chest and arched one brow. "You still blame me for the rumor I invented about myself and William?"

"Actually," Sarah said slowly, trying not to wince at the reminder. She inhaled a steadying breath. "What I wanted to say was that I forgive you. I understand a little better now why you did it, and I want you to know that it was wrong of me to hold a grudge against you for so long. So, sorry."

Jade looked like she needed a minute to process this, or she was deciding whether or not to believe her sincere, albeit reluctant, apology. Whatever the case, Sarah let her have a moment and then asked softly, "Why haven't you told Will you're alive?" She didn't know why it mattered so much, but it bothered her that Jade hadn't said anything during the months that Will pondered the death of his childhood friend.

Jade's eyes flared. "Because there is no point in him knowing."

"But there is," Sarah insisted, trying to keep her voice from rising for Damien's sake. "Do you know how horrible he felt, thinking he'd let you die? The guilt he's experienced all winter wondering what he might have done differently to save you?"

Jade's anger wavered, and Sarah thought she might have gotten through, but then it returned full-force, her eyes blazing.

Advancing until she stood directly before Damien's prone form, Jade hissed, "That is *not* your secret to tell or care for. And *you*"—she pointed a finger at Sarah's chest with a look of such utter contempt that she wished she could escape from the couch—"you pretend that you care and extend your mercy to me, but where is your forgiveness for my *brother*? He could have run and made a new life for himself, but he remains and continues to risk his life to protect you. Yet I see no gratitude or mercy for him."

Sarah gaped at her, trying to come up with a response as the implications weighed heavy on her. Had she even thought about what Damien was risking by coming back for her?

At her prolonged hesitation, Jade shot her one final glare and in a swift movement, unlocked the door, threw it open with flare, and slammed it shut.

Damien's head jerked off his pillow, his eyes hurriedly roving the room. They landed on Sarah's guilty face, and with a wince, he dragged himself into a sitting position, blinking rapidly against the morning light streaming through the small window.

"Are you all right?" he asked, voice rough as he surveyed the room.

"Everything's fine," she reassured hurriedly. "Jade was just leaving."

He rubbed his temple and nodded, his shoulders relaxing some. "Ah, so she is in a mood."

Sarah couldn't exactly deny that, and she didn't feel like explaining why *she* was the cause of said mood. Instead, she asked, "How's your side?"

He touched it gently. "Better, I think, though a bit tight. My arm is already closing up nicely, so I will not have to fret with cleaning that much longer." The scratches she had made on his face were almost gone, too, but she decided not to remind him of how she had assaulted him.

"Good."

Silence reigned, and Sarah bobbed her head, trying to think of something to say. She was saved from doing so as Damien rose stiffly to his feet, rotating his shoulder. He gently twisted to the side in a stretch, being careful of his fresh wound, and the movement caused the muscles on his stomach to bunch. Before she could avert her gaze, he glanced down and caught her eyes on him. They dropped their gazes simultaneously, and Damien quickly moved across the room to pour himself a cup of wine, which seemed a bit premature to her. He took a sip, and Sarah tried pulling her fingers through her hair before she remembered that looking presentable to him shouldn't matter, and her hands fell to the cushion.

They'd had a heart-to-heart last night, and she had wanted to assure him that he was worthwhile, even though she still struggled to forgive him herself. But in the light of day, it felt strange to acknowledge what had been said when ambitions were lessened in the dark; they both appeared to awkwardly fight between carrying on as the "almost" friends they had been hours before, and returning to the roles of captor and reluctantly agreeable captive.

With his back to her, Damien remarked in a tight voice, "I was thinking of checking in on what few connections I have left—see if anything new has come to light. I shall return in a few hours."

"Are you sure it's safe for you to run around town?" Sarah bit her lip, remembering the fact that Cadius was after both of them.

He glanced over his shoulder, his eyes dragging over her face. She clenched her teeth together, feeling heat rise to her cheeks as she questioned if he knew they had held hands in the night. With an unreadable meaning beneath his miniscule smile, he said, "I believe it best if I go."

"But you haven't eaten breakfast yet." Why was she mothering him?

Setting his goblet down on the tray, he shook his head. "When I return." He slipped into Jade's room, leaving Sarah alone. She shook her head at herself, wondering why she vacillated between hating him and wanting to be his friend. Unknowingly, he practically begged to be taken care of, and Sarah had a weak spot for those in need of help.

But she couldn't play both fields—the friend *and* the bitter hostage—and she had been telling the truth when she said she would be out of there the second they found enough evidence against Cadius. But would that mean Damien would return to captivity? The sudden ache in her chest reminded her that it was inevitable, but after seeing how he had been treated as a prisoner, the thought was almost unbearable.

Damien slipped into the main room again, wearing a black tunic tucked into his trousers, and she tried to mask her inner torment. "She saved some of my old clothes here." He leaned down beside the couch and pulled his boots on, looking like he was hurrying about his task, and winced as he lifted the leg that tugged on his fresh stitches.

Moving quickly to the door, he unlocked it with a copy of the key Sarah hadn't known he possessed. Then he paused, the door half-open. He cast a wary glance her way, and Sarah gave him an exasperated look.

"I won't run away; you don't have to lock it."

"It is not you with whom I am concerned," Damien said under his breath. He looked hesitant to leave her, and then he said reassuringly, "I won't take long." And then he left, and the door was locked from the outside.

Sarah fell back onto the couch cushions, releasing a heavy breath. "Get it together, Matthews," she muttered to herself. Damien had done some terrible things, and though she understood why he did it, she still found his logic flawed in kidnapping her. But then she reminded herself that she had preached forgiveness last night, and he was doing this to keep her safe—to his own detriment, no less. Was she only holding onto her grudge out of pride and stubbornness, or was it foolishness to let him off so easily?

"You make this look a lot easier than it is," she whispered to the ceiling. She had told Damien mere hours before that God forgave worse sins than his, but she was having a difficult time forgiving and forgetting. But was she even supposed to with this?

She longed for Karen's wisdom, the familiarity of the Jones family, and the comfort of Will's presence. Sarah sighed heavily, closing her eyes against the pain, knowing they must be thinking all sorts of terrible things had happened to her. She knew Will well enough to be assured that he had gone looking for her within the hour of her capture. What must he be going through right now, what terrible, macabre scenarios had he conjured in her absence? If only to reassure them that she was fine, she considered trying to escape, though she knew that would put them all, especially Will, at risk. And she couldn't do that to them. As long as remaining in Damien's company kept the rest of them safe, then she would stay with him.

☙❧

Thomas placed a hand on his shoulder, his look concerned. "Son, we've been searching all night; the rain washed away the tracks, and there is no way the hounds can pick up any scent after the storm. You're wet and tired, and I am concerned you might collapse if you don't allow yourself a few hours' rest. We can resume before noonday."

His eyes bloodshot and swollen, Will blinked, shaking his head slowly. The queen had been absent when Thomas came, and he had been unable to procure a search party from the king. They were Sarah's only hope now.

He dragged a hand through his dew-covered hair, slicking it back from his forehead. "No, I have to continue the search. The more time that passes—"

"You won't be any good to her if you die of exhaustion," Seth said, thrashing through the bushes on his way to them, Richard just a few paces behind. He attempted to sound teasing, but he looked as worn and concerned as Will did. "For her sake, my friend, have a care for yourself."

"And if it were Karen out there?" Will shot him a pointed look, and Seth cringed. "You see, then, that it is not so easy to give up."

"We are hardly requesting that you relinquish your search," Thomas interjected evenly. "Only that you rest so that we can resume with fresh eyes and clear heads."

Seth sidled up next to Will, and he saw the red-haired man drag in a deep breath. "You're correct. If Karen had been taken and I had no notion as to what might come of her, I wouldn't cease searching until I found her."

At Will's impertinent look at his uncle, Seth added, "*But* you would tell me the same thing I am telling you, and that is to listen to Thomas and rest; two hours is all I ask. You'll be worthless soon if you continue on this way, but rest for awhile and in short order, we will return to our search with renewed strength and fervor."

Will felt like his friend had betrayed him, and the emotion must have shown on his features, because Seth placed a comforting hand on his shoulder, giving a quick squeeze. "And I will be by your side, as you would be by mine."

His shoulders sagging, Will clenched his jaw, knowing both men spoke the truth, though he felt a physical pain in his chest at the thought of ceasing his task for even a moment. "Two hours, and not a minute more." All three men appeared to relax visibly, and Will hadn't noticed their exhaustion until that moment.

Richard said quietly, "We shall find her, William. You said that she is smart and strong."

"We will reconvene at my home and resume our search then." Thomas gave his nephew a small nod of encouragement and then they split up, walking alone to their houses for a few hours of reprieve.

As Will made his way through the forest and up over the rise, guiding his black stallion by the reins, he was haunted by images of what she might endure, what harm could come to her, in the short time that he wasn't searching for her. He was almost certain it had been that derelict Spaniard who had taken her, though his intentions varied depending on if he had been sent or sought her out of his own volition. The fiend's affection for her had been obvious, and Will did not believe—forced himself to deny—that the man would do her harm. But then there was the notion of the second party. Cadius was surely gone, but someone else could have sent the man to collect Sarah, and he did not imagine they would be as lenient as the Spaniard.

A bird stopped its chatter somewhere overhead as he passed, allowing him to hear the faint but unmistakable sound of human voices. On instinct, he released the reins, placing a reassuring hand on the animal's nose to get it to stay behind and allow him to travel undetected. He hastened his steps until he was nearly upon the unknown owners of the voices—two, he realized—and then he slowed, tucking his body behind a hulking tree and cautiously peering around it. A secret rendezvous in the forest was not entirely uncommon, though it was cause for suspicion.

A man stood not twenty feet away, arms folded across his chest. He was facing Will's direction but paid him no mind, as his attention was on the hooded figure before him.

"What more can I do?" the man asked, looking perturbed. "We have tried everything, and still you have been unsuccessful in ultimately changing the course."

Will realized he was eavesdropping on a private quarrel and pushed off the tree to leave when the other man spoke, freezing him to the spot. Though he couldn't place it, there was something so familiar about that voice that it sent a chill over his back.

"One last time," the cloaked figure said lowly. "I was unable to change my past, but I can ensure that my future and that of my son stays on the course I have designed. It was not our original scheme, but no one shall wield the power to change things as we have."

Of what do they speak? Will wondered, narrowing his eyes. He didn't recognize the first man, but the other he felt certain he would know his face if he would simply turn his way. . . .

"So destroying the machine is your aim?" The man unfolded his arms to pinch the bridge of his nose. Something was strange about the way he spoke, as though there was an underlying accent that had faded over time.

"'Tis the only way to prevent others from correcting what we have done, Guy."

That man dipped his head. "I will do as you wish, my lord. Although," he mused, hesitating. "I must ask why you never killed Charles to put an end to all of this. It would be just as successful, since it would eliminate the possibility of him creating the machine to begin with."

"Do not think that I hadn't considered that option." The cloaked figure shifted, hands flexing at his sides. "It was why I originally took him, and to design a working version of the contraption *here*. But if I had taken care of him sooner, I might not have had my son." He clicked his tongue in consternation. "We mustn't be too hasty. Once the machine is inoperative, then it will be safe to do with him as I will with no affect on the current timeline, according to your theory."

Was it murder they spoke of? Will narrowed his gaze as the one man dipped his head and they departed, turning in opposite directions. Will considered trailing one of them, wondering whom they planned to attack, and he even made a move to follow, his old instincts urging him to action. But then he remembered that Sarah was out there, somewhere, and he couldn't afford distractions. Praying God could forgive him for putting Sarah's life ahead of that of their possible victim, he turned in the opposite direction the men had gone.

A bush thrashed nearby. Will froze instinctively, though he told himself it was most likely his uncle or Seth returning. He forced himself to unclench his fists as he narrowed his eyes to see through the mist that rose from the wet earth. The last person he expected to come stomping through the trees, muttering nonsensically to himself, was the very snake he sought.

Lisandro froze, his hand braced on a nearby tree for balance as he stepped over a small hole. Their eyes connected, one filled with surprise, one with hatred. Then the cad's muddy brown eyes widened.

"Well, I did not expect to make any social calls today." His voice dripped sarcasm and false confidence.

Hands shaking with suppressed rage and the desire to do something with them, Will took a step toward him and then another. "Where is she?"

The Spaniard drew himself up to his full height, though he was still inches shorter than Will. "Am I supposed to understand to whom you're—?"

Will had the man's shirt in his clenched fists, nearly lifting him from the leaf-strewn earth as he slammed his back into the tree, vaguely registering the fact that the man weighed less than he had during their last altercation. "Shut up!" he ground out. "She disappeared the day after your escape had been discovered, and your last promise to her was that you would never give up. *Tell me where she is*."

Lisandro tried to break his hold, but it only tightened at his struggle. "She is safe," he returned, eyes flaring.

"You risked her safety in the first place!" he roared.

"And how do you expect to protect her?" The Spaniard grabbed Will's fist, as though that might lessen his grip. His expression was mad, gloating. "The things I know will keep her safe, while you don't even realize that both your lives are in danger. *I* am the right choice for her safety."

Will's fist connected with his jaw, sending the man to the ground in a heap. The throbbing in his knuckles was satisfying. "She will never be safe with you. Where—?"

The man was quick, and Will never saw the hurled object until it was too late. The rock smacked into his temple, causing him to stagger and the edges of his vision to blur for a mere moment, but it was enough time for the coward to lurch to his feet and stagger off into the forest, favoring his right side. Will shook his head like a dog and then ran after him, swiping at branches and leaves to keep his eyes on the man's distant form. He ran like a frightened rabbit, quickly scurrying through the trees, and Will began to lose sight of him. His slight form disappeared around the thick trunk of a tree, and by the time Will came around it, he was gone.

Will cursed the man, leaning his back on the tree to catch his breath as he studied his surroundings, listening. Not a sound reached his ears, save that of the occasional thrush twittering somewhere nearby. The man had been Will's hope of finding Sarah, and he had let him slip right through his fingertips. There was no reality in which he could sleep after having the reprobate in his grasp and then losing his chance of wringing Sarah's whereabouts from him. He had to find her—now.

Will made his way in the direction the Spaniard had disappeared, but there was too much underbrush to trace any identifiable impressions in the wet dirt. But he had to try. Sarah was depending on him, and that thought renewed his strength, his determination and desperation to find her. He would never stop until she was back in his arms.

Chapter Sixteen

"Sometimes we are less unhappy in being deceived by those we love, than in being undeceived by them."

François de La Rochefoucauld

The door opened slowly, admitting Damien's upside-down form.

Driven to total boredom, Sarah had spent a few minutes examining Jade's living area from a different perspective on the couch, with her hair brushing the floor and the blood rushing to her face. At his entrance, though, she nearly fell off the sofa as she scrambled to right herself and her tangled skirt, sure her red face belied her efforts.

"What were you doing?" he asked, a note of strange curiosity in his voice as she shoved her skirt down over her knees.

She lifted one shoulder in a casual shrug, smoothing the twisted folds of fabric that were half trapped beneath her. "Did you learn anything?" she asked, hoping to shift the conversation.

With a slow nod, Damien released the door, closing but not locking it before he moved over to the small window. Keeping the left side of his face to the wall, he peered outside. "Yes, actually."

Sarah perked up a little at this news. She didn't want to get her hopes too high that it might be the kind of information that would give her the freedom to leave, but she couldn't help the spark of excitement at his words. "So?" she prodded eagerly.

As if she hadn't spoken, he remarked, "I'd have thought you would have spoken up before now. The instant I heard of your return, I assumed you would do something to put yourself at risk, and so I found my way into Cadius' good graces to keep you out of the crosshairs as much as possible." He peered at her from the corner of his eye, assessing. "I am surprised you said nothing."

"What are you talking about?"

"The true heir, Richard."

Sarah's mouth dipped in surprise before she could school her expression. "*How* do you know about that?" She had threatened Cadius with her knowledge of their being an heir to the throne besides Adrian, but she hadn't said Richard's name, nor had she admitted that Meredith's child might be alive.

Damien turned to her, the side of his face not masked in shadows twisting in bafflement. "The letter—I assumed you would have used it as soon as I gave it to you."

Now it was Sarah's turn to crinkle her nose in confusion. "I have no—Wait, your apology letter?" He nodded. "I didn't read it. How do you know about Richard?"

Damien stared at her as if she had suddenly sprouted wings. "Oh. . . . You did not even open it?"

She expelled a heavy breath. "I was a little angry with you at the time, kind of like how I'm starting to feel right now."

"All right, but the—the note. Surely you read the note I put inside, at least."

"I barely even glanced at it!" she burst, getting annoyed that he wasn't answering her question outright.

"Well, we have to get it. Where did you last leave it?"

Sarah flexed her lips and glanced around the room, stalling. She narrowed her eyes at a speck on the wall. "That's a little difficult to explain."

Damien blinked. "It isn't with you?"

"No, and why is it so important?"

Taking a deep breath, he answered with forced calm, "It is the letter with instructions *from* Cadius, sealed with his own insignia, telling the recipient to eliminate the child recently borne of Queen Meredith of Serimone."

A slow dread crept into Sarah's mind, settling in the pit of her stomach. "Oh." She racked her brain for the whereabouts of the missive. It had fallen on her floor, hadn't it? She hadn't touched it after opening Damien's letter, or had she thrown it across the room with his? She couldn't remember. "Well, I think it's safe."

"I sent it for safekeeping. . . ." he murmured, voice drifting off as he rubbed his jaw.

"It's not like it's lost," Sarah defended. "It just isn't with me. Here." She narrowed one eye accusingly. "And why is it all right to use your letter, but you kidnapped me just so I wouldn't give the one I had to the queen?"

With a sigh, Damien said, "It is too risky to use your letter between Queen Alexis and Cadius, as it is only speculation as to their motives and what they planned—hardly concrete evidence. If the king or queen did not believe your theory, then your only piece of evidence would be confiscated and wasted too soon. I only kept it from Cadius so that we might have *something* against him, if it came down to it. But the letter I sent with you contains direct orders and is not some note between lovers containing a few seemingly idle threats."

"Oh," Sarah said again, wincing.

His shoulders seemed to sink. "I was hoping we might stop him before . . ."

She waited for him to go on, but he appeared to be deep in thought. "Before what?" she asked impatiently.

With a great sigh, Damien said, "I overheard Cadius speaking of his plan to destroy whatever it is that allows the travel between this place and where it is that you hail."

She blinked, surprised. "But breaking one watch won't stop time travel," she reasoned, half to herself.

Waving a hand as if to help him explain, he said, "No, no. As I recall, he said something about a machine and how it would maintain the corrections he had made and cease any interference."

"But that would mean . . ." Her voice drifted off, horror turning into a brick in her throat. If Cadius intended to destroy the machine that Karen and the professor had built, then would all the changes he had made—everything he had done up to this point—become permanent? And no one would be able to stop him, Sarah could never return home, and she couldn't say what sort of affect this might have on the future.

"You can see why I wished to keep you here," Damien was saying, and she dragged her eyes up to his face. "If he succeeded in stopping travel between our two lands, then you might have become trapped somewhere in between. I have to keep you safe, because if he killed you, I could never correct it, could never undo the past, as he has done." His lips pursed in distaste at the thought, and his eyes filled with pain.

Sarah shook her head. "Even if I am safe here and won't *poof* into nonexistence when the future changes permanently, do you have any idea what this could do to the place where I'm from? And what of Professor Charles—what will Cadius do to him once he no longer needs him, once his plan is finally complete and Charles is just another loose end?"

Damien's face said it all.

"But if Cadius' watch doesn't work anymore," Sarah reasoned, more to reassure herself than anything else, "then he can't get to the future, anyway, so really he can't do any harm. . . . Right?"

Slowly, he said, "Cadius has no intention of returning to your land. However, it appears that he has discovered another who is willing to play part in this final scheme."

"Who?"

"I don't know," he answered, and she knew he was speaking the truth.

"Well, you have to stop him," she insisted.

His voice oozed sarcasm and false bravado when he spoke. "Ah, but you seem to be forgetting, my lady, that I am simply a man living by my own code who hangs on the coattails of others, undertaking whatever means necessary to reach my goals by lieu of pleasing my masters. And you well know that those means oftentimes include underhanded schemes and murder, so who am I to do such a good deed?" He laughed without humor, eyes dimming, voice softening dully. "Yes, I have done terrible things and threw my kindness to the wind when I sold my soul to Lucifer himself."

Sarah shot to her feet, giving him a challenging look. "Then make up for it by stopping him, or at least letting me get word out."

"You would not be protected out there alone, and I cannot go," he said softly. "I cannot leave my sister behind until she is settled."

"A good deed," she whispered suddenly, catching his total attention with her earnest tone. "I'm asking you to do one good thing to earn back my faith. You know Cadius won't stop until he's either succeeded and has silenced everyone involved, or when someone finally brings him down. We can do that."

His eyes were filled with such regret, and Sarah already saw the answer written in his gaze. "I cannot."

Her whole being seemed to deflate. "Then you are just as much a coward as I thought." The harsh tone her words carried causer her to cringe once they were out, but she was too angry to take them back.

It looked as though she had physically slapped him, and he scrubbed a hand over his jaw. "How can you still not trust me after all this time? We were friends once, and I believe you fell for me, in your own way." Damien stumbled over the words, immediately looking like he regretted speaking them aloud.

"That's where you're wrong," she said quietly, her heart feeling weighted by the truth of what she was about to say. "I thought we were friends, but that was mostly a lie, wasn't it? I was tricked into being your friend. And, yeah, I might have felt . . . something for you at one time," she added carefully. "But I didn't fall for you on my own—you tripped me."

He winced and pulled his hand back from his jaw, shifting another inch into the light. For the first time, she noticed the fresh bruise on his left cheek.

"How did you get that?" Had Cadius encountered him after Damien overheard his newest plot?

But the way he froze caused Sarah to narrow her eyes in suspicion. "Who hit you?"

He appeared to war within himself, and then he took a hesitant step toward her, which made her all the more wary of his answer. "I will not lie to you," he whispered. Taking a steadying breath, he answered, "It appears the blacksmith and I overheard the same conversation, and he did not take too lightly to my refusal to reveal your whereabouts."

Sarah gaped at him, her anxiety sparking at the mere mention of Will. "You saw Will? Is he okay?"

"He might have double vision for a day or two, but otherwise he will be fine." He paused and then added, almost dully, "Other than Cadius having him followed."

They had fought once before, Sarah knew, but the idea of him hitting Will back caused her eyes to flare. "What did you do to him?"

"He threw the first punch," Damien defended, absently touching his jaw.

"Because he *knew* you had kidnapped me!" she retorted, glaring. "He was only trying to look out for me."

The gold flecks in his eyes danced with irritation. "He should be looking after his own well-being."

"Why didn't you bring him here, then?" she asked in challenge. "If this has suddenly become a haven for people in danger, as you constantly remind me I am, then why didn't you bring Will here to me?"

The distance Damien put between them was almost imperceptible, but Sarah saw the way he pulled back from her. "I suppose you would like that." He spun on his heels and stomped to the door.

"Where are you going?" she called, still aching for a fight that she knew wouldn't end well, but she was past reason. Will still thought she was in great peril, and Damien had done nothing to protect him when he knew Will might also be in danger, even going so far as to keep them apart.

He threw the door wide and twisted back to face her, lips tight. "To put some distance between us. Hopefully, you will see some reason before my return."

Jade appeared on the stoop and had to lurch aside to avoid her brother as he stormed out.

"I won't!" Sarah shouted after him, realizing her retort was not only petty but a personal insult.

Jade raised a perfectly arched brow at her. "And what, pray tell, was that about?"

Sarah glared after his retreating form. "Your brother got into a scuffle with Will and is refusing to help me stop a madman, going for the passive technique. And he won't let me do anything!" she burst out, chest heaving in frustration.

Jade eyed her for a long moment. "Believe me when I say that I understand your frustration over feeling powerless."

Sarah huffed. "I wish that I could do something. Damien knows that what Cadius is planning could harm my home and will definitely destroy other lives, but he won't *do* anything."

Silence reigned for a long moment, and Sarah raised her head to find the other woman studying her. "Hmm, would that I could help you." Jade shrugged, closing the door behind her. "But my brother would not appreciate my interference, though I know he despises having blood on his hands."

She suddenly gave her a pointed look that Sarah couldn't decipher. "Although he cares, I sometimes I feel that he does not always know what is best for others and forgets that he cannot control their actions." That said, she breezed into her room, and the door clicked shut.

Sarah stared after her, confused by her words and the unreadable message she had tried to convey. Something gnawed at the back of her mind, and she glanced at the front door. Had Jade locked it? She tried to remember the woman pulling her key out and realized she never had.

With bated breath, she moved quietly to the door, listening for a moment, and then carefully inching it open. She shot a look over her shoulder, but Jade's door was still closed. The woman was a lot of things, and helpful had been the last thing Sarah had expected, but she knew without a doubt that Jade had kept it unlocked on purpose.

Stepping outside, Sarah closed the door behind her and set off. If Damien wasn't going to do anything about it, then she had to. She might be the only person left who could save the future.

☙❧

Helplessness was sinking in. Will had lost track of the Spaniard over an hour ago. He was supposed to regroup with the search party soon, and he was no closer to finding Sarah than he had been last night.

Will ceased his aimless stomping through the woods, dragging both hands through his hair in frustration. He hadn't found a single trace of anything that might lead him to her, and he felt too panicked with each passing moment to think clearly about what was right before him; perhaps he had found a clue and had been too distracted to pay it any mind. His best hope for Sarah right now was that she was with the Spaniard and he had enough scruples to do her no harm. The thought, meant to comfort him, was a dismal one.

"Where are you, my love?" he whispered, eyes scanning the forest. The haze that had settled between the trees was lifting, providing for better visibility, but the warm sun streaming between the branches only served to remind Will of the passing of time and his own exhaustion. He was desperate to close his eyes, knowing he was pushing his body too far, but how could he consider his own comfort when Sarah might be at the mercy of that Spaniard?

Will's chest rose and fell with a deep breath. No, he would find her today if it killed him, and together they would tell the queen of her son's possible existence.

Almighty, I know you exist from what my mother taught me, and we both know that Sarah holds complete faith in You. Will closed his eyes, feeling the words form in his mind reluctantly. I know you care for me not, but Sarah is pure and blameless. I am pleading with you to help me find her.

Will waited for . . . what? An answer? He didn't know, though nothing happened, anyway, much to his dismay.

He closed his eyes, feeling pain and exhaustion wash over him. Aloud, he whispered, "I am not sure if You can hear my thoughts, and perhaps I am too informal and You will reject my plea because of my ignorance. But Mother often prayed to You that way, and Sarah says that she has a personal relationship with You. All I ask is that You keep her safe and return her to me—*prove* that all power is in Your hand." Will winced at his words, knowing he was venting his anger at a deity, goading him into doing his will.

With a wavering, defeated voice, he added quietly, "I was supposed to spend the rest of my life with her."

He couldn't say if it was because he felt alone and was in need of Someone to speak with, or if he tried again because it was the last hope he had, but he sent one final plea heavenward. He hoped it would be enough, but his confidence in her swift return was failing with each passing moment. The wondering was eating him alive.

Shoulders lowering and chin dipping toward his chest, Will moved onward, reminding himself to not give in so quickly to despair. He could hear a creek babbling nearby and told himself he could have ten minutes to drink and rest, and then he would be off again.

A shout halted him in his tracks. Will strained his ears, listening intently for any other sound. He thought he might have heard thrashing among the distant trees, but he couldn't be certain with the sound of the creek marring the clarity of his hearing. Then someone shouted again, words this time, and though their meaning was indistinct, Will was certain it had been a woman's voice.

Heart quickening, he moved lithely through the trees in the direction of the noise. A flock of birds abruptly took flight south of him, and he spun that way, hastening toward whatever had disturbed them.

"You're being unreasonable!" The words reached his ears, the first clear ones he had been able to hear yet. It sounded so much like Sarah that his stomach clenched anxiously. He quickened his pace, distinctly making out the sound of someone—no, two bodies—moving rapidly up ahead. Someone responded to the woman, though his words were muffled.

Frantically, Will's eyes scanned the trunks in the distance, and he could just make out a hurried form heading in the direction of the clearing, with a slower pursuer only a few lengths behind. Instinctively, Will knew it was her even before he saw Sarah's auburn waves flying in the wind as she fled. His heart lurched within his chest, and his only thought was that he had to reach her.

"You know I have to stop him." Her call reached his ears, though he was still too far away to make out the face of the man chasing her, though he was almost certain it was Lisandro; she sounded less frightened and more like she were reasoning with the man, which seemed out of place in the midst of their pursuit.

She stopped in the clearing directly ahead of Will and turned to face the man, though he didn't advance on her. Seeing he didn't mean her immediate harm, Will slowed enough to keep his advancement hidden.

"I cannot allow you to do that," the man said lowly. The voice, clearly belonging to the Spaniard, struck a nerve in Will, and he gritted his teeth as he moved through the trees. Though his face was obscured by branches, Will saw plain as day the bow the man lifted and the string he drew back with quaking fingers. His pulse stopped.

"I see you kept your bow at her place," Sarah remarked drolly, breathing heavily as she leaned on her knees. "What're you gonna do? Shoot me?" She spread her arms, giving him a look that dared him to do just that. "Yeah? Well, then go right ahead. You're going to have to if you want to keep me from stopping him." She frowned suddenly, lowering her arms. "You broke your stitches."

"My lady," Lisandro muttered. It was quiet now, and Will had to move carefully through the bushes so as to not be overheard. The dark, wet patch on his shirt was slowly spreading, but the Spaniard didn't put the weapon down, though his arms were shaking. "I said I would never again tell you a lie, and I give you my word that I will set this right."

"Too late," Sarah said, reaching for her wrist.

In the moment that he reacted, Will wasn't thinking about whether or not the man would fire, didn't consider assaulting the Spaniard first—though he was sure that later he would have wished he'd socked him for good measure. No, his only consideration was of getting Sarah to safety and removing her from the crosshairs.

He sped through the trees and burst into the clearing, though Sarah appeared so focused that she didn't notice him at first. But Lisandro did. Out of the corner of his eye, Will caught the way the man's jaw hung open and his fingers holding the string taut suddenly slackened.

It all happened so fast that Sarah looked up and only managed a gasp before he collided with her the instant her face was obscured by a blinding white light, and the arrow sailed through nothing but air.

Chapter Seventeen

"À la folie"

To insanity

All she remembered was Damien pretending that he would shoot her and seeing Will's face for a brief second before she met the ground with a *thump*. The light layer of powder barely lessened the impact, and they both grunted as Will landed on top of her, his arms wrapped tightly about her. When the light was no longer blinding, he unfolded himself and got to his knees, shaking his head like a dog and squeezing his eyes closed. Sarah recalled the sick feeling she'd had the first time she had traveled and knew he must be experiencing the same thing.

But while Will held his eyes closed, waiting for his vision to clear, Sarah's vision was just fine. A knot of dread formed in her stomach as she stared at the gas station over his shoulder, taking everything in. She gaped at him as she rolled onto her back and propped herself up on her elbows, waiting for the world to stop spinning and for Will to disappear from this modern landscape. A part of her was incredibly relieved to see him and for Will to see with his own eyes that she was safe. But that sensation was overshadowed by the fact that he now knew her secret, and she was *definitely* freaking out when she realized that a twelfth century blacksmith had just hitchhiked a thousand years.

"Oh, Lord," she murmured.

At the sound of her voice, Will opened his lids. He seemed to drink in the sight of her for a long moment with his weary gaze, and then he cradled the back of her neck in his hands. His eyes searched hers. "Sarah, I thought the worst might have come of you." He brushed his thumb along her cheek, grazing the corner of her slackened mouth. "Where have you been?"

"I—Damien," was all she managed, mouth working mindlessly. But it seemed enough.

Will's eyes hardened. "I'm going to see the Spaniard hanged for taking you, if I don't kill him myself first."

"How did you follow me?" she whispered, aghast.

He didn't seem to understand her plight and smiled softly, causing the fresh nick by his eye to crinkle. He reached into his pocket and retrieved her necklace, tying it securely behind her neck. His fingers purposefully brushed the skin behind her ear. "Richard found this, and I knew something was wrong. I mended the clasp, knowing that I would soon find you and give it back to its rightful owner. I haven't stopped looking since."

"No, I mean how did you—?" A horn blared on the road, causing her to flinch, though Will lurched back onto his heels and watched with enormous eyes as a silver SUV swerved around a Smart Car and sailed along the asphalt, countless cars following in their wake on the street.

"What the devil!" Will gaped after the two automobiles, and Sarah grimaced at his reaction. A man clad in all leather exited the station, and the dull jingle announcing his exit caused Will to turn that way. He watched in open-mouthed shock as the man threw his leg over his motorcycle, shrinking back into himself as the hog roared to life and the man drove off, past glass high-rises and brick buildings.

Sarah cringed, sitting up. "Um, Will, I think I might need to explain." As though he wasn't dealing with enough already, a large plane sailed low overhead, its engines stirring the trees along the pavement and causing them to sway back and forth.

Will stretched his arm out in front of her, as though to shield her from the roar of the unknown threat. "That was not a falcon," he whispered, sounding awe-struck.

"It's called a plane."

"Where are we?" He glanced around frantically, as though searching for something. His eyes flared. "Did that Spaniard do something?"

"No, Will, it was—I did this." She flinched when he met her gaze, his own completely baffled. "I, um, well." Sarah bit her lip, at a loss for words. Was there any easy way to explain where he was? For the first time, she really got a look at their surroundings and realized with a jolt of panic that she didn't recognize them, either.

"But how—?"

Sarah stood, dusting off her skirt. "I don't know *exactly* where we are," she answered carefully. Spotting a hill up ahead, she said with more confidence than she felt, "We need to get to higher ground."

It seemed that Will rose on shaky legs, and together they made their way to the crosswalk. She pressed the button on the pole, waiting for the light to change, glancing at Will every other second as he took in everything around him—a girl riding her bike, the group of scarf-clad gentlemen smoking outside of a cigar shop, the girls in fashionable wool coats eying the racks of clothing outside a brightly colored store.

Sarah bit her lip. When Damien had found her, she had run, thinking to escape into her own world to buy time—if he wouldn't give her the note he'd taken, then she would find the letter Damien had written and use that against Cadius, and if it came to it, she would stop whoever had been sent to destroy the machine. Damien could play the "safe" card and hide out at Jade's cabin for the rest of his life, if he wanted. Sarah was tired of running and wanted done with it.

But she was supposed to have gone right back to Oklahoma, to the place she had left, as she had every other time before. A note of panic filled her when she realized that nothing appeared familiar.

At last the light changed, and she grabbed Will's hand, dragging him behind her. He gaped at every car as he passed. "Are those *carriages*?"

"Sort of."

They trekked up the hill. The watch had always returned her to nearly the exact spot she had left, and she told herself that she would recognize something as soon as she reached the top. But she didn't. All she saw was a valley with overgrown trees and a smattering of broken-down stone buildings that looked like they were centuries old. Where they once might have served as a home, they were now nothing more than scattered monuments to the past.

"I just—I don't understand." Now it was her turn to look panicked. "I thought I knew where we were, but I don't recognize anything, and I can't—this isn't supposed to be here."

"Locksley," Will breathed, sinking to his knees in the snow.

Sarah spun around to face him. "What?"

He pointed with a quavering finger. "Those buildings—this is Locksley Village, where I grew up."

Will had shown her the village once, but it had been from a distance, and she had barely been able to make out the outlines of houses and trees. She squinted at the dismal scene. "How can you even tell?"

He swallowed. "I just know." Sarah's heart twisted. If this was Locksley, what must he be going through, to see the place of his childhood reduced to nothing more than his memory and a valley of wreckage?

She crouched beside him, at a loss. But if that were true and this valley *had* been the place where he grew up, then the fact that they had landed somewhere in England was a new concern for Sarah, and she had no idea what to do next. She didn't have her passport with her, let alone the connections to get one for Will, and she couldn't head right back into Damien's clutches with empty hands.

In silence, they stared at the rubble—Will lost in thoughts of his past as he tried to adjust to his foreign surroundings; Sarah occupied with her own distress and notions of how to travel to Oklahoma, get Will back, and find what she came for, prospects that had all seemed slightly less complicated thirty minutes ago when she escaped Jade's house.

But as they watched the dilapidated village, the scene shifted in front of their eyes, wavering and wobbling like it was under water. The ground seemed to roll beneath them, and Sarah fell onto her backside; the sight before her blurred like she was on the Tilt-A-Whirl she had ridden at the fair last summer. She felt as sick now as she had then, unable to rise to her feet in search of steadier ground.

Will gripped her hand, and his wide eyes were on her, so he missed the way that the skeleton of Locksley dissolved until it was nothing but a blurry gray-green canvass. Sarah squeezed her eyes closed against the growing pain in her head, like it was filling with pressure that had no way of escape. They were suddenly jerked apart, and Will lost his grip on her, though the fading sound of him crying out her name echoed for a second or two before it was replaced by a deafening roar in her ears. Then all was silent.

Sarah opened her eyes, wincing at the sun reflecting off the snow. Gradually, the ringing in her ears stopped, replaced by the sound of scattered conversation and laughter and traffic moving along the road. Though she had expected it to be completely deserted by now, nearly a week later, she immediately knew she was back on campus.

With a spark of hope at the familiarity of it all, she turned to Will and found the space beside her empty. Dread filled her as she wildly scanned the few students milling about, jumping to her feet to get a better view of their faces. Where had he gone when they'd separated? A sickening feeling of panic filled her senses as she wondered if it was possible for him to have been lost in another place . . . or time.

There! Sarah felt knee-weakening relief as she caught sight of the back of him up the slope, a head taller than the rest and dressed in his trousers and cloak. She hurried to catch up to him, though her steps slowed as she paid attention to everything that was going on around her, like re-watching a film you had nearly forgotten you'd seen before.

Two jocks were moving their mattress out of the dorm, a couple of girls were admiring them nearby, and Professor Demetrius was headed her way. Not Sarah's way, she realized with a mingling of shock and dread as her eyes shifted to the right. Correction: he was headed to the spot where Sarah had stood nearly a week past.

And she was still standing there, dressed in her turtle sweater.

"No," she whispered as she stared at herself standing in the snow across the lawn. How was this even possible? There was never supposed to have been *two* of her in the same place. Karen had said the watches only deposited people in the past age of Serimone as they left their own time, and then returned them to the nearly exact spot in the present from which they had originally left. And the time frame between worlds was supposed to continue moving along, as though the two centuries lived nearly parallel lives with time that moved side-by-side—one sometimes faster than the other—but never touching. So she couldn't have truly gone *back* in time.

But isn't that what Cadius did when Robert's watch malfunctioned? Sarah reminded herself. That's how this whole business had started, with one faulty watch finding its way into unaware hands.

Her eyes widened, realizing with growing horror that someone was, or would, or maybe they already *had* tampered with the machine. If the watches were already malfunctioning, could that mean that at some point in time someone had corrupted the machine, and it was just now catching up with them? She needed Karen for the scientific aspect of all that was going on, knowing she might be able to shed some light on it. But Sarah didn't need to be a scientist to know that one thing was certain: if they didn't stop Cadius and get Will back soon, Sarah wasn't sure they ever would.

Drawing her gaze back to him, she was surprised to find Will making motions with his hands, his eyes wide. Sarah's own gaze turned the size of saucers as she looked over at herself, standing there with a confused look on her face as she watched him. Sarah's pulse quickened, knowing she couldn't shout at him and risk alerting her past self to her presence—there was no telling *what* might happen if they met or saw each other, and she had seen too many science fiction movies to test the theory that they might both implode into nothingness if two versions of herself encountered each other.

Then she spotted the boys making their way across campus with the mattress, suddenly recalling the way Will had disappeared behind it.

Sucking in a breath, Sarah bolted for him, keeping low in hopes that the few students milling about would offer her some cover. Less than a minute had passed, and Sarah knew Professor Demetrius would meet her any second. She tamped down some of her trepidation with the reminder that if she truly *had* seen Will here a week ago, then that meant that this version of herself had been there as well, and she would have remember spotting . . . herself.

Or, at least she assumed so, but she hadn't exactly studied general relativity or the theory of time travel in school.

Bolstering her confidence, she hoped the Sarah on the hill was paying too much attention to Will to notice her doppelganger sneaking up on him from the side. The instant the mattress passed in front of Will, she lurched out from behind a passing student and grabbed his hand, knowing that Professor Demetrius had just caught her attention. She yanked him back, which was easy to do in his stupefied state, tugging him around the corner of the main building.

"What do you—?" Will's eyes bulged at her. He glanced over his shoulder and then back at her. "How did you do that?"

Sarah flexed her hands nervously. "It's kind of difficult to explain."

"We must go back." He gripped her arm and tried to pull her from behind the building. She dug in her heels with a grunt, earning a confused look. "You're—she—y-you're in danger." He managed to frown severely, eyes still wide. "*How?*"

She couldn't answer that just yet. Not knowing what had him so alarmed over her safety, she shook her head, wanting to remove at least one thing from the full plate she had dished him. "No, no, I'm fine. It's just my teacher, and we only talk for a minute. Karen's just about to come and get me for the wedding." She pursed her lips, realizing that she sounded like she was telling the future, which probably wasn't helping matters.

Will couldn't have looked more baffled if he'd tried, and he seemed to be deciding what to focus on. Finally, he pointed in the direction of Professor Demetrius and Sarah as they broke apart and she made her way up the hill, with one final, longing glance over her shoulder. "That man—he cannot be trusted."

"Will, you're being paranoid. You don't even know him."

"But I do," he breathed. Sarah blinked in surprise, and he went on quietly, watching the man's every step as he went to speak with Todd. "I saw him in the forest, with a man whose face was hidden by the cloak he wore. They spoke of destroying some machine and of eliminating a man called Charles in the future, and from what I gathered, it sounded as though they had further dishonorable plans in mind."

Will closed his eyes, looking suddenly pained. He swore quietly under his breath. "Oh, I am a fool. Charles is such a common name, I did not think they meant *him.*"

Charles. The professor. She had assumed he might be in danger at some point, but hearing that there were already plans in the works turned her stomach.

Sarah shook her head, letting the instinctive alarm fade with a dose of reality. "He couldn't have been the one you saw in Serimone. Professor Demetrius lives . . . here," she answered carefully.

Will gave her a pointed look. "I know what I saw. The other man might have called him Guy, but I assure you they are one in the same."

Sarah gauged his reaction to seeing her teacher, considering the fact that Will's mystery man and her professor shared a name. Charles had said he'd had a colleague, but if Professor Demetrius really had been in league with him, then that meant that Demetrius had been ostracized before the watches were in full working order. How had he found himself in the past?

"You're sure?" she asked slowly, contemplating how her life had become so complicated.

"I observed them together just before that Spaniard revealed himself." His gaze darkened as he turned it back on her professor, who was now headed toward his car. "It sounded as though he would be the one to do the deed, whatever that might be."

Sarah pressed her back against the wall now that he could see her fully, as though flattening herself would help to conceal her. She grimaced, wondering how her teacher, adored by all, could be working with Cadius. "Damien told me about a meeting."

After a brief hesitation, Will's shoulders slumped. "I still cannot believe he managed to secrete you away." His look turned hard and self-reproaching. "I should have gone with you to the queen. It was an important task, and I knew Lisandro was uncontained, and I should not have allowed myself to become distracted. . . ."

Sarah took his hand in both of hers. "You left because Robert needed actual help in that moment and because I told you to go. There is absolutely nothing you need to be sorry for. I'm fine." She held her arms wide so he could assess her. "Damien kept me safe."

His wince was so slight that she almost didn't catch it, the nick on his brow twisting. "But I should have been the one to care for you."

"If the bruises under your eyes are any indication, then I'm assuming you stayed up all night trying to find me."

"I never stopped," he assured her again, his piercing indigo gaze searching her face.

Sarah sighed. "And the fact that you never gave up on me means more than you can know." She swallowed, forcing emotion back so she could whisper, "I missed you, Will."

Before she realized he had moved, she was suddenly enveloped in his arms, her head pressed firmly against his chest, the sound of his pounding heartbeat roaring just beneath her ear. She held onto him for dear life, closing her eyes.

"I promise you, love," Will said into her hair, his voice intense and quavering, "that you will never be forced to regret my absence again, nor I yours."

You can't promise that, Sarah wanted to whisper back, the pain in her chest intensifying, vying for attention. As soon as he discovered what this place was, where she came from, then she imagined he would see the same thing she did—that *this* might be impossible. She refused to acknowledge the fact that it was very likely impossible, having once promised to herself that she would not give up on hope. But seeing Will here, so out of place and almost terrified by the small portion of modern life that he was seeing, only served to remind her that he didn't belong in her world any more than she belonged in his.

With a small sniff, she pulled back just enough to look at his face, so earnest and pained and relieved. She touched the scratch by his eye. "What happened?"

"The Spaniard and a rock." It was said so simply, with a surprising lack of inflection or offense in his words, but Sarah grimaced, pulling her hand back.

"Well, if it makes you feel any better, you clocked him pretty good," she said in a dry tone, awkwardly trying to make light of the situation, still avoiding the urgent topic at hand.

The smallest of smiles touched the corner of Will's mouth. He planted a gentle kiss on her lips. "It does." They took a moment to revel in the other's company before he slowly removed his arms from around her waist. "Now I believe we should try to discover where we are." He paused, eying her suspiciously, though there was no admonition in his gaze. "But I suppose you already know that, don't you?"

Biting her lip, she glanced around them. The campus was nearly empty now, though a girl dragging a rolling suitcase through the snow eyed their clothes strangely as she walked past them on her way to the parking lot.

Sarah looked back at Will and carefully replied, "I'm not sure you're ready to hear the truth." And she wasn't sure she was ready to have him look at her differently, to know that she was a freak from the future.

He shook his head. *How crazy and impossible must this all sound to him?* she wondered. "I have no idea where I am and have just seen you appear in two different places, though you do not appear as shocked as I. If you know something, then please feel free to enlighten me."

Sarah heaved a great sigh, wondering what he would think of her once she admitted where she came from and the secrets she had kept from him. But he deserved to know. "Fine, I'll tell you everything, but you can't interrupt me. It won't make any sense, and so you just have to let me get it out and then I can explain the details after. Deal?"

Looking more apprehensive than ever, Will nodded slowly. "All right."

She swallowed. "And can we walk while we talk? I have something I need to get, and I'd rather not get caught by my past self."

❧

Will's face was a mask of confused concentration as she explained, going all the way back to how she and Lilly had been sucked into the past when Karen damaged her watch. Despite the fact that he had agreed to not interrupt, each new event or person that Sarah spoke of sparked a fresh question from Will as he listened with rapt attention. They made their way up campus and to the dorms, and though there were a sparse number of students and teachers left at the school and even less who would be interested in what they spoke of, she kept her voice low, rambling through her explanations as quickly as possible.

She told him that Karen and the professor had created these watches—she held hers out to show him, and though it wasn't much to look at, it appeared to fascinate him—that allowed people to travel through time, from the present to the past and then back again; she told him of landing in the forest that first day, of meeting him, though he had been disguised as the Shadow at the time; how she stayed to help Karen and sent Lilly home with no way of knowing whether or not she would ever see her again.

Sarah hiked her skirts and then climbed the narrow staircase, Will just behind her. "And we assumed that Serimone was just this place in time that appeared out of nowhere," she whispered in the quiet stairwell as they ascended. "That the machine had somehow created it—at least, that's what we hoped."

"Why?" came the soft question behind her. Sarah glanced over her shoulder at Will, whose expression was deceptively blank, save for the subtle widening of his eyes. "Why would it matter if it was fabricated or truly the . . . past?" He stumbled over the word.

Her steps slowed as they reached the upper landing on the second floor. "Because if it was actually the past, then that meant we could mess it up and that our actions there might have consequences in the future. So thinking Serimone had no place in history justified our actions, I guess, but I know now that it was foolish thinking. And I think deep down, Karen knew all along, too."

She didn't go on to admit that's why she had distanced herself from him at first, because she feared leaving him as she would have to do one day, and that her desire to remain with him or bring him home with her could have grave consequences. Instead, she told him of Richard and how Damien had practically confirmed her suspicions of his lineage, and Will appeared completely amazed.

Sarah opened the door to her and Clara's room, which was still a complete wreck, with music playing softly in the background. She had forgotten she'd left it on when she stormed out of her room after receiving Damien's letter. Though she remembered that she would return later to turn it off before leaving with Karen, she did so now, wanting to disturb Will as little as possible.

"What was that?" he asked, pointing in awe at the small CD player, having already heard the music before she could press the OFF button.

"Uh, it's a music player." Sarah pressed her lips together, trying to recall where exactly she'd thrown the note in this disaster. Littering the floor were balls of old homework Clara had insisted on crumpling and leaving strewn about the room to "defy the system." However, she had already finished and turned in those projects, so there really was no point to her act of defiance other than the fact that it satisfied her rebellious desire.

Will touched the ON-OFF button on the CD player, as he had seen her do, his lips parting in surprise as the clear sounds came on and disappeared at his fingertips. Her phone was on the nightstand next to it, and he gingerly touched the screen. It came to life with a small chirp, and he flinched in surprise as the lock screen prompting him to type in the passcode. Abruptly, a rumbling sound issued from the machine as it vibrated against the wood, whistling a happy tune that signaled an incoming call that Sarah was sure she didn't want to accept just then. Will gave a small gasp at the noise and the way it rumbled and moved across the table. He waved her over, the screen casting his face in white light. "Sarah, come have a look at this."

"I can't see a thing," she muttered distractedly. The morning outside was gray and wintery, and the frost-coated window let in little light. While he tapped the numbers on the lock screen, she walked over to the wall and flicked the switch by the door to brighten the dim room.

Will started at the sudden illumination and gaped at the ceiling, seeming to completely forget his fascination with the phone.

"An instant torch," he breathed in amazement, reaching up to touch the bulb. He winced at the heat and retracted his hand. "It's hot but contained; there would be no more accidental fires. . . . Remarkable."

"They still happen, but not as often. Nobody uses torches anymore," Sarah informed him absentmindedly, picking up one piece of crumpled paper after another, though she knew Damien's letter would be on weathered lambskin and look nothing like the rest. But she wanted to leave no stone unturned, and so she continued to sort through her piles of clothing and textbooks and even a few old Starbucks cups. She frowned. "Gross."

"It cannot be possible," Will whispered behind her, drawing her attention as he sat on the edge of her messy bed. He paused, pressing his hand into the plush covers, feeling the mattress spring back as his eyes remained fixed on the white light. "It is before my very eyes, but I can hardly believe they see the truth."

She suddenly realized she hadn't been paying much attention to the impact even the smallest exposure to things Sarah saw everyday would have on him. She stopped her search for a moment, reminding herself that this had to be incredibly overwhelming for him. "That's how I felt when Karen explained everything to me." Feeling like a mothering hen but unable to stop herself, she added, "And you'll go blind if you stare at that too long."

He looked at her in surprise and then proceeded to blink the spots from his vision. "It can make one loose their sight?"

She shrugged. "That's what my mom always told me, but you'll be fine in a minute."

Will nodded, trusting her. "So Karen was the one to lead you here—does Seth know of her origin?"

"No, and I don't want to be the one to break her trust, and I would appreciate it if you let Karen be the one to tell him; she's kind of trying to forget this part of her past, anyway."

"Oh."

Sarah waited. And waited. But he only stared silently at the floor, absorbing every word she had spoken, which had been a lot. She knew he was processing, but his silence unnerved her.

"I thought you'd have more questions about this," she remarked carefully. Actually, *dreaded* his questions sounded more appropriate. She had hoped he would never find out where she came from, wanting to go on prolonging the inevitable. Now she had been forced to throw everything at him at once, and she had expected something more than his quiet, thoughtful look. She hedged, "You don't think I'm crazy, claiming to be from the future?"

Will turned his gaze to her, looking as though he had forgotten she was in the same room. "There is no doubt it sounds preposterous, and yet here we both are. The cloaked man with Guy said he had designs to change the past, but I never thought—at the time I couldn't believe he actually meant it was possible." Will went back to staring at the floor.

Biting her lip, Sarah added, "The guy you saw . . ." He looked up at her then, and she reluctantly admitted, "It was Cadius."

He stared at her, his hand falling slowly to his lap. "What?' he breathed.

Nodding reluctantly, Sarah supplied, "He faked his execution, with some help, and is trying to get himself back on the throne. When he surprised Damien and me at Gabriel's shack, I could hardly believe it myself." She shook her head at the memory of hearing Cadius' voice, seeing his cold eyes again after believing him dead.

With a cringe, she watched Will's face, the emotions and shock passing over it in waves. "I'm sorry. I know this is a lot to take in."

"No, discovering that Cadius still lives and wishes to . . . *alter* history and that the Spaniard is now working against him is almost too much to comprehend," he answered wryly, giving her a dull smile that faded almost instantly. "But finding that I have just traversed through a millennium and you have done so several times before feels like insanity. It certainly outweighs even the latest revelation." Pausing, he said in a halting voice, as though her words had just reached his ears, "Dunlivey—you said it was his cabin. He isn't—what I meant to say is that his body was destroyed."

"No, he's not coming back to life like Cadius." Sarah watched him swallow in relief at her assurance. "But he knew about where I'm from." At his startled look, she nodded reluctantly. "The place where Damien kept me that first night was full of all sorts of things from this world that Karen and the professor had sent back as a test—a small, hand-held torch that doesn't have a flame, supplies used for letter writing and offices that haven't been designed yet. Cadius collected them and told Gabriel about everything, though it didn't sound like he entirely believed him. But it's why Gabriel was after Karen, because he knew she had something to do with what Cadius had told him." Sarah realized she was rambling and pinched her lips together, eying the floor.

Silence reigned, and then Will asked abruptly, "What were you searching for?"

"A letter. It's the reason why I came."

"Is that it?"

She started at his innocent remark and followed the line of his finger to the pile of clothes under her window. The crumpled paper was tucked between a tan sweater and a pair of jeans so it was almost hidden among the folds of fabric. Snatching it from the ground, Sarah let out a relieved breath.

"Who is it from?" Will asked as she sat heavily on the bed next to him.

"Damien," she replied, smoothing out the wrinkles in the paper and trying not to tear the bent edges. She glanced up to find him frowning.

"Is that the letter he had me give to you?" It had been the last wish of a dying man, or so they had originally thought, and so Will had begrudgingly transferred it to Sarah's possession.

"Yes, but I haven't read it yet," she said distractedly. "There's supposed to be evidence against Cadius in here, according to Damien. It's the whole reason why I came—well, that and stopping Cadius from destroying the machine so we can't return to the past." With anxious fingers, she pulled the folds of paper apart to expose the smaller, crumpled missive within. The words My Dearest Sarah beckoned to her on the page, but she ignored them, setting Damien's apology on the bedside table and devoting her full attention to the weathered piece of parchment.

Unsure what to expect, she opened the letter slowly, her eyes dragging over the short request with rapt attention. The crease between her brows deepened as she read.

"What does it say?" Will asked, leaning over her shoulder to better see.

In a voice tinged with amazement, Sarah said, "It's a letter asking for the queen's child to be 'purged from this earth,'" she quoted with disgust. "There's no date on it, but the letter is addressed to Malcolm Devlin."

"The physician?" he said in confusion, referring to the man Damien and Cadius had framed and put to death. "The man delivered the child. Why would he agree to dispose of it?"

Her eyes turned suddenly bright. "Exactly! I don't think Malcolm did. What if he was the one to leave Richard on Dagwood's doorstep?" she mused, half to herself. "He would want him to be safe, but he wouldn't want to keep him within Cadius' reach."

"But the physician was hanged, you'll recall," Will reminded gently as her enthusiasm increased. "There is no one to confirm that he was the one to do it."

She was already shaking her head, refusing to let her excitement be squashed. "It doesn't matter; this is the evidence we need against Cadius. It's sealed with his ring and has his *signature* on it."

Will's mouth hung open. "He sealed his own fate. . . ."

Grinning in a self-satisfied way, Sarah added, "Damien said he slipped it into his letter in hopes that I would use it against Cadius, and I have plans to do just that."

He shook his head. "I cannot believe the Spaniard would give us something so precious to our cause."

She held it out to him. "See for yourself."

Though he masked his embarrassment fairly well, Sarah could still make it out in the hesitancy in his eyes as he pulled back. "Ah, no. I—my reading is not what it ought to be."

"You can't read?"

At her look of surprise, Will added softly, "I can, but it is so uncommonly needed that I don't practice as much as I should; I generally only apply the skill toward lists and orders at the shop. As the children of a gentleman and lady, my parents ensured I had an excellent education, so I read better than most in my class, but still . . ." His voice faded, and he dropped her gaze, clearly uncomfortable.

Sarah dropped her hand to her lap, clutching the letter. "Wow. I mean, I remember reading that only monks and that a few of the upper class knew how to read and write, but even hearing about that in my history class made it hard to believe. Kids here are taught their alphabet as early as two years old," she explained, hoping she hadn't offended him with this insight.

He nodded thoughtfully, and his next question caught her off-guard. "So in this world, Serimone has been reduced to nothing but oral tales?"

Sarah winced. "Actually, I'd never heard of Serimone before, only Locksley, and even then it's sort of an urban legend that nobody thinks is real."

"And me?" Will met her eyes with his piercing indigo gaze. "I don't exist in your world, do I? I am certainly not important enough to merit a tale about my life."

Dropping his gaze, she took his hand and held it on the bed between them. "You're important to me, and I'll never let the world forget you." And so long as he remained in Serimone as the Shadow, she doubted it ever would.

When she looked up again, he was smiling softly, though it faded as quickly as it had come. "So if we do not stop this Demetrius from destroying the mechanism that Karen and Charles designed, then by your assessment, we will be unable to return to Serimone. Which means that we could not submit this evidence against Cadius, Richard might be assassinated, and the man behind it all will have succeeded in getting a direct line to the throne, having used King Adrian and the manipulation of time as the means to do it."

Cringing at his accuracy, she nodded. "That's a little more tangled than I originally thought, but, yeah, that pretty much sums up the situation."

With a heavy exhalation of breath, he said, "Well, then I suppose we have to do something about that."

Chapter Eighteen

"Still round the corner there may wait
A new road or a secret gate."
J.R.R Tolkien, *The Lord of the Rings*

With the incriminating letter stuffed up Sarah's sleeve and her car keys gripped in one hand, they jogged down the staircase and hurried across campus to the gated parking lot. They both kept their eyes peeled for any sign of Sarah's former self and Professor Demetrius, but he was long gone by now and Sarah hadn't yet returned from her conversation with Karen at the coffee shop. Were there two versions of him wandering around Oklahoma, too—one going on Christmas vacation after finishing grading assignments and the other plotting to destroy time? Did the Demetrius from Serimone even have the means to come back to this time?

"Sarah, hold up!"

She stopped dead in her tracks, Will slowing beside her. Todd walked over to her with a smile, and she barely held back a groan.

Stuffing his hands into his coat pockets, Todd grinned at her. Normally it was charming, but today it grated on her nerves. "Nice dress. Did I miss a Renaissance party for medieval history, or something?"

Forcing a pained smile at his joke, Sarah said hurriedly, "Hi, Todd. We're actually just going, but tell Clary I expect a full report after you two get back."

He reached out and touched her arm before she could walk away. Will shifted an inch closer to her, catching Todd's eye for the first time. He raised a brow at Will's hulking form and blank expression. A flicker of disappointment made its way over the other man's face. "Oh. Are you two . . . ?"

"Yes," Will answered firmly at the same time Sarah said, "It's complicated."

The grin came back to Todd's face. "Well, when it becomes *uncomplicated*, you can consider my offer for coffee." She gaped at his boldness, an inherited trait to be sure, since both siblings possessed a knack for catching Sarah off her guard.

"Actually," Will cut in, the muscle in his jaw quivering with annoyance, "we have larger issues at the current juncture and must be on our way this instant. You will excuse us." He took Sarah's hand and guided her away from Todd, whose jaw still hung slack.

Sarah chuckled as she hurried to catch up with his long strides. "You enjoyed that way too much."

His mouth twitched. "Yes, his expression was certainly worth it." His brow furrowed as he turned his gaze her way. "Is that kind of impertinence common here?"

Rolling her eyes heavenward, toward the gray clouds above, Sarah answered drolly, "Unfortunately. Now come on, we gotta get out of here before I—I mean, *she* comes back, since she and Karen should be finishing up soon." She screwed up the left side of her face in consideration as they stepped onto the asphalt of the lot. "That'll take some getting used to."

"Why do we not speak with her? We should warn her about Guy."

"Because," Sarah said. She sighed, realizing she didn't really have an explanation for her paranoia. "I don't know what might happen, which is why I want as little contact with *my* past as possible. I've seen too many movies, but things always go badly if you tamper with the past or meet a former or future version of yourself. I'd hate to find out if those theories are actually true."

Will furrowed his brow, gazing at every car they passed in wonder. "What is a movie?"

"Oh." Sarah paused with the key in her driver's side door. "Like pictures—uh, paintings that tell a story, I guess, but they're always moving and can be about anything. It's like watching real life in this little box, like having your very own theater performance in your house on a small screen. Or big, if you like."

Will looked as amazed as he did confused. Sarah pulled her door open and hiked her skirts to get in behind the wheel. Putting the key in the ignition, she glanced over and found his hand gliding along the doorframe, trying to figure out how she had gotten inside. She reached over and unlatched the door from the inside, and he put his finger in the crevice and pulled it open slowly, folding himself and his long legs into the seat.

"Pull this over your shoulder," she instructed, dragging her own belt across her body and locking it in place. Will searched over his shoulder until he located the metal end, dragging it carefully from its resting place and pulling it forward. "Good, now put that end into this flat gap here." He did so, grinning slightly when it *clicked.*

"What are the restraints for?" he asked, freezing as she started the engine, revving it a few times for it to warm up.

"In case we crash," she answered automatically, then pursed her lips together. "Not that we will."

He nodded slowly and was silent as they drove out of the lot and found their way to the highway. They were both consumed by their thoughts, and Sarah could only imagine what he must have been thinking just then as he watched the frosted landscape blur past.

"It's faster than even my steed," he whispered, then pulled back as his breath fogged the glass near his mouth.

"What?" Sarah asked absentmindedly, pulling herself from her own mind. "Oh, yes, cars are much faster than horses."

Will tapped the window and blew his breath on it again, causing another patch of fog that faded quickly from the glass. He glanced at her. "It's so clear."

"It's glass." She couldn't help smiling at his astonished expression. "You think that's cool, then just press that button—the one with the arrow facing down."

With a single finger, he tapped it and gave a startled laugh as the window lowered an inch and then stopped. He pressed the button and held it until the glass disappeared completely. "Where does it go?" he asked, putting his head half out the open window so he could see in between the seals where it had disappeared.

"Into the door. You can put it back up, if you like."

But he shook his head. "No, I need fresh air." Sarah chuckled. Without looking at her, he reached out and took her idle hand from the center console and held it in his own. "Your world is both incredible and terrifyingly strange," he mused quietly.

Her mirth faded, and she gripped his hand a little tighter. "Yes, it is."

After his reaction, his fascination and acceptance of the modernity of this place, she had been able to convince herself of the possibility of their future—that maybe he *could* fit into her world more than she fit into his. But the more time that went by, the more she realized she was holding onto a delusion that wouldn't last. Will might not realize the full implications of time rifts and split selves and other worlds, and though Sarah understood little of it herself, she knew it meant the end of them was approaching. Faster than she'd ever dreaded.

Tears welled in her eyes, and she bit her lip to keep them from falling. One thing at a time: they had to prevent Demetrius from destroying the machine, *if* he was there already, and then stop Cadius once and for all. Sarah would deal with their relationship later—it was too painful to consider what might become of it just then—but for now she needed to make sure that Will got back home. She loved him too much to jeopardize his safety and his future because she was too distracted by her own emotions to pay attention to what was most important.

After another hour of driving, Sarah pulled off the highway and guided the car down several neighborhoods. A snowplow truck drove by, and Will nearly blocked her view of the street as he leaned over her in an attempt to get a better look as it gathered a wall of snow along the sidewalk.

"Astounding," he murmured.

Biting back a grin, Sarah pulled up along the curb and set her parking break. "Where are we?" His gaze wandered the neighborhood, as though searching for something significant that would explain why they'd stopped.

"My parents' house." Will started and caught her eye, a spark of excitement in his own. Sarah swallowed. "You can't meet them, Will. I haven't really . . . told them about you

His face fell. "Oh. Of course."

"It's just that you're difficult to explain over dinner," she hurried to add. "It's not that they wouldn't love you, but we're crunched for time today." Instinctively, she wanted to assure him that someday he *could* meet her mom and dad and Lilly, but she couldn't make any promises. Although she was tired of vacillating between hope and despair of their fate, it was looking more and more likely that there would never be a reason for him to come back to this place. As it stood, things were complicated enough without adding her parents' concern to the mix.

Her hand hovered over the doorknob, hesitating. She had considered leaving him in the car so she could get in and out quickly, but since this would be the only time he would ever come to her world, she didn't want him to leave without seeing a glimpse of where she'd grown up, as he'd done for her. Especially if it was her only chance to share it with him.

Sarah looked over her shoulder at him. "Do you, uh, want to see my house? I can't take you around too much, because my parents are probably home, but . . ."

His head tilted in confusion. "I thought we had just been to your home."

"I live there when I'm going to school, but this is my home," she replied softly.

Deep blue eyes warmed at her words, and he nodded. "I would love to."

Sarah released a breath, feeling a spark of nervous excitement as she stepped outside. She couldn't exactly say why it mattered so much to her, but her family and this place were a big part of her life, and maybe Will's presence here, for however long, would linger in the days when she would be without him.

By the time she made it around the car, Will had figured out how to open his own door, and together they made their way down the sidewalk.

"Why are we here?" He stepped around a mailbox shaped like a horse's head, looking baffled.

"I need Karen's address. If we're going to stop Demetrius, then we have to know where he's going."

"Ah. Then which cabin is yours?" Will asked, his eyes roving the colored houses along Bethany Lane, some two- or three-stories high. The lane had an ongoing competition for best yard décor this time of year, and Christmas decorations littered nearly every yard. Though it was early afternoon, a few of her neighbors had their timers set to come on—already there were blow-up Santas, animatronic reindeer comprised of nothing but pure white lights bowing their heads up and down, light-up penguins riding stationary sleds, and one yard had a full-fledged manger scene. Even the least festive houses were covered in multi-colored gingerbread lights, icicles, and flashing bulbs that flickered to the rhythm of some unheard tune.

Sarah had become so distracted by the warmth this place filled her with that it took her a moment to remember Will's question. "My house is just a little further down. I didn't want anyone to recognize my car if I parked near the house and try to find me."

"Is this typical of your land?" He looked at her, his eyes raised in astonishment.

Sarah laughed. "Around Christmastime, yeah." At his blank look, she explained, "Christmas Day is December 25th; it's when entire countries honor Jesus' birth with friends and family and gifts." She frowned. "Well, the gifts are more for us, but my family and I always celebrate it as a reminder of the sacrifice He made for us. We usually go to my grandparents' house, but this year with me at school, we didn't have time to travel and are just having some friends and relatives over in a few days for a big party here. It's quite the production."

She was rambling, but Will smiled down at her. "Not many of us celebrate the holiday with such festivities. That sounds like a marvelous tradition."

"It is."

He frowned suddenly, as though something had just occurred to him. "But why do they bedeck their properties so early? I am aware of the date of the celebration, but the year's not yet half past."

Sarah started before she remembered she hadn't told him that time moved inconsistently between their worlds. She was saved from answering as they came upon her house. "This is it." She cut through the grass of the Langdon's property so she didn't walk directly in front of her own—the driveway was empty, but her parents always parked in the garage, which was under a strand of large, multi-colored bulbs that cast blue, green, and red shadows over the pure-white driveway.

Though he was slowed by his interest in the electric bulbs, Will followed closely behind her as she came to the side of the house. Sarah exhaled a sigh of relief that her mom had thought to crack her window open to let some fresh air into her vacated room. The house was on a risen foundation and the window, which was outlined with pale blue lights, came up to her shoulders. She popped the screen out and set it against the side of the house, peering inside her room. Glad to find it empty, she quietly slid the window to the side.

"Give me a boost, will you?" She grabbed his shoulder before he could respond, and Will had no choice but to take her boot and heave her up to the sill. Sarah grunted, maneuvering her skirts through the tight fit, and then emitted a frightened squawk as she lost her balance and tumbled into the room.

Will's face popped through the window above her, aghast. "Are you all right?"

She rolled onto her side with a grimace, hoping no one had heard. "Maybe a bruise or two, but I'll be fine," she whispered, rising to her feet. She looked around her room with a quirked brow. Her mom had done some serious cleaning and organizing while Sarah had been away, which meant that her fall had not been cushioned by a mountain of dirty laundry, or whatever she'd left lying around before she went off to college.

She rubbed her sore hip as Will crawled through with far more agility and grace than she had managed, but then again, he'd had more practice sneaking into places.

"Can you check that box on my dresser?" she asked quietly, pointing to the opposite wall. "There are some keepsakes in there, and I wrote Karen's address down at some point on blue paper."

Because Sarah was the only one living in the modern world where the machine was stored, before she'd left Serimone the last time, Karen had thought it wise that she know the whereabouts of her and the professor's latest home. Sarah had thought it overkill, since she'd believed she would never have a use for it, but she had dutifully memorized the address long enough to come home to write it down. Now she was grateful for Karen's foresight.

Will moved through her room, his eyes taking everything in. Crouching on the floor, Sarah reached under her night table and began sorting through the basket of random letters and cards she'd received the past year. She could hear him moving things around on her dresser. A blue corner of paper stuck out from a wrinkled old envelope, and she pulled it out, smiling to herself to find a Kansas address hastily scribbled on the paper. *Gotcha.*

A door creaked somewhere in the house, and they both froze as Sarah's bedroom door slowly opened. Lilly poked her head through and started when she saw her big sister. Then her expression faded into a smile as she ran into the room and dropped to the floor to give Sarah a bear hug around the shoulders, nearly offsetting her balance.

"Merry Christmas, Sarah!"

With a cringe at the height of her voice and a twist of her heart that said she'd missed her baby sister, Sarah said quietly, "Merry Christmas, Kiddo."

Lilly pulled back with a laugh. "Why are you whispering? Grandma and Grandpa aren't here yet. I didn't even hear you knock, but I'm glad you're home early, because I'm making the gingerbread men today, and Dad says we don't need to do the Hershey Kiss hats, but I know you'd agree that they'd look naked if we didn't, so I wanted to wait to decorate them with you." She frowned as she considered the older girl, whose cringe deepened with every passing moment.

"Can you keep your voice down, Lil?" Sarah asked quietly, rising to her feet, the paper held tightly in her hand.

Lilly's eyes suddenly bulged as she surveyed the open window and the missing screen. "Did you come through the *window*?"

Sarah waved her hands to quiet her. "Yes, because I didn't want Mom and Dad to know I'm here just yet."

"But why not?"

Will's body had frozen in place and his hands hovered, almost comically, over the blue box as they spoke. Sarah considered trying to distract Lilly somehow and get him to jump out the window, but then Lilly followed her gaze and gasped, jumping back a step. "Who are you?"

His gaze flickered between Sarah and her little sister, and no one seemed to know what to do for a time. Finally, Will cleared his throat and took a hesitant step toward her, then gave a curt bow. "My name is William Taylor, Miss Matthews. I am a friend of your sister."

Lilly giggled at his gallantry and then her eyes bugged out once more. She turned her shocked gaze on her sister, who flinched, seeing in her face that she'd just put it together. "He's from that place," she deduced excitedly. Really taking in Sarah's clothing for the first time, she fairly exclaimed, "You've just come from there, haven't you?"

"Shh." Sarah softly closed her door so their parents wouldn't overhear; Lilly's high voice had a way of making words travel far. "Yes, I went back for Karen's wedding."

Lilly's smile could have brought electricity to Serimone. "You told me she was engaged, but I didn't know you were going *back*." She held up a hand, immediately looking inquisitive as she turned her gaze on Will. Her mouth opened and closed, then opened again as she asked, "Then what are you doing here?"

"It's a long story," Sarah hurriedly said, and Lilly frowned at being left out. "One that I *promise* to explain when I get back. I shouldn't be more than a day or two, so Mom and Dad won't even know I'm missing."

Looking reluctant to let them go, Lilly nodded slowly. "Okay. I guess you have to put him back in his world before he meets his future self and time implodes."

Sarah winced. "A bit dramatic, don't you think?" But was it? She motioned Will over and said to her sister, "I'll be back soon with awesome stories, I'm sure." Because they *would* stop Demetrius, and they *would* foil Cadius' plan, and everything would be fine, she told herself.

"He's so tall," Lilly whispered in awe so her sister alone could hear. Sarah smiled to herself as Will came over to help her through the window, being careful this time not to release her arms until her feet were safely on the ground. She looked back inside and saw Will bent over Lilly's hand in farewell.

"It was a delight meeting you, Lady Lilly." She gaped at him like he was a knight on his steed as he hopped over the sill and landed lightly on the snow outside.

"You found it?" he asked as they made their way back to the car. Sarah showed him the slip in her hand, and he nodded. "Well, then, Lady Sarah, I suggest you lead the way."

Chapter Nineteen

"She could no longer borrow from the future to ease her present grief."

Nathaniel Hawthorne, *The Scarlet Letter*

The drive to the Ashmore residence in Wellington, Kansas, would take a little over three hours, Sarah discovered as she keyed in the address into her car's GPS. She sighed, feeling a fresh spark of anxiety at the time that would pass—each minute meant that Demetrius was one step closer to enacting Cadius' plan.

But maybe he hasn't come here yet, she thought with a spark of forced hope, then bit her lip anxiously.

They hit the freeway headed north, with Sarah focusing on the road and Will absorbing every car and sign and overpass they drove by.

"What are you thinking?" she asked after too much time had passed in silence, sneaking a peek at his profile out of the corner of her eye. She could practically feel him processing, but her apprehension was increasing with each mile-marker they passed, and she couldn't stand the total quiet for much longer.

Will gripped the top of the window, which he'd rolled down halfway. "It's a lovely community—the air is even cleaner here."

"Really?" Sarah asked in genuine surprise. "I'd have thought the sheer population alone would make is less pure."

He shook his head thoughtfully, angling his body toward hers. "You don't have much of a forest to freshen the air, but there are no fish markets nearby, nor butcher, nor refuse in the streets." Sarah wrinkled her nose at that. "The smells of dirty living linger in the air of Serimone."

"I hadn't really thought about it before."

After a few more minutes of what was now comfortable silence, Will asked quizzically, "Why did you not wish for your parents to see you?"

Sarah sighed and flicked on her blinker to merge into the fast lane. "Because I haven't told them anything about my little vacations through time."

He nodded silently and then asked, "What we do here or in Serimone—could we truly do irreparable damage, as your sister said and as you've implied?"

Biting her lip, she gave a miniscule shrug. "I honestly don't know if this is the way things have always been or if we're changing history or the future. But we can't take any unnecessary risks."

"Understood. But—" Will paused. His expression turned suddenly open and probing. "But why keep this from me?"

Shooting him a wry look, she replied with, "If you hadn't seen this for yourself, I doubt you would have believed me."

"I might have." But his voice was quieter, unsure.

"Yeah, maybe," Sarah allowed, then she sighed. "It's not exactly the way I wanted you to find out, but I am glad that you know."

Will smiled softly. "As am I. It explains so much and why I found you so fascinating that first day you stumbled into my shop."

"Oh, yeah?" She chuckled. "And how did I make myself seem so intriguing?"

"You had the look of another world about you."

She swallowed at his warm, gentle tone, gripping the wheel a bit harder than necessary. When she glanced up, she saw their exit was coming up and signaled to get over. "We're nearly there," she said, her voice tight.

The GPS guided them off the freeway and to a new housing development in Wellington. Thin, recently planted trees sat in the center of each front yard, shaped like a perfect square, the edges of the AstroTurf perfectly trimmed at the corner of identical cement driveways. Karen and Professor Ashmore had lived there for years, but it didn't appear as though the open fields would be developed anytime soon.

Sarah eased off the gas, her eyes scanning the house numbers.

"1240," Will said suddenly, pointing to a ranch-style house painted a dull shade of beige. Sarah pulled off to the right and parked the car in front of the neighboring house to ease suspicion. Her eyes instinctively scanned their surroundings as they stepped out of the car, looking for any sign of her former professor. But the street was devoid of life.

"Has he arrived yet?" Will asked quietly, his voice cutting through the stillness of the neighborhood.

Sarah eyed the cars parked along the lane, shaking her head. Sucking in a lungful of cold air, she rubbed her hands up and down her arms. "No idea. Let's just hope that we're here first."

"And if not?"

She considered this and then opened the rear door of her car. Reaching into the backseat, she removed the club she used to lock her steering wheel in place; its weight was reassuring in her hand as she closed the door and faced Will. "Then he's already done what he needed to do or we're going to meet him face-to-face."

Will's expression suddenly became that steely, determined mask she had grown accustomed to. He stepped in front of her and made his way slowly up the driveway, his eyes shifting this way and that. Sarah followed close behind, feeling just as mindful of their surroundings as he was.

There was a gnarly, leafless tree in the front yard and overgrown juniper bushes left untended for so long that the brown-and-green overgrowth obstructed the pathway to the door. They had to turn sideways and shimmy through the powder-coated branches.

"What do we hope to gain by beating him to this machine?" Will asked quietly, his words not much more than a white cloud escaping his lips. "Are we supposed to stand guard and fend him off?"

Sarah pursed her lips together as she shoved her way through the tangled junipers, using the club to push aside particularly sharp branches, and she yanked her skirt free when it caught. Her voice was soft but hitched on a high note, her anxiety growing as she considered her plan—or lack of. "Umm, well, I was more focused on getting us here and stopping Professor Demetrius, so I'm really just hoping the machine's pretty compact."

He shot her a quizzical look. "How large is it supposed to be?"

"I don't remember Karen giving its exact dimensions, but I'm hoping 'enormous' isn't bigger than my trunk or backseat." *Oh, Lord,* she whispered, casting a quick look heavenward before returning her eyes to the green- and white-wall before her. *I think we might need your help tonight.*

Will offered her a hand and pulled her free of the bushes. They stood before the door in a 3x3 space where the bushes had yet to reach. He reached for the knob, and Sarah grabbed his forearm. "Wait," she whispered. "It can't be that easy."

"What do you mean?" He watched her as she mused aloud.

"Charles Ashmore is a paranoid, scientific genius hiding ground-breaking technology in his house." As she spoke, her eyes roved the cement slab they stood on, the door, the side of the house. "He has plans never to return but still needs to keep his creation safe for his and Karen's welfare. The professor only wanted to get a first-hand look at history, not change it, and I imagine he'd want to keep it out of the hands of people who'd wish to use it for their own gain."

There was an odd splice in the doorframe, and Sarah ran her fingers over it, feeling metal instead of wood. With baited breath, she dug her nails into the crevice and heard a satisfying pop as the small cover swung open, revealing a hidden circuit board.

"Bingo," she whispered, pleased with her skills of deduction. Her grin faded as her eyes took in the jumble of spliced and disconnected wires and the portion of the green circuit board that looked as though it had been fried. Her grip on the club tightened when she noticed the chips in the paint around the lock, as though someone had used a crowbar to force open the door.

"What is it?" Will asked quietly behind her, leaning close to see the tangle of blue, green, black, and red.

"It's a security system that the professor must have designed to prevent people from breaking in . . . and it's been disabled."

"What does that mean?"

"It means that someone got here first," she answered dully. Heart beating anxiously, she placed a tentative hand on the knob and twisted, pursing her lips when it moved a fraction, the broken lock rattling faintly as she released it.

Will frowned. "Demetrius?"

Swallowing, she said, "I hope not."

They shared concerned looks. "Perhaps I should go through the roof and see if everything is safe," he proposed.

She immediately shook her head and said quietly, "That's gallant of you, but the siding is too slick, and there aren't any windows in the attic. Besides, you won't know what you're looking for or how to get it out; I have to go with you. We're in this together, remember?"

"Together, then," he whispered. At Sarah's nod, he turned the knob, cracking the door open a few inches. He peered inside and then stepped through the door, motioning for her to follow as his eyes scanned the dark foyer. The house was mostly silent, though an eerie creak from the upper rooms made itself heard every few seconds. He closed the door without a sound.

She crept to Will's side along the hardwood floor, feeling gooseflesh break out over her arms. It felt like the heat hadn't been run inside the house in years, and she realized that it probably hadn't.

"It's just the house settling," she said softly, trying to convince herself of that fact. A part of her chastised herself for being so easily disturbed as she was reminded that Professor Demetrius was an *educator*, not a serial killer. But just knowing that he was sent here at Cadius' bidding made him a loose cannon, and Sarah didn't feel the need to run into him and discover just how far his talents reached beyond the school.

"It has to be in the basement," she whispered close to Will's side. He nodded, and quietly they wandered the main level of the house in search of a door or staircase leading down.

The house wasn't large, and they soon found themselves in the sparsely decorated living room, where the unnerving sounds of the house weren't as audible. There was an outdated sofa on the left, a standing lamp next to it, and a piano covered in several layers of dust sitting in the corner on a square checkered rug. No pictures, no television, no board games or magazines sitting on the end table. It was minimalist to the extreme, and Sarah felt a pang in her stomach knowing that Karen had grown up here without much of a childhood. Maybe the upper floor had more signs of life, but after having met the obsessive professor, she doubted it; his mind had room for science only, and she couldn't imagine him thinking of such frivolities as movie watching or game night.

There was a doorway on the wall behind them, the baseboard looking like many a boot had kicked it shut. With a shared glance, Will gripped the greasy knob and turned. They peered down the stairs, which were barely discernible as their bodies blocked the only light coming through the partially drawn blinds.

Sarah gave the light switch a couple flicks before realizing that the house didn't have any power. "After you," she murmured.

He cast her a faint grin and, taking the heavy club from her hand, made his way slowly down the steps. With a wary glance over her shoulder, she lightly trailed behind him, wishing she'd thought to bring a flashlight or her cell phone to brighten the eerie darkness. The air became cooler and seemed to dampen with each step that brought them closer to the bottom. She shivered, squinting ahead, and was just barely able to make out the outline of an open doorway at the bottom of the stairs.

Will saw it too, and his feet stopped on the last step. He inclined his head to the side, listening, and Sarah peered over his head, though she couldn't make anything out inside the room. Not wanting to lose him in the dark, she grabbed the back of his shirt as he stepped inside, following close behind him. She was so focused on what might lie inside the room that she didn't look down to notice the faint but unmistakable red line running the width of the doorway, just a few inches off the ground. Will had unintentionally stepped over it with his long legs, but her skirts caused the wavering line to flicker and disappear, retreating back into the electrical sockets on either side of the doorjamb.

A single, prolonged wail filled the shadowy room, and they both stiffened. Something heavy grated against the floor behind them, and Sarah spun, making out by the faint light upstairs a large metal door sliding over their entrance. She gasped as it *clanked* closed, sealing them in and cutting off any light.

For an instant, they both froze, and then Will was at the door, using the club like a machete and hacking at the door to break it down—little good it did.

"Stop," she said loudly to be heard over the clang of metal-on-metal.

He drew his arm back to his side, panting. "Is this door made of *iron*?" he ground out in frustration.

"I guess the professor had other security measures installed." Sarah felt along the wall near the door, desperate to find a light switch, forgetting that there was no power as her panic heightened with each additional second they spent without light. A barely discernible hiss and crackle reached her ears, coming from somewhere deeper in the room, and she jerked. *Calm down,* she told herself as the sound faded, though her heart rate increased in the oppressive darkness. *Charles isn't malicious and would only want to safeguard the machine, so there won't be anything down here that can hurt us. . . .* She hoped.

Her fingers touched the cold metal of the door, and she felt along the edges, praying for a release switch of some kind. A spark of anticipation jolted through her as she felt the tiny crack of open space, realizing that the old mechanism, probably rusty from disuse, hadn't fully closed the door. The gap was only a sliver—too small for her to fit her finger into and try to jimmy it open, though she certainly tried—but it *was* enough for her to hear the gentle creak of the stairs as someone descended them, taking their time as though they knew their pray had nowhere to go.

She sucked in a breath, a cold sweat breaking out on her neck from the humidity and anxiety. Unable to tear her eyes away from the indiscernible, shifting shadow that was slowly becoming larger, she instinctively reached behind her with one arm, searching for Will but only touching chilly, dank air. Suddenly, a hand pressed against her back, and, nerves taught, her body jerked reflexively.

"I heard it, too." Will's low voice brushed against her ear, and her muscles relaxed a fraction.

The shadow came to a stop just before the doorway, and though she knew they were immersed in total darkness and should be invisible to the newcomer, she took a step back into Will, imagining that the faceless intruder was looking right at her.

"I see you've met with Charles's paranoia." The voice sounded amused.

It took Sarah several beats to register its owner. Her initial surprise passed in an instant as she recalled that Professor Demetrius was the man they had been searching for, had been trying to beat here. She remembered the noises upstairs and knew he'd been there the whole time. The notion caused her to shiver, picturing him stalking them through the house. She wasn't sure if they should play dumb and quiet in hopes that he would leave, though it seemed absurd that they could trick him into thinking the basement was empty after they had triggered the security door. But Will hadn't responded to his remark, either, so she remained silent.

"Created it originally to keep *me* out," Demetrius went on casually, his voice sounding as though he were admiring the door that separated them. "To protect his creation, that is. What an interesting turn of events that it should trap the two people who are trying to halt the destruction of the very thing he loves the most."

Though Sarah was frightened and trapped, she felt a small spark of satisfaction in the fact that as long as they were behind this door with the machine—she hoped it was there, at least—then Demetrius wouldn't be able to touch it.

There was silence on the other side of the door, and then came a dry, amused, "Honestly?" Demetrius chuckled. "I watched from the upper floor as you two pulled up. And you think I didn't hear you come down here? Although I must admit," he added, sounding vaguely impressed, "I *was* a bit flummoxed to see you, Miss Matthews, as I had no notion of your involvement, though your seemingly first-hand knowledge of the Middle Ages has begun to make sense."

Sarah released the pent-up breath she'd been holding, knowing it was useless to pretend. First Damien, and now even her college professor was in bed with Cadius. Who *wasn't* mixed up in this mess?

"Which version of you am I talking to?" She tried to make her voice sound hard, sure, and she cringed at the faint tremor her words carried.

A chuckle. "Ah, yes, it was a bit surprising to come back and find I was already here—*had been* here. But the professor you know has yet to return to Serimone for instructions, though he will soon, I assure you."

Will placed a hand on her back, and she could feel his tension through his fingertips. There was a faint squeak, and Sarah knew his hand had tightened around the rubber handle of the club.

"You know you're on the wrong side, Professor Demetrius," she remarked. Even as she said it, she knew the hope that he didn't realize he was involved with a murderous madman was futile. There would be no reasoning with him.

"Yet I am not the one caught in a snare," he retorted, his accent making him sound both amused and condescending. "No, I believe I'm on the correct side of *this* door."

She ground her teeth, feeling more annoyed than frightened, though somewhere in the back of her mind, she vaguely recalled that she and Will weren't exactly on the sunny side of this circumstance. Although as long as they were in here behind a sealed door, that meant that Demetrius couldn't get to the machine . . . if it really *was* down there with them, a fact that they had yet to confirm in the darkness.

"How did you become involved with Cadius?" Sarah jumped a little at the sound of Will's deep voice so close to her ear.

"Quite an interesting story," Demetrius remarked conversationally, seemingly unimpressed with their knowledge of his connections. "I was at the school several years back, after having been betrayed by Charles"—the sudden, intense bitterness in his voice was startling, ringing out in the darkness before he collected himself—"when I saw a man stumble from the park and onto campus. He was oddly clothed and looked completely distressed by everything he saw. The man confided in me that he didn't belong here and was in his own land when he picked up a watch—a fact that I deduced from his description—and was suddenly transported to this world."

Sarah could hear the smile in his voice when he said, "He was stranded, but I had a watch of my own and told him I would take him back under one condition: that he would share what he had seen in those moments he spent between worlds and that, when the moment was right, he would help me exact my revenge."

His story certainly corroborated with what Cadius had told her and Damien. Sarah blinked at the tiny sliver of light and the shifting shadow just outside the door. "That's it? You're working with Cadius and going through all this trouble—destroying an incredible invention and possibly wrecking your body by traveling with an unstable version of the watch—all because the professor *fired* you for acting like a loon?"

A fist slammed against the door, the metal clang echoing in the stillness. Sarah flinched and swallowed, pressing her back against Will's chest, trying to put a little distance between her and the man on the other side of the door.

"He *destroyed* my career in England," Demetrius ground out. "I managed to track him as far as the state of Kansas in hopes of finding the machine and taking it for my own. An entire life's work and passion, endless hours of research—all lost the moment he threw me out because we disagreed on how the machine should be used. But though I used every resource I had at my disposal, I never discerned his exact location, nor, consequently, that of the machine."

There was a small, sly smile in his voice when he spoke. "But Cadius had seen two possible worlds in which Charles and Karen lived, and I realized that only one of them led to the creation of the machine with which we both could get what we desired."

Sarah sucked in a breath as understanding hit her. "You," she breathed. "You came up with the idea to kill Karen's parents, not Cadius."

"The reality in which they survived left the girl unmotivated." Demetrius' voice hardened as he spoke. "The only conclusion was that she needed *incentive* to assist in Charles's efforts—a little nudge to encourage her to explore her natural talent in the sciences. It was the only way."

Murder. That seemed to be Cadius' answer to everything, too. "Why couldn't you just leave Karen and her family alone?" Sarah asked quietly, steadying her voice when it threatened to quake with anger and sadness over her friend's unnecessary loss. *The greed of man. . . .* "If you had a watch, instead of going through the hassle of getting Cadius back to Serimone and planning a fatal car accident for an innocent couple, why didn't you just go back yourself? You could have traveled to the time when you were working with the professor and stolen the machine and designs yourself. Obviously, it isn't as impossible as we thought to travel back." Sarah pressed her lips together, kicking herself for giving Demetrius an idea he might not have thought of already.

"Ah, but I tried many times after I left. But *it would appear*"—it sounded as though he forced the words out through clenched teeth—"that Charles later designed a safety feature within the machine that affected all functioning watches; they then allowed for travel between worlds, but prevented apparation within a single realm. We could visit the past and return to our own time in the future, but it was never intended for us to alter either one, constantly moving side by side with no room for interruption.

It should have reassured Sarah that, from what he was saying, her presence in Serimone wouldn't change the past. But Cadius had, she was instantly reminded, and though it had been a fluke, there were still too many variables to feel secure. Nothing seemed impossible these days, even altering history.

Demetrius went on, saying, "I searched the house up and down for his original designs so I might correct his lack of foresight, but it appears he has destroyed them."

"Clever alchemist," Will murmured above her, catching on quicker than Sarah would have expected. Louder, he observed, "He made precautions to ensure that you would never be able to change history, wondering all along if you might betray him."

Demetrius chuckled, though there was rancor in it. "Other way around, I'm afraid, lad. He destroyed my career and turned his back on the empire we could have built together, and now I will destroy everything that is precious to him."

Sarah shook her head, confused. "So that's it? The two of you did all this and spent years plotting out your revenge just to come here and stop anyone else from traveling through time? That isn't much of a plan," she said, finding it hard to believe that *this* was Cadius' end game. There had to be more, but she couldn't understand what else he had in mind other than taking over the throne, a theory that had become more muddled the instant she discovered Adrian was his son.

Another low chuckle from Demetrius sent a shiver down her spine, breaking through her distracted thoughts. "Of course not. Cadius has always desired control of Ridlan, and if starting a war is the way to begin the process, then imagine being able to predict your enemy's next move and reverse the clock to anticipate it before he has the thought."

"Wait, no." Though he couldn't see her, Sarah waved her hands in the air, trying to dismiss his words even as a knot of apprehension formed in her stomach. "Cadius told me his watch is no good, and the one that you have is unstable—it would be too risky to keep traveling back days or hours in battle. Even Karen and the professor had to stop before they became too sick to continue—you won't be able to keep it up. *And*," she insisted, "you just said that Charles made it so someone can't keeping going back in history, and destroying the machine would make it impossible to travel in the first place."

She could hear the frown in his voice as she spoke. "Yes, that did present complications to his original plan, which we were forced to revise. However, we soon realized that Cadius' return to Serimone put him amazingly *back* in time, to before he had left, and that one jump allowed him to change nearly two decades. He has already altered all that is necessary, allied himself with and eliminated the right people. We just used time's own momentum and are simply ensuring that no one can undo what Cadius has done."

"You're making a mistake," she tried again, a little desperately. "You don't know what kind of repercussions destroying the machine might have."

"I care not for your theories, I only want the retribution I've been promised." He sounded flippant about the whole thing. "Now, if you'll excuse me, I believe I have to change history. And, it would seem, the future as you know it." Sarah could almost picture him tugging on the end of his sweater in a self-satisfied way, as he did sometimes in the classroom when he was getting ready to share a new piece of information with his students.

Demetrius tapped his finger against the door, as if in contemplation, and the sound was irritating and eerie in the silence that followed. "Ah, yes," he said finally, lowly. "I imagine this should keep you."

Infuriated and terrified, Sarah shouted, "So you're just going to leave us here to die?" It came out as a near-shriek, knowing he planned to do just that.

"Even if by some miracle you found a way to escape and returned to Serimone at some point in history, it wouldn't matter: if you return, you will be found. Cadius informed me the blacksmith is being watched constantly, waiting for a lady—whom I now realize is you—to seek out his help. Then the pair of you would be taken in for questioning, found guilty, and executed, I presume."

Demetrius clicked his tongue in consternation. "My understanding is that the both of you have been quite bothersome to plans that are centuries in the making, comprised of hard work and dirty tasks. Lord Lisandro still lives, as I suspect from your confirmed presence, Miss Matthews, and the fact that Cadius' men were sent to kill the pair of you and only one returned. Lisandro's whereabouts are still *un*confirmed, as of yet, but you should know better than anyone that time erases the impossible."

"So we're dead either way." Sarah's voice was dull, echoing in the quiet basement. That strange *pop-hiss* sounded behind them again, and she pressed her lips against her mounting alarm.

Demetrius' low chuckle caused Will to stiffen beside her, and gooseflesh broke out over her arms. "You were a good student once, Miss Matthews. I believe you should be able to conclude that answer yourself, though I do wish you the best."

"Were a good student." As in past tense. He's already written us off. Sarah shut off that destructive train of thought before it caused her panic to heighten. "And what if we know something you don't know?" She tried to sound confident and coy, hoping he bought her bluff, hoping he didn't test her knowledge right away.

There was a pause on the other side of the door, a long inhalation of breath, and then: "I doubt that very much. But if you do become useful in time, I believe I know just where to find you." His shoes scuffed against the dirt- and dust-crusted cement floor as he turned on his heels and made his way up the stairs, each groaning out a note that plucked Sarah's raw nerves.

Will was stiff and silent behind her, even when the upper door creaked closed, sealing off their only source of light. Then he sprung into action, stepping away from her. She tried not to miss his presence as she heard him shuffling around the outer perimeter of the room, though it was terribly hard not to as she fought back the paralyzing darkness.

"There must be another way out, a trapdoor or secret tunnel—*Ouch!*" He collided with something that fell to the floor with a dull clatter.

Sighing, Sarah shook her head, though he couldn't see. "It's not like Serimone Castle—houses don't just have secret passageways or hidden escapes. People use *doors* here." But as her eyes adjusted to the total darkness, she saw, a foot to the left of the door, a blinking red light about the size of a pea. Squinting, she moved in front of it, a little baffled to find that the basement had electricity. But she reasoned that the professor must have installed a backup generator to keep the machine functioning.

Though the natural light from above had been miniscule through the crack in the door, it had been enough to prevent her from spotting that faint little spec. Feeling around it, her fingers traced the outline of cold plastic, though there were too many buttons for it to be a light switch, and she didn't want to press anything willy-nilly in case the professor *had* booby-trapped the place. Tentatively, she slid her hands along the cold stone wall, hoping against hope that—

"Yes!" She flipped the switch and staggered back a step in surprise, closing her eyes against the light that flooded the basement, feeling half-blind after being immersed in complete blackness. Her eyes adjusted to the light coming from the numerous recessed bulbs mounted into the ceiling. She gave a perfunctory glance over the shelves lining the walls, the worktable with the metal lamp poised over the mass of papers littering the surface, the overturned chair by Will's feet, him blinking rapidly, a bulky object covered in a dust-blackened tarp, and to the left . . .

Her heart dropped to her feet, and she wondered at the prospect of feeling such instant despair. It hadn't mattered that the door had sealed Demetrius off, because the evidence that he had already been down there was before her very eyes.

The machine was smashed to bits. It looked like someone had taken a baseball bat to it, though there were no weapons lying around. Oil leaked onto the floor around the mangled heap of metal that had once been among the greatest inventions in history, designed by an old man and a girl who should not have been orphaned. A spark popped from the exposed circuit board, which explained the faint hissing noise she'd heard earlier. Will jumped at the sound and the tiny burst of flame that came from the smoking hardware, but she felt rooted to the spot. While it had once been the very first working time machine stabilizer, now it was nothing more than a dilapidated mass of broken hopes and wrecked dreams.

Sarah's knees threatened to give way. Not wanting to explain why the sight distressed her so, she averted her eyes as Will examined the mechanical corpse. Instead, she chose to lend a critical eye to the massive, round object obscured by the tarp and the faint pulsing glow beneath. To distract herself with a task, and also driven by her own insatiable curiosity, she pulled the covering away. The heavy tarp slid to the floor, upsetting a cloud of dust that settled all around her, small particles hanging in the stuffy air and clouding her vision. She blinked the grit away and stared in surprise at what she instinctively knew was the first machine the professor had designed, the very first creation that allowed objects to travel between times and realms.

It was covered in layers of dust and grime, and the rounded face of the enormous, bulbous machine that came up to her chest was covered in a confusing array of knobs and short levers and buttons, which carried the faded marks of writing, as though they had been pressed countless times over the years and the words had been rubbed clean. A small hatch stood open a crack, and Sarah imagined numerous office supplies—and one ill-fated guinea pig named Chester—going inside that hatch and finding themselves in a new world.

Her mind was blessedly, though temporarily, distracted by her fascination with the machine as she envisioned Karen and Charles working side by side, him directing her to input codes as he read from his notes that were currently scattered about the desk. There was a round plastic face, about the size of a child's fist, that rose a few inches off the board where Sarah assumed commands were input. The small green bulb under it blinked faintly beneath the hard-packed dust covering the old plastic.

Sarah felt a spark of excitement run through her, only to have it be submerged in an ice bath that was the reminder that *this* machine had never transported human beings anywhere safely—only small creatures and some pencils and paper—and that the one thing keeping her hope alive lay in shambles to her left.

Swallowing hard, she dragged her eyes away from the pain the sight of either machine caused her and moved closer to study what she now realized was a security system in the wall. Her hands shook as reached out to touch the faint red light she'd seen earlier, her mind not on her task at all. She pressed her lips together, closing her eyes.

Don't give up yet, she reminded, though her usually strong inner voice sounded far away, like it had already done just that. Karen had told her that when the machine was down, each watch had one built-in time jump that could get them home to amend the issue. But if the machine lay in an *obliterated* heap and the rusty old model couldn't transport human beings . . . Any previous hopes that Sarah had been clinging to were dashed, just like the brains of that hunk of metal behind her.

Karen had said before that her home was in Serimone, with Seth and his family, and that she never intended to return to her proper time. Sarah knew that once she used her last jump to get her and Will back to Serimone, she could use Karen's—the only other functioning model—to come home, but after that she would have no way of ever returning to their land.

No, she told herself, don't think about that yet.

"Is this what we have been searching for?" Will's voice cut into her tortured reverie, and she sucked in a steadying breath and tried to paste on what she hoped was a neutral expression as she turned.

"Yes." Her voice sounded lifeless, and she cleared her throat.

His look was wary. "And the fire . . . I'm assuming that is not supposed to be there."

Sarah shook her head slowly, eyes fixed on the wasted genius on the floor. "No. We were too late." Tears pricked at the back of her vision, and she quickly focused on the security system again, keeping her back to him. "We had a lock system like this at my house a few years back," she observed aloud, though her voice thickened in a tell-tell way. Will was silent as he came up behind her, and she cleared her throat. "It was a nightmare with two young kids who didn't know how to operate it, so we got rid of it, but it looks like Karen and the professor haven't updated it in awhile." Not that they'd been around *to* do any improvements. "It has an auto-locking system that closes everything up for an hour or two until the right four-digit code is entered or until the police arrive."

"The what?"

Having gained control of her emotions enough that she felt safe to turn around, Sarah caught his confused expression and supplied, "They're like guards. The security system is supposed to keep someone trapped inside until they're caught or keep intruders out long enough for them to give up."

Shaking his head at the absurdity of it all, Will raised a brow. "And we are the intruders."

"But I can't imagine that the professor would want the cops barging in on his experiments while he was away," she mused, "so I'm almost positive he disabled that feature. At least, I *hope* he did," she amended.

Biting her lip, Sarah looked about the room, trying to find some evidence of the code to get them out of here, hoping the professor had used something in plain sight to remind him of the numbers. But the walls and floor were only cement, with no pictures or posters, and the desk was fairly clean, save for the papers with formulas and diagrams scattered about. No obvious codes that she could tell.

"Each time you left, when you went to be with your family or had an emergency that kept you away . . . You were returning to your home, weren't you?"

Face twisting in pain at his quiet musing, Sarah nodded slowly. Knowing it was useless to try thousands of possible combinations when the door would unlock by itself in a few hours, she sank to the floor with a sigh. He dropped down beside her without a word.

"When I left that first time, I wanted to say goodbye to you, but I didn't have any intention of returning—I was supposed to go back to my time and stay there. But then Karen asked for my help again, and I . . . wanted to see you," she finished quietly. "I had left Serimone only a couple weeks before, but when I came back, so much time had passed, and I realized you had moved on."

She jumped at Will's genuine laugh. "I think we both know I had not quite forgotten about you." Then his face fell with sudden comprehension. "But you left for months before you returned. How was it such a short time for you?"

"Karen explained to me once that time moves differently in our worlds, usually faster in one than the other, though it's never completely consistent on which timeline increases." Although she had dreaded the time when Will found out where she came from, it was a relief now to be able to talk about it with him, and it distracted her from their current circumstances. Now she could tell him why she had done things and been absent for so many months and not have to invent poorly crafted stories or family emergencies to convince him of her need to be away.

She shivered against the cold cement, and Will shifted closer to her, draping an arm about her shoulder. She suspected it was both to keep her warm and to feel nearer to her. After nearly a full minute, he said softly, his voice tinged with sadness, "So it could be months before I see you next."

Sarah closed her eyes against the painful welling of salt water. "It could be, or it could be days for you and a year for me." She didn't say just then that with the machine in utter disrepair and neither Karen nor the professor in this era to fix it, this next trip to Serimone to return Will would be her last.

It's too soon, she whispered to herself, then dropped her gaze. It would always be too soon.

He brought his other arm around her and tightened his hold, releasing a shuddering breath against her hair. "I don't like letting you out of my sight for so long."

"Why do you always feel such a need to protect me?" She grinned despite the gravity of their situation and the things Demetrius had said. His heartbeat thumped under her ear when she pressed it against his chest. "I mean, I know I've gotten myself into trouble more times than I care to count, but I'm not going to disappear if you take your eyes off me for a second." Her eye twitched as she fought a grimace, realizing that her disappearance might soon be a reality.

Another long pause, and then Will drew in a deep breath. "Because in Serimone—in my world, people die of disaster and petty accidents, sickness and disease without warning. You accept the fact that when you bid farewell to someone you love, you may never have the chance to see them again. And if your family wasn't directly affected by an instance, then it struck your neighbor and their children, permanently shaking their lives. Death is not as uncommon as it should be, and it never stays its fickle hand for long in my land."

Her heart clenched at his words. What must that be like for him? Disasters struck in the modern world more often than they should, but it was nothing compared to the odds of Will's era, where only half a family's children would survive to adulthood and "old age" was when someone reached their fortieth birthday. In the Middle Ages, starvation wasn't uncommon in poverty-stricken families and disease ran rampant from the uncleanliness of living. How much loss did those people experience everyday?

Placing her hand on the forearm around her waist, she whispered in a tight voice, "I've read that the survival rate was low, but hearing it from you and seeing it first-hand—those people were never real to me before. I didn't understand. . . ." Her words faded, and she closed her eyes.

Will kissed the top of her head. "I know, love, and I hope you never do."

She sighed, her expression bleak as her gaze wandered their temporary prison. "Things aren't looking great right now for us, are they?"

"Haven't we been through worse, my love?"

"What?"

"We have weathered storms and death, you and I. You were nearly lost to Allan's poison and again in that lake—" He paused for a moment, and she gave his hand a squeeze, reminding him that she was still here. Clearing his throat, he added, "And we were meant to burn alive, as well. You can't tell me that you harbor a fear of being briefly sedentary in this basement after all you have overcome."

Sarah was so taken aback that she just stared up at him. Then she smiled, her tiny laugh bouncing against the walls. "I guess you're right."

He drew her tight against his chest once more. "In the morning, things will be different. You shall see."

She sighed again, placing her cheek on his chest. "Since when did you get so filled with faith?" she teased softly.

"The day I met you." Pulling back, she looked up into his face, making out his eyes and soft smile. At her look, he added, "It seems that since that day, one of us or the other has had their life frequently put in imminent peril, which forces a man to acknowledge a Higher Power."

"But you don't believe He cares for *you*," she filled in quietly, knowing exactly what he was thinking. How many times had they had similar conversations, always leaving her dissatisfied?

He caught her hand, trapping it over his heart. "I want you to know—" He inhaled a large breath and let it out in a huff. "I am sure the Almighty exists and aids others, but I have yet to fully realize Him and feel that He would pay me special attention." He raised her hand, kissing the back of it before laying it on his chest again. And, as he had said once before, he added, "This topic always upsets you."

Sarah swallowed and snuggled back against him for warmth. After a few seconds of silence ticked by, she whispered, "I know I sound like a broken record, but He *does* love you, Will, more than you could ever love me, if that gives you an idea of how great it is." Hadn't she said nearly that exact thing to him before? How many times did she need to say it for him to understand?

Leaning his cheek against the top of her head, Sarah felt him smile. Softly, he said, "I very much doubt there is a love that could ever match mine."

She knew it was meant to soothe and praise her, and a small part felt pleasure at his affection. But the rest of her being was filled with heavy sorrow at the fact that he might never know how dearly he was loved.

To change the subject, she remarked, "I guess this place is pretty different for you, huh?"

His soft chuckle echoed in the room. "Yes, your world is a bit estranged from eleven hundred and eighty-two."

"Yeah, well—" A gasp escaped her lips as she sat bolt upright, taking Will by surprise. "It couldn't be that simple," she whispered excitedly, jumping to her feet. Her fingers trembled as they hovered over the keypad. With a deep breath, she typed in 1-1-8-2. A single *beep* emitted from the system, and the red LOCK symbol stayed a steady green. The door slid open slowly, the hideous shriek of rusty hinges the best sound in the world.

She let out a startled laugh and turned to Will, who was rising to his feet slowly, a disbelieving grin on his face. She smiled in return. "Let's get you back where you belong."

Chapter Twenty

"And I'd choose you; in a hundred lifetimes, in a hundred worlds, in any version of reality, I'd find you and I'd choose you."

Kiersten White, *The Chaos of Stars*

They jogged up the basement steps and into the fading light of day outside the Ashmore's home. Sarah hesitated at the curb, eyes scanning the nearly deserted lane until she spotted an empty plot set behind the other homes and headed across the street toward it. Will came up beside her. "Would it not be more expedient to follow him in your car?"

Shaking her head, Sarah answered, "I'll pick it up later." She didn't mention that this next time, she'd be coming back alone. "I don't want too much time to pass, and I bet Demetrius transported the second he found a spot private enough." She felt a sinking in her gut as she tried to count back. How long had they been trapped down there? An hour, maybe more? It was still too much time, and who knew what kind of a head start Demetrius had in Serimone—perhaps a day had already passed there.

The thought caused Sarah to move a little quicker down the sidewalk, and she moved between the silent houses, their boots crunching in unison against the icy snow. Behind the houses was nothing but undeveloped land stretching on for at least a mile, only a field with the frame of a house or barn just beginning to rise in the distance. The skeleton of the soon-to-be building sat twenty feet back from a thin, willowy tree that stood like a lone sentinel on the piece of land.

Sarah tucked herself behind it, waiting for Will to follow before pulling her sleeve back. "Would we not have more cover near one of those cabins?" he asked.

The tree did little to conceal them, so she understood his concern, but Sarah shook her head. "I don't want to be too close to somebody's house in case something goes wrong."

"What could possibly go wrong?" His innocent question turned her stomach. Now that the machine was destroyed, there was no telling how bumpy their return trip to Serimone would be, and she didn't want to accidently suck a family—and their home—back to the twelfth century in a terribly *Oz* moment. Unless, of course, the house landed on Cadius, then that would be an entirely different story.

Instead of answering, Sarah asked her own question, her hand hovering over the watch. "You ready?" Will nodded silently, and she pressed the small dial on the side.

Instantly, she knew something was wrong.

It was worse than ever, that feeling of being split from her body as the white light burst forth, blocking out all else as it consumed them. The dull roar was still there, as it always was, but this time it felt like an ear-splitting wail that was wracking Sarah's senses. Then she realized *she* was the one screaming. Dully, she registered the fire-like burn that coursed through her veins as her body was broken down against its will and every law in nature. Above the rushing in her ears, she heard Will cry out beside her, and she reached for him but found nothing to cling to.

She gripped her side where the pain was, closing her eyes against the splotches of white-hot light that danced across the backs of her lids. With the stabilizer destroyed, whatever ability to transport humans that remained in the mechanics of the watch didn't seem to be enough; instead of some fantastical journey through worlds that held a little bit of wonder and magic in the feat of what she was doing, it felt as though Sarah's body was being dragged through a bog, slow and unwilling, as it was wrenched this way and that, each movement painful. Her head felt muddled, and her veins seemed to be filled with fire, pulsing it through every limb. Each breath that she managed to drag into her paper-thin lungs burned like she was choking on acid.

Sarah was thrown to the ground as blackness slammed into her, bringing with it total silence, save for the lingering roar in her ears that was already beginning to dissipate. Eyes still closed tight, she retched, her stomach giving up nothing but her mind begging her to do something to make the stress on her body cease. She choked, dragging in ragged breaths as she opened her watery eyes. The intense pain had disappeared nearly the second the light went away, but the memory of that horrible trip wracked her body, refusing to fade, lingering in the form of aching limbs and a quivering stomach. Her pulse thumped uncomfortably in her feverish cheeks.

Swallowing hard, she glared at the sunlight overhead as her senses returned to her and her ears began to register sound once more. She could hear traffic nearby, children laughing, someone shouting out a greeting to a friend, a dog or two barking somewhere in the distance. Her hand instinctively reached for Will before she realized what she was doing, and when she felt nothing, her head jerked to the left, searching. The abrupt action caused her head to pound terribly, but that fact was lost on her in the absence of his presence.

Heart thumping in her chest, Sarah rose on shaky legs, eying the swing set in the distance, the children playing on the monkey bars, their parents sitting on benches, the autumn leaves scattered over the grass. The scene wavered around the edges, as though it was playing on an old projector, giving this place a dreamlike quality, like it wasn't quite real. She swung around, taking in her surroundings and the fact that she had no idea where—or *when*—they were. At least, she hoped Will was somewhere around here. The thought that he might have landed in another place or time sickened her.

She stumbled forward, blindly hoping to somehow run into Will in the grassy area, but she had no idea where to start. Was he safe in Serimone? That was a best-case scenario, and she imagined him in some random timeframe with no way of finding her or returning home, stranded, confused . . . alone. She could never forgive herself if her foolishness led to the destruction of his life. And she'd have no way of knowing what happened to Will unless she *found* him.

Her feet stopped almost of their own accord, planting themselves firmly in the grass an instant before she realized her eyes had caught on something across the way. She couldn't say what made her stop and stare at the woman whose back was to her, but there was something about her that pulled at Sarah, stirring awareness in her for no rational reason. But then the woman turned around, and Sarah felt the world stop as she glimpsed another version of herself.

It wasn't like earlier that day, where she had known she was on campus and what her former self was going to do the next instant. This woman appeared a little older, more mature than anything, really, as though she had lived more of life than Sarah had in her eighteen years. Maybe she was in her late twenties now, bouncing a contented baby on her hip and laughing at the antics of a dark-haired child as he squealed on his way down the slide. It was difficult to judge her age exactly, since we can only ever see a mirror reflection of ourselves and never the *real* thing—an exact living version of herself that looked the same and yet not. What was this place?

Everything listed to the right, though the woman and the children continued on as though the world wasn't tipping onto its side. Sarah's knees weakened, gut flipping along with the sinking and tilting of the scene before her. Or maybe she was the one falling onto her side.

She squeezed her eyes closed, gripping her stomach as she rolled over, head feeling like it was spinning on her shoulders. Somehow, she managed to rise to her knees, blinking as her vision blurred.

Hands gripped her shoulders, and she jerked her eyes open to find Will staring down at her. "Thank heaven. I thought I'd lost you again." He dropped down beside her, face drawn in a mixture of concern and relief.

Feeling shaken by what she had seen and what she still had questions over, Sarah shook her head quickly, trying to keep him from spotting what she had. But his gaze had already moved over her hair, and she whipped her head around in alarm, surprised to find that their surroundings were turning to soup.

The scene of Older Sarah and the two children, and everything else around them, was strange and distorted now. It was like watching melting candle wax or a wet painting that had been doused with a bucket of water, causing all the colors to drip down the canvass in a strange, deforming fashion. The noises around them became garbled, like they were underwater, and Sarah's legs started to feel like Jell-O. A loud clap emanated from all around them just as a new frame slammed into place and fanned outward, taking over the sweet melting park with that blinding light.

Will hurriedly wrapped his arms around her, as though afraid they might be separated again. When the unearthly noise no longer reverberated in her chest and her head felt like it was void of cotton balls, Sarah tentatively opened her eyes, shock and relief causing her to sag against him as she recognized Glendale Forest.

Pulling back, Will placed a hand on either side of her face, examining it. "Are you all right?"

She nodded silently, though her response was false.

He exhaled in disbelief. His face was pale, and his hands shook as much as her own did. The final lurch into Serimone hadn't been as painful as the trip to that in-between world where Sarah had seen her future self, but it had felt entirely unnatural—more so than usual, that is.

"What *was* that?" he asked.

Clearing her throat, Sarah answered honestly, "I won't really know until I talk with Karen. I'm assuming that because the machine was destroyed, travel isn't as smooth or easy as it once was; it was like we couldn't break down properly and the watch didn't know which world to drop us in." She didn't mention the fact that there wasn't supposed to have been *two* versions of herself running around or that she had seen a glimpse of her own future; it would only cause more questions, ones that she didn't have answers to.

"That was—" Will shook his head. He stared at her with wide eyes.

"A lot to process, I know." She exhaled and glanced around them. "I promise we'll talk about this later and get all the answers we can from Karen, but right now we have to find a way to stop Demetrius from getting back to Cadius and from them finalizing whatever plan they have in mind to start a war with Ridlan."

She frowned, wondering what the point was, anyway, now that the machine was destroyed. Cadius had already gotten what he wanted, though she reminded herself that there were still some loose ends he intended to tie up. She considered what Demetrius had said about Cadius' desire to seize control of Ridlan, but how would he even do that?

A sudden, dreadful thought filled her mind, and she grimaced in distaste. "And Charles. Now that keeping him around is no longer useful and their plan is coming to an end, I'm worried he'll be next on their list. What do we do to stop them?" she asked a little helplessly.

Will followed her shift in priorities, offering up, "The quickest way would be to go directly to King Adrian before we do anything else. Cut the snake off at the head, so to speak."

Nodding, Sarah agreed, "You're right. Cadius can't do anything if the king is expecting an attack on himself or with Ridlan, and with his resources, hopefully we can track Cadius and Demetrius down before they can enact whatever remains of their plan."

They were reacting purely on instinct now—Cadius was the bad guy and needed to be stopped, and they intended to do just that—but what could he possibly have in mind next? She felt like he had exhausted the majority of his plan and was already on the run from the king, but he had shown time and time again that he would stop at nothing to bring about his endgame, whatever that might be. The fact that they didn't yet know what that was unnerved her.

"So we're in agreement that we go to the king first?" Will clarified.

"It's the only way. He's made sure that no one can change the past or future now that he's done what he wants with it. And I still feel like Cadius will come after the king; I think he plans to kill Adrian and take control of his resources to start a war with Ridlan, and then overpower the small city to control its weapons forges. Though knowing Adrian's his son . . ." She sighed, feeling unsure about nearly everything just then. "I just don't know what his next move is, which makes me want to tell the prince *right now*." She turned around, and Will caught her arm.

"Wait." She stared up at him in confusion. Gently, he said, "You know it has to be me."

Sarah blinked, feeling a little hurt when she realized he was thinking of leaving her behind. "You want to go alone?"

"If Cadius is watching the castle and sees you there or in town—"

"But he's got it out for you, *too*," she reminded.

"Let me worry about that." He gave her a faint smirk, and she somehow knew he was planning on sneaking into the castle. "I am not as high on his list of priorities as you are. And as soon as King Adrian knows about Cadius and the fact that he seduced his mother Alexis, lied about his heritage, while also reminding him that he killed the only father he ever knew, then I don't believe anything would stop the new king from ensuring that Cadius sees the grave this time."

Sarah hated to admit it, but it did make sense that he should be the one to go. There was just one problem with his plan. "Where should I go in the meantime?"

"Oh." Will frowned. In the perfect silence that followed, they both heard the far away but unmistakable sound of a sudden heated argument.

With a shared look, they quietly moved through the thick underbrush. Up ahead in the fading light, they could just make out two figures clad all in black, one holding a sword menacingly toward a lone man. His hands were behind his head in an act of submission, his brown hair falling over his eyes.

"I said *on your knees*!" The man's sword slashed through the air, and the brown-haired man had to jump back to avoid the blade catching him across the chest.

"Let's not be hasty gentlemen." Sarah sucked in a breath at the sound of Damien's nervous chatter and mock bravado. She tugged on Will's sleeve, pulling him forward, and mouthed Damien's name to him, unknowingly carrying a pleading look in her eyes. Will appeared surprised, and then his shoulders sagged in displeasure, knowing what she was asking even before she was fully aware of it. She wasn't exactly asking him to save Damien, but she couldn't just walk away while he was in danger.

"From one thing to the next." Will's words were so quietly muttered that she had to strain to hear him, but it was true; he had just returned from a shocking trip to the future only to come back home and have to save his enemy. With a sigh, he pulled free of her grasp and instinctively reached over his shoulder for an arrow that wasn't there. He frowned as he quickened his pace, despite his lack of defense.

"Wait, no!" she whispered harshly. He held a finger to his lips as he moved ahead of her through the trees, crouching low as he circled up behind the men. Sarah tried to follow quickly, but she wasn't nearly as practiced as Will and was slowed in her attempt to keep quiet.

The one with his sword still sheathed came up behind Damien, grabbing his joint hands at the back of his head and kicking him behind the legs. With a grunt, Damien fell to his knees, gritting his teeth as his head was jerked back and a knife was pressed to his throat. "The master sends his condolences that he couldn't be here to finish ye off himself," the man hissed near his ear, loud enough for Sarah to hear. He spat onto the ground at his captive's boots.

"Oh, well, that is a shame." Damien's casual tone was forced. "Shall we wait for Cadius to join us before we proceed? Although it *is* a tad muddy down here, and I could use a stool or even a crude carpet to sit on, if it isn't too much of an impertinence."

The man laughed, a sick, menacing sound low in his throat. The action caused the scar that ran from his lip to his ear to stretch, turning his grin into a grotesque sneer. "Ye'd be one of them loose ends he wants to shore up, and I don't think he'd take too kindly to us forcin' a sit-down between the two of ye."

All pretense gone, Damien glared at the man across the way, though his words were directed to the scarred brute at his back. "You are aware that I was once in the same position as you two parasites, shoring up Cadius' 'loose ends,' as you called it. How long do you think it will be before you find yourselves in the same position I am in now?"

Both men frowned, and Damien cringed as the knife was pressed deeper against his throat. "Let those be yer last words, *m'lord,*" Scarface jeered lowly. Damien closed his eyes, lips pursed.

A branch snapped beneath Sarah's boot as she rushed past Will in her sudden haste to reach the bound man. She froze as the sound echoed like a gunshot in the quiet forest, and every head snapped her way. Damien's eyes widened, and Scarface appeared momentarily stunned by her presence. But the other man reacted quickly, gripping his sword as he took several threatening steps toward her. Sarah retreated a few feet, keeping her eyes on his gleaming weapon.

Will burst out of the trees then, a short knife suddenly in hand, temporarily drawing all attention his way. The man holding Damien was distracted long enough for his captive to shove the knife away and jerk an elbow into his rib cage. Scarface doubled over, gripping his side as Damien lurched to his feet, grappling for control of the weapon.

The other man held his sword out toward Will, who circled him slowly, his dagger no match for the massive steel sword. And judging by the man's cocky sneer, he knew it, too. He reacted first, lunging forward and slicing his weapon in an arc that would have gutted Will had he not quickly dropped into a roll beneath the swinging blade; it passed over his head, going too wide for the man to correct its path in time.

Will came up on the man's other side and, before he could react, slammed the hilt of his knife into his temple. The man's legs gave out beneath his weight, eyes rolling into the back of his head as he crumpled to the ground at the base of a tree. Will prodded the unconscious man with the toe of his boot and received no response.

Sarah was so focused on making sure that Will bested the man that she hadn't realized Scarface had overpowered Damien off to the right and had come up behind her. Damien rolled onto his side with a groan as the man's arms circled around her shoulders, and she ground her teeth, shocked and annoyed that he had snuck up on her.

At some point in the skirmish, Damien must have managed to get the man's sword free of its sheath, and he quickly jumped to his feet now, shaking his head as if to clear it and pointing the weapon at the man who held her. He and Will advanced cautiously. Scarface stiffened, and the tip of the knife pressed deeper, breaking skin. Sarah gritted her teeth as a trail of blood ran down her neck.

Will stopped abruptly, but Damien kept coming. The man's gripped tightened about her shoulders, and the blade shook uncomfortably against her neck. She flinched as it scraped the tender spot on her skin. "I'll kill her."

"You idiot," Will hissed at Damien, raising his hands in a submissive gesture, though he still had a grip on his dagger. "Hold your ground."

Damien's angry, calculated gaze rested on Sarah's pained features, and he quickly halted, albeit reluctantly.

They were at a stalemate. The men couldn't come any closer because Scarface might harm her, but her captor couldn't kill his only bargaining chip.

Okay, Matthews, you can do this, she coached herself. During senior year, she and her friend Janice had taken a class in self-defense at the urging of their parents, who insisted it would make them feel more reassured with their daughters going off to different colleges and living on campus. They hadn't taken it very seriously at the time and had goofed off for the majority of the tutorial, but Sarah had paid attention to a particular hands-on portion she'd been coached in: How to break your captors hold from behind. She couldn't have been more grateful for that training now, her lips barely moving as she mentally ran through the steps.

"What do we do now?" Will asked diplomatically, keeping his hands in the air. "I can't allow you to take her as your hostage, and I know you wish to walk away from this. If you release her, you can, and neither myself nor this man"—he flicked a hand in Damien's direction—"will try to stop you."

His gaze darkened at the man's scoff, and his foul breath brushed her cheek. "Or you could take your chances and run, but rest assured I will gut you before you take three steps."

As he talked, Sarah positioned her feet a little wider on the ground as she slowly slid her fingers beneath Scarface's forearm. He didn't seem to notice, too distracted by his contemplation of the situation he'd gotten himself into and his consideration of Will's words. But she didn't care to wait for his decision.

Taking a deep breath, she used her hands to break his hold about her shoulders, pulling hard in a downward motion to give her the freedom to quickly reach over and wrench the hand holding the knife far from her throat. He was caught off-guard by her force, and Sarah yanked his arm straight over her shoulder and bent his wrist back at an uncomfortable angle. His howl of surprise ended in a winded gasp as she drove her elbow hard into the tender spot of his ribs that Damien had wounded just moments before.

He dropped to his knees, and she jumped away from him as the men surged forward. Will's expression was a mixture of shock and pride, and Sarah felt a flicker of a grin on her lips, just as surprised as he that her brief training a year ago had actually paid off.

Damien reached him first and jerked the man's arms behind his back. Scarface hissed. "Stings, doesn't it?" Damien ground out as he pulled just a little harder, and the man's face whitened.

"Don't be hasty." Will advanced, shaking his head, his look severe. "We need him conscious."

Damien glared at him, though he loosened his grip. "Are we working together now, blacksmith?"

The man's face lit with sudden recognition, and he grinned at Will. "I thought I recognized ye. We've all been takin' turns watching yer place and shop, hoping for the lady to turn up." His laugh turned a little desperate and crazed as Damien pulled back an inch, his expression stony. This time Will didn't correct his rough treatment.

"How long do ye think ye all can last?" Scarface's voice was tense and cracked with pain. His beady gaze flickered between Sarah and Will, though they knew Damien was included in the conversation. "The master has ev'ry man at his disposal lookin' for ye lot, and he won't stop 'til every last one of ye is dead."

"He's tried that before, as you'll recall," Damien said mockingly through gritted teeth. "Yet here we are, living and breathing." Will's eyes were dark, his expression blank except for the pulsing at his temples as he watched the man.

Unable to unnerve either of the men, Scarface turned his head toward Sarah, careful not to disturb Damien's hold on his arms. His eyes were wide and desperate, and though his position was rather bleak at that moment, rattling their courage seemed to be his only defense. "And what of ye, girlie? Yer his true prize. Ye might kill me today, but there are countless others who would take my place. The master won't rest until yer six feet underground—"

Will rammed the hilt of his knife into the top of the man's skull, silencing him. He appeared momentarily stunned and wavered on his knees, then suddenly dove face-first into the ground as Damien released him. He lay motionless at their feet, and Damien gave Will a look that was a mixture of mock condemnation and amusement. "I thought we needed him conscious."

"We don't anymore." Will's jaw flexed as he stared down at the man. A drop of blood slid down over the fiend's temple.

"I thought *I* had issues," Damien muttered, his easy grin coming out just then. He appeared to enjoy the fact that Will had lost his temper.

"How did you manage to get yourself caught, anyway?" Will asked, quirking a brow as he regained himself.

Damien's mirth quickly faded, and he glared at him. "You must forgive me for not having wasted my youth sneaking around dank sewers and learning to silently scale trees like some barbarian."

Will advanced a step, fists clenched. "Some of us had to learn useful skills instead of riding on the murderous success of others."

"Oh, shut *up*, both of you," Sarah fairly shouted. They gaped at her in surprise, and she pointed at the two bodies they appeared to have forgotten about. "We need to talk about what to do with them, once you guys are finished flexing your muscles."

"Leave them." Will shrugged, recovering first from her outburst.

Damien looked reluctant to let him take the lead in the decision-making process. "Won't they report back to Cadius as soon as they regain consciousness?" he asked condescendingly.

"And what would they say?" Will countered. "Cadius already knows we are all alive. All they can report is that they saw us in the forest and were overpowered. Are you suggesting we kill two men in cold blood while they sleep?"

Damien's shoulders seemed to stiffen in indignation. "No, I am not."

"Then we are agreed." Inhaling deeply, Will let out a high-pitched whistle that caused Sarah to jerk in surprise. To her, he said, "What we need to decide on is where to go next. Obviously, we cannot return to my home just yet, and I don't wish to leave you alone when I go."

"Making travel plans, Taylor?" Damien seemed far too pleased with the idea, but they ignored him.

"I could go with you, you know," Sarah suggested.

"We both know it would be simpler if I go alone," Will reminded her quietly, trying to keep the other man out of the conversation. "It is far easier to sneak one person into the castle than two."

"I'll hide out somewhere for a time, then. I can take care of myself."

A small smile played at the corner of his mouth as his gaze landed on the man near their feet. "So I've noticed."

"Sarah should come with me." Both their heads whipped around at Damien's words.

Will's eyes narrowed at him. Through gritted teeth, he said, "That will not happen." He turned back to Sarah. "You could stay with Thomas."

But she shook her head. "If they're watching you, they'll be watching your uncle." She hated admitting it, but the truth of it was impossible to ignore.

"What about the Seth and Karen, or the Joneses?"

Sarah didn't see the problem with this plan and opened her mouth to agree, then snapped it closed at Damien's amused chuckle. "It took me all of two days to discover who Sarah's acquaintances were. You don't believe that Cadius has done the same, perhaps before I myself thought to look for them? The only place he *isn't* having watched is my refuge, because they have yet to discover where I have been staying."

Will looked annoyed at the interruption, but then his gaze wavered; he actually appeared to be considering his words.

They all turned at the sound of thrashing in the bushes, and Sarah's pulse slowed as a dark stallion emerged from the thicket. It quickened into a canter when it spotted its master, prancing nervously near Will. He rubbed it between the eyes in a soothing gesture, and it let out an anxious shriek at being left alone for so long. The man "napping" in the shade of the tree moaned but didn't wake at the sound, though he would soon.

"Time is running out, blacksmith," Damien taunted when he was silent too long.

Will's eyes narrowed, and Sarah sighed. "Don't provoke him."

"But he knows I am right." The cockiness had faded from Damien's face, and his expression was all seriousness now. "You know as well as I that the only safe place for her right now is with me."

Will's keen gaze assessed him, and the pulse below his jaw throbbed underneath his skin. "He's right." The words were low and choked, as though he'd had to force them out. His hand dropped to his side, and the animal exhaled loudly in protest.

"You're agreeing with him?" Sarah asked, appalled that he was suggesting she return with Damien and annoyed that her—sort of—grand escape from Jade's cabin had been in vain.

Sighing at her obvious displeasure, Will said, "You heard Demetrius; they haven't found where Lisandro is hiding, though everyone we know is being watched until we slip up and show ourselves. Though it pains me to say it, wherever he is might be the only safe place for you right now." The words appeared to leave a poor taste in his mouth, and he swallowed.

Sarah reluctantly admitted to herself that he was probably right, but still. . . . "So you're asking me to *willingly* go back with him? After he drugged and kidnapped me?"

His nostrils flared, and it looked like he was trying very hard not to look at the other man. "God help me, but yes. I believe his twisted regard for you to be genuine, and I know we both have the same goal in mind, and that is keeping you out of Cadius' hands." His steady gaze landed on Damien. "Isn't that right?"

"Of course." Damien looked offended and irritated at Will's underlying suggestion that he would risk her safety.

Will just watched him for a moment longer, his eyes narrowing as his expression darkened. "Good, because if any harm comes to her under your care, I *will* end you, Spaniard. Make no mistake."

There was no pretense in Damien's features as he nodded. "My only thought is for her protection."

Seemingly satisfied, Will turned to Sarah and wrapped her in a crushing embrace. "I will come for you when it's safe," he whispered against her temple.

"If the guards were unsuccessful in uncovering our whereabouts, what makes you think you will be able to find us?" Damien asked. Will had given an inch in admitting that Sarah would be the most protected with him, and clearly he wasn't ready to let him forget it.

As if Sarah had been the one to present the question, Will pulled back slightly, brushing his thumb over her cheek. Quietly, he said, "I *will* find you." His eyes were intent, full of promise, and Sarah felt the tiniest bit of her trepidation fall away, though the majority of her fear still clung to the edges of every thought.

Slowly, she nodded. She reached into her sleeve for the letter, but Will touched her elbow. “Keep it for now. In case . . . Just in case.” *In case I don’t come back, he’d meant to say*. If he wasn’t able to get to the king and warn him, then he didn’t want the evidence to disappear with him.

Sensing her fear, Will leaned down to give her a gentle, lingering kiss, and then her eyes bulged as he lifted her up so she was sitting side-saddle on the back of his horse. She gripped the horn with suddenly clammy fingers, still wary of the great beast. She’d ridden the animal with Will before at break-neck speeds as they’d fled Damien and the royal guard, but he wasn’t coming with her this time, and that old fear slipped through once more. “But what about you?”

His hand resting on her knee, he nodded over his shoulder. “The castle isn’t too far off, and I would rather you have the horse.” The barest flicker of a secretive grin passed over his lips just before he whispered, “I can track my steed’s shoes anywhere.”

Sarah bit her lip to hide her responding grin, and he gave her knee a reassuring squeeze before releasing her. As Damien passed him on his way to the horse, Will grabbed his arm suddenly. Damien cast a casual glance down at the hand that held him in place and then up at its owner.

“Protect her at all costs,” Will said lowly, “or I will finish what I started in the woods that day.”

Damien jerked free of his grasp, though his expression wasn’t angry. Actually, he looked rather sad. “I care for her as you do and will guard her with my life.”

That seemed to pacify Will somewhat, and an unreadable look passed between them before he nodded. They still hated one another, that much was certain, but they appeared to have come together in agreement on one thing: they loved Sarah and wanted to see her safe.

Damien threw himself into the saddle behind her and grabbed the reins. He didn’t huddle smugly against her, as she had expected, but rather kept a respectful distance, sitting as stiff as a board in the saddle. To Will, he said, “Do what you must, Taylor, and know that I will ensure her safety until you return to claim her from me.”

Chapter Twenty-One

"Blot out his name, then, record one lost soul more,
One task more declined, one more footpath untrod,
One more devils' triumph and sorrow for angels."

Robert Browning, "The Lost Leader"

Dusk had settled thick and heavy by the time Damien halted Will's stallion beside the cabin. He helped Sarah down, though she barely noticed that she was moving off the horse as she chewed her lower lip, wondering how things were progressing at the castle. Was Will inside? Had he told King Adrian? Maybe the king had already sent out a search party to stop Cadius. The thought filled her with some hope as she reentered her former prison and helped to stave off the oppression she might have felt just then.

Jade sat on the couch, patching a hole in a shirt that must have been Damien's. She glanced up, and her look of indifference instantly turned to one of annoyance as Sarah filed in behind her brother.

"Oh, honestly!" she cried in frustration. Stabbing the needle into the fabric, Jade dropped it into a pile on the floor and threw her hands into the air, looking completely exasperated. Apparently, she wasn't happy to see Sarah return after having helped her escape. "I don't know why I bother." With a huff, she stomped off to her room and slammed her door.

"Glad to see she hasn't changed while I've been away," Sarah muttered to no one in particular, though she felt a pang of guilt as she recalled how Jade had helped her—whatever her motive might have been.

Sarah fingered the watch on her wrist mindlessly, her thoughts turning to Serimone Castle.

"So what grand business does the blacksmith have in town today?" Damien asked, his mockery barely detectable as he removed his cloak and tossed it onto the couch.

"If you *must* know," Sarah replied in a rather self-satisfied tone, snatching an apple from the basket on the short counter. She took a bite, flinching at the mealy texture, though she was too hungry to reject it. "Will should be at the castle now, letting it be known that Cadius is still alive and is Adrian's father, and also that there is another heir. Which means I should be out of here before nightfall when Cadius is captured and executed. Again," she added, as though it were a small detail. She grinned around another bite, feeling like a winner. Soon they wouldn't have to look over their shoulders, and it would finally be *over*.

Damien's head shot up. "Taylor is going to speak with the royals on this matter?"

She nodded, not quite understanding the alarmed look in his eyes. "Well, just the prince—*king*. He's going to sneak in past the front guards, hopefully undetected by Cadius' men, and request an audience with King Adrian. Will has to tell him that Cadius might be coming for him next. As soon as the new king hears everything, we'll finally be safe." She had only been on the run for a couple days, but the idea of being able to go outside or travel the land without worry of Cadius hacking off her head sounded almost too good to be true. They had spent months tracking his schemes, and she felt eager to put the chapter of her life involving Cadius to rest for good.

She pushed aside the reminder of the fractured machine and her lost ticket to ever come back here, focusing instead on the good for now.

"It will make no difference."

Sarah pulled back in surprise as his softly spoken words and dismal tone broke into her idyllic reverie. "Are you kidding me? As soon as it's discovered that Cadius is *still alive* after he killed the former king, then King Adrian won't spare any effort to find him and have him executed. Permanently, this time."

His lips turned white as he pressed them together. Damien swallowed hard, looking as though he were fighting within himself. He closed his eyes, his head drooping toward the ground. "You had to tell me this. . . ."

"I don't get it." Sarah waited until he raised his head, and her excitement sank a little at the look of pain and indecision on his face. Warily, she asked, "What aren't you telling me?"

He exhaled slowly, seemingly releasing whatever was holding him back from speaking. His eyes were dull, his voice reluctant. "If he goes to the king with this information, he will not have to concern himself with Cadius finding him: He will be sentencing himself by playing right into his hands."

"I already said that Cadius wouldn't even know he was there—"

But Damien was shaking his head, eyes suddenly imploring. "I told you he has eyes everywhere, but can you not see? That day in the wagon and countless other times—it was why I told you to keep your theories a secret, why I feared you would reveal them to the wrong people. Surely if . . ." He nodded once, slowly, as though coming to a realization. "Ah, yes, I forget you did not read my letter."

"Can you not speak in riddles for a second!" Sarah snapped, pulse quickening in dread. She set the apple on the counter and clenched her fists, sounding calmer when she asked, "Now, what do you mean Will's in trouble?"

"Just that," he admitted grudgingly, then he sighed. "Yes, Cadius was the mastermind behind the entire plot, and he arranged the murder of the king." He paused, as though the words were difficult to form. A muscle in his jaw spasmed as he seemed to take a moment to decide on something, and then he met her eyes. The look of sympathy in them stopped her heart. "But if the blacksmith goes forth with this information, it will mean his death sentence. And since they know of your association, yours as well." His jaw clenched.

"But *why*?"

His voice softened, as though he didn't wish to tell her something she would not like to hear. "Because King Adrian already knows that Cadius is his blood-father."

"No, that's—why hasn't he said anything?" she breathed in shock, then shook her head quickly. "But it shouldn't matter that Will tells him something he already knows. Once he informs the king that Cadius is alive and still trying to see his sicko plan through, then he'll be forced to do something with him. He can't just let a murderer go free!" she said, a little desperately.

Damien lowered his voice, as though it would help her see reason. "He can and he will. Cadius carried out the plan, but it was King Adrian who ordered the death of the king."

Sarah felt like she'd been punched in the gut, and the apple turned sour in her stomach. "No, but . . . he couldn't have."

"But he did." His tone was gentle, and he looked like he wanted to touch her and offer comfort, though he didn't. "Cadius earned the prince's trust and told him that he had sired him, how much he had loved his mother when Josiah had not. He slowly corrupted the prince's mind over the years, setting his design into motion. Though I suspect that Cadius continued with his scheme out of some twisted love for his child and a desire for him to rise, not simply retribution against his better brother—not *entirely*, at least."

Sarah stared at the ground, eyes unseeing. But Will was at the castle, probably speaking with the king and telling him that they knew everything. If he was not only involved but had instigated the death of the man who'd raised him—

Oh, God, don't let it be true, she pleaded silently. She met Damien's gaze—hers filled with horror, his with compassion. "Will. He'll be at the castle by now." She wrung her hands, nervous energy coursing through her body. "We have to warn him and tell him that Adrian knows everything and was the one to kill the king. He's walking into a trap."

Damien sighed, shaking his head sadly. "I am afraid it's already too late. He will discover these things for himself soon enough."

଒ଓ

A knot of pain twisted in Will's gut as he watched Sarah ride off in the Spaniard's arms, but there was no time to dwell on that now—he would finish his duty to the king's life, and then he would come for her. Although he loathed the man for every twisted word he had spoken to Sarah and the torment he'd put her through, Will knew that, unfortunate though it might be, Lisandro was one of the few people with whom she would be safe.

But that would change as soon as Will told King Adrian what his uncle—father—had done and the madman was stopped once and for all. With that objective in mind, Will's feet pounded over the forest floor on his way to the castle.

It must have been mid-evening, though the clouds hung low in the sky, casting gray, hazy light over everything. His steps slowed as he neared the castle's backside, taking a moment to get his bearings, and he spotted the mossy outcropping hanging low over the rock face, just a little deeper into the forest. He pushed aside the tangle of vines and moss and thorns to reveal the tunnel into which he'd once secreted Sarah away.

Focusing his attention on the path before him, he hurried down the tunnel and let the curtain behind him close, plunging him into total darkness. The lack of light was oppressive, but he had traveled this secret passage countless times as a child and young man, and he didn't need an ounce of light to guide him as he slid his hands along the cold stone walls.

He paused at the door, feeling along the jamb until his fingers brushed the hinges, prying at the jagged nails with gritted teeth. At last, the door broke free of the old rusty hinges, and with a grunt, Will shoved it open. The door squeaked loudly in protest as it swung outward on the support of nothing but the chain-lock, and it hung there awkwardly as he jumped down into the room.

He made his way through the underbelly of the castle, pausing at doorways to listen to the sound of a guard's footsteps until they receded down the hall, and after a time, he miraculously found himself in the upper wing to which the royals typically kept themselves. With bated breath, Will moved quietly along the corridor, unnerved by the fact that numerous torches lined the walls, casting him in perfect light. There was nowhere to hide, though he quickly realized that no guards were stationed in this wing to spot his lurking form. This fact disturbed him, and he wondered how many guards under Cadius' thumb had been sent to look for them. He knew of two, both of whom were lying on the forest floor.

His steps quickened, along with his pulse, as he moved beyond several open doors with a brief glance inside that told him they were unoccupied. He continued onward, passing a door that was barely cracked open. Voices carried to him, and he halted his search as he heard the king's voice. He had only seen the gray-eyed king a few times and had only really ever heard his voice during the knighting ceremony, but Will was certain it was he.

"Give him my response immediately. You are dismissed," King Adrian said, his normally lifeless voice tense.

"Of course, Majesty," came the response. Will flattened himself against the wall as the door opened, his entire body as stiff as a board as a guard emerged. Holding his breath, Will watched the man's back as he hurried down the hall, a missive clutched in one gloved fist. By pure luck, he never glanced behind him.

Will released the breath he'd been holding back. He took a moment to steel his nerves and then slipped inside the room. He found himself in the king's study, with floor-to-ceiling bookshelves lining the walls, countless maps and charts scattered about the desk, and His Royal Highness himself staring out the far window as he warmed himself by a roaring fire. It was springtime, but the bitter cold of winter lingered in the drafty stone castle.

"Your Majesty."

He spun around, his look of total detachment turning to one of utter shock. "What in God's name—?"

"Please, Highness, I must speak with you." Will closed the door quietly behind him, trying to look as non-threatening as possible.

King Adrian gripped the windowsill, looking more like a frightened child and less like a newly crowned ruler of a kingdom. "How did you get in here? There are no jewels in this room."

He thought him a thief, Will realized. Concerned that the situation could quickly escape his control, he said, "I swear I am here to save your life, not harm it."

"How—?" The look of fear on King Adrian's face momentarily faded in recognition. He pointed at Will. "I know you. I knighted you." Will tried not to sigh. Clearly, his past efforts to stop Cadius hadn't made quite the impact he had thought. Then the king's expression cleared. "Taylor," he breathed.

Will nodded, hardly impressed that he had remembered his name. "Yes, and I have urgent news. It concerns your father and the fact that his death was no accident."

The young king's expression froze. He said blankly, "We have already established that, as I recall," referring to his sentencing Cadius for his involvement in the death of King Josiah.

Will hesitated, wondering how to begin and how much to share outright. He knew that if he was unable to convince King Adrian of his true origin and Cadius' unrelenting plot surrounding the kingdom of Serimone, the king might consider his actions today as treasonous and have him imprisoned. Yet Will had come here with one purpose in mind, and they would never be free of Cadius until someone put a stop to his plotting once and for all.

Whatever his tact, it would come as a shock to the king, and so he took a deep breath, hoping for the right words to remove them from this mess. "I know you are aware of his true nature, Your Majesty, forgive me. But recently some new evidence has appeared. . . ."

"Out with it," King Adrian sighed in frustration.

Will said as delicately as possible, "My lord, Cadius lives."

King Adrian blinked, and then his face slowly fell into an unreadable look as he stared at the rug beneath his feet. His swallow was audible in the heavy silence permeating the study. "That cannot be possible."

"Your uncle somehow survived the noose. His continued existence has been confirmed through eye-witness accounts."

The young king's head snapped up. "Who are the witnesses?"

Sarah's face came to mind, and for an unexplainable reason, Will felt that he needed to keep her name out of the conversation. "They wish for anonymity just now, Majesty. But although Cadius was originally convicted for murdering your predecessor, we have proof that his involvement goes much deeper than that single act; I fear he plots for the throne, more than just retribution against his brother."

Slowly, the color drained from the king's face, his lips parting in a look of vague alarm and surprise, as though he couldn't quite believe what he was hearing. The youthful freckles on one cheek stood out on his pale features, a stark contrast against the aging effect of the dark circles and squint lines around his stormy eyes.

Will nodded reluctantly, responding to what he assumed was the unspoken question he saw in those eyes. "I believe that you are the only thing standing between him and total control of the throne."

That strange, blank expression remained on his features for a moment longer, then the king grinned disbelievingly. "And who would allow a dead man onto the throne? Do use your head."

Will exhaled slowly, asking for patience. He hadn't been sentenced to the gallows for breaking into the king's private study uninvited, but breaking *through* King Adrian's density and cockiness was more of a challenge than he had thought. He reminded himself that Cadius' plan and sudden reappearance would seem a bit far-fetched, so he tried once more, trying to keep the impatience from his tone. "I understand how it must sound, Majesty, but I assure you it is true: he has been plotting for your father's throne for years and will stop at nothing to get it. I only come here because I have great cause to fear that a threat to your life is imminent."

A hand fluttered in the air in a dismissive gesture. "I am constantly guarded. I fear no sudden attacks in the night."

"Have you not noticed how your force has dwindled?" Will fairly barked, losing patient with the arrogant new king who, in his ignorance, was attempting to dissuade him from his task. "I practically grew up in this very castle, and never have I seen so few guards stationed in the royal wings. And I was able to outmaneuver your sentries moments before I found you. Do you not believe that Cadius and his minions could find their way inside undetected, as well?"

The king seemed to consider his words, pursing his thin lips. Suddenly, he said, "I require a drink." Seemingly in a daze, he turned his back to Will and went to the table beneath the window, on which sat a short decanter and several silver goblets. He poured himself a hearty cup of dark wine, drinking deeply as he stared out the window.

Will hesitated, knowing that there was no way to cushion what he was about to say. "There is more, my lord." A muffled *"Mm"* was all he received as the king downed the contents of his goblet and began pouring another, his hand shaking as he tipped the pitcher. His behavior was odd, and though Will knew he needed to reveal the full truth, he wasn't sure now was the best time for it.

With a sigh, he admitted reluctantly that it would never be well timed for a king to hear that he was illegitimate, with no right to the throne.

"There is a letter from Cadius himself indicating your . . . true heritage." King Adrian's back stiffened at his cautious words, hand tightening around his goblet. Taking a step toward him, Will went on gently, "There are a series of missives between Cadius and your mother, Queen Alexis, that discuss how he seduced and then fell in love with her. They shared a mutual hatred of the former king and conceived a child together. . . . You."

He didn't believe it was wise to tell the new king that there was another living heir to the throne, a *true* heir. No one would take kindly to hearing their position could be stripped from them at a moment's notice by a total stranger—raised as a peasant, no less—and so he decided to hold back the information he had on Richard. Let the king absorb all that he had been told already, and Will would fill in the rest in time.

A prolonged silence filled the room, and Will shifted uncomfortably, waiting for a reaction from the king. At last, that man set his goblet back down, slowly, as though with deliberate calm, and he filled another glass, offering it to Will. He could tell the king was trying to maintain a dignified façade as he processed it all, and Will didn't want to seem ungrateful, so he accepted the wine with his murmured thanks. Taking a polite swig, he managed not to wince as the bitter brew slithered down his throat.

Though the young king before him must have had hundreds of questions, he asked only one: "And who else knows of this lurid affair between my uncle and Queen Alexis?"

"No one, my lord." Will blinked, unsure why he had told the falsehood. Yet he felt an unexplainable urge to protect Sarah from any involvement in the unraveling of Cadius' plan, however secure this conversation with the king might be. Even if the king did what they hoped he would with the information, Will didn't feel as protected by these walls as he once had; there were too many listening ears for him to entrust them with his secrets.

King Adrian nodded. "Good, good," he muttered. Then louder, "I suppose all that is left are a few questions for you."

A side door leading into the study opened suddenly, and Will spun around as three guards entered. Two of them carried the weight of a man between them, his knees dragging on the floor, head dipping forward as though his neck could no longer support it. They dropped his body unceremoniously at Will's feet.

He jumped back, eyes widening in surprise. He looked at the guards' blank faces for an explanation and then narrowed his suspicious gaze on the king. "What is this?" The man on the carpet moaned, and Will's heart stopped at the familiar sound.

He dropped to his knees, taking great care as he gently rolled the body over. A startled gasp escaped his lips at his uncle's bloodied face, the split lip and swollen eye, the blood matting his salt and pepper hair. Will had seen him only just that morning, but he was nearly unrecognizable now, his features distorted by knuckles and fists. His own hands bunched in anger.

"Did you do this?" he accused the guards, his murderous gaze shifting between them. His toes clenched and unclenched in his boots, ready to sprint into action and strangle the first person to open his mouth and admit what he had done.

"They tried . . . to make me talk, son." Thomas's whisper was strained and broke off in a gurgling cough that caused Will's heart to lurch painfully in his chest.

He placed his hands gently on either side of his uncle's battered face, rage and fear and distress vying for attention in his body. "*Who*, Uncle?" he demanded gently. In that moment, he felt capable of murder and was certain he would not hesitate to do to that man as he had done to his uncle. "Who did this to you?"

Thomas shook his head, and it rolled from side to side. "I gave them nothing of you and Sarah." His voice was intentionally quiet so that Will had to lean his ear against his lips to hear his next words. "And they questioned me of another son, a true heir. . . ."

Will's lips parted, and his chest clenched painfully. He closed his eyes, dropping his head in regret. "Oh, Uncle, this is all my fault."

"I must say," a voice remarked conversationally as the last man Will had expected entered the room with a flourish. The smooth, cold, self-satisfied voice grated on every one of Will's last nerves.

He raised his head slowly, hands shaking, jaw clenching and unclenching as he stared up at the man who had put everyone he cared for in harm's way.

Cadius *tsked.* "The girl and Lisandro have put up quite a fight, though we *will* find them, rest assured. But it was so kind of you to bring yourself to us."

Will's pulse sped up in shock and anger. "Your Majesty," he said to the king, his voice full of urgency and rage, "this man is a murderer and a traitor to the crown."

"I know," came his whispered reply. The king's eyes were dull, his expression blank once more as he came to stand beside Cadius. The older man placed a hand on his son's shoulder, grinning as though Will had fallen directly into his snare. And, Will realized, he had.

He shook his head in disbelief. He stared at Cadius and the king, whose eyes were as cold and stormy as his father's. The guards quietly placed their backs to the wall, watching the scene with looks of detachment. "You knew he was alive," he whispered.

"Of course." King Adrian shot a quick, searching glance at his father, who nodded in assent that he could speak on the matter. The scene was so familiar it hit Will like a battering ram: the young king, hesitant to sentence his uncle to the gallows for crimes of treason, and Cadius' quick nod of assurance. At the time, Will had thought it was the action of a caring uncle letting his nephew know that he would not blame him for the justice he must dole out, but now Will realized that Cadius had been letting the then-prince know that it was all part of the plan.

Will speared an accusatory glare at the king—no, simply Adrian, for this child had lost any respect Will might have had for him. "What business could you possibly have with the man who murdered your father?"

Adrian narrowed his dull eyes, and the hatred burning there lent them a spark of life, though his twisted expression of repressed sorrow and crazed fury sent a shiver down Will's spine. "My predecessor was even less a father to me than he was a good king to Serimone. I will excel where he failed and take control of Ridlan with my *true* father by my side."

The look of strangely tender pride on Cadius' face sickened Will. "At what cost?" he asked, disturbed that they would start a war with an ally simply to expand their control over the land.

The older man turned his gaze on Will, who gently placed his uncle's head in his lap, as though he could shield him from Cadius' stormy gaze. The action also gave his hands something to do so they didn't pummel Cadius and his cowardly son into the stone floor.

Cadius ignored his question altogether, casting a passing glance at Thomas before returning his gaze to Will. "Though we interrogated him using multiple tactics," he droned, "Thomas Greene was unhelpful in revealing what we wish to know. However, King Adrian"—he seemed to speak the title with great relish and pride—"reminded me that he can still be of use in getting *you* to speak."

Will's face fell, his chest rising and falling in steady, practiced breaths that helped to focus his mind. "Son, no—" Thomas admonished softly, then lapsed into a weak coughing fit that wracked his bruised frame. The wet sound echoed through Will's head.

His hold on Thomas tightened protectively, and Will stiffened his spine. "What do you wish to know?" Simply a question, not a promise that he would give Cadius the information he sought.

A look of surprise passed over Cadius' gray features at what he imagined to be quick acquiescence, then he smiled—a cold, calculated tip of his thin, pale lips that said he had just discovered something. "Ah, Lady Matthews is not your only weakness." As always, that underlying threat to Sarah's life was there, unspoken but ever-present.

Will's carefully sculpted expression of ambiguity slowly turned into a glower, his lips curling as his eyes betrayed the threat he wished he could make good on that instant. His voice was low and deadly. "If you lay a hand on her again, I will personally ensure that you do not survive this. Not that you will ever find her." The reminder of her well-being and the fact that Cadius had yet to find her gave him no small amount of assurance. He grinned confidently, the action small but genuine.

One white-gray brow rose derisively on Cadius' forehead. He returned Will's grin, though his held menacing promise. "But soon," he intoned. Will clenched his jaw as he added in that grating voice of his, "We have reason to believe your little troupe of outlaws has an inkling as to the identity of Meredith's child. Now, tell me, does he still live?" Will narrowed his eyes and gave him a dead stare, masking his surprise that Cadius thought they knew anything about Richard.

When he remained silent, the older man tried again, taking a step closer. His voice dropped its false saccharine tone, turning acerbic as he narrowed his eyes. "Is anyone else privy to the true events behind the child's demise, then?"

A flicker of alarm coursed through Will at the turn in conversation, though he tried to keep it from showing on his face. "No. But the next time you attempt to have a royal infant murdered, you should really do a better job of covering your tracks," he mocked, nostrils flaring in his attempt to keep his temper at bay. It would only get him into more trouble, but he could not resist taunting the blaggard who stood before him now.

Cadius speared him with a deadening glance, which Will returned with as much gusto and hatred, perhaps more. Though he did his best to hide it, Cadius' next words sent a chill over his whole body. "If you do not open your foul mouth and tell me what I wish to know, then I will have my men break every feeble bone in this weathered tracker's body."

Will's tongue curled, ready with a heated reply, when he felt a weak tug on his arm and looked down at Thomas, who motioned feebly for him to come closer. Will leaned in, his uncle's cool breath tickling his ear.

"Richard, Seth—they're safe. We had separated before I was . . . taken." Relief spread through Will's muscles at the reassuring words, having wondered if they were trapped somewhere under the castle being questioned as his uncle had. He felt himself relaxing an instant before Thomas whispered, "Tell them nothing, son. I am too far gone to save."

"Uncle, no. You are strong—" Thomas lifted a shaky hand and barely placed his fingertips against his nephew's cheek to silence him. Two of his fingers were obviously broken, bent at odd angles that wouldn't straighten like the others as they pressed against his skin. Will bit his lip to stifle the broken sound of rage and agony that welled up within him. But his uncle's gaze was bright with a light he could not comprehend.

"My body is broken, but not . . . my spirit. I pray that someday you might feel the peace I know now." He broken off, the effort of speaking throwing him into a coughing fit. The hand dropped from Will's cheek, and he noted with alarm that his uncle had coughed a few specks of blood onto his shirt.

"Oh, Uncle, forgive me. I never meant for this to happen," he whispered brokenly, no longer caring if Adrian or his father were witness to his torment.

"No." Thomas's voice was feeble but resolved. "No, son, this . . . is *not* your doing; I made my own choice. Forgive yourself," he whispered. "Do not let your pride keep you from Great Love."

Will didn't understand what he meant. "Uncle, you know I love Sarah."

But Thomas just shook his head. He had to pause for a breath before he could continue, his voice softer and more distant than before as he switched topics, seemingly unable to keep a steady train of thought. "You were my only child, and I am so proud . . . of all you've done. Never forget the goodness she unlocked, for I have always seen it, as does Sarah. . . . Love you—so proud . . ." His voice faded. Though his one good eye remained open, he stared at nothing, and Will knew he had already lost him.

Though everything in him rebelled at any display of emotion or weakness before these murderous fiends, he couldn't help it. A sound like that of a keening animal welled up within him, and Will allowed his sorrow and rage to bleed out into one horrific, wailing scream that rattled the windowpanes. A sob wracked his frame, and he clutched his uncle's broken body to his chest, cradling it there as Thomas had done for him when his parents died. He buried his face in his uncle's neck, letting the tears fall as he did his best to hide from Cadius and his son how thoroughly they had broken him.

"Well, that is a shame." The sound of Cadius' flat voice sent a flash of rage through Will. He raised his head slowly, eyes murderous, body shaking with sorrow and something else. Will blinked, hard, his gut burning with a sudden fire.

Cadius moved toward the guards standing against the wall. "And who led the interrogation of the prisoner?" The eyes of the man on the right widened guiltily. It was the only indication Cadius needed, and he struck the man across the face, the clap of flesh on flesh sounding like cannon fire. "We needed him alive, you fool," he hissed. "Next time, employ greater caution."

Will's tear-filled and suddenly burning eyes rested on Adrian. That man watched him cradle his uncle's body with a confusing look of pity and grief—perhaps his compassion had not been completely wiped away under his father's influence. Abruptly, Will's head clouded and ducked forward without warning. He jerked it upright, shaking it to clear his foggy mind. "What did you do to me?" he whispered.

Reaching for one of the jeweled rings on his hand, Adrian flipped the top off to reveal a secret compartment. White residue coated the inside. He snapped the clasp closed, obviously deeming the action enough of an explanation for Will's condition, which worsened by the minute, shocking Will at his sudden decline. "I was going to let you go, in hopes that you would draw Lady Matthews from hiding. But when you revealed your knowledge of the correspondence between Father and my mother, the late queen, I knew you were too much of a risk to allow you to roam free. I do wish you would have drunk more; it would have made this so much . . . quicker for you."

Any notion he'd had of the young king being the lesser of two evils was washed away with those words. "You don't deserve your title. You had your own father killed," Will ground out, then clutched his gut in pain. Somehow, he managed to get out the last arrow he had, hoping it would put a chink in the man's deluded armor. "Will you do the same to your own mother so that you might rule alone?"

"She is not my mother!" Adrian shrieked. The first spark of life in a long time flared into his stormy gaze just then, and his anger burned like that of a frightened, frantic child. He looked half mad as tears filled his eyes, nostrils flaring, and Will wondered how long Cadius had been corrupting him, poisoning his memory of his father and mother.

Cheeks flushed, Adrian came forward, wrapping his slender hand around Will's throat until he choked. "I never knew my mother, and that was thanks to Josiah's cruelty and the way he cast her aside, unloved; his indifference killed her. Now, we have yet to find the correspondence between my parents," he said suddenly, abruptly changing topics, as his father had. "Tell me where you discovered them."

But Will shook his head. If these were his last breaths, he was not going to spend them giving this petulant king and his sadistic father what they wanted. "That wasn't why she died," he managed, his voice hoarse.

His vision blurred, and the effects of his drink began to overpower him. Shaking his head, he managed to glare at the childish king's wavering image. He clenched his fists, hoping his next words would wound him, though Will knew that it could never be as painful as the loss he had just experienced.

"No, the late Queen Alexis is not here to cajole this ridiculous excuse for a leader because *that man*"—he felt too weak to turn his head in Cadius' direction—"filled her with child, and she died because she gave birth to a revolting coward. You brought about her death, *Highness*." He spat out the title with mockery and loathing, driving the truth home like a hunter might plunge his blade into the heart of a stag. Will only hoped the man bled slowly.

A brief flicker of pleasure shot through him at the look of torment and intense rage that filled Adrian's pale features. Will narrowed his eyes, which was easy enough considering they were already drooping closed of their own accord.

"Have the body burned and dispose of the rug," Adrian commanded suddenly, his voice cracking. The stunned guards hesitated until the request was barked again, and then they slowly moved toward the corpse on the floor.

Will growled as two men tried to take Thomas's body from his arms. "Don't touch him!" he shouted. He put all his fading strength into holding onto Thomas, though he knew his uncle was gone and he clung only to a shell of what he once was.

One of the guards rammed the side of Will's face with a fist, breaking his hold as they dragged Thomas from his arms. He collapsed onto his knees once more, back hunched in exhaustion, pain, and grief, lacking the strength to hold back the lone tear that leaked from the corner of his eye. He watched, helpless, as the man who had raised him was carried to the side door between the two guards. Thomas's head lolled back, and his unseeing eyes watched his nephew until he disappeared through the doorway.

Adrian turned to Will, whose face was pinched in torment. He stared up at the king, knowing that he'd ordered his uncle stripped away to cause him one last moment of pain as payback for Will's accusations. *An eye for an eye*. Will wondered how he could be as cold and demented as his father, who watched the scene with a gloating, insatiable look in his eyes.

"Fear not, Taylor," the boy-king said, his voice cold and flat. "Lady Matthews will be joining you shortly."

Will's throat closed up and his chest constricted in agony—no doubt caused by the poison coursing through his bloodstream and the realization that his uncle was dead, and he and Sarah might soon follow.

"You're the devil," he muttered, wavering on his knees. Unable to resist any longer, his eyes rolled back and he slumped to the floor.

Chapter Twenty-Two

"Though much is taken, much abides; and though
We are not now that strength which in old days
Moved earth and heaven, that which we are, we are;
One equal temper of heroic hearts,
Made weak by time and fate, but strong in will
To strive, to seek, to find, and not to yield."

Alfred, Lord Tennyson, "Ulysses"

For the next thirty minutes, Sarah pleaded with Damien to let her go. He reminded her again and again that the second she stepped into town, Cadius would claim his hold on her. "You would be putting yourself at risk, and he would have you questioned until you turned over every last one of us. You'd be dooming us all, your innocent friends included."

Sarah quieted then, biting her lip as she slumped onto the couch. She wanted to snap back at him that she could never betray any of them, but how could she know that she was able to withstand such torture until she was put in that position? She shivered, not wanting to test her theory.

As her head cleared, she admitted he was right: she couldn't risk their lives by being so hasty. She stared up at Damien with tortured eyes. "I get that, but I can't do *nothing*. Please, Damien." His name slipped out, and she realized it was the first time since his return that she had said it without rancor or animosity.

He closed his eyes. "Sarah." He had dropped the "my lady," seeming to sense, as she did, that their dynamic had somehow shifted from prisoner and detainee to something else entirely—something softer, though Sarah wasn't quite ready to call them friends just yet with all the water that still churned under the bridge.

Shaking his head, Damien sighed. "What if I sent someone to investigate Taylor's whereabouts or see if they can safely remove him from the castle? Would that appease you for now?"

Sarah nodded eagerly, feeling a small rush of relief that weakened her knees and made her glad she was already sitting. At least now she would have answers.

"All right." Damien whipped his cloak back on, explaining that he'd send his man into the castle and wait for word to come, and then return as soon as he could.

"Thank you."

Damien paused at her quiet words to his back. He looked at her over his shoulder, his expression hooded as the moonlight outside hid it from Sarah's view. "You might not thank me when I return." Then he threw the door open, not bothering to lock it behind him; Sarah wouldn't go anywhere until she heard news of Will, and he knew it.

Hours passed as Sarah waited on the couch, back rigid in expectation, hands clasped anxiously in her lap. *What's taking so long?*

At some point, Jade emerged from her room and urged her to eat something, at Damien's insistence, she was sure, but she refused. "I can't. Not until I know Will's safe."

Jade had shaken her head, her eyes distant, though her gaze said she understood Sarah's fear. "Hope is a dangerous thing, little one—a slippery slope that claims many prisoners." Silently, she had gone back to her room with her meager supper and closed the door. She hadn't seen Jade since—once she thought she heard the other woman crying softy, but Sarah imagined it was just the wind playing in the trees outside.

ଓ଼ଃ୬

The earth rolled and dipped unnaturally, attempting to lull him back into a fitful slumber even as the chill and the cloying stench of human waist and saltwater brought him back to his senses. Will moaned as he rolled onto his side, the action shooting fire through his still-tender nerves and setting his head spinning. He sucked in a deep breath, hoping to let the nausea pass, but the overpowering smell of sea and excrement had him gritting his teeth to keep from vomiting.

With his eyes closed, he replayed the last day back in his mind, trying to focus his senses and discern what had happened: Adrian's betrayal, Will's tainted drink, Uncle Thomas dying in his arms, Sarah back in the Spaniard's clutches, Cadius' triumphant face. . . . How had everything gone wrong so quickly?

Knowing he needed to focus, he swallowed the burn of fresh tears as he pushed aside the memory of his uncle's bruised face and the peace that had been on it even on the throes of death. The look in his eyes had disturbed Will more than he cared to admit. His uncle was gone, the last bit of family he had left. After Will's parents died, it had just been he and Thomas, and Will had no idea what he was supposed to do without him.

When at last the world stood still and his stomach did not threaten to empty itself with each breath, he propped himself against the wall and cast his gaze about the room, blinking in the darkness, attempting to get his bearings. He tried not to let himself panic over the fact that he was at sea, an undeniable circumstance as he listened to the rumble and splash of the vessel as it glided over choppy waters. When he craned his neck, he could make out the stars dotting the black sky through the tiny round window above his head.

The ship pitched forward slightly, sending a spray of saltwater through the hole in the wall, and a chill shot down his spine. For whatever reason, Cadius and his son had spared his life, though that was another concern entirely, as it meant they still had a use for him. But to where were they sending him? To some strange torture?

After a few moments, he saw that the wall at his back extended down a long corridor into inky blackness. His end of the hall was closest to a set of stairs, the base of which was lit by a single lantern that swayed with each bob and dip of the ship, barely lighting a ten-foot circumference that glided from one wall to the next as it shifted. The light hurt his eyes every time it swung his way, making it difficult to see much outside of the circle of light.

Focusing his gaze against the near blackness that was only broken up by the tiny flecks of moonlight shining through few windows, he was able to make out the bars that lined the sixteen or so small rooms on either side of the walkway. One contained small stacked barrels, leaking some sort of black fluid, he noticed, before his eyes drifted onward.

He missed them at first, but then one of the black lumps shifted and he squinted harder, discerning in each cell the shapes of men huddled on the floor against the cold, though they were all eerily quiet. His eyes focused up-close, and it was only then that he realized the space he occupied was similarly barred-in.

Will sat up straight like a bolt of lightening, only vaguely aware that it didn't send his senses reeling this time. The drug must have been wearing off, a fact that would have given him relief had he not just realized that he was on a vessel transporting prisoners, and he was part of its cargo.

Rising to his numb legs sent needles of pain down them as the blood flooded back, but at least his strength and senses were returning. He stood before the bars, hands roving the metal in search of a weak spot, his eyes doing the same each time the lantern swung his way, though he found no loose bars or fragile points.

Feeling like a caged animal, Will gripped an iron in each hand and tried prying them apart. He held his breath, veins standing out on his neck as he pulled, but the reinforced bars held. Someone did not want their prisoners escaping.

Growling in frustration, he forcefully shook the bars again and again, more to vent his anger than anything. The sharp motions jarred his head, which was still recovering, and he stopped abruptly, panting hard. His hands slid down as he leaned his forehead between the bars, though the gap wasn't large enough for him to slip his head through, and rested his forearms on the horizontal rod that stretched the length of his cell. There was nothing left for him to do, and his unoccupied mind wandered to his uncle in his arms.

The agony hit him afresh, washing over Will in a sudden, breathtaking wave of sorrow. He squeezed his eyes closed, grinding his forehead against the rough bars as he thought of Thomas as he lay dying, always so brave and selfless. Knowing that Seth and Richard were unharmed offered him some consolation, but his uncle had given his life to protect all of them and to hide a secret he had not known himself.

And then there was Sarah. The king and Cadius had outright admitted that they had yet to discover where Lisandro was hiding, but it was only a matter of time before they joined Will in a similar fate. Or worse.

Fury and helpless frustration rising, he slammed a palm against the bars, letting out a growl of rage.

"I have tried similar tactics, but believe me, you will only earn yourself blisters."

Will whipped his head to the left. A man emerged from the shadows of his cell, grinning, not unkindly, as he gripped the irons adjoining their prisons. As the light swung their way, Will could discern weatherworn features and brown hair that was beginning to go white around the temples. The sight of another human being set him on edge, but there was something about the stranger's eyes, a noticeable kindness in those brown depths, that caused his anxiety to subside, though his heart twisted a little in his chest. The man reminded him of his uncle.

"How did I get here?"

The man scratched his neglected beard, his grin fading. "Same as the rest of us—carried onboard unconscious and then tossed into one of these cells." He tapped a finger against one of the bars, as though Will needed reminding.

Will frowned as he took in the man's bedraggled appearance. "How long have you been in here? And when did I arrive?" Had it been hours, days, since Adrian had drugged him? Will was *mostly* certain the Spaniard would do whatever it took to protect Sarah, but what he could not withstand was the legion Cadius would surely send if he found their location. Will couldn't waist any time in getting as much information as he could before he found a way to escape.

"Oh, it's been nigh a fortnight for myself," the man answered after a moment's pause, rubbing his thick beard again in contemplation. "Last thing I remember is being near the docks on the outskirts of Ridlan, and when I came to, I had already been smuggled aboard a smaller vessel that brought me here. But you arrived only a few hours ago."

Will's shoulders sagged. Knowing a full day had not yet passed was a small relief, but he was still trapped in an unfamiliar vessel. "Do you know our destination? Has the crew mentioned anything to you?" The man did not appear entirely malnourished, and after spending two weeks on the ship, *someone* must be feeding the prisoners to keep them from wasting away, so it was impossible he had not encountered another soul while onboard.

The man shook his head regretfully. "Sorry, no, but I believe it is safe to remark that Avalon, Cockaigne, and Arcadia will not be possible destinations." All utopias that Will agreed they would not find themselves disembarking on.

Tilting his head to the side, he eyed Will curiously. "And what great offense might you have done to earn yourself a place among such great legends as myself?" he asked, his voice at once inquisitive and sardonic.

Strangely, knowing that they were in the same boat—quite literally, Will mused—he found he trusted the man. "I crossed Serimone's new king." The man raised a brow and had the gall to chuckle. Will narrowed his eyes, perturbed at his callousness. "I don't *deserve* to be here, unlike you lot."

Shaking his head, the man's laughter slowly faded, though the grin remained. He sounded amused when he said, "Boy, *none* of us belong here." He motioned around the cavernous underbelly of the ship, to the other cells. "A few petty thieves, yes, but most of these pathetic souls are victims of circumstance, present company included."

Will narrowed his eyes and asked skeptically, "An entire vessel of innocents? Forgive me, but that seems a little unbelievable."

"And yet here you are." Will frowned. The man leaned closer to the bars, peering through. "After conversing with the others these past weeks as more and more unwilling passengers were added, we discovered that there is a common thread linking us all: At one point or another, every last one of us was involved to some extent with either Cadius or King Adrian—whether in direct service to them, double-crossing either one, or because we had discovered something about the current regime, however large or small, and decided to speak out."

"Tying up loose ends," Will remarked quietly, thoughtfully. If others were catching wind of their deception in Ridlan, then the extent of the damage done went far beyond their small town and the forests of Serimone. No one was safe.

Taking a deep breath, he turned his gaze back on the man across from him, who watched him back with a curious, peaceful look of his own. His calm in the midst of their current circumstance was faintly irritating and unnerving. "What great trespass against the boy-king might you have done to find yourself on a prisoner transport?"

"I was caught preaching about God and the Christ in a public square in Ridlan."

Will blinked in surprise. "I know the concept of religion can be quite caustic as of late, but it seems a bit extreme to ship you off to some foreign land. And why would the king even bother to meddle in such a petty cause of another kingdom?"

The man chuckled softly. "You would assume so, wouldn't you?" A shadow shifted in the man's cell, and for the first time Will noticed the sleeping form huddled in the corner, propped up against the wall and the next set of bars. His new companion glanced over his shoulder at the slumbering man and lowered his voice as he turned back to Will. "The king of my homeland detests religion of any kind—Protestant, Roman Catholic, Reformed—and forbids open discussion of it."

Narrowing his eyes in confusion, Will asked, "Then why express your opinions so freely? Why not just remain silent? God knows all, does He not?" It was one of the very reasons why Will was so adamant that he would never find absolute forgiveness. "I am sure He would not fault you for protecting yourself when your heart is loyal to Him."

"But how loyal would I truly be, then, if I lived my life and remained silent about what He has done?" The man shook his head. "The Almighty has brought me through many trials—most of them self-inflicted," he added a bit wryly. "Now, tell me, how could I deny God when I have been given everything by Him?"

"And yet you find yourself a prisoner," Will reminded, feeling a little piqued. Why did the mere mention of God seem to stir up repressed anger and guilt and a feeling of insecurity that he could not quite account for?

The man quirked his head to the side, that strange, peaceful look on his weathered features again. "But my soul is not captive, boy, you can be sure of that. And if I can help encourage even one to believe or lighten the burden of another, then it will have all been worthwhile."

Shaking his head, Will said with more bitterness than he intended to reveal, "Do not waste your time with me."

A keen, brown-eyed gaze assessed him. "How is it that you believe there is a Savior but do not know him personally?"

Will wasn't exactly certain how he could be taken hostage in a conversation about God on a *prisoner* vessel, of all places, and he fidgeted uncomfortably in place. Finally, he shrugged. "The Almighty has simply never been real to me."

"Hmm," the man murmured thoughtfully. "That seems so strange to me now. To deny God's presence in my life and His mercy would be like rejecting a part of myself. He makes me whole," he added quietly.

Will cast his eyes to the ground, thoroughly humbled by the man's honest declaration, so similar to words he had heard before. Sarah, Uncle Thomas, this man—they all seemed to carry such undying faith within them, like some inner light that guided their path and caused them not to feel such crippling fear and despair. His uncle had even shown greater strength than Will had felt as the man lay dying in his arms. What was wrong with Will that he could not accept the kind of peace he glimpsed in their features? He thought of Sarah and her watery eyes whenever she spoke to him of God's mercy, recalling how *he* had pleaded with the Almighty to save Sarah from Allan's poison. She and his uncle had professed it to be a miracle.

"You sound like friends of mine."

"They sound entirely wise." Will couldn't stop the reluctant tip of his lips that emerged at his words. Grinning, the man nodded once. "Merek Hildebrand of Ridlan."

Will gave his name, and Merek smiled. "Any enemy of Cadius is a friend of mine."

"You said that everyone here crossed either Serimone's king or Cadius in some way," Will remarked thoughtfully. "What is your reason? You mentioned sharing your beliefs, but what is your connection to Cadius?"

"Ah." Merek's smile faded. He shook his head. "I own—well, *owned* an inn that Cadius bedded down at frequently whenever he came to Ridlan. One day, he arrived at my inn fully intoxicated, rambling on and on about some great discovery and his plan to control both Serimone and Ridlan in the future. It was many years ago, and I thought nothing of it—simply the ranting of a drunkard. But as of late, I have noticed men watching my every move, and these sentries were not part of *my* kingdom, though I recognized a few as having escorted Cadius to Ridlan during his sojourns there. I am suspicious by nature, mind you, and so hearing about some of the strange things that were occurring in Serimone and knowing that I was being followed . . . Well, I certainly began to suspect, though I did not refrain from going about my day to day life. But when he caught word of my public testimonial those weeks past, and the fury of my own king, Cadius was only too pleased to offer up his vessel as the solution to both their problems. As you said, they are tying up loose ends."

Will paused, realizing what he had just said didn't make sense—few in Serimone knew that Cadius was still alive, so how had this man discovered that he had escaped the noose? "What makes you think that it was Cadius who placed you here? He's dead, is he not?" Will bated, testing to see what the man knew as his own suspicion mounted. "This could be anyone's ship, then."

"I saw him," Merek remarked matter-of-factly. Will pulled back, and the man nodded in confirmation. "I began to come-to before they managed to put me in this cell, and I overheard Cadius and the captain speaking about the arrangement." His eyes darkened. "Cadius was not three meters from me, and I was too weak to do anything."

Will knew the feeling, knew the regret and anger the man must feel toward Cadius and the hatred he felt for his own helplessness. Yes Will knew it only too well.

His head jerked toward the stairs at the sound of shouting above deck. The ship dipped sharply to the left, and Will stumbled against the bars, gripping them tightly as it tipped precariously in the other direction. A series of thuds sounded above them, and joining the increased shouts was the metal clang of swords.

"What the devil—?" Will swore as his face slammed into the bars with the sharp pitch of the boat. The lantern swung free of its hook, the case shattering as it smashed to the floor and set a small scattering of hay aflame in the far corner. The fire seemed insignificant and would most likely burn itself out, not that Will even had time to fret or register relief as they dipped again.

Merek gripped the edge of his tiny window and pulled himself up to peer outside, ignoring the hard spray of seawater in his face. He scowled. "Pirate ship," was all he said, but it was enough to strike a chord of fear in Will. They were completely defenseless down here.

"What are we supposed to do?" he asked, still clinging tightly to the bars, though they appeared to have regained control of the ship. Several of his fellow passengers had risen to their feet in the commotion, wondering, as he was, what was happening.

Staring out through the window with an unshakable gaze, Merek said in a firm voice, "Nothing right now, boy, though I believe now is as good a time as any for you to see how real God is."

Footfall *thumped* against the stairs, and Will's spine stiffened as heads turned to watch the small opening. The tiny fire in the corner made the fear in the boy's enormous eyes perfectly clear as he rounded the corner, and he fumbled with the ring of keys in his shaking hands, dropping them once on the floor. He was so young and scrawny that Will knew he must have been a cabin boy, youngsters that were oftentimes forcefully brought aboard ships for hard labor. The boy jammed a key into the lock of Will's cell and twisted—nothing happened, but Will's heart still sped up in anticipation, pushing aside his confusion over why they were being released.

"What's going on?" he asked as the shouts and sounds of sword fighting increased above deck.

Large, frightened eyes met his. "Pirates, sir," he answered nervously, his voice high and yet unchanged. Will tried to place his accent—Scottish, perhaps? "They came up quick and boarded us before the Cap'n and watch could 'lert us. Ten dead on our side, 'lready, sir." That seemed to remind him that time was wasting, and he went back to ramming keys into the lock. "You don't gots no weapons down 'ere; I gots to get you out in case she goes down, see, though the quartermaster says you don' matter. But you can help us fight, make it fair." The key in his hand turned as he rambled nervously, surprising them both. He grinned a gap-toothed smile.

"We'll help, boy," Will assured him, knowing it would be in their best interest to be rid of whatever foreign threat had boarded the ship. It might also prove the perfect distraction to find a way off of it.

The boy nodded and removed the key, pulling the door open.

"*What are you doing?*" someone roared. Will whipped his head toward the stairs to see a large man glare at the boy. A slash of red across his chest marred the perfect white of his tunic, and he held a sword in his hand, looking fierce and furious.

The boy paled. "Q-Quartermaster, sir. I was only tryin' to save 'em. If she goes down—"

The quartermaster silenced the boy with a backhanded stroke across the cheek. "They are *our cargo*," he spat. "What happens to them doesn't matter, but it is imperative that we defend the ship. We need all hands on deck."

Though the boy was nodding, his words were contradictory. "But, sir, they're still peoples, an' they can help."

A snarl was his response, and the cabin boy flinched. "Lock them back up," was his command.

Will didn't have time to think up a plan or be cautious—this might be his only opportunity. A brief moment of hesitation passed, and then he threw his full weight into the closing door, accidentally sending the boy reeling backward. Will cringed as his head connected with the bars of an empty cell behind him, and he slumped to the floor, stunned.

The quartermaster shouted for Will to stop, waking the remaining passengers who called out encouragement and foul curses against their captor. Will flattened his palm and thrust the side of his hand against the man's neck. He dropped to his knees, choking as he clutched his throat. But Will knew it would only temporarily stagger him and keep him from following, so he pushed aside hesitation in lieu of freedom.

He scurried toward the stairs but halted on the first step, the sound of his fellow prisoners shouted pleas tugging at his conscience. Yes, some of them were guilty of minor crimes, but many of them, like Will, were only trapped down there because of one man's greed and fear. If he left them to face whatever was coming, he would be sealing their deaths.

With gritted teeth, Will turned back, slipping on the wet floor as he hastened to the dazed cabin boy, who was shaking his head and had only just risen to his feet. He held out his hands. "Keys." The boy only stared up at him. Will took a breath. "What is your name, boy?"

"Gilcrest," he whispered.

As patiently as he could, Will said, "Gilcrest, I am sorry, but I need those keys *now*." There was a pause from the boy, and Will realized what held him back. "We will take you with us as a free man, if you wish." The cabin boy nodded eagerly and handed them over. Will grabbed the keys from his grasp and scurried back toward the prisoners. The shouts suddenly became cries of joy as he went from cell to cell, twisting keys in the locks until every door was open.

When he had freed every last one of them, he turned and saw that they had all congregated at the base of the stairs, the cabin boy included, waiting. Will swallowed. He had been their savior, and now they looked to him for guidance. Taking a deep breath, he slipped through the small crowd to stand at the base of the stairs, facing the dirt-crusted but grateful, expectant faces before him. *Twenty lives in my hands,* he thought after a quick head count, feeling the burden weigh down on him. He met Merek's eyes and his nod of encouragement.

Clearing his throat, Will spoke loudly to be heard above the crashing of the waves and the sounds of battle above them. "I am an innocent, as are most of you, and none of us deserve to be put to death or shipped off to some foreign land to be treated as slaves." A murmur of agreement went up through the gathering, rumbling through the hollowed-out ship just as more shouts sounded from above. Will gripped the railing to steady himself as the boat rolled on the waves, the men all dipping to the left to regain their balance. Gilcrest, however, barely leaned to the side, having most likely spent a good portion of his life at sea. The boy looked up to him as though he held all the answers.

Will swallowed. Rain began pattering the deck above, joining the sounds of shouting and swords clashing. "We must first defend this vessel from whatever outside force has boarded her."

"You expect us to fight alongside our captors?" a man cried out in protest from the back. Some muttered questions they were too frightened to voice, as though seeing the man's reason.

Will met his eyes with a steady gaze of his own, spearing the man to the spot with its fierceness. Then he allowed his eyes to travel over the group, making a point to meet each man's gaze in turn, trying to instill in them a bit of the confidence he was far from feeling but hoped he conveyed with his firm stance and unwavering gaze. These men needed hope, and he knew they were all looking to him for it.

"The ship is our only chance to return to our homes," Will said, "and as the quartermaster revealed, they will be protecting her at all costs and will not waste their time with prisoners who are assisting them in reclaiming their vessel. Once she is secure, then we will find a way to overpower the crew and force them to deliver us to land. It is our only chance. *But*," he added, "we are without weapons or any mode of true defense, and there are great risks in going up these stairs."

"The other option is to remain in our cells, trapped," Merek threw in loudly so all could hear. "We would be awaiting an unknown fate either way, but at least we will have a fighting chance of survival if we try to claim the ship." Will nodded at him, grateful for his support. But would it be enough?

There was a pause, a few beats where Will's heart roared in his ears in the sudden silence that enveloped the belly of the ship. He waited, wondering what they might choose, imagining a hundred different scenarios in those few seconds. Then one man shouted in a fierce tone, "Better to have a chance at life than to live this death another day!" It took a moment, but soon every man was crying out, the sound of defiance reverberating in the open and resonating in Will's chest with a spark of hope.

It felt strange to command such a large group after being a recluse for so many years, but the responsibility he felt for these lives—while it filled him with a sense of gravity and foreboding—it also gave him purpose. Knowing that these twenty-odd bodies would all be working together to fight for a shared cause was the most empowering feeling he had ever experienced. If they worked together, they could survive this.

His eyes traveled one final time over the group of men whose gazes had turned fierce, their resoluteness visible even in the dim light. "Then let us fight!" His voice rang out over the noise above, though the cries of assent drowned out his shout as they charged after Will up the stairs.

They emerged from below deck to find nothing but chaos bathed in rain and moonlight. Though they were obviously losing, judging by the number of seamen's bodies scattered about the upper deck, the crew fought valiantly against the sea pirates, who looked more like barbarians in the eerie lighting that cut through the low-hanging fog—scarred faces, odd, mismatched attire, knives strapped across their chests, and a string of sharpened bones tied about their waist all lent them a terrifying fierceness that was meant to intimidate their opponent. It appeared to be working, as nearly every crewman, equipped with a weapon or not, had wide, frightened eyes as they defended themselves.

The issue, Will quickly realized, was that they had been unprepared for an attack and the majority of the crew were left weaponless, having to use their fists and random items to defend themselves against the swords and knives wielded by the pirates.

A young seaman *thumped* to the deck near the opening of the stairs, the knife that had been thrown into his back sticking straight up. A growing red stain appeared on his tunic as rainwater pooled in the corner of his eye. The barbarian who had slain him lost his triumphant sneer as Will met his eyes, and he didn't need to tell his body to move as he sprung into action, diving for the knife in the man's back and throwing it at the pirate. He wasn't as skilled with daggers as he was a bow—a weapon he ached for now—but the tip landed in the pirate's inner thigh, just as he had intended.

With a cry, the pirate dropped to his knees, his sword clattering to the deck. Will rushed forward, thrusting his knee upward and into the man's chin before he could react. He crumpled, unconscious.

Will collected the sword and gripped the hilt tightly, his palm slick with rain. He used his free hand to wipe the wetness from his eyes. "They aren't trained fighters, so use whatever you can find to defend yourselves," he called out. "There might be weapons on the dead." Though he winced at how callous his words sounded, he knew it was a reality they had to face: they needed whatever defense they could lay hold of, and the dead had no use for a weapon.

His men, none of whom looked as though they'd held a weapon in their lives, all appeared stunned at his quick reflexes in battle. His calm seemed to remind them of the urgency they were facing, and they scattered to join the fight, some pausing to heft lighter crates that hadn't been strapped down as they ran into the melee. Perhaps it was madness, but there was no time to ponder another route to ensure their freedom.

With gritted teeth, Will moved over the prostrate body of the pirate and worked his way to the other side of the ship, seeing an unarmed crewman in distress. Will's heart fell, seeing the boy was not more than thirteen and was corned by two pirates, who were obviously toying with him. One of them flicked the tip of his sword across the boy's chest, and he cried out as a thin red slash joined the others already crisscrossing his shirt.

Anger blazing, Will stealthily came up behind them. The young man caught the movement, his wide eyes alerting the pirates to his presence. They turned, one of them barely deflecting a harsh blow from Will's sword, the force of which had him stumbling back into the boy, who shrieked in protest as he was shoved against the railing. The other barbarian advanced, his sneer stretching the scars on his face, just as the first regained his footing. The bones about their waists clanked eerily, seeming to keep rhythm with the steady spatter of the rain against the deck.

Will narrowed his eyes, widening his stance in preparation of an attack from both men. He had the advantage of training and years of practice, but there were two of them, and both held long swords, bloodlust hanging in their gazes.

"I've your back, sir." Suddenly, Gilcrest was at his side, and in his hand was . . . the remains of a torch that had sputtered out in the rain. His only weapon was a mass of burnt, damp wood, yet his gaze was shockingly ferocious on his young face. The pirates shared an amused glance and didn't spare the boy another look.

Will wanted to tell him to get back, that his loyalty, while touching, would only get him killed. But he gritted his teeth, jumping back as another blow came from the first pirate. Their weapons clanged, and he grunted as their swords crossed, each vying for the advantage. Gilcrest let out a high-pitched battle cry as he smacked the other man across the face with his torch. The sound momentarily startled Will's opponent, drawing his gaze away for a second too long.

With his attention diverted, Will grabbed for the man's wrist, steadying their joined swords, and shoved him backward to get him off-balance just before he landed a kick to the man's midsection that sent him reeling. Arms flailing, the pirate smacked into the railing, losing his balance as he stumbled overboard with a shout.

Breathing heavily, Will turned to find the young crewman watching the scene with a shocked look on his face, half forgotten in the midst of the melee. He met Will's eyes, looking startled and baffled at his assistance. "You're one of the prisoners," he said shakily.

"Get out of here!" Will shouted, hearing the boy scramble away as he turned in time to see the remaining pirate, whom Gilcrest had foolishly and bravely assaulted, lifting his sword high; he was certainly paying attention to the cabin boy *now.*

With a cry, Will dove forward, extending his sword as Gilcrest closed his eyes and braced himself for the blow that arced downward. The pirate's weapon glanced off of Will's, though the impact jarred the sword from Will's hand and sent it clattering to the deck. The bottom of a boot connected with his stomach, and Will fell with a grunt as the air left him.

Gilcrest launched himself onto the man's back, trying to strangle him with his scrawny arms. The man grimaced as he tried to break free, and suddenly the boy was thrown to the deck. He lay there, groaning, as the pirate advanced on Will. His sadistic smirk twisted Will's insides as all the reasons he had to fight for life flooded his mind—Sarah, protecting Serimone and his friends, returning to avenge his uncle's death. But his chest heaved with each breath as he fought for air, wheezing as he propped himself up on his elbows. His eyes madly scanned the deck in search of a weapon, but his sword was several feet out of reach of either himself or Gilcrest, who was just rousing.

Will narrowed his eyes up at the pirate, trying to see him through the torrents of rain. Shock ran through him, turning his blood cold and weighing his mind down with the same fog that enveloped them. This couldn't be the end, he thought distantly—he would not die at the hands of a *barbarian.* There was no glory in a death such as this, and for the first time in his life, he wondered what came after it.

The pirate's anger-filled face suddenly turned blank as a crate was smashed over his head, crumpling him to the ground.

Will blinked through the fog in surprise, and Gilcrest rose shakily to his feet, mouth agape. Merek stood above him, soaked from head to toe, his features grim. "With age comes wisdom," he remarked wryly—probably more out of habit than actual amusement, as his serious expression did not lighten. He held a hand down to Will, appearing to ignore the man he had knocked unconscious at their feet. "Come. We've found a small boat and are loading what remains of us onboard—the battle's already lost, boy," he added when Will hesitated. He nodded slowly, accepting assistance and rising to his feet with a grimace.

The three of them ran together, which was difficult on Will's recovering lungs, though he did his best to keep up as they followed Merek. Though a few of the pirates had been slain, many of them were still moving about the deck, calling out orders as the new captain took over. They seemed more intent on taking control of the ship and discovering what sort of booty they had uncovered than in slaying the stragglers. Perhaps they intended to make them part of their crew of marauders.

Will steeled his jaw, knowing they would not trade their freedom to become prisoners under a new command.

They hurried along, trying to maintain a low profile, but Will's steps slowed as he took in the aftermath of what could only be described as an outright slaughter. Countless crewmen lay in pools of their own blood, and Will recognized several unseeing faces, having known them for only a few brief moments below deck. *How many have we lost?* he wondered as he tried taking in a count of the men who had followed him and now lay facedown on the deck or stared up at the falling water with blank eyes.

"Here," Merek whispered loudly to be heard over the rain and the shouts coming from the new captain and crew. Will jerked his eyes from the macabre sight in time to see Merek disappear behind a tall stack of barrels that had been strapped securely to the deck by thick ropes. Will and Gilcrest found him carelessly hopping over the side of the ship, and the younger boy squawked as they both surged forward to peer overboard.

Will blinked in surprise as Merek peered back at him, standing on a small boat where several of the prisoners sat looking up at him anxiously. It drifted gently from side to side, suspended by a mass of ropes that were connected to a pulley system. The men sat waiting for him, and perhaps the next step in his half-cocked plan.

"I'd forgot we had a dinghy," Gilcrest murmured, his look one of admiration. He launched himself into the boat much as Merek had, landing with a muffled grunt amidst the sound of the men hissing at him to have a care.

If Will was not so out of breath, he might have chuckled in relief. He gripped the railing, intending to haul himself over, when strong hands grabbed him from behind, yanking him back. Gilcrest cried out as Will grappled with the pirate who was trying to wrestle him from the side. His fingers slipped from the rain-slicked railing, and he spun to fight the man.

"Lower the boat." Will grunted the command. But the men hesitated, and some were even attempting to climb back onto the main vessel, despite the fact that it was out of reach. "Detach her quickly!" he shouted this time, landing a blow to the man's jaw that had him reeling into the crates. A single rope snapped from its latch under the force of his weight, and the crates, along with the man, loudly toppled into a heap on the deck. One shattered at the impact, and the man groaned amidst the splinters, caught beneath a large crate that had his legs pinned down. The cacophony drew the attention of several pirates nearby, and some left their stations, coming to see what the commotion was about.

Will realized that the men still had not gone, and he knew with more pirates headed their way that it might be their only chance. He threw an arm to the side, urging them away. "I'll swim to you. Go, *now*!" After a pause, he heard the faint squeak of the pulleys as the boat was lowered into the water with a small *plop*.

As his opponent rose shakily to his feet, he risked a glance over his shoulder and saw with great relief that they had rowed some twenty feet away. The men sat, waiting for him in the rain, Gilcrest standing at attention near the front. Will grinned at the staggering pirate, knowing he could have this man overboard before the other barbarians could offer assistance. He would join his fellow men shortly.

Warning shouts came from the prisoner holding area down below, and Will saw over the pirate's shoulder two of his barbaric crewmates emerge from below deck. They looked frightened and were screaming for everyone to take cover. A loud crack sounded above the cries of the wounded and the shouts of the new crew. Will jerked his head toward the sight of the screaming men abandoning ship, their bodies landing in the choppy water.

It happened in a mere instant, and he didn't have time to wonder what had frightened them as he turned in time to see the vessel crack and split wide open before it exploded in a gust of fire, smoke, and blazing wind.

ଔଓ

It was hours before the front door creaked open, spilling hazy moonlight onto the floor of Jade's main room. Sarah sat up quickly on the sofa, where she'd been watching that very door, waiting for the instant Damien and Will stepped inside. Her tired eyes blinked against the pale light, trying to make out two forms. But it was only Damien who entered, his posture rigid as he reluctantly came inside, closing the door behind him.

Sarah's heart pounded expectantly, though it hiccupped in dread as her eyes readjusted to the darkness and she could at last make out his expression. She stood on shaky legs. "Why isn't Will with you?" she asked, wanting to hear him contradict her terrifying thoughts.

Damien's handsome features were twisted with compassion. "I am so sorry."

Every hope she'd ever had and lost and dared to hope for again came crashing down with those words. Worse than the sight of the time machine lying in an irreparable heap was the look on Damien's face now. She shook her head in denial, though she had feared this very thing when Will had gone to the castle to free them all. It was supposed to have been a simple in-and-out excursion, and then he would return for her. How had everything gone wrong so quickly?

"What happened?" she whispered, her voice catching. She managed to swallow, though the action pained her.

Damien cringed, and he gently took her arm. "Perhaps you should sit down."

She shook off his hand, clenching her jaw to keep the tears at bay. They gave her tone a sharp, broken edge. "Please, just tell me what happened to him. I have to know."

He hesitated. "How much?"

"Everything," she answered softly, though she wondered if she truly wished to know. She tightened her fists. "Tell me what happened at the castle."

Damien watched her face closely, and then reluctantly admitted, "It took some time for my informant inside the castle to glean anything. However—" He stopped, licked his lips, and sighed. "I do not have every detail, but my man discovered that Thomas Greene was questioned yesterday, though it sounds like their efforts were wasted. I don't know precisely what they were hoping to learn from him, but I think we can presume the same thing."

"What happened to Thomas?" she interrupted, her voice was barely above a whisper in anticipation of news of Will that she felt certain would come. Ignoring the facts wouldn't change reality, but she was still hesitant to hear Damien out even as the wait increased her anxiety. She cleared her throat. "Is he okay? Did they release him when they figured out he didn't know anything?"

"Sarah," he said gently. His fingers brushed the back of her hand, as though the contact might offer her brief comfort, before his arm fell to his side. "The tactics they used to question him . . . He did not survive."

She was breathing heavily now, staring into Damien's eyes, which looked nearly black in the low light. She felt fearful of the truth she saw in his gaze. Swallowing, she voiced the question she most needed and feared an answer to. "And Will? Did they interrogate—?" She clenched her jaw and ground out, "Did they do the same thing to him?"

The faint shake of Damien's head sent a small shockwave of relief through her, and she nearly collapsed to the ground. Her relief was short-lived with his next words. "But he was apprehended."

Her lips parted as she processed this, and then her head shot up. "We have to get him back. It's been a few hours, but if we can find out where they're keeping Will, then you can help me rescue him."

"No."

Sarah blinked at the softly spoken word, though his unwillingness only heightened her resolve. "Fine, if you won't help, I'll find a way to save him myself." She started for the door with a determined stride, but Damien's hand shot out to stop her. Confused and more than a little perturbed, she looked up at him. If he wasn't going to help her, then at least he could let her make her own decision about it.

"What?" she snapped, urgency tugging her heart and mind toward the door, to the woods and castle beyond. "Why can't I go and bring him back?"

"Because there is nothing to retrieve." His quiet, matter-of-fact words sent a chill through her. The question in her eyes caused him to wince, but still he said softly, "Taylor was put on a prisoner transport vessel that set sail, presumably for Africa, immediately after his capture. . . . I was informed that the ship he was on was attacked by barbarians, and somehow the ship went down—an onboard explosion is suspected. The report came from a fishing vessel returning to port that stumbled upon the carn—the remains of the ship."

Carnage, he had been about to say, Sarah was sure. The realization sent a shiver through her. "They saw the barbarians and crewmen in the sea and went to offer assistance to the survivors, but . . . there were none." Though she could tell his honest words were carefully selected to cause her the least harm, it did little good, since the truth was too painful to bear in any form.

"Are—?" She halted as her vocal chords grated, clearing her throat to shed the sound of sandpaper rasping against her words. "How can they be sure it was the ship Will was on?"

But Damien was already shaking his head at her proposition. "They could not bring in all of the lost, but the body of the captain was brought to land, and one of the dockworkers recognized him. He knew what vessel the captain had been sailing on, and the same one that went under was the very ship on which Taylor and many others had been placed."

No survivors, he had said. Sarah's chest clenched. Her chin lurched up and down in an attempt to choke back her sobs as the reality of what he had told her at last sank in. She gripped her stomach, trying to quell the agony that rose from within her even as she chanted that Will was all right, he would come for her. She bit her lip, drawing blood in her effort to hide her pain. But who did she have to be brave for anymore?

"He isn't gone," she whispered to no one in particular. Then she dragged her watery gaze to Damien's face, eyes pleading for him to make her understand. Brokenly, she said, "He was going to come for me. Everything was going to be fine once he . . . I wasn't supposed to lose him so soon."

That thought caused several tears to slip down her cheeks, and once they were out, her sorrow could no longer be held back. She choked on her sobs, sinking to the floor slowly when her legs could no longer support her. The thought of choosing to let him go at some point in the future had been terrible enough, but she had been preparing herself for it for months, knowing that it might be inevitable. But losing him like this . . . The sudden force of her pain surprised her, and she gave into her shock and sorrow.

There was a moment of hesitation where she knew he was deciding if his comfort would be welcome, and then Damien's arms were suddenly around her as he kneeled beside her.

"*No*," she moaned in protest—of his embrace, of Will's death, of the fact that the villains had won. She pulled back, weakly hitting Damien in the chest again and again with her palm, her fist. He winced but let her hit him, having known the kind of agony and helpless rage that she was experiencing.

When she gave him a feeble shove, he only tightened his hold on her, pressing his cheek against her temple. He had held her when Edith died—at his own hands, a fact that she hadn't known at the time—but this instance she didn't push him away. She sobbed against his shirt, clinging to him, needing his embrace to hold her upright. For a moment, she pretended they were Will's strong arms surrounding her, but then she remembered that those arms were lost at sea and would never hold her again, and the sobs began afresh as she cried against Damien's shoulder.

Will's okay. He has to be—Oh, God, please. Her silent, simple plea floated in the air between her and heaven, and for a brief second, she wondered if anyone heard. Or cared.

She closed her eyes, awash with guilt, and shook her head at the distress-fueled doubt in God's mercy, something she had preached to Will about time and time again. *I'm sorry. I know You're listening, but I'm scared and hurting, and I just—I don't know what to do now that Will's gone.*

She fisted Damien's shirt in her hands, knowing it would be a long time before she felt okay again. Tears rolled down her cheeks and dripped off her chin, soaking through the fabric on her forearm. *We were a team and now . . . God, what am I supposed to do?*

No clear answer came, but the crippling hysteria was beginning to pass, though the ache was still there, burning inside her chest a little every time she breathed. Her lips had grown numb by the time she composed herself enough to pull back. She looked up at Damien with a quivering chin and found his gold-flecked gaze swimming.

"Y-you're crying," she observed shakily, taken aback at this display of emotion over a man he had detested. "But you hated Will."

His smile was sorrowful. He used a finger to brush away the tear that had slipped over his lid and landed on her cheek. His palm stayed there, thumb rubbing under her eye. "But *you* loved him," he replied softly. "My tears are for your sorrow."

Fresh tears welled up, making the outline of Damien's features wobble. But she bit her lip, somehow managing to hold most of them at bay as she found a modicum of strength when her hands curled around her necklace—something solid to cling to. The letter crinkled faintly in her sleeve, half forgotten.

She swallowed the pain in her throat and whispered regretfully, "I never told him."

The moon was at its height, allowing her to see his expression in the gray-white light. The faint tip of his lips was a mixture of pain, chagrin, and wry amusement, though the wetness clinging to his lashes belied the latter emotion. "Ah, but he *knew*, my darling. He knew."

ଔ

Damien watched her shoulder rise and fall, assuring himself that she would find more peace in unconsciousness than she would in this reality. His head was turned to observe her as he leaned his back against the couch, though he could only make out the outline of her features in the dark: her head resting in the crook of her bent arm, auburn hair spilling over the side of the sofa. He was only ever allowed to truly study her as she slept, and though she always fell asleep in the same position, somehow it never failed to fascinate him—even if his memory of her had to piece together her features in the faint moonlight coming through the tiny crack in the shutters.

When they had both become too sore and cold sitting on the floor, Damien had urged her to lie down, and her silent acquiescence as she let him guide her to the sofa had saddened him; he had never seen her so broken, like a hollow shell of the woman she had once been. He did not have to see Sarah's face now to know that her expression would be more peaceful than it had been earlier, having seen the torture and denial, sorrow and disbelief as they washed over her features until she fell asleep from pure exhaustion.

It had pained him to tell her that the blacksmith knew of her affection for him, but it was the truth, one that visibly helped to lessen the guilt he saw weighing her down. Damien witnessed her love for the man in nearly everything she did: it was in the way that a special light could be found in her eyes every time she was around Taylor or spoke of him, how she smiled for him alone, or in those instances where they seemed to silently understand one another, conveying some message outsiders would never understand. And if those and countless other truths weren't reasons enough, the depth of her affection was obvious in the fact that, without a second thought, she had been willing to risk her safety and her life to rescue Taylor. It was achingly clear that a part of her had died with the man tonight, and Damien knew a piece of her heart was floating in some dark part of the sea, never to be recovered.

Holding her and having her cling to him for comfort had been a horrifically tangled experience. For a few seconds, Damien had taken no small pleasure in holding her and imagining that nothing stood in their way, but pain had laced every spark of joy that tried to surface, knowing that she was only in his arms seeking comfort in the wake of losing the love of her life.

Empathy for her sorrow, sweet joy at her need for him, and bitter guilt for taking *any* pleasure in a man's death, even Taylor's, all vied for attention, marring his time with Sarah. Damien did not want to be the kind of man who would capitalize on a woman's loss, and so he had told himself to focus on her need for comfort and friendship, forcing all other thoughts aside and turning his full attention on simply being present when she needed him the most, even if nothing came of it for him.

But being selfless did not come easily to him, he acknowledged as he leaned his head against the sofa, examining Sarah's profile in the dark. If letting her go to be with the man she loved had been a selfless act, then Damien had to admit to himself that, if given the chance to redo the past week, he would be terribly selfish all over again if it meant having these last few days with her once more. He was fairly certain that keeping Sarah from precious hours with a lover who would soon die made him a horrible person, a man undeserving of a woman such as she.

He sighed.

"So it is true?" Isabella's voice was soft, and he looked up at her. How long had she been standing there? "William is dead?"

Damien nodded solemnly. His voice was a faint whisper to keep from waking Sarah. "I am afraid so."

"Oh." She sank to her knees, gazing at the floor with an unreadable gaze. She whispered another simple, "Oh."

"I am sorry, sister. I know you were close once."

Her gaze was distant even as she looked her brother in the eye. "Our friendship was a lifetime ago. I have long given up on caring for him in that way." Her words were filled with quiet firmness, but he sensed they were partly false. He didn't press her, though, knowing she would grieve in her own way.

Isabella's eyes landed on Sarah's sleeping form, and a flicker of sympathy caused the corner of her mouth to twitch. "How is she?"

Another long sigh escaped him. "I can hardly say, but seeing how broken and lost she looked . . . It tore at me," he whispered, staring at Isabella with a gaze tortured by more than Sarah's current grief.

For a long stretch of silence, she only observed him. Then she said, her words faint with disbelief, "You still care for her, after all this time. How?"

Damien lazily rolled his head from side to side. "I do not know, truly. From the moment I met her, I knew she could teach me to love again." He paused. "Yet I never thought it was possible to love someone so much when they care so little for you in return—to continue in your affection even when all hope is lost."

"I have seen how she looks at you," Isabella said, her voice the tenderest he had heard in a long while. He met her eyes, and moonlight danced off her beseeching gaze. "I assure you, brother, she does care. Do not think yourself so beneath her returned affection."

Damien's exhalation of breath sounded hopeless to his own ears. His voice was so quiet, almost like he hadn't meant to say the words aloud, though he had to admit them to someone other than himself or he feared he might go mad considering them in silence. "She has only just lost the love of her life. I could never—" He stopped, clearing the emotion from his throat. "I know that she could never care for me as she did Taylor, and I would not force my love on her now—not when she is so destroyed by her loss. What sort of man would that make me?"

"Even though her weakness almost guarantees that she would fall into your arms?" Isabella looked at him incredulously, though there was a bit of admiration in her gaze that caught him off-guard. He could only stare back at his sister and nod slowly. "But you still wish to woo her, no?" she pressed softly.

A small, strangled laugh broke the quiet, and Damien shot a quick glance at Sarah's sleeping form to ensure she hadn't woken. He lowered his voice. "Of course I wish to win her. I do not believe I can ever cease loving her, but I know I cannot pursue it just now." He exhaled a controlled breath through his nostrils. "Perhaps not ever."

"I can respect your compassion and regard for her feelings, brother, but she deserves neither you nor your honor." Her voice was laced with the edge of a protective sibling, and he had to smile at an emotion he hadn't glimpsed from her in what felt like ages.

"Oh, Isabella," he said quietly. Sarah stirred, and his hand brushed her hair back from her face, careful not to wake her. "Someday I hope you know a love like this, one that makes you willing to sacrifice for the better of the other."

"I thought I did," she whispered, voice pained. The hand on Sarah's head paused, and Damien's brows drew together as he watched the anger and hurt fill his sister's lovely face. "I gave up everything for you, as you risked it all for me after I killed Father. I joined this life of a self-selling woman—a life I *detest*—to get information for *you*, hoping that the quicker you finished your duties for Cadius, then perhaps you might end your association with him sooner. Then we could finally be a family again." Her voice wavered with hurt. Quietly, she added, "Though that is not entirely the reason."

He felt staggered. "Isabella, I—I had assumed you took up that . . . practice to spite me. You said you wanted no part of my dealings or to take handouts from a murderous scoundrel such as Cadius."

"That is not precisely what I said."

"I know, but I would rather censor the exact words you used in regard to both myself and Cadius." He thought he might have caught a flash of a grin in the dark. Lowering his voice, Damien asked gently, "What else, then?"

Her silhouette remained stoic in the moonlight, and she would have given no hint of the hurt she had carried all this time had it not been for the tiny sniff that came from her general direction. "It was, in some small part, to spite the men in my life and assert control over my own future. But you know I never approved of your involvement with Cadius, and my main motivation for selecting that profession was because I believed I could help you." Isabella gave a quiet, uncaring laugh to cover the emotion in her voice that hovered just beneath the surface. "And I am sure my pride and sense of self-preservation was a factor in choosing a more 'lucrative' field than seamstress work."

There was a pause on Damien's part as he absorbed what she had admitted and the cavalier sense of vanity she had thrown in at the end. He had been under the impression that his little sister was ungrateful for his care and all he had tried to do to make their lives better. And now she was telling him that she had participated in a life he disapproved of to protect *him*? Though her façade had hardened over the years, he knew it was just that—a mask—and he could see how the derision and disgust of the townsfolk had hurt her. Isabella had done an excellent job of pretending to be vain, conceited, and indifferent, but Damien saw how she had been affected—being ostracized by polite society and made the subject of the town gossips' whispered exchanges in the street as she passed by.

As the silence lengthened, her shoulders dipped noticeably. "I suppose it was foolish of me to imagine that either of us could ever leave these lives—that of a worthless tramp and the lackey of a cruel blaggard." The shift in her expression was unreadable in the darkness, but he could picture her face with the sound of forced bitterness her words carried.

Damien winced at her words and the truth they carried on his part, even if it was a little harsh. "You are *not* a worthless tramp, little sister." His hand left Sarah's head, and he rose to his knees to wrap his sister in a tight embrace. Her arms immediately wrapped around his middle, seeking his comfort. "But haven't we left them behind, dear heart?"

A bitter laughed escaped Isabella's lips, though her voice was despondent. "No, we both carry the stench of those lives with us wherever we go. If neither of us can forgive ourselves for what we've done, how can we expect to let them go?"

He was silent a long time, searching for the answer. Finally, he sighed, resting his chin on top of her head. “I wish I knew.”

Chapter Twenty-Three

"You call it hope—that fire of fire!
It is but agony of desire."

Edgar Allan Poe, *Tamerlane*

Sarah lay awake staring at the ceiling after they left and until the sun began to rise, pondering what she had overheard. Yes, she'd felt guilty when she awoke in the middle of the siblings' conversation, but she had felt too tired to let them know she was alert and then too embarrassed when she realized they were talking about her.

Damien's words tapped on her consciousness for the rest of the night and into the morning like a bothersome woodpecker. He had claimed he loved her before, but Sarah had brushed it off as some twisted affection or dire need of his to feel close to someone, anyone. But overhearing his words, filled with such tenderness and longing . . . It was undeniable.

Damien was truly in love with her.

Certain that he wouldn't consider leaving her alone after the distressing news he had relayed last night, Sarah rolled onto her side and found him on the floor, exactly as she had expected, knowing that he would want to be there if she needed anything. He looked as he had the other night she had studied his sleeping face, with his tousled hair, mouth parted slightly. But this time she saw him with different eyes, unclouded by her own anger.

A knack for shutting down her defenses, that's what he had; Damien had a way of making her feel pity, even when she wanted to hate him after she'd found out who he was working for. Her thoughts and feelings for Damien had never been cut-and-dry, turning into a jumbled pile of indiscernible mush whenever she tried to sort them out and make sense of who he was. He had been a friend that evolved into a romantic interest who caused her toes to curl and her breath to catch unexpectedly, and then he had become a murderer and a kidnapper concerned for her safety. But this . . .

With a quiet sigh, Sarah planted her hands under her temple and closed her eyes, though she couldn't fall back to sleep. Her compassion stirred for Damien when she thought about his proclamation of love and the selfless way he told his sister he would protect Sarah, knowing she might never feel anything for him again.

"I have seen the way she looks at you, brother. . . . She does care." Jade's words haunted her now, contradicting the anger she wanted to hold

onto when it came to Damien. But it was the truth. Despite everything, Sarah *did* care, and some small part of her still wished she were different and that she could return his feelings, if only to give him the love he had always longed for and never had. But Damien had been right when he said her heart belonged elsewhere, and she could not betray Will's memory.

She closed her eyes, agony washing over her as she remembered him, and though her eyes filled, she had shed too many tears last night for them to begin falling again. A part of her was disbelieving that someone so vital to her life could be lost so quickly, but the look on Damien's face—the guilt, regret, and empathy—had spoken volumes. She knew he hadn't been lying when he said the men on Will's ship had all died in the attack and the ensuing explosion. And coupled with the constant pain in the gap in her chest where Will's memory rested was a single question: What now?

This was all supposed to be over by now. The plan had been for Will to tell the king that Cadius was alive and was his corrupted father, the king would have Cadius executed—and check for a pulse this time—and then they would be free to live their lives outside of fear of Cadius' sadistic plotting. But Will was gone, and with Cadius and King Adrian—Sarah still felt a shock of surprise at the reminder of his involvement—on high alert, and not to mention the practically endless resources at the kingdom's disposal . . .

Sarah sighed, knowing it would be impossible to convict *anyone* at this point, not that the king would do anything about it, seeing as he'd been the one to have his father killed, according to Damien. Though this mess had begun on a petty vendetta and twisted loyalty, it had moved onto something much bigger when Cadius decided he wanted control of Ridlan. Nobody was higher up than a royal, she reasoned, so there was no one left to make them pay for what they had done.

Cadius and his son had won, which meant that all of Serimone had lost.

She temporarily pushed aside the reminder of the true claim to the throne they assumed Richard had in favor of her own misery and hopelessness. *I deserve an hour to wallow.*

She realized it was a ridiculous thought and felt a spasm of guilt over her selfish behavior, but she couldn't help feeling a sense of total hopelessness. Will was dead because she had dragged him into this mess, failed in her original objective in remaining in Serimone, put Damien in prison—though she wasn't so sure that getting him out of Cadius' clutches had been a *bad* thing—and her involvement had caused people to die, though her more logical side argued that Cadius probably would have killed them regardless of her presence in the twelfth century.

Sarah wanted to tell herself to be strong—for Wills' memory, if nothing else—but despondency swallowed her up, every negative thought she'd been trying to keep at bay surging to the surface at once.

Both she and Damien were wanted either for treason or meddling, and the authorities and the current regime would all be after them, which meant that neither of them could get within spitting distance of Serimone Castle without someone spotting them. Even if they did manage to find someone who would help them stop Cadius and *the king*, they would be apprehended the second they revealed themselves, being the only ones who had evidence against the evil father-son duo. And if she and Damien did nothing and remained safe . . . Either way, it was over, and they had failed miserably.

A door creaked on its hinges, and Sarah propped herself up on an elbow and watched as Jade quietly emerged from her room. "Morning," she whispered sleepily. Her eyes were red-rimmed and puffy, and Sarah knew she hadn't imagined her sobbing the night before as she took in her emotion-wearied features. Sarah assumed she looked the same, if not worse.

"Hey."

"Why are you awake so early?" Jade asked, her surprise leaking out into her words. She pulled the shawl about her shoulders a little tighter, and her boots were on, to keep her feet warm, Sarah assumed, since Jade still wore her nightclothes. "I had expected you to sleep until midday."

Sarah gave an awkward half-shrug from her position on the couch. She pulled her blanket up a little higher against the early morning chill and opted for Jade's usual tactic of blatant honesty. "Just pondering all the lives I've screwed up, including your brother's."

"I cannot disagree with you on that count," Jade remarked dryly, though her lips tipped almost imperceptibly with fondness as she gazed at her sleeping brother.

Sarah was too tired to take offense at the remark. Seeing Jade's face and recalling the protective distrust in her voice last night, Sarah thought that Jade and the Will she had first met had something in common: they pushed people away as a form of self-preservation.

The reminder of Will stung, and she sucked in a shuddering breath. She would trade nearly anything for even an hour with the old, aloof Will, if just to see his face one last time and say goodbye. The watch strapped snugly to her wrist mocked her, completely useless. What was the point in being a time traveler if she couldn't go back and save those she loved?

Her chest clenched. Yet another reminder of things left unsaid.

Damien stirred, blinking, and scrubbed a hand over his face to wake himself up. He looked first to his sister, whose face had turned blank once more, but then his gaze landed on Sarah, and he sat up quickly. "How are you?" His tone was soft and gravelly from sleep.

Her throat tightened at the note of compassion in his voice. It felt strange to have Damien asking how she felt after the man she was in love with had just died, but the look of genuine openness in his sleepy features and bleary eyes put her at ease, reminding her that he truly did care how she had been affected.

A shaky breath was dragged into her lungs. "I'll be all right." She sat up, swallowing back the sudden tears that attempted to belie her words.

Though he didn't look as though he believed her, Damien nodded.

"Thanks for, um, last night." She stared awkwardly at her hands in her lap, reminded of the blubbering mess she had been reduced to. But she felt no shame as she met Damien's eyes, knowing he had lost loved ones, too.

"Of course." He nodded once and rose to his feet. "Now if you will excuse me . . ." He made his way out of the house, surprising Sarah at his obvious embarrassment and abrupt departure. Then she remembered the inconvenience of not having indoor plumbing, an amenity that she would never again take for granted back home.

Jade sat on the floor and stared off at some distant spot on the wall, her lips pursed. "I am sorry."

Sarah started, surprised at her apology as much as she had been that Jade was *choosing* to remain in the same room as her. The words had seemed reluctant and had been forced past a clenched jaw, but still. "For what?"

"For—" Jade sighed and met her gaze. For the first time since Sarah had met her, Jade appeared to have completely let down her guard; all haughty guise had fled her face, making her look young and exhausted. "For treating you so poorly when I first met you. And recently," she added.

The apology seemed sincere, but it took Sarah a moment to recover from her shock over the fact that it was coming from *Jade*. "T-thank you."

Jade nodded curtly. "Well, yes." Her eyes skirted anxiously about the room. Sarah waited, sensing she had something else to say and wondering if she was expecting an apology in return. Her red-rimmed eyes filled, though she refused to meet Sarah's gaze. "All my life, I have been controlled by men; they have told me what to do with my own life and how to act, how I should dress. I know much of it was self-inflicted by the profession I chose, but it stung all the same. It was like living with my father once again."

The corner of Sarah's mouth tipped downward in sympathy, though she wasn't quite sure what had caused the other woman to open up to her.

Moved, she lowered herself to the floor. It was a small thing, but it put them at eye level, and she didn't want Jade to feel that Sarah was placing herself above her. "I'm sorry for judging you and for thinking you were so heartless."

Jade winced, and Sarah realized how her words must have sounded. "Thank you, I suppose."

To try and make up for the offense she might have caused, Sarah added, “Will told me you were a good person, and I’m sorry I let my jealousy cloud my judgment.”

“But I have not been,” Jade whispered, dropping her gaze. “William was the first man, aside from my brother, to treat me as an equal—as though I were a person. We met when we were both children, and he quickly became my only loyal friend. When the other girls would tease me or the boys made obnoxious advances, William was always there for me, leaving a few sharp words or bruises in his wake.”

Sarah smiled despite the pain in her chest. “Sounds like Will.” Though their mutual affection for and loss of Will seemed to have given them a safe ground on which to speak, it felt too soon to think about him in the past tense. She swallowed.

Jade nodded. “Even after I joined this life to help my brother and earn an honest living—” She halted, chuckling is a self-deprecating way. “I suppose *honest* is not quite the right term. Regardless, William came by day after day, asking me to leave my new profession. He said he would find me a job elsewhere, not realizing that all I wanted was *him* and not some second-rate way of living.”

Wincing, Sarah shook her head, feeling genuine compassion for this woman who had driven her nuts and tried to wedge her and Will apart. She was surprised by her desire to mend the rift between them, but she touched Jade’s arm, anyway. The woman jerked in surprise but didn’t pull back. “We both lost him, Isabella, and I’m sorry.”

Jade blinked, seemingly taken aback by the use of her given name. Then she nodded slowly. “He was never mine to lose,” she whispered. A moment passed before she collected herself, smiling faintly as she focused on a good memory. “When we first met, I refused to give him my true name, because I wished to forget my old life and the girl I had been. So he gave me a new one instead, saying it reminded him of springtime.”

“What was it?”

She smiled softly with fond remembrance. “Marian.”

The sweetness of the story turned sour in Sarah’s stomach. Marian. *Marian?* Jade was Marian? She and Will were supposed to be together? The pain in her chest intensified. It looked as though Sarah and Will had never been meant to fall in love, and somehow she was certain that her meddling with the past had ruined any future Jade—*Marian*—and Will were supposed to have. If she hadn’t come back here to try and stop Cadius, she wouldn’t have enlisted Will’s help, which meant she never would have driven a wedge between he and Jade, and he never would have gone to the king and ended up a prisoner on that boat. She’d rewritten history without even realizing.

The horror on her features was lost on Jade as she turned toward the opening door. Damien strode in just as his sister rose to her feet, quickly masking the emotions that had passed across her face just moments ago. She was once again the blank-faced sister, and Sarah wondered if she felt embarrassment over expressing so much emotion with her brother the night before.

"I believe I will take a stroll before we break the fast." And then she was gone, closing the front door softly behind her. They didn't bother to lock it anymore; Sarah had nowhere else to go, and they all knew it.

Damien shook his head at the closed door. Something had shifted inside of Sarah sometime during his conversation with Jade last night, and she felt like she was gazing at the old Damien—if not a little more battered and rough around the edges, she thought as he touched his wounded side. That confident swagger she remembered so well was practically non-existent, but once more she saw him as the friend he had been before he shot Edith.

Her compassion stirred when she looked up at him, now knowing how the loss of love made you feel empty and confused inside. Although Damien hadn't physically lost her, he'd never really had Sarah's affection, and that kind of unreciprocated love could be just as painful as what Sarah was experiencing. Her heart ached for him, and she wanted to relieve the burden that made his gaze heavy, if even just a little.

"Your sister loves you, you know."

Damien let out a long breath. "Yes, but some days I do not understand her."

"She's a lot like Will." He met her eyes, curiosity flickering across his espresso gaze. Sarah bit her lip for a moment, gathering herself so she didn't break down again, and then added softly, "I used to get so frustrated that he couldn't express his feelings and would shut down when given the chance. It took me awhile to understand why he did, but now I know it was because he was afraid of letting people in and then losing them as he lost his parents."

Damien blinked and sat on the floor near her, close enough to touch as he propped up his knees. "I do not understand; Isabella knows that I am here to support her, so why should she fear our parting?"

Sarah fought for words before giving up with a shrug and a sigh. "I don't know exactly. But I'm telling you that your sister doesn't want you to see how much you mean to her because she's afraid to let you in. Maybe she's scared another man in her life will reject her or she'll lose you someday. I don't know." Her fingertips grazed his knee in a comforting gesture, but she quickly pulled back, not wanting him to read into it. "But I'm positive Isabella loves you and only wants to be loved by you in return."

Propping his chin on his hand, Damien mumbled, "We are a confusing lot, are we not?"

A laugh escaped her lips, startling her. The sound felt like a betrayal to Will's recent departure from this earth, and her shoulders drooped. "Yeah, I guess we are. Just be honest with your sister and don't get discouraged when she acts like she doesn't care." She shot him a faint, encouraging grin. "You'll break her down like you broke me down."

He winced, and she realized he had taken her comment the wrong way. She had meant to make a joke of the fact that he made everyone adore him, but she could tell from the look in his eyes that he was reminded of the time when she had said he'd broken her spirit.

"She told me she took part in an unsavory occupation to protect *me*, to help me remove myself from Cadius' grip as expediently as possible." His tormented gaze met Sarah's. "My only goal in uniting with Cadius was to earn enough to make a life for us, and in so doing, I was the cause of my own sister selling herself for information and money." His Adam's apple bobbed in a guilty swallow.

"You know that was her choice; she didn't have to join that life."

He shot her a wry grin, though his gaze was weary. "It must be a family trait, jumping into foolish ventures."

Sarah chewed on her lip in the silence that followed. Quietly, she asked, "Was protecting Ja—Isabella—the only reason why you started with Cadius?"

He looked like he was about to say something and then changed his mind. He sighed. "That . . . and the fact that it is easier to embrace the darkness than to become one with the light."

"Damien." Sarah stopped and shook her head, unsure how to phrase her thoughts. He had always been able to confuse her, to make her feel a hundred things at once—hatred and kindness, joy and fear. Even now as she stood his mostly willing captive, she knew that he was simply a lost boy who had done what he thought best to protect her, and Sarah's heart truly opened to him for the first time in months, without hesitation or indecisiveness.

"Look at me," she insisted when his glazed eyes remained on her dirty hem. Dark brown eyes met hers, and she saw him swallow. She muttered, "How can you be so darn complicated and puzzling?"

He blinked in surprise. "I am sorry, I don't mean to be."

A frustrated breath escaped, realizing she'd voiced the thought aloud. "No, I'm sorry. Damien, you might have allowed yourself to be manipulated and to believe that you are only worth what others tell you, as Jade does, but believe *me* when I tell you that you are kinder than you give yourself credit for."

He scoffed, and she shook her head. "I mean it. You have done bad things—you can't deny that—but you have shown me greater gentleness than most others here and considered me a friend after having only known me a day. You cared for and comforted and encouraged me." A small grin turned the corner of her mouth. "And at the ball, you acted like a total idiot to lighten the mood."

His lips twitched with suppressed humor. "Yes, well, playing the buffoon is something I do quite well. I find it rather easy to lapse into the role at parties."

"But you didn't do it to entertain the others," she countered softly. "You did it for me, just so I wouldn't feel out of place. You put your reputation of being this mysterious Spanish lord on the line and made yourself look like a fool so I would feel like less of one. I *know* that you're a better person than you give yourself credit—than you'll allow yourself to be to reach your potential. You are brave and courageous and truthful." Wryly, she added, "When it suits you."

A grin twitched at the corner of Damien's mouth, though it faded at her next words. "And don't for one second believe that your soul is lost to Cadius. It doesn't belong to him, and it isn't lost because of him."

His eyes sparkled with suppressed emotion. "You can say these things and make such boasts of my character after all I have done? After the things I have put you through? You should loathe me."

"Yeah, well, you still have a knack for ticking me off." His grin at last emerged, although reluctantly, the movement sending down his cheek one lone tear that had been building in his eyes. Sarah's heart softened once more, twisting inside her chest at the pain permanently etched into his features.

"But I forgive you." She sucked in a breath at the same instant he did. Though she hadn't meant for their conversation to take this turn, as she spoke the words, she realized they were wholly true. At some point during this journey, perhaps months or moments ago, she had forgiven him without even acknowledging it. Steadying her quivering chin, she whispered, "I forgive you, Damien, for everything. With my whole heart, you have my forgiveness."

He didn't quite seem to know what to do with that. He divided his attention between her face and the fascinating floorboards. "It seems impossible," he breathed after several painfully silent minutes floated by with Sarah anxiously biting her lip.

"Well, believe it." She let out a choked laugh, the emotions of the past day making her feel a little out of control. But seeing the look of relief on Damien's face was worth hashing-out old wounds.

Slowly, another thought took root, a fear she hadn't considered before.

"What is it?" he asked.

Sarah scrunched up her face in concern. "Robert."

Damien looked confused. "What?"

"Will's assistant at the livery. Robert knows a little bit about what's been going on." She thought about hiding the fact that he knew just about *everything*, but then she realized he was already involved. Sighing, she elaborated, "It's Robert's watch that caused Cadius to travel to my world, and he won't know that Will's gone. They've been eliminating everyone close to us, and if Cadius were to recognize Robert . . . I don't know what would happen to him." Sarah gnawed on her lip, wondering and worrying. Would Damien let her go long enough that she could sneak into town? Would she be spotted and killed if she did? The door might be unlocked, but she doubted Damien would let her out of his sight now, anyway. Maybe Jade would help distract him.

Damien finally looked directly into her eyes, bafflement evident in his own gaze. "You truly wish to alert this man, Robert?" Sarah's head bobbed vehemently, her eagerness and mounting disquiet making her skin crawl.

Dipping his head once in acknowledgement, he said softly, "Then I shall do my best to ensure his survival. Isabella was planning on sneaking into town this afternoon for supplies. Would it suffice if she were to give him a warning?"

"Oh, yes," she agreed readily, grasping at any straw of hope he might hold out to her. Her apprehension eased a degree at his words. "Anything so that he knows Cadius might be out to get him. There's no one to look out for him with Will gone. . . ." She looked away, pain creasing her brow.

"You know that if he were alive, he would do everything in his power to return to you," Damien supplied with a grimace. His eyes softened sadly as he whispered, "I did." The instant the words left his lips, he appeared embarrassed that he'd admitted it aloud.

Sarah lowered her eyes to her lap in shame. He had done terrible things in the past, but he was trying to make up for them now in his search for some sort of perverted justice against Cadius. And though he was going about it in a completely deranged way, he had sacrificed his freedom to come back to Serimone, risking a worse sentence than before, so that he could keep her safe.

She placed a hand on his arm, and though she couldn't admit it aloud, she hoped it conveyed her appreciation for his efforts.

He swallowed thickly as he gazed at her hand, looking as though he longed to brush his fingers across her skin. But he appeared to still carry respect for her and resisted the urge. Sarah quickly, awkwardly, removed her hand.

Clearing his throat, he called out, "Isabella!"

She started as the door opened and Jade peeked around the corner; Sarah hadn't heard her loitering outside as Damien must have. His sister quirked a brow as she entered the room, her heirs making her seem superior even in her nightgown. "Am I cattle that I should be summoned thus?" she snapped, speaking grandly—to annoy her brother and make up for her "weakness" the night before, Sarah was sure.

Damien shook his head, appearing at a loss. The dark-haired woman's nose twitched, and Sarah wondered if she might have regretted speaking so harshly when he had lately been making an effort to change.

"What is it, brother?" Jade inquired, more calmly this time.

"When you go into town, I need you to inquire after the blacksmith's assistant, Robert. You must inform him that a certain *watch* that escaped his possession was recovered by Cadius. He is in grave danger and needs to be watchful of suspicious characters—possibly even encourage him to hide away for a fortnight—"

"Pardon?" Jade nearly screeched. Her mouth hung open in shock. "You wish for me to ruin my new identity by revealing myself to a man who works the *forge*?"

"It's not as though you know him," Damien answered simply, clearly not understanding that her cap was about to burst.

"He is *William's* assistant." Her tone suggested that he was perfectly stupid for not realizing this sooner. Their heart-to-heart the night before appeared completely forgotten. "He, along with the whole of Serimone, is under the impression that I am dead. *How* can I begin a new life for myself if I am still tied to the former?"

"It's not like Will's going to be there to recognize you," Sarah supplied, though her heart clenched a little at the reminder. She wallowed back the instant reminder, eyes beseeching. "I know you care for Will, and he would never want his friends harmed. Please, Isabella, I'm certain Robert's life will be in danger without you to tell him to watch out for himself." She hoped using Jade's given name—a reminder of a gentle young girl with compassion—would help to seal the deal.

Narrowing her eyes, Jade tapped a finger on her thigh as she considered the sincerity of her features. Sarah swallowed a little nervously beneath her gaze, but she stared back at her, unflinching, knowing that she would find the truth to her words written there.

"Fine," Jade announced at last, exhaling, the sound sharp and a bit haughty. Though her mask was back up, it was cracked, and there were small traces of the soft-spoken woman Sarah had glimpsed just that morning.

But then Jade bustled into her room and slammed the door, and Sarah winced. *It's definitely a convincing disguise, though,* she thought dryly.

Several minutes later, Jade emerged from her room tying an expensive gold sash about her shoulders. She was supposed to be blending in with the common folk of Serimone, but it looked as though old habits of dressing to impress were hard to shake.

She looked irritated as she pulled the sash up to cover her head and hiked her chin superciliously. "If I have to recreate another identity because of this Robert, then I shall kill him myself before Cadius has a chance to discover him." And then she swept through the doorway, slamming it behind her.

Chapter Twenty-Four

"Between two worlds life hovers like a star,
'Twixt night and morn, upon the horizon's verge,
How little we know that which we are!
How less we may be!"

Lord Byron, *Don Juan*

The sound echoed through the building as Robert brought the hammer down on the glowing horseshoe to properly mold it. He used the prongs to inspect it by the light of the forge's fire and saw its imperfections—the dents and pockets that made it pointless to reshape. He sighed, knowing it wouldn't help to reheat the piece of metal, and dropped the mangled shoe into a bucket of cold water where it hissed in objection.

There were two iron rods warming in the fire, and he pulled out one of them with a gloved hand. He inspected the jaggedly sharpened end of the iron—each piece was to become a curved hook for the butcher's order—and frowned, knowing he'd only served to bend the metal into a distorted point. Both rods would have to be completely reworked, which he would attempt, and probably fail, to do later.

Gritting his teeth in annoyance at his own incompetence, Robert set the cool portion of the handle in between two metal clamps and turned the crank until the clamps tightened around the rod, holding it firm without his help. It was an invention of Will's, like a pair of extra hands to hold objects that would need two free hands to mold it.

He ripped off the thick gloves he wore, angrily throwing them to the table. He was no good at this part of the job—making and bending metals was *Will's* forte, and he had no idea where he'd gone off to. The man had come by the livery to collect his stallion, told Robert to watch the shop until he returned, and then he had simply taken off. At first, Robert had thought he might have found a trail leading to Sarah and would return soon. But too much time had passed, and he hadn't seen his employer since.

Feeling restless, Robert walked over to one of the mares at the back of the building. It pranced around the space, pawing at the ground in an anxious sort of way that caused him to wonder if the animal sensed his own agitation. Clicking his tongue, he called her over and rubbed his hand up and down between the eyes to soothe her. The mare seemed to calm some, though it snuffed loudly from time to time, letting him know that she still sensed something amiss.

"Where are you, Taylor?" Robert mumbled. The horse whinnied in response.

"Hello?"

Robert spun at the light voice. Coming around the corner, he saw a woman with a sash over her head enter the livery, her steps hesitant. Taking a deep breath to recover from his concern over Will's absence and telling himself to act professional, he pasted on a smile that he hoped appeared earnest. "Can I help you, miss?"

She started, her full, painted lips parting. Releasing the sash, it fell back to reveal dark hair and an anxious expression on her staggeringly beautiful face. The woman cleared her throat and said with great importance, "It is I who am here to help you." Her voice was soft and somehow husky.

Blinking, Robert glanced behind her, wondering if she was alone or if he should have been expecting her. Did Will send the woman? "Beg your pardon?"

"You are in grave danger," she whispered. She made it seem as though she was delivering some great, impacting news.

"I believe you have the wrong man." Robert took a step back from the woman. She was lovely to look at, no doubt about that, but she appeared to have a screw or two loose.

Heaving a disgruntled sigh of annoyance, the woman appeared to drop her look of self-importance, though it was immediately replaced by one of exasperation. "Honestly," she breathed, sounding vexed. She advanced a step toward him, as if to make him see reason. "I was asked to come here by someone who values your safety; they believe you are in danger. Something about Master Cadius discovering an item of yours and setting out to find you." She narrowed her eyes in thought. "Or something of the sort. I could not hear the entire conversation."

Robert racked his brain for some kind of hidden message in the words, wondering who had sent the woman and what she was even talking about. Realization punched him in the sternum. The only thing of value he owned—or *had* owned, as the case may have been—was the watch Professor Charles had given him. He'd lost it in Ridlan years ago and had assumed it had been trampled or buried beneath layers of muck somewhere, safe and unfound. If it had been discovered by someone from this time . . .

"Whatever the case may be," the stranger went on, taking no notice of his sudden change in expression, "I have done my good deed by informing you that you are in great peril, and now I may—"

"Was it a watch?" Robert interrupted. She stared blankly at his urgency. "The item he found—did the person who sent you mention it being a watch?"

She seemed to think this over and then said slowly, "Yes, but I have no idea what that is or how it applies to your imminent death."

But he wasn't listening, even at the cavalier implication that he would soon die. His heart quickened with horror at what she didn't even realize she was saying. Sarah must have sent the woman to warn him; she was the only one aside from Karen who knew about the watches, and he didn't think Karen would contact him so soon after settling into her new life. Robert's mind worked quickly. If Cadius had been the one to find his time watch all those years ago . . . Had he used it?

Better question: Cadius was *still alive*?!

Robert suddenly gripped her thin arms, staring her hard in the face. "You know where Sarah is." It wasn't a question.

Her eyes widened up at him before she could school her features into a look of innocence. "I don't know what you—"

"Take me to her at once."

She shot him a practiced glare that looked like it could wither stone. Removing his hands with surprisingly strong fingers, she said airily, "I cannot."

He was about to disagree when the livery door burst open. A beast of a man strode in, a sword strapped to his right hip and a long dagger not-so-subtly concealed in his boot. The hilt stuck out a good three inches and caused the woman to take a step back when she took note of it.

"Can I help you?" Robert asked, trying to look congenial as he shrewdly moved so that half his body covered hers.

The man's smile looked more like a sneer, pulling on the ugly scar that stretched along half his face. "I believe ye can. See, I met some friends of yers earlier an' have been sent to relay the same message to ye as I did them." The dagger was drawn from his boot and in his meaty hand, poised to throw, before Robert could blink.

Thinking on his feet, Robert threw gentlemanly rules out the window as he shoved the woman to the floor. She squealed in shock and annoyance, tumbling to the ground and out of the path of the soaring dagger, which Robert narrowly avoided as he jumped to the right. It sailed inches from his shoulder, and he knew the man had been aiming for his heart.

His assailant lunged suddenly, his body moving lithely across the floor for so large a man as he drew his sword. He followed Robert's retreating form as he stumbled toward the table near the forge, a purpose in mind.

He dove for the long iron rod left heating in the fire and removed it from the flames, barely spinning around in time to deflect the downward stroke from the man's curved blade. The impact drove him to his knees, sparks flying at the contact of the sword against the glowing iron.

Robert scrambled to his feet an instant before the next strike came, this one to his side. He twisted, shoving the iron straight toward the ground to block the blow, but the man was stronger, and the rod was forced against his side, the blade slicing a hole in his shirt. The man's face was strained as he tried to drive the blade in deeper. It nicked Robert's skin, and he cringed.

Grunting for purchase as his boots slid across the ground, he launched his shoulder into the man's chest, sending him backward, if only half a foot, and he nearly lost his own balance. Robert hadn't realized the woman had risen to her feet, but she was suddenly there, launching herself onto the back of his assailant with a cry. She reached around his head to scratch at his face, and the man roared, gripping her shoulders and throwing her against the wall. The woman curled in on herself, shaking her head and looking unsteady as she planted her palms on the ground, as if to rise.

The instant the man turned back to him, Robert launched himself into the air and hiked his knees to his chest, quickly extending them and planting his boots against the man's stomach. It was a move he had only ever seen in action movies, but, incredibly, it worked. The man stumbled backward, arms windmilling for balance as Robert landed unceremoniously on his back, the wind leaving his lungs in one great *whoosh.*

Coughing, he tried to get back to his feet, knowing he had to prepare for the man's next attack, though he only managed to prop himself on his rear and palms as he waited for the newcomer to make his move.

The man's eyes were wide and alarmed as he stood with his back near the table Robert had been working on before. The sword clattered to the floor, and he jerked as though to break hold of something, stumbling forward as he lost his balance.

Robert scrambled back as the man came at him, then dropped suddenly to his knees. Over his head, Robert caught a glimpse of the pointed rod sticking over the side of the table, steadied by the clamp. A good four inches of the tip was now covered with blood, and a piece of shirt fabric clung to the point.

Robert balked as the man let out a groan and fell, face-first, onto the wood planks. Dark red stained the back of his shirt around the gaping hole the rod had left, and blood flooded out to stain the floor in a small pool.

Shaking, Robert rose to his feet, his wary gaze trained on the man. He half expected him to lurch to his feet and run Robert through with the sword near his sprawled legs. But the man's arm had been twisted at an uncomfortable angle beneath his body when he fell, and his eyes were closed, his back completely still and devoid of breath. The blood was starting to slow, and the ring of red near his left arm no longer expanded over the floor.

Trying to still the trembling in his limbs at the sight of a dead body, Robert turned to the woman and found her propped against the wall, eyes wide as she stared at the man's lifeless form. "Are you all right?" he asked. Her lips trembled like his fingers did, but when she met his gaze, he visibly saw her spine stiffen as she squared her jaw.

The woman's saucy glance vacillated between a glare and gratitude as he helped her to her feet. Her wavering voice belied her set-chin and the practiced look of strength that wobbled on her features.

"What did I tell you?"

ଔଓ

The man, Robert, quirked a blondish brow. "What about?"

In an attempt to cover her increasing anxiety, she bent to retrieve the sash she had lost in her fall. Her fingers trembled. "I told you someone would hurt you." But then her eyes returned to the man sprawled across the floor, and Isabella's shock was suddenly too strong to mask. She stared, wide-eyed, at the body of the man, at the blood pooled around his chest and abdomen. There was a hole on the back of his shirt, and she thought she detected faint bits of torn flesh peeking out between the gap in the fabric.

"I might be sick," she whispered, not having meant to admit it aloud to this stranger.

"Put your head between your legs," Robert advised, though he looked as nauseated and pale as she felt. Isabella wondered if the only reason he managed to hold back the contents of his own stomach was because he didn't want to clean up any more bodily fluids that day.

Though she still felt as though she might retch at any moment, her gaze automatically flickered with haughty annoyance as he took her elbow and guided her around the corner so the man was out of sight. She sucked in a deep breath, steadying her nerves and her steely pride. "It's not as though I have never seen a dead body before." She tried to sound strong when she said it, hating to appear so weak in front of a stranger—especially one with such piercing eyes and an endearing smile to boot—but images resurfaced, and with them a floodtide of fear and emotion.

She imaged her mother as she had discovered her, lying bloody and beaten beneath her father's heavy fist. Then only a short time later, her father lying at the base of the stairs, red liquid bubbling from the gash in his head. Isabella had been angry when she shoved him, but she had not meant to kill him. She still felt the confusing weight of guilt and grim assurance when she thought on that moment of decision, certain she would not alter her choice, if given the chance. And that frightened her most of all.

"A simple 'thank you' would suffice, my lady," Robert replied dryly, breaking into her dark reverie.

She snorted, an automatic response that surprised her, considering the circumstances. "For what, pray tell?"

He gave her a look that said she was a fool for not understanding. "I saved your life back there."

Her eyes widened in mock innocence. "Oh, are you referring to when you assaulted me? The man was after *you*, and I can protect myself." Isabella attempted a steady glare, but her heart was beating quickly as she relived the moment she watched the man accidentally impale himself, the tip piercing through his back and into his heart, and then his collapse as blood poured from the wound. Her vision clouded around the edges as her stomach churned and knees buckled.

Robert grabbed her around the waist just before she collapsed, holding her upright as she struggled to straighten her spine. "I can see that," he said wryly.

Looking up at him sharply, Isabella clenched her teeth together to keep her lips from parting at his nearness. He was even more handsome up-close, with a crystal-blue gaze and perfectly formed lips that were stretched into an amused grin, despite the corpse just around the corner. His nose shouldn't have matched the rest of his handsome features, but the up-turn at the end was actually rather adorable.

She reprimanded herself when she realized she was admiring him, lowering her lids until she was staring at him through mere slits. It made it easier to form thoughts when she couldn't properly see him. "Unhand me."

"When you can stand on your own two feet," he responded simply, and the corner of his mouth quivered with suppressed humor. He seemed to be enjoying her struggle, tightening his hold when she nearly slipped through his grasp.

Glowering, she tried to suppress her mounting panic. The only time she had ever been in a man's arms—aside from a hug from her brother or when her father would beat her—was when she was being used, and she was *not* going back to that life.

Isabella planted her hands against his solid chest and shoved him away from her, barely managing to remain on her feet. "I have been manhandled my whole life," she grated out between clenched teeth as she willed her legs and spine to stiffen. "I left that behind and I *am not* going to allow myself to be used by a man again."

"Used by—hey, lady, that's not what this is." He looked as shocked by her outburst as she was, but then his blue eyes seemed to clear. The hands, raised in defense, lowered slowly. "I thought you looked familiar."

He appeared to search his brain. “Jade, isn’t it? I’ve seen you around town, though not for a while. Where have you been?”

She stared at him, expression blank, unsure how to respond. She hadn’t expected him to *know* who she was, and she waited for a look of realization and disgust to cloud his handsome features, or shock that she was not dead. It never came. He only looked expectant and curious, his expression open.

“Actually, my name is Marian,” she answered quickly and blinked, not quite sure why she had used the name William had given her. But Isabella carried dark memories with her, and Jade held the stench of desperation and sorrow that she had lived with for far too long.

Hiking her delicate chin, she added, “I left that life behind some months ago.”

“Marian,” he whispered, his shoulders drooping a little in what looked like disappointment. Isabella didn’t know why that name would strike a chord with him—Will never would have shared it with him, would he?—but Robert seemed to recover from his surprise. “I almost didn’t recognize you with an expression on your face.” He looked as though he were contemplating her features, a slight, teasing grin at the corner of his mouth once more.

“I am a bit out of practice in ambiguity, as of late,” she mumbled, knowing it was true. She had been hiding from society and her old life and hadn’t needed to pull out her cold, unfeeling performance for months. Except with her brother, that is. “So sorry to disappoint.”

Robert shrugged, smiling unrepentantly. “Don’t be. I like you more when you let your fire show.” He immediately appeared embarrassed and chuckled nervously.

Her eyes widened in disbelief before she remembered to school her features. Voice filled with false indifference, though it hitched with bitterness at the end, she remarked, “Most men prefer a pliable woman to kick around. We women must accept it as the way of the lesser sex.” She couldn’t say why she did it, precisely, but she knew she was testing him for a reaction, curious how he would react. And ready to lash out at the typical response she received.

His severe frown was unexpected. “Well, some men are shameful and get their delight from being as vile as possible.” His blue gaze softened when he caught her surprise at his extreme reaction. “I’m sorry. One of my foster fathers was, well, the kind of person you’re talking about, so I know that there are plenty of men like him out there. But—” Robert hesitated, appearing to consider her as the silence stretched to nearly a minute. It made her squirm on the inside, but she refused to look away as she contemplated what type of father a “foster” might be.

"*But*," he started again, rubbing behind his ear thoughtfully, "there are good, honorable guys out there. I mean, look at me! I'm the perfect male specimen," he announced gaily, trying to make light of it.

Despite the fact that a body lay just around the corner, she felt herself grinning—a genuine smile that she had not felt on her lips in months. "That remains to be seen," she returned sassily, trying to drop her smile.

He grinned at her another moment, eyes roving her features. For the first time in what felt like an eternity, Isabella wasn't afraid or uncomfortable beneath a man's gaze. His eyes were a clear blue that she felt could hide nothing, and there was no malice or lust or ill intent in his features. She could only find friendly curiosity that faded to concern as his mirth fell away.

"I suppose I should figure out what to do about *him*," he sighed out, gaze wary as he gave a look in the general direction of the dead man. His eyes returned to her face, and he shot her a crooked grin of gratitude. "Thanks for the warning, by the way, and for distracting him. I'm not sure I could have gotten the drop on him without your help."

His smile and open expression, his humility when complimenting the assistance of a *woman*—though she couldn't truly say she had been much help—was foreign to her. He was not the typical man with whom she'd formerly spent her days—and nights—all the same slimy, dull creatures. Robert had shown her kindness and revealed modesty, desirable traits that not a single man in her life had possessed.

She contemplated her feelings toward this man and found she did not *want* to hide from him or disguise her features. A light smile curved her lips, painted out of habit, though the sensation was genuine. "It was a pleasure rescuing you, even if your gratitude did come a smidgeon late." He laughed, not out of cruelty or some perverse notion, and Isabella found she liked the sound of pure, innocent delight.

Though it was perfectly improper—a thought that was ironic coming from her own mind—Robert stretched his hand out to her, that easy grin tipping his mouth. "The pleasure was mine entirely, Lady Marian."

He calls me a lady, she whispered to herself, feeling both confused and delighted at his high opinion of her, even though he had made it clear he knew of the illustrious history that the name Jade carried. She delicately grasped his hand, amazed that for the first time in a long time, a simple touch could be friendly and unforced, and she didn't question whether or not he wanted something from her.

"I'm sure I'll see you again." She couldn't be certain, but his words held a note of hope.

"Perhaps," she responded slyly and turned to leave, sashaying her hips as she moved toward the door.

"Wait!" he called out suddenly. Isabella paused, biting back a grin as she turned, glad to see that she was not rusty after so many months in seclusion. He scrambled over to her, face pulling into what she imagined was supposed to look austere—an expression she assumed he didn't often employ. Sternly, he said, "You're taking me to Sarah." It was not a question.

She blinked, not having expected *that* sort of declaration. "I thought you had a corpse to attend to," she responded smartly, an old habit that seemed to be the most difficult to break.

He seemed to consider that a moment, then said in a rush, "I'll deal with him later, since I can't leave him to rot by the fire for long. But it'll take too long to get the situation cleared up, and you have to show me where Sarah is. Or else."

Isabella bit the inside of her cheek, considering her options. Though she hardly knew this man who had assassins appearing on his doorstep, she did not believe he would do her harm and so there was no real threat to his words. Damien would see it as a betrayal to reveal their hideaway, and she felt poorly over that fact, but she doubted Robert would allow her to leave with the unshared knowledge of Sarah's whereabouts on the tip of her tongue.

With a sigh, she flicked the gold sash over her hair. "Come with me."

ଔଡ

Sarah's knee bobbed up and down as she waited for Jade to return with news of Robert's safety. She hoped he had listened to the woman and heeded Jade's words. And had she told him that Will was dead? The reminder settled hard in Sarah's stomach, and she worked out the knot in her abdomen by wringing her skirt in her lap.

It had been like that for over an hour, trying to distract herself and then, abruptly, thoughts of Will would push their way into her consciousness, and she was nearly overcome by despair when she was reminded of the fact that she would never see him again. Somehow, she would recover herself by sheer will and focus her thoughts elsewhere, but always, unbidden, Will's image was there.

Once she tried to lighten her spirit by telling herself that she would go home soon and could forget about this place, leaving her torment behind. But the idea made her feel so instantly guilty and horrible that she nearly lost her meager lunch all over the floor. Will was as much a part of her as the heart that beat inside her chest and the lungs she had been struggling to fill with air all day.

No, there would never be any leaving him behind, even if it was easier to forget about the ache that accompanied his memory; she would rather feel her heart squeeze painfully each time she thought of Will than try and live without him each day. She'd heard people say that the pain of lost love fades in time, and Sarah knew in her heart that they spoke the truth, but the idea was so hard to imagine in that moment that she couldn't even comprehend a day where it wouldn't hurt to breathe.

"Are you certain you do not wish to have some warm tea?" Sarah jerked and glanced over at Damien, who she had forgotten was in the room with her. He had managed to get her to eat some stale bread and dried meat, and then proceeded to watch her with a wary gaze as she fidgeted on the sofa, her eyes glued to the door or filled with tears of sorrow.

"No, thank you," she said.

She saw Damien nod in acknowledgement out of the corner of her eye. He sighed audibly, and she looked at him in question. "What can I do to divert your mind from it? Would conversing help?"

Sarah stopped her head mid-shake. So many thoughts gnawed at her, and she focused on all the questions she had been holding in for months. "Actually, I have a few things I need answers to."

He looked surprised that she'd agreed, but relieved just the same. "All right."

"The day you killed Edith," she began, and Damien flinched. "That's not—I mean, I know it was an accident." That was true, but it was still difficult to picture Damien as her killer, even if he hadn't meant to release the bowstring that had led to the life being slowly drained from her.

"What is your question, then?" He looked wary and curious.

"*Why?* Why sneak into the castle dressed as the Shadow?" Sarah wrung a fistful of skirt fabric in her hand. "I've been wracking my brain for months, and I can't figure it out."

"Oh." Damien dropped her gaze and swallowed thickly. "I required a disguise no one would ever suspect myself to employ, and many had heard me speak poorly of Serimone's vigilante." His eyes met hers, guilty. "At Cadius' insistence that he was working against his cause."

"But a disguise for what?"

"I suppose it matters not at this point." Damien let out a gusty breath. "I had been searching for weeks for the alleged letters you found, hoping that some incriminating evidence against Cadius might be there, as he had been too cautious to leave a trail everywhere I looked. Eventually, I came accross a hidden compartment in the late queen's room but was interrupted before I could investigate further. I managed to convince the guard who discovered me that I was on business from Cadius himself, and he allowed me to go, but I knew that if I returned and was caught once more, Cadius would surely hear of it—I believe we both can imagine how he would handle *that.* So I snuck into the castle in disguise to find the letters."

Sarah drew her brows together. He had tried to get away from Cadius months ago? She was amazed but not unbelieving, and it only served as a reminder that Damien had never entirely approved of Cadius' dealings—he had only been a means to an end for Damien, and though she couldn't say she *approved* of the way he'd gone about it, she felt she understood him a bit more each time they spoke of his dealings with the man. "But obviously you didn't get the letters, because I found them."

He nodded. "I was spotted before I could reach the room and tried to escape downstairs to the servants' entrance, but a maid spotted me and screamed, and I was forced to think of a new route. But when I returned upstairs to use the secret passage leading to the dungeons . . ." Damien lowed his gaze, shame washing over his features. "You know the rest of the story."

Sarah chewed on her lip. She did know, reminded of her chase after the false Shadow, his trembling fingers as he accidentally loosed the arrow that sailed over her head and ended Edith's life.

Choking back her own guilt, Sarah said quietly, "One time Edith spoke to me about keeping off Cadius' radar, but the way she said it made it sound like she'd been punished by him at some point. And then when I knew her husband and boy died . . . Do you know what happened to them? Was it some kind of punishment from Cadius?" She winced. "I never got a chance to ask her."

Damien shook his head regretfully. "I'm afraid I hadn't heard her name or paid her any attention until you requested she become your personal maid." His gaze hardened around the edges. "But if Cadius was involved in her life to any extent and she displeased him, then I've no doubt that any tragedy that followed was on his orders."

Swallowing, Sarah nodded, having suspected and dreaded the same thing.

A handful of minutes passed between them in silence, and then Damien asked, "There must be something else that plagues your mind that you wish for answers to."

She shot him a tiny grin. "Does the silence make you uncomfortable?"

"*Yes*." They both chuckled, though it died too soon. His expression turned helpless, and he seemed to fight for the right words. "I simply—I cannot *stand* wondering what you are thinking and how I might make it right."

Sarah was touched, but still she asked, "Doesn't it drudge up a lot of pain for you, though?"

"If it keeps you speaking to me, I will endure whatever questions you might have."

Taking pity on him and moved by his earnest response, she nodded. "Okay." She thought for a moment, sorting through all the questions that had tangled themselves together over the months. "That day when we went into town, what were you doing when you said you were going to Will's shop? He and Robert never saw you go inside."

Damien seemed to look to the past, and then his expression cleared. "Oh, well, I *had* been planning to pick up an order for steel buckles and place an order for a few more items. But then I saw Isabella across the street and went to speak with her about . . ." He hesitated for such a long time that Sarah thought he had given up on the conversation until he finished with, "She had been involving herself with a certain guard to retrieve information for me. As she had ignored my previous missives requesting that she not risk her safety for me, I went to speak with Isabella in person."

Sarah remembered the letter Jade received with Damien's seal on the front. It had seemed so incriminating at the time, but now she realized it was simply a brother trying to protect his sister. Yet another reason to release her old grudge against him.

"I never thanked you for saving Will and I from Allan," she said as it occurred to her, voice lowering in a flood of gratitude. Damien dropped his gaze bashfully. "I mean it. Will got us out of that burning building, but if you hadn't stopped Allan, he wouldn't have had any qualms about revealing the Shadow's identity and making sure whatever sick execution he had planned would succeed the next time. His only goal was to appease Cadius and satisfy his own demented mind."

Sucking in a deep breath at the surprising pain as she thought of Will, she finished with, "So, just thanks for saving us." Her voice wobbled as she attempted a smile.

"I only wish I could have saved him for you this time."

She could tell he meant it, and her lip quivered. "Me too."

His arms wrapped around her in a flash, pulling her against his side. She shuddered there for a few minutes, savoring his warmth against her cold flesh. It felt strange to seek comfort from Damien and she didn't want to give him the wrong idea, but although she still ached inside, he was like a balm to her raw nerves. "Thanks for being here with me, muck and all," she added wryly.

"I vow to always wallow with you in the mire." His voice was so sincere it twisted her insides.

"But that's just it." She pulled back from him, and his arms dropped from her shoulders at her expression. "I need someone who will lift me up out of it." She turned her eyes to the ground, only just catching Damien's flinch, and whispered, "Even though I knew it was impossible, a part of me imagined that Will and I would have forever."

"Sometimes eternity can be captured in an instant, a lone memory to which we cling." Sarah looked up into his piercing eyes, surprised by his words. His voice wobbled at the edges, though his gaze was steady. "I know it is difficult now, but if you loved him"—he stumbled over the word *loved* before collecting himself—"then hold onto whatever instant captured your eternity together."

Sarah swallowed thickly, moved by the beauty of that sentiment, knowing what it took for him to say it. "Thank you, Damien." Their gazes stayed locked for several long seconds, and she tilted her head in sympathy and pain, knowing she was the reason for the tormented look in his eyes. She wasn't sure if it was cruelty to give him even the slightest hope, but she quietly admitted, "Sometimes I wish things were different."

A wry tilt of his lips. "If only for my sake."

"Yes," she whispered, cringing. But they both knew it was true.

Taking a long drag of air, Damien let it out in a rush, the gust wobbling from deep within his chest. He tried to smile. "I believe you know I will never give up on you, and I would not mind being your second choice as long as I had you. . . . *But*"—the muscles in his cheeks spasmed—"I also know that you do not deserve a half-life, torn between loving a man and wishing you could love another, purely out of sympathy and to appease him."

"Oh, Damien." Her mouth worked, throat burning with suppressed emotion. She met his gaze, her eyes beseeching him to understand. "It isn't like that." She flinched, knowing that wasn't entirely true. She wanted to touch his arm to make him understand, but she didn't think physical contact would spare him any pain at this point. "I just know that you deserve to be someone's first choice and are worthy of being fully loved. I'm just sorry that it couldn't be me."

A small flicker of a grateful smile graced Damien's lips. "You might not have given me the love I wanted, but you have given me the love and friendship I needed most."

"But it can't be enough," she whispered, having known what real love felt like.

"No," he answered honestly, and then added when her face fell in sorrow, "but it is enough for now."

Sarah's heart softened. That fickle, life-giving organ in her chest always seemed torn between giving him the love he had proved he was worthy of, and accepting the reality that she could never care for him outside of friendship. "Thank you," she breathed.

The door swung open then, and both heads swung with it. Jade entered, looking both annoyed and unnerved, her cheeks flushed. Sarah gasped audibly as Robert strode into the room behind her, and his eyes met hers at the sound. Relief flooded his face, and he barely glanced at Damien as she jumped to her feet, meeting him halfway. They didn't know each other that well, only having grown a friendship because of their mutual connections to Will and Karen, but still they collided together, each beyond reassured to see the other in good health. Their first hug was a little awkward, but Sarah clung to him, glad for a familiar face.

Robert's chuckle was a breath of assurance near her ear. "I can't believe I found you. Will's been gone for a few days searching for you, but I'll try to get him a message to let him know you're safe."

The air seemed to flee the room in a rush, and she felt lightheaded as she fought back a fresh floodtide of emotions, knowing exactly why Will was missing. She didn't think Jade would have revealed this fact to him, and Sarah regretted the fact that she had had to be the one to tell him. But there was no one else: Thomas was dead, and this small group—along with Damien's informant and the fishermen who had pulled Will's body from the sea—were the only ones who knew of his death.

Pulling back from Robert, she bit her lip. "I have something—" But she couldn't finish, trying desperately to keep her tears at bay. She had been the one to break the news of Will's death to him before when it had appeared he had been killed by a harrowing tumble over a waterfall, but she didn't think they would be so lucky this time as to find that someone had merely jumped to conclusions. She wished beyond anything that poor information had been given, that Will was out there somewhere, coming for her.

Robert's face fell at the look on her own. Twisting his neck, he watched her suspiciously out of the corner of his eye. "What's happened?"

Her chin quivered. "Oh, Robert," she choked out. "He's gone."

Chapter Twenty-Five

"If I never see you again, I will always carry you
Inside, outside, on my fingertips
And at brain edges, and in centers of what I am
Of what remains."

Charles Bukowski

Robert kept scrubbing a hand over his face as he paced back and forth, lips moving as though he was talking to himself.

Sarah's hand twitched in her lap, feeling jittery at his anxiety. She knew there was no reason for her agitation at his own concern as he processed Will's death, a fact that she was still trying to sort out herself. But her nerves were fried, every emotion heightened, which, in this case, was mostly frustration and anger at the unfairness of it all, though she felt constantly on the verge of tears, which annoyed her all the more. Unfortunately for Robert, he was the easiest target available for her wrath.

"Stop that!" she snapped at last, chest rising and falling quickly.

Abruptly, he halted, giving her a surprised look. Hurt filled his eyes. "Sorry. I'm just trying to absorb all this. At least what you told me explains why someone was sent to kill me."

Damien was sitting on the couch beside her, and his hand shifted to her knee, a gentle reminder that she was being too harsh. Some of her needless anger faded at his touch, and her shoulders sagged, realizing that Robert was as hurt and shocked as she was. And no one had tried to kill *her* . . . that day. "No, I'm sorry for biting your head off. That was uncalled-for, and I shouldn't direct my anger at you. You lost Will just like I did."

"Not quite like you," he whispered. Sarah dragged in a shuddering breath, chest constricting as she nodded. Her hands quivered as she held back a fresh onslaught of tears. She was tired of crying, but the wound was still too fresh, and each breath was an effort. She never thought loving someone could be so painful, and she *certainly* never imagined that she would lose Will. Even when she thought he had died before and imagined that John's body had been his, Sarah had still been hopeful, numb to the concept of Will's death. But now, it was too real and left her feeling empty.

Jade stood silent in the corner and had been that way since she'd brought Robert back. Her continued presence had surprised Sarah, who had thought the woman would take off the instant she returned, since she had been so perturbed when she'd left. But her gaze followed Robert's movements as he paced about the room, her mind obviously working over thoughts that Sarah couldn't read on her features. Although she had overheard some pretty shockingly unbelievable things that day, so it wasn't exactly surprising that she appeared to be deep in thought.

"So, the machine is really destroyed?" Robert asked suddenly, breaking into her thoughts, and Sarah turned her gaze on him. He looked confused and crestfallen at once. "No more between-world jumps?" Sarah shook her head stiffly, trying to control her emotions that seemed wayward, as of late.

"That means once you leave, you'll be gone for good." She bobbed her head again, somehow managing to breathe past the building ache in her chest. With a gusty sigh, Robert raked a hand back through his hair, and she grimaced, the movement all too Will-like.

He froze, his head rising to meet her gaze once more. His expression turned guilty and pained, and his voice lowered an octave as he asked, partly of Sarah and partly of himself, "With Greene and Will gone, who takes over the shop? He has no next of kin, and I don't think Will had any sort of instructions written down. Do I try to sell it, take control of it?"

Sarah rose from the couch, coming over to place a hand on his arm. She looked up at him, swallowing past her own resurfacing emotions. Ten minutes. She could be strong for Robert for ten minutes. "Just keep going on as you have been. We'll—we'll figure things out in time. Nothing has to be decided right this second."

Shaking his head, Robert said quietly, almost in a daze, "I have to get back to feed the horses." Sarah gave a slow nod, sensing he needed time to process as she had—*still was*—and pulled her hand back. His next words caused her eyes to bulge in shock and curiosity. "And I have a body I have to report to the authorities, which will be a mess to explain."

"Wait a sec—"

"I will show you out," Jade volunteered quickly, surprising everyone in the room and distracting Sarah's mind from the fact that Robert was apparently stashing a corpse somewhere in town. Jade blinked. "What? I can be a generous host."

Sarah almost blurted out that she hadn't exactly *volunteered* to be helpful a single instance in all the time she had known Jade. Somehow, Sarah managed to bite her tongue, though Damien still appeared suspicious, eying his sister warily.

Robert, however, just smiled. "I'd like that." Jade stood by the door, but he hesitated. Turning back to Sarah, he tipped his head to the side, eyes darting between her and Damien, who had just risen from the couch but stood away from the group like an outsider. Lowering his head and his voice, Robert asked her, "Are you all right here? I don't think Will—"

“It was his idea,” Sarah whispered back, recalling the look in Will’s eyes just before he’d run off into the forest. He had been sure he would return to find her, and now she wondered how he would feel about the situation. She shook her head at the question she’d never have an answer to. “I’ll be fine. I just need to figure out some things for awhile.” Like what to do about Cadius and the king, how she alone could help right the kingdom, and when the right time would be for her to return home for the last time. What more could she do here, anyway?

Robert’s gaze swept her features, catching on the uncertainty and utterly drained look on her face. But he nodded slowly and straightened. “All right. But if you need anything”—his eyes flickered over her shoulder to Damien for an instant before returning to her face—“don’t hesitate to come for me.”

A ghost of a smile, though it was genuine, twitched at the corner of Sarah’s mouth. “Thanks. And if you hear anything—” She pursed her lips together, wondering what news he could possibly have, but that niggling remainder of fruitless hope refused to depart entirely. “Just, please, let me know.”

With a nod, he turned and followed Jade out of the cabin. The door closed but not before Sarah heard him say, “So, have you ever seen how ironworking is performed?” She didn’t catch Jade’s low response, but her tone sounded flirtatious.

Silence reigned in the room, though a crackle of awkward electricity sparked in the air in light of the conversation Jade and Robert’s appearance had interrupted. Her eyes found Damien’s, and she thought he might have grimaced when she met his gaze, though it was meant to look like a smile. “Your friend is all right, and now you know he can defend himself.”

“Yes,” Sarah agreed slowly, and Damien appeared to steel himself against the lead-in her tone carried. “But there is someone who can’t. Professor Charles is at the heart of this.”

Damien’s shoulders stooped in exasperation. “Did we not save your friend only moments ago?” He sighed. “We cannot protect everyone in the kingdom. . . .”

“I’m not asking you to,” she hurried to clarify. “But the professor is the only one who can replicate these watches, and if Cadius wants to be the only person in history to ever alter it, then you can bet the professor will be just as ‘safe’ as the rest of us. Jade warned Robert, and just in time, it seems, and now we have to get Charles out of the castle. It seems farfetched that he could even create another watch here, but I *know* he’s in danger from Cadius and the king.”

Pinching the bridge of his nose, Damien mumbled, “Anyone else we need to rescue? Her Majesty the Queen, perhaps? The gamekeeper?”

Sarah curled her hands into fists, grinding her teeth in frustration that he didn’t see how important this was. “This is serious. I know I’ve asked a lot of you, but Karen's guardian *will* be murdered if we don't do something about it. Now."

His expression was difficult to read, and she felt a spark of hope in her stomach that he might agree until he said, "It's not possible for me to get into the castle with Cadius and the king on high-alert, let alone sneak another person *out*."

"Then I'll do it." The defiant words slipped out before she'd thought them through, but as they rang through her ears, she realized it could work. She stood a little taller, hiking her chin. "Will showed me some of the secret passages leading in and out of the castle . . . and I accidentally discovered a few myself when I got lost in the dungeons. I can be in and out with the professor before anyone realizes—"

"*No*." Damien seldom raised his voice with her, and she reared back, surprised. Then her brows lowered in annoyance, and her fists were suddenly on her hips.

"No? What do you mean, *no*?"

He looked as though the deep breath he took was meant to offer him some patience. What does he have to be annoyed over? Sarah thought, her eyes narrowing to a challenging glare.

"He put himself in the center of this mess," Damien said, "and he will have to find a way out of it. Perhaps he already has." She was almost positive he was just saying that to placate her, which only stirred her irritation.

"And that's the attitude that keeps you from being one of the good guys." She bit back a grimace at her harsh tone, knowing it wasn't true and that she was completely destroying any progress they'd made such a short time ago. But the thing that kept her from apologizing was the assurance that Will would have fought her on the matter, wishing to protect her, but in the end, he would let her make her own choice. Damien was taking her thoughts and feelings out of the equation, and she didn't like it.

"So, *why*?" she pressed. "Why won't you let me warn one of the few people left in my life here?"

"Because I am going to lose you!" he fairly shouted. His chest heaved as he stared at her, worked up even as his eyes softened in grief.

She blinked. "What?"

Damien collapsed onto the couch, staring up at her with a miserable gaze. "That machine you and Robert spoke of—that is the only thing allowing you to go home and return to Serimone. From what I understand, that ability to bring you there and back is gone. No matter what I do, whether I help or hinder you from going, you *will* leave one day for a final time, and I can never make you love me enough to stay. Now I am expected to let you go before your time?" He dragged in a breath that shuddered past his lips. "Yes, I hold you here for selfish reasons, but if you leave now, I will lose you forever, and sooner than I should have to."

"That's what you're forgetting, Damien," she said quietly, hating herself a little as she drove in the final dagger, using similar words to ones she'd spoken to him before. "You can't lose something you never had." Maybe it was her own pain that caused her to say it, but it was the truth, and that fact seemed to hurt him most.

Instant pain filled his eyes, and he dragged in a sharp breath as though he'd been stung. Sarah did her best to ignore the guilty tightening in her chest at the look on his face, vacillating between shame at what she'd said and fresh anger that Damien wouldn't let her decide her future, let her *choose*.

Jade came back in then, silencing any reply he might have had and the apology Sarah felt more compelled to give with each passing second. She locked the door out of habit, and when she turned there was a tiny, thoughtful smile quirking the corner of Jade's painted mouth, but her expression turned defensive when she saw the curious looks she was receiving. "What?" Blank stares met her, and she hiked her chin. "You are the one who told me to find him, brother. I was simply befriending our guest—*playing nice*, as you wanted me to."

Pressing a finger against his temple, Damien muttered, "I don't believe I meant *that.*"

"You and Robert seemed to hit it off," Sarah remarked, doing her best not to look at the man in the room. She wouldn't exactly call she and Jade friends—far from it, actually—but somehow in the last couple days, they had become civil, and Sarah wanted to keep it that way. It was definitely a plus that she could avoid talking with Damien for a few more minutes, but she also suspected that Jade could use a friend around here.

Sarah bit her lip, marveling at the irony that she was trying to befriend the woman who had attempted to break up her and Will, and who, in a fit of crazed passion or depression, had nearly killed him as she took him over the falls. *Will wonders never cease?*

Jade's gaze swung from her brother to Sarah in surprise, but then a tiny tremble gained control of the corner of her mouth. She casually rubbed her lips together, but Sarah—a fellow girl—knew it was to buy time and swipe the growing smile from her lips. "If you mean he is not as odious a creature as most men are and that we engaged in a perfectly congenial conversation for a few moments, then yes, I would have to agree."

Rolling her eyes, Sarah quipped, "Way to suck the romance right out of a connection, Isabella." It felt surprisingly good to joke with someone for a minute to ease the guilt and frustration tensing her shoulders.

Jade didn't quite seem used to Sarah using her given name, but she recovered quickly. "I am not precisely sure what you mean, although I can assure you there is nothing romantic about watching a man impale himself upon a fire poker . . . or whatever it was."

Grimacing, Sarah asked, "What happened? Robert mentioned something about it earlier, but I didn't really hear what went on."

Jade's countenance subtly shifted as she told the story of how the brute had come into the shop and attacked Robert, and how the man had slipped and skewered himself on a sharp rod.

"Wow," Sarah breathed. "Isabella, who knows how it would have turned out if you hadn't given him a heads-up. Maybe he wouldn't have been prepared for the guy, and Robert could have been hurt."

Jade's gaze shifted uncomfortably around the room, and one of her slender shoulders lifted in a shrug. "Well, I would hate for such a sweet boy to lose his head, so . . ."

Sarah was a little taken aback at her sudden show of embarrassed humility, but it was a nice side of Jade, even if the woman was still trying to maintain some essence of her prickly facade.

The room turned silent as Jade removed her boots by the front door. She paused, looking up to find both Damien and Sarah studiously avoiding each other's gaze. "What went on in the hour I was away? Anything noteworthy?"

"Nothing," they said in perfect unison, then shot the other a look before quickly turning away.

Jade *harrumphed* but didn't press them.

"Actually," Sarah said slowly as the need to get some space from this tiny cabin quickened her pulse. "I was just going for a walk. Clear my head a bit."

"Sounds lovely—" Jade began, but her brother shot to his feet.

"Absolutely not!"

Sarah whipped around to face him and cast a glare his way, though she hadn't really expected any other reaction from him. "I am *not* here as your prisoner anymore, remember? I only came back because Will thought it would be the safest place for me, and he was supposed to come back." Her snippy tone wavered at the mention of Will, and she cleared her throat, trying to steady her nerves. "I have no idea where we are, and I don't think I could find my way out—even if I had been paying attention on the trip back—which also means the odds of someone finding me out here are slim. No one knows where this place is, you said so yourself."

Damien looked like he was wavering, but she could tell he wasn't going to relent entirely.

"Oh, come now, brother," Jade reprimanded with a wave of her hand, somehow sounding both flippant and perturbed. "You know she speaks the truth, and she will stay nearby, if she knows what's best for her."

"I will," Sarah agreed quickly, ready to accept any terms so long as they allowed her *outside* of the house.

With a gust of breath, Damien shook his head, and her hopes sank only to shoot right back up when he let out begrudgingly, "I suppose."

"Now that wasn't so difficult, was it?" Jade patted her brother's shoulder approvingly, receiving a wary look from him, as if he didn't quite know what to do with this display of mild, albeit sarcastic, affection. "It is out of your control, and you must let others decide their own fate." She said it almost as a gentle admonition, no sign of the resentment or sarcasm her tone typically carried when she spoke to her older sibling. But what was the most unsettling was the conspiratorial wink Jade threw her way, like they were old friends sharing a secret. Sarah's eyes widened as the woman sashayed to her room . . . *humming* to herself?

She needs to hang out with Robert more often, Sarah thought wryly.

Turning to Damien, who was watching her intently, she said, "I know you don't like the idea of me running off into the forest alone, but I promise I won't leave permanently without letting you know." It had been implied before, but hearing the words from her lips, his tense posture relaxed, and she realized how much he had been dreading her doing just that.

"I need to . . . process everything," she finally added, and she certainly had a lot to think about. "I'll stay close and be back soon."

"Yes." He nodded reluctantly, stiffly. "All right." She could tell he wanted to say more, but to his credit, he held his tongue and remained silent.

Damien unlocked the door for her with a final, "Be cautious," and with a nod, Sarah stepped outside, dragging in her first free breath in what felt like days. Daylight glinted off the forgotten sword that was half-buried in the grass, the dried blood looking like rust on the blade. The sun warmed her face and hair as she wandered gratefully through the trees, dead leaves crunching beneath her feet. She stared up at the light breaking through the fresh springtime growth in the trees and pressed her back against a young oak.

Closing her eyes, she let everything wash over her: the sound of birds calling to each other overhead, how the breeze wove through her unbound hair, the way the shadows cast on her face by the leaves wavered back and forth in the wind, throwing muted yellow and then bright orange over her eyelids.

A patch of sunlight was suddenly cast over her hand, touching her skin with warmth. She closed her eyes tighter, drawing her fingers toward her palm as though she was holding onto something precious. These were the sights and sounds that Will loved so much, and being a part of it in that moment, Sarah could almost pretend that he was there, whispering her name in the breeze. Her chest spasmed in bittersweet pain as the word *Sarah*, spoken so reverently again and again like an exquisite treasure, rustled through the branches above her, tickling her ears.

"I'm here, Will," she said, her voice a mere breath. "Come back to me."

But though she clung to that fantasy, as hard as she willed it to be true, when she opened her eyes as the clouds drew in overhead, the empty space beside her and the lack of warmth in her hand reminded her that it had been nothing more than the wind.

Chapter Twenty-Six

"I acknowledged my sin to you, and my iniquity I did not hide. I will confess my transgressions to the LORD; and you forgave the guilt of my sin."

Psalm 32:5

The earth was cold and black, like a frozen blanket clung to his body and covered his eyes. He had floated so long, his body weightless and all sensation leaving his limbs before everything went completely and blessedly blank. When his consciousness began to return to him, he fought it off, wanting to remain in the warmth of oblivion. But the longer he stayed there, the more the real world began to fade, filling him with a strange, inexplicable sense of foreboding at the uncertainty that he sensed lying just beyond the dull blackness.

If he let go completely, what awaited him? His spirit sank as he realized that there was nothing waiting for him in the blank oblivion up ahead, nothing of worth or meaning.

He became aware that his spirit seemed to be calling out a word, a name he couldn't quite grasp, as though he was unconsciously trying to remind himself of a vague recollection that was supposed to carry immense meaning. Perhaps enough significance to desire to return.

"Come back to me."

Suddenly, in his mind's eye, all he could see was a pair of almond-shaped eyes, crystal clear and blue, softening in a smile that was for him alone. His heart lurched to a stop. That voice and the image of those eyes reminded him of . . . something he could not put a name to, but he was certain that he had to get back. He fought desperately against the sweet oblivion, swimming through the blackness, knowing there was something—some*one*—he must return to, even if he could not recall their name. He wasn't yet done fighting, and though he did not know who or what awaited him on the other side, he was certain he had to return to *her*.

Feeling slowly began to return to his extremities one by one, sending needles of shooting pain through his body, making him wish he had not chosen to come back, even with the uncertainty and vague sense of fear that had flooded him in the darkness. Will opened his eyes slowly, coughing on the smoke that burned his lungs, which appeared the most adversely affected, save for his head as it burned furiously.

He blinked up at the man leaning over him. "What happened?" he croaked.

"Do you remember who I am, boy?" the man asked.

Will racked his memory bank. His face was terribly familiar, but the name . . . "Merek?" he tried, tasting the name on his tongue as though it would help him match it to its owner.

Merek's shoulder's sagged in relief. "Yes, that's good. You were under for a long time—wasn't sure if you would have your full memory. The lantern must have rolled to the barrels of pitch below deck," he explained, and the memory of the explosion suddenly came back to Will. His muscles twitched as he again felt the gust of heat and glimpsed the glaring possibility of his death in the burst of light. "It was not a large blast, but enough to sink the ship. Instead of being lost at sea or consumed by the brunt of the flames, you were somehow blown clear off the deck and into the water with the first blast. Other than a few bumps and bruises, you came out fairly unscathed, though I did have to reset your shoulder after the impact of hitting the water jarred it loose."

Will swallowed against the sting he was suddenly aware of that pulsed in his shoulder. He cringed, his thick saliva barely coating his parched throat. He felt as though he had swallowed half the salty sea. "How . . . did I get here?"

Relaxing back onto his heels so he was no longer leaning over him, Merek rubbed at the angry cut on his own chin. "When I saw what happened to the ship, I told the men to go ahead and dove into the water hoping to find you, and it seems we were both blessed this morning. I discovered you and a piece of the ship large enough for us to stay afloat, and *somehow*"—he said it with a grin and some kind of secret meaning—"we practically washed up on the closest shore, as did a few of the prisoners onboard who abandoned ship before the explosion. It was the same piece of land that our little motley crew found, as well. We washed up a little while ago, and I was going to call out to the others to help drag you further ashore when you came to."

Will thought of the last thing he had seen: the growing fissure in the center of the vessel, the ominous *boom* an instant before he glimpsed the flames and felt the hot breath of a dragon against his face. "I should be dead," he whispered in amazement, shivering in his sopping tunic.

Merek's grin softened, turning teasingly smug. "Is the Almighty real now?"

Will swallowed hard, shaking his head in denial. "No, but He—He did that to save you all."

"Our survival had *nothing* to do with getting you off that ship safely, and you know it. You are simply too frightened and pig-headed to accept that He cares and would pay you special attention."

Will balked at the man's candor, but Merek had that perpetual grin on his mouth, and his tone had not been unkind. It was a tone his uncle would have used, blunt and matter-of-fact but understanding.

The older man watched him now with an open, expectant gaze that slowly turned into a questioning stare. “What is it that you fear?”

When he remained silent, Merek went on softly, “I remember a time when I refused to acknowledge His love for me because I was *scared*; I knew I could never do anything deserving of a mighty love like that, and so why pretend that I was good enough for it? Most of all, though, I was terrified at the prospect of anyone knowing me entirely, knowing my darkest thoughts and feelings and fears. We cannot hide from Him, and I was certain that if someone knew me to my core and my innermost being, then they could certainly never love me.” Merek took a wavering breath, giving Will a moment to process his words. When he did, he was surprised to realize that the man’s thoughts very much mirrored his own, however much he wished to pretend it was not fear that held him back.

Merek went on. “I felt that if I were stripped bare, completely exposed for all to see, I would only find rejection and pain.” Tears welled in his eyes, and the growing light danced in their watery depths as he gave Will a beautiful smile. “I could never have been so wrong: My earthly father never loved me because of what I could offer him, and neither does my Heavenly Father hold my worth in acts. He loves unconditionally, even through my darkness and my shortcomings, and best of all is that not *once* has He ever left my side.” He wiped his eyes, and his voice cracked with emotion and joy, a sound that caused fissures in Will’s remaining defenses. “*That*, boy, is love in its purest form.”

“Do not let your pride keep you from Great Love.” His uncle’s words as he lay dying settled like a weight on his resisting spirit. At the time, Will had assumed he was referring to Sarah and being closed off to love with her, which had seemed absurd, but now he was certain that Uncle Thomas had been referring to the love that Merek spoke of now. It was a love that Will had told himself time and again he did not need nor deserve, but now he knew with startling clarity that it was exactly what was necessary to fill the empty hollow deep within his chest, a void that even Sarah had not been able to completely fill.

Heart pounding wildly within his breast, Will slowly brought himself up into a sitting position. The muscles in his jaw flickered and spasmed in protest of what he was about to do, but with a calming exhalation of breath, he released all remaining doubt and resistance. His vanity would not keep him from Great Love, and tears burned the backs of his eyes at the thought that he wished Uncle Thomas could be there for this moment. He had never given up hope on his nephew, though he had every reason to for nearly a decade. Will only wished that his uncle could know that after so many years, he had at last come to the conclusion that he wanted—*needed*—God in his life the way Thomas and Sarah did.

Swallowing hard, Will met Merek's eyes, his look expectant as he watched the inner battle the younger man fought. "Tell me what I have to do," Will said, quiet but demanding.

Merek grinned, and his eyes again filled, this time in delight and pure joy. "Boy, all you need to do is ask for His forgiveness for your transgressions and make the Almighty the master of your life. Let Him take control for once. I tell you, He is quite a bit more gracious with our lives and has more forethought than we do."

Will tucked his chin in surprise, feeling abashed. "It cannot possibly be so simple."

Tipping his head to the side, Merek's grin widened. "Aye, but it is. It is far more difficult to forgive ourselves than it is for God to extend His mercy to us." He planted his palms on his knees, grunting as he rose. Pointing just over the small, rocky rise, he said, "You can see the fire about twenty meters inland. That's where I'll be." He placed a comforting hand on his shoulder and squeezed. "I will give you some time."

He stepped away, and Will felt a spark of desperation in his gut. "How should I—what do I say?" he called out.

Merek turned. "As little or as much as you like, so long as it comes from the heart."

"But what if I don't do it properly?" Will asked, genuinely concerned and a little panicked that he could muddle something so important, so long in coming. He could not let down Sarah or Uncle Thomas . . . or himself.

A slow grin curved the older man's mouth. "As long as it is earnest, He will never reject your request." And then he disappeared over the mound of sand and rocks, sending a few pebbles cascading down the hill in his wake.

Rubbing his hands together to instill warmth back into them, Will suppressed a shiver. He felt bereft and at a loss for words in Merek's absence, unsure what he needed to say or do to earn forgiveness.

"All we must do is acknowledge our transgressions, and in the Almighty's gentleness and compassion, He washes them away. We have a clean spirit, a fresh slate, with no stain of our former sins because of His grace and Great Love." His uncle's words had been long-forgotten until that moment, and Will heard the man's voice with aching clarity, as though Thomas was there with him.

Swallowing was suddenly difficult, and Will tried not to let the pent-up guilt and pride choke out his words. Sincerity, Merek had remarked. Will dragged in a lungful of brisk air and let it out, along with his pride and inhibitions that held him back.

"All right," he whispered, eyes cast out over the dusky horizon. It felt so strange to speak informally to the Almighty, but he had done it once or twice before, when he wanted something. Still, the words tried to choke him, and he had to swallow hard before he was able to drag them out. "I suppose You want me to apologize first. I cannot even count the sins I have committed against You and others, and I don't know if I must admit them all."

Will considered Merek's words: *"Acknowledge our transgressions."* It didn't sound as though he needed to provide a litany of his sins, but simply admit that he *had* sinned.

His shoulders slumped a little, humbled. He stumbled over the words at first, feeling awkward and uncertain, but then it became easier to admit everything to Someone whose face he could not see. "I understand that You know what I have done, have seen my pride and foolishness and stubborn behavior. And I-I am truly sorry for the doubt and resentment and bitterness that I have clung to these years past. I want—"

He bit his lip, feeling the need to express the fear in his heart. Softly, he admitted, "But there is nothing I have done to earn this love others tell me of, one that I glimpsed years ago in my own home when my parents were alive. I desire to find it, but the thought that You could love me . . . unconditionally . . ."

Years of self-rejection and anger and hurt swelled to the surface, resulting in the tears that dripped down his cheeks. He didn't bother to stop them, for once not ashamed to cry in front of Someone who, he now realized, had always known his innermost thoughts and feelings. "I want to be free—make me free of my past." He sucked in a deep, shuddering breath. He was no philosopher, and his words came out sounding stilted to his own ears, but they were earnest, and he felt an unexplainable certainty that the sincerity of his words was more important than what came from his lips.

"So," Will breathed softly. When he closed his eyes, one final, cleansing droplet tumbled over his lid and down his cheek. He had never felt such a need to be accepted, to be whole. Sarah's presence had filled a void in his life and his heart to bursting, but this was different: what he wanted was *true wholeness*, a kind of purity that he suspected could only be found in one Being. "If You will have me, I want You. I desire the peace that I saw in my uncle's face and have glimpsed in Sarah's. I want—I want to *know* You," he said earnestly. "My uncle said that you were a friend and comfort to him in his darkest times. I have known what true isolation feels like, and I don't want to ever feel alone like that again." Will tucked his chin to his chest, ashamed of his own shame.

"Please," he whispered at last, his heart in every breath he took, eyes tightly sealed. "I need You in my life, Almighty God . . . *Father*—" He nearly choked on the word, which had surprised him when it escaped his lips, feeling both foreign and natural. Once more, he was moved to tears at the thought that, after so many years of feeling alone, he was no longer an orphan.

It was overwhelming, thinking that so many wrongs could be mended and made right with a few seemingly inadequate words, but something assured him that the repentant sincerity in his heart was enough. Though it felt strange and unexplainable, in that instant, Will was confident that, despite his blundering words, everything had changed. "I—thank you," he breathed. What more could he say?

Will opened his eyes, blinking a few times to expel the remaining water from his sight. He waited for several beats—for a miracle, a strike of lightening, some ordinary sign that his forgiveness had been granted. There was nothing obvious on the horizon, though the very tip of the sun was barely visible at the edge of his sight. Yet it brightened its surroundings nonetheless, chasing away the blackness.

That was how Will felt in that instant, he realized with a small tilt of his lips. There was no dramatic shift in his world, nor earth-shattering realization that made him sure that he would never again experience hardship. But he *felt* different in his core, as though this new light within him had begun to cast away the darkness that had swallowed him whole all his life—slowly at first, and then all at once as the light within him grew stronger and larger. Yes, there had been no physical change, but he felt lighter than he had in a long time, and he knew his earnest plea had been answered.

Peace, he whispered to himself, naming the feeling deep within him. His smile grew as he inhaled his first deep breath in his new life and rose to join the others.

They had built a fire, the sun just rising as they huddled around it talking in muted tones, maybe thirteen total—*sixteen*, Will corrected as he did a head count. His heart sank a little. So few had made it off the ship in the end, and even fewer had survived the fight and explosion and the swim to shore. Will reminded himself that there were still sixteen safe, sixteen lives to be grateful for.

Merek was sitting on a rock just outside the circle of crewman and had taken off one of his own weathered boots, turning it over to allow the sand and seawater to slide out, the muck splashing at his feet. He glanced up at the sound of Will's boots crunching over the gravel and sand. A slow grin spread over his face as he approached, and Merek slipped his empty boot back in place.

The boy, Gilcrest, was on the other side of the group looking downtrodden and entirely putout, but the instant he caught sight of Will, he jumped to his feet and scrambled around the fire to stand before him. Will thought the boy might launch himself into his arms as he fidgeted there, eyes huge, but somehow Gilcrest refrained, though he immediately launched into a hurried explanation of the reason for his surprise.

"Sir, when Master Merek appeared and said that you were unharmed, but that you wished to remain on the beach and would join us when you were ready, I was greatly concerned. He said you were all right, but I assumed you might've lost one of yer legs or an eye, the way you didn't wish to be seen. What happen to ye?" His accent had thickened the more harried he became, and he paused for a breath. Will's lip twitched, suppressing a grin of amusement.

"Give the man some air to breathe, boy." Merek had risen to his feet, and his full-fledged grin caused Will's own smile to emerge.

Gilcrest's eyes widened even further, and he looked fully reprimanded at the comment. Dipping his head, he retreated a step. "Beggin' your pardon, sir. Didna mean to cause a stir."

Will placed a hand on the boy's scrawny shoulder before he could run back to his place by the fire. He smiled down at Gilcrest, and the boy seemed to relax some at his gently amused expression. "You were very brave back there on the ship, and I am terribly grateful for your assistance. You may have even saved my life."

Once more, the boy's eyes bulged, making him look like an adulated bullfrog. "Oh, you had everything handled yourself, sir; I only did what I could. I'm fairly scrappy, sir." He puffed out his chest, taking on a serious expression.

Giving his shoulder a final squeeze, Will turned his gaze to the circle of men, their faces aglow in firelight in the early morning hours. One by one, they rose, each nodding their head in turn, as though in salute. Will felt his throat constrict at the looks of appreciation on their faces, all of whom he had helped to free from their prison aboard that ship. If he hadn't obtained the keys to those cells, none of these men would have survived the explosion that wracked the underbelly of the vessel. The thought flooded him with gratitude that these few had made it out alive and also filled him with a sense of responsibility for this "motley crew," as Merek had called them.

He glanced down, realizing that Gilcrest had taken hold of his arm to guide him to the fire. Will tried not to wince as the movement tugged on his recently set shoulder. "Come and warm yourself by the fire, sir."

The men parted as they neared, revealing the warmth their tight circle had been masking, and Will had to resist plunging his chilled and aching limbs into the warmth of the flames. He reached his hands out toward the bright glow of the strong fire, curling and flexing his fingers as near to the flames as he dared, trying to remove the ache from his bones. Will ducked his head to stare at the flames, feeling uncomfortable beneath so many watchful eyes, all looking to *him* for guidance. Only when Merek came to stand beside him, stretching out his hands toward the flames, did Will's shoulders relax.

"How are you, boy?" Merek asked softly, or as much as that deep voice of his allowed.

Rotating his shoulder, Will answered honestly, "I have a terrible headache from the blast, my lungs still burn a little when I breathe, my bones feel cold, and my arm aches after being forced back into place—thank you for that, by the way."

"That was not what I meant."

Will's chest contracted as he released a large breath. "I feel . . . confused." He rubbed the back of his neck with one hand before stretching it out toward the warmth of the fire once more. "I cannot honestly say what I am thinking at the moment: I feel anxious and at peace, excited and filled with happiness all at once. It's terribly muddling."

His head whipped around in surprise at Merek's chuckle. The older man clapped him on the shoulder. "Well, it sounds as though you did it right."

"I am *supposed* to feel baffled?" Will was not sure he had heard correctly.

Merek gave him a sympathetic look, though the amusement still lingered there at the corners of his eyes. "Boy, you gave your life over only a few moments ago. You will be battling with the fears and emotions of your flesh for some time yet, if not for the rest of your life."

An ember popped in the fire, launching itself at Will's feet and quickly burning out. He dropped his gaze to it, feeling a little disillusioned. "Oh."

"But, William." Something in Merek's voice caused him to look up, and when he did, the older man smiled softly. "You must understand that your life will not be perfect now, and you should *never* expect yourself to be. But what you just did, what you allowed the Almighty to do in your life, ensures that you will never be forced to walk alone. Someone will always be at your side, One whom you can turn to for guidance and peace. And I can with a clean conscience guarantee that your life will never be more complete than it is this very morning."

Will stared thoughtfully across the flames at the growing light beyond. A moment later, he realized he was smiling and turned his sincere gaze on Merek. "Thank you."

"I felt you were fairly close and would get there on your own someday, but I did not mind giving you that final push. Granted, getting blown clean off a vessel recently overtaken by pirates and surviving the blast might have had some influence over you." Merek winked, causing Will to shake his head.

"You are a strange man."

With an indifferent shrug, Merek said, "So they tell me."

They lapsed into silence for a time, and Will found the murmured conversations around the fire, the soft buzzing of hushed chatter, comforted him. They had survived false accusations and imprisonment, barbarians and explosions, and an intense sense of peace flooded him; he felt immensely grateful that they were all here, safe. Even young Gilcrest, who had been so timid with the quartermaster, was smiling and conversing with the older men, gazing up at them as though he had finally found people who accepted him. The sight warmed Will's heart.

One of the men on Will's left mentioned to another that he had been away from his fiancé for over a fortnight and was anxious to return to her and let her know he was all right.

Instantly, Will remembered the blue eyes that had pulled him back to this earth, and he felt a moment's guilt that he had allowed himself to become distracted and dawdled here on the beach, enjoying this peace and camaraderie he found with these men. But as delightful as it was listening to them talk about their lives back home as he warmed himself by the flames, their words stirred in him an intense desire to return to his own home and assure himself that Sarah was safe. He knew he couldn't stay a minute further and had to find her to warn her about the king. He also felt as though he had been away from her for an eternity and was excited to share about his newfound faith, knowing that she would be overjoyed to hear his news. A spark of anxious hope shot heat through his middle.

"I have to go back," Will announced.

Merek pulled back in surprise at his sudden declaration. "We've only just narrowly escaped death. Are you sure you want to be running off so—?"

But Will was already shaking his head. "You don't understand. Sarah, she—my friend is in trouble. I have to go to her." His eyes met Merek's, and though his words had been tangled and vague, the man seemed to understand. He nodded slowly.

"Do you know where we are?"

After nearly an hour of staring at the horizon, Will had begun to recognize some of the hillsides as those on the outskirts of Serimone. This very beach Will had visited as a child, he now realized, and he told Merek as much.

Lifting his brows, Merek remarked, "If you intend to go to Serimone Castle, it would be over a day's trek on foot, perhaps more."

"I will not be on foot," Will responded confidently.

Merek cast a pointed glance around him, taking in their barren surroundings. "We don't exactly have a wagon at the ready."

"On our way to Ridlan one year for a visit with some distant relatives, my parents and I stopped on this beach, but only a few miles from here, one of our horses tossed a shoe. We were forced to find a livery to repair it, and I believe I remember where it is. I can lease a horse and be on my way."

Lifting a brow, the older man asked, "And what sort of leverage do you have to rent a horse?"

"I'll find something." Will's look must have appeared as stubborn and unyielding as he felt, because Merek's shoulders sagged.

"Fine, boy. You have dried yourself out by the fire, and if you feel this is something you must do, then who am I to stop you?"

Will gave him a nod of thanks and turned his gaze out over the men, who had heard a bit of his declaration and were all staring. Clearing the last bit of smoke from his throat, Will said loudly to the group, "I must return to my home, and I urge you to do the same. Return to your towns, your wives and children."

"But what about Cadius?" one of the men directly across from Will asked, posing a question that many of them seemed to be thinking, judging by the concerned nods of agreement. "He had us imprisoned and put on that ship without any sort of evidence against us. How are we supposed to live our lives when he is still out there, ready to blacken our family names?"

Will steeled his jaw and stiffened his spine, meaning every word when he announced, "Cadius will no longer be a threat to you, I give you my word." He tried to not let revenge guide him and had to remind himself to reign in his murderous thoughts. However, after everything that Cadius and Adrian had done to harm Sarah and the kingdom—add to that list the death of his uncle Thomas—Will could make no guarantees about how he would react when he again met those men. Yet whatever the case, after today, he made an oath that the boy-king and his father would never again harm another soul.

The men cast searching glances at each other for half a minute, seeming to silently discuss whether they believed Will's words or not. But their desire to return home appeared to outweigh their fear, and slow nods greeted him around the circle. That same man who had spoken up earlier nodded once at Will. "God's speed, and thank you for all that you did."

Will swallowed, his throat constricting as he gazed around the circle of men. Suddenly, he wished he had taken the time to learn all of their names. Now they were just faces, soon to be nothing more than vague memories of a great escape in the night, though he sensed it was more than that. This day would be with him forever, and Will shared a special camaraderie with these men, nameless though they were. They would forever be a part of his life and, he sensed, he would be a part of theirs.

Gilcrest was suddenly beside him, gazing up at him as though he was the most venerated man in the world. Will felt a jolt of concern for this boy who had experienced such a difficult childhood, wondering if he would be all right out on his own, free though he was. Then he felt Merek's presence over his shoulder and glanced back at the man, who smiled slightly and nodded once.

Turning back to the boy, Will placed both his hands on his thin shoulders. Bending down so he was at eye level with Gilcrest, he said, "Stay with Merek, he will look out for you."

Gilcrest nodded slowly, all seriousness. "But what will you do, sir?"

Will straightened, staring over the boy's head at the rising sun. Taking a deep breath, he answered, "I am going to end this madness." He gave Gilcrest's shoulders one final squeeze before taking a step toward the forest, his heart urging him to hurry. He halted abruptly, hesitating. Will turned toward Merek one final time, and his voice lowered with gratitude. "Merek, I—I don't know how to thank you for what you did back on the ship and . . . what you helped me to be willing to finally see."

Perhaps he imagined it, but Will thought the flames reflected off fresh water in the older man's eyes. "I would not have had it any other way."

Will gave a curt nod before his own stirring emotions could choke him and spun around, ignoring the fading pain in his skull as he jogged off into the forest as the sun rose overhead. There were only three thoughts in his head, instructions that ran through his mind again and again, reminding him of his purpose: charter a horse, stop Cadius once and for all, and find Sarah. That last thought caused his long legs to pump faster, carrying him through the trees and drawing him closer to the blue-eyed woman and the end of this terrible race.

Chapter Twenty-Seven

"Treason doth never prosper, what's the reason?
For if it prosper, none dare call it treason."

John Harrington

There were a few hiccups in Will's plan: nearly dying had sapped him of strength, his legs were shaking after having run several miles through the hilly terrain, and it had taken precious time to convince the proprietor to lend him a horse with nothing more than a promise that he would return the next day with the animal and a sizeable fee. Yet after three excruciatingly long hours, Will was on a horse galloping at lightening speed through the forest on his way into the heart of Serimone. To Sarah.

His meager progress was slowed far more often than he liked as he let his steed rest. The animal was sturdy and well muscled, but after almost an hour of urging the animal to its limit, its back was slick with sweat, froth sprayed from its mouth, and the look in the animal's eyes was one of pure panicked exhaustion. Feeling sorry that he had pushed it too hard, Will let up before it keeled over from beneath him and soon found a small brook by which he let the animal rest. He did not push his horse as hard after that, knowing they were making good time and that the animal would die if he did, though the frequent pauses in his journey were like torture as the sun rose steadily overhead.

As the horse sniffed the grass beneath it in search of more succulent blades, Will looked the perfect picture of a traveler taking a much needed reprieve as he sat with his back against the trunk of a tree. But on closer inspection, one of the knees pulled toward his chest was bouncing anxiously, as though even the exhaustion setting into his limbs couldn't keep him from moving.

Will planted his forearms on his knees, trying to still his jittery movements as he envisioned seeing Sarah again. The one positive aspect of these frequent stops was that it gave him a moment to think, though it also provided him sufficient time to overanalyze the events that would occur in the coming hours. Had someone told Sarah that he had been taken and the ship had gone down? He hoped not, recalling how terrible it had been for her before as she wondered if he had been killed. Will knew what it was like to question if he would ever see *her* again, and he never wanted to give her that kind of pain.

The image of his uncle's dying face suddenly surfaced, and he closed his eyes against the sheer agony that twisted his insides, knowing he was the cause of his death. There was no doubt in his mind that Uncle Thomas would not want him to cast blame, and there had been no sign of it in his uncle's eyes, even though he must have known that he had only been questioned because of the situation in which Will was involved. However, despite Will's internal reasoning, the death of his uncle still hung over him.

Suddenly, he was reminded of the way Uncle Thomas had said to not cast blame upon himself, and Merek had said it was easier to be forgiven than to absolve oneself of guilt and shame. He was beginning to see the truth in that statement.

Will paused when he recalled that only just that morning, he had asked to have his life and perspective changed. Taking a deep breath, he tried to recall the peace he had felt as he gave his life over to God during that sunrise.

"All right," he whispered, becoming more bold in his perfectly new faith, though the knowledge that he could speak to the Almighty and have Him *listen* did not make his words any less stilted. Yet there was something entirely freeing and surprisingly natural about speaking his thoughts aloud, and Will felt no shame as he rested his head back against the tree and said to the limbs above, "I suppose You already know the thoughts I hold in my heart, the guilt I harbor over my uncle's death."

He bit his lip, pushing back another wave of sorrow. "Uncle Thomas clearly did not hold me accountable, and from what I have heard, I honestly believe You have forgiven me, as well." The truth of the statement was staggering, and it was a moment before Will could go on with a steady but soft voice. "Help me to forgive myself for involving my uncle. I believe—what I mean to say is that Thomas was too intelligent to ignore the facts for much longer, and I think, perhaps, they eventually would have questioned my uncle in regards to Richard, anyway. I need . . ." He grimaced when the words faded. It was difficult for him to admit when he was wrong to *himself*, much less some perfect deity, but then he recalled the peace and love that had overwhelmed him in its clarity that morning, and somehow he felt an assurance that he would not be judged for his self-condemnation.

Exhaling slowly, Will closed his eyes and whispered with an open heart, "I am tired of holding myself accountable for every ill in my life. I am not sure I can, but help me to forgive myself if I had any part in my uncle's death. Help me . . ." But his voice faded as he wiped a tear from his cheek, and he knew there was nothing more to say.

He recalled a few instances where he had found his mother praying and crying softly, memories he had not thought about once since the day they occurred. But now he remembered the look of utter peace on her tear-stained face when she had finished, and he felt it now—the heaviness was still there, but something was different, and the weight bowing his shoulders down felt lighter, as though an invisible hand had removed a portion of it to make the burden less. A small smile tugged at his mouth, and he knew something very much like that had just occurred.

But the smile pulled downward as thoughts of his uncle turned to thoughts of Cadius, and he marveled at the way his disposition could be so easily shaken. But Will was new to such faith and trust, and so he tried to maintain some of that peace as he considered Cadius' next move.

He was systematically eliminating players in the game, as Sarah had pointed out, and, unbidden, Will envisioned Charles Ashmore—*the professor,* as Sarah had called him—as he stood before Karen on her wedding day, love for her guardian apparent in her eyes. If Cadius had come after the rest of them, why would he not concern himself with the creator of the very thing around which Cadius' master plan revolved? Will was almost certain the man was next on Cadius' list, if he had not yet been removed as a threat to their plan, but his mind kept straying to the sweet idea of having Sarah in his arms as soon as possible.

He raked a hand through his hair, slightly damp from the last stop near a shallow stream over an hour ago. While the horse grazed nearby, he had done his best to scrub the dirt and sand from his exposed skin, wanting to look presentable when he saw Sarah next. But how could he spend all of his time searching for the place where Damien kept her safe if he was almost certain that Charles Ashmore was in imminent peril? His conscience wouldn't allow him to be so selfish, and with a grunt of annoyance, Will shoved away from the tree and mounted his horse, knowing that they were near enough to push the rest of the way.

The forest was eerily silent as the trees blurred on either side of him, as though every creature in this wood sensed something he did not. His stomach clenched from such a long ride without food and the absence of sound, the hairs on the back of his neck standing on end. He urged the horse faster, and it obeyed despite the spittle flying from its mouth each time it exhaled a small squeal.

The trees parted to reveal a small one-room cabin with a stack of chopped wood adorning one side. Will pulled back abruptly on the reins and threw his right leg over the horse's neck before dropping to the ground and dashing into his cabin, not wanting to waste a moment on his way to Serimone Castle. He would ensure Charles Ashmore's protection, and then he would *find Sarah.*

Opening the lid of the chest at the end of his bed, he pulled out a green cloak, which was just beginning to fray around the edges. Fingering the cloth softened by years of use, he allowed himself a brief minute to ponder his next move. Which fate was worse and earned a harsher punishment: to be discovered as a treasonous escapee or as the Shadow, the vigilante whose once spotless repute was now stained with murder? Although he was the same man with a hood or no, wearing it somehow made him feel invisible, invincible, like no one could catch him if he were found out. Will needed that assurance now.

He draped the cloak about him, throwing the pack of arrows over his shoulder and picking up his trusted bow in movements as familiar to him as breathing. He had forgotten the power that came from holding his weapon, and he realized he had missed it terribly.

Steeling himself for what was to come, Will flipped the hood over his head and made his way outside. The stallion pawed anxiously at the earth, and he placed his boot in the stirrup and threw himself into the saddle. At little urging, the animal shot off in the direction of the castle, as though it had spent so much time running that it had a difficult time sitting still. Will sympathized with the creature.

He realized just then that he had not given a thought as to how they could overcome Cadius and his son and put a stop to this insanity. The evidence they had against Cadius was weak at best, and it would do little good if everyone, save the king, was under the assumption that he was dead. Knowing he was spiraling, Will took a deep breath and murmured into the wind, "One objective at a time." Once he ensured Ashmore's safety and found Sarah, they could come up with a plan together, he was sure of it.

Gritting his teeth, he leaned into the wind with one thought on his mind: Evidence or no, he was going to end this once and for all.

Above the trees, the tallest spires of Serimone Castle rose to meet the darkening sky, the purple flags bearing the royal crest flapping in the breeze. Faint thunder rolled overhead, and he knew a storm was blowing in from the east, not that it mattered. Nothing would keep him from finding Sarah *today*.

Will slowed the horse's pace and kept to the tree line to avoid being spotted by the additional guards walking up and down the parapet at equal intervals. It would be easy enough to distinguish a penetration point in their observation patterns, but he didn't waste his time; he needed to get *beneath* the castle, not go above it.

When he reached the backside of the castle where he knew there was less protection, he quietly dismounted and tied the horse to a low branch, then counted his long steps under his breath until the earth groaned faintly beneath his weight. Crouching down, he brushed aside the layer of dirt, leaves, and dead twigs to reveal a trapdoor cut into the earth. He grabbed the rusty iron rung and grunted as he pulled up the door, letting it fall unceremoniously to the ground.

He peered inside the dark, forgotten passageway, wondering if it had been discovered in Cadius' paranoia to ensure his son's and his own safety. As a curious boy with nothing better to do, Will had discovered several secret passageways leading into and out of the castle, so this was not his only option. However, he reminded himself, the other secret corridors were more easily discoverable, if one chose to look hard enough, and the coating of debris that had covered this trapdoor gave him cause to imagine that no one had been through here in ages. Perhaps he had been the last to use it, which—he hoped—meant it would not be filled with snares and pitfalls. And, most importantly, it would take him exactly where he needed to go.

Knowing hesitation would only stir up more doubts, Will slipped down into the passage, landing lithely on his feet. He listened for any sound of movement in the dank, quiet corridor, as he couldn't see beyond the small circle of light filtering down from the cut in the ceiling above him. Only a faint *drip drip* reached his ears, and he moved quickly and silently, counting off the turns and steps. His heart rate slowed as his boyhood wanderings came back to him—the adventure of getting lost in the labyrinthine halls and having to find his way out—and creeping in the dark suddenly became second nature once more.

Will stopped, his hands searching the cold stone until they found a seam in the wall. Pressing as he once had did little good, the hinges refusing to budge after years of neglect, a fact that reassured him some as he put his shoulder into it and heaved the false wall open. He would have stumbled into the hall as it gave way if he had not run into the heavy tapestry that concealed the hidden passage. Placing his palms flat against the fabric to still it, he strained his ears to catch any movements and then peered out to find the corridor empty.

Quietly, he closed the door behind him and exited his hiding place, heading down the hall to the right. His hood had fallen back at some point, and he flipped it up to obscure his features as he passed under a lit torch. The corridor was still deserted, but that did not mean it would remain that way for long.

A shout of pain reached his ears, and the ghostly sound that echoed through the silent passageway set every unsuspecting nerve in Will's body on high alert. He scurried ahead and turned when he hit the fork in the corridor, vaguely aware that the usual guard hadn't been patrolling that area as he rounded the bend, following the sound of shattering glass and wood shelves clattering to the ground. He jerked to a stop in the doorway to the alchemist's chamber, surveying the damaged beakers and parchments scattered across the floor, the overturned worktable.

Movement to the left caught his eye, and he turned to find a man standing over a crumpled form, chest heaving as the knife in his hand dripped blood onto the stone floor. The man didn't look pleased to have bested his opponent, but rather his face was tormented. He whipped his head at the sound of Will's sharp intake of breath as he recognized Lawrence, an old friend of his father's who had let Will have the run of the castle as a boy. The guilty expression on his face, as though horrified at what he had just done, let Will know that this man was another victim of Cadius' blackmailing.

Lawrence's shocked eyes narrowed as they took in the Shadow. "How did you get in here?" he demanded, managing to sound panicked as he said it. But Will couldn't answer, both from fear that his voice would betray his identity and total disbelief that this man he had known nearly all his life had—

Will jerked at the small gasp Charles Ashmore released, and it took him a moment to realize the man was trying to call out to him for help. When he instinctively took a step toward him, Lawrence raised the knife in a defensive posture. Will questioned if this old family friend would still threaten him if he were not dressed as a supposed traitor, and he swallowed, wondering what he was supposed to do when someone he was once close to suddenly became involved with Cadius.

But Lawrence removed his questions as he lunged, and instinct kicked in for Will as he grabbed the hand holding the knife and slammed his fist into the side of his head. Lawrence staggered to the side, and the dagger went clattering across the floor. It was close enough for Will to snatch, but he couldn't use it against him, regardless of whether or not this mission to attack Ashmore was by choice or force.

When he had regained his balance, Lawrence threw a hard fist in Will's direction, but he quickly ducked as his arm shot overhead. Thinking quickly, Will grabbed him behind the neck and brought his face down to connect with his upraised knee, hoping the pain of a broken nose would stop him. But Lawrence only slumped to the ground, rolling onto his back and lying still as a trickle of blood ran from his nostril. Will froze, panic seizing him as he wondered if he had killed him by accident, but then Lawrence's chest rose slightly, and Will's shoulders slumped as he exhaled his fear in a wavering gust.

He hurried over to Charles Ashmore, who lay on the floor, both hands clutching his bloody abdomen as he watched Will with enormous eyes, one of which was exaggerated by the circular piece of glass held together by the strange metal wiring connecting it to his ears. One of the pieces appeared to be missing, and the crunch of glass underfoot made Will suspect he had just stepped on it.

Pressing his palms over the man's own bloody hands, Will said in a voice steadier than he felt, "You will be all right, but I must find you help."

But Charles was shaking his head faintly from side to side. "No, Cadius . . . I *saw* him." He grasped the front of Will's cloak in a grip surprisingly strong for his frail fingers, smearing blood across the fabric. Eyes flecked with gray bore into his own. "I saw him." He seemed to realize who was hovering over him, and his grip slackened as amazement filled his gaze. "It can't truly be you."

Will hesitated, finding it difficult to break the old habit of keeping his identity a secret, but then he realized that Charles might die feeling unsafe with a hooded vigilante looming over him. Wanting to put him at ease, Will pulled back his hood, keeping one hand over the man's wound. "It's William Taylor, sir."

Eyes widened even further as Charles stared up at him in awe. "William," he breathed. "How can—?" He grimaced, clutching his free hand over Will's as his expression turned urgent. "I don't know who else to tell, but Cadius . . . is alive. There is so much you don't know, William. . . ."

Shaking his head, Will admitted, "I know everything."

Charles blinked, his pain momentarily forgotten. *"Everything?"* he clarified.

"I know that Cadius and King Adrian are working together to become an unstoppable power, and somehow—" Will paused, still amazed at the fact himself as he said quietly, "I went into your future with Sarah. I know everything, Charles."

The man's pale face brightened a fraction. "That's marvelous!" His sudden cry brought about another cringe of pain, and his expression fell abruptly, gray-flecked eyes clouding over. His voice was faint but insistent, sentences disjointed as he faded. "You must go. Cadius is here."

"Where?" Will pressed.

As though he hadn't heard, Charles whispered in a fading voice, "He and the king must be stopped. I was so foolish, so blind, and I didn't see . . . his plan until now. But you must stop them."

Will balked. He thought of Karen and her broken relationship with Ashmore, which Sarah had told him had yet to be mended, the fact that he would never see her and Seth's children grow. "I cannot leave you here alone."

"Never mind what happens to me!" Charles gritted his teeth as his outburst sent a fresh bubble of his own blood over their joined hands. "Man wasn't made to play God," he rasped. "In my arrogant pursuit of knowledge . . . I tried to change the world." His voice was barely above a whisper now, though the hand covering Will's tightened. A shaky breath punctuated each word. "Stop them, William. Whatever it takes, amend this horrible wrong I've done and *stop Cadius*."

It was so similar to the instant his uncle lie dying in his arms that Will froze for a moment, fear seizing his body. One by one, he forced his muscles to unwind. As much as the idea tempted him, he could not kill Cadius in cold blood, if that's what the man was suggesting. Yet although Sarah had Damien's letter, Will was certain he could find evidence against the man in this very castle.

"With everything that is within me," he declared firmly, feeling the heat of his passion to end this madness burgeoning inside of him once more. "I swear to you that Cadius will be stopped."

"And my girl," Ashmore suddenly choked out urgently, his strange gray-flecked eyes large and unfocused as they gazed up at him. "Make sure she's safe."

Will swallowed, seeing in the dying man's eyes that this was the most important thing to him, and he gave a small nod. Reluctantly, regretfully, he removed his hand from Charles's stomach, seeing that the blood had slowed some, though it still seeped through his weathered fingers. He stood.

"Go, William," Charles whispered urgently. "Go and save this city from the evil I created."

It was horrible to leave him lying there, alone and bleeding on the floor of his destroyed alchemy chamber, and Will wondered if he would survive such a wound. But there was determination in the old man's eyes, letting Will know that he could not sway him and would only waste time arguing. He could do nothing more except keep his promise to everyone and put a stop to Cadius' plan.

He shot a quick glance at Lawrence to ensure he was still out cold, sensing that even if he awoke, the guilt in his eyes when he had stood over Charles meant that he would not have the courage, or the stomach, to finish him off. When he drew his gaze back to Charles, the man's hands were shaking, though his expression was resolute, strong. "We will not lose you to Cadius," he said firmly, though even as he spoke, he wondered how he could get help to Ashmore without exposing himself—the entire kingdom might be at stake if he didn't end this today, and he could not risk any delays. But he knew he had to try to save him, somehow.

Will felt a stab of guilt, thinking that he should have pushed harder or come for the man sooner, then perhaps . . .

But Charles Ashmore shook his head, his voice sounding steady for one moment. "*You* are the hero in this story, William, and it's about time Cadius discovered that villains never win."

ଔ

The darkening clouds had opened and began loosing a light mist over the earth by the time Will found his way to the upper floor. He spent nearly half an hour sneaking through corridors and searching for secret passageways, backtracking when a guard or servant came his way, and he hoped that someone had found Charles during that time. At last, he neared the former queen's chambers, knowing that it was there that Sarah had found the incriminating notes between Alexis and Cadius nearly a week past.

As he neared the door leading to her room from the side entrance, he sniffed the air, detecting the faint stench of burning parchment. Suddenly wary, he advanced on the partially cracked door with cautious steps and peered into the other room. He forced himself not to react thoughtlessly when he saw the backs of Cadius and his son standing near the fireplace, silently watching a small fire. It was odd to find them in there together, though Will's suspicion turned to panic as he saw that one of the drawers in the desk had been ripped out, its contents spilled carelessly on the floor.

They were burning the letters, and he felt suddenly sure, from the look of the heap of ashes in the fireplace, that there was nothing left to be used against Cadius. Will felt like collapsing to the floor and giving up, something that was in opposition to everything he was. He stood just behind the door, frozen in shock and despair, as the malevolent father spoke above the crackling of the flames.

"It is finished," Cadius whispered in satisfaction, placing a hand on his son's shoulder. "So many years have come down to this moment, to our success."

Adrian turned his head to look at his father, his eyes distant, sad. "In so many ways, Father." He reached inside his vest and produced something from a hidden pocket. Will narrowed his eyes, though they widened as the firelight glinted off the reflective surface of a watch not unlike the one Sarah constantly wore.

Carelessly, Adrian tossed it into the flames.

"What—No!" Cadius fell to his knees before the fireplace. He reached for the watch without forethought and hissed, yanking his hand back as the flames began to melt the device; the wristband crumbled a few seconds before the black glass face cracked and shattered. It was consumed by the fire, almost dissolving as it molded together with the heap of ashes that had once been love letters between Cadius and the former queen.

Cadius stared up at his son with wide, confused eyes, accusation hanging in his gaze. "Do you have any idea what you have done?"

"This contraption"—Adrian motioned to the fireplace and what little remained of the watch—"cannot fix what we have done or amend the past and bring about a new future, as you have claimed it can. The only way to secure my future as king—to fulfill this desire of ours—is to eliminate all threats to it." He hesitated and then squared his shoulders. "Our plan *shall* prevail, Father, even if your death is the only way to ensure its success."

The door leading from the outer hall opened into the room, startling Will from his own thoughts as he tried to discern what he should do now that the letters were destroyed. He had just been contemplating the difficulty in finding Sarah and retrieving the Spaniard's letter *and then* returning back to the castle unseen before time ran out, but then Adrian's words reached his ears. Cadius appeared surprised and suspicious at his tone, but then he cast his gaze to the door and his eyes widened in alarm as he took in the faces of the four guards that entered.

Will pressed against the wood to allow himself another inch of viewing space, wondering what he was watching transpire. He wanted to stay and watch, unseen, but now that the evidence he'd come for had been destroyed, he was tempted to give up and run back to Charles to ensure he received proper care and find the place where Sarah was being safeguarded. But then Cadius spoke, and Will knew something was wrong.

"Adrian, those are not my guards." His voice held a note of concern, but then his expression became disbelieving as he caught his son's regretful gaze. "What have you done?" he whispered.

"You always told me that love is weakness and weakness must be eradicated," Adrian said diplomatically in answer, though his eyes tipped in sorrow as he added softly, "And I have discovered that *you* are my only weakness, Father."

There was a pregnant pause, the guards looking uncertain as they glanced between their king and the uncle, who, until a moment ago, had been presumed dead. Will, too, was having difficulty placing the look on Adrian's features and the expression of betrayal in his father's. Then the boy-king said quietly, "Guards, arrest my uncle and tell the executioner to prepare for his hanging early this evening. Inform Captain Quinn that he is to read his crimes." His voice was eerily calm for a man who had watched innocents die and had just sentenced his father to death . . . for the second time.

The guards hesitated a moment, and then as one they reached for Cadius. There was no struggle, no pleas for his life; his look was utter betrayal and disbelief. One guard wrenched Cadius' hands behind his back, causing him to wince, though his gaze did not waver from his son's withdrawn face. Adrian lifted a hand before they could drag him from the room. "After everything," Cadius breathed, hurt evident in each word. "How *could* you? I am your father." Countless emotions clouded Cadius' expression and strangled his voice.

"I have no father," Adrian whispered, for the benefit of the guards, Will was sure. "Now there is nothing left to be used against me. I will find strength in my solitude—surely you of all people understand this." Adrian's voice cracked, as though he desperately wished his father *did* understand his reasoning. Will shook his head as much to dismiss his deranged words as to clear his own muddled mind. He didn't believe Cadius ever intended to lose his life to his own scheme—no, that addition to the plan had been the young king's doing alone.

Rolling his head in unbelief, Cadius suddenly looked horrified, his eyes tortured as he whispered, "Oh, my boy, what have I done to you?" It was the first bit of remorse Will had ever glimpsed in the man's features.

Adrian closed his eyes, seeming to need a moment to collect himself as his actions sank in. But Will felt no pity for the child who had become king, knowing that Cadius had created a monster and would live with the consequences.

Having put his emotions in check, Adrian glanced down at him. His hands shook but his voice remained steady as he said, "I have become what we designed. Take him away."

There was no resistance from Cadius as he was jerked backward and dragged from the room, his eyes pleading with his son for a better answer, though he said nothing as he was pulled around the corner and out of sight to await his hanging less than two hours away.

Will was so intent on watching the entire shocking scene that he did not hear the guard come up behind him. A hand gripped his arm, and he spun around to find an unfamiliar man staring at him with a gaze that vacillated between professional anger and shock that the vigilante had been caught snooping around Serimone Castle once more. "You are wanted by the Crown," the guard informed, as though Will was not aware of the fact. He wondered why he had chosen such an obvious disguise until he remembered that his face was still hidden beneath the hood.

He wasn't caught yet.

With swift movements, Will's left hand shot out and broke the man's hold on his arm. Before he could react, Will crouched and kicked his leg out, spinning so that it caught him behind the knee and sent the man sprawling onto the floor. Will was already on his feet, and he dashed to the hall, trying to recall the quickest way out as adrenaline and the startling event he had just witnessed tried to take over his logical processes. He didn't get very far, though, before someone slammed into him from the side.

Two guards wrestled Will to the ground, and he growled in frustration as he tried to jerk free, lifting his knee in defense. A howl of pain as it hit one of the crouched guards between the legs sent a small spark of gratification through him, though it immediately died when a fist rammed into his abdomen and it was all he could do not to shout.

A shadow passed over him, and he stared up at Adrian with all the disgust and hatred he could muster. The boy-king watched him struggle with a blank, disinterested gaze, and then recognition passed across his features as Will's hood fell away. "Knight Taylor," he whispered in surprise. "After word of the vessel's destruction reached me, I did not expect you to be alive, and least of all did I expect you to be the masked vigilante who has been causing such trouble."

His features, which had paled considerably during his betrayal of his father, brightened a modicum, though he still appeared older than his years and drained of life. "I suppose it is just as well to have you be the murderous Shadow. My fa—*uncle* will love to watch this," he said carefully, for the benefit of the guards, no doubt.

Will was tempted to remind him that it takes a murderer to recognize one, but he was too busy trying not to wince at the throbbing in his gut.

Adrian turned his back and walked down the hall away from the guards who struggled to hold Will down. In a dismal tone, he said over his shoulder, “Have him ready for this evening.”

At his words, Will thrashed wildly, knowing that he was sentencing him to hang, along with his father. His legs kicked madly, and his fists flew, connecting with shoulders and jaws, anything he could touch as the guards shouted to each other to hold him down. There was nothing heroic in a death such as an execution, and he couldn’t leave Sarah this way, not now. He tried to wrench free, knowing there was an open window in the room just past the stairs that he had taken note of earlier, thinking he might be able to launch himself outside and catch one of the trellises leaning against the side of the castle.

But then the burly guard landed a fist to his head, and everything went dark.

Chapter Twenty-Eight

"If it is true that there are as many minds as there are heads, then there are as many kinds of love as there are hearts."

Leo Tolstoy, *Anna Karenina*

Damien was sitting on the couch exactly as she'd left him, though he was slumped over his knees, rubbing a hand over his mouth. He looked up sharply when she entered the room, appearing surprised that she had returned, and she couldn't blame him. The walk had cooled her temper, and she felt guilty for the things she'd said.

"Listen." Sarah closed the door behind her, casting her guilty gaze about the room before she could meet his eyes. On a sigh, she said, "I'm sorry for how I treated you earlier. I shouldn't have said what I did, and you didn't deserve my anger. *Although,*" she added, "you *were* acting like I was your prisoner, so that was a little overbearing—"

"He is alive," Damien whispered, his gaze and voice expressing his shock. She halted midstride, a little alarmed at the look on his face. He let out a small, shocked laugh as his hands made random motions in the air, as though they might help him understand something. But he went silent, his fingers turning into knots in his lap.

"Damien," she said cautiously, advancing one step, then another. Her heart sped up anxiously, though she tried to tell herself not to get her hopes up. It could be anyone, she told herself. Plenty of people had died since she'd come to Serimone. . . . "Who are you talking about?"

His stunned and reluctant eyes met her apprehensive gaze. "You said you would return quickly, and so I became anxious when you were gone for nearly an hour. I went in search of you near the castle in the event that one of Cadius' men had found you, or you had wandered too far." One of Sarah's brows shot up, as if to say this had been the overbearing problem she had just spoken of, and he raised a hand to stop her admonition.

"I inquired of my informant if he had seen you." He let out a quick breath through his nose. "Not you, but he had seen that blacksmith I'd previously inquired after being led out of the castle in shackles."

If her heart was a racehorse before, it was now trying to place first in the Indie 500. "Will's alive? Someone actually saw him?" she whispered, voice quaking with uncertainty and an unwillingness to believe her building hope, lest it let her down again. But Damien nodded slowly, and Sarah's knees buckled. She sank to the floor, tears immediately filling her eyes, and she was having difficulty catching her breath. But then a stupid grin broke out on her face as she stared at the farthest wall. Will was alive. A lone droplet spilled over her lid as she closed her eyes, dragging in her first deep breath in a day. When she saw him, she was going to punch Will for almost dying twice.

She opened her eyes as something Damien had said registered. Meeting his gaze, she whispered, "Shackles?"

Another slow, reluctant nod. In the midst of her delirious haze, she felt a spark of sympathy for him that he always had to be the bearer of bad news for her. She swallowed the sudden pain in her throat as she remembered that there was bad news. But as long as Will lived, there was hope.

When he remained silent, Sarah burst out, "Oh, come on, say something! We've been in worse scrapes. Will's alive, so how bad could it possibly be?"

After a brief hesitation, Damien came over and crouched down beside her. The situation was so painfully familiar that her hands began to quake, and she gripped the fabric of her dirty skirt to keep them steady.

"Yes, he is alive, but not for long." At his words, Sarah's pulse halted for a full two beats before pounding heavily against her throat. Cringing, he went on softly, "He must have survived the blast aboard the ship and came back to the castle, only God knows why. Taylor was caught and apprehended shortly after his arrival."

Sarah was silent as she stared, unseeing, over his shoulder as he spoke. Then her eyes snapped to his as a sudden, desperate idea filled her mind. "So we just have to stop Cadius and the king, right? I mean, the queen will release him when she realizes that he's being held under false pretenses."

But Damien was already shaking his head. "Taylor was discovered disguised as the Shadow, and considering general distrust of his alter ego and the Shadow's illustrious history of being a murderer . . ." He cringed at his own words, no doubt recalling the fact that one of these murders falsely tacked to the Shadow's hood had been his fault. "Although the king was the one to discover Taylor and wants him gone for his own purposes, in the eyes of the law, the man wearing that mask *is* guilty of terrible crimes. They plan to have him hanged as a traitor at the earliest opportunity, before nightfall, I suspect." His voice faded, and he watched her with a sad, wary gaze.

Shoulder's bowing under the weight of this, Sarah stared at the floor. She shook her head, willing his words to disappear from her memory. Her tortured gaze met Damien's, and his eyes softened at the tears in her own. "No," she whispered brokenly. "I can't find out he's alive only to lose him again. I just can't."

His arms came around her, and he held her tight against his chest. "I know," he whispered, chest falling as he released a deep sigh. "But there is nothing we can do from here."

"Then, please, *let me go*," she whispered, throat closing as she pushed away from him. The muscles in her neck worked as she swallowed. "I have to save him. A part of me will die if I don't get to him in time, and I'll never be able to forgive *myself* if I don't try to stop them."

He was so silent, his body so completely still, that she wondered for a second if he might have turned to stone at her words. But then he exhaled slowly, his shoulders drooping downward even as his lips tipped up in a sad smile. "You are asking me to release the woman I am in love with so she might save the life of the man she loves, at the risk of her *own* life?" He quirked a brow, hinting at the absurdity of her request.

Sarah's chin quivered as she nodded, accepting the truth of his statement. For the first time, she truly allowed herself to admit that she was desperately in love with Will, and he would be dead soon if she couldn't get to him and . . . But she didn't have a plan other than reaching him before—

Tears slipped unhindered down her cheeks at the visual she snapped off before it could fully form, but the idea of his hanging was there, tainting her mind. "And I haven't told him," she whispered. They were words she had said before, but now they held a greater terror because she could do something about it, and she might still fail.

Her heart quickened in panic, realizing she might never have the chance to tell him how she felt if she didn't go to him *now*. Her beseeching gaze returned Damien's tortured stare. "He has told me countless times that he loves me and said that I should take my time. But my time is almost up, Damien. If I don't get to him and stop the execution . . . I've lost him so many times before, and I can't let him die wondering if I ever truly loved him."

"He knows," Damien whispered. He met her gaze. "I have told you before, have I not? It's impossible to ignore, the way you look at him. I knew you were in love with someone when you rejected my advances at the ball, though I wasn't certain it was Taylor at the time. You did not realize it then, but I did." The breath he inhaled seemed to shudder in his chest before he let it out, adding softly, "Isabella said I need to stop choosing the future for others. I cannot protect you forever, and this is your choice."

Sarah blinked, half-shocked that he was . . . agreeing? But she saw it in his face, knew he was letting her go, and tears of pain and gratitude rushed to the surface, making several watery Damien's dance before her eyes. "I don't know how to thank you for keeping me safe and for . . . everything," she breathed. She didn't know what else to say. A painful band squeezed around her chest as Damien's gaze swam and the gold flecks danced in their depths.

He pressed his forehead to hers, eyes closed tight against the similar pain that she imagined constricted his heart. His breath wobbled in his chest as he held back his emotion, but she felt it rolling off him—felt it in the way he held onto her as he pulled her into a tight embrace, pressing his face into the crook of her neck as though she would dissolve and drift away if he dared let go. Sarah felt the wetness on her neck and didn't know if it was caused by her own coursing tears or Damien's. Maybe it was a little of both. She knew that each needed the other in that moment to release the tension and emotion they had both been holding in for too long. It was an instant of friendship and mutual pain, and Sarah knew it would be one of their last shared memories.

They stayed like that for several long moments, grieving together, though it felt like an eternity to Sarah, who heard the sound of Damien's heartbeat like the oppressive ticking of a clock, reminding her that Will was running out of time. But Damien . . . A part of her wondered if she could leave him like this. Even as the thought that Will was out there, *alive*, urged her to move, she felt such terrible agony thinking that Damien might never get his happy ending.

"Go to him." His voice was so quiet that Sarah jerked back, unsure if she'd heard correctly. Damien reached inside of his jacket and produced the key to the padlock on the door, though it wasn't secured. But she knew it was symbolic of him relinquishing his hold on her freedom as he held it out to her with trembling fingers.

"I cannot insist you remain here in the name of safety, fooling myself into believing that we could make a life together. I love you too much—" His voice cracked, and he turned away for a second to collect himself. When he looked at her again, tears pooled in his dark gaze once more, and the flecks of gold in his eyes looked like drowning stars. "If there is any purity left within my body, then it is my love for you that burns white, and I *will not* lie to myself by imagining that I can force your affections. It is my very love for you that begs you to stay and pleads with you to go to him. Save him and be happy."

Sarah wiped the tears from her cheeks, nodding slowly, reluctantly even as her heart thanked him for revealing that Will was alive and letting her go. Needing to touch him one last time, to feel that connection she'd sensed so quickly with him, she placed her palm against his wet cheek, hoping that her touch would be a comfort and not cause him further pain. "You aren't the unlovable man that you think you are. And—and I know it isn't what you want to hear, Damien, but you have been a true friend."

To her surprise, he gave her a soft, crooked smile as he clasped her other hand in his own. "As you have been."

Slowly, she drew back her hand, and his own raised a fraction as her fingertips slipped from his, as though he wanted to prolong this final connection for as long as possible. Because, they mutually acknowledged but refused to say aloud, that once Sarah left, she was never coming back.

"Say goodbye to Isabella for me," she said quietly, and then moved for the door.

"Sarah?"

She spun around in the doorway, impatience and surprise melting when she saw the tears slipping down Damien's cheeks as he sat on the floor. He looked anguished, amused, and tortured all at once. "What sort of plan do you have to stop the enactment of the law?"

"I don't know," she answered honestly. "But I'm all that Will has left and the only one who will try to set things right." She paused, thinking. "You could come with. With all the evidence you've been willing to give me, I'm sure they'd see your help as cooperation. You might even be a free man, after all."

But he was already shaking his head, eyes distant. Softly, he murmured, "No, I wish only for this to end." His lips pulled into a tight line, and he closed his eyes, as if fighting back a wave of pain. When he opened them, his golden-espresso gaze bore into hers. "Go. For both your sakes, go."

Sarah felt as though her heart was pulling her in two different directions—the one leading her toward Will, and the other part of her heart that hated to leave Damien behind, when she knew letting her go must be costing him. "How can I leave you here like this, though?" she whispered, throat tight.

Instead of answering her question, he gave her a small, beautiful smile. "I want you to know that you were the light in my darkest hours, and every dream I ever had pales in comparison to the brightness you shone into the darkness of my heart, defying every shadow in residence. I shall forever carry a piece of you with me, Lady Sarah Matthews." His smile wavered, but his eyes were luminescent. "I am better for having known you, my darling."

Sarah felt herself drowning in his sorrowful yet resolved gaze. With an aching heart that urged her to hurry, she allowed herself a moment to give her friend one last glance that she hope revealed her genuine gratitude. "I'll never forget you, Damien Lisandro."

He placed a hand over his heart, eyes welling once more, though he looked as though he was desperately trying to hold them at bay. "Then for my sake, let that memory you carry be of the man you once knew. Remember the friend you cared for and with whom you laughed. . . . No matter what happens to me, remember that man." His gaze burned with a need for her to understand something that she wished she had more time to decipher.

"I will."

His soft whisper barely reached her ears. "Go and save your heart before it is too late. Take his horse and head east; it will be faster. You *will* find him, my lady," he offered up as final encouragement. Damien lifted his head and met her eyes one final time, giving her the tiniest of encouraging smiles that she knew was for her sake alone.

Sarah swallowed and said farewell to the lost boy who was no longer unloved. "Goodbye, Damien," she breathed, knowing that these would be the last words she ever spoke to him. With great certainty, she *felt* that after that day, her eyes would never rest on Damien again. Judging by the way he closed his eyes and hung his head, looking pained, he knew it, too.

Dragging in a deep, shuddering breath, she forced herself to turn away from him and dashed through the door and into the misty forest, doing exactly what Damien had told her to do: Whatever it took, she was going to save the man who held her heart.

Chapter Twenty-Nine

"I have been astonished that men could die martyrs
for their religion—
I have shuddered at it, I shudder no more.
I could be martyred for my religion.
Love is my religion,
and I could die for that."

John Keats

The stallion watched as she hesitantly neared, showing no anxiety at the approach of a near stranger after being left so long unattended. Though Jade had fed him while he'd been tied up outside the small cottage, Sarah half expected the animal to act wild with hunger and try to snap at her as she neared. But the animal was as calm as she remembered, though a little larger, and stood black as night against the dimming light of day.

"Okay, buddy," she whispered, flinching as the stallion's ear perked at the sound of her voice. But she didn't slow as she raised her hands, splaying them wide to show they were empty. "I come in peace." He was still saddled and the bridle was on, waiting for her. She swallowed as she came to a stop before his enormous face, freezing.

You've ridden him before, she chastised herself to bolster her courage. But then her shoulders sank when she remembered that Will had been the one guiding the horse as they flew through the woods, recalled the way the world had blurred and it was just the two of them soaring above the earth on a black cloud of muscle and strength.

Sarah said under her breath so as to not startle the animal, "I need your help to get to him, and I'm—I'm scared of you and a lot of other things. The truth is I'm terrified of being too late to save him, but I'm afraid to go and find that Will is already gone." Her voice shook, and she realized it was easy to admit her fear to a horse that would keep her secrets, the very same animal that would bring her to Will.

A wave of surprise coursed through her as the animal lowered its head, moving forward an inch. She hesitated, but then her quivering hand rose hesitantly, her fingertips barely grazing the animal's black hair. It seemed to lean into her touch, and her fear of the creature ebbed away as she drew her palm from the tip of its midnight mane down to its nose, gently rubbing him between the eyes with her fingers. His coat was softer than she remembered, though she couldn't recall ever really *touching* it outside of wrapping her legs around its middle like a wet cat trying not to drown.

You're braver than you think. Will's words whispered through the trees, pricking the hair on the back of her neck, and she tried not to cry.

The animal watched her as she pet him, eyes grave as though he sensed her temper. And, she supposed, he did sense her anxiety and eagerness. "Let's go get him, boy," she said softly.

Though Sarah felt they had bonded, she still walked cautiously around it, wishing she could muster Will's grace as she bent her leg high and hoisted herself up into the saddle. Her skirts became entangled around her body, and she tried not to upset the animal as she fidgeted until she hiked her hem up to her knees to keep it from toppling her. She felt perfectly confident for all of five seconds until she glanced down and realized that she was up and the ground was *way* down there.

Mustering all the courage she could, Sarah gripped the reins. "Go easy on me, buddy," she mumbled, giving the stallion a gentle squeeze in the side with her heels. It didn't jerk like she'd thought it would but trotted easily forward, though he appeared more eager than she to quicken their pace.

She was doing a good job of staying in the saddle, but she continually pulled back on the reins and muttered a gentle "Whoah" to keep the animal at a more comfortable pace. But then she remembered that Will didn't have all the time in the world, and if she could remain upright in the saddle, then she couldn't really justify moving through the forest at a snail's pace. Speed equaled saving Will, and it was worth the possibility of breaking her neck to get there in time.

"Try not to get us killed." With a deep breath and Will's words guiding her on, she flicked the reins. A screech left her lips as the stallion blasted forward, darting through the trees as though it knew precisely where it was going. Sarah was a little less confident and resisted the urge to close her eyes until they reached town. Her thighs burned as they squeezed the animal's side, hands gripping the leather straps so hard her knuckles turned white. But while it was terrifying, she couldn't help feeling a spark of that exhilarating freedom she'd experienced before and knew that, as strange as it seemed, she wanted to do this again. With Will.

She gritted her teeth and leaned into the wind, giving up all hope of steering and let the animal race like a bullet as its hooves at up the distance to town.

It began raining as they charged through the forest, heading east as Damien had directed—just a light discharge of excess water from the sky. But by the time they reached the town and broke through the tree line, her dress was fairly soaked and her hair was plastered to her forehead. She shivered, wiping the moisture from her face as she broke through the forest and headed toward civilization, almost having forgotten what the small town looked like after so long in the forest and Jade's cottage.

As Sarah rode, she had wondered where they would be holding Will, but all doubt fled her mind when she heard the shouts coming from the courtyard of Serimone Castle. With a racing heart, she urged the panting animal to the left and charged through the ghost town the square had become. Carts were left unattended and barrels stood with half-closed lids, as though everyone had fled suddenly.

Quickly and carefully, she pulled up her left knee and fell from the horse, managing to land on her stiff legs with a grimace. Hands shaking from her life-or-death grip on the reins and the adrenaline coursing through her body, she dashed through the unguarded gates, gasping nearly as hard as the animal that she left just outside. Despite the rain, there was a large crowd gathered, forming a tight circle around the public execution stands, a hangman's noose at the ready, though no prisoners were in sight. Yet.

Her anxious gaze darted left and right over the throng and then passed over the few standing on the platform to the side of the noose that waved in the breeze, awaiting its first neck to snap. Beneath a small covered shelter off to the right sat the queen in an ornate chair made from bronzed wood and gold-dyed fabric. Sarah could see from this distance that Queen Meredith appeared the perfect picture of queenly grace in her fine gown, hair neatly braided over her shoulder. But the hands clutched in her lap were pale to match her face, and her eyes darted over the gathering anxiously, as though she didn't wish to be there and wanted to dismiss them all. Sarah wished she would—no one deserved a public execution.

Just then King Adrian appeared on the stairs, and her eyes narrowed. *Except maybe him*. It was tempting, so tempting, to call out that *he* was the murderer and should be punished for *his* crimes. But then she reminded herself that Adrian and Cadius both wanted her dead, and it wouldn't help Will if she got herself executed right alongside him.

She bit her lip, swallowing back the angry bile rising in her throat as Adrian sat down by his mother in a chair slightly larger than her own, a constant reminder that he held more power than anyone in the kingdom. The queen leaned toward him, whispering anxiously, her face strained, but the arrogant king waved his mother off, casting his own gaze to the stand where the execution would take place, fidgeting eagerly in his seat. His face conjured images of Damien's pain and Thomas dying and Will awaiting his fate.

Hands shaking and stomach quivering as she suppressed the desire to claw his eyes out, Sarah turned her gaze away from the royals and saw a familiar redhead above the crowd. Seth looked surprised to see her, but he moved quickly through the congregation of townsfolk, speaking to some unseen figure at his side, and Sarah felt a spark of relief that Karen was with him.

Her friend shoved two people aside with more force than one might suspect for someone of her size. Karen hurried to her side, and the two girls squeezed each other tight. Sarah's throat burned as her friend's presence disarmed her. She couldn't remember ever being so relieved to see Karen's face as the girl pulled back, giving her a panicked look as she drew her gaze over Sarah's body in search of some physical scar.

"We were so worried!" she said loudly over the curious conversations that rolled like waves around them, her voice hurried. "Seth went searching for you with Will, but then *Will* went missing, and there was no word from either of you for days. And—Sarah, what is going on?"

Sarah wanted to make a joke that, of course, it would take a crisis to get Karen in public again after so long, but now wasn't the time for jesting. She was trying to figure out a way to describe the past week in a single sentence to save time, but was jostled by the growing crowd. Someone shoved Karen forward in their eagerness to reach the best vantage point of the stand, and Seth glared at the man's back as he disappeared through the mass of bodies. He took his wife's arm and pulled her aside, out of the main congestion. Sarah followed.

When they were out of the thick of it, he opened his mouth to say something and then Sarah was suddenly wrapped up in a quick, crushing hug. He pulled back, looking like he wanted to grin, though the current circumstance kept his mouth downturned. "We're glad you are all right, but what happened to you?"

She shook her head, unable to explain everything just then. "What are you guys doing here?"

"We were in town when everyone started dispersing, saying that a sudden execution would begin soon," Seth offered, face darkening. "They all wanted to see why it was being held so publicly, and Dagwood said it was Will." The crowd suddenly grew to a deafening roar, and his eyes shot over her shoulder. His face paled. "Oh, Lord, is that him?"

Sarah spun, heart stopping as she took in the two prisoners being led up the stairs, their hands in shackles before them. Each wore a black hood over his head, but there was no doubt in her mind that Will stood on the left, his tall, strong frame unmistakable to her as he cautiously shuffled up the steps. He was directed by a stony-faced guard to stand facing the crowd near the center of the platform, and his hood was yanked off his head with a flick, making his hair a mass of spiky black on one side that quickly flattened in the rain. He glared at the sudden light, though it was gray and hazy as the rain began falling in earnest.

Sarah almost cried in relief when she glimpsed his familiar face and saw with her own eyes that he was alive, and she wanted nothing more than to rush onto the stand and kiss him. But it wasn't the time or place, and she was still frantically scrambling for a way to get him released as they led him to the noose that swung back and forth. Will appeared to flinch when he saw the slip that would fit over his head, and she could see the wheels in his head spinning as he searched for some way to free himself.

With a start, she remembered that she had Cadius' letter ordering Malcolm Devlin to dispose of Richard as a baby. It didn't necessarily prove Will's innocence, but declaring Cadius guilty of this act would—hopefully—cause a domino effect that would unravel everything he and Adrian had done, and she prayed that Will's release would be a part of their plan crumbling. At the very least, it would buy him more time to figure something else out.

She shoved a hand up her sleeve, though her expectancy was overcome with alarm as she realized the letter was no longer there. Her hands shook as she searched both sleeves, stomach twisting in panic as she realized it must have fallen out somewhere. She stared up at Will, useless hands falling limp at her sides. What could she do now? She couldn't fail him after everything he had done to protect *her,* couldn't let him lose his life without knowing how she felt about him.

Karen took her hand to get her attention, and Sarah managed to draw her gaze from Will's face, pulling her mind from thoughts on how to get his attention without drawing the king's. Her friend's green eyes bore into hers. "How do we stop this?" she shouted over the crowd. Strands of dark red clung to her cheeks.

But Sarah could only shake her head, wondering the same thing herself. Then she froze in utter shock as the hood was removed from the other prisoner and Cadius blinked against the rain. He turned and caught his son's eye, and Adrian gave him the look of a child searching for reassurance that his actions were justified. As if in offering, he flicked his fingers toward Will, but Cadius merely shook his head as the roar of shock at his presence broke out over the gathering, drowning out any response he might have had.

There was no time for Sarah to process how *he* had found himself on the execution stand that day as she slipped out of her friend's grasp and moved through the crowd, which was nearly impossible as the bodies all pressed together in anxious anticipation. She thought Karen might have called out to her, but her focus was on Will's face as she called his name over and over, trying to be heard above the noise. His head was bowed slightly as he stood directly beneath the gibbet, and she thought his lips might have been moving. She knew the instant he heard her, because his head shot straight up and his eyes frantically scanned the crowd. When they met hers, she thought his features might have lightened for an instant, though panic quickly replaced his expression.

He shook his head violently. *"No,"* he mouthed, eyes flicking pointedly to Adrian sitting on his throne chair, wearing an anxious expression. Sarah knew he didn't want her to expose herself, but she also wondered if part of Will's insistence was his fear that she would see him hanged.

Tears flooded her vision as she advanced, making the world a wash of bodies and wood. "I won't leave you, Will," she said loudly, though her voice cracked; she couldn't abandon him now, would never forgive herself if she wasn't there for him. There was no way he heard her, but he must have read her lips because he closed his eyes against the pain that flooded his features.

A man appeared at the top of the stairs, and it took Sarah a moment to recognize Captain Quinn, his crooked grin replaced by narrow, white lips and a grim expression. His look shifted to controlled fury as he passed Cadius, who lifted an indignant brow and shot him an arrogant smirk to annoy him further. The man was set to hang, by the looks of it, but his conceit appeared unshakable even in the face of death.

Quinn appeared to shake off the encounter as he moved toward the king and queen, giving her a salute of respect as he clapped his free hand over his heart and dipped his head. Though she gave him a nod and a tiny smile, she appeared uncomfortable with the situation, her face drawn with regret.

His countenance changed completely when he turned to address Adrian, and there was no respect in his posture as they shared harsh whispers for a full minute. It lasted until the young king raised a fist for silence, and Quinn shook his head as he moved to the edge of the platform. His regretful gaze landed on Will as he slowly unraveled the scroll in his hands, which seemed to be a sign for the executioner, a large man with the hood of his black cloak drawn, to slip the noose over Will's head.

Sarah placed a hand over her mouth, frozen in terror.

The mob began to quiet in expectation of his sentence, the swelling tide quelled only by curiosity over the words that would be spoken over Will.

Quinn's voice was loud and clear as it rang out through the courtyard, though it was clear he was distressed at the words he was forced to read. "William Taylor, you are hereby charged with several accounts of traitorous activity, as follows: breaking and entering into restricted areas of Serimone Castle, falsifying documents against King Adrian the Great of Serimone—" Captain Quinn's eyes actually widened, as though the addition to Adrian's name was entirely humorous, despite the circumstances. "For these crimes, you were given a sentence and were in the midst of being relocated when you escaped. This offense alone is punishable by life in prison."

"The ship *sank*!" Will shouted in outraged disbelief, the first sound he had made since entering the courtyard, his gaze not on Captain Quinn but on the king.

In that pause, Sarah threw caution to the wind and cried out, "He's innocent!" along with a few others, and she thought she might have heard Seth shouting in agreement. She couldn't read Will's expression as his eyes searched her face, and she wished there was something more she could do as her panic mounted, their cries going unheard as Quinn read on, his tone regretful and his eyes sorrowful when he recognized Sarah standing there. There was a hitch in his voice, and he averted his gaze back to the false parchment, which Sarah had a sneaking suspicion had been written by either Cadius or his son.

"In addition to these offensive crimes is murder committed under the deceptive identity known as the Shadow. William Taylor, you are here today because you were discovered masquerading as this . . . *traitorous* vigilante"—Quinn stumbled over the word—"and carry the guilt of the Shadow's crimes, as well as your own."

It didn't appear that Quinn believed a word of it, and he actually shook his head at one point, to which the king gave him a glare and an order to continue. Quinn's chest rose and fell, and his last words had quieted considerably so the multitude collectively leaned closer in order to hear. Voice shaking with repressed anger, he said, "These acts are considered treason against the Crown, as well as an absolute betrayal to the sacred agreement of the Knight's Oath. Your guilt in these duplicitous crimes has been determined, and this justice will be swift, merciful, and right in the eyes of the Law and the Church. The penalty for these collective crimes is death, to be enacted immediately."

A rumble went up over the crowd once more, turning into cries of dissent against the ruling, claiming his innocence, while others shouted for a quick execution; they only wanted blood, and it didn't matter that it was Will's they were spilling. Though Sarah knew the accusations weren't true, she had no way of proving it, and Will wasn't trying to deny it. Instead, he stared straight ahead, his gaze steady, refusing to plead for his life when he must have known it would do no good. His silence was his final act of defiance.

She fought her way through the throng of curious and bloodthirsty onlookers until she stood just behind the barricade that had been set up to keep the crowd from charging the stands. She wiped the rain from her face as she stared up at Will, every sound fading to the back of her mind as she looked into his eyes. There was fear there, and she was sure it wasn't for his life but because he would leave her behind, unguarded and broken. She had never felt more worthless or helpless in her life.

God, help him. She realized she had spoken the words aloud, though no one noticed her plea.

The tears she had been trying desperately to hold back joined the raindrops coursing down her cheeks. She wanted to tell him that she would think of something to get him out of this mess and scream at anyone who would listen that he was innocent, but she couldn't speak past the pain in her throat, couldn't breathe in the press of bodies. Unable to say what she wanted, she kissed her fingertips and spread her palm over her heart, praying he understood. Will's chest shuddered as he held back his own emotion and mouthed the words *I love you.*

She nodded, biting down on her lip. She couldn't lose him like this, and she dragged her eyes over the crowd, looking for an opening to squeeze through. Not wanting to lose sight of him, her desperate gaze flickered to Will and then to the wall of bodies in front of her, and then back to the man on the stand. She tried forcing her way in between the people closest to her, but she was immediately shoved back, a few townsfolk pressing closer to her as more entered the courtyard to see what was happening.

Queen Meredith leaned in toward her son, expression speaking the urgency of whatever she had to say as she motioned toward Will. But the king merely stared straight ahead, his gaze both cruel and anxious, as though he couldn't rest easy until all threats were eliminated. Which, in this case, included Will.

King Adrian gave a small signal to the executioner, and the man in black moved past Quinn, who looked instantly panicked and lurched for Will a second too late as the lever was unceremoniously released and the bottom of the platform dropped out from under Will's feet.

Sarah screamed in horror. In a single second, she felt shock and agonizing dismay that it had happened so quickly, without warning, giving her no time to interfere. She hadn't expected it to be over so soon, she thought in the instant that he dropped . . . and landed in a heap on the ground below the stand.

Everyone was looking around in bewilderment, and Sarah realized why when she saw the arrow sticking out of the wood, the frayed bit of rope swaying from the gibbet in the breeze. It had sliced through the long chord just in time to save Will's neck, and her knees nearly gave out at the sight.

He was dazed as he tried to rise with his hands behind his back, only to fall to his knees. Heart in her throat, Sarah scrambled over the barricade as the crowd went wild in confusion and stumbled to Will's side, dropping down beside him. Hands shaking, she loosened the noose and slipped it over his head, tossing it away in disgust, wondering briefly at the fact that his life had just been spared. Then she cradled his face, trying not to ruin this moment by crying again a she took in the scrapes on his cheeks and forehead, the yellowish bruise near his hairline. She didn't know if he had received them in the explosion at sea or wherever he had been held before being brought before the crowd. But in that moment, she told herself it didn't matter.

"I thought—I can't believe you're safe," she breathed.

"And you," he whispered, eyes scanning her own face, chest rising and falling quickly. His lips found hers, soft and disbelieving. She clutched him so tightly her muscles quivered, but she didn't care, focusing on the fact that he was back in her arms.

"Curse these shackles," he muttered when he pulled back, and she let out a breathless laugh. Suddenly, a cacophony of shouts sounded out behind them, and when Sarah glanced over her shoulder, they were all watching something overhead with shocked expressions as a commotion sounded above, and heavy boots hurried across the hastily erected platform. She looked up and saw someone jump over the trapdoor Will had just fallen through.

"What's going on?"

Will planted one foot on the ground and rose. "Let's find out."

Seth was there suddenly, and he helped him over the barricade, which was an awkward process with his hands behind his back, and then wrapped him up in a brotherly hug when he was steady on his feet. Karen's smiled flickered on her face as she stared off at something overhead. Sarah and Will turned to look with the rest of the crowd on a scene no one understood.

The Shadow stood on the parapet walk behind the platform, his bow at his side, and Sarah knew he had been far enough to the right to make the shot that saved Will's life. His wet hood sagged over his head as he gripped the shoulders of a man whose hands were tied before him, and it took several beats for Sarah to recognize the face of her college professor through the rain. *What was happening*?

The guards, executioner, and Captain Quinn, along with everyone else in attendance, gaped between the Shadow standing there in his masked glory and Will, who had just been "hanged" for being that same vigilante.

A switch seemed to flip, and suddenly three guards broke into motion and hopped onto the staircase that the execution stands had been built against, racing up the steps despite the fact that the Shadow didn't appear to be going anywhere. Sarah observed that he was almost . . . waiting for them to come for him and Guy Demetrius. The bow was ripped from his grasp and the two men were grabbed and dragged down the steps, though her old professor was the only one who tried to fight, appearing weak as he attempted to throw a punch with his hands bound.

Once on the dais, both were kicked to their knees before the king and queen's chairs, and Demetrius winced as he landed. Sarah took note of the bruises and grime on his face, but her attention was diverted as the hood of the other man was pulled back. For a brief second, she feared that Robert had heard about Will's sentencing and had gotten it into his head to be a hero and try to save Will. But then her heart dropped to her feet as the hood fell back, revealing an all-too familiar face she had thought she would never see again.

"Damien," she breathed, shooting a worried glance at Will, who appeared just as shocked and wary to see him there dressed as the Shadow once more. A few bruises marred Damien's cheeks, and there was a nasty cut on his lip, though it appeared from the look of Demetrius that he had been on the losing end of that fight.

"That's *your* Damien?" Karen asked, leaning close to her ear. Sarah nodded mutely, though Will stiffened at the remark. Her friend gave her an alarmed look, knowing how much Damien had meant to her, even after his betrayal. And she was probably surprised at the fact that Sarah *wasn't* surprised to find him roaming around the city.

The queen stood slowly, appearing as though she was still reeling from the events. "Damien Lisandro," she said in surprise when she recognized the man who had charmed the entire court last winter, including herself. She looked down at Will and then back at him. "Surely this must be some sort of mistake." Sarah couldn't have agreed more.

"I fear it is not," Damien replied grimly. His gaze caught Cadius' eye, and he did a double take at finding him shackled and ready for the gallows. When he recovered, Damien shot a flash of a grin in the man's direction.

Shaking her head, Queen Meredith asked in disbelief, "*You* killed one of the castle servants last winter?"

Sarah sucked in a breath, and she was sure everyone heard it in the silence as they waited for Damien's response. He clearly had not expected that issue to be addressed so quickly, but he bowed his head even as his hands were tied in front of him with rope. Quietly, he admitted, "Yes." He didn't try to deny it or explain how it had happened, and at his look of grave acceptance, Sarah's confusion turned to panic as she realized he had just admitted to murder.

"It was an accident!" she shouted. Though part of her reminded herself that his admitting to Edith's death freed Will of it, she was terrified that he was outright revealing himself. Half the crowd turned at her outburst, but those on the dais didn't appear to know who had spoken. That is, except for Damien.

He shot her a look to quell her brewing anxiety. Something in his gaze silenced her, and though she wanted to throw her body onto the stage and free him herself, she bit her tongue. The paralyzing shock of seeing Will up there had faded, allowing her to use her head again, and she told herself to not be hasty.

"My Queen," he began hurriedly, "I have urgent information I *must* share with you this instant."

The father and his royal son shared an alarmed glance at the recent shift in control, and even Sarah pulled back in surprise. *What is he doing?*

King Adrian seemed to regain his senses and was suddenly on his feet beside the queen, looking rattled. "This—this man speaks falsities!" he accused.

Appearing almost amused, Damien quirked a brow. "I have yet to level any charges, my lord." But then he turned to the queen, and his face became grave. "But these accusations do involve the king, Your Majesty."

She looked shocked, seeming unsure what to believe. But her curiosity won out over the outrage of the boy-king, and in a composed tone she said, "Proceed."

Sarah couldn't be certain, but she thought Damien's shoulders might have dipped a little in relief. "This man I have brought before you this day is Guy Demetrius, and he has been employed by the king's *former* advisor"—Damien lifted his bound hands toward Cadius, who looked suddenly panicked and without a plan—"for many years now. Under Cadius' careful instruction, Guy devised the idea to . . ."

His voice drifted off, and Sarah wondered how much he could admit without them dismissing him as crazy. He couldn't exactly tell them that Demetrius had been trying to help Cadius change the past. She released the anxious breath she'd been holding when Damien finally said, "He provided him with the concept of putting his *own* child on the throne and eliminating all obstacles that might stand in the way, including your own son, My Queen." His tone had softened at the end, as though trying to be delicate with the matter.

Queen Meredith looked momentarily confused, presumably thinking that he was referring to Adrian. But then her pale lips parted in comprehension. "What?" she whispered, but it didn't matter; they could have heard a pin drop in the silent courtyard as everyone listened with piqued interest and bated breath.

Damien nodded, but his eyes darted nervously to Adrian's face, which was becoming increasingly red. Sensing he was running out of the king's "patience," he hurried to add, "Guy also attempted to murder Lady Sarah Matthews and William Taylor." It was a bit of an over-dramatization, since Demetrius had simply planned on just leaving the two of them trapped in Professor Ashmore's basement, but she would be the last to correct him. "I apprehended this man and brought him here for you today so that he might testify to the blackness of Cadius and King Adrian's character." He shot each of them a steely look in turn.

The queen flinched, as if shocked and hurt by his accusation, but she quickly recovered. "Do you not realize," she began slowly, her tone almost curious, despite the underlying threat her words carried, "that what you speak is heresy against the Crown?"

Sarah inched closer, seeing the way Damien's throat contracted in a swallow. "I do, My Queen, but is it not a worse crime to let murder go unpunished when it has been brought to light?"

There was a pause, and then the queen directed the smallest of nods at Demetrius. "What do you wish to say?"

He shook visibly, and he shot an apprehensive glance at Cadius, who was barely masking his rage. Sarah recalled the cruel look in her professor's eyes and the coldness of his laugh when she and Will encountered him, his bold confidence and terrifying calculation. The man before them now was a stark contrast to that self-assured mastermind, and she realized that his obvious distress was just further evidence that Cadius could manipulate and strike fear in anyone. The thought wasn't exactly comforting.

When Queen Meredith's expectant look turned annoyed as his silence dragged on, Demetrius hurriedly began, stumbling over his words as he seemingly tried to expel them before he lost his courage. "Cadius, he—I encountered him many years past. He was distressed and after speaking with him, I discovered that our acquaintance could be . . . mutually beneficial. What Lisandro says is true, and when Cadius and I—when we returned to this land, I—"

"Continue, please." The queen's voice was soft, but it was a command.

Demetrius bit his lip and stared at the boards beneath his knees, and it was unclear if he was refusing to speak or merely hesitant about admitting his part in Cadius' crimes. But Damien elbowed him in the ribs, his muttered words carrying to Sarah's ears. "Everyone here will catch their death if you don't get on with it. He is powerless now."

The reminder seemed to unlock Demetrius' stiff muscles. Lifting his head, he breathed in deeply. His expression was beseeching as he admitted, haltingly, to the queen, "With my knowledge of a certain form of alchemy, I was able to . . . devise a concoction that would render King Josiah . . . ill. But I had no notion of him wishing to *kill* the king," he was quick to add, a look of fright crossing his face.

Queen Meredith looked visibly shaken, and the muscles in her neck bunched, though she managed a stiff nod, urging him to continue. During it all, Cadius' look remained stony, though Sarah could see the cogs in his mind working furiously, trying to decide if it would be better to remain silent and indifferent, or if he should speak out against the accusations—which would make him appear less guilty?

Looking vaguely relieved, Demetrius detailed a few events, much as Damien had, being brief in his statement as he exposed his part in helping Cadius "inadvertently" murder the king, how he put the idea in his head to put his own child on the throne to spite his brother, though he swore that Cadius acted on that of his own accord; that Cadius and his son wished to conquer Ridlan and seize control of its weapons to become the largest ruling power in England.

Hearing it all said aloud, with so many listening ears and not spoken in hushed tones amongst themselves, Sarah's heart sped up, feeling that the end of this was closer than she'd ever imagined. She reached back for

Will's hand without even realizing it, and he gave hers an encouraging squeeze, his shackles rattling faintly as he shifted closer to her.

"And why, pray, should I believe any of this?" Queen Meredith asked calmly, though her voice wobbled near the end. She added in a dry tone, "Even if I am inclined to do just that." Sarah exhaled the breath that had caught in her chest, surprised the queen was even listening to this. But maybe she had already suspected for some time, seeing how her son had been slowly corrupted day after day.

Demetrius hung his head. "Because, Highness, I have nothing left to lose." To Sarah, his abrupt betrayal suddenly made sense: Cadius had lured him back to this time under false pretenses, but he had only been another pawn, cast aside like all of the other worthless pieces in this game.

His head jerked up and he glared a Cadius with sudden ferocity. "*Admit* that I was only helping you. Admit that you betrayed me and left me stranded in this place, threatened to have me killed if I came within a hundred yards of this castle."

But Cadius at last managed to recover himself, and he schooled his expression into one of indifference. "And who is this man to accuse us? I have never seen him before in my life." Guy's expression of appeal had slowly faded as he spoke. A look of acute fury masked his features now, and he swore foully under his breath when he realized he had just been betrayed again.

The queen lifted her brow imperiously at her brother-in-law. "You are a convicted traitor and had a hand in murdering this land's king, an unforgiveable crime that you were *unsuccessfully* executed for. I believe that, whoever Guy Demetrius might be, his word is far more trustworthy than that of a criminal."

"*He* is a criminal, as well!" Adrian pointed out in a childish voice, pointing at Damien, who only quirked a brow at his antics, looking far more confident in the outcome of this event than he had appeared earlier. "And an escaped one at that."

"And how did this man discover you?" the queen calmly asked Demetrius, completely ignoring her son. But Sarah could tell she was doing her best to focus on the facts so she didn't fall apart . . . or ask about her *true* child.

Damien answered, "Cadius has a hideaway in the woods, Majesty—" The queen lifted a hand, and it was all it took to silence even the birds that had sought shelter from the rain in the castle spires.

"I wish to hear it from him."

Reluctantly, Demetrius admitted, "Lisandro and I have encountered one another briefly before, and when he discovered that Cadius had abandoned me, he went in search of me. I was found at this cabin that he mentioned, as I tried to create a plan to find my way home. When I refused to come with him, I was . . . overpowered"—he practically muttered the word, and the queen inclined her ear to hear him better—"and he promised that my sentence would be reduced, eventually convincing me that it would be best if I turned Cadius *and* the king over to you, Your Highness." He shot a look at King Adrian, though he didn't appear as fearful of him as he was of his father. "I've never met the king until this moment, Cadius made sure of that, but I did discover that this newly crowned royal was aware of everything, even devising some parts of the plan himself."

Queen Meredith was careful not to look at the boy on her right, and she squared her jaw, ever the picture of queenly grace, even if Sarah did notice the way her lips quivered as she licked them. Diplomatically, she said, "Lisandro cannot promise such things, but perhaps I shall consider leniency. But surely you have some residual sense of loyalty to Cadius," the queen reasoned, sounding as though she were goading him into admitting something more. "Or at the very least a sense of fear of how he might react to your betrayal. So I ask you, why have you turned on him?"

Demetrius nodded, seeming to straighten a little from his submissive position. "I admit that I joined him because I wanted revenge against another party, and helping Cadius would, I was certain at the time, allow me to find it. And I did, in a way, but at a great cost as Cadius betrayed me and left me here, a fact that I revealed to you before." His gaze hardened as he leveled a look at Cadius and ground out, "He took my future from me."

"As you helped take my husband's," the queen said softly, sorrow in her brown eyes. She seemed even smaller in that moment, and her voice was nearly a whisper when she added, "And my son's, and my own."

For the first time, Guy Demetrius looked guilt-stricken—maybe because he had finally been confronted with the consequences of his selfish actions—though fear had also entered his gaze.

"My Queen," Captain Quinn said boldly in the silence that followed. She inclined her head toward him, appearing surprised that he had spoken. He placed a fist over his heart and quickly dipped his head in respect. "Forgive my impertinence, and I know your thoughts and judgments are elsewhere, but I must ask you about the man accused here today." He pointed at Will, who stiffened beside Sarah. "In light of these events and as we see before us the vigilante to whom these crimes rightfully belong, I must beseech you to reconsider the sentence of William Taylor, asking that he be found guiltless in the eyes of the law."

Although the queen appeared dazed as she stared at her son, she managed a nod. "Release him," she said, her faint voice somehow sounding out over the crowd as she gave the command. A ripple of confusion rolled through the gathering, though the cheers drowned out everything else—for Will's freedom or for the capture of the "true" Shadow, Sarah couldn't say.

Quinn hurried down the stairs and into the crowd, which parted to make way, watching with eager eyes. He grinned as he unshackled Will, who rubbed his naked wrists. "You're free, boy."

"Thank you, Captain," Will said softly, his voice barely audible above the spontaneous roar and congratulatory shouts that broke out. Quinn smiled at Sarah as Karen squeezed her elbow in excitement, and Sarah could have hugged him in that moment as she nodded her gratitude.

As Quinn turned to go, Will grabbed his arm. "Wait, the alchemist—I found him wounded in his alchemy chamber, along with the guard, Lawrence Ochencia. Suspend all judgments, and I will explain what I can later, but Charles requires *immediate* attention. The guards would not listen to me and offered no aid, so I pray he has already been found." The captain of the guard looked surprised, but he nodded quickly and broke through the crowd to provide whatever assistance he could.

Sarah was shocked to hear this, but she didn't have time to dwell on the fate of the professor as her eyes were drawn back to the platform. Her face fell as a guard grabbed Damien under the armpit and began dragging him away, though Demetrius was left kneeling on the dais to be further questioned.

Sarah jerked forward out of instinct. Will gasped her name in surprise, gripping her hand to hold her in place. When she looked at him, he shook his head, then his eyes immediately returned to the stage and she could see his mind working for a way out of this. For Damien, a man he claimed to despise.

"I have a letter," Damien shouted, suddenly desperate as he yanked his arm free to reach into his pocket. He dropped to his knees in his haste, stretching his arm to hold out a note to the queen. One guard gripped his shoulder while another reached for the letter, though Queen Meredith waved him off, taking the small missive from his hands with a curious look.

Eyes widening, Sarah realized that it was *the* letter; it must have slipped out of her sleeve and Damien had to come and deliver it himself. But the longer she considered it, the less likely it became as she recalled the spotless floor in Jade's cabin, and she knew she hadn't lost it there, nor did she think she had woken with it on her person. She bit her lip, wondering if she had ever lost it in the first place.

A sleep-clouded memory surfaced, and she vaguely remembered Damien touching her last night, the faint crackle of shifting paper almost causing her to wake even before his conversation with Jade. She looked up at him in sorrow as she realized that he must have taken the letter from her sometime in the night. *This* had been his plan, to keep her out of harm's way by accusing Cadius and Adrian himself. He must have known it would cost him dearly, yet he still came to finish this. *For her.*

Damien began with, "It is a request written in Cadius' own hand and sealed with his mark that your child, Your Majesty, be disposed of to protect this"—he pointed at the young king, who recoiled at the look of rage in Damien's eyes and the increase in his tone—"*bastard*, a product of the departed Queen Alexis of Serimone and *not* King Josiah, but rather his deceitful brother, Cadius." A collective gasp and confused murmurs rumbled through the throng.

The king shot to his feet, the furious flush that brightened his pale features completely hiding the boyish freckles along one cheek. "You are out of line!" he fairly screeched. Damien grinned subtly, his gaze shifting between Cadius and Adrian in a self-satisfied manner, as though savoring this moment of rebellion.

Damien elaborated, "When you gave birth to your child, Majesty, Cadius panicked, knowing that his son would have no right to the throne if ever it were discovered that he was sired out of wedlock with a *peasant*." He paused meaningfully as he let Adrian's heritage sink in with those gathered, resonating until they began murmuring amongst themselves. His voice softened as he looked at the queen. "Years of planning gone if he did not amend this potential threat. And so, upon the birth of your and King Josiah's son, he sent a letter to the deceased physician, Malcolm Devlin, to dispose of the child."

Damien was a master storyteller, and he allowed another potent pause for Cadius' torture alone. Finally, he said lowly and directly to the older man, "But Devlin did not obey the order."

"It's . . . it isn't true." Sarah wasn't sure if Cadius was denying the accusations or the fact that the physician had gone against his instructions. He had been relatively calm for someone who was awaiting his own execution, but at Damien's words, his gaze widened in alarm, and he looked panicked for the first time Sarah could remember in . . . Actually, she couldn't ever recall him wearing the look of total uncertainty that weighed his features down. The king appeared completely unsure what to say or do, and he looked to his father for guidance, though that man was staring at the Spaniard, aghast.

Damien's expression was goading, eyes bright, knowing he was dragging Cadius close to the edge and looking as though he expected the older man to take the final step all on his own. All Damien needed to do was give him a little nudge. "You only seduced Alexis so that you might have a direct line to the throne, and if your child should die, then perhaps you might become King Regent one day."

"*I loved her!*" Cadius cried in outrage, chest heaving as he advanced a step. The guard closest to him grabbed his arm and yanked him back, but Cadius' eyes stayed on Damien, trying to sear him to the spot. "How dare you question my loyalty to her or my son?"

There was no disguising Damien's surprise that his plan had worked, but then he grinned slowly like he'd just caught a mouse in his trap.

The queen whipped her head toward the prisoner. "Excuse me?"

"*What?*" Cadius spat, appearing genuinely confused in the midst of his rage, and then his face cleared and panic set in as he realized he had just confirmed everything he'd been accused of. He looked caught off-guard and stumbled over his words. "I did not mean—"

"Lady Sarah was the one to discover this, Highness," Damien hurried to interrupt Cadius' explanation with a quick, concerned glance at her. "After being drawn into your confidence, she was the first to discover Adrian's true heritage and that your child is alive. All I request is your protection over her, and she will tell you all you wish to know about your lost son." He didn't beg for his own life, but used these precious moments to bargain for hers.

Sarah felt sick. She shivered, soaked to the bone.

Queen Meredith stepped to the edge of their little shelter, her gaze wandered over the strangely silent gathering, though there was no masking the eager hope in her expression. "And where is this other child?" Her eyes met Sarah's, and though her voice remained steady, Meredith's watery gaze stood out through the rain. "Where is my son?"

No questions, no denial or insistence that he was dead and that they had no way of proving he was alive. Sarah wondered if the queen had sensed her child was out there all along, waiting for her to find him. Her eyes drifted back to the letter, expression a tangle of confusion, sorrow, and hope.

Sarah felt a spark of excitement at being able to reunite the mother and son, but it quickly died in her stomach as a knot of dread took over.

At a silent command from the king, no more than a downward flick of his fingers, one of the guards moved toward Damien. But the rest of the guards hesitated, uncertain whom to obey.

"Hang him!" the king screamed, looking mad as he stood in the pouring rain, trying to cling to the last of his power as he commanded Damien's silence once and for all.

One guard hesitantly moved from Cadius' side when everyone appeared frozen in shock, and another—one who Sarah had seen with Adrian before—joined him as they hefted Damien to his feet. Knowing where they were taking him, he kicked and pulled and thrashed, trying to yank free of their grasp. It was a struggle for them to hold him steady, though all too quickly he was standing below the slipknot the executioner had hastily tied at the king's order.

Damien jerked his head left and right, trying desperately to avoid the noose as they slipped it over his head. He tried to elbow one of the guards in the stomach, but couldn't get enough leverage to cause any damage, and he winced as the rough rope cut into his neck as another guard yanked on the end.

Sarah was just as frantic and shouted that he was innocent, Edith's death had been an accident, but the mob had found their voice, and countless townsfolk shouted for his blood. They called out that he was a traitor, had pretended to be their savior and then had gone around murdering innocents, while others cried out for a fair trial. The sounds echoed through Sarah's head, the noise and the thirst for blood and false justice made her sick. It was all she could do not to retch on the stones beneath her feet or slap the man nearest her, who had proclaimed Will's guilt and was now calling out to Damien as though he were a traitor. The tides had shifted, as had the delegation of guilt, but the thirst for death that day was the one thing that remained the same.

"This isn't right, Your Majesty." Will's voice stood out from the others as he called up to Queen Meredith. Sarah looked at him, momentarily taken aback that he would defend Damien, but she reminded herself that he wouldn't wish to see the man executed after he saved his life.

The queen looked up from the letter with a dazed expression, mouth working as she looked out over the crowd and appeared to notice the position that Damien was in for the first time. Sarah could see a hundred thoughts being processed in the three seconds she stood there, frozen: raising her sister's son and swallowing his recent betrayal, which had been right under her nose, the recent revelation that her true son was alive, that they were hanging a semi-innocent man who had just provided her with evidence of her son and Cadius' guilt.

She moved out into the rain, her face a tangle of fury, pain, and confusion. "Release him," she commanded, and after a beat, the guards shifted as though to remove the noose from Damien's neck.

"I am *your king*!" Adrian's cry echoed through the courtyard, and a few of the onlookers drew back in silence as the guards froze, looking between the two royals, trying to decide who to trust and obey.

"According to these accusations—" Queen Meredith's voice cracked, but she managed to say in a strong voice that begged no argument, "You are *not* the rightful heir to the throne. Until we can sort this ordeal out, you have no power here."

Adrian spun on her and growled like some feral animal, "You are not my mother. She died because *your husband* cared for her not, and she was too frail when she gave birth to me. That is why I made sure his death was slow and painful, because he did not deserve to live a life that he erased her from. I always knew—"

"Silence yourself, boy," Cadius hissed, but in the growing silence of the crowd, the queen heard every word.

She turned on him, her face at once disbelieving and filled with comprehension. Water ran down her face in a steady stream, and strands of red-brown hair stuck to her cheeks and forehead. Her hands shook and voice wavered as she realized that the boy she had raised had killed her husband.

"So it is true, then?" Her gaze landed on Adrian once more, expression overtaken by pain. In the deafening quiet surrounding them, she said softy but clearly, "What has he done to you?"

But her question was not answered just then as the king let out a war cry that startled everyone, and he hurtled toward the gallows. Seeing that the control of power had shifted, one of the guards pulled himself from his shock and tried to stop Adrian, though the king flailed like a fish and slipped free. Another guard left Damien and joined the other to restrain the rabid man, but it was as though the adrenaline coursing through Adrian's veins gave him superhuman strength as he fought back the men with fists and elbows and legs, thrashing like a caged animal.

"Stop him," the queen demanded, though they were doing their best to subdue him. Cadius tried bolting down the stairs, and several guards were detained as they attempted to conquer him.

Seeing that the wrathful king was nearing, Damien tried wriggling free of the ropes that had been hastily tied around his wrists to no avail, and his movements only tightened the noose about his neck. Sarah realized with mounting panic that he was trapped, a fact that he seemed to acknowledge himself as he gave up his escape and met her gaze. Will tried to shove his way to the platform, shouting for people to get out of his way as he pushed them aside.

Catching the movement, Damien's eyes snapped to Will's. "Leave. Get her out of here!" he shouted to be heard over the panicked cries and the senseless calls for his blood, the sound of the king screeching and thrashing to free himself.

Will shook his head, but the other man shot him a pleading look, and he suddenly stopped his fight to get closer. Sarah saw how his profile tightened in confusion and then reluctance, and she struggled to move forward as he slowed. But everyone pressed her back as they vied for a better view of the entertainment above them. Panicked, she elbowed someone in the ribs, not caring who she hurt as she tried to get to him, moving deep into the throng as her friends became swallowed up by the wall of bodies behind her.

Not like this, not like this, she chanted over and over as she shook her head at Damien. He had freed Will for her and provided the evidence needed to stop Cadius, put the wheels in motion to convince the queen of Adrian's guilt in the plan. He couldn't die *like this*. "Stop him!" she screamed, as though her voice alone could subdue the king.

"Sarah, don't!" Will somehow managed to get through the mass and spun her around, shaking her to get her attention. She stared up at him in shock and betrayal. "He is doing this for you. Don't let his sacrifice be in vain."

But Sarah just shook her head, wanting to deny the fact that the king was nearing the lever that would drop Damien several feet, and the additional guards were still trying to make their way through the thick crowd. They'd never make it in time.

She yelled for Damien to be released, shouting that he was innocent. "Someone help him!"

"Adrian," the queen cried, aghast. "Stop this at once!" But he was beyond reason, his look determined and feral as he dragged two guards with him.

"Leave, now," Damien commanded her with a pleading glance at Will. A look passed between them, and Will pursed his lips, jaw twitching in displeasure as he gave a single, regretful nod.

Suddenly he was fairly dragging Sarah out of the gathering, carelessly shoving bodies aside to make a path for them. She was too shocked to fight him off, head bobbing left and right to see around the heads blocking her view, heart and mind racing as she tried to decide how to help Damien, how long it would take her to rush the platform and free him. Her body felt separate from this moment, as though she couldn't think properly and was watching everything from a distance.

A gap parted in the crowd suddenly as she and Will fled through the gates. In a flash, she saw how Seth, unable to flee the mass of onlookers, wrapped his arms around Karen to shield her from the sight of the gallows, how the queen shouted at someone to stop the king, saw the look of acceptance in Damien's gaze.

"It's all right," he said calmly, and she read his lips just as the king lunged for the lever with a crazed screech. Sarah stopped breathing when Damien looked at her in that piercing way of his, placing his fisted hands meaningfully over his heart. And then he closed his eyes an instant before the floor fell out beneath him and the rope pulled taught.

And then she found her breath and screamed.

Chapter Thirty

*"It is a far, far better thing that I do than I have ever done;
it is a far, far better rest that I go to than I have ever known."*

Charles Dickens, *A Tale of Two Cities*

Will didn't stop until they were around the corner, past his anxious horse, and then he leaned on the outer wall and pulled her against him. His arms were tight around her, like a protective shell, and she squeezed her eyes closed, planting her fists against her ears. But she couldn't drown out the muffled roar of the crowd, nor did it block the image of Damien falling, falling, *falling*. And this time, there was no one to set him free.

She trembled in Will's arms as she stared off into the distance, seeing Damien through the rain and recalling the way he had tried to tell her it was okay to let him go, how he had thumped his hands to his heart. "*Oh*," she moaned, trying to block out the image as she buried her face in Will's chest. But there was no denying the look in Damien's gold-flecked eyes, ones that would never gaze back at her ever again—acceptance of his fate and all the love he felt in his heart.

"I am so sorry," Will murmured against her hair, and she heard his voice crack.

Somehow, Sarah managed to speak through the unshed tears that clogged her throat, feeling too shocked to let them fall. "I couldn't help him." Her small voice was muffled by his shirt, and she turned her head to place her cheek against his dirty tunic, her arms clinging to his back. "I said bad things about him," she ground out past her chattering teeth, her voice akin to a groan. "I rejected him and was angry at what he'd done. But I-I never thought he . . . that he would . . . He wasn't supposed to *die*."

Will's hand stroked comforting circles along her back. "I know you never wanted that," he replied softly.

She pulled back, blinking up at him against the rain, gratitude and grief vying for control. For a moment, she couldn't say what she wanted to, and he just touched her cheek in the silence, neither caring that they were standing in the center of the downpour. "Damien gave you back to me," she whispered in amazement, fully recognizing the sacrifice he had made, must have *known* he was making. Will leaned his forehead against hers, releasing a wavering breath that spoke of every moment they had been apart and the way they had been reunited. "He traded his life for yours, and I'm—I'm grateful for what he did. "

Her eyes dropped to his shirt, and she shook her head in anguish and chastisement of herself as a new wave of grief took over. Will pulled back, though his hands remained around her waist. Quietly, Sarah admitted, "But I can't help but think that if I had realized he'd taken the letter, then I could have . . . He shouldn't have been there," she finished in an distressed whisper.

"I am alive because he *was*. He knew what he was doing, and I don't believe that he came here with his eyes closed." His soft, gentle words cut her to the core. But she still shook her head, unable to accept that this wasn't at least partly her fault.

"I should have known he'd try to protect me. I could have delivered the letter to the queen myself, and I—I—"

"Damien did it for you," he said again, and somehow hearing Damien's name spoken on Will's lips—not the derisive *Spaniard* or Lisandro—made his sacrifice so much more real: even *Will* admired him for it. "He was a man of his own mind and knew what he was walking into, and, Sarah, he *chose* to come," he reminded. "Do not cheapen what he did by pretending as though you could have swayed his decision. Damien knew the cost and was willing to pay it, regardless."

Will's words resonated in her mind and heart: *he* chose *to come*. Free will. It was a concept she had become well acquainted with, and as much as it pained her to admit, it had been Damien's choice to come there that day, to expose the king and Cadius and free Will.

At her prolonged silence, Will placed his hands on either side of her face, staring deep into her eyes as he enunciated each word as though to better make her understand. "He did it for *you*."

She dropped her head to his chest and listened to the sound of his heart pounding against her ear, beating with the life in his body, life given back because of what Damien surrendered. His hand came up to stroke the soaked hair from her face, but she hardly noticed the rain anymore, shuddering as she repressed a sob of sadness and gratitude. "I know he did."

They clung to each other in the downpour, waiting until their friends were able to join them, each consoled by the shared embrace of the one they loved and found, each feeling a different kind of sorrow for the life that had just been lost.

After several moments, Will observed wryly and in disbelief, "You rode my horse here."

Sarah looked up into his eyes, seeing that ring of lighter blue that she hadn't realized she had missed so desperately until then. "It was the only way I could get to you in time. I was terrified to ride alone, but then I kept hearing your voice telling me I was strong and brave."

He dropped his head and kissed her softly, their lips slick with rain. "Because you are, love."

She dragged in a breath of damp air, taking his words to heart. She needed that strength now. Quietly, she said, "It seemed like the queen believed the letter and what Damien said. What do you think will happen from here?"

Will exhaled. "I don't rightly know."

A shadow passed quickly among the trees, and Sarah squinted through the rain, eyes going wide as Jade burst from the forest and started running toward the castle. In a daze, Sarah slowly pulled away from Will, and he followed her eyes. His mouth opened in astonishment as he saw the old friend whose "death" he'd felt responsible for, but Sarah could only watch the woman with a heavy heart, knowing she had to be the one to tell her that her brother was dead.

When she was only ten feet away, Jade finally glanced up and saw them, skidding to a halt in surprise. She shot Will a quick, apprehensive look and then directed her gaze to Sarah, her expression urgent. "Where is he?" she panted, cheeks flushed despite the fact that the rest of her face was terribly pale. Her eyes were wide and frightened, panicked, but then she saw the regretful look in Sarah's own gaze.

"Isabella," she began, moving toward her, throat tightening in empathy.

The color was instantly sapped from Jade's cheeks, and her arms hung limply at her sides as she collapsed to the ground with a moaned "*No.*" In that moment, she appeared to lose all desire to hide or keep her emotions behind a glass wall as she placed her soaked hands over her eyes and wept.

Sarah felt she was the last person in the world that should comfort her, but Will was frozen in place, and so she took an uncertain step forward, and then another until she was crouched next to Jade. Tentatively, she wrapped an arm around the woman's shoulders, wondering if she would cast her aside or scream that it was all Sarah's fault that her brother had come there that day. But Jade surprised her by throwing herself into Sarah's arms and sobbing against her shoulder.

Sarah's throat burned as she wrapped her up tight, closing her eyes against their shared pain, though she couldn't compare her brief months having known Damien to the lifetime the siblings had spent together.

Though her body shuddered every now and then, Jade's sobs faded quickly, and she went quiet in her arms. Softly, Sarah asked, "How did you know to come here?"

Sniffing, Jade responded in a broken whisper, "He told me what he planned to do, that he had another letter that would expose Cadius once and for all. My brother said there was a man he had to find, one who would speak out and reaffirm the evidence he planned to present. He—" She broke off, swallowing hard as she met Sarah's guilt-stricken gaze. "He said he had not even attempted to save William before, and he had to try now.

Damien—he told me he wanted to prove to himself that there was still good in him." Sarah bit her lip against the agony burning behind her eyes and in her chest.

Oh, but there was, Damien. She hoped her whispered thoughts could reach him.

"I tried to stop him, tried to catch up to him," Jade went on, straightening her spine, though Sarah still kept one arm around her. "But you know how stubborn and quick he is." She attempted a grin, but it fell flat. "I became lost tracking him in the forest when he went to find that man, and I knew it had been long enough that he would be on his way to the castle by then. By the time I found my way . . . I suppose it was too late."

She dropped her gaze, and Sarah gave her shoulders a comforting squeeze. "We tried to get him released, but there was nothing we or you could have done." The words were difficult to get out, but once they were, she realized they were true, a fact that didn't bring her the reassurance she had hoped.

Will took a hesitant step toward them. "Marian?" he whispered, sounding as though he expected a different explanation.

Jade managed to roll her eyes through her tears, appearing annoyed to be interrupted, though Sarah knew her well enough now to see that part of her response was habit. "Yes, William, I am alive." She said it dryly like it was old news, sounding a bit like her snappy self, and Sarah almost wanted to smile. Almost. "Sarah mentioned that you felt ill about my death, but, well, I suppose you shouldn't, considering I never died," Jade said in her typically flippant tone. But then she grimaced, adding softly, "I am sorry I did not tell you before now."

"You knew?" Will asked Sarah. He looked as shocked at this fact as he had in discovering that Jade was alive.

Sarah nodded slowly. "Yes, and I'm sorry, but I didn't feel it was right to tell you without her consent."

Sniffing, Jade looked at her with a soft kindness in her gaze that Sarah had never seen before. "Thank you."

"But how do you *know* her?" Will clarified, looking between them with confusion evident through the water and haze. None of them truly seemed to take note that the clouds had cracked open and were still raining the heavens down upon them; there was too much to say to notice something as insignificant as the weather.

"Damien was my brother." Jade's whisper froze the expression on his face. She turned to Sarah, wearing a look somewhere between panic and regret. "I'd not told him I loved him for so long. What if he—?" She bit her lip and turned away, barely managing to whisper, "He died thinking I did not love him."

Damien's words came back to her, spoken in reassurance that Will hadn't suffered thinking she didn't care about him. Sarah bit back a sob at the guilt and pain at the reminder and seeing Jade in the exact position she had been so recently when she thought Will was dead. Only this time, Jade's ending would not have a happy twist concerning her brother.

Taking up her hand, Sarah told her, "He knew you loved him, Isabella—you wouldn't have risked coming here and exposing yourself if you didn't. And he . . . loved you, too," she managed past the tears that threatened to choke her.

The cries of the crowd were dying down, and people were slowly filing out through the gate. The excitement had been over for several minutes, and everyone was heading home for the night. Sarah was so exhausted that she was beyond thinking about what might have become of the king or Cadius, or even Demetrius. All that she cared about was that Damien wasn't there with them now, and those three were to blame.

"Is it my fault?" Jade whispered, sounding like she desperately needed and didn't want to know the answer to her question. "His death—is it my fault that he came here, because he did not believe he mattered to me?"

It was the oddest thing, but seeing her own emotions and unnecessary guilt play across Jade's features, Sarah felt that she was able to see more clearly. Suddenly, Will's words made sense and her self-blame seemed foolish. Though the words were difficult to say and it felt wrong to dismiss her guilt so quickly, she spoke honestly and from the heart when she said, "No, Isabella, your brother chose to speak the truth. The only ones to blame for his death are in there." Sarah pointed to the wall, to the courtyard where it had all happened. Her voice shook as she added, "And we'll make sure they pay."

Realizing she sounded just like the men who had been on the stand today—seeking revenge at whatever cost—she shook her head and sucked in a breath of heavy air, redirecting her thoughts to what Jade and she needed to hear. Reminded of Will's words, she said, "Damien made his own choice today, and we can't dishonor his sacrifice by throwing the fault of what happened on ourselves. He came here of his own free will to make sure bad people couldn't hurt anyone else ever again."

There was a long pause that hung heavily in the darkening gray light, and Sarah let it sink in. "My brother was a hero," Jade said quietly. The way she spoke, it sounded like a question.

The tears Sarah had been too shocked to cry now filled her eyes and spilled over as she stared off into the distance, letting the rain wash over her. A shudder passed over her frame hearing Damien referred to in the past tense, but though rainwater and emotion coursed down her cheeks, she managed to give Damien's sister a comforting smile. When she spoke, her words were honest.

"Yeah, Isabella. He really was."

ଓଃ

When the mob dispersed, Seth and Karen were finally able to join them. Upon seeing her friend, Karen outran her husband and dropped to the wet stones beside Sarah, taking up her hand. "We thought you were still in there, and when I couldn't get out of the crowd—" But then she noticed that there was a stranger in their midst as Jade stiffened at Sarah's side.

"I'm Karen." She gave Jade a faint smile, her voice soft after what they had just witnessed. Or, rather what Seth had shielded her from. The big man stopped beside Will, placing his hand on his friend's shoulder as they watched the women in silence, their faces drawn in concern.

Sarah had mentioned Jade to her friend before when the woman had been out to get Sarah, and she wondered how Karen would react to meeting her for the first time, especially since she had supposedly died months ago.

"My name—" Jade swallowed, looking small and uncertain with her dress clinging to her slender shoulders and her hair hanging in a limp, damp curtain around her pale face. But then her eyes cleared, and she almost smiled, as though just coming to a realization. "My name is Marian."

Karen's lips parted in recognition as she cast Sarah a concerned glance, knowing that the name meant something to her—and would someday mean something to Will, if their hunch was correct. Sarah's left eye twitched as she fought back a cringe, nodding to assure her friend that she already knew. Later, she would explain to her that Marian and Jade—and Isabella—were all one in the same.

"It's nice to meet you," Karen said slowly, sounding like she was trying to decide if that was actually true.

Then she turned back to Sarah, her green eyes filling with tears of sympathy, the kind that only a best friend who knows you to your core can shed when the other is in pain.

Sarah's own eyes filled as Karen threw her arms around her neck, unconcerned of the rain that fell around them in earnest. She didn't press her to go inside: Karen was just there for her in that moment, and that meant the world. "I'm so sorry," she whispered near her ear. Sarah could only nod mutely as she held on.

"How did you know my brother?" Jade asked in curiosity and confusion.

Karen jerked back. "Your *what?*" She looked to Sarah for clarification, and she could only sigh and shake her head.

"It's a long story."

"Well," Karen began. She shot Seth a glance through the sheets of water that fell around them, and they seemed to share some silent conversation in that single look that lasted no longer than three seconds. Then she said decidedly to Sarah, "You and Will are spending the night at his parents' house, and we'll stay with you. It will be just like old times." Her tones softened. "I think you need this."

Sarah blinked away the rainwater and tears that clouded her vision, knowing she *did* need the comfort and distraction they could provide.

"Why don't you come have supper with us?" Karen asked Jade kindly, and Sarah smiled through her tears as pride for her friend filled her heart. "Do you have somewhere to go?"

Jade's eyes widened considerably, and she seemed to have momentarily forgotten how to conceal her reactions as she stumbled to her feet. The other girls followed, both a little surprised at her adverse reaction.

"Oh, um, no. Thank you, but I cannot. I must be getting back."

Karen nodded and didn't press her, though Sarah knew her tenderhearted friend was probably dying to bring her back and feed her some of Ruth Jones's solid cooking, or make her smile at Leah and Josh's antics around the fire.

Wiping strands of red from her cheek, Karen gave the woman a small smile. "All right." To Sarah, she whispered, "Take your time," before leaving to join the men, seeming to sense that they needed a minute alone.

"I'm sorry, Isabella," Sarah said. Somehow she managed to grin past the tightening in her chest. "Or should I say, Marian?" Then her smile fell, and there were too many tangled emotions to decide exactly what made her forced mirth falter.

Jade stared at the puddle her hem was soaking in. "For so long my brother was the only one to call me Isabella, and it is . . . nice to hear it spoken."

Sarah nodded, understanding. But then concern filled her, and she marveled that her rancor toward this woman had changed so abruptly into compassion in such a short time. Once again, she considered the fact that breaking someone's defenses down appeared to run in the Lisandro blood. "What will you do now?"

Jade stared off into town, though she couldn't have seen anything beyond ten yards in the gray mist that was quickly fading into night. "Take up an honest living, I suppose. I still have my cabin, but I have never been completely on my own before." Her voice broke, and she swallowed. "Before Damien left, he said that he had been saving the majority of his earnings and had put them aside for me. He told me where he had buried them." Her pale lips curved a tiny in a smile of fond remembrance. "My brother, always taking care of me."

A moment of silence passed between them, but Sarah didn't feel she could leave just yet. "Isabella?" She met her eyes, and for a moment, Sarah felt staggered by their similarity to her brother's. But she sucked in a breath and said quietly, "I'm glad I met you, and I wish you the best."

Now Jade appeared taken aback, but then that small smile returned. Sarah felt, not for the first time, that she was glimpsing a whole new side to her. "As am I. And—" Jade hesitated, appearing almost embarrassed as she revealed, "What you said before, to my brother, about forgiveness? Well, I want you to know that I have been considering it. I am . . . *trying* to forgive myself and allow your God to show me how to do it." Once the words were out, she seemed to breathe easier. "I make no guarantee," she hurried to add at Sarah's blank stare. "But I will try."

Sarah blinked at her in surprise. She had been trying to tell Damien to forgive himself, but he hadn't listened. Yet somehow his sister, whom Sarah had despised at the time, had heard every word and taken it to heart. Sarah's smile quivered at the edges, knowing she had tried so hard to help one person while ignoring the other, thinking that Jade's heart was too hardened and stubborn to redeem. How wrong she had been.

"You don't know how glad I am to hear that," she whispered, the sound of her voice nearly drowned out by the heavy splattering of the rain. She felt incredibly grateful that her own stubborn pride hadn't kept Jade's ears from hearing what her heart needed to know.

But perhaps the most shocking thing of all was when Jade—Isabella, Marian—gave her a tight hug and murmured, "Take care," before pulling back and jogging back toward the woods.

Standing alone in the rain, Sarah let the water wash over her as she watched the woman go until she became nothing but a wobbly blur and then nothing at all. Sarah turned to join her friends, her eyes scanning over their water-slicked faces, the sight of them standing there silently, completely drenched as they waited patiently for her, thawed her frozen core.

Karen wrapped her arms around her middle, meeting her halfway. "Come on, let's get you home."

Sarah knew she was not referring to her own time, but rather to the Joneses' house. And somehow, after everything that had happened, the word was fitting for that place. "Yeah," she whispered, leaning her head against the top of Karen's. "Let's go home."

Chapter Thirty-One

"I do not know if I will ever be complete,
but I know whatever I am,
You will always be the rest of me."

Tyler Knott Gregson, "Typewriter series #616"

Karen and Seth led the way in their wagon, each holding onto one corner of a tarp slicked with pig fat to repel the rain. They had offered to drive the others, but Sarah just wanted to be alone with Will for the journey and revel in the fact that he was here with her now. Her arms were wrapped around his waist as they rode his horse through the forest, and he kept one of each of their hands linked over his heart, pressed together like he was never letting go. Before they left, he had collected another horse from the backside of the castle, and its reins were tied to the saddle horn as it trailed obediently behind them.

The canopy of trees overhead acted as a semi-effective umbrella against the deluge still pouring from the darkening sky, not that it really mattered, since they were already soaked to the bone before they reached the Joneses' house. Though it hadn't been all that long since the wedding, Sarah felt reassured that this, at least, had not changed—the barn off to the side of the sweet house, with its covered porch and welcoming light glowing faintly from within.

The girls hopped off near the house and dashed under the covering while Seth and Will went to feed the horses and get them settled for the night. They found the main area empty, though a hefty fire warmed the small room, and the comforting smells and the sound of Mrs. Jones loudly humming a jaunty Irish tune eased Sarah's taught nerves. Despite everything, she felt more at peace just being around this familiar place.

Ruth's humming stopped at the sound of the door being sucked closed by a gust of wind outside, and it was her husband who came to see who had just entered. His rust-colored eyebrows rose on his forehead when he saw the two bedraggled, drowned rats just inside their door.

"Ladies!" he exclaimed in surprise. But then his face softened as he absorbed Sarah's presence. "Karen and Seth said that you had gone missing. I'm so glad to see you are all right."

She wasn't sure if that was an entirely accurate depiction of her current state, but she nodded, knowing that she felt safer here than she had in what felt like a long time.

Ruth popped her head out of the kitchen, released a screech upon spotting Sarah, and rushed to give her a hug, mindless of the sauce-coated spoon she was holding. But Sarah shrugged it off since her dress was ruined, anyway, and she would much rather have a hug from the petite woman who was trying to squeeze the life from her.

Mrs. Jones pulled back, the front of her dress wet from Sarah's clothing, and gripped her upper arms as brown sauce dripped onto the wood floor. Her face was a perfect mask of motherly concern. "*Where* have you been, dear?" But she rushed on before Sarah could think of a simple way to answer that. "When we heard you had been taken, we were so worried. I have done nothing but bake and cook, I was so beside myself—half the town is fed and plump because of my concern. Have you eaten? Well, I made plenty tonight. Don't you fret, we'll get some meat back on you soon enough."

Sarah didn't think she had lost too many pounds at Jade's cabin, but she bit back her smile as the woman gasped. "What am I thinking? Leah is upstairs, go and find her; Karen gave her so many of her old dresses when she moved out, bless her heart, and you both must change before you catch your death. Joshua is tending the animals and—Where *are* those men of yours?"

Then she took in the trail of gravy she had created along the floor and threw her hands in the air, sending more droplets of brown everywhere. "Would you look at what I've done?" She shooed them away, saying that she needed to clean up, though Samuel was already rubbing a rag over the floor with his boot, grinning.

The girls did as they were told, though it wasn't easy lifting their waterlogged skirts to get up the stairs, and Sarah felt guilty about the wet trail they left behind. Leah was just opening her door by the time they reached the landing, and her eyes went wide at the sight of them. When her shock passed, she threw her arms around Sarah's neck and squeezed her tight. The girl always reminded Sarah so much of Lilly that she felt a tightness in her throat as she returned her embrace.

But Leah pulled back abruptly, wrinkling her nose. "Why are you all wet?"

Karen laughed. "Mind if we borrow some of my old things while these dry out?" She held up her dripping skirt for emphasis.

Leah nodded and went back into the room, rummaging through the chest near the wall and murmuring half to herself, "But I get to hear *everything*; I don't want to be excluded again because I'm too young. Nothing interesting ever happens, and it isn't fair that I get left out."

"Is it safe to talk about everything?" Karen whispered as they stood in the doorway, but Sarah just shook her head, shooting Leah's back a meaningful look.

"I'll tell *you* everything later," Sarah replied in a hushed murmur.

It took them ten minutes to peel off their soaking layers, but the dry skirt Sarah slipped on felt wonderful, even if it was a little snug around the hips and didn't quite meet her ankles. Her hair was a tangle around her face, and Leah jumped at the opportunity to braid her hair, inspired to do so as Karen expertly wound her own wet mane into a sloppy braid behind her back. Sarah knelt on the floor and relaxed as the younger girl's fingers combed through her hair, gently tugging and separating strands as she knotted it and let the braid fall over her shoulder. Water fell off the end and made some splatters on the floor, but Sarah felt dry, and she felt safe.

Will was just coming out of Seth's old room down the hall, wearing a fresh gray tunic. As soon as he saw her, he was instantly at her side. He took up her hand, and his was freezing cold from holding the reins for so long. Though he didn't say anything, countless questions hung in his gaze, and there were so many things she wanted to ask him in return. But she didn't know which question to pose first, thinking that some things couldn't be said in front of everyone.

Instead, she simply gave his hand a quick squeeze and whispered, "We're both all right." And that seemed to be enough as he smiled tenderly down at her, and they shared a look that spoke of their fear in losing the other and their joy in finding them again. No words were needed in that moment, and somehow that was more meaningful than any conversation they could have had just then.

They walked down the stairs behind Karen and Leah, following the sounds of chatter and the clanking of wooden utensils. The others were already gathered around the table, and Will and Sarah sat in the two empty seats on the opposite side. Seth smiled at his wife and motioned to the chair beside him. Karen planted a quick kiss on his smiling lips and then, grinning, plopped down in the empty chair on Sarah's left. Seth feigned a look that said he was entirely putout, but Karen ignored him, which only made his grin widen as his sister took the place between her two brothers.

As Mr. Jones blessed the meal and gave thanks for the safe return of Sarah and Will, Karen held her hand under the table, and Will had yet to let his grip on Sarah go. Tears burned her throat as she stared at her empty plate, feeling the love of her friends like a reassuring embrace.

Although she was feeling more herself after the harrowing evening, Sarah could only manage a few bites of the meal, though Will ate his share and then some, which caused her to wonder if he'd eaten at all since he had been taken. But Mrs. Jones didn't appear to mind as she scooted the bread a little closer to him and ladled more vegetable stew into his bowl and sliced another piece of roast chicken when the bottom of his plate became visible.

Leah was like a jumping bean at the table, and she was the first to crack. "Someone has to tell me what happened before I explode!" Samuel grinned, and his wife chastised their daughter, though Leah just stared

Sarah and Will down, her brows lifted high on her forehead. "We knew Sarah had gone missing, and then Seth said Will disappeared, but no one has said *anything*."

There were plenty of harrowing and sorrowful events to detail, and Sarah released a startled laugh. "I don't even know where to begin." She looked to Will, waiting for him to jump in with his own story, one that she didn't know yet. But he shook his head.

"You first, and I can fill in the gaps from where I stood."

"But where should I start?"

Karen was the one to answer as she gave her an encouraging nod. "Back to when it all began."

Sarah pursed her lips, realizing her friend was saying it was all right to discuss her involvement, as well, something that she had never even shared with Seth before. It was a big leap for Karen, though bringing everything to light also gave a sense of finality that this entire mess was at last closed up tight.

Sarah took a moment to gather her thoughts, and then she took a deep breath and began, knowing there were some details that would have to be omitted. She told them how she had "come" to Serimone, and she and Will had joined Karen's investigation of the king's murder. She opened her mouth to say more but was cut short by Seth's exclamation.

"You did what?!"

Karen grimaced, but hiked her chin in defense of her actions. "I was afraid it would put you all in danger if I revealed what I was doing, but I couldn't just let a murderer run free when I had a hunch that—"

"'A hunch'?" Seth mimicked in disbelief, looking around the table for support, though his mother just waved a hand.

"Karen, dear, you should not have endangered yourself in such a way"—she looked between Sarah and Will—"and neither should the two of you. But what's done is done. Now, be quiet, Seth, so we can hear the rest of the story." She pushed her empty plate aside and leaned forward on her elbows.

Mr. Jones stood, commanding everyone's attention. "Since we are all finished with supper, why don't we let this brave group warm themselves by the fire, eh?"

Sarah wasn't so sure she agreed that *she* had been brave. But then she thought about all they had fought to accomplish and everything they had overcome, and she couldn't help feeling that, though she'd felt frightened and anxious more times than she cared to admit, she *had* found bravery and strength during this journey. A small spark of pride filled her that together, she, Karen, and Will had accomplished so much, and what she felt in that instant was something she would never forget.

They all ended up in the main room crowded around the fire, sitting cross-legged on the floor as they listened to Sarah talk about finding the letters and discovering that Richard was the true heir, a revelation that caused a collective gasp to ring up from the group. She opted for the brief version of her kidnapping and being held in the shack, trying to paint Damien in the best light possible and ignore the way her throat tightened at the thought of him. But Will took up her hand, adding his perspective of events while she had been away, allowing her a moment to collect herself before they gave a *very* abridged version of what had occurred after he'd found her.

"But how did you discover where she was being held?" Leah asked breathlessly, eyes big, enraptured by the true, but vague, version of the incidents. Sarah considered the fact that it should have been strange to discuss these things and their investigation after it had remained such a well-kept secret among so few. But mostly it was a relief to be able to speak of it in the past tense, because that meant it was actually over and there were no more shadows lurking over their shoulders to threaten their loved ones.

"She had already escaped all on her own," Will began, pride in his voice. "I was wandering the forest in search of her and—" He looked at Sarah then, and a small, tender smile curved his mouth. "It was the strangest thing, but I just . . . found her."

Sarah placed her other hand over his. "Yeah, you did." Then she laughed in surprise as Leah sighed dramatically.

Since the majority of her story involved Damien and being trapped at Jade's cabin or "implored" to remain there, she let Will take over and explain how he had come to the king with information that Cadius was alive, but Will ended up being the one betrayed. His voice thickened with emotion as he quietly told the part where his uncle had been killed.

The room had gone completely silent except for the crackling of the fire, and Sarah unconsciously tightened her grip on his hand, pressing her knee against his. He shot her a quick, grateful look for her offer of silent comfort, and he hurried on to tell of how he had been drugged by the king and awoke on the boat. A spark of shock ran through her as he laid out the events of rallying the prisoners and fending off the pirates who had overtaken the ship, gritting her teeth as he described the explosion and being thrown into the sea. She told herself to relax her shoulders when she heard that he had been fished out, but her hands still quivered against his, knowing how close he had come to death not once but twice.

"If you escaped from the ship," Seth interjected, looking confused, "then how did you come to get yourself hanged today?"

Mrs. Jones gasped. "And you *did not*"—she punctuated the word with a slap to her son's shoulder, receiving a whine of protest—"tell us?"

Rubbing his injured shoulder, Seth answered, "We didn't exactly have time, Mother." But she just huffed and muttered under her breath.

To Sarah, Will supplied, "I knew I had to stop Cadius and Adrian before this went any further, even before I could find you." By the look in his eyes and the way his tone softened as he spoke, she knew that's all he had wanted to do. He kept all mention of the Shadow from his story as he said, "I was apprehended after I witnessed them burning Queen Alexis's letters, and then Adrian turned on his father, saying that his love for him was the only thing that could foil their plan." He shook his head at the twisted mind that Cadius had created.

"And the professor?" Karen asked softly. She had absorbed everything in silence but spoke up now when the one thing that really mattered to her was omitted. "You told the captain that he had been wounded. Do you—what happened to him?"

Will gave her a remorseful look. "I am sorry, but I don't know. I'm sure he is being taken care of as we speak."

Karen nodded, stiffening her spine, and Seth reached out to rub her back. Sarah wished there was something she could do, and she prayed that Charles would not be lost to Karen so soon after the man had come back into her life.

It was late by the time they concluded their shared tale, having received a fair amount of interruptions and exclamations from their listeners. Near the end, Josh punched a fist against his palm, calling Damien a "scheming rapscallion who got what he deserved," for which he received a hissed reprimand from his mother.

Sarah's gaze fell. Though she knew they couldn't understand why Damien had done all that he did, it still hurt to hear him referred to in that way.

Will's hand found hers, and he said in a strong, steady voice, "I cannot say I agree, Joshua."

"But the Shadow was wanted for murdering someone at the castle, correct?" he countered.

Will answered carefully, "He was the one to kill Edith, yes, although it was an accident from improper training. But—and I thought I would be the last to admit this—the man changed in the end; he kept Sarah safe and traded his sentence for mine. I owe the man my life." When he looked down at her, Sarah could only give his hand a squeeze of gratitude, unable to speak past her unshed tears.

Mrs. Jones gave a firm nod and said in a tone that left no room for argument, "And we shall be forever grateful for his sacrifice, William, because he gave you back to us."

Now Will was the one to look emotional as his gaze wandered the sober faces around him, all nodding their agreement. "I am glad to be here with you all," Will said in a thick voice. It was not a grand speech, but the look of open gratitude and love on his face caused everyone to smile, because Sarah knew that, in a way, he had found his home, too.

Just a little while later, when Sarah and Leah started yawning, everyone began to break up, the youngest Joneses heading for bed upstairs. Seth accepted a kiss from his mother, crushed Sarah in one of his famous bear hugs, and shared a brief "man-hug" with Will that caused Sarah to grin. Seth mumbled something to him, and the two men shared a long look, emotion pooling in Seth's gaze, but then he just nodded, as though that spoke a thousand words. Will clapped his friend on the shoulder, and then they parted.

"Boys," Karen whispered to Sarah in a stage whisper. Louder, she said, "Us three girls will share a room tonight. No boys," she said sternly, as though that had been an option. Seth gave her a pouty look, and she rolled her eyes, resisting a grin. "I believe you can do without my presence for one night, my darling, and I can *certainly* survive without your snoring." Seth didn't deny it but merely laughed that deep, jovial sound of his. The entire room smiled.

Karen gave Sarah a backbreaking hug, a trait that she must have learned from her husband, and whispered, "Take your time," before darting upstairs on light feet in front of her husband.

Mrs. Jones suddenly had a stack of blankets and a straw pillow in her arms, and Sarah realized she hadn't seen her leave or return. "These are for you, William," she said, placing them on the floor near the fire to warm them. Under her breath, she muttered, "Though heaven knows why he cannot stay in Seth's room." She shot her husband a look. Reaching high on tiptoe, the petite woman waited for Will to lean down so she could give him a motherly kiss on the cheek. It had been so long since he'd had anything close to a mother, and Sarah felt tears prick the backs of her eyes, knowing how much these simple moments and touches meant to him.

Mr. Jones gave Will a steady look, and Will actually appeared intimidated under the big man's gaze. "That bed does *not* get unrolled until she is safely tucked in her own bed. *Alone*," he added hurriedly, like it needed clarification.

"Oh, heaven help me, he's already sleeping on the floor on a separate level of the house from everyone else." Mrs. Jones huffed a breath and grabbed her husband's hand. Sarah pursed her lips together to keep from laughing at Mr. Jones's severe expression and the look of alarm in Will's eyes. It was kind of fun to watch him squirm.

As she pushed him right up the stairs, ignoring her husband's protests that they shouldn't be left alone, Mrs. Jones said, "Honestly, Samuel. We have left them unchaperoned before."

"But now their relationship has progressed," he interjected, as though this made all the difference.

Sarah could practically hear her rolling her eyes as the woman's fading voice said, "You are being absurd. They need to speak alone, and Karen will find us if she does not come upstairs. But *I trust them*."

Sarah didn't hear Mr. Jones's muttered response at the top of the stairs, though it sounded like unenthusiastic agreement. Their faith in her caused her heart to constrict, but in a nice way that reminded her she was loved by so many here, and she would miss them all.

Her thoughts were beginning to turn dark, and the reminder that she would return home soon turned her stomach, so she quickly pasted on a teasing grin. "What was that whole nearly silent exchange between you and Seth?"

"Oh." Will sat against the wall near the fire, and he held out his arm, waiting until she snuggled up against him. His voice was quiet and humble when he said, "He wanted me to know that he was proud of all I had accomplished as the Shadow, and he would not tell a soul."

She smiled, glad that the two friends had become reacquainted this past year, giving back to Will the friends and sense of family he hadn't had for so long. "I knew he was too smart to believe along with everyone else that Damien could have done all those good things." At the mention of Damien, she swallowed, closing her eyes as she leaned her cheek to his chest and tried desperately to put up a wall in her mind, stopping all thoughts of him when even the good memories led to the reminder of his death.

"Tomorrow," Will began, "I have to return the horse I borrowed. Would you like to come with me?"

Sarah nodded eagerly. A moment of quiet ensued, and her mind wandered, stomach turning as she was reminded that she had something important to share with him and had spent too long contemplating if she should or not. *Well, several bombshells to drop,* she amended, *but one at a time.*

"Will?"

"Mm hmm?"

She swallowed. "When Cadius held Damien and I at that shack—I told you it was Gabriel Dunlivey's hideaway when I explained everything that happened, right?"

He immediately bristled at the name. "Yes, I recall the conversation at your university."

There was no easy way to say it, and she closed her eyes, stomach in knots, wondering if she was doing the right thing in telling him. But he deserved to know, and she couldn't keep him from the answers he had sought for years. Taking a deep breath, she said, "When Cadius revealed his plan to us, he talked about Gabriel and . . . your parents." She exhaled and looked up at him, and she saw in his pinched gaze that he already knew. Reluctantly, she admitted, "I'm sorry, Will, but you were right all along."

He released a shaky breath, his eyes on the wall opposite them. After a long moment, he said in a low, strained voice, "It does not come as a shock, as I suspected Dunlivey all along, but . . ." His throat worked in a swallow. "I thought I had moved past it once he was killed, but I suddenly wish the man were still alive so I might . . ." He shook his head. "I don't know what I might do." He glanced down at her, expression questioning. "Does that make me a terrible person?"

"It makes you human," Sarah whispered. Softly, she said, "I know it doesn't bring them back, but your father was brave and he stood up for what was right. You got that from him."

A small smile graced his lips, and he gave her a single nod. Sadness hung in his eyes as his parents' deaths were brought back to the forefront of his mind, but there was a new clarity to his gaze, as though a burden that had been clouding it for so long had been lifted. "After so many years wondering, I can finally lay that demon to rest."

Sarah rested her head against his chest once more, sighing out her relief that it was a weight removed from both their spirits. They lapsed into silence for several minutes, and she held onto him, breathing in his scent, reassuring herself that he was there. It felt strange to be so at peace in this home, so relaxed and safe after all they had been through, but she did; it was as simple as being with these people and having Will's arms around her. But as much as she wanted to savor this moment of stillness and comfort, she couldn't remain silent when there was so much to say.

She pulled back to look into his face, trying not to cry and make it harder on him. "I was so sorry to hear about your uncle, Will."

The contented expression on his face dimmed some, and his chest rose and fell beneath her shoulder, but he only nodded.

"When you were telling the family that he'd died," she began cautiously, "I could tell you were leaving some things out. Do you want to tell me about what really happened to him?"

Will rested his head against the wall, turning to watch the fire. His eyes were dark and distant, and his voice was thick with pain. "I went to find the king, but he drugged me without my realizing, and then when Cadius was brought in, it became clear that they were working together. And Thomas—" He closed his eyes, and Sarah pursed her lips at his sorrow, feeling her own build for the kind man who had been like a father to Will and who had saved her life last August. "They had beaten him, believing he had information about Richard, and perhaps they were trying to see if he knew of our whereabouts. He died in my arms, his body broken, and there was nothing I could have done to ease his pain."

Tears filled Sarah's eyes due to her own sadness and the knowledge that being helpless to save others was Will's Achilles' heel. She wished there was something she could say to lessen his obvious pain, but his eyes met hers, and he seemed to need only her presence as he drew her tighter against his side. With a ragged breath, he admitted, "I blamed myself for involving him at all, feeling I was just as guilty as those who had shattered his body."

"Oh, Will," she whispered brokenly.

But he shook his head. "It took some convincing, but at last I was able to accept that Uncle Thomas did not hold me responsible. I . . . forgave myself." It looked like he wanted to say more on the subject, but something held him back.

"And it really *isn't* your fault," Sarah felt the need to emphasize, wondering if his silence meant he wasn't entirely convinced of his innocence in the matter. She sat up a little straighter against him, so they were more at eye level as he slouched against the wall. "You can't be blamed for bad men getting it into their heads to hurt Thomas the same way I'm not to blame for Edith's death because the arrow was meant for me. You told me that, remember?"

One corner of Will's mouth curved upward at her vehemence. "Yes, I do."

"Good," she said. Her body softened against his, the events of the day—and if she was being honest, the past week—weighing down on her. It was as though every emotion and thought she'd had in that time poured over her, some being purposefully ignored, each flashing by in an instant until she remembered the feeling of almost losing Will.

"When Damien told me that you'd been taken and the ship had gone down," she began, pursing her lips to resist their quivering.

He grimaced. "I'd hoped you had not heard."

Sarah's voice was small and shook as she whispered, "It wrecked me, Will. He said that your uncle had been killed, and I wished I could have been there for you. And then thinking that you had died tragically and alone, and I never got to say goodbye in the way I wanted . . . I couldn't imagine my life without you in it."

The breath he expelled brushed the top of her head, and he kissed her forehead. "You don't have to."

But I do, she was tempted to say back. The words were on the tip of her tongue, ready to reveal that all too soon she would leave him one final time and return to the place where she belonged. But as much as she wanted to get it over with and blurt out the truth of their remaining time, she closed her mouth, her eagerness to admit their lack of future outweighed by her desire for one of them to be able to enjoy these few precious moments they had left together without a dark cloud hanging overhead. She wanted him to enjoy these moments without the desperation to remember every detail and the taint reality left to it. She would be doing enough memorizing for the both of them.

But tomorrow, Sarah told herself. You have to tell him tomorrow.

Though she knew it was foolish, she hiked her chin and kissed him, selfishly needing these moments with him even as she knew that each second would only bring them closer. Her fingers slid into the tangled curls at the nape of his neck, her mouth lingering over the scar on his lip as one of his thumbs brushed over the white crescent on the back of her hand—constant reminders that they had come close to losing one another so many times.

Will shifted so he leaned into her, closing the space between them as his hand found the small of her back, drawing her to him. "Sarah," he whispered breathlessly against her mouth, and she knew it was just a reassurance that she was there.

Reminded that Mr. Jones and his disapproving brow were right upstairs, she pulled back reluctantly. Will's eyes opened slowly, and he grinned lazily down at her. "Oh, yes, you *certainly* will not have to do without that."

The pain in her chest slowly started to fade as she pushed it to the back of her mind, and despite herself, Sarah laughed.

Will's hand dragged up her neck, fingers tangling themselves in her braid, his face suddenly serious. His Adam's apple bobbed in a swallow, and he kept her face close to his. "When I saw you there—oh, I was terrified," he whispered, voice wrought with emotion. "I was so relieved to see you one last time, but then I thought about how watching *you* die would—" He broke off, grinding his teeth for a second before saying, "I knew what it would do to you to watch me die, and I was also afraid you would be taken if you revealed yourself. I saw that you were thinking of a way to save me, and it was horrible imagining that you might get yourself hurt to protect me."

"Now you know how it feels," she said back, smiling softly as she took up his hand and kissed his knuckles, pressing his fist over her own heart. "You're always saving me, Will, and I hope you know that I would do anything to protect you."

Sarah looked into his dark eyes, hoping he couldn't see the undercurrent of sadness in her own. Nodding slowly, Will said, "I suppose we are even, then." A strange look passed over his features, and he hesitated a long moment before tentatively saying, "Lisandro—Damien . . . Do you wish to tell me what happened while you were with him?"

She sighed, unconsciously leaning into Will a little more as her lids grew heavy. "There really isn't much to tell that I haven't already said. Except for Jade," she thought to add, feeling Will nod. "It was definitely a shock to see her alive and find out she was Damien's sister, Isabella. But she—I know it sounds strange, but she really changed while I was there. She . . . softened."

"I knew she was not completely hardened," Will said, and she could tell he was smiling. She tried not to focus on the knot in her stomach when she wondered at the possibility of the two of them together, reminding herself that it might not happen and right now was *her* time with Will.

Quietly, she said, "And Damien did as you told him: he kept me safe. He let himself be beaten by Cadius' henchmen in that old shack, and—oh, Will," she whispered, recalling how Damien's body had looked that first night at Jade's as he lied on the floor. "I saw him, and he was thin and bruised and had been branded as a traitor. He was so ashamed of what he had become, but that wasn't him. Not really."

"I realize that now," Will assured her softly.

She bit her lip, holding back tears. "He cried when he told me about the pirates and the ship because he knew how it hurt me. And when he let me go so I could get to you before the hanging"—she stumbled over the word—"it was like he was *really* saying goodbye, like he knew he wasn't coming back."

His finger idly wound around the tip of her braid. "Your friend knew what he was walking into, and while I think he hoped he might be pardoned, I don't believe he thought there was much of a chance of him escaping with his freedom . . . or his life, if it came to it."

"And it did," Sarah whispered, expelling a ragged breath. Will's arm tightened around her waist, and she felt safe enough to admit, "You know how, despite the bad things he did, I still cared for him." He stiffened a little, but she felt him nod. "Well, I saw such a change in him after he, um, kidnapped me." There was no way to sugarcoat it, so she didn't try. "I was so angry at him for hurting all of us, but through my own pride and hurt, I still saw this boy who just needed to see his purpose in the world and know that he was loved. . . . Sorry, I know this topic bothers you."

Will rested his chin on her head. "No, I do not feel threatened that you cared. Your heart is too big for you to not allow everyone inside." She thought he might have been smiling and was relieved, afraid he would be wounded that she could say she "loved" Damien when she hadn't yet told Will she felt that way for him.

"Well," she went on softly, "it wasn't easy, but I managed to forgive Damien, and Jade too, when I saw just how . . . *wounded* they both were. But I knew he had changed when I saw how strong he had become these past months, gaining the courage to stand up against Cadius. And when I discovered how much he cared about me and was still willing to help find you—" She sighed, at a loss to describe how much Damien's sacrifice meant to her, and how dearly he would be missed.

But Will surprised her, rubbing his thumb over her knuckles as he said, "You are right, he did change."

Sarah looked up at him. "How do you know?"

He smiled tenderly down at her and seemed to hold her hand a little tighter. "Because the selfish Spaniard I met last winter would never have had you within his grasp and willingly let you go; he could have whisked you away somewhere, allowed me to die, and eventually won you over.

Your presence here is evidence that he *did* experience a transformation of the heart."

"Did you really mean what you said about him to Josh?" she murmured, closing her eyes as she leaned into his side. "That he traded his life for yours?"

After a brief pause, as though ensuring the words were true, Will said, "Yes, I am sure of it. And you know," he added slowly, thoughtfully, "in a way I believe we may have saved all of Serimone with Damien's help—perhaps Ridlan, as well, if Cadius and Adrian had tried to conquer it." Sarah let what he said sink in. Damien had kept her safe, helped her and Will, and in the end, he had been the one to find Demetrius and give up the final evidence so Sarah didn't have to risk herself. Hopefully Cadius and Adrian would be behind bars because of his courageous choice.

She smiled past the tightness in her chest. "Just a team of ragtag time travelers saving a kingdom. Now *that* makes a pretty great story, doesn't it?"

"And we did it together." There was such pride and contentment in his voice that she closed her eyes.

"Yeah, together," she whispered after a pause, knowing that she wouldn't be able to say that about them for much longer. Biting her lip, she strove to take control of her emotions, and her old defense mechanism kicked in. With a tired grin on her face, she teased, "You know, if I wasn't so relieved to see you, it would be a little redundant that you keep almost dying and then coming back. Is this some ploy to make me like you more?"

Will chuckled softly, but the sound soon faded. "And do you?" he whispered so quietly she almost didn't catch the words.

She stiffened as his full meaning sank in, and if she wasn't so tired, she might have responded with a witty reply to divert his attention. Unable to keep silent but knowing it wouldn't be fair to say what was on her heart, she simply whispered, "I do." She looked up at him, and he grinned in a self-deprecating way. As she had suspected, those were not the words he had longed to hear.

"We should get you to bed."

Sarah was about to protest that she'd rather spend the night talking with him, but then he scooped her up in his arms and carted her up the stairs, and her words fled. "I—I can walk on my own," she managed, surprise widening her tired eyes.

"I know," was his response. That and the mischievous grin on his lips. Sarah laughed softly, and his smile widened.

He set her down on her feet, and Karen must have heard them coming because she opened the door, pressing a finger to her smiling lips. "Leah's asleep. *Goodnight*, Will."

Sarah rolled her eyes just before Karen slipped back inside the room. Will waited until she was out of sight before placing a gentle kiss on Sarah's mouth. "I will be just downstairs if you need me." His breath played with the hair around her face, and he pulled back at her nod.

She slipped inside the room and softly closed the door as Karen kicked off her rather rustic looking fur slippers. She waited to blow out the candle until Sarah slipped into the makeshift bed on the floor, her exhausted limbs turning to Jell-O. There was a rush of cool air as Karen crawled in beside her, and they pulled the blankets up to their chins.

"I made sure Leah got the bed," Karen whispered. As her eyes adjusted to the dark, Sarah caught her friend studying her face. "In case you needed to talk."

The tears Sarah had been holding back slipped down her temples and soaked her hair. She rolled onto her side to face her friend. In hushed tones, she told Karen everything, leaving no details out—from Damien taking her after she discovered Richard was the queen's son to the very hanging they had found themselves at that day.

Karen said nothing, seeming to sense that she just needed to get it all out, though she gasped when Sarah told her about going to the future with Will and finding the machine in pieces; Karen took up her friend's hand when her voice became choked as she talked about Damien's kindness and thinking that Will had been killed at sea. And she was shocked to discover that Cadius had kept all those modern trinkets she and the professor had sent back. "Just further evidence of Cadius' obsession with the future," Sarah said.

Karen let her cry, though Sarah tried to be quiet for Leah's sake as she revealed how much Damien had suffered, the way he protected her and sacrificed his life to keep her safe, arriving at the execution as the Shadow to draw suspicion away from Will, though she couldn't tell her that the allegations that Will had an alter-ego weren't entirely false. Seth might have figured it out, but it didn't mean everyone had to know, even if Sarah was *dying* to tell her.

Though Karen didn't say much in regard to Damien, Sarah could tell she was amazed at all he had done for them. And finally, Sarah gently and reluctantly relayed what Damien had told her about how her parents' death had not been an accident, how Demetrius and Cadius had plotted to change her future just so they could alter the past.

Tears glistened in Karen's eyes by the time she finished. "It makes me hate Cadius all the more, and the man who gave him the idea. The fact that Cadius tried to ruin my life just so he could selfishly take the crown . . ."

Sarah squeezed her friend's hand, her own throat thick with tears. But Karen was stronger than she was, and she nodded against her pillow, as though accepting things as they were. "But they've been gone for a long time, and although I can't help wondering what my life would have been like if my parents had survived that car crash, I know that everything would be so different. It's true that I never would have helped the professor create the machine if they were alive, and I wouldn't have come here and found a family and a man who loves me. I wouldn't have met you"—she grinned at Sarah—"and you never would have come to Serimone and helped to stop Cadius and the king's plan."

"Cadius sealed his own fate," Sarah whispered in sudden realization. "He did all of this to change the past and to get Alexis and put his own son on the throne, but *because* he messed with the future and history . . . His actions are what brought you here, and you shared your suspicions with me, we got Will onboard, and together we were able to unravel his plan. His selfishness was *literally* his undoing."

Karen shook her head in shock. "Cadius was never meant to succeed, and history seems to have a way of correcting itself."

Her words brought back the reminder that only Sarah's return to Oklahoma—to school, to normal—could right whatever ills her presence had done to this timeline.

"Sarah," her friend said softly when she saw the fresh tears that rolled over the bridge of her nose. "You think that Will and Jade—*Marian*," she corrected, shaking her head at the reminder, "are supposed to be together, and I get that some little legend about a guy in a hood makes that seem like it should end with the two of them riding off into the sunset. But it's impossible to ignore how in love the two of you are, and there's no way that he can ever feel that way about someone else, not after—"

"I haven't told him," Sarah whispered.

Karen's eyes widened. "What? Still?"

Her friend's shock hurt, reminding her that her love was written all over her face, but she couldn't admit it to Will. "I just keep thinking that it's selfish of me to say, 'I love you and I always will, but I'm leaving you forever and you're supposed to marry someone else or history as I know it might crumble.' It sounds dramatic, but that's basically how it is."

Karen winced. "Well, when you put it like that . . ."

Wiping her eyes, Sarah gave a shuddering sigh when the tears continued to fall. "It's killing me not to tell him, but if he knows how much I love him, then he might not try to love anyone else after I'm gone, and he'll live his future alone because my love gives him hope that we'll be together. Somehow. And I know he'll try to make me stay here."

"And you're scared you'll want to," Karen filled in softly.

Sarah nodded slowly. "Either way I'm breaking both our hearts." Her lips quivered as a dismaying thought struck. "And, Karen, with the machine broken, I can never come back and see any of you." It had been implied, but the full force of the pain didn't hit her until she said it aloud.

Karen's body stiffened, though she was quick to say, "We'll figure something out. We still have my watch—"

"But I used mine to get here," Sarah reminded her gently. "Robert's was too far gone to be useful, and Will told me that Adrian destroyed it, anyway, and Demetrius used his watch after he ruined the machine, so it's safe to assume it's useless, too. Which means I have to use yours to go back."

Karen's entire body seemed to sink into the blankets in defeat. "That's right. . . . Well, what about the professor? If he's—" She pursed her lips. "I know he lost his, but if he's all right, then maybe he can recreate a watch." But her voice drifted off in doubt, and though it was unnecessary, Sarah said what they were both thinking.

"But his plans for the watches are a thousand years away, he can't safely travel, and it is definitely a few centuries before electricity will be created."

"Maybe, though?"

Her words sounded hopeful, but Sarah could tell that even her positive friend was losing confidence that they could make it work. "It looks like you were wrong to worry: time seems to have a way of correcting itself, despite my presence here. It's just fixing itself by making sure I can't come back." Glumly, Sarah mumbled, "So short story of this week is that I'm having to dump a boyfriend I'm in love with—who, incidentally, doesn't know that— to make sure he marries someone else, a friend of mine was hanged to protect me and the aforementioned man, and the only chance I ever have of seeing you again has gone up in smoke." She winced, noticing how everything had been about her feelings.

She could hear Karen crying softly beside her. "This week was kind of the worst."

"Your wedding was a highlight, though," Sarah hurried to add, striving for a light point in the gloomy conversation that she had begun. She kicked herself for casting a dark shadow over what should have been a happy night, knowing they were safe and had stopped Cadius' plan from taking root. But some things were too important to ignore, and she knew Karen wouldn't want her to keep her fears to herself to spare her. Yet another reminder that Sarah was going to miss her.

"That was a pretty great day." Karen tried to grin, but her tears caused it to waver. They spilled over in earnest now, and she barely choked out, "I'm going to miss you."

Sarah bit her lip and nodded, her friend having read her thoughts. "You know, this place and these people, you—Serimone has become a little piece of home, and I'm going to miss you all so much."

Karen held their joined hands between them, and their tears spilled onto the pillow they shared. "But I want you to know that you changed all of our lives here, Sarah, and we'll never forget our friend."

Choking back a sob, Sarah whispered, "And you'll all live in my heart for another thousand years."

Chapter Thirty-Two

"Ah, when the King comes home!
That's music—all the birds of April sing
In those four words for me—the King comes home."

Alfred Noyes

Sarah cracked open her heavy lids, glaring at the muted light. It had been the best night's sleep she'd had in days—surprising considering she'd slept on the floor and had been a complete wreck just before crashing. But allowing her body to have a full night of rest meant that getting oriented in her exhausted state was not easy as she propped her groggy self up on her elbows, examining the room. The spot next to her was empty, as was the bed that Leah had slept in, and with a groan, she rolled off the bed—floor—and stumbled to her feet. Running her fingers through her hair proved her braided tresses were in tangles, and she gave up trying to re-braid it and simply unwound the strands to let her auburn waves do what they willed down her back.

The doors upstairs were either cracked or open to empty rooms, and she knew she was the last one up as she walked down the stairs, rubbing the corners of her eyes and wearing the dress she had slept in. Will's blankets were neatly folded by the sleeping fireplace, as though he had never touched them. After having a good cry with her friend last night, her heart, though still burdened, was a little lighter, and Sarah felt a smile as she remembered being in his arms, his kiss on her lips.

Karen exited the kitchen and looked surprised to see her, though she hurried over to her side. "I was just coming up again to see if you were awake." Her voice was low.

Sarah resisted a yawn. "Yeah, sorry, I was out of it."

Eyes softening, Karen nodded. She looked over her shoulder to the kitchen, and they both heard Ruth humming. Taking Sarah's arm, she moved her to the corner of the room nearly out of reach of the woman's soft tune. "I wanted to catch a second with you before they know you're up, and I didn't want them to overhear."

"What's wrong?" Sarah whispered, sensing the urgency in her friend's tone. "Where's Will?"

Karen shook her head. "He decided to let you sleep, and at dawn he went to see Captain Quinn about what happened yesterday. He'll return any minute, and I wanted to ask before he came back . . . Well, when are you going to tell Will and everyone that you're leaving?"

She posed the question as gently as possible, and it was a valid one, but the weight instantly returned to Sarah's shoulders, and there was no denying that a decision had to be made. And soon.

The lump of dread returned, settling in her middle. "I've been putting off telling Will for days now, and I'm just terrified of how he'll react—how *I'll* react," she mumbled. With Karen's sympathetic eyes trained on her and a comforting hand on her arm, Sarah felt safe to quietly admit, "It's not like keeping it a secret will change the situation, but I just feel like the second I tell everyone I'm going and can never come back, then it will really be true."

Sarah bit her lip, fighting back tears. "And after so many people have walked out of Will's life, how can I expect him to understand that I'm doing what's best for him? How do I tell him that abandoning him isn't a betrayal after I convinced him to let his guard down and let me in? He's going to be crushed. . . . And if I'm being honest, so will I."

But then she sighed in resignation, answering her own questions before Karen could respond with her usual wisdom. "Delaying the inevitable isn't going to help matters, I know." She released a pent-up breath. "We have to return a horse that he borrowed, and I'll tell him then." Her words were as much a promise to herself as they were an assurance to her friend.

Karen tucked a strand of perfectly straight, red hair behind her ear. "Do you want me to tell the family while you're gone? Would that make it a little easier?"

Her shoulders sinking in relief, Sarah nodded. Yes, she still had to tell Will and say goodbye to everyone, but not having to tell an entire household that she was leaving was definitely a portion of the burden lifted. "Thank you."

"Do you . . . need to leave soon?"

Sarah sucked in a breath, feeling acutely the sad hesitancy in her friend's green eyes. "Probably. When Will and I were, you know, in 2016, it sent us back so no time had passed from when I originally left with you. But that was a glitch, and I know how inconsistent the time realm can be, or whatever you want to call it; I've been gone for over a week, and who knows how many days or weeks it's been back home. I need to go back soon, maybe even tonight." She rubbed under her eye at her friend's surprised look. "I know, I know. I want to put it off as long as possible, too, but at the same time I'm afraid I'll eventually lose my courage to leave if I stay much longer. And with the stabilizer destroyed, I'm nervous that something could go wrong if too much time passes."

They both spun as the front door creaked open. Will stepped inside, wearing the same gray tunic from last night, and when he saw her, his mouth immediately tipped in that tender way, his eyes softening. His look turned Sarah's insides, pleasing and guilting her all at once, and she didn't know whether to run from the room or kiss him good morning.

"We've been summoned," he said, his voice low as though he was sharing some intimate secret.

Sarah blinked. "What?" She glanced at Karen for an explanation, but she looked just as baffled.

"I didn't wish to wake you," Will went on, "and set off early to speak with the captain of the guard about the previous day, asking all that I could. I have been pardoned, but I felt it safest to speak with Quinn before encountering anyone else," he added dryly. In case the queen's ruling on his release had somehow been overturned, he meant.

"And what did he say?" Sarah clutched her hands in front of her, not bothering to disguise her eagerness. "Why are they asking for us?"

"To testify," he said, then sighed, scrubbing a hand over the neglected stubble that had thickened over the last few days. "Apparently, even after the statement Guy Demetrius provided, the queen still wishes to hear from other witnesses. And it would appear that we are the only ones left willing to testify."

"What's this, now?" Mrs. Jones stood in the kitchen doorway, a rag knotted between her hands. "You are going to testify against that horrible man and King Adrian?"

Will nodded, and his eyes darkened a little as he said, "They are both terrible men, and I will do my part to ensure they are punished for what they have done."

"That I do not doubt." Mrs. Jones huffed, her Irish spunk coming in earnest as her motherly anger took over, like a mother bear whose cubs had been threatened. "They nearly took you two children from us, bless your hearts, and I know it's not very Christian of me, but I would like to see them both hanged for the trouble they caused." She worried her lower lip. "I'm only wondering if Sarah is strong enough to see them again."

Mrs. Jones looked so concerned, and when Sarah glanced at him, Will's lips turned up faintly. "You are strong enough," he said lowly, "but I can testify alone. Our appearance is really more of a formality than anything."

"I'll go," she said quickly. She hadn't been there the first time they had convicted Cadius, and it had been so anticlimactic to discover that he had been hanged—unsuccessful as it had been—instead of being a part of his trial. Maybe it was out of anger or retribution or simply a desire to see with her own eyes that he wouldn't hurt anyone ever again, but she wanted to be there when they revealed the evidence they had risked their lives to obtain, and support Demetrius and Damien's statements.

Will watched her face closely and then nodded, as though seeing the truth of her strength in her eyes. Turning to Karen, his look became cautious. "I believe you should come, as well."

Karen stiffened. "Why?"

"While I was there, I inquired of Quinn if he had found Charles Ashmore in time." Karen sucked in a breath, expecting the worst, but he touched her arm reassuringly. "Quinn discovered he had already been found and was being cared for, but your professor . . . he was very bad off and will need to recover for some time. Charles is resting at the castle now, and I asked if you could see him while we gave our testimonies."

Karen's eyes widened, and Sarah wondered at her reaction before realizing what might have held her back. Lowing her voice, she said, "You don't have to worry about being seen anymore. No one can hurt you now."

Slowly, Karen nodded, accepting the fact that Dunlivey and Cadius were no longer out to get her and couldn't harm her if they wanted to, since the latter was dead and the former might soon join him. But then her look became suddenly faraway. "Of course, you're right." Her voice was steady, but Sarah could tell she was trying to keep it together as her mind worked up all sorts of possibilities, wondering what condition the professor was actually in or if he would make it at all. Their relationship had never been full of expressed love or emotion and was a bit tenuous to navigate, but Sarah knew the quirky genius and his "daughter" loved each other, and this sort of bomb couldn't have been easy for Karen to hear. "Of course I'll see him. I just—I'll need a few minutes before we go."

Mrs. Jones placed a hand on her shoulder, seeming to sense the same thing that Sarah had. "Why don't you help me make a basket for the journey? William, you and Sarah should take the wagon into town."

"Come for us when you are ready to leave," he said to Karen, his voice gentle. And then Mrs. Jones guided Karen in her glassy-eyed state into the kitchen, one arm about her shoulders, murmuring words of encouragement and comfort.

Outside, Sarah filled her lungs, savoring what felt like her first free breath in ages, though a part of her was still inside with her friend, torn between comforting Karen and giving her the space she needed to collect her thoughts.

Will took up Sarah's hand, looking content as they strolled into the barn. "Where are the others?" she asked.

"Seth and his father are mending a roof leak at his and Karen's cabin, and I believe the youngest Joneses are taking a walk."

Sarah grinned. "Leah will love to hear the stories we come back with." Her smile dimmed a little when she remembered that soon Karen would deliver poor news to that girl and her whole family. But Sarah shoved the thought and the burning in her stomach aside, wanting to have just a few unburdened hours with Will before she told him she was leaving.

"She will," he agreed as Sarah plopped down on a bale of hay in the corner. Will guided his horse and then the other from the large stall, a gentle hand on their noses the only coaxing they needed. She smiled at the way the big man with the calloused hands softened with the creatures.

As he placed a bit in his horse's mouth, he said, "I went to see Robert on my way to the castle. He was relieved to find me alive"—Sarah knew the feeling—"and he told me a rather strange story involving an *assassin* and . . . Jade?" He said it in questioning disbelief and looked to her over the animal's back.

Sarah held up her hands, smiling at the simple joy of having a conversation with Will in the barn. "I kid you not. I figured someone would come after Robert eventually, since he was connected to both of us, and Isabella—Jade—was willing to go." It was a stretch of the truth, since Jade had practically stormed out of her little cabin. "I'm assuming it was one of Cadius' goons, but a man came into the livery, and Robert and Jade fought him off. I guess he skewered himself on something and bled out."

Will tightened the leather harness leading to the wagon, shaking his head. "That was what he told me, though with a few more embellishments."

Sarah's grin faded as her mind turned over a thought, and she said, "Hey, do you mind if we stop somewhere before we go to the castle?"

"Of course. Where?"

She smiled. "I'll tell you on the way."

☙❧

He grinned in return, not minding one bit that she was keeping a secret from him, unable to know that she was keeping far more than just that one. He made one final adjustment and came to sit beside her on the hay, pressing his shoulder against hers. But his body was too stiff, he knew, and he tried to relax his shoulders.

"I can *literally* hear you thinking," she teased.

"Sarah," he began hesitantly, "there is something I did not tell you last night. About the ship and what happened after."

Her look was instantly concerned.

"I felt—embarrassed, perhaps? I can't honestly say why, but it is so new to me."

She placed a hand on his arm, and he relaxed under her touch. "Will, what's wrong?"

"Nothing, truly. But I . . . On that shore, after the explosion . . ." He swallowed and exhaled slowly, feeling unaccountably nervous. But then she gazed up at him with an open, expectant expression, and he touched her cheek, his awkward anxiety fading away as he stared into her blue eyes. The corner of his mouth quivered in a faint, disbelieving smile, and suddenly the words were not so difficult to find. "The man I told you about, Merek?" She nodded. "He helped me to see that I was spared for a reason, and after so long running and fearing to admit that I was *afraid* to open myself up to love, I realized the truth at last."

Sarah sucked in an audible breath, and he knew that she was daring to hope for something he imagined she and his uncle had both prayed over for a long time. He smiled down at her. "Yes, love, I gave my life over to the Almighty."

Instant tears filled her eyes, but her face was magnificent and bright as she whispered, "Really?" At his nod, she gave a choked laugh. "Oh, Will, I just . . . I never thought it would happen. This was the best news you could have given me today." She waited half a beat in delayed shock and then spun onto her knees, throwing her arms around his shoulders and planting a kiss on his neck. Drawing back with her arms still twined behind his head, she smiled at him, and the way her teary gaze searched his face warmed his insides. "I'm so happy for you."

Her smile was infectious, and Will grinned, feeling like this was the most perfect moment in history. He twisted so he faced her, resting his hands on her waist. "Thank you for waiting patiently for this mule-headed blacksmith to finally see that it was all right to love and accept it in return. It took so many years, but I believe my love for you opened my heart to the idea of being forgiven and allowing someone to care for me."

She didn't say it, her expression turning suddenly hesitant, though he had not expected her to. But then she surprised him by pressing her soft lips against his, and he used his hands to pull her against him. Silence reigned in the moments that followed, but he tasted the words on her lips and in the breaths that passed between them, heard them in the way she brushed her fingertips through the hair at the base of his skull, sending shockwaves through him and an almost agonizing need to never let her go. And it was there in the way she curved into him, clinging to the back of his neck as though the thought of losing him had been unbearable for her.

But she pulled back too soon, as she always did, and he tried not to let his disappointment show as she broke the kiss. He would never force the words from her lips, which were a satisfying deep pink from their prolonged kiss, though he wished he could know what held her back.

Her smile wobbled and her eyes were glassy. "Sorry," she mumbled, cheeks flushed. "I was just *really* happy." The dazed expression on her face caused him to forget his concern that she hadn't declared her love for him as his stomach warmed once more. It was all he could do to keep his hands *only* on her hips and not draw her in again as she planted herself in his lap, staring up at him with wide eyes. She brushed the backs of her knuckles against the stubble under his chin, and he closed his eyes, savoring this moment.

"Uncle Thomas would be happy for you, too." Will looked down and caught her small, sad smile. She gave him an encouraging nod, though the way her gaze watered was unmistakable. "He loved you so much and wanted you to know what it's like going through life knowing you're loved in unbelievable ways. To know you don't have to live this life alone." She bit her lip, appearing momentarily pained as she looked away, and he imagined the underlying meaning in her tone was in regard to the loss of his uncle.

Will dragged in a breath, thoughts of Thomas still difficult to manage without feeling the ache of his death. "He spent years praying for freedom from my past and my own self-loathing, and I know he would have loved knowing that all those years weren't for naught. That he planted the seeds, and I . . ." He broke off, the notion of what might have been too painful to concentrate on.

Without a word, Sarah's arms wrapped around him, and he drew her close, releasing a shuddering breath as he planted his chin atop her head. Several long minutes passed as he found unmatched comfort in her embrace, and then Will felt a smile tugging the corner of his mouth.

"What?" she mumbled, somehow sensing it.

"I was just thinking . . ." Will shook his head. "It sounds mad, but I believe I hear my uncle laughing."

ꙮ

They rolled through the gates and into Serimone, an unlikely trio of friends and allies—a medieval blacksmith, a time traveler, and a twenty-first century college freshman. It sounded like the beginning to a poor joke, but to Sarah, these people on either side of her meant the world, and there would forever remain portions of her heart dedicated only to these friends who had stood by her side through the good, the bad, and the unimaginable strangeness they had encountered.

Will pulled the horses to a stop just outside the open castle gates and helped the girls down. No threats to her safety remained, but Karen had been silent and wary the entire ride, although her anxiety could have been caused by the uncertainty of Charles Ashmore's condition. A guard simply glanced at Will and, recognizing him, opened the main doors.

"We will be expecting two men soon," Will told him. "Please ensure they are allowed entrance." The guard nodded, and they stepped inside.

Karen's eyes were large as she took in the castle interior for the first time, the tapestries and stonework and windows high on the walls. Sarah grinned, wishing she could give her a quick tour, but Terrance was already hurrying down the hall toward them, smiling.

Sarah recalled his kindly presence at the knighting ceremony, and the thought caused her to gaze up at Will, at the hero who had fought for her heart and won it, unbeknownst to him. He was a knight and a blacksmith, he had been Serimone's vigilante and an adventurer like his father. But most of all, he had become a friend to Sarah, a partner, and she knew his presence in her life would be unmatched, no matter how many centuries she traveled through.

"Lady Sarah, Knight Taylor." Terrance dipped his head at each of them in turn, grinning broadly, but it dimmed some as he said, "They are waiting for you now." Then he turned to Karen, his lips fully tipping down, though his eyes were curious. "And who might this be?"

"Karen Ashmore," Will answered. "The alchemist, Charles Ashmore, is her father. She wishes to see him while we give our testimonies."

Surprised, Terrance's weathered forehead creased as his brows lifted. "I had no notion of his having any living relatives." Karen winced, obviously hurt that the professor hadn't talked about her much, but Terrance was already waving a hand in the air. "No matter." He snapped his fingers at one of the guards and told him to escort Ms. Ashmore to the room the alchemist had been moved to during his recovery.

The guard motioned up the stairs. "Right this way, miss." Karen squared her shoulders, though Sarah noticed the way her friend's hands trembled faintly, and she gave her an encouraging nod before Karen followed the guard up the staircase.

"Let us not leave Her Majesty waiting." Terrance bustled down the hall, and they had no choice but to follow.

It appeared the majority of the guard was stationed about the throne room as they entered, standing stony-faced and silent along the walls and on either side of the doors leading to and from the room. The last time Sarah had been in there was for Will's knighting ceremony, but the heavy mood inside reminded her that unlike that day, there would be no celebration after, no joyous proclamations. They had gathered for no other reason than to mete out justice.

And today, there was only one monarch sitting on the throne, with three well-guarded prisoners kneeling before her, a good ten feet away.

Terrance stepped back near the door, and a guard escorted Will and Sarah to the side of the dais where Captain James T. Quinn stood, his expression grave as he nodded at them. Hesitantly, Sarah turned to look at the three men whose hands were shackled before them. Her heart thrummed a wild beat against her ribcage when she realized they were all looking at *her*—Adrian with a look of childish rage, Demetrius with a beseeching gaze, as though she was the deciding vote on his fate, and Cadius with that cold, steady gaze of his, daring her to speak out against him. But she lifted her chin, letting him know that he was done intimidating others to get what he wanted.

"Are you aware of the reason why you were called here this day?" the queen asked Will and Sarah, her voice smooth and collected, echoing through the perfectly silent throne room that sizzled with tension. She angled her body to look each of them in the eye, and they nodded, but still she clarified, "Your presence was requested to corroborate the stories of

Guy Demetrius and Damien Lisandro, whose statements I believe you both observed one day past."

Sarah's throat tightened, knowing that Damien had sacrificed his life for his testimony, and her gaze landed again on his killer. Her swallow was thick as sorrow and fury raged within her, and she wanted to claw out Adrian's eyes for ending the life of her friend. But then she remembered that she was surrounded by guards and attacking a king, even a deposed one, would only get her into trouble. So she sucked in a shuddering breath, praying for calm in the face of these enemies.

Beside her, Will was stiff, carefully avoiding Cadius' gaze as his jaw clenched and unclenched. The queen allowed each of them to give a brief account, in their own words, of what they had witnessed of the king, Cadius, and Demetrius, and also what they wished to say against them. Will's voice was strong and steady and reached the far corners of the room as he gave his testimony, and Sarah wished he had shared some of his own confidence with her. But then she heard the faint tremor in his voice as he told of his uncle's torture and death, and when she looked down, the fingers of his right hand shook before he drew them into a fist.

She knew it must be killing him to be in the same room as the man who had devised his uncle's death and to pretend that he wanted justice for the man when, she assumed, Will only wanted to strangle him for all he had done. He took a deep breath when he finished, his gaze darkening as he stared Cadius down, and though there was still rancor in that man's stormy gaze, it was obvious his confidence was flagging.

Her speech was much quieter than Will's, voice turning wobbly at points in her story that produced bad memories. But saying aloud all that these men had done to her and to others caused her conviction to grow, slowly and steadily, until her voice strengthened and she became bolder in her declarations, pointing to each man as she told of what she had observed and heard of their deeds.

Through it all, Queen Meredith remained silent, simply nodding in agreement at points or pursing her lips when either party spoke of Adrian's betrayal or her husband's death. When she felt she had been given enough information, she lifted one hand in a graceful request for silence, and Sarah sucked in a breath, realizing she hadn't stopped talking for what felt like ten minutes. Though her confidence had increased as she spoke, her nerves were still a little frayed after her long-winded explanation, and it was a blessed relief to be able to close her mouth and stop jabbering.

"I thank you both for your honest testimonies." The queen's voice was no longer firm and commanding. She sounded worn-out and weighed down, and for once the sweet queen looked like a ruler who had lost her sister, husband, and child, and who had an entire kingdom looking to her for guidance.

With a single finger, she tried to subtly rub her temple as she pretended to fiddle with her hair, and then she sighed, the first sound of genuine dismay she had made since discovering that the man she had raised as her own had betrayed her. "First, I wish to address the matter of Guy Demetrius."

His back straightened, eyes widening in trepidation.

Queen Meredith's gaze bore into his, her stern countenance returning as she stared him down. "Your testimony yesterday assisted in the judgment brought against the king's former advisor and . . . Adrian," she said, appearing pained to say his name so informally, the absence of a title serving as a reminder that he was no king. "I am tempted to heed Lord Lisandro's advice and lighten your sentence for your cooperation. One year imprisonment, and because Cadius abandoned you without a home or employment, after your character has been tested during this era, we shall assist you in finding an honest occupation in Serimone." Demetrius balked at his sentence, but then he ducked his head, probably realizing that the queen was being extremely lenient, considering he had been the one to provide Cadius with the idea and means to take the kingdom for himself.

The queen looked directly at Sarah as she said, "You were wronged by this man, as I understand it. So, what say you? Do you agree that his sentence should be reduced?"

Sarah flinched, caught off-guard, and she felt Will's entire body turn to stone. But although she knew her word wouldn't carry much weight against the decision of a ruling monarch, she realized that in asking for her opinion, the queen was showing that this kingdom would no longer be ruled with an iron fist; she was attempting to get justice for those specifically wronged by the men before them today, and she was giving Sarah the chance to change Demetrius' fate, to show him mercy.

Sarah looked at her former professor, wincing a little as she stared at a man who had stayed after hours to advise her on projects, and then had left her and Will to die. She bit her lip, staring into his pleading eyes, thinking that one measly year was too good for him.

Mercy, she whispered to herself, wondering at the fact that grace and compassion were some of the hardest characteristics to muster. "I do agree, Your Majesty," she said quietly, unsure whether she liked the look of utter relief on Demetrius' face or if she wanted to take back her statement.

Queen Meredith gave a decisive nod and turned back to the man in question, her face steely once more. "Your sentence has been pronounced, but do not quickly forget my clemency or the benevolence of Lady Matthews this day."

"I will not, My Queen," Demetrius said hurriedly. When he glanced Sarah's way, she thought there might have been genuine remorse and apology in his gaze, but it dropped quickly when he encountered Will's deadly glare.

The queen's eyes suddenly turned sorrowful as she considered Adrian, betrayal unconcealed in their golden-brown depths, and Sarah wondered if maybe the queen was tired of pretending that she was untouchable. Then the woman's gaze landed on Cadius, and a single brow lifted, face becoming suddenly pinched with repressed anger. Her voice was tight and low as she said, "You have tried to control my life for so many years—took my sister and her son from me, stole my husband and *our child.* So believe me when I say I would like nothing more than to watch you hang at the end of a rope, assured that you will never again torment those I care for or anyone else in this beloved kingdom."

Her lips trembled, and she seemed to compose herself, sitting a little straighter in her chair, though her voice was still tight. "But such swift justice would be too good for you, and there has been enough bloodshed for a lifetime, I feel."

"My Queen?" Captain Quinn appeared confused, awaiting clear orders.

She eyed the criminals before her, each driven by their own lust for revenge or power, and shook her head. To Quinn, she said calmly, simply, "Adrian and the man he calls his father shall spend life in prison. It will be a fitting judgment to allow them to live out the remainder of their days with the question of *what if*—to spend an eternity considering their actions and where their plan went awry, how they were overthrown by a single letter and the courage of so few." She appeared vaguely relieved once it was out there, as though she hadn't wished to dwell on their sentence for too long.

The three felons were brought to their feet, a guard on either side of them. Demetrius kept his head bowed in capitulation, but once again Adrian thrashed like a wild animal, though his hands were bound, unlike yesterday, and this time he did not slip through their fingers. Sarah stared him down as he shot her a seething glare, and she tried not to savor the look of terror that hung in his frantic gaze.

"This is an outrage," Cadius called out as they carted him away, his feet slipping against the floor as he resisted. "You were not raised to be queen. How do you expect to rule an entire kingdom alone?"

"You have given me no other choice," the queen whispered, but he was too panicked and enraged to hear her.

"You will fail, Meredith!" he shouted, spittle flying from his mouth as they dragged him from the room. The words hung in the air, and the queen closed her eyes, an anxious line creasing her forehead.

Sensing that they were about to be dismissed, Sarah took a step forward, urgency causing her lips to move. "Your Majesty." The queen opened her eyes slowly, as though surprised she had spoken up. "I hope it isn't impertinent of me to ask, but what are they going to do with Damien Lisandro's body?" Her heart sped up, unable to ask if they had 'disposed' of it already. "You remember that we were friends once, and I want—I want to make sure he's respected."

Queen Meredith watched her sadly, a look of empathy in her brown eyes. "He was a kind man with a gentle heart, which is why it came as such a shock." She shook her head, and it was all Sarah could do to tell her she wasn't wrong about him and that he *was*—mostly—innocent.

The queen squared her delicate shoulders. "I do not believe his intent was malicious, and in the end, I would have wished him pardoned for the information he brought forward. My son—" She flinched and corrected herself. "*Adrian* was out of turn, and I am incredibly sorry for your loss."

It was nice to hear that someone else had seen the good in Damien, but Sarah wasn't sure if it helped to know that the queen would have been on his side or if it hurt more to hear it said aloud that Damien had been hanged unjustly; he could have been standing there beside them now. But the queen hadn't exactly answered her question, so Sarah waited, holding her breath.

Eyes softening, Queen Meredith nodded once, decisive. "He will have a proper burial out of respect, at the edge of the forest on castle grounds. Perhaps a yew tree to mark his grave and ensure it will remain for many eras, as will his memory."

Will placed his hand on the small of her back, and Sarah swallowed past the tears in her throat. "Thank you," she whispered.

"Now." The queen cleared her throat, face apprehensive and expectant as she said, "Lady Sarah, there is a matter I wish to discuss with you. What Lord Lisandro mentioned—"

Hurried footsteps sounded down the hall, and they turned to see a guard enter the throne room. He knelt on one knee before his queen, bowing as he clapped a hand over his heart. "There are two men who have just arrived at the request of William Taylor, Your Majesty. Should I allow them entrance?"

Surprised, the queen looked to Will and then Sarah, who smiled softly. "Do you want to meet your son?" she asked.

Sarah had never seen such a look of terror and apprehension and shocked excitement on the woman's face as she rose slowly to her feet, eyes glued to the open doorway. Though she nodded to the guard, her expectant gaze never left the empty hall. The man returned just moments later, Richard and Dagwood hesitantly following behind, identical looks of suspicion and concern on their faces. When they had stopped in town to invite them to the castle, Sarah had assured them they were being summoned for good news, but clearly they were both wary of coming into the presence of Serimone's sole monarch.

The queen sucked in a breath, looking suddenly like she might need to sit back down. But she moved forward, one step and then another until she was standing before Richard, her eyes searching his face so high above her own. "Is it true?" she asked, though surely she saw the similarities between them—the gold-brown eyes, straight nose, and red-brown hair.

He recoiled some, clearly wondering why he was being addressed by the queen, and Sarah bit her lip, wondering if she should have told him why he was coming there today. But Will had said this was something that needed to be shared between the queen and her son, and she knew he was right, so she remained silent.

"Is what true?" Richard asked cautiously.

Queen Meredith's gaze was wistful, though an ounce of disbelief clung to the corners of her eyes. "I remember you—your name is Richard, yes? We met only a week past."

He nodded, still appearing confused. "I recall, yes."

"This must all seem so strange to you." For a moment, the queen looked indecisive, her hands twisting in her skirt as she glanced in Sarah's direction for guidance, though that girl could only shrug. Turning back to her son, Meredith's voice softened. "Over twenty years past, I gave birth to a child I was told had died from disease shortly after his entrance into this world. However, I have recently been informed that my child, *my son*, was taken from me and placed in the home of another. It was the kindness of one man that saved his life. I—" She couldn't seem to find the words, her gaze drifting downward. What must she be feeling, Sarah wondered, to have lost and found so much in so little time?

But Dagwood's expression had shifted as she spoke, realization dawning on his weathered features. "The gold, the seal on the note," he whispered in disbelief. The queen jerked her head up, meeting his eyes, which instantly turned apologetic. "Oh, My Queen, I did not—If only I had realized sooner . . . Please forgive my ignorance."

She was already shaking her head. "No apologies, please."

"What is going on?" Richard asked, casting his suspicious gaze between the two of them. But he was no fool, and hesitant comprehension crept into his gaze, though he still appeared shocked and uncertain at what had been implied.

Sarah held her breath, knowing his world was about to change forever.

The queen took one step forward. "My son had a birthmark behind his ear, shaped like a crown. May I . . . ?" She reached up tentatively with one hand, her fingers trembling. Richard looked as though he wanted to pull back, but he nodded stiffly instead, allowing her to gently part the hair behind his ear. Sarah could barely make out the small, distorted scar, though she clearly saw the way the queen's shoulders fell.

"When I was seven, I burned myself with a fire poker," Richard explained. The queen nodded, eyes distant as she pursed her lips, clearly considering what the absence of a birthmark might mean. "*But*—" Richard dragged in a breath, brow knitting anxiously. "My mother made something for me before I was cast aside, and it was placed in the basket in which I was left on Dagwood's doorstep. If you are, truly, that woman . . . *my mother*, then perhaps you will recognize this."

He reached inside his shirt and pulled the hand-carved pendant over his head, handing it to her, his eyes scanning her features as though seeing her for the first time. Maybe he was finally noticing that he had her eyes, and Sarah knew his passion for justice was passed down from her, as well.

Meredith took it with a choked laugh, her smile wobbling as she gazed down at the carving of the lion. "You were a squalling babe when you were born, and I used to call you my little Lion Heart," she whispered in fond remembrance. "I knew even then that you were strong." When she looked up at her son, a tear slipped down her pink cheek. "How right I was, as you have survived so much."

Richard was breathing hard, and he still looked a little fearful of believing what was before his very eyes. "Mother?" he whispered in doubt. Then he swallowed, and a disbelieving smile curved his lips. "Mother."

She touched his cheek, lips trembling in a smile. "Yes, my son, I have found you."

"I would have brought him straight here if I had known, My Queen," Dagwood said, his gaze remorseful. "I should have realized something was amiss when the letter left with him when he was abandoned—something so seemingly unimportant—was recently stolen. I am incredibly sorry."

The queen shook her head. "No. I thank you that you kept such gentle care of my son until the day when I could reclaim him." She looked to Richard, her eyes drinking in the sight of the child she had lost over two decades ago, and smiled softly. "We have much to discuss, but first . . . Will you sit and speak with me for a time? I long to hear about the years I missed."

Sarah grinned as the big man nodded silently, wondering if he knew what was to come, that he would someday rule beside his mother with all the passion for truth and justice that Sarah had witnessed. She knew it didn't make up for losing Adrian the way that she did, but Sarah could see how the queen's heart had been filled with Richard's presence.

The queen turned to Dagwood and held out her hand, which he kissed. "Please join us," she encouraged softly. "I wish for you to remain in his life, and I would like to learn more about the man who raised my son."

He nodded quickly, appearing both surprised and honored.

The queen moved over to Sarah, tears falling in earnest down her shining face. She kissed both her cheeks, holding onto Sarah's shoulders as she whispered, "Thank you for bringing my son back to me. You do not know—" She broke off. But Sarah did know, her heart swelling with joy for this woman who had shown her such kindness.

"Consider us even—for you looking after me at that awful dinner party," Sarah quipped, though her voice was tight with emotion.

Queen Meredith squeezed her hands. "Oh, my dear, we shall never be even, but I thank you nonetheless." The queen looked to Will. "And I owe you my gratitude for enduring much to ensure that justice was brought to this land." Will nodded once, appearing too overcome to speak.

The queen strolled back to her son, and Richard stared at his friend in shock, as though he might be able to tell him if this were a dream. Will just grinned slowly, giving him a slow, teasing bow. Richard laughed in disbelief, gave a dazed smile in Sarah's direction, and then allowed his mother—the queen—to take his arm and guide him and his father from the room.

࿇

They followed the guard down the corridor in silence, the joyous mood the reunion had caused fading with each passing step as they were led to the professor's sickbed. The door was open a few inches, and Sarah flattened her palm against the wood and slowly opened it.

Karen's back was hunched over their joined hands, eyes full of concern glued to her guardian's face. The room was kept warm by the continual kitchen fires directly below, and the professor's coverings had been pulled down some to reveal his bare chest and the large bandage circling his ribs. Though no blood was visible on the fresh dressings, his face was chalky and his closed lids were an unhealthy gray tone. The pink-tinged water on the bedside table had yet to be changed. Sarah's stomach flipped a little in memory, and she forcibly pushed aside the reminder of tending to Damien's wounds.

Tentatively, they entered the room, and Sarah whispered her friend's name.

Karen hastily released the professor's hand and wiped the tears from her cheeks, pasting on what appeared like it was supposed to be an encouraging look. "They said he'll be all right. He's going to be fine." Her voice was rough with emotion, and she nodded abruptly again and again, as though the action gave each word greater merit. She cleared her throat as Sarah neared, and her redheaded friend looked like she was desperately trying to hold it together. "He's going to be fine, right?"

Sarah bent to wrap her arms around the girl, who seemed smaller in that moment, and felt her shudder. "I know he will." Karen made a small sound that said she was trying to keep from crying, and something in Sarah's heart clenched as she whispered, "You don't always have to be strong for everyone."

Those words appeared to be her undoing, and Karen's shoulders shook as she cried softly. "I thought he would be awake when I came. It was perfect in my head, with us apologizing and making up for lost time, him telling me how proud he was of me." Sarah stroked her silky hair, pursing her lips as she shared in her friend's pain.

Will crouched in front of Karen's chair, and she pulled back a little from Sarah in surprise, as though noticing his presence for the first time. "I was there after he had been wounded," he began in a low, smooth voice that caused both girls to hold their breath to better listen. "He was brave, telling me to leave him there to stop Cadius, knowing that he could perish if I did not assist him that instant. And, Miss Ashmore—Karen," he said earnestly, staring into her eyes. "He used what we both thought might be his last breaths to beg me to make sure you were kept safe and to tell you that he loves you."

Karen's eyes filled once more. "Really?"

"It's true."

Three heads swiveled in the direction the raspy voice had come. The professor's lids were crackled open, a crooked, tired grin twisting his pale lips. He braced himself as though to sit up and then sucked in a breath, freezing. "Probably unwise," he rasped.

Karen rose to adjust the pillow behind his head, and he gave her a grateful smile. But then his gaze traveled down over his exposed chest, and his eyes bulged. "Oh, my."

"I have it." Karen unfolded the covers and pulled them up to his shoulders. He shot her another look of thanks, and then his expression turned serious.

"What William told you—" He cleared his throat, and Sarah was reminded that expressing emotions had never come easy for the man. "I meant every word I said to him."

Sarah's left eye narrowed, a little disappointed that *this* was the best he could do, but Karen was smiling through her tears, nodding as though she understood. And Sarah supposed that after years of living with the eccentric scientist, she did.

With a strange expression on his face, like a scientist studying a puzzling problem, the professor turned his gaze to watch Will, seemingly unaware that he was grinning faintly in what looked like awe.

"Professor," Karen said, face falling a little. "There's a lot to tell you, and I'll come back and let you know what you missed, but first I have some . . . bad news." Sarah knit her brows in confusion until she went on gently, "The machine was devastated. Sarah saw it herself."

The professor's eyes widened meaningfully at Will, though he was a little too obvious about it. Karen shook her head. "Don't worry. I'll explain how he knows later."

He stared at the door, his mouth gaping slightly before shaking his head in denial. To Karen, he said, "I cannot believe the machine is ruined. It can't be . . . *gone.*"

"But it is," she said softly. "And there's something we need to know about travel." Sarah touched her arm, shaking her head when she understood what her friend was getting at. She was moved, but Karen shouldn't give up this moment of reunion with Charles so soon to mend something that was probably unfixable. With a quick look at her, Karen said to the professor, "I know your body can't make the trip back, same as me, but I was hoping there might be another way for you to create a watch here, or sustain the one that's left."

She was careful to speak, and Sarah knew she was trying to not clue Will in too early before Sarah could tell him what the dilapidated machine really meant. But for once, the clueless professor understood the subtle context of the situation, and his sad gaze flitted between the two girls as he said, "Would that I could, my dears. I have the plans stored in my head, the one place that my old nemesis could never touch"—Sarah flinched, knowing that Karen had a lot to catch him up on—"but it would take years to recreate what came about after decades of research, and the impossibility of it being done without any modern tools or electricity, not to mention the stabilizer . . . The damage to the machine would cause the same irreparable harm to the watches in our possession, and I can do nothing to fix them while I am here."

"Your watch, then?" Karen insisted, desperation creeping into her small voice. "Did you ever find it?"

"You know it was confiscated some time ago, and in such ill-repair that even if it could be found, I've no hope of mending it." He looked directly at Sarah, his tone regretful as he finished with, "It is impossible."

"Why is that a concern?" Sarah's entire body stiffened at Will's question, his innocence in this matter. "Yes, it made the journey uncomfortable, but not entirely unbearable or impossible." She couldn't look at him. Instead, she found the professor's gaze, which slowly cleared until he gave her a look of sympathy.

"Ah," the professor whispered in comprehension, eyes closing. "Of course."

Karen placed a hand on his arm, her smile trembling slightly as he pried his lids back open. "Why don't you get some sleep? I'll come visit you again in the morning." He nodded, lids pulling down once more in exhaustion.

Karen watched him a minute longer, then she took up Sarah's hand. Her tone was low and urgent as she whispered, "Don't lose faith yet. We'll think of something."

Though Sarah nodded, she was afraid her hope in the impossible had been gone for a long time.

Chapter Thirty-Three

"Come to me in my dreams, and then by day I shall be well again.
For then the night will no more than
pay the hopeless longing of the day."

Matthew Arnold, "Longing"

Sarah swallowed as they rolled down the overgrown trail leading to the Joneses' land, her throat parched and her tongue thick for no reason. She knew it was all in her head, her body reacting to her desire to never say what she knew she must tell Will, but that didn't lessen the tightness in her chest.

"Would you like to accompany me?"

Sarah shook her head, drawing her gaze around to find Will standing on the ground and offering a hand to her. They were in front of the barn, and she hadn't even realized they'd stopped. Karen was beside her still, and she touched her arm. Lowly, she said, "I'll go tell them. Good luck."

Sarah sucked in a breath, knowing she would need it, and her friend headed toward the house. She turned to Will, shaking her head. "Sorry, what were you saying?"

"I was asking if you would accompany me as I return the horse." His brow drew together. "I thought I had mentioned it last night. . . ."

Sarah nodded. "Of course, I remember. Sure." And she did, she just hadn't thought the opportunity to tell him that she was leaving would come so quickly.

He put away the wagon and saddled both horses, making quick work of it. Sarah was tempted to tell him not to rush, though she knew he was eager to be on the road and have this business done with.

It was less than half a day's ride up, he'd said, and they rode most of it in silence. Sarah's mind was filled with anxieties, doubts, and questions, and somehow these feelings overshadowed her typical fear of a strange horse. Or maybe it was her forced reliance on Will's animal yesterday that had sapped her of her anxiety for good. While she panicked in silence, Will merely seemed content to have her riding so near to him, their knees nearly brushing as he enjoyed the fresh air and the company beside him, the peace of the countryside and of the sweet birdsong echoing through the trees. Yesterday's storm seemed to have exhausted the sky of its anger, and lazy white clouds parted in the breeze, allowing golden light to warm the earth.

Everything about it was idyllic and should have lessened her nerves, or given her enough peace that she could at least enjoy these fleeting hours with Will and the beautiful land that she would soon leave. But she was so wired with anxiety that twice she considered pulling over so she could heave her nerves onto the grass, and she barely managed to keep from yelping when her horse whinnied.

"Is something wrong?" She looked up at Will, alarm shooting through her, those three words making her question if he knew what she was about to tell him. But his face was only curious, and she exhaled.

"Sorry, just a little anxious," she replied honestly, and when he nodded, she knew he was thinking of her past trouble with riding.

His look turned a little roguish as he leaned toward her, his knee bumping hers, but his tone was filled with false innocence. "I would be more than pleased to have you ride with me. If it would put you at ease."

Sarah's grin was slow in coming, but when her surprise at his boldness faded, she tossed her head back and laughed, her worry finding momentary release in the action. "You're ridiculous."

"Incorrigible," he corrected, then lifted a brow, waiting.

"I think I'm safer over here, thank you very much."

Will shrugged. "Suit yourself. I get you on the way back, though." He swayed contentedly in his saddle, and her smile fell as she watched his profile. Her Will was happy, and she was going to take that from him. *But he will be happy again one day,* she reminded herself, the only thought that, while it twisted her heart and made her hate this even more, it gave her hope.

They weren't pushing the horses too far and only had to stop once to give them a break, so they made it by early afternoon. The livery was a tiny building on the outskirts of a small town in the middle of nowhere, and Sarah imagined that she could see the ocean stretching out like a wavering blue line in the distance.

While Will returned the horse and thanked the man, she wandered the one-room shop, realizing that she would never see Will's own business again. Her fingers brushed idly over the shoeing tool on the bench, recalling the first time she had seen him and her intimidation at his hulking, brooding presence.

A faint smile tugged at her lip-ends as she thought about the kindness he had revealed in his shop the very next day, doing his best to erase the fears of a perfect stranger. Every event in that livery came back to her, images that flashed by like the cars of a speeding freight train, and she brought one back before it could disappear, holding onto it: Will working over the table, his shirtsleeves rolled up, the fire casting a warm glow over his handsome features. And when he glanced up at her, the smile he gave and the open look in his eyes . . . She should have seen then that he loved her.

"Sarah?" She yanked back her hand, losing her grip on the memory as she realized she was staring at a blank wall. The man had gone to put his horse away, and Will was holding his hand out to her. "It's time."

Sarah swallowed as she took it. "I guess it is."

Only his horse remained, and Sarah sat bone-straight in the saddle, strangely uncomfortable with their closeness. How was she supposed to break the man's heart if she was leaning on him for support?

Will placed a kiss on the back of her neck, sounding amused as he said lowly, "Relax, love. Everything is all right."

How wrong he was, but she couldn't tell him that—at least, not yet. So she forced her body to unravel muscle by muscle, leaning back into his chest with reluctance. Instantly, she softened against him, surprised how the contact made her realize that her brief denial had caused her to miss it. How much worse would it be to go forever without him?

This time Sarah couldn't stand the silence, and she filled it with idle talk and observations about the weather or the proprietor of the shop, how that woodpecker in the distance sounded like a jackhammer. She questioned Will about the types of trees and which ones would bloom later in spring, and he obliged her, a grin in his voice.

"What about your old friend, Lawrence?" she blurted at one point. "You said he was the one who stabbed the professor."

Will inhaled deeply, and she tried not to notice how her body rose with his or how his heart beat near her ear. "I asked Captain Quinn about him earlier, and he said he listened to Lawrence's entire story, how his family had been taken and held captive. Apparently, that was his first dalliance with Cadius, though at the time he had been under the impression that he was being ordered by the king himself to kill Charles; he was surprised to learn from Quinn that Cadius was even alive."

"Did they find his family?" Sarah was genuinely interested, and it wasn't her anxious need to fill the silence that caused the question.

"His family is safe, thank God. Cadius had been holding them in the dungeons, and they were released late last night."

"But what will happen to *him*?"

Softly, Will said, "I saw the look in his eyes as he stood over Charles. He was . . . horrified at what he had done. I asked the captain to be lenient with him, and Quinn said that he must serve his community as a sentence, with constant monitoring on his behavior for six months' time. But he will not serve a sentence in prison, and his family will remain free." He hesitated. "I wanted to tell you earlier, but I was unsure if I should mention it in front of Karen, seeing as he did attack her guardian."

She nodded, appreciating his sensitivity in the matter. Though Karen was forgiving by nature, Sarah wasn't sure how she would feel about Lawrence's "cozy" sentence after seeing the professor ashen and bandaged. "I'm glad he'll be all right," she said.

There was a moment of silence, and her heart rate kicked up as she took note of it, racking her brain for another topic, anything she hadn't already covered. Will took advantage of her brief pause and suggested that they give the horse a break and walk for awhile. She hadn't realized she had talked away so much of the afternoon.

At her distracted nod, he helped her down from the sweat-slicked horse, keeping one hand wrapped around hers and the other on the reins as they strolled through a field of tall grass. It made a *swooshing* sound as it brushed against their clothing, some stalks slipping beneath Sarah's skirts to tickle her legs. Will's hand was familiar, rough, and warm in hers, and she wondered if this would be the last peaceful moment they had together.

Wanting it to go on forever, she said, "It's a beautiful day. Why don't we take a break ourselves, enjoy the afternoon for a little bit?" She was being a coward, she knew, but the closer that moment came when she would shatter both their dreams, the more she wished this sweet afternoon would never end.

Will smiled softly. "Perfect." She guided him to a tree she spotted not too far off.

"Did I ever tell you my uncle was married?" Will remarked suddenly, his voice thoughtful as he swung their hands between them.

Sarah shook her head, surprised but glad for any excuse to delay what she had to say. "Who was she?" she asked.

He released the horse to graze nearby and sat in the shade of the tree, propping one knee up to rest his forearm. Sarah pressed her back against the rough bark, her shoulder brushing his as she stretched her legs out in front of her.

"She was a tavern girl he met in Ridlan. They were both young, and as my uncle told it, he fell in love instantly." Will's lips tipped in fond memory. "Uncle didn't speak of her much, but he once claimed she was the most beautiful angel put on this earth by God." When he looked at Sarah, his expression turning soft and serious, her heart gave a lurch. "I now realize he was wrong."

She swallowed at the look of unmasked love and admiration in his gaze. Her voice was small when she asked, "What happened to her?"

Will squinted at the tree line in the distance. "Typhus. She was gone quickly after they had married, and as she did not believe in God, my uncle always wondered whether he would see her again."

"Oh." Saddened over Thomas's rough life, Sarah stared at her hands in her lap and watched as his larger one came to rest over her fingers. She looked up at him and observed the subtle brightening of his features, curious about what had changed his mood.

"He warned me to never enter a relationship unequally yoked, and that phrase always grated on me. But I see now that a relationship cannot be successful if the two are never on equal terms on issues of the greatest import." His voice was low and suddenly tinged with an uncertainty she couldn't account for, and he spoke quickly as though to mask the nervous twitching of his fingers over hers.

"That makes sense," she said, wondering what he was getting at.

His Adam's apple bobbed, and there was a flush to his cheeks now. He didn't seem to be able to hold her gaze for more than two seconds at a time. "What I mean to say is that I know it concerned you and my uncle that I did not believe as you do. But, well, now that I *do* . . ." His eyes shyly met hers as he gave her the most adorable, uncertain smile. "I suppose that there is nothing left for us to fret over."

The tender look in his eyes sent a jolt of panic through Sarah, and she wondered if he might propose then and there. *This is it,* she thought, pulse increasing. She realized she couldn't let him say another thing, each word like a dagger through her heart. She could only hope that his would bleed less.

"Will." At the trepidation in her tone, his expression fell some as he studied her face. "When the machine was destroyed . . ."

"Go on," he urged, giving her hand a tiny squeeze.

Dragging in a wobbly breath, she felt the acid squirting in her stomach, making her sick. "I was upset because that machine was what made these watches work and allowed us to travel back and forth between my time and yours. Now it can't do that anymore."

His brow pulled together in confusion, though awareness was slowly creeping into his gaze. "But we returned here without issue."

"Remember how rough the trip was?" she reminded him. "It isn't supposed to be like that. Each watch can store one jump, but once it's used, the watches are useless."

Will's hand stiffened over hers. "What are you saying?" His voice was tight with apprehension. She had said goodbye to him before, and it was no wonder he sensed it coming now.

"I'm saying," she heaved out on a gusty breath, brow knitting as she tried to fight back her tears. "I'm telling you that Karen's watch is the last one, and it can only be used once. I have to return to my own time, and when I do . . . Will, I won't be able to come back," she whispered.

He was shaking his head in denial, and then his movements stilled. "Karen asked Charles if he could create another," he whispered in realization, and then to himself, "How could I be so stupid?" His dark eyes dragged over her face, desperation filling his gaze. "But why must you go?"

Though she wanted to close her eyes against the sting in her chest, she held his gaze, needing him to understand. "I have a home and a family I have to return to. I don't belong here, Will. I never did, and I know things about this time that . . . We don't belong *together*," she finished, knowing any excuse would never be enough for him.

"I disagree," he said plainly, stubbornly. His jaw twitched, and he tried to calmly ask, "When were you planning to leave?"

With a wince, Sarah answered, "Tonight, as soon as we get back."

She had been dreading this moment since she discovered the wrecked machine in Charles's basement, building it up in her head. The burning anxiety low in her stomach did not lessen after the words were out, and her fear was legitimized when she saw the look of betrayal and panic that clouded Will's eyes.

He lurched to his feet, startling her, and paced a foot one way and then another. "*Why* did you not tell me sooner?" he heaved out, breaths coming ragged in frustration and alarm. "How am I supposed to take this? You say you are leaving once more, never to return, and you allow no time to convince you to stay."

"That's just it!" she shouted, rising as tears of anger and sadness pricked her eyes. "I was terrified that if I told you I couldn't come back here, you would convince me to stay. And—and *I can't*." The word left her lips like a moan. "It's what's best for the both of us."

"Then I will come with you."

He said it like it was such a simple thing that Sarah laughed in astonishment. Pursing her lips together, she strove to remember all the reasons why that was impossible. "That can never happen."

Will frowned, his eyebrows pulling up and together in distress. "I have done it before, haven't I?"

Seeing that look of betrayal and fear in his eyes caused her heart to wrench painfully, and she clenched her fists to keep from reaching out to him, nails biting into her palms. "Your life is here, and someone has to be this town's hero. Where I come from, you're too important to be erased from history. And it *would* erase you, Will," she said pointedly, hoping to make him understand.

"I don't care." She opened her mouth to protest, and he quickly added, "Cadius and Queen Alexis were not together, and look at how it tore them and an entire kingdom apart."

Sarah shook her head, already seeing large flaws in his hurried logic. "All those things happened because they were both selfish after their lives were turned upside down, and they decided to do to others what had been done to them; they betrayed so many in an attempt to right the wrongs in their life, instead of making the choice to rise above their circumstances and move on. I've known all along that I would have to make a choice, and I choose to be selfless. To save both our futures." Her voice wavered, and she bit her lip.

Will came to stand before her, and his voice cracked as he whispered, "But I could have carried that burden with you. You should have let me, given me the choice in my own fate." A guilty tear slipped over her lid, and he pressed his lips together, seemingly deciding that he didn't want to fight with what time was left. Shoulders squaring, he said stubbornly, "You believe you must go, but you can't possibly imagine that I will not try to find you." Of course, the only way that he would let her leave was if he thought he could come for her one day.

"You can't, Will," she whispered brokenly.

"And why not?"

"*Because!*" she exploded, throwing her hands into the air, all the fear and pain and frustration at their circumstances coming out in that one word. "Because someday you and I—this thing between us—is going to blow up in our faces. I knew from the beginning that it wouldn't work and that I shouldn't get involved with you." Her voice hiccupped, turning pained as she said, "I knew better, and now I'll ruin your future if I stay and hurt you if I go. This is all my fault, and I am so s-sorry."

Will placed his hands on either side of her face, kissing her soundly, his lips hard and desperate against hers as he pressed her back against the tree. Stupidly, she allowed the taste and scent of him to cloud her senses even as she knew he was desperately trying to convince her to stay, using the only defense he had yet to try. They were both breathless when he drew back to whisper against her lips, "Why won't you let me tell you that you are worth the pain?" He pulled back, looking into her eyes. "I learned something on that ship, and that is the fact that I never wish to be without you."

She rubbed her lips together, the feel of his kiss lingering there. "You don't know how much I want to stay, but—"

"Then stay." Will's thumb brushed the soft skin under her neck where her pulse rushed painfully. "*Stay with me*," he breathed.

A shudder passed through her as she forced back the desire to do just that. "But I have a home and a family to get back to, my sister, and I haven't graduated from college yet. I have a *life* in the future, and my presence here—gah, how do I make you understand?" she groaned in frustration, feeling helpless.

"You cannot leave like this." He looked positively crestfallen, and Sarah's chest clamped around her heart.

"I have to," she said, wrenching the words past her own mounting agony. "I wish there was another way, but I can't just abandon my family back home and everything I've ever known. I don't belong here," she said again, then whispered, "Someday you'll be able to forget about me."

Will's shoulders rose and fell as he tried to control his breathing. "Is there nothing I can do to convince you to stay?"

She gave a slow shake of her head, eyes sorrowful. "I have to go back, and once I do—" Her voice cracked, unable to say that she couldn't return someday. When she dragged in a stiff breath, her heart ached with the effort.

"No," he replied firmly. "I will see you again."

"Oh, Will," she breathed, pained. This would be so much easier if he would just accept the way things were and the reality that they could never be together. The fact that he kept bringing it up and denying the obvious only prolonged the inevitable, only lengthened the agony of saying goodbye once and for all. "I really wish that you could accept the fact that this is both of our futures I'm protecting here. And I hope that someday, when your life has fallen into place, you'll look back on what I did and realize that it was the right decision."

Will held up a hand to stop her protest, then used it to gently tuck a stray tendril behind her ear. His large palm covered her cheek as his fingers entangled themselves in her hair. "I know I cannot keep you here, nor should I prevent you from returning to where you belong. What I meant is that I will carry you with me each day and I will see you in everything I do. So, no, this is not the last time I will glimpse your face, love. *But* should the clarity of your image fade—" He seemed to choke on the words, clearing his throat during a long pause. When he spoke again, his voice was low, full of fierce determination.

"If, God forbid, I should begin to forget the little things that make you the woman you are, then I shall fight to recall these moments we've spent together, the good and the bad—the way your eyes nearly turn green when they fill with emotion, how your laugh seems to come so easily, so carefree; the feel of you in my arms, as though we were designed to fit together."

"Like puzzle pieces," Sarah whispered, not having meant to speak up and break into his musings. But she had thought the very same thing so many times, and she almost smiled. "A few jagged pieces of wood that look broken, but when you put them together, they just make sense. Like they were designed to fit together."

He smiled at her quoting of his words. "Precisely." The hand on her cheek dropped to wrap around her fingers. His voice lowered, turning soft, like a loving touch, as he examined their twined fingers. "And then there is the way your hand fits in mine, like those puzzle pieces you spoke of. This simple touch speaks a thousand words, even before we gained the courage to speak of our feelings for one another. It gave me *hope*." He met her eyes again. Sarah fought the intense desire to close her own and savor this moment, but she was afraid to look away from his face for even a second, wanting to remember every last detail of him.

There was a hesitation on his part, and a shaky breath seemed to give him the courage to continue, though his voice wavered with repressed emotion. "Forget me if it makes it easier for you to cope with our parting, but I cannot bear a day without the thought of you, without recalling to mind your smile or hearing the sound of your laughter when I see something you would find amusing. And so, even if it causes me intense pain . . . I will forever carry your memory with me, refusing to lose hope that someday I will not have only mere recollections of a love gone by. Perhaps, one day, I will be able to gaze into your eyes once more—eyes that captured me the moment you stumbled into my livery that fateful day—and tell you that I waited a thousand years to glimpse them again."

It was the most beautiful thing anyone had ever said to her, and, she assumed, the most perfect thing a man had *ever* said to a woman. But the thought of him holding out for her only caused her immense grief. "You know it would be easier on both of us if you forgot about me altogether. Move on with your life."

"Because I can simply forget about you? After all we have been through and what you mean to me?" Will looked amazed and a little hurt that she would even suggest such a thing.

Softly, Sarah whispered, "Everyone's forgettable with enough time." She stared up into his dark, expressive eyes, which welled with pain at her words. *Well, maybe not everyone.* "Here." Reluctantly, she reached behind her, knuckles scraping against the rough bark as she tried to unclasp his necklace from around her neck, though her shaking fingers refused to comply.

Will took both her hands in his and gently pulled them down. "Please, keep it. Then I'll know that you will have a piece of me with you."

Her eyes welled with tears that she desperately tried to press back, throat burning with the effort. "I know that"—she swallowed hard, blinking away the water that made his image swim—"it will be easiest on both of us if we can move on, but I don't want you to think that I'm just one more person abandoning you or that I won't be thinking of you. *Everyday* of my life I'll carry a little piece of you with me, Will Taylor, regardless of whether or not I have this to tether me here." Carefully, she disentangled her hands from his and removed the necklace, pressing it into his palm and closing his fingers when he refused to accept it. "*Please.*"

He opened his fingers to stare at the necklace in his hand, his look despondent. "So you wish to leave it behind."

Sarah smiled softly through her tears. Her neck felt naked without the familiar weight of the chain and the promises it had held. "You're impossible to leave behind." Words she had spoken to him so long ago, but now they carried a deeper meaning. "But you deserve to have it back."

His gaze met hers suddenly, grip tightening around the pendant. "One day—one day I will put this back where it belongs."

Sarah didn't bother to tell him that she knew it belonged on the neck of another woman. She felt sick at the thought that anyone else should wear it and considered, for one selfish moment, taking it back—a small token to bring home with her as a memento of every beautiful and heartbreaking second they'd spent together. But she had spoken the truth when she said that she didn't need it to remember him; she knew it would be nearly impossible to move on as it was, and it would only hurt each time she looked at it. Maybe it was a mistake to leave it behind, and maybe she was supposed to bring it back with her, but right then, Sarah knew that it would be easier to create a life devoid of Will's presence—she clenched her jaw at the thought—if she didn't have a constant reminder of him hanging around her neck.

Instead of admitting the tortured thoughts that caused her stomach to clench and the fist around her heart to do the same, she strove for her last shred of bravery. In a choked whisper, she said, "So we should say goodbye, then. Before we get back to the house."

A soft shake of Will's head sent that stubborn lock in motion across his forehead, which she brushed back. It was such a small, silly thing to miss, but Sarah ached at the thought that she would never again see it fall out of place. "No, love, this is not goodbye."

"Then what should we say?" she asked, voice hitching with desperation. She wished she could say what was on her heart, and now more than ever she wanted to tell him that she had fallen in love with him so deeply, that leaving him was shattering her inside and she would never forget the way she felt when she was with him. But she couldn't; if she said it out loud, she knew he would follow her to the ends of the earth until he found her again. The thought that he loved her so much both thrilled and terrified her, because his dreams were here, and she would never take his home from him, nor would she knowingly destroy the future that was supposed to be. Saying those three words would be selfish, and after he had given her everything and offered up all that he was, how could she ask him to give up his home for a lost girl who was torn between two worlds?

But he didn't ask to hear those words for the first and final time. With his finger, he trailed the path of a wayward tear down her cheek, smiling softly. "I shall see you soon."

She closed her eyes, feeling broken. Her pulse thumped painfully in her chest, and she no longer had to wonder why they called it a broken heart; she felt as though it would crumble at their feet any moment. "Will." His name was a pained moan on her lips.

His finger, wet with her tears, raised her chin. She opened her eyes to find that his indigo gaze was swimming, as well. Will's smile wobbled, and she knew that she would never forget the look in his eyes just then. He kissed her, soft and wet with both their tears pressed between their lips. The hand that spread across her cheek trembled as he pulled back, and he pasted on what she assumed was a brave smile. Two tears dropped in perfect succession, rolling down over his cheekbones and falling off his chin.

"But I *will* see you soon." He pressed a finger to her lips, which had opened in protest. "If it is all I have, then tonight I shall see you in my dreams, love."

Sarah used her thumb to brush the wetness from his chin, knowing that he must be wrecked inside to be brought to tears. This once silent and brooding blacksmith had turned into a man overflowing with compassion and love that he poured out on *her*, even though he must have known it was the end for them. She didn't think she would ever miss someone as much as she would this man, her first love, and the only person who would hold onto hope when all hope was lost. In that moment, Sarah was certain that there would never be a day that love for this man did not keep her heart pumping the memory of him through her entire being, however painful each beat might be and regardless of whether she bled a little each time.

A breath shuddered past her trembling lips, but somehow she managed to say it back, meaning it with every inch of her shattering heart. "I'll see you in my dreams, Will."

Chapter Thirty-Four

"Ah God, that love were as a flower or a flame,
That life were as the naming of a name,
That death were not more pitiful than desire,
That these things were not one in the same!"

Algernon Charles Swinburne, "Laus Veneris"

The ride back was pure agony, and Will tried to memorize every detail of it. He would never forget the feel of her back pressed against his chest, his hands abandoning the reins so his arms could wrap tightly around her waist, how her shuddering sighs tore at him. When he turned his head to peer at her face, she was watching the shifting sun on the horizon with a look of such grief and palpable misery that Will felt his heart break for them both. He saw in her eyes that she cared for this land, and he still did not fully understand why she must leave it. Or him.

He leaned down to press his cheek to her hair, closing his eyes as the dancing sunlight played over his face, breaking through the leaves overhead to bathe them in warmth. The happy orange shadows that danced over his closed lids were a stark contrast to his current mood, a painful reminder of warm memories among the dreary reality in which he found himself. How cruel it was to have opened himself to the greatest love he had ever known only to lose it after so brief a time.

Lord, how do I make her stay? he beseeched silently, hoping for some obvious response from the Almighty. But the only words in his head were Sarah's as they listed all the reasons they could not be together, and surely that was not the answer to his question. He would not accept that this woman in his arms would leave his life forever even as her abandoned necklace burned a hole in his pocket.

She sighed, sitting a little straighter in his arms, and he glanced up and saw the house looming in the distance. When Will had asked her how she was going to break the news to the family, she said that Karen was going to do it for her so she could leave just after their return. His throat tightened, knowing that all too soon she would be gone.

He pulled back on the reins near the porch and threw his leg over the back of the horse, landing on the ground with an exhausted *thump*. Taking her waist in his hands, he drew her down, pulse throbbing at her nearness and the memory of their first ball together, holding her near as he was now. She must have been thinking the same thing, because her chest rose and fell quicker, eyes softening as the hands resting on his biceps slid upward, making a trail of fire along his arms and shoulders until they came to rest behind his head, and she drew him down.

Her lips trembled as they met Will's, and he knew she was holding back her tears. One arm came to encircle her waist and he placed his other hand on the one around his neck, curling his fingers over hers. He marveled—not for the first time but perhaps the last—at the perfect way they fit together, how moments like these made him feel as though his hands had no purpose until they had found hers.

"What am I to do without you?" he whispered, pressing his forehead to hers, feeling as though his world was crumbling to the very ground on which she stood.

A wobbling breath slipped from her lips, and Sarah gave him what he thought was supposed to be a brave look. Her voice was soft as she answered, "We're going to be okay, Will. It's going to take some time, but *you will be all right*. I promise."

Placing a gentle kiss on the tip of her nose, Will smiled softly. "Haven't I told you before that you have more courage and strength than you allow yourself credit for?"

"I just know what has to be done." But her words were quiet and shook with repressed emotion, her conviction waning. She appeared drained, and he knew his earlier outburst had not helped her exhausted state. How long had it been eating at her to keep all those secrets bottled up inside, feeling as though she could not tell him the truth for fear he would attempt to change her mind?

Guilt filled him at the reminder that he had beseeched her to stay against her better judgment—thoughtlessly *begged* was a better term for how he had acted. She said she was leaving to protect them both, and though his heart felt like it might stop beating forever the moment she left his side, perhaps she was right in saying that she was the one who had to selflessly walk away, because he was certainly too weak-willed in regards to Sarah to make that decision himself. But how could he ask her to give up her family and home and all she had ever known for *him*?

He took up her hand in his own, kissing the backs of her knuckles. "Come, let's get you inside." Two sets of heavy-burdened boots stomped drearily up the porch steps and into the house, neither seeming to have the strength to pick up their feet.

It was obvious that Karen had told the family Sarah was leaving the instant they entered, because the main room was filled with every last Jones, wide-eyed and anxious. They all sprang to their feet when the door opened, and immediately Sarah was swept away from him in a tide of hugs and well wishes and tears from Leah and Mrs. Jones.

Seth found Will and drew him aside, pulling him into a quick embrace. "I am so sorry." His face was filled with concern for his friend, and Will's throat tightened at his sympathy. Seth's gaze landed on his wife, lips turning downward, and Will knew he was considering what it might be like to lose Karen. He envied his friend and the security Seth had in the fiery, tenderhearted redhead.

Then his eyes found Sarah's across the room as they searched him out, and he reminded himself that he would not switch positions with any other man in the world. Though he wished their situation were different, in spite of all the pain they had endured and the agony that was to come, he would not change what they had for anything. Their time together had been brief and riddled with ups and downs, but he was certain these past months would be the greatest of his lifetime, and he would never forget the warmth she had brought to every corner of his once dead heart.

"Karen said you must be off immediately, but surely you can stay for a light supper," Mrs. Jones insisted, eyes flooding as though she might burst into tears without warning as she studied Sarah at arm's length. "Your parents will understand, I'm sure."

Sarah shook her head, and though she pasted on a brave smile, he could see how wrecked she was inside. "I wish I could." Her voice quavered for an instant, smile wobbling before she secured it back in place. "But I really can't stay any longer." The expression in her eyes caused Will to wonder if she was trying to save them all more pain by leaving quickly and with as little fuss as possible. His heart fell a little, realizing he had asked more time of her, not considering how tortuous this must be for her.

"I'll go with you," Karen said quickly. "See you to the edge of the forest." The two women shared a look, and Sarah nodded.

It took close to half an hour for her to receive another round of goodbyes, but Will was in no rush to have her go. Seth's crushing bear hug brought tears to her eyes, and Leah's watery gaze caused Sarah's smile to waver. Twice, Mrs. Jones insisted on her taking a basket for the journey, but Sarah just shook her head. "It will be a quick trip." Her voice was small and tight, and he saw her composure slipping as she gave each of them one last hug and tearful kiss on the cheek.

When her gaze met Will's in question—asking if he would accompany her—he shook his head and followed her and Karen out the door. The entire Jones clan stood on the porch, Leah and Mrs. Jones crying softly, as they all waved them off, standing outside the door until they disappeared into the forest.

Sarah's fingertips brushed the back of his hand, and he suddenly realized how stiff and silent he was. He glanced down at her to find her forehead creased with uncertainty and concern. "You don't have to come, Will. It might . . . Maybe it will make it harder for you."

But he shook his head. "No, I want to spend every last moment I can with you."

Biting her lip, she nodded, and he heard her steady intake of breath.

Karen led them to the edge of a clearing and stopped, turning to Sarah. "You'll have to change once you get there, and it should take you right back to school. The ride shouldn't be too bumpy, but if you get sick, the professor would always make me saltines and hot limewater after a rough trip. And say 'hi' to Lilly for me." She was babbling, taking control of the situation to divert her mind.

Sarah touched her hand, and Karen's voice cracked. No longer distracted, tears instantly set her green gaze swimming. "I knew you'd have to go someday, but not like this," Karen choked out. She grinned, and it wobbled at the edges. "And I definitely didn't expect the stranger who fell into this time to become my best friend."

Sarah made a choking sound and wrapped her friend in a hug. Will's ribcage ached, and he looked away momentarily, the sight reminding him of his own forthcoming parting with her.

"I almost forgot." Karen's voice was thick with tears, and she swiped at her damp cheeks before reaching into her sleeve. She pulled out a letter and handed it to Sarah. "For you, but don't open it until you get back."

"What is it?"

Karen's eyes softened. "Just something to remember me by."

Sarah nodded gravely, and with a deep breath, she turned to Will. The air seemed to catch in his lungs, and words felt impossible. He had done all the pleading and convincing within his power, and there was nothing left to do to make her stay. She would not be the woman he loved with everything that was within him if she was easily swayed against something she believed she must do. He loved her all the more for her selfless conviction even as he wished he could change it.

"I will not ask you to remain with me," Will said. He swallowed and touched her face, his fingers like a whisper across her skin. Blessedly, Karen turned away, giving them a sense of privacy. His voice lowered to an intimate level even as his tone thickened with determination. "Ours is a timeless love; it cannot be broken or shaken. Rest assured that as long as there is breath in my lungs, as long as stars spread across the heavens, I will never give up on this love."

"But wouldn't it be easier to let go?" she whispered brokenly, desperately.

"Would it be easy to carve out a piece of my heart?" He shook his head. "No, you are a part of me now, and whether or not you are in this world, know that I will forever carry a piece of you with me."

Sarah's lips trembled as she nodded, clearly moved by his earnest passion. When she had found her voice, she whispered, "And you can be sure that when I see those stars you mentioned, I'll be thinking of you."

Knowing that there was nothing left to say but farewell, he took both her hands in his, savoring the feel of their soft warmth, and drew his face down to hers. Her lips were gentle against his, the kiss speaking of past joys and all the agony that was in their joined hearts. And like this thing between them that had only just begun, it was over all too quickly.

"I'll see you soon, Will," she said to him, a look of hope in her eyes that broke his heart.

"I shall see you in my dreams, love," he repeated, his voice cracking with emotion.

Sarah stepped away from him, their arms stretching the growing distance until their fingers parted and his hand fell, empty, to his side. It was pure torture to watch her walk into the center of that clearing alone, her back straight with brave determination as her shoulders shook from repressing her sobs.

She reached the center of the clearing and slowly turned. Tears streamed down Karen's cheeks, and she raised her hand in farewell. Sarah managed to give her friend a faint smile and then turned to Will, her face a pale mask of uncertainty and sorrow.

He was not powerless to stop her this time, but rather he had to choose to let the only woman he had ever cared for with such a burning, all-consuming love walk out of his life forever. It was the most painful thing he had ever experienced, and he was letting it happen because Sarah was certain this was how things needed to be.

For a long moment, she simply searched his face, as though memorizing his features in the same way he was cataloguing every detail of her own. Then she lifted her fingers to her lips and pressed them to her chest as she had at the execution ceremony. Will's jaw spasmed with restrained emotion, though a lone tear slipped over his lid as he did the same, kissing his fingers and spreading them over his heart, knowing that if he opened his mouth, he would beg her to stay. And he feared she might do just that, against her better judgment. It was pure agony to stand there and do nothing, feeling torn between getting what he wanted and doing what was best for Sarah's future.

Her hand drifted to her wrist and the watch he hadn't noticed she wore. She closed her eyes, as though the sight of him was too painful to bear, sending tears streaming down her cheeks. There was a blinding flash of white, and Will threw up a hand against it. Panicked that instinct had made him lose sight of her, he quickly opened his eyes and took an involuntary step forward. But the clearing was empty, and there was no trace that she had ever been there other than the sudden fissure splitting his heart in two.

His legs felt like they might give out beneath him as the realization that she was gone, perhaps forever, washed over him in torturous waves. A tiny hand came to rest on his arm, and with a dazed expression, he stared down at Karen's tear-streaked face.

"I'm so sorry, Will," she hiccupped, biting back a sob.

His entire body was shaking, and he wrapped his arms around Sarah's friend and let her cry, sharing in her pain. Silent tears fell down his own face as he stared off into the forest, recalling the first time he had ever seen Sarah as she gaped up at the Shadow in shock, a young woman lost in the woods. How could he have known that day would change his life forever?

Karen shuddered against him. "She's gone."

He squeezed his eyes closed against the pain coursing through him and the throbbing that was pulsating in the sudden void within his chest. "I know she is," he whispered, wishing more than anything that his words held no truth.

Chapter Thirty-Five

"Time and tide wait for no man."

Geoffrey Chaucer

Time is a strange concept.

It is the one thing in the universe that is always moving, but in a moment can stand perfectly still. Some days it seems to drag on endlessly, but the simple presence of enjoyment can cause it to pass all too soon. Meaningful instances register in the memory of someone for a lifetime even as other, more painful images fade away, only to be recalled to mind in some far-off day when the pain of loss is not so fresh. And though time cannot be stopped or captured, moments can.

There was no denying that the kingdom of Serimone and its people were some of those forever things—sweet memories that would cause her to smile and some that she would repress to survive. But even if some things needed to be forgotten until they became less agonizing to think of, Sarah knew her love was unshakable by distance and time, and that was the one thing she could take home with her.

She clung to the security of her feelings as she jolted abruptly through a blaze of white and pain, landing on her knees in the snow. Her head jerked up, eyes desperately searching out the faces she knew were no longer there, half hoping it hadn't worked. But instead of forest, she saw her dormitory standing tall and bright in the sun, the light reflecting off the snow to glisten on the windows that streaked the front of the building.

And the awful fact of time is that, in a single instant, everything can come crashing down.

Sometime during her journey, the face on the watch had cracked, and the tiny fissures spreading out over the glass released a steady stream of pale smoke. The reality of what she had just done and the fact that she would never again have a whispered conversation with Karen late at night, or find herself in Will's embrace as he kissed her and told her he loved her, caused that familiar band to cinch around her heart. Serimone was safe because of her help, and Richard would soon rule beside his mother, both just and passionate monarchs who would help their kingdom rise into glorious power once more. And she would never get to see any of it happen.

With clumsy fingers, Sarah untied the steadily heating watch from her wrist and yanked it off, heaving it into the snow twenty feet away with a cry. It left an angry welt behind, wrapping all the way around her wrist.

Because time was unstoppable, she knew that her life would go on, though it would never be the same and there would always be an open hole in her heart, waiting for it to be filled by the presence of one man that she would never see again. Although the thought was still a jab, the idea that she was doing what was best for Will was the only thing that brought Sarah any comfort.

Agony wrapped around her like a cold blanket, and she collapsed onto her side in the snow and let the tears come in the middle of the deserted campus, no other sound but that of the wind echoing her cries back to her.

Yes, time would move on, but in that instant, Sarah didn't feel that her heart would ever recover.

Chapter Thirty-Six

"If the past were offered me again,
And choice of good and ill before me set,
Would I accept the pleasure with the pain,
Or dare to wish we had never met?"

Augusta, Lady Gregory, "If the Past Were Offered Me Again"

Two years later

The day was unusually hot and sunny, though a cool breeze dried the sweat on the back of her neck as Sarah trekked up the hill, her breath coming fast and ragged in anticipation. The English countryside was different than she'd remembered, and she reminded herself that years of changes could do that to a landscape.

A lark called out its song nearby, and her heart gave a familiar lurch, old memories surfacing at a single trigger sound. She glanced down at her phone's GPS to distract herself, comparing it to Karen's letter. Her old friend had done all the calculations over the course of a few days and sent her a fair estimate of where it should be. Sarah just hoped she could find the spot before her flight later that evening.

The trees thickened suddenly, no longer sporadic as she dove into the overgrown forest, swatting limbs out of her way and stepping over dead trees lying in her path. The sun was all but blocked out above her, and she was so focused on watching her footing that she didn't see the forest's edge until she passed through the trees and entered a large clearing. It was no wonder so few knew about this place, since she had been given near-exact directions and still had difficulty finding this old treasure.

Her breath caught in her throat as she stared at Serimone Castle and the ruin that it had become. Though the outer walls were all standing for the most part, hardly any portions of the ceiling remained, having caved in ages ago to make room for the tree that was just peeking out over the tallest wall. No flags greeted her from the towers, though she saw the ghosts of them waving at her in the breeze. The parapet walks were gone, the very ones that she had seen countless guards pass over as they made their rounds, and she almost imagined that she could hear the sound of their boots moving over the stones.

It wasn't as though she had expected it to be exactly as she'd remembered after a thousand years—it was a miracle it was standing at all—but seeing it so broken down and forgotten twisted her heart in painful ways. Somehow it didn't seem right that the world should forget this place that had meant so much to so many.

Sarah suddenly realized that she was just standing there, in the middle of what should have been the cobbled road, staring at the remains of a once great kingdom. She had saved for months for her trip to return to this very place, and she had already spent four days wandering the city and countryside, debating if she should try to find it or not. She didn't want to waste another minute of the precious ones that remained here, and so she stepped inside the ruins of a castle long forgotten by all but one.

The main gate was gone, and she walked right over the grass-covered courtyard, avoiding the large stones and debris littering her path, and through the open archway leading inside. Stale air greeted her. She shivered as the oppressive cold of the castle's innards soaked through her T-shirt and jeans, though daylight spilled through openings in the ceiling and warmed patches of the main room. Her eyes gazed up the length of the thin tree sprouting toward the open sky—burgeoning life in the midst of this dying relic. It was strange to see the crumbling walls of the castle and still picture, vividly, a memory on each of the cracked and fragmented stones.

The passageway near the stairs had caved in, blocking off the recollection of Damien comforting her in the little alcove when she'd thought Will had died, so she wandered under the collapsing archway and into what had once been the ballroom. Half of the outermost wall had fallen down in a sort of V-shape to expose the woods beyond. Chunks of the floor were missing and what remained of it was broken up and half-risen by overgrown roots, but it didn't distort the image of the night Sarah had discovered Will was alive—how the stones on the dance floor had held a nearly polished sheen as Will snuck into the room, surprising her by taking her hand and guiding her in a dance.

Her hand twitched, and for an instant, she could feel Will's fingers wrap around hers, his hand pressed to the small of her back as he guided her along the dance floor.

When she closed her hand over the imaginary one she held, Sarah could almost picture the expression behind the black mask he wore, and her heart quickened in remembrance as she recalled that was the night he had admitted he loved her. She would have snuck into the corridor just off the ballroom to be in that place where he had kissed her for the first time, but the entire passageway had fallen down, and it was impossible to get back there.

Sarah winced, pained at the symbolism of it—that this part of her past was broken and there was no way to get back to it.

Carefully, she picked her way up the stairs, avoiding the broken patches, though it felt sturdy enough for her to make it to the upper level.

Briefly, she wondered if there was any way to get *under* the castle, to the dungeons and the secret passages Will had taken her through. But then she shook her head, knowing that even if they hadn't caved-in yet, it wouldn't be safe for her to go down there alone.

She wandered the second floor aimlessly, unable to go down some hallways where the walls had come down. The servants' wing that she had briefly lived in was inaccessible due to an absence of a large expanse of the floor. She considered vaulting it to reach the other side and continue her trip down memory lane, but then she reminded herself that she hadn't come there to die and went back the way she'd come.

The upper staircase was in worse shape, and as she ascended, she saw the perfectly open sky above and how all the outer walls had nearly crumbled to pieces at this height. Stones littered the floor, some piles building in the corners near the walls. She could see all the way down a series of broken-down passageways that she knew would lead to the guest wing she and Damien had stayed in, but something told her seeing her old room and Damien's completely decrepit would only darken her melancholy mood.

Instead, she found herself looking out over the forest, the waist-high outer wall giving her a good view of the land. Biting her lip, she thought for a moment and then turned north, her eyes finding the spot where the Joneses' house had once stood. The expectant look on her face fell a little as her eyes found nothing but trees and untended brown grass growing wild in the open field, and the hill on which Seth had built his cabin and a life for he and Karen was completely bare. Sarah consoled herself by bringing to mind her chat with Karen in the living room while Seth and Will discussed that creature on the roof. It had been a good day, and Sarah held onto that memory for a moment longer than necessary, steeling herself before she turned east and stared into the distance.

After the changes she had seen, she wasn't sure what to expect, but it was disappointing to find nothing the same. Will's cabin would never have survived so long, not that the overgrowth of trees and new forest would have allowed her to see it from this distance, but even Glenborough Falls had dried up to nothing more than a large rock bed above a sloping hill.

A sort of despondent panic filled her as she saw with her own eyes that, though her memories had remained the same, everything here was different. Had anything remained unchanged?

Suddenly, she thought of the trees that were still growing despite all odds. Queen Meredith had said she would plant a tree to mark his grave, but nearly a thousand years had passed, and Sarah wasn't sure if it was possible that it would still be there.

She made her way quickly down both staircases, slowing to a more cautious pace when she heard small stones dislodge from the underside of the stairs as she passed over, clattering to the floor below. Jumping over the last three steps, which were almost entirely missing, she landed on the jagged stones of the entryway and hurriedly walked into the open. She dodged around hunks of fallen stone and piles of rubble that had tumbled from above, cutting a path straight through the courtyard and the protective "outer wall" that was no longer there.

The forest was on her left, and on her right was the symbol of a fallen kingdom as she moved quickly along the overgrown, rubble-strewn path. Her pulse quickened with each step until she heard nothing but the anxious anticipation of it roaring in her ears. For a brief moment, her steps slowed as she wondered if it would even be there after so long, or if it would be just another absent reminder of the past.

Her breath caught when she saw it, and she exhaled in relief, her entire being seeming to relax as the pent-up tension she'd been holding inside was released in that single exhale. The other trees had died or fallen down or been recently replanted, having grown into adolescence all on their own. But there, exactly where it should have been at the forest's edge, was Damien's grave-marker, standing taller and more beautiful than all the others. At least one symbol of Serimone remained, not unaltered, but changed for the better as it aged and grew. The certainty of it before her warmed her heart.

The yew tree was eye-catching, as he had been, with an enormous trunk that Sarah could never hope to reach around, just like she could never hope to hold onto Damien forever. She thought of his laugh and devilishly teasing grins, the way his eyes warmed when he looked at her or opened wide with surprise over how she tended to him when he was sick. He had looked like a carefree child that day they "escaped" the castle together, his smile bright as his eyes watched her beneath the pile of snow atop his head. At times he had been a welcome distraction for her, and despite his poor choices, he had grown into an incredible, loyal friend who would do anything to keep her safe.

The scar on his chest had marked him as a traitor, but in the end, unbeknownst to him, Damien had become a hero. Even after Sarah was dead, this tree would go on living despite the fact that no one would remember its purpose—a reminder of a man who had selflessly sacrificed his life to save an entire kingdom and the man she loved.

Sarah smiled, unsure whether it was curving in melancholy or joy as nostalgia set in. Her feet seemed to move with a mind of their own until she stood before the yew. Slowly, her fingers slid over the rough bark of the massive tree, its branches spreading out wide above her like a lush green canopy, protecting her.

"Hey, Damien," she whispered, the sound of his name feeling strange on her lips after years of being unable to express it, but it felt right to say it aloud, like he could hear her. For a flicker of a moment, she wondered if Will or Karen or the Joneses had similar graves marked somewhere in the countryside, but she knew it would be impossible to find them. She flattened her palm against the tree, closing her eyes as that old pain caused her chest to swell.

For two years she had tamped down the memories, shoving aside the pain and tears nearly the instant they surfaced, throwing herself into her academics and friends and work during the summer. Only on her weakest days did she allow herself to dwell on her time in Serimone for an hour of melancholy remembrance, but each time left her feeling emptier than before. Eventually she became tired of the emotional ups and downs and strove to not dwell on the past. But that afternoon, she allowed herself to fully recall her too-brief visits to the twelfth century, remembering each face and memory with details she thought she had forgotten.

Beneath the shade of the solid yew tree, with its strength at her back reminding her of Damien's care of her, she felt it safe to recall the danger and excitement, the slow-building love between her and Will, her friendship with Karen. As she sat there, she recalled every laugh and tear shared with Karen, as well as that girl's courage, Seth's infectious laugh and his mother's big heart, the quick kindness Mr. Jones and his children had shown her. The clarity of her memories surprised Sarah, and she regretted holding them back for so long, feeling as though she had betrayed the memory of her friends to spare herself pain.

Reaching into the back pocket of her jeans, she produced one of her favorite letters from Karen, glad they could still communicate. The note Karen had passed into her hand as Sarah was leaving had been detailed instructions on how to stabilize the power cell of the old machine created by her and Professor Charles. It had taken months of weekend trips to her dad's hardware store and the Ashmores' basement, but Sarah had managed to get the old clunker operating again. Though it would never be able to safely send a human being through time, it did allow them to pass letters back and forth.

Once a month or as often as she could manage it, Sarah traveled to that house, each time fearing that the house might be discovered as vacant and torn down or sold by the bank. But it was always standing there, the hedges growing further over the pathway, the security system still disabled, though Sarah had replaced the lock on her first visit back. And each time she brought a small stack of outgoing mail and went down into the musty basement, heart beating in excitement. She pressed a button on the machine, waited for the flash of white, and opened the small compartment on the side of that rusty old machine to find a small pile of letters waiting for her. Those notes from her friend—strategically placed in the first clearing where everything had begun and drawn to the future by the simple press of a button—kept Sarah tethered to that land and prevented the pain of absence from overtaking her completely.

The letter she held now was nothing more than a quick summary of a humorous week, with some embellishments to make her smile, Sarah imagined, though they did the trick every time she read it. Karen was always in high spirits in her writing, telling her about what had happened that week and ending with a quick note saying how much she missed her.

In her first letters, she had been hopeful, telling her that Will was holding out for her and to be patient, that maybe there was still a chance, though Sarah had told her not to let him know they were still communicating, as she feared it would give him unnecessary hope. But then Karen started mentioning him less and less, and he hadn't been in her last few letters at all. Though reading his name had pained her, and she *was* partly relieved that the absence of him in the notes meant that he might be moving on, it was that very idea that made Sarah wish her friend would give her some kind of update on how Will was doing.

Then again, she thought, maybe she didn't want to know.

She considered the dead trees she had stepped over in her path, the overgrown land and broken-down castle that no one but her seemed to remember. This place was just a shell of memories and an era long gone, and being here hadn't made her feel closer to the time and people she had left behind, as she had hoped. Rather, it served as a reminder that time never stopped moving forward.

But although her heart was heavy, for the first time, Sarah felt that soon she might be able to move along with it without dragging her feet in the past. She assured herself that someday, though she had difficulty imagining it, her heart would heal completely.

Sarah pushed away from the tree, rising on stiff legs. Placing her palm against the trunk of the tree, she whispered, "Goodbye, old friend."

And with a deep breath, she left that place behind.

Chapter Thirty-Seven

"There is no past that we can bring back by longing for it. There is only an eternally new now that builds and creates itself out of the best as the past withdraws."

Johann Wolfgang Von Goethe

"And I would like to relinquish my cloak and bow to you, Robert." That man looked completely taken aback.

"I'm not sure I understand," he responded carefully, looking as though he didn't want to get his hopes up.

They were standing in the livery, a week like any other, despite the fact that Will had just announced that he was departing Serimone and wished to leave his business in Robert's capable hands. However, the blond man appeared even more shocked that Will was also attempting to bestow the role of town vigilante to him.

Will grinned, sensing his repressed eagerness. "You are the Shadow now, and enough time has passed that I believe there will not be such animosity attached to that name when a reborn Shadow arrives. You have been a true friend and partner, Robert, and I hope you know how grateful I am for all you have done for me."

Shaking his head and appearing as though he could not believe his luck, Robert countered, "But what about you? *You're* the Shadow."

"I have decided to retire," he replied with a casual lift of one shoulder. Quirking a meaningful brow, he said wryly, "I believe you know where I store my bow."

Robert nodded guiltily, a slow smile revealing perfectly straight teeth. "It's me," he whispered, looking suddenly awe-struck. Will didn't have a moment to contemplate his expression, because the next beat he asked his former employer, "So, then, do you mind if I take things a bit further with Marian? We've been spending a lot of time together, but I felt I needed your permission first."

Although he was aware of their growing friendship, Will was surprised to find that Robert had been seriously pursuing her. Perhaps he had not been paying much mind to anything outside of the realm of his own concerns. But then Will searched his brain for a reason why they should not get their happy ending and found none. "I don't understand why you would feel the need to consult with me first."

Rubbing his chin, Robert mumbled, "I had my reasons. So . . . ?"

Will smiled. "By all means."

Robert looked perfectly pleased. "What's your plan, then? Now that you've given your shop away and are relinquishing Shadow duties to me." His mouth twitched, appearing as though he was holding back a childish grin of delight.

With another shrug that expressed his complete uncertainty, Will answered, "I took on the livery and forge because it was what my father did, and the Shadow was a way to avenge my parents' deaths, a task that is now complete. I suppose all that's left is to find my new dream."

"Where will you go?"

With an uncertain sigh, Will answered, "I truly don't know. Nothing seems certain at this point."

Robert nodded in understanding, and he grinned in that contagious way of his. "I hope everything works out for you, Taylor. I really do."

"As do I, Robert." He gave his old friend a nod and, with a breath of courage, forged ahead on his new life and the mysteries that it might hold.

ꕤ

Jade entered the livery late that evening, her feet aching. The sun was just beginning to set, bathing the interior of the shop in warm light. Following the sound of nickering and murmuring, she walked around the corner of the room and paused, planting her hip against the wall to watch Robert, as she often did.

He spoke softly to the rust-colored stallion, rubbing a brush over its back. The fading sunlight bounced off Robert's yellow hair, and Jade imagined what the light would do to his eyes: the pale blue would be cast with golden-green embers that burned brightly with affection. The image brightened her gloomy mood.

Sucking in a staggering breath, she marveled at the way her feelings had grown for this man, turning into a confusing tangle of emotions that had taken her months to properly understand and sort out, as she had never felt such a slow-building passion for anyone.

She had never been in love.

The horse whinnied, sensing her presence and causing Robert to turn her way. *Traitor,* she thought toward the animal, as she could no longer study his handsome features unobserved.

Robert's smile put the sun to shame when he spotted her, and her heart hiccupped, making her feel ridiculous and self-conscious. He closed the stall door and made his way to her, grinning in pleasure. "How did it go?"

Jade groaned at the reminder. Her brother's saved funds had lasted for some time, but she would soon run out, and Robert had insisted she allow him to find her proper work. Briefly, she had wondered if he was concerned she might resume her old occupation and prickled at the suggestion. But then she had seen in his eyes the earnest desire to get her on her feet, and somehow she knew that it was not her tainted past that caused him to quickly offer help. Swallowing her pride, she allowed his assistance, and within a day, he had found her and declared, rather self-importantly, that he had secured her a comfortable position at Serimone Castle. She had started that day.

Pushing away from the wall with a grimace, she said dramatically, "Long and tiresome, and I feel as though I perished around mid-day only to be brought back to life to beat the drapes." Under her breath, she muttered glumly, "And if that Terrance corrects my work one more instance . . . Dearest," she crooned sweetly. Robert raised a brow, sensing a favor was about to be requested of him. "Would you allow me to borrow that fire poker you shaped the other day? Only for a bit."

He threw his head back and released a laugh, and her lips twitched in response. Shaking his head, he chuckled. "No, there will be no threatening your overseer on your first day . . . *Maid* Marian."

She rolled her eyes at him, though he had said her name with such unexpected tenderness that her cheeks warmed against her will. It was still so new and strange when he gazed at her, his sweet smiles and soft eyes never demanding anything of her; he looked at her as though she was something precious and unique to be cared for. The feelings he stirred in her with his assuredness and tender heart were still a novelty to her, and gave her no end of pleasure.

On impulse, Jade took one step forward and then another, her hands clasped behind her back and a coy expression on her face. She waited, but Robert only lifted a brow, and she bit her lip to suppress a laugh. When they both acknowledged that their friendship was evolving into something more, he had declared that he wished to respect her and would never initiate a kiss, waiting until she was ready. It was terribly sweet and considerate, but also annoyingly inconvenient at times.

With a tiny grin on her painted lips, she raised herself on tiptoe and kissed him soundly. When she pulled back, she murmured, "Care to reconsider your vow?"

"It was a stupid rule, anyway." Robert swallowed thickly, and Jade gave him an expectant look, which caused him to grin. "Technically, you initiated it, so—" He wrapped his arms around her, silencing her laugh with a kiss that left her breathless.

That self-satisfied grin was back on his face when they broke apart. Robert wrapped her up, and she tucked her head against his solid chest, allowing him to rock her softly back and forth. "How are you?" he asked after several minutes.

Jade sighed. Today was also the anniversary of her brother's death, and she still missed him terribly everyday, more than she had expected she would. "In need of distraction," she whispered, closing her eyes.

After a moment, he said, "Taylor left today."

She shook her head at that, a little in awe of William. "I believe he is so brave to go out there on his own."

Softly, so she almost did not hear, Robert mumbled, "I could use some of his courage."

Confused, Jade pulled back from him, and he shoved his hands into the pockets cut into his trousers. She narrowed her eyes, seeing that he was playing with a tiny object.

"Would you care to go for a walk during the sunset?" he blurted, looking anxious and eager at once.

"Where do you wish to take me?" she asked, sure her excitement was palpable. Wandering through the forest beside Robert was one of her favorite pastimes.

He still appeared unaccountably nervous, but then he touched her cheek, and his gaze seemed to clear. "To see where our future will take us."

Despite all her bravado and the pride that she struggled to overcome everyday, Jade had somehow opened herself to the possibility of love. It had taken months to accept that others—like Robert and William and a few kind townsfolk—did not hold her past against her, and even longer to forgive herself for the things she had put herself and her brother through. Some days she still felt history fast on her heels, the reminder of past sins ready to choke her. But then she recalled what Sarah Matthews had said about forgiveness and the love of the Almighty, and she made an effort to remind herself that she was not beyond redemption if she chose to change.

And each day Robert had managed to thaw her once cold heart, revealing to her a kind of compassion and selfless love she had never before glimpsed. He surprised her time after time with his patience and tenderness, and she had come to trust and care for him more than anything.

Taking up his hand, Jade said earnestly, "Let us find out where it goes, shall we?"

Chapter Thirty-Eight

"So come with me where dreams are born, and time is never planned."

J.M. Barrie, *Peter Pan*

Sarah kicked her legs back and forth as she sat on the fence, staring off into the expanse of flat land as she contemplated the letter she was writing to Karen. She bent over her paper and told her about the start of her new job on Monday at the historical museum outside of town. Sure, it wasn't one of the big national museums on the east coast or in Europe, but she could use the experience. Though she imagined, with a wry tip of her lips as she paused in her writing, that she had more experience in that area than anyone else.

When she had announced at the end of the spring semester that she had switched her major to history at dinner her first night back home, her parents had been supportive. But when she added that her emphasis would be in the Middle Ages, their looks had turned to confusion, while Lilly's lips tipped in a knowing grin as she stared at her plate, trying to mask her secretive smile. She had no doubt recalled all of her older sibling's stories, the only person in this world with whom Sarah could confide, since Lilly had experienced Serimone first-hand. The sisters had grown closer after Sarah's return, her adventures having taught her one important thing: time is precious and family is rare, and neither should be wasted.

A contented snuff caught her attention just before the mahogany-colored stallion practically shoved her off the fence post as Archer tried to nuzzle her arm. Sarah laughed as she caught her balance, holding onto the horizontal piece of wood and rubbing the side of the young horse's face with her other hand. "There's a good boy," she cooed softly. Her thumb rubbed over the arrowhead birthmark between his golden eyes, the very mark for which she had named him. And if she was being totally honest, his determination reminded her of someone.

Shortly after her return, the empty plot behind the houses in Karen's neighborhood had slowly been converted into a horse ranch, and Sarah had watched it grow a little bit each time she came to drop off her letters. As soon as the main stables were built and horses brought in, Sarah had volunteered. Once she overcame her initial anxiety, being around those animals had taken away some of the sting of separation, making her feel like she was still a part of the past. But when this wild lad had been born with a crooked hind leg and its owner had wanted to put him down, it had become more than a mere balm for her slowly healing wounds; she dedicated every spare minute she had that summer to tending to the animal and helping in its rehabilitation, adopting him the minute she had enough cash.

The owner of the ranch had said their bond was unique and strange, but Sarah knew the tight link she had fostered with the animal was due to the security they found in one another, the way they helped ease the pains of the other. Focusing on Archer's needs had forced her to put aside her own, and that more than anything had helped to mend her own bent and broken injuries.

"Wanna go for a ride?" she whispered. As though he sensed the meaning of her words, Archer's ears pricked and his head shot up. Sarah laughed, slipping the pen and paper on her lap into her backpack that dangled from the fence post. Standing on the lower bar of the fence, she threw her leg over the prancing stallion's back.

He was still in training, and like he always did the minute she was seated, Archer gave a massive shake before prancing wildly off. Sarah gripped the reins in preparation of this, knowing he was still young and needed to get out his pent-up energy before he would settle down. It took less time than usual for her to coach him into a slow walk around the perimeter of the corral, and sensing he was under control, Sarah let her mind wander, her thoughts far away as her eyes drifted over the landscape.

The house and barn were modern, dirty but new trucks sat in the paved driveway, and when all was nearly silent, she could hear the faint sounds of the freeway in the distance. She was unable to stop her observation that this place was so different from another, but when she closed her eyes and tipped her head back, she imagined that the shadow of a plane passing over the sun was the light playing through a canopy of leaves overhead. Her jeans were warming in the sun and her bare shoulders were starting to burn, but if she concentrated hard enough, she felt the feathery-soft kiss of snow on her cheeks.

Time seemed to pass some by, she thought as her mood turned reflective. And yet it was inescapable for others, drawing them into its embrace and dragging them along for the ride. As Sarah had promised herself on her trip not too long ago—a fact she sometimes conveniently "forgot"—she wasn't supposed to be digging her heels into the dirt. She knew there was no capturing or rewriting or speeding up time, and she reminded herself to enjoy the ride as the world passed endlessly by.

Her words to Will suddenly flooded her mind, as though closing her eyes opened herself to past memories she'd thought were long gone. Lips tipping contentedly, she suddenly felt assured that they would both be okay. She wished she could do this feeling justice in her letter to Karen, letting her know she was all right.

Archer released a disgruntled sound and jerked beneath her. Eyes flying open, Sarah gripped the reins a little tighter and leaned forward to keep her balance. "Whoah, boy." He let out a nervous huff, and she ran a hand over his neck soothingly, feeling his muscles quiver in irritation. Her sight wandered over the landscape in search of what had startled the animal.

A quick, sudden breeze blew in from the south, pieces escaping her braid to tickle her face, and she squinted in that direction as the wind died down. There was a flickering silver light a ways off, like the reflection of the sun against glass, and it shivered for several seconds before she thought she heard the faint sound of a car backfiring in the distance. The light disappeared in a flash, and Sarah narrowed her left eye in confusion as she slowly dismounted, her gaze glued to that spot as she came around Archer to stare at the wavering shape. Her pulse quickened in disbelief, afraid to trust what she was seeing as the shadow slowly morphed into the outline of a man walking toward her.

Heart in her throat, Sarah moved without thinking as she dropped the reins and climbed over the fence, her movements slow as though she was in a trance. She didn't dare to believe what her eyes were telling her as the distance between them lessened and his features began to take shape—the dark wavy hair above a brow raised in anticipation, broad shoulders accentuated by the white tunic he wore, long legs that ate up the space between them. His face was older, more mature, but his smile was as brilliant as she remembered.

She stared at him, having frozen in place at some point, and watched as he made his way to her. At last, she saw his dark, emotion-filled eyes reflecting the light of the sun as he stood before her. They watched each other, gazes searching, feeling hopeful and anxious and awkward after so long apart.

Finally, she broke the silence. "Please tell me I'm not going crazy," she said breathlessly.

Will grinned slowly, softly. "No. I told you I would find you, did I not?"

"But—but *how*?" she stammered, sure her eyes must be huge. "I used the last of the watches, and I've been to Karen's old house—the machine that powers them is still in pieces."

He scratched the back of his neck, and it was such a *Will* thing that her breath momentarily caught. "I would have come sooner, but there were difficulties."

"Like what?" She wanted to keep him talking, fearing he might disappear the instant he closed his lips.

Will's eyes met hers again with such a burning intensity that she clenched her fists, afraid to touch him and ruin this perfect mirage. "A few months after you left"—he stumbled over the word, as though the wound was still fresh, and Sarah wondered how long the separation had been for him—"I remembered what Ashmore had said about his timepiece being taken, and as no working watch remained, I knew it was my only hope. It took us months to find the watch Cadius had seized, locked away in a hidden compartment in his chambers, and it was in such poor condition that I was uncertain if Charles could ever get it in working order again."

He inhaled a steadying breath. "Too long it took to repair the old timepiece, though I dedicated every waking minute to our venture. We failed time and again, even with the help of Robert and Karen—Charles called it a 'downside to the simplicity of this life.' We became desperate one day, or rather I did." He grinned faintly. "Charles and I created a structure made entirely of metallic elements, a device that would carry electrical currents into the watch when it was charged. The only issue was that we had to wait months for the right lightning storm to create electricity with a high enough intensity to power the watch for a single trip. Or so I am told."

"Like Frankenstein," Sarah breathed, suddenly aware that a smile of disbelief had curved her lips.

He nodded. "That is precisely what Karen said when she started crying, 'It's alive!'" Though he shook his head in bewilderment, Sarah could only laugh, picturing her red-haired friend standing beside the professor as she flipped a switch, bringing the watch to life in a black-and-white version of a Mary Shelley novel.

Laughter fading, Sarah let her mouth fall open a little as she shook her head. "I just don't understand how you're *here*, though—as in, this ranch."

"Oh, of course." Will's brow furrowed, as though trying to remember. "Karen informed me that the watch had no capability for . . . '*GPS*' and that it would simply return me to a piece of open land closest to the machine, drawn like a magnet to its original source. She said once I arrived, I would need to find her home and wait for you there, that you would come for one of her letters." His lips softened. "But it seems I found you before that was necessary."

Sarah swallowed, still in shock. "She thought of everything," she said vaguely.

"Karen even insisted on 'future prepping,' as she called it." Will blushed a little as he admitted, "I went to their cabin nearly every evening while we tried and failed to restore the watch, and she taught me to read as you would, teaching me the arithmetic and sciences she said are basic but common here." There was a tinge of pride in his voice, and Sarah's eyes filled unexpectedly. "And I learned about things like moving portrait boxes called *televisions* and small devices that allow you to communicate with and hear anyone in the world."

Sarah was absolutely amazed that he had gone through the painstaking trouble of learning all that, and she felt a jolt of gratitude toward Karen that she'd had the foresight to prepare him for this world . . . as much as she could.

"But it's so different here," she whispered, then frowned. Why was she trying to dissuade him when he had come all this way to find her? Because, she realized, she had recovered from the loss of him before, and she wasn't sure she would be able to again if her hopes were dashed.

He grinned slowly. "I am fairly adaptable." Tipping his head to the side, that stubborn lock of hair fell over his forehead as he studied her. "You kept saying 'someday,' so I decided that today could be yesterday's someday."

"So you're staying?" Sarah dared to ask, fear and hope apparent in her eyes.

"Unless . . . you are spoken for?" Though his expression didn't change much, the set of his shoulders and jaw were suddenly stiff, and his voice had hitched in pain at the end.

"No!" she blurted, aghast at the thought. A look of absolute relief came over his features, and she realized he'd been afraid of a different answer.

His hand lifted slowly, his fingers pausing an inch from her face. He seemed to hold his breath until he spread his palm out across her cheek, and only then did he exhale, as though he had waited for this moment as long as she had. "Then, yes, love, I am staying. I knew it was a one-way trip going in, and not once did I look back."

"I never thought—" Blinking, she shook her head, still having difficulty believing in what was standing right before her. Her movements stilled, dread filling her senses with a metallic tang and overriding the bliss of that moment. "Wait, you have to go back. You can't be here; it's why I left you behind in the first place."

Will placed calming hands on her bare shoulders, his touch warmer than her sun-kissed skin. He smiled softly. "Karen explained your fear to me—that your presence in my era or mine in yours would somehow upset time. And she insisted I tell you that it's about time *you* received your happy ending."

It sounded like something she would say. "What about Serimone, though? The Shadow, the *kingdom*? You're supposed to be a knight, remember?"

"I took an audience with Queen Meredith and informed her that I had to follow my heart, and she was quite understanding as she released me of my duties." He grinned. "Actually, she wanted me to relay her well-wishes for our future and gave me a *sizeable* amount of gold, enough to settle down while we figure out our situation." Sarah took note of the bulging pouch strapped to his buckle, and her eyes widened. "And anyway, Robert can handle the rest."

"What do you mean?"

"I signed ownership of the shop over to Robert, and now that the bounty on the Shadow has been forgotten and his debt paid, I left him in charge of the duties of town vigilante, as well. Something tells me he was more than happy to comply."

Sarah's mouth worked until she managed, "But you're supposed to be the Shadow. You can't just leave. . . . Can you?"

He looked rather pleased with his cleverness as he replied, "You said *someone* had to be Serimone's hero for the sake of history, and I decided that as long as someone took over my place, then history would not lack for any legends." He chuckled softly. "He and Jade also appear to be spending quite a bit of their time together, so I think he will be just fine."

Robert and Jade. *Robin and Marian!* Sarah couldn't believe she had been such an idiot, with Robert's fascination in the Shadow and his quick interest in Jade. The smile steadily growing on her face fell in an instant as she realized that she had let years slip by because she thought she was protecting history. Though she could never have known that Robert was supposed to take over the legendary torch, it still burned to realize that so long had passed when she could have been with Will.

"I wasted years," she whispered, pained. "I thought I was doing what was best for everyone."

Will's face softened, and he tucked a loose strand of hair behind her ear. "As difficult as it was to be apart from you—" He broke off, a breath shuddering through his chest as he cringed in remembrance. Softly, he admitted, "I felt broken and lost in your absence, but I don't like to think of all those years as wasted or that we grew apart during that time. Rather, I choose to believe that time and distance only proved that our bond is strong enough to endure any obstacle. While we were separated, we grew parallel with one another instead of apart, and I only hoped for the day when I might close that distance between us."

As if in response to his words, her feet inched closer until she had to tip her head back to see him. Placing a hand over his heart, she found the steady thrum of it turn to a rushing pulse beneath her palm. "You said all those years," she began slowly. "How long *has* it been since I left?"

His throat worked in a swallow. "Four years." Sarah's expression froze on her face, shocked, as his hand cupped her cheek. "But this moment makes every tireless day spent working on that contraption worthwhile."

So long! That this man would wait years for her was baffling and did strange things to her stomach. "You left everything behind," she breathed, amazed. She gripped the fabric of his shirt in her hand, needing to understand. "Why?"

Will brushed the backs of his knuckles across her chin, smiling tenderly. His eyes filled with warmth. "Because I have waited a thousand years to hear you admit that you love me."

She gaped at him, choking out a startled laugh. "You risked your future, and possibly your life traveling here, just to hear me say that?"

"You *are* my future, Sarah Matthews, my life's blood." His eyes darkened, burning with a sudden intensity that made her toes curl in her sneakers. "Wherever you go, you carry my heart with you. You said Serimone is where I belong, but it is in you that I find my home."

She closed her eyes, letting his beautiful words wash over her. Silence reigned, and she knew he was waiting for her to speak. Taking a deep breath, she opened her eyes, working to keep her voice steady as tears blurred his patiently expectant face. Her voice was small as she ashamedly admitted, "I didn't want to tell you because I was afraid it would only make it harder on you when I left. I thought you might not follow me if you had no reason to."

He grinned. "It appears you were wrong. You know I can be as mule-headed as Seth, when necessary."

Sarah gave a faint laugh. Sucking in a breath, she returned his steady gaze. "William Taylor, I love you. I have for awhile now, and I'm sorry I didn't tell you sooner."

Face breaking out in a huge, relieved smile, Will nodded firmly. "Then I made the right choice, love." He wrapped her in a crushing embrace, and she choked back tears of joy and fear. "I only wanted to hear you say it so I might tell you of my certainty that I belong here with you."

She leaned back to give him a teasing grin. "And how did you know that?"

With his calloused thumb, he brushed a tear from the corner of her eye. The action was so familiar that Sarah closed her lids against the sweet ache building in her chest. "Because I saw us together that day, with our children."

Her eyes flew open. "What?"

Nodding slowly, Will said, "When we were returning to Serimone and were separated, I saw you—a bit older and with two young children, a boy and a girl." She saw him swallow, his face momentarily pained. "When I imagined you had wed another, I felt the acutest grief. But then a man joined you, and I knew, I *knew* that I was glimpsing a possible future for the two of us. One I wanted very much."

"You saw the two of us together," she breathed in disbelieving joy.

"I had hoped it was, at least."

His words sank in, and she gaped at him. "You mean, you didn't know? You risked everything thinking that it *might* be you?"

Will's gaze darkened, softening around the edges, the light blue circle around his iris drawing her deeper in. "Did you doubt that I would fight hell on earth to get back to you? It was always supposed to be me at your side, and seeing that it could be that way one day only urged me to make that future a reality. I wanted to be that man, and I did everything I could to ensure that I would take over his place."

Choking on a laugh, Sarah reached behind his neck, pulling him to her. His lips were familiar as they pressed softly against hers, and his arms encircled her waist, drawing her closer. She imagined his lids were closed tight like hers, knowing they had both waited too long for this moment. One hand slid into his hair, her fingers tangling themselves in curling locks as soft as silk, though a little longer than she remembered.

A tear slipped down her cheek, overwhelmed with emotion, as she placed her other hand over his pounding heart, trying to put a little distance between them as her fears took over her need to be near him. "But your life is there, Will," she whispered brokenly. "How can you leave it behind?"

He placed his hand over hers, pressing it against his chest. "You are my life, Sarah, and with Thomas gone, my only family left. Wherever you are, there I shall be."

"You feel that way now." Her voice was small as she dropped her gaze, feeling torn between elation and agonized guilt that she had drawn him from his world. "But what happens when you wake up one day and realize that you gave up everything to be with me? When we have a fight or this life becomes too strange for you, won't you want to run away into the forest?" Her eyes met his, dipping in sorrow. "You'll suffocate here."

"I seem to recall many an argument back in Serimone, and yet we still find ourselves in this spot." Will's wry tone surprised her. Then his mouth softened, curving in a tender smile. "I am tired of running. The greatest voyages will pale in comparison to the adventure of starting a life with you. And I am sure that will be quite the challenge with your temper," he teased, just to make her smile.

She scoffed. "*My* temper?"

His smiling eyes turned serious once more. "I never wish to experience another thrill unless you are there with me. Let me show you that our life together will be grand and exciting all on its own."

Sarah's fears had slowly melted away during his speech, and she felt the corner of her mouth twitch. "You'll still get bored."

"Ah, love," he whispered, shaking his head. "Life with you will never be dull." His gaze drifted to her lips, and he brought his head down and kissed her, long and gentle.

"I thought I'd never get this," she said breathlessly against his mouth,

She felt his chest rise and fall faster, and his deliberate control disappeared as he leaned into her, his lips moving with a sort of desperate hunger that surprised her, though she felt the same agonizing fire burning within her. Although Will had seen the possibility of their future together, there was no way he could have known for certain, and the two of them had been left to wonder if this moment would ever exist or if they would truly live an existence without the other.

Seeming to sense her thoughts, as they were probably his own just then, Will cupped the side of her face with his large hand, the other pressed against her back. The fingers behind her neck drew her nearer, and she clung to him, never wanting this moment to end. She felt his smile spread against her own lips before he put a hair's breadth between them. "Sarah." Her name was a mere disbelieving breath on his lips, but that one word was filled with all the love in his heart and every unspoken promise that she was sure he would keep.

Gazing into his eyes so close to her own, they looked like dark pools she wanted to fall into and float in for the rest of their lives. And she could now.

Sarah pressed her forehead against his, touching his cheek, taking her time after their hurried kiss. She savored the feel of stubble against her fingertips, his breath on her face, the lingering feel of his lips on hers. "This is real, isn't it? Because I've dreamed of this before."

Will was too close to see his smile, but she heard it in the satisfaction of his voice. "So you *did* see me in your dreams." She felt a little embarrassed that she'd admitted it out loud, but then he brushed the hair back from her cheek so tenderly it stopped her apology. "As I dreamed of you, whether waking or sleeping."

"We aren't making a terrible decision, are we?" Her breathless words were muffled as she buried her face in his chest, breathing in his earthy scent.

His deep chuckle rumbled against her cheek, and she smiled, no longer fearing that the sound of his laughter would be taken from her. "No. I believe that together we can take on the world—*any* world."

Sarah jerked her head back suddenly, keeping her arms about his waist, eyes bright with excitement. "I'm going to have to teach you how to drive a stick and to use a cell phone. And the movies! Karen told you about the T.V., but—oh my gosh, Will, you're going to love seeing movies at the theater! And I have to take you to Disneyland."

He was shaking his head, looking entirely amused at her enthusiasm. "I have no idea what you just said, but I look forward to you showing me everything your world has to offer."

She grabbed his hand, pulling him, laughing, back to the ranch. "You have to meet my horse, Archer."

"A horse? Archer?"

She stopped abruptly, staring up into his grinning face. Earnestly, she said, "He reminded me of you, and I haven't been afraid of horses for a long time." She didn't have to say that it was the thought of him at her back or his hand on her waist that encouraged her to push past her fear. Somehow, he seemed to sense that she had taken pieces of his memory with her everyday, as she imagined he had done the same with her.

Will's smile turned tender, thumb gliding over her knuckles. "Braver than you believe, remember?"

Excitement fading, Sarah's eyes widened as reality sunk in and she considered the future. "How am I going to introduce you to my parents?"

But his gaze only brightened. "Your family? And your sister, as well?"

"Yeah," she mumbled distractedly. "They'll totally love you, don't worry about that, and my mom will probably smother you with questions and food the second you step foot in the house. But we might have to integrate you slowly into the family, otherwise they'll know something's up if we act like we know each other too well; I haven't exactly mentioned any devilishly handsome, slightly older blacksmiths yet—"

"I am certain we'll figure everything out. In time." His answer was so simple that Sarah stared at him for a full minute, and his grin only grew as the seconds passed. He finally laughed. "I have waited so long to be with you, and I believe my patience can extend to a slow and steady introduction to your family. We can take as much time as we need." He took her hand. "I can withstand anything as long as we are together."

She had to smile at him, still waiting for the fact that he was here, *permanently*, to sink in. "I guess you were right: anything is possible with God and enough time." She laughed. "I guess a thousand years is enough time for miracles."

Touching her face gently, Will stared into her eyes, his filled with promise and deep emotion. "Yes, anything. The future is uncertain but it is ours, my love, and I cannot wait to discover what God has in store for us."

"Together, right?" She smiled, heart skipping in her throat.

He touched her face tenderly, looking like he was finally home. And maybe all of their wandering *had* led them to this exact moment, this chance to discover what laid in store for them. "Yes, love, together."

Will kissed her then, soft and unhurried, as if they had all the time in the world. After all the running and chasing and fighting against time itself, Sarah let herself melt into that blissful moment, unrestrained by the pressure of the passing hour or the setting of the sun. It was one of those forever moments that time could never erase from her memory, and she dove headfirst into the security of knowing that this now was theirs and would never be taken from them.

They had faced so much in the past, but now they had the chance to grow side-by-side in the present, defying the restraints of time and the passing of shadows between worlds. And, uncertain though it may have been, in that instant, their future began.

Epilogue

"The purpose of life is not to be happy. It is to be useful, to be honorable, to be compassionate, to have it make some difference that you have lived and lived well."

Ralph Waldo Emerson

Mary crept into the room, her steps light as she entered the small attic. Sunlight snuck through tiny gaps in the ceiling and revealed a wall of floating dust particles that drifted off the old furniture and uncovered storage chests. She bit back a shriek as her hand brushed over a spider web, and she wondered why her mother had spent so many hours up here, returning with a wistful smile on her face. It was that very question that had caused her to explore the upper level of the cabin that day, while her father tended the field and her mother went on one of her thoughtful walks.

The chest she sought was no taller than six inches, but twice as wide, and she snatched it from the top of her aunt's old desk. Months ago, she had caught her mother sitting in the middle of a ray of light in the attic, crying softly as she read a letter, hunched over the very chest Mary held in her hands. A floorboard had creaked beneath her slipper, and her mother had hastily wiped her eyes, pretending as though nothing were amiss as she placed the letter in the box and closed the lid.

Later that night, Mary had asked her father about what she had seen. With a soft, sad look in his eyes, he had placed a big hand on his daughter's shoulder and said, rather cryptically, "I believe she is remembering an old friend."

In the months that followed, her mother had only returned to the attic a scarce number of times, and Mary's insatiable curiosity had been eating at her ever since. Now, she dropped to her knees and placed the chest before her, swiping a lock of bright red hair behind her ear. Her fingers hovered over the clasp in reverence, wondering what treasures this chest might hold, before she turned up the lid. Her face fell a little in confusion as she took in the letters beneath a pile of . . . tiny paintings?

Mary's hand reached inside and drew out the stack of color, moving them back and forth and watching the rays of light play across the glossy tops. She rubbed her thumb over the surface, marveling at how it was smoother and held more clarity than the greatest artists in the world could hope to capture in their portraits. But despite their strange texture and thinness, they *were* pictures of some kind, and Mary held her breath as she carefully sifted through the stack, placing them facedown when she was finished to keep them in order.

The uppermost image was of a young woman with a tan, freckle-sprayed face surrounded by waves of long auburn hair. A man had his arms around her as they sat atop a horse the color of mahogany, land stretching out behind them for miles around. Her smile was bright as she stared back at Mary, but the dark-haired man had his head tipped to watch the woman, grinning at her enthusiasm. Mary turned the parchment-thin painting over and squinted to make out the faded words scribbled over the white back of the image. *Archer loves the new farm!* she read at last. Love, Sarah.

The remaining images were all of this Sarah and the big man, some far away paintings clearly done by another, while others were strangely close to their laughing faces, as though the portrait had been commissioned to freeze a random moment in time. One was of a house and barn on the large piece of land Mary had seen in the first image, though this one captured the two standing beneath an iron archway and a sign that proclaimed TAYLOR FARMS. She came to one that had been placed in the stack backward, and she read the note first: *Thinking of you under Damien's wings.* She turned it over and saw Sarah sitting on the ground with her hand wrapped around a featherless quill, her back against the enormous trunk of a yew as its branches stretched out above her.

Then a child suddenly appeared in one image, a tiny sleeping babe in the arms of a tired-looking Sarah, who was reclining in bed dressed in a white gown. Despite the fact that the frame was tilted oddly to the left and nearly cut off the woman's head, her face was glowing as she leaned close to the child and pointed away from herself, toward Mary. That girl did not fully understand the long note on the back of it, but it mentioned *Our little Thomas* and the fact that Will was still learning how to work a camera, though his *selfies* were improving, whatever that was.

As Mary went through each image, some of which were beginning to peel and yellow around the edges, she realized that this couple had commissioned their entire lives to be catalogued. She flipped through years and years, watching time pass for Sarah and Will, whose name appeared in the small notes on the back of each image. Mary saw their son and daughter grow into adulthood, how Sarah and Will's hair slowly became streaked with gray and white, lines appearing around their eyes and mouths, though their smiles did not dim and Sarah never lost that mischievous glint in her eyes. Although she did not know them, Mary felt an immense sadness when she reached the last moment captured of their lives, and she stared back at their bright faces aged by time as they sat on their porch, arms around one another, watching small children play in the grass.

She wondered who this man and woman were to her mother and why she had these portraits of them—these people whose entire lives Mary had just watched fade away in a few minutes. She knew with absolute certainty that reading the letters would be the only way to find out.

Mary dove into the missives, eyes devouring the words. Sometimes they were long, other instances the note was short and a mere expression of how much Sarah missed the girl's mother, whose name was inscribed at the top left corner of every letter. Her nose wrinkled as she tried to make out the strange, informal language that Sarah used, and some of her words made no sense to Mary; it sounded as though her mother and Sarah had been separated years ago, and every word she read was exciting and a mystery. Certain passages of each letter stood out to her, resonating in her mind until she could better understand what they meant:

"Preparing for graduation has been hectic, but I can't wait for it to be over! Will is taking me to our favorite spot out of town after the party tonight. He said he'd wait to propose until I graduated, but the poor guy's waited so long I thought he might crack before now. Don't tell him I know, though, it'd ruin his fun. . . ."

Mary grazed over the next few letters, knowing that her mother would be returning soon and she didn't have much time.

". . . farm is coming together. Will was so excited to put the gold to good use! It gives him purpose to work the land and help these kids while he goes to school. It's taking him awhile to get his degree, and I know it's trying his patience."

"Being in England and standing in the place where (I think) your house stood on the hill made me ache to laugh with you again. I can't talk with you in person, so Will took a picture of me under that tree I told you about while I write this letter. I'll send it along with my note, and it'll be like I'm there saying this to you!"

There was a letter telling of their children, Thomas and Allison, and how their Aunt Lilly spoiled them. A hastily scribbled note at the bottom said, *"And Will asks that you punch Seth in the shoulder on behalf of him, for whatever stupid thing he'll do this week."*

Mary frowned, skipping ahead once more and wondering why an assault on her father was supposed to be amusing. The furrow in her brow deepened as she read an excited letter from Sarah that appeared to be a response to something her mother had written. It expressed her joy that her mother was having a "miracle child" and stated that, no, she did not think that having a baby at thirty was strange, especially considering their circumstances, which went unspecified and only left Mary feeling more curious.

". . . scares me how time has shifted, moving faster over here. I'm afraid that one day you'll wake up and I'll be gone. . . ."

Shaking her head at Sarah's strange talk, Mary wondered if she was attempting the use of a metaphor as she reached inside the chest for the next letter.

"What are you doing here?"

Her head shot up in alarm at the sound of her mother's voice, wondering if she would be terribly upset with her for prying into her personal belongings. "I-I wanted to see . . . I found this?" She pointed at the open chest and the mess of letters, and winced.

But instead of revealing that inner fire Mary knew was inside, her mother sat on the floor beside her, smiling softly as she took in the scattered paintings and letters. "I haven't looked at these in ages."

"Who were they?" Mary breathed, excitement sparking at the openness in her mother's gaze. "Who was Sarah?"

"She was my best friend in the entire world." With a sigh of remembrance, she said, "Sarah moved away many years ago, long before you were born."

"Does Father know of her?"

Her mother hesitated, then said slowly, "Yes, she lived with his family for a short time, and I told him everything. Updated him on the family, I mean," she was quick to add. Mary could tell she was keeping something from her, something her father knew, but she had too many questions that she needed answered in order.

Mary fidgeted eagerly in place. "Can I meet her, Mother? Looking at all these strange paintings and hearing about her entire life . . ."

Her mother's lips curved into a sad, wistful smile. There were tears in her eyes as she said, "No, dear. Twenty years is quite a long time for some, and I am afraid she passed away several months ago, just one year following her husband. Her sister sent me a letter informing me of their passing."

Mary slowly frowned. "Oh." After a pause, she said in disappointment, "So then she did not live such a long life after all. That is so sad."

"On the contrary, she and her true love lived for many joyous years together, having children and seeing their grandchildren grow and mature. They were old and gray before their time came."

"She looks so happy," Mary remarked softly.

Her mother selected an image from the floor and studied the two older faces with a tiny, wistful smile. Their expressions were brightened by the lit candles in the shape of a 5 and 0 on the cake before them. Mary tilted her head and was just able to make out the words *We owe it all to a little puddle and you* written on the back.

"Yes, dear," her mother said softly as she set the image down to wipe a tear from her eye. "I believe they would both agree that it was worth the wait."

"So they did love each other, then?" Her mother nodded, stroking Mary's hair, which was the same shade as her mother's, except for the streak of white near her temple. Decisively, the girl announced, "Someday I want to find a love like that."

She didn't quite understand the look in her mother's eyes, but the soft smile that graced her lips caused the girl to wonder if she was pondering another lifetime. "A love like that can last forever."

"And did it?" she asked curiously.

Her mother's green eyes drifted to the lone window, and it looked as though her mind was suddenly a thousand miles away. "Yes, my dear. Their love broke the boundaries of time, and I only wish that others could know of their story."

Mary paused thoughtfully, then said, "Aunt Leah said that true love never fades and cannot be ignored; it simply remains in the hearts of those they touched. Their story and love won't be forgotten, Mama, it will just live on in others."

Tears welled in her mother's eyes, though the girl couldn't account for their presence. "Yes, my darling, I believe you are right."

Acknowledgements

This trilogy has been in the making for a decade (nearly to the week), building slowly from an eight-page creative project to a full-fledged series over the years. I imagined what it might be like for Sarah to become trapped in Serimone, what adventures she might encounter, and most of all, I wondered what it would be like to make her a part of history. As I wrote the last few lines of Defying Shadows, I'll admit that there were quite a few tears shed (and during several other scenes, as well). A big part of my life that existed for ten years only in Serimone was finally complete, and it suddenly hit me that I would never get to write about shenanigans at the Joneses' home, choreograph a swashbuckling/arrow-shooting battle, create a heart-wrenching scene with Damien, or pen a beautiful moment between Sarah and Will. I am excited to get to other projects that have been begging for attention, but the gang in Serimone will forever remain in my heart, and I hope in yours, too.

But it wasn't all fun and games. Similar to raising a child or making a proper cup of coffee, it takes a village to produce a novel. Through the entire process, I had an incredible team that kept me going and encouraged me to finish this project.

All the love and thanks in my heart to my incredibly supportive parents! DeAnna, Elizabeth, and Katie, the Three Musketeers and the best sisters a girl could have—thanks for always letting my freak flag fly, for never thinking my eccentricities were too kooky, and for accepting the fact that a writer's mind isn't always a safe place when they're in the zone. But most of all, you guys pushed me to keep writing, and I can't thank you all enough for helping me over self-doubting funks (and for providing caffeine).

To Cassie for always being there and for your unexpected passion for Sarah's story. And to my AMAZING Team of Shadows (#TeamHood!) for beta-reading Defying Shadows in its most tragic state, and still somehow falling in love with it. Cassie, Sarah E., Crystal C., Carleigh, Krystal, Sarah B., and Deborah, you ladies were so fun to get to know. Your questions and gushing about these characters always made me smile, and your endless encouragement and advice were invaluable. I do believe I've found a forever friend in every last one of you bibliophiles!

To the creative, stupendous, and drool-inducing Lisa M. (@TheElegantStylus) for designing this cover and redesigning the one for Rising Shadows. You made me fall in love with every single aspect of these fangirl-worthy covers, and I can't express how much I adore having these on my bookshelf. *fireworks* *explosions* *squeals of delight*

And to you, dear reader, for stumbling upon the tale of Serimone. Storytelling isn't something for the faint of heart. Every book is the product of hundreds of hours of joy and tears, the pages filled with the blood, heart, and soul of the writer in hopes that we might entertain you for a few hours or days. But if you're like me, then Sarah and Will's story found its way into your heart, and I hope that you will join me in Serimone again and again, finding new adventure and meaning on each page. While I wish that I could continue writing out their story for the rest of my life, I know that it takes a leap of faith to discover something amazing. We just have to be patient, make a choice, and trust that we are braver than we believe.

P.S. Look, Ma! I'm still totally unscathed by my childhood obsession with thieves (Robin Hood, Aladdin, etc.). And to think, you were worried about me joining a gang of hooded do-gooders. . . . Now I just write about them!

www.ingramcontent.com/pod-product-compliance
Lightning Source LLC
Chambersburg PA
CBHW020633020726
47494CB00001B/168

9781939156792